Collected Stories

BY TENNESSEE WILLIAMS

PLAYS

Baby Doll (a screenplay)
Camino Real
Cat on a Hot Tin Roof
Clothes for a Summer Hotel
Dragon Country
The Glass Menagerie
A Lovely Sunday for Creve Coeur
Small Craft Warnings
Stopped Rocking and Other Screenplays
A Streetcar Named Desire
Sweet Bird of Youth

THE THEATRE OF TENNESSEE WILLIAMS, VOLUME I
  Battle of Angels, A Streetcar Named Desire, The Glass Menagerie
THE THEATRE OF TENNESSEE WILLIAMS, VOLUME II
  The Eccentricities of a Nightingale, Summer and Smoke, The Rose Tattoo, Camino Real
THE THEATRE OF TENNESSEE WILLIAMS, VOLUME III
  Cat on a Hot Tin Roof, Orpheus Descending, Suddenly Last Summer
THE THEATRE OF TENNESSEE WILLIAMS, VOLUME IV
  Sweet Bird of Youth, Period of Adjustment, The Night of the Iguana
THE THEATRE OF TENNESSEE WILLIAMS, VOLUME V
  The Milk Train Doesn't Stop Here Anymore, Kingdom of Earth (The Seven Descents of Myrtle), Small Craft Warnings, The Two-Character Play
THE THEATRE OF TENNESSEE WILLIAMS, VOLUME VI
  27 Wagons Full of Cotton and Other Short Plays
THE THEATRE OF TENNESSEE WILLIAMS, VOLUME VII
  In the Bar of a Tokyo Hotel and Other Plays
27 Wagons Full of Cotton and Other Plays
The Two-Character Play
Vieux Carré

POETRY

Androgyne, Mon Amour
In the Winter of Cities

PROSE

Collected Stories
Eight Mortal Ladies Possessed
Hard Candy and Other Stories
The Knightly Quest and Other Stories
One Arm and Other Stories
The Roman Spring of Mrs. Stone
Where I Live: Selected Essays

Tennessee Williams

Collected Stories

With an introduction by Gore Vidal

A NEW DIRECTIONS BOOK

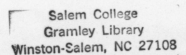

The introduction by Gore Vidal appeared in a somewhat different form in the *New York Review of Books*.

Grateful acknowledgment is made to the editors and publishers of the following magazines and journals in which many of these stories first appeared: *Antaeus, Christopher Street, The Columns, Esquire, Flair, Mademoiselle, Manuscript, ND Fourteen—New Directions in Prose and Poetry, The New Yorker, Partisan Review, Playboy, Playgirl, Story, Town and Country, Vogue,* and *Weird Tales.* (Details of the publishing history of individual stories will be found in the "Bibliographical Notes" at the end of this volume.)

Thanks are also due to the Harry Ransom Humanities Research Center, The University of Texas at Austin, and to the University of Missouri Archives (Record Series C:6/20/1, English Department, Literary Prizes and Awards) for permission to use manuscript materials in their possession.

A special note of thanks to Andreas Brown and Lyle Leverich for their assistance in dating the stories.

Manufactured in the United States of America
First published clothbound by New Directions in 1985
Published simultaneously in Canada by Penguin Books Canada Limited

Library of Congress Cataloging in Publication Data

Williams, Tennessee, 1911–1983
    Collected stories.
    (A New Directions Book)
    I. Title.
PS3545.I5365A6   1985   813'.54   85-10642
ISBN 0-8112-0952-0

New Directions Books are published for James Laughlin
by New Directions Publishing Corporation,
80 Eighth Avenue, New York 10011

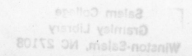

Contents

v

Preface:
The Man in the Overstuffed Chair

He always enters the house as though he were entering it with the intention of tearing it down from inside. That is how he always enters it except when it's after midnight and liquor has put out the fire in his nerves. Then he enters the house in a strikingly different manner, almost guiltily, coughing a little, sighing louder than he coughs, and sometimes talking to himself as someone talks to someone after a long, fierce argument has exhausted the anger between them but not settled the problem. He takes off his shoes in the living room before he goes upstairs where he has to go past my mother's closed door, but she never fails to let him know she hears him by clearing her throat very loudly or saying, "Ah, me, ah, me!" Sometimes I hear him say "Ah, me" in response as he goes on down the hall to where he sleeps, an alcove sunroom connected to the bedroom of my young brother, Dakin, who is at this time, the fall and winter of 1943, with the Air Force in Burma.

These months, the time of this story, enclose the end of the life of my mother's mother.

My father's behavior toward my maternal grandmother is scrupulously proper but his attitude toward my grandfather Dakin is so insulting that I don't think the elderly gentleman could have endured it without the insulation of deafness and near-blindness.

Although my grandmother is dying, she is still quite sound of sight and hearing, and when it is approaching the time for my father to return from his office to the house, my grandmother is always downstairs to warn her husband that Cornelius is about to storm in the front door. She hears the Studebaker charging up the drive and cries out to my grandfather, *"Walter, Cornelius is coming!"* She cries out this warning so loudly that Grandfather can't help but hear it. My grandfather staggers up from his chair by the radio and starts for the front stairs, but sometimes he doesn't make them in time and there is an awkward encounter in the downstairs hall. My grandfather says, "Good evening, Cornelius" and is lucky if he receives, in answer, a frigid "Hello, Mr. Dakin" instead of a red-eyed glare and a grunt.

It takes him, now that he's in his eighties with cataracts on both eyes, quite a while to get up the stairs, shepherded by his wife, and sometimes my father will come thundering up the steps behind them as if he intended to knock the old couple down. What is he after? A drink, of course, from a whiskey bottle under his bed in the sunroom, or the bathroom tub.

"Walter, watch out!"

"Excuse me, Mrs. Dakin," my father grunts breathlessly as he charges past them on the stairs.

They go to their bedroom, close the door. I don't hear just what they say to each other, but I know that "Grand" is outdone with Grandfather for lingering too long downstairs to avoid this humiliating encounter. Of course Grandfather finds the encounter distasteful, too, but he dearly loves to crouch by the downstairs radio at this hour when the news broadcasters come on, now that he can't read newsprint.

They are living with us because my grandmother's strength is so rapidly failing. She has been dying for ten years and her weight has dropped to eighty-six pounds. Any other person would be confined to bed, if not the terminal ward of a hospital, but my grandmother is resolved to remain on her feet, and actively helpful about the house. She is. She still does most of the laundry in the basement and insists on washing the dishes. My mother begs her to rest, but "Grand" is determined to show my father that she is not a dependent. And I have come home, this late autumn of 1943, because my mother wrote me, "Your grandmother has had to give up the house in Memphis because she is not strong enough to take care of it and your grandfather, too."

Between the lines of the letter, I read that my mother is expecting the imminent death of her mother and I ought to stop in Saint Louis on my bus trip between the West and East coasts, so I have stopped there.

I arrive there late one night in November and as I go up the front walk I see, through the curtains of the front room windows, my grandmother stalking across the living room like a skeleton in clothes. It shocks me so that I have to set down my luggage on the front walk and wait about five minutes before I can enter the house.

Only my grandmother has stayed up to receive me at this midnight hour, the others thinking that I had probably driven on through to New York, as I had so often before after promising to come home.

She makes light of her illness, and actually she manages to seem almost well for my benefit. She has kept a dinner plate on the stove for me over a double boiler and a low flame, and the living room fire is alive, and no reference is made to my failure in Hollywood, the humiliating termination of my six-months option as a screenwriter at MGM studios.

"Grand" says she's come here to help Edwina, my mother, who is suffering from nervous exhaustion and is very disturbed over Cornelius's behavior. Cornelius has been drinking heavily. Mother found five empty bottles under his bed and several more under the bathtub, and his position as sales manager of a branch of the International Shoe Company is in jeopardy due to a scandalous poker fight in which half of his left ear was bitten off, yes, actually bitten off, so that he had to go to a hospital and have a plastic-surgery operation, taking cartilage from a rib to be grafted onto the ear, and in spite of elaborate precautions to keep it under wraps, the story has come out. Mr. J., the head executive and my father's immediate superior, has at last lost all patience with my father, who may have to retire in order to avoid being dismissed. But otherwise everything is fine, she is telling me about these things because Edwina may be inclined to exaggerate the seriousness of the family situation when we talk in the morning. And now I ought to go up to bed after a long, hard trip. Yes, I ought to, indeed. I will have to sleep in brother Dakin's old room rather than in my usual retreat in the attic, since the bed in the attic has been dismantled so that I won't insist on sleeping up there and getting pneumonia.

I don't like the idea of taking Dakin's room since it adjoins my father's doorless appendage to it.

I enter the bedroom and undress in the dark.

Strange sounds come from my father's sunroom, great sighs and groans and inebriate exclamations of sorrow such as, "Oh, God, oh, God!" He is unaware of my sleepless presence in the room adjoining. From time to time, at half-hour intervals, he lurches and stumbles out of bed to fetch a bottle of whiskey from some place of naive concealment, remarking to himself, "How terrible!"

At last I take a sleeping pill so that my exhaustion can prevail over my tension and my curiously mixed feelings of disgust and pity for my father, Cornelius Coffin Williams, the Mississippi drummer, who was removed from the wild and free road and put behind a desk like a jungle animal put in a cage in a zoo.

At supper the following evening an awful domestic scene takes place.

My father is one of those drinkers who never stagger or stumble but turn savage with liquor, and this next evening after my homecoming he comes home late and drunk for supper. He sits at one end of the table, my mother at the other, and she fixes on him her look of silent suffering like a bird dog drawing a bead on a covey of quail in the bushes.

All at once he explodes into maniacal fury.

His shouting goes something like this: "What the hell, why the hell do you feel so sorry for yourself? I'm keeping your parents here, they're not paying board!"

The shout penetrates my grandfather's deafness and he says, "Rose, let's go to our room." But my grandmother Rose remains at the table as Edwina and Grandfather retire upstairs. I stay as if rooted or frozen to the dining-room chair, the food turning sick in my stomach.

Silence.

My father crouches over his plate, eating like a wild beast eats his kill in the jungle.

Then my grandmother's voice, quiet and gentle: "Cornelius, do you want us to pay board here?"

Silence again.

My father stops eating, though. He doesn't look up as he says in a hoarse, shaky voice: "No, I don't, Mrs. Dakin."

His inflamed blue eyes are suddenly filled with tears. He lurches up from the table and goes to the overstuffed chair in the living room.

This overstuffed chair, I don't remember just when we got it. I suspect it was in the furnished apartment that we took when we first came to Saint Louis. To take the apartment we had to buy the furniture that was in it, and through this circumstance we acquired a number of pieces of furniture that would be intriguing to set designers of films about lower-middle-class life. Some of these pieces have been gradually weeded out through successive changes of address, but my father was never willing to part with the overstuffed chair. It really doesn't look like it could be removed. It seems too fat to get through a doorway. Its color was originally blue, plain blue, but time has altered the blue to something sadder than blue, as if it had absorbed in its fabric and stuffing all the sorrows and anxieties of our family life and these emotions had become its stuffing and its pigmentation (if chairs can be said to have a pigmentation). It doesn't really seem like a chair, though. It seems more like a fat, silent person, not silent by choice but simply unable to speak because if it spoke it would not get through a sentence without bursting into a self-pitying wail.

Over this chair still stands another veteran piece of furniture, a floor lamp that must have come with it. It rises from its round metal base on the floor to half a foot higher than a tall man sitting. Then it curves over his head one of the most ludicrous things a man has ever sat under, a sort of Chinesey-looking silk lamp shade with a fringe about it, so that it suggests a weeping willow. Which is presumably weeping for the occupant of the chair.

I have never known whether Mother was afraid to deprive my father of his overstuffed chair and weeping-willow floor lamp or if it simply amused her to see him with them. There was a time, in her younger years, when she looked like a fairy-tale princess and had a sense of style that exceeded by far her power to indulge it. But now she's tired, she's about sixty now, and she lets things go. And the house is now filled not only with its original furnishings but with the things inherited from my grandparents' house in Memphis. In fact, the living room is so full of furniture that you have to be quite sober to move through it without a collision . . . and still there is the overstuffed chair.

A few days after the awful scene at the dinner table, my dearly loved grandmother, Rose Otte Dakin, bled to death in the house of my parents.

She had washed the dinner dishes, had played Chopin on the piano, which she'd brought with her from Memphis, and had started upstairs when she was overtaken by a fit of coughing and a lung hemorrhage that wouldn't stop.

She fought death for several hours, with almost no blood left in her body to fight with.

Being a coward, I wouldn't enter the room where this agony was occurring. I stood in the hall upstairs. My grandmother Rose was trying to deliver a message to my mother. She kept flinging out a wasted arm to point at a bureau.

It was not till several days after this death in the house that my mother found out the meaning of that gesture.

My grandmother was trying to tell my mother that all her savings were sewn up in a corset in a drawer of the bureau.

Late that night, when my grandmother had been removed to a mortuary, my father came home.

"Cornelius," said Mother, "I have lost my mother."

I saw him receive this announcement, and a look came over his face that was even more deeply stricken than that of my mother when she closed the eyelids of "Grand" after her last fight for breath.

He went to his overstuffed chair, under the weeping-willow floor lamp, like a man who has suddenly discovered the reality in a nightmare, and he said, over and over again, "How awful, oh, God, oh God, how awful!"

He was talking to himself.

At the time of my grandmother's death I had been for ten years more an irregular and reluctant visitor to the house than a member of the household. Sometimes my visits would last the better part of a year, sometimes, more usually, they would last no more than a week. But for three years after my years at college I was sentenced to confinement in this house and to hard labor in "The World's Largest Shoe Company" in which my father was also serving time, perhaps as unhappily as I was. We were serving time in quite different capacities. My father was the sales manager of that branch that manufactures, most notably, shoes and booties for kiddies, called "Red Goose Shoes," and never before and probably not to this day has "The World's Largest" had so gifted a manager of salesmen. As for me, I was officially a clerk-typist but what I actually did was everything that no one else wanted to do, and since the boss wanted me to quit, he and the straw boss made sure that I had these assignments. I was kept on my feet most of the time, charging back and forth between the office and the connecting warehouse of this world's largest wholesale shoe company, which gave me capable legs and a fast stride. The lowliest of my assigned duties was the one I liked most, dusting off the sample shoes in three brightly mirrored sample rooms each morning; dusting off the mirrors as well as the shoes in these rooms that were intended to dazzle the eyes of retailers from all over the States. I liked this job best because it was so private. It was performed before the retailers came in: I had the rooms and the mirrors to myself, dusting off the sample shoes with a chamois rag was something that I could do quickly and automatically, and the job kept me off the noisy floor of the office. I regretted that it took only about an hour, even when I was being most dreamily meticulous about it. That hour having been stretched to its fullest, I would have to take my desk in the office and type out great sheaves of factory orders. It was nearly all numerals, digits. I made many mistakes, but for an amusing reason I couldn't be fired. The head of the department had gotten his job through the influence of my father, which was still high at that time. I could commit the most appalling goofs and boners and still I couldn't be fired, however much I might long to be fired from this sixty-five-dollar-a-month position. I left my desk more often than anyone else. My branch of "The World's Largest" was on the top floor but I had discovered a flight of stairs to the roof of the twelve-story building and every half hour or so I would go up those stairs to have a cigarette, rather than retiring to the smelly men's room. From this roof I could look across the Mississippi River to the golden wheat fields of Illinois, and the air, especially in autumn, was bracingly above the smog of Saint Louis, so I used to linger up there for longer than a cigarette to reflect upon a poem or short story that I would finish that weekend.

I had several enemies in the office, especially the one called "The Straw Boss," a tall, mincing creature who had acquired the valuable trick of doing nasty things nicely. He was not at all bright, though. He didn't realize that I liked dusting the shoes and running the errands that took me out of "The World's Largest." And he always saw to it that the sample cases that I had to carry about ten blocks from "The World's Largest" to its largest buyer, which was J.C. Penney Company, were almost too heavy for a small man to carry. So did I build up my chest and slightly damage my arterial system, a damage that was soon to release me from my period of bondage. This didn't bother me, though. (I've thought a good deal about death but doubt that I've feared it very much, then or now.)

The thing I most want to tell you about is none of this, however; it is something much stranger. It is the ride downtown that my father and I would take every morning in his Studebaker. This was a long ride, it took about half an hour, and seemed much longer for neither my father nor I had anything to say to each other during the ride. I remember that I would compose one sentence to deliver to my father, to break just once the intolerable silence that existed between us, as intolerable to him, I suspect, as it was to me. I would start composing this one sentence during breakfast and I would usually deliver it half-way downtown. It was a shockingly uninteresting remark. It was delivered in a shockingly strained voice, a voice that sounded choked. It would be a comment on the traffic or the smog that enveloped the streets. The interesting thing about it was his tone of answer. He would answer the remark as if he understood how hard it was for me to make it. His answer would always be sad and gentle. "Yes, it's awful," he'd say. And he didn't say it as if it was a response to my remark. He would say it as if it referred to much larger matters than traffic or smog. And looking back on it, now, I feel that he understood my fear of him and forgave me for it, and wished there was some way to break the wall between us.

It would be false to say that he was ever outwardly kind to his fantastic older son, myself. But I suspect, now, that he knew that I was more of a Williams than a Dakin, and that I would be more and more like him as I grew older, and that he pitied me for it.

I often wonder many things about my father now, and understand things about him, such as his anger at life, so much like my own, now that I'm old as he was.

I wonder for instance, if he didn't hate and despise "The World's Largest Shoe Company" as much as I did. I wonder if he wouldn't have liked, as much as I did, to climb the stairs to the roof.

I understand that he knew that my mother had made me a sissy, but that I had a chance, bred in his blood and bone, to some day rise above it, as I had to and did.

His branch of "The World's Largest" was three floors down from the branch I worked for, and sometimes an errand would take me down to his branch.

He was always dictating letters in a voice you could hear from the elevator before the door of it opened.

It was a booming voice, delivered on his feet as he paced about his stenographer at the desk. Occupants of the elevator, hearing his voice, would smile at each other as they heard it booming out so fiercely.

Usually he would be dictating a letter to one of his salesmen, and not the kind of letter that would flatter or please them.

Somehow he dominated the office with his loud dictation. The letters would not be indulgent.

"Maybe you're eating fried chicken now," he'd boom out, "but I reckon you remember the days when we'd go around the corner for a cigarette for breakfast. Don't forget it. I don't. Those days can come back again . . ."

His boss, Mr. J., approved of C.C.'s letters, but had a soundproof glass enclosure built about his corner in "The World's Largest". . .

A psychiatrist once said to me, You will begin to forgive the world when you've forgiven your father.

I'm afraid it is true that my father taught me to hate, but I know that he didn't plan to, and, terrible as it is to know how to hate, and to hate, I have forgiven him for it and for a great deal else.

Sometimes I wonder if I have forgiven my mother for teaching me to expect more love from the world, more softness in it, than I could ever offer?

The best of my work, as well as the impulse to work, was a gift from the man in the overstuffed chair, and now I feel a very deep kinship to him. I almost feel as if I am sitting in the overstuffed chair where he sat, exiled from those I should love and those that ought to love me. For love I make characters in plays. To the world I give suspicion and resentment, mostly. I am not cold. I am never deliberately cruel. But after my morning's work, I have little to give but indifference to people. I try to excuse myself with the pretense that my work justifies this lack of caring much for almost everything else. Sometimes I crack through the emotional block. I touch, I embrace, I hold tight to a necessary companion. But the breakthrough is not long lasting. Morning returns, and only work matters again.

Now a bit more about my father whom I have come to know and understand so much better.

My mother couldn't forgive him. A few years after the years that I have annotated a little in this piece of writing, my mother became financially able to cut him out of her life, and cut him out she did. He had been in a hospital for recovery from a drunken spree. When he returned to the house, she refused to see him. My brother had returned from the latest war, and he would go back and forth between them, arranging a legal separation. I suspect it was not at all a thing that my father wanted. But once more he exhibited a gallantry in his nature that I had not then expected. He gave my mother the house and half of his stock in the International Shoe Company, although she was already well set up by my gift to her of half of my earnings from *The Glass Menagerie*. He acquiesced without protest to the terms of the separation, and then he went back to his native town of Knoxville, Tennessee, to live with his spinster sister, our Aunt Ella. Aunt Ella wasn't able to live with him, either, so after a while he moved into a hotel at a resort called Whittle Springs, close to Knoxville, and somehow or other he became involved with a widow from Toledo, Ohio, who became his late autumn love which lasted till the end of his life.

I've never seen this lady but I am grateful to her because she stuck with Dad through those last years.

Now and then, during those years, my brother would be called down to Knoxville to see Dad through an illness brought on by his drinking, and I think it was the Toledo Widow who would summon my brother.

My brother, Dakin, is more of a Puritan than I am, and so I think the fact that he never spoke harshly of the Toledo Widow is a remarkable compliment to her. All I gathered from his guarded references to this attachment between Dad and the Toledo Widow was that she made him a faithful drinking companion. Now and then they would fly down to Biloxi and Gulfport, Mississippi, where Dad and Mother had spent their honeymoon, and it was just after one of these returns to where he had been happy with Mother, and she with him that he had his final illness. I don't know what caused his death, if anything caused it but one last spree. The Toledo Widow was with him at the end, in a Knoxville hospital. The situation was delicate for Aunt Ella. She didn't approve of the widow and would only go to my father's deathbed when assured there would be no encounter between the widow and herself in the hospital room. She did pass by her once in the hospital corridor, but she made no disparaging comment on her when I flew down to Knoxville for the funeral of my father.

The funeral was an exceptionally beautiful service. My brother, Aunt Ella, and I sat in a small room set apart for the nearest of kin and listened and looked on while the service was performed.

Then we went out to "Old Gray," as they called the Knoxville Cemetery, and there we sat in a sort of tent with the front of it open, to witness the interment of the man of the overstuffed chair.

Behind us, on chairs in the open, was a very large congregation of more distant kinfolk and surviving friends of his youth, and somewhere among them was the Toledo Widow, I've heard.

After the interment, the kinfolk all came up to our little tent to offer condolences that were unmistakably meant.

The widow drove off in his car which he had bequeathed to her, her only bequest, and I've heard of her nothing more.

He left his modest remainder of stock in the International Shoe Company in three parts to his sister, and to his daughter, and to my brother, a bequest which brought them each a monthly income of a hundred dollars. He left me nothing because, as he had told Aunt Ella, it didn't seem likely that I would ever have need of inherited money.

I wonder if he knew, and I suspect that he did, that he had left me something far more important, which was his blood in my veins? And of course I wonder, too, if there wasn't more love than hate in his blood, however tortured it was.

Aunt Ella is gone now, too, but while I was in Knoxville for Dad's funeral, she showed me a newspaper photograph of him outside a movie house where a film of mine, *Baby Doll*, was being shown. Along with the photograph of my father was his comment on the picture.

What he said was: "I think it's a very fine picture and I'm proud of my son."

Tennessee Williams
c. 1960 (Published 1980)

Introduction

I

Thirty-seven years ago, to the day that I am writing this note, Tennessee Williams and I celebrated his thirty-seventh birthday in Rome, except that he said that it was his thirty-*fourth* birthday. Years later, when confronted with the fact that he had been born in 1911 not 1914, he said, serenely, "I do not choose to count as part of my life the three years that I spent working for a shoe company." Actually, he spent ten months not three years in the shoe company, and the reason that he had changed his birth date was to qualify for a play contest open to those twenty-five or under. No matter. I thought him very old in 1948. But I was twenty-two that spring of the *annus mirabilis* when my book *The City and the Pillar* was a bestseller and his play *A Streetcar Named Desire* was taking the world by storm; as it still does.

In 1973 Tennessee wrote a book called *Memoirs* (published 1975). He was not, as he was quick to warn us, at his best mentally or physically when he wrote the book, and though he purported to tell the story of his life, he chose, instead, to write about sexual adventures and glancing encounters with the great, ignoring entirely the art and inner life of one Tennessee (born Thomas Lanier) Williams. Fortunately, in "The Man in the Overstuffed Chair" (which I hope you have just read), he has given as dry and precise an account of his early life as we will ever have. Here he introduces most of the characters that he will continue to write about for the rest of his life. The introverted sister, Rose, on whom a lobotomy is performed, erasing her as a person. Whose fault? He blames their mother, Edwina, who gave the order for the lobotomy—on the best medical advice, or so she says. Then there is the hard-drinking, extroverted father, Cornelius, at odds with relentlessly genteel wife, sissy son, Tom, and daughter, Rose, who may or may not have accused him of making sexual advances to her, which he may or may not have made. There is the grandfather, Reverend Dakin, who gave to strangers all the money that he had put by for reasons not made clear (though Tennessee once told me that his grandfather had been blackmailed because of an encounter with a boy); and, finally, the grandmother, yet another Rose, known as Grand, the survivor, the generous, the non-questioning. The son, Tom, is shadowy here: after all, he is creator. But, as he has just told us, over the years his sympathy shifted from mother to father while he was never to be out of love with Rose or Rose. As you are about to see, he will spend a lifetime playing with the same vivid, ambiguous cards that life dealt him.

The stories are arranged in chronological order. The first was published (in *Weird Tales*, no less: a sister avenges her brother) when Tom was seventeen; the last was written when Tennessee was seventy-one. These stories are the true memoir of Tennessee Williams. Whatever happened to him, real or imagined, is here. Except for an occasional excursion into fantasy, he sticks close to life as he experienced or imagined it. No, he is not a great short story writer like Chekhov but he has something rather more rare than mere genius. He has a narrative tone of voice that is totally compelling. The only other American writer to have this gift was Mark Twain, a very different sort of writer (to overdo understatement); yet Hannibal, Missouri, is not all that far from Saint Louis, Missouri; and each was a comic genius. In any case, you cannot stop listening to either of these tellers no matter how tall or wild their tales.

Over the decades I watched Tennessee at work in Rome, Paris, Key West, New Haven. . . . He worked every morning on whatever was at hand. If there was no play to be finished or new dialogue to be sent round to the theater, he would open a drawer and take out the draft of a story already written and begin to rewrite it. I once caught him in the act of revising a short story that had just been published. "Why," I asked, "rewrite what's already in print?" He looked at me, vaguely; then said, "Well, obviously it's not finished." And went back to his typing.

Many of these stories were rewritten a dozen or more times, often over as many years. The first story that he ever showed me was "Rubio y Morena." I didn't like it (and still don't). So fix it, he said. He knew, of course, that there is no fixing someone else's story or life but he was curious to see what I would do. So I reversed backward-running sentences, removed repetitions, simplified the often ponderous images. I was rather proud of the result. He was deeply irritated. "What you have done is remove my *style*, which is all that I have." He was right.

It has been suggested that many of the stories are simply preliminary sketches for plays. The truth is more complicated. Like most natural writers, Tennessee could not possess his own life until he had written about it. This is common. But what is not common was the way that he went about not only recapturing lost time but then regaining it in a way that far surpassed the original experience. In the beginning, there would be, let us say, a sexual desire for someone. Consummated or not, the desire ("Something that is made to occupy a larger space than that which is afforded by the individual being") would produce reveries. In turn, the reveries would be written down as a story. But should the desire still remain unfulfilled, he would make a play of the story and then—and this is why he was so compulsive a working playwright—he would have the play produced so that he could, like God, rearrange his original experience into something that was no longer God's and unpossessable but *his.* The frantic lifelong desire for play-productions was not just ambition or a need to be busy, it was the only way that he ever had of being entirely alive. The sandy encounters with the dancer Kip on the beach at Provincetown and the dancer's later death ("an awful flower grew in his brain") instead of being forever lost were forever his (and ours) once translated to the stage where living men and women could act out his text and with their immediate flesh close, with art, the circle of desire. "For love I make characters in plays," he wrote; and did.

I called him the Glorious Bird. I had long since forgotten why until I reread the stories. The image of the bird is everywhere. The bird is flight, poetry, life. The bird is time, death: "'Have you ever seen the skeleton of a bird? If you have you will know how completely they are still flying. . . .'"

There are some things of a biographical nature that the reader should know. Much has been made of Tennessee's homosexual adventures (not least, alas, by himself); and, certainly, a sense of other-ness is crucial to his work. Whether a woman, Blanche, or a man, Brick, the characters that most intrigue him are outsiders, part of "that swarm of the fugitive kind." Although there is no such thing as a homosexual or a heterosexual person, there are, of course, homo- or heterosexual acts. Unhappily, it has suited the designers of the moral life of the American republic to pretend that there are indeed two teams, one evil and sick and dangerous, and one good and normal and—that word!—straight. This is further complicated by our society's enduring hatred of women, a legacy from the Old Testament, enriched, in due course, by St. Paul. As a result, it is an article of faith among simple folk that any man who performs a sexual act with another man is behaving just like a

woman—the fallen Eve—and so he is doubly evil. Tennessee was of a
time and place and class (lower middle class WASP, Southern airs-and-
graces division) that believed implicitly in this wacky division.

Thirty years ago I tried to explain to him that the only way that a
ruling class—any ruling class—can stay in power and get people to do
work that they don't want to do is to invent taboos, and then punish
those who break them while, best of all, creating an ongoing highly
exploitable sense of guilt in just about everyone. Sexual taboo has
always been a favorite with our rulers though, today, drugs look to be
even more promising, as alcohol was in 1919 when old-time religionists
prohibited it to all Americans. But Tennessee had been too thoroughly
damaged by the society that he was brought up in to ever suspect that
he had been, like almost everyone else, had. He thought he was wrong;
and *they* were right. He punished himself with hypochondria. Happily
and naturally, he went right on having sex; he also went right on
hating the "squares" or, as he puts it, in "Two On a Party," where Billy
(in life the poet Oliver Evans) and Cora (Marion Black Vacarro) cruise
sailors together: "It was a rare sort of moral anarchy, doubtless, that
held them together, a really fearful shared hatred of everything that was
restrictive and which they felt to be false in the society they lived in and
against the grain of which they continually operated. They did not
dislike what they called 'squares.' They loathed and despised them, and
for the best of reasons. Their existence was a never-ending contest
with the squares of the world, the squares who have such a virulent
rage at everything not in their book. . . ."

The squares had indeed victimized the Bird but by 1965, when he
came to write "The Knightly Quest," he had begun to see that the poor
squares' "virulent rage" is deliberately whipped up by the rulers in
order to distract them from such real problems as, in the sixties, the
Vietnam war and Watergate and Operation Armageddon then—and
now—underway. In this story, Tennessee moves Lyndon Johnson's
America into a near-future when it seems as if the world is about to
vanish in a shining cloud. In the process, the Bird now sees the squares
in a more compassionate light; he realizes that they have been equally
damaged and manipulated; and he writes an elegy to the true American, Don Quixote, now an exile in his own country. "His castles are
immaterial and his ways are endless and you do not have to look into
many American eyes to suddenly meet somewhere the beautiful grave
lunacy of his gaze. . . ." Also, Tennessee seems to be bringing into focus
at last the craziness of the society which had so wounded him. Was it

possible that he was *not* the evil creature portrayed by the press? Was it possible that *they* are wrong about everything? A lightbulb switches on: "All of which makes me suspect that back of the sun and way deep under our feet, at the earth's center, are not a couple of noble mysteries but a couple of joke books." Right on, Bird! It was a nice coincidence that just as Tennessee was going around the bend (pills and booze and a trip to the bin in 1969), the United States was doing the same. Suddenly the Bird and Uncle Sam met face to face in "The Knightly Quest." What a novel he might have made of this story! instead of that flawed play, *The Red Devil Battery Sign*. He was, finally, beginning to put the puzzle together.

Although Tennessee came to feel a degree of compassion for his persecutors, they never felt any for him. For thirty years he was regularly denounced as a sick, immoral, vicious fag. *Time* magazine, as usual, led the attack. From *The Glass Menagerie* up until *The Night of the Iguana*, each of his works was smeared in language that often bordered on madness. "Fetid swamp" was *Time* critic Louis Kronenberger's preferred phrase for Tennessee's mind and art. Then, in the fifties, the anti-fag brigade mounted a major offensive. Ironically, most of these brigadiers were Jews who used exactly the same language in denouncing the homosexual-ists that equally sick Christians use to denounce Jews. Tennessee turned to drink and pills, and then, worse, to witch doctors. One, a medical doctor, hooked him on amphetamines; another, a psychiatrist, tried to get him to give up writing and sex. Although the Bird survived witch doctors and envenomed press, they wore him out in the end.

II

"I cannot write any sort of story," said Tennessee to me, "unless there is at least one character in it for whom I have physical desire."

In story after story there are handsome young men, some uncouth like Stanley Kowalski; some couth like the violinist in "The Resemblance Between a Violin Case and a Coffin." Finally, when Tennessee wrote *A Streetcar Named Desire*, he inadvertently smashed one of our society's most powerful taboos. He showed the male not only as sexually attractive in the flesh but as an object for something never before entirely acknowledged, the lust of women. In the age of Calvin Klein's steaming hunks, it must be hard for those under forty to realize that there was ever a time when a man was nothing but a suit of clothes, a shirt and tie, shined leather shoes and a gray felt hat. If thought attractive, it was because he had a nice smile and a twinkle in his eye. Marlon Brando's appearance on stage, as Stanley, in a torn sweaty T-shirt, was an earthquake; and the male as sex object is still at our culture's center stage and will so remain until the likes of Boy George redress, as it were, the balance. Yet, ironically, Tennessee's auctorial sympathies were not with Stanley but with his "victim" Blanche.

Let us now clear up a misunderstanding about Tennessee and his work. Yes, he liked to have sex with men. No, he did not hate women, as the anti-fag brigade insists. Tennessee loved women, as any actress who has ever played one of his characters will testify. Certainly, he never ceased to love Rose and Rose. But that makes him even *worse*, the anti-fag brigade wail, as they move to their fall-back position. *He thinks he is a woman.* He puts himself, sick and vicious as he is, on the stage in drag; and then he travesties all good, normal, family-worshipping women and their supportive, mature men. But Tennessee never thought of himself as a woman. He was very much a man; he was also very much an artist. He could inhabit any gender; his sympathies, however, were almost always with those defeated by the squares or by time, once the sweet bird of youth is flown—or by death, "which has never been much in the way of completion."

Three relevant biographical details. Tennessee's first love affair was with a young dancer named Kip, in 1940. Kip gave up Tennessee for marriage, died of a brain tumor in 1944. Tennessee was at the death bed. This is the stuff of high romanticism or, as Tennessee quotes Elizabeth Barrett Browning in *Streetcar*, "'I shall but love thee better after death.'" He certainly carried if not a torch a showy flambeau for Kip to the end. Pancho was second; they met in New Orleans in 1946, the first year of Tennessee's success. They quarrelled; they parted in 1947. Tennessee was guilty, as he shows us in "Rubio y Morena." But, fearful of the ever-vigilant anti-fag brigade, he changed Pancho to a woman, something that he almost never did.

The third and most lasting affair was with Frank Merlo, an Italo-American prole. They began to live together in 1948. During Tennessee's great years, Frank was his anchor. But after drink and barbiturates altered Tennessee's character, they parted. A year or two later, in 1963, Merlo died of cancer. "I shall but love thee . . ."

The stories fall into four groups. First, those written up to 1941 when, at thirty, he became a professionally produced if unsuccessful playwright with *Battle of Angels*. The second period was from 1941 to 1945, when he became a hugely successful professional playwright with *The Glass Menagerie*. During this time he lived in Hollywood; worked for MGM; enjoyed "the wonderful rocking horse weather of California." Third, the great period, 1945 to 1952, when all the ideas for the plays were either in his head as stories—or on the stage itself. Fourth, the rest of his life when he wrote few stories; and play-productions became more and more difficult. To this period belongs "The Knightly Quest," one of his best stories. "I slept through the sixties, Gore," he said to me, in an exchange much quoted. "You didn't miss a thing," I am quoted as saying, which is true; but then I added, "If you slept through the sixties, God help you in the seventies." God did, to a point. He wrote a number of good stories; but then came the eighties—and death.

Tennessee's stories need no explication. So here they are. Some are marvelous—"Two On a Party," "Desire and the Black Masseur"; some are wonderfully crazed—"The Killer Chicken," "The Mysteries of the Joy Rio." So what are they *about*? Well, there used to be two streetcars in New Orleans. One was named *Desire* and the other was called *Cemeteries*. To get where you were going, you changed from the first to the second. In these stories and in those plays, Tennessee validated with his genius our common ticket of transfer.

Gore Vidal
26 March 1985
Rome

Collected Stories

The Vengeance of Nitocris

I. OSIRIS IS AVENGED

Hushed were the streets of many peopled Thebes. Those few who passed through them moved with the shadowy fleetness of bats near dawn, and bent their faces from the sky as if fearful of seeing what in their fancies might be hovering there. Weird, high-noted incantations of a wailing sound were audible through the barred doors. On corners groups of naked and bleeding priests cast themselves repeatedly and with loud cries upon the rough stones of the walks. Even dogs and cats and oxen seemed impressed by some strange menace and foreboding and cowered and slunk dejectedly. All Thebes was in dread. And indeed there was cause for their dread and for their wails of lamentation. A terrible sacrilege had been committed. In all the annals of Egypt none more monstrous was recorded.

Five days had the altar fires of the god of gods, Osiris, been left unburning. Even for one moment to allow darkness upon the altars of the god was considered by the priests to be a great offense against him. Whole years of dearth and famine had been known to result from such an offense. But now the altar fires had been deliberately extinguished, and left extinguished for five days. It was an unspeakable sacrilege.

Hourly there was expectancy of some great calamity to befall. Perhaps within the approaching night a mighty earthquake would shake the city to the ground, or a fire from heaven would sweep upon them, a hideous plague strike them or some monster from the desert, where wild and terrible monsters were said to dwell, would rush upon them and Osiris himself would rise up, as he had done before, and swallow all Egypt in his wrath. Surely some such dread catastrophe would befall them ere the week had passed. Unless—unless the sacrilege were avenged.

1

But how might it be avenged? That was the question high lords and priests debated. Pharaoh alone had committed the sacrilege. It was he, angered because the bridge, which he had spent five years in constructing so that one day he might cross the Nile in his chariot as he had once boasted that he would do, had been swept away by the rising waters. Raging with anger, he had flogged the priests from the temple. He had barred the temple doors and with his own breath had blown out the sacred candles. He had defiled the hallowed altars with the carcasses of beasts. Even, it was said in low, shocked whispers, in a mock ceremony of worship he had burned the carrion of a hyena, most abhorrent of all beasts to Osiris, upon the holy altar of gold, which even the most high of priests forbore to lay naked hands upon!

Surely, even though he be pharoah, ruler of all Egypt and holder of the golden eagle, he could not be permitted to commit such violent sacrileges without punishment from man. The god Osiris was waiting for them to inflict that punishment, and if they failed to do it, upon them would come a scourge from heaven.

Standing before the awed assembly of nobles, the high Kha Semblor made a gesture with his hands. A cry broke from those who watched. Sentence had been delivered. Death had been pronounced as doom for the pharaoh.

The heavy, barred, doors were shoved open. The crowd came out, and within an hour a well-organized mob passed through the streets of Thebes, directed for the palace of the pharaoh. Mob justice was to be done.

Within the resplendent portals of the palace the pharaoh, ruler of all Egypt, watched with tightened brow the orderly but menacing approach of the mob. He divined their intent. But was he not their pharaoh? He could contend with gods, so why should he fear mere dogs of men?

A woman clung to his stiffened arm. She was tall and as majestically handsome as he. A garb of linen, as brilliantly golden as the sun, entwined her body closely, closely, and bands of jet were around her throat and forehead. She was the fair and well-loved Nitocris; sister of the pharaoh.

"Brother, brother!" she cried; "light the fires! Pacify the dogs! They come to kill you."

Only more stern grew the look of the pharaoh. He thrust aside his pleading sister, and beckoned to the attendants.

"Open the doors"

Startled, trembling, the men obeyed.

The haughty lord of Egypt drew his sword from its sheath. He slashed the air with a stroke that would have severed stone. Out on the steep steps leading between tall, colored pillars to the doors of the palace he stepped. The people saw him. A howl rose from their lips.

"Light the fires!"

The figure of the pharaoh stood inflexible as rock. Superbly tall and muscular, his bare arms and limbs glittering like burnished copper in the light of the brilliant sun, his body erect and tense in his attitude of defiance, he looked indeed a mortal fit almost to challenge gods.

The mob, led by the black-robed priests and nobles who had arrived at the foot of the steps, now fell back before the stunning, magnificent defiance of their giant ruler. They felt like demons who had assailed the heavens and had been abashed and shamed by the mere sight of that which they had assailed. A hush fell over them. Their upraised arms faltered and sank down. A moment more and they would have fallen to their knees.

What happened then seemed nothing less than a miracle. In his triumph and exultation, the pharaoh had been careless of the crumbling edges of the steps. Centuries old, there were sections of these steps which were falling apart. Upon such a section had the gold-sandaled foot of the pharaoh descended, and it was not strong enough to sustain his great weight. With a scuttling sound it broke loose. A gasp came from the mob—the pharaoh was about to fall. He was palpitating, wavering in the air, fighting to retain his balance. He looked as if he were grappling with some monstrous, invisible snake, coiled about his gleaming body. A hoarse cry burst from his lips; his sword fell; and then his body thudded down the steps in a series of wild somersaults, and landed at the foot, sprawled out before the gasping mob. For a moment there was breathless silence. And then came the shout of a priest.

"A sign from the god!"

That vibrant cry seemed to restore the mob to all of its wolflike rage. They surged forward. The struggling body of the pharaoh was lifted up and torn to pieces by their clawing hands and weapons. Thus was the god Osiris avenged.

II. A PHARAOH IS AVENGED

A week later another large assembly of persons confronted the brilliant-pillared palace. This time they were there to acknowledge a ruler, not to slay one. The week before they had rended the pharaoh and now they were proclaiming his sister empress. Priests had declared that it was the will of the gods that she should succeed her brother. She was famously beautiful, pious, and wise. The people were not reluctant to accept her.

When she was borne down the steps of the palace in her rich litter after the elaborate ceremony of coronation had been concluded, she responded to the cheers of the multitude with a smile which could not have appeared more amicable and gracious. None might know from that smile upon her beautiful carmined lips that within her heart she was thinking, "These are the people who slew my brother. Ah, god Issus grant me power to avenge his death upon them!"

Not long after the beauteous Nitocris mounted the golden throne of Egypt, rumors were whispered of some vast, mysterious enterprise being conducted in secret. A large number of slaves were observed each dawn to embark upon barges and to be carried down the river to some unknown point, where they labored throughout the day, returning after dark. The slaves were Ethiopians, neither able to speak nor to understand the Egyptian language, and therefore no information could be gotten from them by the curious as to the object of their mysterious daily excursions. The general opinion though, was that the pious queen was having a great temple constructed to the gods and that when it was finished, enormous public banquets would be held within it before its dedication. She meant it to be a surprise gift to the priests who were ever desirous of some new place of worship and were dissatisfied with their old altars, which they said were defiled.

Throughout the winter the slaves repeated daily their excursions. Traffic of all kinds plying down the river was restricted for several miles to within forty yards of one shore. Any craft seen to disregard that restriction was set upon by a galley of armed men and pursued back into bounds. All that could be learned was that a prodigious temple or hall of some sort was in construction.

It was late in the spring when the excursions of the workmen were finally discontinued. Restrictions upon river traffic were withdrawn. The men who went eagerly to investigate the mysterious construction returned with tales of a magnificent new temple, surrounded by rich green, tropical verdure, situated near the bank of the river. It was temple to the god Osiris. It had been built by the queen probably that she might partly atone for the sacrilege of her brother and deliver him from some of the torture which he undoubtedly suffered. It was to be dedicated within the month by a great banquet. All the nobles and the high priests of Osiris, of which there were a tremendous number, were to be invited.

Never had the delighted priests been more extravagant in their praises of Queen Nitocris. When she passed through the streets in her open litter, bedazzling eyes by the glitter of her golden ornaments, the cries of the people were almost frantic in their exaltation of her.

True to the predictions of the gossipers, before the month had passed the banquet had been formally announced and to all the nobility and the priests of Osiris had been issued invitations to attend.

The day of the dedication, which was to be followed by the night of banqueting, was a gala holiday. At noon the guests of the empress formed a colorful assembly upon the bank of the river. Gayly draped barges floated at their moorings until preparations should be completed for the transportation of the guests to the temple. All anticipated a holiday of great merriment, and the lustful epicureans were warmed by visualizations of the delightful banquet of copious meats, fruits, luscious delicacies and other less innocent indulgences.

When the queen arrived, clamorous shouts rang deafeningly in her ears. She responded with charming smiles and gracious bows. The most discerning observer could not have detected anything but the greatest cordiality and kindliness reflected in her bearing toward those around her. No action, no fleeting expression upon her lovely face could have caused anyone to suspect anything except entire amicability in her feelings or her intentions. The rats, as they followed the Pied Piper of Hamelin through the streets, entranced by the notes of his magical pipe, could not have been less apprehensive of any great danger impending them than were the guests of the empress as they followed her in gayly draped barges, singing and laughing down the sun-glowing waters of the Nile.

The most vivid descriptions of those who had already seen the temple did not prepare the others for the spectacle of beauty and grandeur which it presented. Gasps of delight came from the priests. What a place in which to conduct their ceremonies! They began to feel that the sacrilege of the dead pharaoh was not, after all, to be so greatly regretted, since it was responsible for the building of this glorious new temple.

The columns were massive and painted with the greatest artistry. The temple itself was proportionately large. The center of it was unroofed. Above the entrance were carved the various symbols of the god Osiris, with splendid workmanship. The building was immensely big, and against the background of green foliage it presented a picture of almost breathtaking beauty. Ethiopian attendants stood on each side of the doorway, their shining black bodies ornamented with bands of brilliant gold. On the interior the guests were inspired to even greater wonderment. The walls were hung with magnificent painted tapestries. The altars were more beautifully and elaborately carved than any seen before. Aromatic powders were burning upon them and sending up veils of scented smoke. The sacramental vessels were of the most exquisite and costly metals. Golden coffers and urns were piled high with perfect fruits of all kinds.

Ah, yes—a splendid place for the making of sacrifices, gloated the staring priests.

Ah, yes indeed, agreed the queen Nitocris, smiling with half-crossed eyes, it was a splendid place for sacrifices—especially for the human sacrifice that had been planned. But all who observed that guileful smile interpreted it as gratification over the pleasure which her creation in honor of their god had brought to the priests of Osiris. Not the slightest shadow of portent was upon the hearts of the joyous guests.

The ceremony of dedication occupied the whole of the afternoon. And when it drew to its impressive conclusion, the large assembly, their nostrils quivering from the savory odor of the roasting meats, were fully ready and impatient for the banquet that awaited them. They gazed about them, observing that the whole building composed an unpartitioned amphitheater and wondering where might be the room of the banquet. However, when the concluding processional chant had been completed the queen summoned a number of burly slaves, and by several iron rings attached to its outer edge they lifted up a large slab of the flooring, disclosing to the astonished guests the fact that the scene of the banquet was to be an immense subterranean vault.

Such vaults were decidedly uncommon among the Egyptians. The idea of feasting in one was novel and appealing. Thrilled exclamations came from the eager, excited crowd and they pressed forward to gaze into the depths, now brightly illuminated. They saw a room beneath them almost as vast in size as the amphitheater in which they were standing. It was filled with banquet tables upon which were set the most delectable foods and rich, sparkling wines in an abundance that would satiate the banqueters of Bacchus. Luxurious, thick rugs covered the floors. Among the tables passed nymphlike maidens, and at one end of the room harpists and singers stood, making sublime music.

The air was cool with the dampness of under-earth, and it was made delightfully fragrant by the perfumes of burning spices and the savory odors of the feast. If it had been heaven itself which the crowd of the queen's guests now gazed down upon they would not have considered the vision disappointing. Perhaps even if they had known the hideous menace that lurked in those gay-draped walls beneath them, they would still have found the allurement of the banquet scene difficult to resist.

Decorum and reserve were almost completely forgotten in the swiftness of the guests' descent. The stairs were not wide enough to afford room for all those who rushed upon them, and some tumbled over, landing unhurt upon the thick carpets. The priests themselves forgot their customary dignity and aloofness when they looked upon the beauty of the maiden attendants.

Immediately all of the guests gathered around the banquet tables, and the next hour was occupied in gluttonous feasting. Wine was unlimited, and so was the thirst of the guests. Goblets were refilled as quickly as they were made empty by the capacious mouths of the drinkers. The songs and the laughter, the dancing and the wild frolicking grew less and less restrained until the banquet became a delirious orgy.

The queen alone, seated upon a cushioned dais from which she might overlook the whole room, remained aloof from the general hilarity. Her thick black brows twitched; her luminous black eyes shone strangely between their narrow painted lids. There was something peculiarly feline in the curl of her rich red lips. Now and again her eyes sought the section of wall to her left, where hung gorgeous braided tapestries from the east. But it seemed not the tapestries that she looked upon. Color would mount upon her brow and her slender fingers would dig still tighter into the cushions she reclined upon.

In her mind the queen Nitocris was seeing a ghastly picture. It was the picture of a room of orgy and feasting suddenly converted into a room of terror and horror, human beings one moment drunken and lustful, the next screaming in the seizure of sudden and awful death. If any of those present had been empowered to see also that picture of dire horror, they would have clambered wildly to make their escape. But none was so empowered.

With increasing wildness the banquet continued into the middle of the night. Some of the banqueters, disgustingly gluttonous, still gorged themselves at the greasy tables. Others lay in drunken stupor, or lolled amorously with the slave girls. But most of them, formed in a great irregular circle, skipped about the room in a barbaric, joy-mad dance, dragging and tripping each other in uncouth merriment and making the hall ring with their ceaseless shouts, laughter, and hoarse song.

When the hour had approached near to midnight, the queen, who had sat like one entranced, arose from the cushioned dais. One last intent survey she gave to the crowded room of banquet. It was a scene which she wished to imprint permanently upon her mind. Much pleasure might she derive in the future by recalling that picture, and then imagining what came afterward—stark, searing terror rushing in upon barbaric joy!

She stepped down from the dais and walked swiftly to the steps. Her departure made no impression upon the revelers. When she had arrived at the top of the stairs she looked down and observed that no one had marked her exit.

Around the walls of the temple, dim-lit and fantastic-looking at night, with the cool wind from the river sweeping through and bending the flames of the tall candelabra, stalwart guardsmen were standing at their posts, and when the gold cloaked figure of the queen arose from the aperture, they advanced toward her hurriedly. With a motion, she directed them to place the slab of rock in its tight-fitting sockets. With a swift, noiseless hoist and lowering, they obeyed the command. The queen bent down. There was no change in the boisterous sounds from below. Nothing was yet suspected.

Drawing the soft and shimmering folds of her cloak about her with fingers that trembled with eagerness, excitement and the intense emotion which she felt, the queen passed swiftly across the stone floor of the temple toward the open front through which the night wind swept, blowing her cloak in sheenful waves about her tall and graceful figure. The slaves followed after in silent file, well aware of the monstrous deed about to be executed and without reluctance to play their parts.

Down the steps of the palace into the moon-white night, passed the weird procession. Their way led them down an obviously secreted path through thick ranks of murmuring palms which in their low voices seemed to be whispering shocked remonstrances against what was about to be done. But in her stern purpose the queen was not susceptible to any dissuasion from god or man. Vengeance, strongest of passions, made her obdurate as stone.

Out upon a rough and apparently new-constructed stone pier the thin path led. Beneath, the cold, dark waters of the Nile surged silently by. Here the party came to a halt. Upon this stone pier would the object of their awful midnight errand be accomplished.

With a low-spoken word, the queen commanded her followers to hold back. With her own hand she would perform the act of vengeance.

In the foreground of the pier a number of fantastic, wandlike levers extended upward. Toward these the queen advanced, slowly and stiffly as an executioner mounts the steps of the scaffold. When she had come beside them, she grasped one up thrust bar, fiercely, as if it had been the throat of a hated antagonist. Then she lifted her face with a quick intake of breath toward the moon-lightened sky. This was to her a moment of supreme ecstasy. Grasped in her hand was an instrument which could release awful death upon those against whom she wished vengeance. Their lives were as securely in her grasp as was this bar of iron.

Slowly, lusting upon every triumph-filled second of this time of ecstasy, she turned her face down again to the formidable bar in her hand. Deliberately she drew it back to its limit. This was the lever that opened the wall in the banquet vault. It gave entrance to death. Only the other bar now intervened between the banqueters, probably still reveling undisturbed, and the dreadful fate which she had prepared for them. Upon this bar now her jeweled fingers clutched. Savagely this time she pulled it; then with the litheness of a tiger she sprang to the edge of the pier. She leaned over it and stared down into the inky rush of the river. A new sound she heard above the steady flow. It was the sound of waters suddenly diverted into a new channel—an eager, plunging sound. Down to the hall of revelry they were rushing—these savage waters—bringing terror and sudden death.

A cry of triumph, wild and terrible enough to make even the hearts of the brutish slaves turn cold, now broke from the lips of the queen. The pharaoh was avenged.

And even he must have considered his avenging adequate had he been able to witness it.

After the retiring of the queen, the banquet had gone on without interruption of gayety. None noticed her absence. None noticed the silent replacing of the stone in the socket. No premonition of disaster was felt. The musicians, having been informed beforehand of the intended event of the evening, had made their withdrawal before the queen. The slaves, whose lives were of little value to the queen, were as ignorant of what was to happen as were the guests themselves.

Not until the wall opened up, with a loud and startling crunch, did even those most inclined toward suspicion feel the slightest uneasiness. Then it was that a few noticed the slab to have been replaced, shutting them in. This discovery, communicated throughout the hall in a moment, seemed to instill a sudden fear in the hearts of all. Laughter did not cease, but the ring of dancers were distracted from their wild jubilee. They all turned toward the mysteriously opened wall and gazed into its black depths.

A hush fell over them. And then became audible the mounting sound of rushing water. A shriek rose from the throat of a woman. And then terror took possession of all within the room. Panic like the burst of flames flared into their hearts. Of one accord, they rushed upon the stair. And it, being purposely made frail, collapsed before the foremost of the wildly screaming mob had reached its summit. Turbulently they piled over the tables, filling the room with a hideous clamor. But rising above their screams was the shrill roar of the rushing water, and no sound could be more provoking of dread and terror. Somewhere in its circuitous route from the pier to the chamber of its reception it must have met with temporary blockade, for it was several minutes after the sound of it was first detected that the first spray of that death-bringing water leapt into the faces of the doomed occupants of the room.

With the ferocity of a lion springing into the arena of a Roman amphitheater to devour the gladiators set there for its delectation, the black water plunged in. Furiously it surged over the floor of the room, sweeping tables before it and sending its victims, now face to face with their harrowing doom, into a hysteria of terror. In a moment that icy, black water had risen to their knees, although the room was vast. Some fell instantly dead from the shock, or were trampled upon by the desperate rushing of the mob. Tables were clambered upon. Lamps and candles were extinguished. Brilliant light rapidly faded to twilight, and a ghastly dimness fell over the room as only the suspended lanterns remained lit. And what a scene of chaotic and hideous horror might a spectator have beheld! The gorgeous trumpery of banquet invaded by howling waters of death! Gayly dressed merrymakers caught suddenly in the grip of terror! Gasps and screams of the dying amid tumult and thickening dark!

What more horrible vengeance could Queen Nitocris have conceived than this banquet of death? Not Diablo himself could be capable of anything more fiendishly artistic. Here in the temple of Osiris those nobles and priests who had slain the pharaoh in expiation of his sacrilege against Osiris had now met their deaths. And it was in the waters of the Nile, material symbol of the god Osiris, that they had died. It was magnificent in its irony!

I would be content to end this story here if it were but a story. However, it is not merely a story, as you will have discerned before now if you have been a student of the history of Egypt. Queen Nitocris is not a fictitious personage. In the annals of ancient Egypt she is no inconspicuous figure. Principally responsible for her prominence is her monstrous revenge upon the slayers of her brother, the narration of which I have just concluded. Glad would I be to end this story here; for surely anything following must be in the nature of an anticlimax. However, being not a mere storyteller here, but having upon me also the responsibility of a historian, I feel obliged to continue the account to the point where it was left off by Herodotus, the great Greek historian. And therefore I add this postscript, anticlimax though it be.

The morning of the day after the massacre in the temple, the guests of the queen not having made their return, the citizens of Thebes began to glower with dark suspicions. Rumors came to them through divers channels that something of a most extraordinary and calamitous nature had occurred at the scene of the banquet during the night. Some had it that the temple had collapsed upon the revelers and all had been killed. However, this theory was speedily dispelled when a voyager from down the river reported having passed the temple in a perfectly firm condition but declared that he had seen no signs of life about the place—only the brightly canopied boats, drifting at their moorings.

Uneasiness steadily increased throughout the day. Sage persons recalled the great devotion of the queen toward her dead brother, and noted that the guests at the banquet of last night had been composed almost entirely of those who had participated in his slaying.

When in the evening the queen arrived in the city, pale, silent, and obviously nervous, threatening crowds blocked the path of her chariot, demanding roughly an explanation of the disappearance of her guests. Haughtily she ignored them and lashed forward the horses of her chariot, pushing aside the tight mass of people. Well she knew, however, that her life would be doomed as soon as they confirmed their suspicions. She resolved to meet her inevitable death in a way that befitted one of her rank, not at the filthy hands of a mob.

Therefore upon her entrance into the palace she ordered her slaves to fill instantly her boudoir with hot and smoking ashes. When this had been done, she went to the room, entered it, closed the door and locked it securely, and then flung herself down upon a couch in the center of the room. In a short time the scorching heat and the suffocating thick fumes of the smoke overpowered her. Only her beautiful dead body remained for the hands of the mob.

(Published 1928)

A Lady's Beaded Bag

Through the chill of a November evening a small man trudged down an alley, bearing upon his shoulders a huge, bulging sack. He moved with that uneasy, half-unconscious stealth characteristic of an old and weary mongrel who realizes that his life can be preserved from its enemies through wariness alone. The profession which he followed was not illegitimate; he had no need of fearing molestation from the enforcers of the law. And yet his manner seemed to indicate a sense of guilt and fear of detection. He kept close to the walls of the garages as though seeking concealment in their shadows. He skirted widely the circles of radiance cast by the occasional alley lights. Whenever he encountered another alleywalker he lowered his head without glancing at the other's face. He had none of the defiant hardness and boldness common among most of his kind. He was oppressed with an almost maniacal sense of lowliness and shame.

He had been a trash-picker for fifteen years. He had spent each day following an unvarying route through the alleys of the city's exclusive residential section, delving among the contents of ash-pits for old shoes, broken and rusted metal objects, and bundles of soiled and ragged cloth. The fruits of his scavangery he sold for a pittance to dealers who could make use of such rubbish. It would have been an intolerably drear and colorless occupation had he not been sustained through all of those fifteen years by the hope of some day discovering among the trash something of great worth accidentally thrown there. A diamond ring or pin, a watch, earrings—something for which he might receive hundreds of dollars, bringing the fulfillment of his beggar-dreams.

There had been times when his heart had been made to leap simply by the sharp glitter of a bit of broken glass or golden tinfoil, glimpsed

13

over the edge of an ash-pit. And though he had found nothing as yet of greater worth than the scraps of metal, leather, and cloth, hope had not died in him.

He had made it an inviolable rule always to complete his route. Therefore, though his sack was already packed to its capacity, he would not turn back this evening until he had traversed the last block of alley. With aching feet and back he trudged from pit to pit, stopping sometimes to exchange one piece of rubbish in his bag for another of slightly more value. He came at length to a pit whose contents were surmounted by a mauve-colored milliner's box, filled with a bundle of wrapping paper. He was prompted by some impulse to pull the box to the edge of the pit to look at it more closely. The sound of something heavy sliding beneath the bundled paper caught his attention. Removing the paper, he peered sharply into the interior of the box. He saw there one of those things for which he had been searching fifteen years. It was a lady's beaded bag.

For a moment greed was stronger than caution. With trembling fingers he seized the bag and started to lift it from its covert. But at that moment a door slammed and he quickly lifted the heel of an old shoe and pretended to examine it, while his heart hammered at his breast and his head swam with excitement. A lady's beaded bag!

The door slammed once more. He dropped the old heel, crouched closer against the pit. He reached once more into the interior of the box and found the beaded bag. He drew his fingers over its soft, cool surface with the lightness of a cautious Don Juan caressing a woman of whom he is not sure. Once more he scanned the vista of backyards before him to assure himself that he was unobserved; then with lightning speed removed the bag from the box and stuffed it into the pocket of his coat. It was done. The treasure was his.

With elaborately affected nonchalance he swung the sack over his shoulder and started slowly down the alley, betraying outwardly no sign that he had found in the pit anything of more importance than the milliner's box and the old heel that he had fingered. But in his pocket his hand was clasping the beaded bag—clasping it tightly, as though only through the cutting of the tiny cool beads into the hot flesh of his palm could he be made really to believe in its reality. With his fingers he found the opening of the bag. He squeezed them into its plushy interior. He could feel the coins and bills which it contained. It was fairly stuffed with them. Enchanting visions of the pleasures which this money could bring him passed kaleidoscopically before his eyes. He pictured himself clad in handsome clothes, dining upon delectable foods, enjoying for a while those luxuries and splendors of life of which he had yearningly dreamt for many years.

Before reaching the end of the alley he glanced once more behind him. And in the instant of that glance all of his rapturous dreams were shattered. Standing beside the ash-pit in which the bag had lain was a tall young man in the garb of a chauffeur. Their eyes met. And though the regard of the young chauffeur was perfectly casual, it brought panic to the trash-picker. He fancied that he could read in that regard a cold and stern accusation. The loss of the bag, he decided, must have been discovered; it had been traced to the ash-pit. The chauffeur had been sent by his mistress to retrieve it. In all probability, he knew that it had been taken by the trash-picker. He would notify the police. And the world of which the trash-picker had always been so insanely fearful would lay its cold, cruel hands upon him for having become a violater of its laws. The thought of that made him sick with terror; frantic as a small animal caught in a trap.

Of a sudden it occured to his distracted mind that he might still save himself by surrendering the bag to its owner. Without another thought he hastened out of the alley and around the corner. He followed the walk until he came before a handsome residence of gray stone which he identified as the one in whose ash-pit he had found the bag. Almost breathless with fear and awe, he scurried up its walk and steps to the grilled outer doors. He found the bell and gave it a brief ring. In a few moments the doors were opened up on a brightly lighted vestibule and he beheld hazily a young woman clad in an austerely cut uniform of black and white.

Barely raising his eyes to her face he lifted the bag, humbly as a priest would lift an offering to the altar of some wrathful god, and mumbled,

"I found this in the trash."

Looking at the bag, the maid recognized it as one belonging to her employer. She realized that it must have been thrown in the trash-pit with the milliner's box which she had removed from her employer's room that morning. She feared, however, that she might be dismissed for carelessness should she tell the true circumstances of its loss and recovery. Therefore, upon bringing the bag to her employer's bedroom, where she was dressing for a dinner engagement, she said,

"Mrs. Ferrabye, I found this lying on the piano."

Without turning from her dressing table at which she was arranging her hair, the woman replied,

"Put it in my drawer, Hilda."

A few minutes later a delivery man arrived with a belated package from a modiste's shop. The maid carried it up to her employer's room, laid it on the bed and gave her employer the bill. It amounted to several hundred dollars. The woman opened her beaded bag. She drew out that sum—practically all that the bag contained—and handed it to the maid. Then she lifted the lid of the box and raised from its tissue wrappings an evening wrap of diaphanous white material, sprinkled with glistening bits of metal. She held it beneath the light to survey it critically a moment; then dropped it upon the bed, marring the refined beauty of her face with a grimace of disgust.

"Honestly, I must have been out of my mind when I bought this thing. Why I could never dream of wearing anything so perfectly ridiculous."

Turning back to the mirror and beginning once more to smooth the golden coils of her hair, her momentary annoyance passed, and her face quickly resumed its former expression of smiling self-satisfaction.

(Published 1930)

Something by Tolstoi

I was dead tired and I felt myself a failure; the place looked like a quiet hole, in which a person could hide from a world which seemed all against him; and, finally, Brodzky wanted his son to go to college; there you have the reasons for my becoming a clerk in the bookshop. The morning I got the job I had been dazedly walking the streets for several hours. In the shop window that neatly printed sign, CLERK WANTED, caught my attention. I walked in and found the proprietor, a gaunt, Hebraic figure of a man, in the back of the shop, seated behind a huge desk piled with books. He looked me over shrewdly. What induced him to hire me is difficult to imagine. My face drawn and my body sagging with sleeplessness, I could hardly have been of a very prepossessing appearance. Perhaps something about me communicated to him the fact that I would work earnestly and faithfully in return for just the quiet and dusky security that his small bookshop had to offer.

At any rate, I got the job and found it very much what I had wanted. My life was dull, but its dullness was compensated, if compensation were needed, by the privilege of being witness to a drama that was no less rich, I am sure, than any contained in those thousands of volumes which crammed the bookshop's dusty shelves.

At that time, Brodzky's son was eighteen. He was the spiritual, contemplative type of young Russian Jew, with slender build, dark skin, delicate, aesthetic features. I never got to know him. No one could, for he was as reticent as a small wild animal—the sort of person it is utterly impossible to come within any companionable distance of. This story is about him—his father died two months after employing me.

17

Young Brodzky was terribly in love and the girl was a gentile. That was why old Mr. Brodzky wanted to get him off to college. Like most other Jews of his generation, he desperately opposed the marriage of his son with a gentile, and it looked as though the two, if, left alone, would inevitably drift into marriage. The boy was with her all the time. He was never with anyone else. They had grown up together; played all their childhood upon the same back fire escape; grown into each other, you might say.

They weren't at all alike. There was, of course, the ordinary racial difference—the difference of Gallic blood from Hebrew blood, which is almost like the difference of the sun from the moon. But there was more than that. There was a complete antithesis of temperaments. He was, as I have said, timid and spiritual and contemplative; she was something of a hoyden—full of animal spirits, life, and enthusiasm.

In spite of that, they had loved each other tremendously since childhood. He had been lonely, I guess, and she had been uncared for.

When I first saw her, she was a lovely-looking girl. Her body seemed a perfect expression of her spirit. It emanated brightness and warmth. But the loveliest thing about her was her voice. Often, in the evenings, she sang to him, and with such compelling charm that I could never help listening, whatever my occupation or thoughts.

Shortly after I had replaced young Brodzky as his father's clerk and the boy had been sent off to college, the old man fell ill. Mrs. Brodzky sent very quickly for her son, but before he had time to return, the branched candles were lighted, and the death chants were being sung in the family rooms above the shop. Mrs. Brodzky's will was not as strong as her husband's had been. The boy refused to go back to college, and in less than a month he and the girl were married and were living together in the upstairs rooms. Then began the tragic drama to which, for fifteen years, I was a spectator.

The conflict between their temperaments was immediately as obvious as their devotion to each other had been.

She had never had anything. It was probable that during her childhood she had often been in want of adequate food and clothing. She should have been satisfied enough, one would think, with her position as the wife of the owner of a fairly prosperous bookshop. But she was an inordinately energetic and ambitious little thing. She wanted more, much more, than the modest bookshop could give. She began urging her husband to sell it and get into some more lucrative business. She couldn't see how impossible that would be. Long as she had known him, she couldn't see that such a dreamy fellow as he could fit nowhere better than in a bookshop. He saw it plainly enough, however. Change was something that he dreaded. He loved the dusky security of that little shop—loved it as passionately as I had loved it. That was why, although we were not companionable, we had come to feel for each other a strong sympathy. We had the same abhorrence of those noisy streets that lay outside the bookshop door.

She kept after him relentlessly; gave him no peace; concentrated all of her immense energy in the struggle with him. But the boy found in his race heritage the strength to stand against her. And this is what happened after nearly a year. She met a vaudeville agent somehow. He discovered the loveliness of her voice and told her the possibilities it might have in the theatrical business. Told her a lot of things, I suppose, and at last bewitched her so completely with expectations that she determined to leave her husband.

I don't suppose I have made clear enough the way that the young fellow loved his wife. It was more than the usual uxoriousness of the Jew. His love for her was the core of his life. There is a great danger to such a love. When the loved one is lost, the life is lost. It crumbles to pieces. That is what happened to the life of young Brodzky when his wife went away with the vaudeville company.

I should describe to you the way she left him.

One morning, after having talked, I suppose, with the vaudeville agent she dashed into the shop and called to her husband, who was unpacking a new shipment of books. She had a wild, hysterical note in her voice, and she held one hand against her throat as though somebody had been choking her.

From the way that she spoke to him you would have thought they had been engaged in a violent quarrel. But it had come out of a clear sky—a sky, at least, that was no more than ordinarily clouded.

She said to him: "I have come to the end of my rope. I can't stand it here any longer. I've told you time and again, but it's no use. I've got a wonderful chance now—and I'm going to take it. I'm going to Europe with a vaudeville show."

The boy said nothing to her at first; he looked as though he had had all the life knocked out of him. He stared uncomprehendingly after her as she rushed up the stairs to their living rooms. Oddly, I recall that he was holding in his hands a red-bound book of which we sold several hundred copies that season, flippantly titled, *Idiots in Love*, and that, despite the real tragedy of the situation, I could hardly prevent a smile at the grotesque pertinence of that title to the dazed, helpless look on his face.

When she came down again he seemed to have come, at last, to understand what was happening.

"You are going away?" he asked dully.

She replied that she was. Then he reached in his pocket and handed her a heavy black key. It was the key to the front door of the shop.

"You had better keep this," he told her, still with complete quietness, "because you will want it some day. Your love is not so much less than mine that you can get away from it. You will come back sometime, and I will be waiting."

She clutched him by the shoulders, kissed him, and then, gasping sharply, ran out of the shop. From the dusky interior, we stood looking after her. Together, we stood looking into the street that we both abhorred and feared; the street, noisy with life and brilliant with sunlight, which seemed to exult maliciously in having swept into its busy stream all that was of any value to the man beside me.

During the months and the years that followed I was witness to a thing which seemed to me worse than death.

As I said, she had been the core of his life. When she was gone, he went to pieces. I thought at first that he would fall into a complete and violent madness. Distractedly he walked the crooked aisles among the bookshelves, moaning and rubbing his hands up and down the sides of his coat. Customers stared at him and hastened out of the shop. I tried to persuade him to remain upstairs. But he wouldn't. He could not stand it up there, I suppose; their living rooms were haunted by the memory of her. For several nights he stayed with me in the room which I occupied in the rear of the shop. He didn't sleep. He kept me awake with a constant muttering—words that were addressed to her. More than anything else, he would say, "You love me—sometime you are going to come back."

Seeing that he was not getting over it, I sent for his mother, who had gone to live with some relatives. She quieted him a little. And not long after that he took to reading.

He took to reading as another man might have taken to drink or to drugs. He read to escape from reality. And in the end his reading accomplished its purpose with a dreadful effectiveness.

Seated at the great desk near the back of the shop, he would read the whole of the day, until his eyes closed with weariness. His mother and I tried to rouse him, to get him to wait upon customers, unpack and arrange books, not because his help was needed but because we felt that he might be benefited by the occupation. He seemed willing to do what he could. But he had become as helpless and awkward as a baby. His constant reading fogged his consciousness, made him increasingly dull. The simplest questions put to him by customers puzzled him. He could not remember the titles of the books they asked for. He stared around him in a ridiculous, bewildered way, as though he had just come out of a deep sleep.

I had hoped—for I had come to feel for him a strong pity and sympathy—that this state would be only temporary. As months and years went by, however, it showed no sign of passing. He was apparently a lost man—a burnt-out candle. There was no hope for ever reviving him. Not unless she should return to him. And even in that case—even if she did come back—perhaps it would be too late.

Nearly fifteen years after she had left, to go abroad with the vaudeville company, the young Mrs. Brodzky returned to the bookshop. It was a mid-December evening; dark had fallen, but the people, shopping for Christmas, were still swarming upon the city walks. Their breath covered the window of the shop, I remember, with a glistening frost.

The shop was closed and all the lights extinguished except the bulb suspended over the desk in the rear, where Brodzky was reading. I was standing at the door, interested in the pageant of the passing people. A handsome chauffeured car drew up to the curb and a woman, wrapped in furs, emerged from its tonneau. A street lamp stood directly above the car, so that when the woman turned her head toward the shop, I knew instantly that it was she.

With an odd feeling of terror, I shrank away from the door, half hiding myself among the shadowy bookshelves. She approached the door, making her way eagerly through the swarm of shoppers. Apparently she was unchanged; in her face and the movements of her body, sharply illuminated by the street lamp, she was as intensely alive as before. Why had she come back, I wondered? Had her husband's prophecy been fulfilled and had she found, after fifteen years, that her love for him had been too strong to escape?

I was about to force myself, with an extreme reluctance, to step to the door and admit her, when a key sounded against the lock. She still had it—the key that he had given her that morning fifteen years before!

In a moment the door had swung open and she was standing within the dim-lit shop. I could hear her breath, coming sharply. She looked about her with glistening eyes, but somehow failed to see me as I crouched foolishly in a corner among the bookshelves. I could see that she was tremendously excited. She was clutching her throat with one gloved hand, just as she had done the morning that she left—as though somebody had been choking her.

In the fifteen years since she had left it, the place had changed little: so little, indeed, that it must have been extremely difficult for her to believe that those years had actually passed. They must suddenly have seemed altogether incredible, like a fantastic dream. The dimness, the queer shadows of the piled tables and shelves, the smell of the paper, the muted sound of the crowded street—it must have been over-whelmingly like those winter evenings, fifteen years before, when she had used to come down from their living rooms above to help him close shop.

She must have had the feeling of one stepping back, literally, into the past.

Pressing a tiny handkerchief against her lips, she seemed to be struggling to contain herself. Softly, she stepped forward. She must have seen, then, that he was seated at the desk. Only the top of his head was visible; the rest was concealed by a large book. His hair, thick and blue-black and uncombed, glistened brightly beneath the electric bulb. It occurred to me, with quickening horror, that she would find him physically almost unchanged. In those fifteen years he had not very perceptibly aged; he was too lifeless, it had seemed, to grow any older.

I told myself that I must step forward and prepare her for what she must discover. But something prevented me altogether from stirring from my hiding place among the bookshelves. I watched her as she slowly advanced to the desk and I seemed to feel the intensity of her emotion. It seemed to bore through me—unendurably.

I often wonder what she was thinking as she stood before the desk, looking down at the man whom she had loved passionately as her husband fifteen years before. She might well have been puzzled, by then, at the strange absorption with which he read, his consciousness apparently unpenetrated by the sound of her entrance and her footsteps, creaking noisily upon the ancient boards of the floor. Perhaps, however, she was too nearly filled with joy, and a kind of terror, to wonder about anything.

In a sharp, trembling voice she called his name: "Jacob."

With a jerk, he raised his head and stared in her direction with blinking, squinting eyes. Moments dragged by, excruciatingly slow, while I watched them staring at each other.

I had expected her to cry out and fling herself upon him; that, assuredly, would have been the natural thing for her to do. But the dullness, the total unrecognition in his eyes must have restrained her. What could she have been thinking? Did she suppose that he was deliberately refusing to recognize her? Or did she imagine that the fifteen years had altered her beyond his knowing her?

When I thought that the very air must snap with tenseness, he spoke.

He spoke to her, in that hollow, quavering voice that had become habitual to him, these words: "Do you want a book?"

She raised her gloved hand to her throat and uttered a slight gasp. I was glad that her back was toward me and that I couldn't see her face. The wracking moments dragged on, while those two continued to stare at each other. She must have come, at last, to some conclusion; she must have determined that the fifteen years had done so much more to her than to him that she was unrecognizable. At any rate, she seemed to gain possession of herself. Her figure relaxed somewhat and she lowered her hand from her throat.

"Do you want a book?" he repeated.

She stammered: "No—that is—I wanted a book, but I've forgotten the name of it."

Before those staring eyes she must have found it utterly impossible to say abruptly, "I am Lila. I have come back to you." She must have seized this pretense of having come for a book as a means of disclosing herself to him with a less awkward directness.

Seating herself upon a stool, close in front of the desk, she said,

"Let me tell you the story—perhaps you have read it and can give me the name of it. It is about a boy and a girl who had been constant companions since their childhood. They wanted to be together always. But the boy was a Jew and the girl was a gentile. And the boy's father was terribly opposed to his son marrying out of his own race. He sent the boy off to college. But a short time afterwards, the father died and the son returned and married the girl. They lived together in a few rooms over a small bookshop which had been left to the boy by his father. They would always have been exquisitely happy together except for one thing; the shop provided little more than a living and the girl was ambitious. She adored the boy—but her discontent grew on her and she was continually urging her husband to enter some more profitable business. But the boy was very different from the girl. He loved her so much that he would do anything for her—but he was incapable, somehow, of giving up the shop that had belonged to his parents. You see, the boy was a dreaming, sentimental, strange sort of Jew. And the girl could never quite see things from his angle. Her people—who had died and left her with a widowed aunt—had been French. She had inherited from them great vigor, practicality, and love of the world. After a time, she received an offer from a vaudeville agent to exercise her talent for music upon the stage. Blinded with the glittering prospect of a theatrical career, she decided to accept the proposition of the vaudeville agent. She returned to the bookshop and told her husband that she was going to leave him. He was too proud to make any effort to keep her, but he handed her a key to the shop and told her that she would be wanting it someday—and that he would always be waiting for her. That night she sailed for England with the vaudeville show. Upon a stage in London she had a huge success. She became a famous singer and traveled through all of the great countries of Europe. She lived a wild and a glamorous life, and for long periods she did not think at all of the dreaming Jew who had been her devoted husband, nor of the small, dusty bookshop where they had lived together. But the key to that bookshop, which her husband had given her the night that she left him, remained with her. She couldn't force herself, somehow, to relinquish it. The key seemed to cling to her, almost with a will of its own. It was an odd-looking key—old fashioned—heavy, and long and black. Her friends laughed at her for always carrying it with her and she laughed with them. But gradually she came to discover her reason for keeping it. The glamor of the new things with which she had filled her life began to fade and to thin, like a fog, and she could see—shining through them—the real and lasting beauty of the things that she had left behind. The memory of her husband and of their life together in the small bookshop came to her mind more and more vividly and hauntingly. At last she knew that she wanted to go back—she wanted to let herself into the bookshop with the key she had been keeping for fifteen years, and find her husband still waiting for her, as he had promised he would."

The woman had risen from the stool; her body was trembling and she was grasping the desk for support.

There are moments of stillness, stiflingly complete. When the woman spoke again there was a note of terror in her voice. She must have begun to realize what had happened—what had become of the man who had been her husband.

"You remember it—you must remember it—the story of Lila and Jacob?"

She was searching his face desperately, but there was nothing in it but bewilderment. He said at last:

"There is something familiar about the story. I think I have read it somewhere. It seems to me that it is something by Tolstoi."

From my covert among the bookshelves, I heard a sharp metallic sound that must have been the key dropping upon the floor. And then I heard her stumbling among the jumble of tables and shelves. She must have been hurrying, with a blind frenzy, to get out of the place. I shut my eyes—not daring to see her face and the horror that it must contain—until the door had closed behind her. When I opened them, the man in the back of the room had covered his face again with the large book and had resumed reading with his customary, dreadful quietness. His wife had come back to him and gone away again, and all was so fantastically the same that I might have believed what had occurred a dream, if I had not seen, lying upon the floor, the heavy black key to the bookshop.

1930–31 (*Not previously published*)

Big Black: A Mississippi Idyll

A gang of Negroes were laying a road south of Jackson, Mississippi. They were breaking rocks. Their picks clanged heavily, monotonously. A hot wind, sweeping at intervals like the spasmodic breath of some monster with a belly of fire, crouching upon the other side of the level cotton fields, brought swirls of yellow dust from the parched ground and groans and curses from the lips of the rock-breakers.

It was late afternoon. The white boss, a giant of an Irishman, wet and fiery red as if he had just been dipped into a tub of blood, had a brown jug of corn "likker" under a clump of weeds somewhere up the road. He had trudged up to it every hour or so during the long day, and now he had begun to stagger a bit; his cursing voice had gotten thick. He was after the men like a mad devil. They gave him no back talk. They kept their eyes away from him. They all knew that he had once burst a Negro's head open for calling him a name, and that he had gotten away with it.

Rhythmically, heavily, they heaved themselves up and down, nothing behind their picks, now, but the weight of their exhausted bodies. Song that usually sticks in the Negro throat as long, almost, as breath, had grown weak and sporadic. And for long periods there was nothing to be heard along the blistering road but the scuffling and thick cursing of the white boss, the murmur of the yellow-hot wind in the cotton, the clanging of the picks upon the rocks, as heavy and as monotonous as Time.

Then a thing happened which had happened often before, but which had nevertheless, an effect that was always startling. One of the men flung his pick violently upon the top of a pile of rocks. He tore his blue shirt open to the waist, laying bare the gleaming black arch of his chest.

He flung his muscular arms high above his up-thrust head and uttered a savage, booming cry.

"YOW-OW. YOW-OW-W-W."

There was a break in the clanging of the picks, even in the staggered cursing and parading of the white boss. This was a cry that could have been duplicated by no other throat. It was a huge, towering cry, beginning upon a deep growling note and veering flame-like into a ululating peak, high enough and sharp enough, it seemed, to split open the sky. A human cry? It seemed, rather, the voice of the flat and blistering land. It was elemental, epical, like a challenge and like a prayer flung at Life.

The clanging of the picks began again. The white boss continued his staggered cursing and parading. But that cry had penetrated and quickened the minds of the rock-breakers; it had shaken them from their torpor.

"Ole Big Black—there he goes agin!" they had said. They had looked at each other and grinned. The aching of their backs and arms, the soreness of their feet, were less acute. Their miseries seemed to have found expression in Big Black's vast utterance and to be accordingly relieved. In a few moments they had caught up a song.

Big Black was six feet and five inches tall. He was prodigiously, repulsively ugly. His great, round face was like that of the "nigger" in the revolving circle of wooden dummies at which baseballs are cast for Kewpie doll prizes at carnivals and amusement parks. His shoulders and his arms were gargantuan. He had, probably, more lifting, and pounding, and dragging power than any two men in the gang. He exulted in the use of that power. When he hoisted to his shoulder some great weight which the strongest of his fellow workmen could barely have raised from the ground, his eyes gleamed triumphantly, like those of a wrestler who has thrown an opponent. He worked feverishly. Work was Big Black's meat, said the men in the gang. And it was a good analogy, for Big Black gorged work as though he were famished for it— as though he could never get enough of it. When he had finished breaking his own pile of rocks, he would shove a neighboring workman roughly aside, and start in upon his. That was why the white boss, who never dared to curse the gigantic Negro, tolerated him in the gang.

And yet Big Black was not a popular character among the men of the gang. He was too strange, savage, inarticulate. He never joined in the

songs or bantering conversation. He never shot craps, told vastly Rabe-
laisian jokes, went into town on Saturdays to drink "likker" and visit a
woman. He never chased after the cotton-picking girls or told tall tales
when he was off the road, or lay with his belly in the hot-soft dust and
laughed with The Love of Life Returning After Toil. He was a black
beast that had taken grotesque human form and had no voice but that
terrible ululating cry . . .

It was quitting time now. "Quittin' Time!" the drunken red Irishman
bawled. He was lurching widely; he would sprawl into the shadowed
weedy ditch, now that it was quitting time, and there he would sleep
for several hours, grunting, still muttering curses, his blue shirt clinging black with sweat to his red barrel chest, flies settling upon his bare
throat, wet and bright red as blood, and upon his arms, red hams
covered with a fuzz of white-bleached hair.

When night came, showing that the coolness of a moon and stars
could still exist above the sun-tortured earth, he would slowly rouse
himself; he would vomit; after a while he would drag himself out of the
stinking, weedy ditch, go lurching down the road, beginning to sing. He
would retrieve the half-emptied jug from the clump of weeds, see that
it was securely corked, and then he would go on staggering, and
singing louder and more cheerfully, till he came to his Ford, parked
beside a fallen tree; cranking and cursing; then a wild spluttering; and
then back to town, singing, veering crazily upon the bumpy road,
shooting up clouds of dust in the white moonlight, thinking blithely of
the things that waited for him at home—a big Irish supper on a
checkered table cloth, a big Irish woman on a brass bed . . .

It was quitting time. The Negroes trudged over the flat dusty fields,
toward the row of cabins which housed them. They trudged wearily,
yet their voices were loud and mirthful. The Love of Life Returning
after Toil was in them. The scent of suppers seeped over the fields,
cotton-picking girls stood in the doorways, their hands on their hips,
their white teeth flashing. Snatches of song and laughter, as free as
birds, danced into the air. There was the rattling churn of a pump, the
joyous bark of hounds to returning masters, the mooing of a cow, the
frantic clucking of a hen seeking to evade its executioner, the blaze of
the day dying out, the white moon turning yellow. Banjos twanged
mellowly—tomorrow was Sunday—Life was forgiven its trespasses—
hugged close hot black bodies. Life—having its way . . .

Big Black did not go with them. There was no one waiting for him in the cabins. And it would be hotter in them than it was upon the road. There would be the stench of sweating bodies, sizzle of frying foods; too many people, too many voices, and none of them for him. He preferred to be by himself. A huge, black figure, a black beast in grotesque human form, he trudged down the road. Where was he going? He didn't know. He kept on down the road; he passed the white boss's Ford beside the fallen tree; he passed a rusted tin sign picturing a bottle of medicine, a cat killed by dogs lying in the ditch, an automobile tire worn smooth and white with frayed edges. He came at length to the wooden bridge that crossed the small river. Up a ways he saw a patch of wooded land upon the shore of the river. The sun hadn't fallen or lost its heat. His body was tired after its orgy of labor on the road. It would feel good lying in the shade—maybe he would bathe himself in the river. It was over half a mile to the clump of trees. But when he got there, the shade was good. He dropped to the ground among some bushes. He groaned, stretched himself, closed his burning eyes. He was too tired to bathe in the river—too tired . . .

His mind was about to sink into sleep when, not far distant, there came the sound of splashing in the river. He re-opened his eyes. He raised himself slightly, and peered between the bushes in the direction of the splashing. Through the tangled leaves and branches he caught a glimpse of white arms flashing above the brown surface of the water. He lifted himself quickly upon his hands and knees, quickly but silently. Like a great black animal, he crouched behind the bushes, peered at the naked girl bathing up there. The river was thickly interwoven with light and shade from the slowly sinking sun. He could see her for a moment; and then she was gone; and then she appeared again. He could see now an arm, now a shoulder, and now her face; once she dove into the shallow water and the fleeting glimpse of her white body curving sinuously above the dark brown stream, catching the sunlight like wet ivory, made him quiver. The mind behind those glistening animal eyes worked slowly, precisely. She was by herself. She was very young—not more than a child. She must have come from the poor white folks' camp on the other side of the river.

The feverish ache left Big Black's body. He felt cool and tense with excitement. He crawled, noiseless as a snake, through the tall grass, behind the thick screen of bushes, till he had come to a point alongside the bathing girl. Watching her from his bushy covert, his breath came so thick and so loud that he feared she might hear it. She was now standing near the opposite bank, only knee-deep in the stream. Her body was just ripening into womanhood; it was delicately beautiful. The low sun, shining through her hair wet by the stream, touched it with prismatic color. Her skin was gleaming white like the inner surface of a wet shell. Big Black devoured her with his eyes, clenched his fists, stiffened in every muscle, felt sick with desire of her.

"She will cross the river," he said to himself, "and then I will get her."

For several minutes she stood in the same position in the unshadowed patch of water, as though she were drinking into her body the dying warmth of the sun. Then she waded deeper into the river and started swimming slowly, gracefully toward the bank upon which Big Black was crouching.

He waited until she was within a foot of the shore; then he plunged through the bushes, dove over the low bank into the water. With his huge hand he throttled her first cry. For a few moments the feel of her wet, struggling body in his arms intoxicated him. He swayed back and forth, clasping her, and uttered low, guttural sounds like a hungry animal tearing at a fresh kill. Then of a sudden the ecstasy fell away from him. Horror replaced it. His eyes fastened upon his black hand clasping the white, terrified face of the girl. Its great spatulate fingers spread wide, gripping the white face, it looked like a hideous, huge black spider. It was ugly—ugly. The ugliness of it sickened him. Still clasping her writhing body, but now standing quite still, all of the desire gone out of him, he stared with fierce loathing at that black hand of his, and he muttered bitterly to himself,

"You big black devil! You big—black—devil!"

He raised the screaming girl high over his head, flung her into the middle of the stream. Then he scrambled madly up the bank and through the bushes. As he ran along, panting, stumbling, for all the world like some great hunted beast, he wondered dazedly what he should do. He couldn't return to the cabins. That evening, as soon as the girl had reported his assault, they would be scouring the country for him. He turned back to the river, dove over the low bank—there was a current in the middle—it bore him away—away . . .

A gang of Negroes were laying a road south of Savannah, Georgia. Their picks clanged upon the rocks, as heavy and monotonous as Time. The wind blew yellow swirls of dust, the men groaned and cursed. Among them was a black monster of a Negro. He was prodigiously big, prodigiously ugly. He worked with a fury, as though he could never get enough of it. They called him Big Black, the strongest, ugliest "nigger" that ever worked for a white man.

Big Black paused for a moment in his orgy of labor to spit upon the pile of rocks. He watched the brown stream of tobacco juice trickling over their white surface, the flies settling avidly upon it. It was ugly, ugly. And as he watched it, a picture flashed sickeningly into his mind of a black hand, like a huge and hideous spider, gripping the white face of a girl! Ugliness seizing upon Beauty—Beauty that never could be seized! . . .

Big Black tore his blue shirt open to the waist, arched his huge black chest, flung his sweating arms above his head, and uttered a savage, booming cry.

"Yow-Ow! YOW-OW-W!"

It began upon a deep growling note, veered flame-like into a ululating peak, high enough, and sharp enough, it seemed, to split open the sky. It was elemental, epical. It was like a prayer and like a challenge flung at Life.

There was a break in the clanging of the picks; wet ebon faces grinned at one another.

"There goes ole Big Black agin!"

In a few moments they had caught up a song.

1931–32 (Not previously published)

The Accent of a Coming Foot

She felt the eyes of the sisters appraising enviously her city clothes, the spring hat of dark blue straw trimmed with red cherries, the gaily printed crepe dress, the brand-new slippers of black suede with silk bows only slightly mud-flecked from the walk across town since she had walked so carefully, taking very huge or tiny steps to avoid the streaming cracks and puddles.

"I can't understand how Bud happened to miss you at the station," Mrs. Hamilton was still lamenting, "he left in plenty of time."

Catharine's lips were dry and she could feel them trembling. Every step of the long walk from the station had been like a relentless crank winding up inside of her some cruelly sharp steel spring whose release would certainly whirl her to pieces. But the release had not come. Bud wasn't waiting on the other side of any door in this house. There were only his mother and his sisters. So the spring had to go on winding itself still tighter till heaven knows what might happen.

"There was such a crowd," she exclaimed bravely, turning to Mrs. Hamilton, "and it was raining so hard that he probably couldn't see me!"

"Such a crowd?" Mrs. Hamilton repeated with justifiable wonder. Hers was not a spirit to accept implausible excuses, and at Mineola seldom more than three or four persons alighted from a single train.

"Well, not exactly a *crowd*," Catharine breathlessly admitted, "but you know how it is in the rain. Everyone looks just alike."

Cecilia cut in sarcastically: "Mother, do you suppose Bud mistook the Moulton's colored cook for Catharine? She's coming back from her cousin's funeral today . . ."

"Cecilia!" Mrs. Hamilton gasped. She turned apologetically to Catharine again. "Cecilia's always poking fun at Bud!"

As usual when visiting the Hamiltons, Catharine felt the necessity of sidestepping some kind of scene.

"Please don't scold him when he comes in," she begged, "because it wasn't his fault and I really enjoyed the walk. The air was so fresh and clean after that stuffy pullman, and the rain . . ."

The sound of a car churning up the road gave a quick tug at the steel spring in her chest. It wasn't Bud, though. The car whined listlessly by and the rain's brisk monody echoed again through the house, through all the dark, high-ceilinged rooms, like the laughter of ghosts.

"And the rain," she went on, glancing toward a streaming window, "has almost stopped."

"It's been raining for five days straight," Mrs. Hamilton remarked impressively.

Through the window Catharine could see the melting green shadow of leaves. There were trees all around the house. It was hidden among the trees. And Catharine felt that somewhere among their dripping greenness the boy must be hidden, too, peeking timidly now and then through the streaked windows, appraising like his sisters her new city clothes, the blue hat with the cherries, the dainty, mud-flecked slippers, but not daring yet to come into the house and welcome her home.

"Five days!" she repeated, "think of that!"

Her voice sounded much too loud, as voices sound in a fever, and she could hear the red cherries dancing vivaciously against the brim of her hat. She added hastily, in a calmer tone: "I thought it must have been raining an awfully long time. The branches were so wet that they hung right down over the walk, so that all the way up Elm Street I had to hold my hands in front of me to keep the leaves from brushing my hat."

"What a pity!" said Mrs. Hamilton, "Well, I told Bud . . ."

Turning heavily around, she spied Catharine's coat on the couch and snatched it up by the collar.

"Evelyn! The idea of putting Catharine's coat down there! It's all wet!"

Holding the coat gingerly before her, she went toward the back of the house with heavy, measured steps and Evelyn skipped shyly behind her. Catharine was left alone in the front hall with Cecilia. That would make it more difficult when Bud finally came in. Cecilia's air of cynical detachment was never any help in a crisis. It was hard to believe that she was really Bud's sister, this placid, housewifely girl bent over the hall grate with a box of matches.

"Our coal gave out in the middle of March and we haven't had the furnace going since. This will take the chill off a little."

Something was certainly needed to take the chill off, Catharine thought. There was nothing about this house that was calculated to warm a visitor's heart. It was uncompromisingly ugly. Its lean yellow shape spoke more palpably of age than its creaking timbers, and its interior, with high ceilings, tall stairways, suspended lamps, and angular furnishings, had a relentlessly vertical look as though one could never lie still in it for a moment but must climb ceaselessly toward some undiscovered summit of darkness. It was uglier and more Ibsenish than ever in the presence of April. It seemed to pucker its yellow face malevolently against the young green gesture of returning spring. Its walls groaned and its windows shrieked a loud denial to the playful wind, and through its dark rooms the echoing rain was transposed to such a dismal minor key that to Catharine it sounded like the sly laughter and whispering of ghosts.

The artificial logs in the grate had burst into blue flame.

"Would you like to go upstairs now, Kitty?" Cecilia asked. Cecilia, the older sister, had been Catharine's chum in the old days. She and Catharine and Bud had played together in the orchard back of the Hamilton's house. They had gone through school together, and after his own graduation from high school, Bud had waited a year for Catharine and Cecilia to graduate so that the three of them could go off to the state university together. Cecilia and Catharine had joined the same sorority, but Bud had failed to make a fraternity. He hadn't reacted at all well to college. It hadn't brought him out of his shell, as they had hoped it would, but had made him even shyer than before. He had sat in the back of his classrooms almost like a deaf-mute, mumbling that he didn't know when questions were asked and staring gloomily out of the window when tests were given with his pencil clasped tightly between unmoving fingers. His tall, loose figure had slipped about the campus with such a swift stealth that some of the students had humorously called him "the galloping ghost." He had dropped out of everything toward the end of the year and the next year he hadn't gone back. Thereafter Catharine had seen him only on vacations, and each time he had seemed shyer and quieter and more remote. He had seemed to be floating out upon the cold lake of his loneliness further and further from the friendly shore upon which she stood waving and calling his name. Each time she had somehow managed to wade out through the deepening waters to find him again and force her way through his pretended forgetfulness. "Oh, it's you!" he would seem to say. He would smile with whimsically puckering eyelids and the cold waters of the lake would recede and he would follow her with grateful sheepishness back to the shore of their old-time comradeship. And how delightful it had always been to so recapture their past: everything being warm and sweet between them again: their hands and even their lips being able to touch with the old-time ease! But now that she was returning from her year of work in the city she wondered if it would be at all possible to reach him again. Perhaps these cold waters had closed completely, this time, over his head.

She felt her throat getting tight with something—pity or longing or fear—as she answered Cecilia's question:

"No, let's stay down for a while. I don't want to miss Bud. He's bound to be back in a minute."

Cecilia put her arm around Catharine and led her into the parlor. She switched on the table lamp whose silver-fringed alabaster bowl gave a milky color to the gloom. Then she sank down on the ottoman beneath Catharine's straight-backed chair. Catharine felt suddenly at a loss for conversation. The two girls seemed strangely removed from each other now. Catharine had been in the city since their graduation last June. She was selling advertising space in a city newspaper, making a career for herself, while Cecilia remained in the small home town waiting for Robert, her fiancé, to get established in the grain business so that they could marry. Now that Catharine and the town were definitely severed by her father's death, over a year ago, she and Cecilia would probably see very little of each other, and the ten months of separation had already somewhat blunted their friendship. When they had gone upstairs and shared a bedroom, it would be easier, perhaps, for them to draw close together again, but now their eyes on each other's face went either too deep or too shallow and there was a touch of self-consciousness in the ultra-casual pose of their bodies. Catharine was anxious to remove it with friendly chatter. She talked for a while about her work in the city, but as she talked her head moved with such a nervous vivacity that the red cherries on her hat kept clinking brittlely together and she was unpleasantly reminded, for some reason, of a time in college when her coatsleeve had brushed against the arm of a human skeleton in the zoology lab: it had rattled like those cherries and she had glanced sharply up to see the death's-head staring straight in front of it with a fixed, grimly patient smile, as if to say: "Don't apologize! It was an accident, I'm sure! Besides, dear lady, we bones have learnt the vanity of pride . . ."

She turned quickly to Cecilia and asked: "How's Robert?"

"All right," Cecilia said listlessly. "The grain business is awfully bad right now. We may have to wait another whole year. Waiting gets to be a habit around this place. You just wait and wait for things to get started."

She laughed a little painfully, not looking at Catharine. Catharine touched the girl's dark hair. It was the only thing about Cecilia that reminded her of Bud.

"Time goes lots faster now that we're out of college!"

"Not for me," Cecilia answered. "It's just the same as it always was only you aren't here anymore. And Bud's got so funny. Really, I don't know what he's coming to. This is just exactly like him, Kitty!"

"What's like him?" Catharine asked.

"Why, not meeting you at the station. Going off somewhere by himself just like he was scared you'd bite him or something!"

"Scared of *me*?" Catharine laughed. "Oh, Cissy, that's absurd!"

But as she laughed Catharine caught herself glancing again through the muddy windows as though she expected to see Bud's face peeking faun-like between the quivering shafts of green vine.

"Bud was always like that," she added gently. "We mustn't expect him to change all at once."

"All at once?" Cecilia mocked. "He was twenty-three last month."

Catharine looked down at her hands, waiting tensely, when she heard the back door slam. But it wasn't Bud this time, either. It was Evelyn, lifting her shrill voice to declare that the butcher's truck had broken down. Then Catharine's eyes, beginning to focus again, observed that her black kid gloves were still on. She started drawing them slowly off, grateful for this small occupation, but alarmed to find that her bare fingers had turned so icy cold with suspense.

"If you had lived here in the house with that boy all this year . . ." Cecilia's voice shrank almost to a whisper, "I tell you, Kitty, you'd be down right *scared*! Most of the time he's up there in the attic by himself, pounding away on that old typewriter of his that he got from the junk shop, not even bothering to put on all his clothes, Kitty, just a sweat-shirt and a pair of old pants like he was training for a championship prizefight or something. . . . I tell you he doesn't act civilized anymore, Kitty! He shaves about once every week, he never combs his hair and it seems like Mother just has to *make* him take a bath! Can you imagine that?"

The steel spring in Catharine's chest was twisting itself once more upon the axles of an approaching car. Once more the car passed on by and the spring snapped back, and the rain momentarily seemed to follow the car down the road. The walls eased their complaint, and from the kitchen came sounds of Mrs. Hamilton preparing lunch. It was going to be round steak *en casserole*, the Hamiltons' company dish. She could tell by the smell of onions, already tickling dryly the back of her throat and making it hard to swallow.

"What is he working on now?" she asked Cecilia.

"Bud? God only knows!" Cecilia laughed shortly. "He has poetry published in the little magazines, you know, but they never pay him a cent for it!"

"Yes, I know," Catharine said gently. It was useless trying to explain to Cecilia that poetry wasn't a commodity, that it could never be bought or sold, that it was, in fact, untransferrable, remaining forever a part of the one who wrote it—the little black trail that his fugitive spirit left behind it on paper. . . . In the days when Bud had read poetry to them both in the orchard back of the Hamiltons' house, Cecilia had sometimes liked the sound of it, but would almost invariably ask them: *What does it mean?* And Bud and Catharine would look at each other and smile over Cecilia's puzzled head because they two had understood so perfectly: but couldn't tell!

"Why should a grown-up man write stuff like that anyway?" Cecilia went on. "It seems so silly in times like these, when people have to sink or swim, to go around with your head up in the clouds, scribbling down little things on paper that don't make sense!"

Catharine tried to laugh: "Maybe that's Bud's way of swimming. There are lots of different ways, you know, and Bud never was the typical man of action!"

"Man of action! My God, I should say he isn't! He does absolutely nothing about everything! Not even his rejection slips seem to bother him much: no more than being beaten at a game of solitaire would!"

"That's what it is: a game of solitaire!" Catharine suddenly cried out, lifting both hands to her face.

"What is?" asked Cecilia.

Catharine flushed: "Bud's kind of life, I guess!"

Cecilia relentlessy watched her deepening flush for several moments before she spoke.

"It seems such a lousy shame! You know what I mean, Kitty. The way we'd always hoped about you and Bud . . ."

Catharine tried to keep from trembling as Cecilia's hand closed with a merciless pity around her ankle.

"Hoped about us? That's silly! Bud and I were never anything but friends!"

"That's a fib!" Cecilia said softly. "All the time that we spent together when we were kids: do you think I was blind?"

Catharine held her eyes ironly against the sympathy in Cecilia's.

"That was a long time ago. We've all of us changed since then."

"It's a good thing that *you* have!" said Cecilia. "He's gotten to be *such* a fool! The craziest thing happened just last week. I found some of his stuff lying around the house. I was kidding him about it being so mushy and all. It made him terribly sore. He got up from the table and ran upstairs and he didn't write anything for a couple of days after that. Just sat in his bedroom, moping, till Mother sent for the doctor. She thought he was sick!"

Cecilia was laughing. She seemed to be expecting Catharine to laugh with her. But Catharine couldn't. She couldn't even smile.

"You shouldn't have done that, Cissy," she said in a tone that seemed absurdly severe. Cecilia's laughter and the smell of onions were getting too much. She had a funny feeling in her stomach. She was really fond of Cecilia. But she had to admit that the Hamiltons, all of them except Bud, were like that. Onions for company and laughter at the worst times. She wanted all at once to stand up and beat her fists against the old yellow boards of the house that were fraily forbidding the spring. She wanted to beat hard against them from the inside like April from the outside till the yellow boards splintered and tumbled down and she and Cecilia stood unsheltered in the leafy wetness outside. And then with no threshhold to push his timid feet across, Bud would surely be there. "Oh, it's you!" his half-averted smile would seem to say. And she would be standing only knee-deep in the cold waters of his loneliness. She would be able to wade out to him again and lead him back to the shore . . .

"Oh, my God, I wish he would come!" thought Catharine.

Didn't he know that she would make it very easy for him? Just as easy as she possibly could! Catharine knew how to make it easy for Bud. She'd had so much practice in the past. She had learned the wisdom of holding herself off at first. She wouldn't run up to him and try to kiss him before all the others. She wouldn't even hold out her hands unless he held his out first. She would lift her hands instead to the bright red cherries on her hat as if to signify by their color something of what she had to offer this time. But no other sign: nothing to frighten him off! She would even pretend to be earnestly brushing the mud-flecks from her slippers as he came thrusting himself desperately forward. She would glance in his direction for only one moment and simply call out very loudly, very brightly, *"Hello, Bud!"* And then she would go on talking to the others as though the year hadn't passed, as though nothing at all had passed between this morning and those times when two young girls and a boy had eaten picnic lunches in the orchard back of the old yellow house; when the boy had read poetry to the girls or lay on his back talking quietly to himself or to her or to the trees, which seemed never to move quite softly enough to keep from jarring the drowsily delicate flow of his voice; when he had driven them, after their lunch had settled, down to the river, where the two girls and the boy had undressed behind separate bushes for a swim and stretched themselves afterwards on a stone-smooth log to get dry . . .

As though nothing had passed since then? Well, nothing *had* passed, really! The book had been closed for a while, but the place marked plainly . . .

"I'll make it very easy for him," she promised herself. "He won't be afraid!"

But the house was now filled with little noises, any one of which might betray his stealthy return. Sudden-soft closing of doors. Footsteps moving along the upper halls. Now slow and now hurried. Footsteps on the stair. Too heavy for Bud and too loud. He always moved his large body with an amazing penury of sound. In her mind's eye she could see him now, moving through a thousand different rooms and places, as she had seen him in the past years, and he moved always like a tall, vague shadow, one hand stretched slightly before him like the feeling hand of the blind, suspicious even of air, groping for things unseen in the path or halfway poised for some defensive gesture as one would move through regions of perilous dark, his eyes very wide but always seeming ready to blink against the full light.

"He's coming *now!*" Catharine suddenly whispered.

The steel spring in her chest had coiled to its quivering limit as she heard, through the gusty rain, the faint slamming of a car door just outside the house. It was slammed twice. He always had to slam it a couple of times to make it stay shut . . .

She jumped to her feet. She was ready in spirit to be quite casual and gay. To be calm because it was necessary for her to be so. But just as suddenly her breath was gone, gone utterly, and it was now her turn, it seemed, to know all of what he had known: the agony of feet coming toward one and of a door thrown open!

"He is coming *now!*" she whispered, half to Cecilia and half to herself.

"What did you say?" Cecilia asked sharply. She was just coming back from the kitchen where the casserole had commenced to burn.

"Nothing!" Catharine gasped, "Only I heard . . ." She stopped, not being quite ready to pin herself down.

"Oh dear, it's started raining harder again," said Cecilia. "Why don't you sit down?"

"Be composed!" thought Catharine. "He's coming now!"

She reached deep into her bones for something that was solid. But now her bones were hollowed out by the running waters of fear. She knew that she couldn't wait for him any longer. The spring had coiled itself too tight this time. She wouldn't be able to bear the intolerable moment of his birth in her presence again. That moment would pass, of course, and afterwards she would be able to hold the precious new life it had given her to an unburdened bosom and breath could go on. But she hadn't the strength for it now. Whatever fortitude her soul had once contained was now gone . . .

She pushed herself up from the chair's clutching cavity.

"I think I shall have to go up for a moment," she gasped.

But Cecilia hadn't heard those coming sounds through the rain. She got lazily up from the ottoman on which she had sunk. She switched out the milky fringed lamp and the parlor was left to the rain's green darkness again.

"Come on up with me!" Catharine called.

She had already fled to the hall and started up the tall steps toward the haven of darkness above.

"Come on, Cecilia! *Please*, come on!" she called again, glancing behind her in terror.

But already she saw Bud's tall shadow drawn against the streaming oval glass of the door. She felt herself impaled like a butterfly upon the semi-darkness of the staircase. She could move neither up nor down and her knees seemed ready to sink.

"Come on!" she called faintly.

Bud's shadow had crouched a little toward the keyhole which rasped now with the small noise a mouse first makes in the night when he comes to your room.

"Come on!" she called despairingly once more to Cecilia. But her voice had shrunk to a whisper and Cecilia, gliding lazily into the hall, had now also caught Bud's shadow drawn against the wet pane and now also stood stock still, hands raised to her hips in the beginning of a sisterly gesture of reproach.

"Here he is *now*!" she called loudly, "Oh, *Bud* . . ."

The door swept all the way open and banged against the hatrack. And there he stood, dripping with rain, his tousled head bare, his shoulders hunched, his face lifted intuitively toward the dark staircase. And all that Catharine could see of him plainly was his eyes: arrow-bright: unable to move from her own till some sign set them free, eyes like a possum's glaring at night from a torch-lit tree with the hounds and the men forming their fatal circle around it.

His hand lifted slightly before him. He made a guttural sound in his throat. He seemed about to start forward . . .

And still Catharine couldn't move from the middle steps of the staircase. She couldn't speak the gay words of greeting nor touch the red cherries that trembled on her hat's brim. She stood with her head held stiffly, like a haughty old dame glaring down the straight line of her nose at some impertinent intruder. Her mind knew only the hard round shape of the banisters and the palpable blaze of his eyes. The moment gathered intensity. Still neither moved. Then it ended with a noiseless splintering like a tree lightning-struck seen falling through a storm. Bud bowed slightly from the waist as though this house were a bathroom which he had inadvertently entered at the wrong moment, finding Catharine there unclothed or in an unfortunate pose. He bowed slightly, stiffly, and with averted eyes he backed noiselessly out of the door and closed it behind him . . .

"*Well, of all things!*" gasped Cecilia.

But Catharine was already flying up the rest of the stairs, her heart beating like a captured bird against the very top of her throat. She plunged into the misty white bedroom and flung herself down on the bed, crying terribly, achingly, knowing that she could never find him again.

And now the rain washed softly against the yellow walls of the house, rather apologetically explaining to all who might listen within that there was no deliberate malice in life: that there was in life only a vast obliviousness, a tranquil self-absorption which boded neither evil nor good for those who lived.

You could almost hear it saying: "Observe our hands, and their gestures, limitless, yes, they are that, timeless, yes, they are that, but whatever they do, it is without thinking or knowing, and so what help can they give you?"

March 1935 (Not previously published)

Twenty-seven Wagons Full of Cotton

It was late in the afternoon. The gin stands were pumping and the pneumatic pipes still sucking. A fine lint of cotton was floating through the sunny air, across the tired gray road and the fields of copper-topped Johnson grass, grown nearly waist-high, and onto the porch where Mrs. Jake Meighan and her guest from the syndicate plantation were seated on the swing. Fifteen wagon-loads of cotton had already been seeded and were being sent on to the compress, a few miles further up the road toward the little Arkansas town, but there was nearly the same number still to go in the slowly creeping line between the scale-house and the portico of the ginnery. It would be an hour or two after dark, ginning at his maximum rate of three or four bales an hour, before Jake Meighan could get through with the syndicate's first September picking.

These twenty-seven wagons full of cotton were a big but not a totally unexpected piece of business for Jake. The syndicate usually did their own ginning. In fact their plant was larger and better equipped than Jake's. It was not fireproof, however, and when Jake, sitting on his porch last night, saw a flickering red glare on the southern horizon he mysteriously remarked to his wife that it looked like he might be doing a pretty big piece of business tomorrow. He was not mistaken.

Mrs. Meighan was now doing her level best to entertain the plantation manager while his cotton was being ginned. But the heat had done something to her head. She had lost the stimulating effect of several cokes drunk during the long, blazing afternoon and now she felt utterly numb.

"You're beautiful," the syndicate man remarked to Mrs. Meighan.

"Naw, I ain't," she objected lazily, "I'm too big."

"I say you're beautiful," he insisted. "I like big women."

Out of the corner of her eye Mrs. Meighan could see him licking his lips and looking down at her body. The look in his eyes shocked her a little. But not unpleasantly.

Feeling a bit faint, she brushed the fuzz of cotton lint from her moist cheeks and leaned back in the swing which she kept lazily in motion with the lopsided heels of her white kid slippers. Her legs were bare. They had been shaved not so long ago but now they needed shaving again. The sweat trickled deviously between the stubbles of dark hair down the bulging calves and lumpy ankles and splashed into little pools underneath the swing. A swarm of flies was buzzing around her. The little man from the syndicate plantation kept brushing them off with his riding crop. Sometimes he struck her bare legs so smartly that it left a small red mark.

"Quit that switching me!" the woman finally protested.

"I'm just shooin' the flies off," said the man.

"Leave 'em be. They don't hurt nothin'."

As a matter of fact she rather liked the tickling sensation that the flies made walking up her legs. She also liked the flicking of the little man's whip when he didn't swing it too hard. Altogether she was rather comfortable. But she wished that she hadn't finished up that case of cokes. She felt so terribly lazy and tired.

"Cotton, cotton," she muttered. "I feel like a big lump of cotton m'self!"

Her eyelids fluttered dreamily shut. But she could feel, it seemed, through the very pores of her skin what the little man's eyes were doing. She felt their desire trickling over her huge body as warm and liquid as her own trickling sweat. It had a pleasant, soporific effect. It was like stretching herself out and relaxing all her muscles in a tub of tingling warm water.

The little man nudged her with his elbow.

"You're tired," he whispered insinuatingly.

"Sure I'm tired," she whimpered. "That damned thing over there'd make anybody tired."

"You oughta lie down," the little man whispered.

She felt her lips curving up in a foolish smile. She tried to force them back down but it was like trying to smash a drop of quicksilver beneath your thumb. She guessed it must be the heat that was getting her like this. It certainly couldn't be anything else. She never had liked little men, especially when they acted fresh. And this little man from the syndicate plantation was hardly more than half her size. Why it would be just the same as . . .

A picture so ludicrous entered her mind that she chuckled out loud.

"You oughta lie down," the little man whispered again.

"You gettin' fresh?" she asked with attempted severity. But the laughter bubbled irresistibly up from her throat. She felt the soft multiple convexities of her chin shaking with it.

"Aw, I know you big women!"

"What makes you rub it in so much about me bein' big? You think I don't know it? Jake says that I'm the biggest woman in this part of the state!"

"I never seen one bigger," said the syndicate man.

"You're a shrimp, that's what *you* are. You're no bigger than a flea."

The man laughed.

"You're no bigger than an elephant. And even elephants have fleas."

The woman could not help laughing too. The laughter spluttered uncontrollably up from her throat like water gone down the wrong way.

"Ticklish?" the man asked.

"Cut it out!" she screamed.

The man drew back his hand and glanced nervously across the field.

"Hell! You don't need to holler!"

He gave the floor a savage kick with the heel of his boot. The accelerated motion of the swing sagged her tremendous shoulders toward him. Her fat arm slid against his bony elbow. She let it rest there a moment. The little man's arm, bare below the rolled sleeve, was hairy and dark as a monkey's. It burned with a sharp animal heat into her flesh. It stung her almost painfully. And now his fingers were edging up the side of her thigh . . .

I oughtn't to let him touch me like that, she thought. But she was too lazy to move. . . . And what difference did it make.

"Hell's fire but you're big!" the man grunted.

She was too tired to say anything this time. She felt her lips falling open and the saliva accumulating thickly inside her mouth.

The man picked up one of her limp hands from her lap and uncurled the helpless pink fingers. With a calloused, stub-nailed fingertip he traced the lines of her palm.

"You're gonna meet a little man who likes you an awful lot. You're gonna set on the porch swing with him while your husban' is ginnin' out his twenty-seven wagons full of cotton. Then you're gonna get tired. You're gonna take the little man inside your house. You're gonna fall for the little man like a ton of bricks . . ."

He started laughing again and so did she.

"Don't it say nothin' about me smackin' a little man for gettin' too fresh?" she laughed.

The woman looked vaguely out across the country. The miles of white cotton, voraciously sucking the life from the soil, seemed to have left it desiccated and dull as an old woman at whose bosom children have sucked again and again and on whose body men have lain till her breasts hang dry as locust pods in the summer wind and her emaciated limbs are crumpled beneath her swollen belly. The woman herself was not like the country but like the cotton. She had grown big upon the land. Like the cotton, too, she had reached her September season. She was full and bursting with ripeness . . .

The sweat trickled down from her forehead, beaded her lashes and entered her eyes. Everything was shifting and swimming before her like images in a wind-rippled pool. She sank back into a voluptuous passivity, feeling only the afternoon's limpid heat and the fingers of the little man pressed almost painfully against her throbbing pulse. He had dropped her palm and now he was trying to circle her sweating wrist with his fingers. He couldn't quite squeeze them around it.

"Ummm! Ummm!" he grunted. "You *are* big!"

"So's America," she answered foolishly.

"Who said anything about America? Did I say anything about America? Hell with America! You're bigger'n the whole southern hemisphere!"

"Quit that!" she whimpered shrilly.

The little man had started twisting her wrist. Now he laughed and struck her smartly with the riding crop.

"You play too rough!" she groaned.

Again she leaned back weakly, feeling the slow drip and tickle of his desire over her mountains of sweating flesh. He leaned closer and she felt his hot breath on her neck. What is he going to do next, she wondered. The skittish muscles of her stomach drew tight as, with two fingers, he plucked a bit of cotton lint from the corner of her mouth. His hand cascaded leisurely down the front of her dress and came to rest on her lap.

"You sure are big!" the man muttered.

She stole a glance at him from the corner of her barely opened eye and saw his lips drawn back and the tip of his tongue caught between his teeth. She shut her eyes again with a deep, luxurious sigh.

"Yes, I'm pretty big," she admitted, "but I guess you like big women."

"Never had no use f'r them small ones," he said.

Her bosom rocked with helpless laughter. What's the matter with me, she wondered. I guess it must be the heat.

"Ticklish? *Ticklish?*"

With a frantic squeal she threw herself away from him and clutched hard at the swing's iron chains to pull herself up to her feet. The brilliant afternoon sunlight swam dizzily in her eyes. She nearly slumped down again on the swing, her body had grown so feeble. But she shoved herself desperately forward. Her feet dragged slowly across the creaking floor.

"Where you goin'?" the man asked sharply. He had also gotten up from the swing. She looked anxiously back at him. Her eyes were so dim with drowsiness and with the oily lint of cotton that she could barely distinguish the outlines of his figure.

"Stay where you are!" she commanded. But her voice sounded indistinct and fuzzy as it did when she was drunk.

"Where you goin'?" he repeated, this time with a slightly menacing tone.

"In," she said.

"What f'r?"

Slowly she looked out over the coppery fields of Johnson grass, across the tired road and at the hazily shifting outlines of the spidergray ginnery. Its steady throbbing sounded in her ears as her own blood sounded against the pillow at night and she felt as though she were upon the verge of falling asleep. If she called out very loudly, at the top of her voice, perhaps her husband or some of the negroes would hear . . .

But she was barely able to open her mouth. Much less utter a cry.

"What you goin' in f'r?" the little man demanded still more sharply.

She shuffled forward a few steps more and leaned exhausted against the screen door. She heard his footsteps advancing but she could see nothing but the watery brilliance of the sun. She turned her great body toward him like a huge, clumsy animal making a last stand against some lighter and more dexterous foe. He stood only a few inches away from her now and he was playfully flicking her with the riding crop. Flicking her playfully across the legs. It didn't hurt her much. But as her eyes focused a little more clearly on the man's dark face she had a fantastic notion that he was planning to beat her severely with the whip. She felt that he was planning to force her into the house where he would give her a terrible beating . . .

"You stay outside! Hear me?" she gasped.

The man said nothing. He just smiled and flicked her slightly harder with the riding crop. Already her muscles were flinching beneath an expected flagellation and her lips were trembling upon the verge of tears.

"I'm just goin' in t' make a li'l lemonade," she whimpered. "You stay out here on the porch, now, an' watch them ginnin' out your cotton."

"I'll go in, too," he said firmly. "I'll squeeze the lemons."

He came forward another step, raised his knee and thrust it against her side. She leaned hard against him a moment, refusing to be pushed inside the door which he had drawn open. Then the riding crop swished through the blindingly brilliant air and came down sharply this time across her flank.

"Get on in there!" the little man hissed. "Get on inside the door!"

She felt the hot tears coming into her eyes and constricting her throat. All the resistance flowed out of her flesh like water and she allowed herself to be propelled by the tip of the riding crop through the door and into the darkness of the hall. She heard the screen drawn shut and the latch fastened.

"It'll be night," the little man whispered, "before they git through."

She retreated further into the dark hall, a tremendous, sobbing Persephone, and leaned against the bedroom door as if to conceal it. She felt his hand sliding past her and heard it twisting the knob and the bedroom door coming open. She tottered backwards a step, thrust herself frantically forward and hung onto the little man's shoulders.

"Oh, my God, it's so hot!" she whimpered, her whole body seeming to melt into a helpless mass. "Please, for God's sake," she whimpered, "don't hurt me!"

1935 (Published 1936)

Sand

The old woman lies awake listening to the sound of his breathing. Night after night it is the same. She cannot sleep for listening to that hoarse, painful rasp. Whenever the sound is interrupted she lies tense, waiting, while the excruciating moments gather upon her own nearly motionless chest like weights of iron. Then slowly or quite suddenly the sound of it recommences. He has not stopped breathing. He has awakened for a few minutes only and then gone back to sleep.

"Thank God!" she breathes. "Thank God!"

During the day she listens, too. While in the kitchen she has always one ear cocked toward the front room where he is reading. She listens for the periodic crinkling of the turned pages and the knock of the pipe bowl against the tray.

These sounds reassure her and she breathes more freely.

She calls him: "Emiel, Emiel, it is time for your drops!"

He comes lumbering back to the kitchen. His feet shuffle clumsily and there is a vague look in his bloodshot eyes. His right leg is slightly stiffened from the stroke. His mind is no longer very alert. His vest is always spotted with grease. He slobbers when he eats. Water dribbles down his chin when he drinks. Often she must speak to him twice before he seems to understand. He sits brooding a great deal. He lies on the couch by the radio and hears nothing. The music is wasted. The comedians, the amateurs, the news-reporters, and the symphony orchestras are all wasted on his ears. He is thinking about his sickness. His face is already like the face of a dead man, gray and expressionless.

"Emiel, Emiel!" she calls to him.

He gets up slowly from the couch or the chair and stares vaguely around him. Sighs or grunts. She brings him the glass of water tinted pink with the five drops. He takes it without a word and drains it. A

49

pink trickle goes down his gray-stubbled chin and spots his vest. She comes close to him. Purses her lips. Makes a soft, purring sound. Touches his chin with the tip of her handkerchief. Brushes the wet spot off his vest. Pats him fondly on the pink and silver dome of his head or runs her fingers tremulously down his slack unshaven jowls.

"Emiel!" she murmurs sadly.

He sinks back onto the couch and she tucks the Indian blanket around him. It is the red and black Navajo blanket that they bought nearly fifty years ago on their honeymoon trip to the West Coast. She remembers how frightened she was, or pretended to be, of the grim-looking Indians gathered around the station platform, how she squealed with delight over the turquoise bracelet and then with terror when the gesticulating grunting squaws formed a greedy circle around her, pushing things into her face. She remembers how Emiel's arm went around her and his fingers kept spasmodically pressing into her side till she became almost faint. She could hardly walk back to the train.

The radio goes on. A political candidate is making a speech. His voice booms out dramatically. He declares that this is a crisis in the affairs of the nation. Vital issues are at stake. But here in the warm interior of their living room neither of them is listening to the statesman's words. Night surrounds them. Black squares of it press against the curtained windows. They are alone. They are sitting close together. There are only the two of them in this lamp-lit interior. They look as though they were posing for a picture. In a minute the camera will click and the cameraman will say "All right" and they will both smile and start moving again.

But now they are waiting.

At ten-thirty she helps him up from the chair or the couch and they go into the bedroom. He bends to remove his slippers.

"No, Emiel, let me," she whispers.

Her hands are amazingly swift and gentle, but ugly to look at, the veins knotted like earthworms under the purplish red skin.

"There now, you old grouch!" she whispers.

Her eyes peer teasingly up at him from under the tangle of frowzy gray hair and he catches a glimpse of a fleeting brightness in them which is the ghost of her youth, appearing with a shy, furtive quickness, as though shamefully aware of its own incongruity, and fluttering quickly off, like a songbird that momentarily rested on a frozen branch, casting a single startled glance at the glittering, icily uncordial season that surrounds it and then receding instantly back into that dim but secure dimension from which it had but for that one moment miraculously appeared.

While he undresses she goes into the kitchen and prepares him a cup of warm milk.

"Emiel, Emiel!" she calls.

He comes shuffling heavily into the kitchen. His felt slippers whisper sadly along the black and white checked linoleum. The loose boards creak. They make small half-hearted complaints beneath the old man's tottering weight. He sinks down in the kitchen chair. He stares for a moment enquiringly at the icebox and the gas range as though they had asked him a question which he had not quite understood.

"Emiel, your milk," she says.

He doesn't seem to see. She lifts it herself to his lips. He sucks it slowly in. Grunts. Her dish towel is barely quick enough to catch the white trickle.

"Emiel," she murmurs sadly.

His mind is not very clear any more. She wonders sometimes if he is really aware of what he is doing. Does he know what she is saying to him? She talks a great deal. Silence seems heavy these days. It is no longer a natural thing as it used to be before he suffered the stroke. Now silence is waiting and waiting is a continual dread.

When the light is out she begins to think again. The thoughts swarm mercilessly into her mind and she murmurs aloud. Sometimes it is the seashore again and he is lying beside her on the warm sand. The bright grains of it are sliding from his palm and trickling over her bare legs and arms. This memory has a remarkable life. It is the most vivid of them all. She hears the sound of waves coming in and her eyes close slowly against the glitter of sun. Prismatic colors flash through her tangled lashes. She hears his voice slow and caressing as the grains of trickling sand. Rose. Rose. Rose. Rose. He is trying to make her smile. But she will not smile. She keeps her lips drawn tightly together. The sand trickles slowly. Then more swiftly. Then slower. It is warm, so very warm against her bare skin. In spite of herself her lips begin to curl up at the corners. She laughs out loud. The earth rises and sways beneath her. Her body grows large. Immense. The moment is timeless.

It forms a perfect arc through space. She whispers his name. Then holds her breath. Yes. He is still beside her. But the warm sand no longer slides from his palm. The glittering sun is lost. It is dark. She turns slowly upon the bed, her eyes closed. If she stretches out her fingers she can touch the sheet that covers him. Yes. She can hear him breathing. Still breathing. The hoarse dragging sound goes wearily on. A tired, heavy thing crawling painfully forward. Desperately pushing and pulling itself still further along. When will it stop? She shudders. No, it must not. Never. Such a thing could not happen to her . . .

And then one day she hears a heavy thud. She drops the soup ladle. She stands motionless by the kitchen stove. There is much to assure her that nothing had happened. The casual ticking of the white enamel clock. The throaty murmur of boiling carrots. The buzzing of an early summer fly blue-winged against shining copper screens. And sunlight on geranium leaves. She forces her fingers to lift the soup ladle again. She holds it rigidly poised like a weapon, her eyes blindly staring. In a moment she will hear the slow crinkling of the newspaper or the clank of the pipe bowl against the glass tray. She waits for these. Still there is nothing. Something inside of her congeals. Grows hard and cold as a rock. She staggers forward. No use to delay. She sets the dripping ladle down upon the cloth-covered table and goes straight forward to the living-room door and pushes it open . . .

"Emiel!" she whispers. She is too breathless to say more than that.

He is standing by the round oak table. It was not him, it was only a large book that fell to the floor.

"I was looking at it. I dropped it," he explains.

It is an album of postcard pictures of places that they have visited together on vacations in younger days. There are pictures of Niagara Falls and Yellowstone Park and Canada and Florida and the Great Smoky Mountains. They started it nearly fifty years ago when they took their honeymoon trip to the West Coast. Since then they have been steadily adding to it, almost each summer when they could afford to leave town, and it is now a large book full of pictures.

Slowly Emiel bends to pick it up.

"No, no," she cries, "let me!"

She darts over to where the fallen book lies. Some of the pictures have spilled out. Her red fingers scoop them quickly up from the carpet. She lifts the book painfully and replaces it upon the table. They face each other. He returns her gaze vaguely. Saliva dribbles from the corners of his mouth. His lips are quivering. How moist his eyes are!

"Emiel, oh, Emiel!"

She flings her arms passionately around him. Draws him close against her shrivelled bosom. In that embrace she must hold him forever. Time must not take him from her. Let the rest slide away like sand. She will have to keep this!

"Emiel!" she speaks commandingly. She will show him that she still has strength enough for them both.

But he will not look in her eyes that have all this force to give him. He turns evasively away from her with those shuffling movements. And her own firmness cracks. It gives way completely and she goes shuffling uncertainly as he does across the room to catch again at his sleeve no longer commanding with a false show of power but only barrenly pleading for something to share.

"What is it, Emiel? Let me know!"

She has followed him into a corner. He doesn't attempt to turn around and escape her. He just stands there avoiding her look till her light touch drops from his sleeve, and then he murmurs—"I was just thinking. That's all."

April 1936 (Not previously published)

Ten Minute Stop

The man whom he went to see in Chicago was not in town.

"He's gone on a lake cruise," said his secretary, "and won't be back till the latter part of the month."

Luke couldn't believe that the man was really gone.

"But I wrote him that I was coming and he promised to see me. It's very important. *Terribly* important. It's about a job. You see, he knows a cousin of mine and my cousin . . . "

"He'll return about the twenty-third of the month," the girl interrupted. "See him then."

She swung crisply back to the machine, her face like a door slamming shut against his.

He felt indignant and couldn't curb his tongue.

"What the hell does that boss of yours think I am? I haven't got money enough to chase him back and forth across the country. Spent my last cent, nearly, making this trip up here to see him and God only knows . . . "

She gripped the phone.

"Shall I call the watchman—or will you get out?"

He took the evening bus back to Memphis. Rented a pillow for fifteen cents because the thought of another sleepless night actually terrified him. He didn't feel like himself. He felt as though the thread of his identity had snapped and he was moving on with nothing at all left behind him.

The bus was a long time loading. Beginning to feel panicky, he clasped the pillow under his arm and darted out of the Blueflyer over to the station drugstore where he purchased a pint of whiskey. Came back with the bottle stuffed in the pillow, hoping that he wouldn't get

54

hungry on the way home. He had thirty cents left. He sat on the back seat. It extended clear across the back of the bus so that if nobody else occupied it he would be able to stretch himself out. But a young Negro came and sat down close beside him. Then a woman with a baby, Italians, and by the smell of the paper boxes which she spread across the remaining vacant space he judged them to be transcontinental travelers. Redolent of soft bananas and unwashed diapers. It was stiflingly close, the bus not yet started. The young Negro looked at him and grinned. He tried to grin back but his lips were stiff. This alarmed him still more. Not even able to crack a smile!

Defiantly he took the bottle out of the pillow and drank.

"Lucky!" murmured the Negro, rolling his eyes at the ceiling.

Luke offered him a drink. Was afterwards sorry, as the Negro waxed voluble. Showed Luke his taped knuckles. Knocked a white boy out last night in the fourth round.

"Did better," remarked Luke, "than Joe Louis."

Which started the Negro off on what promised to be interminable.

"How far you going?" Luke cut in.

"Champaign. That's where I live."

"How far's that?"

"'Bout hundred fifty mile."

Well, from then on, thought Luke, maybe I'll get some sleep.

He started dozing, however, before they were clear of the city. It was a restless, enervating sleep. He woke up at intervals of every fifteen or twenty minutes. Opened his eyes to find the bus moving each time through dusk a few shades deeper, till finally it was quite dark and they were out of the city and only dark, level fields were sliding past with an occasional yellow light of a farmhouse. Voices droned ahead of him. The young Negro committed himself as earnestly to sleep as to battle, snoring upon a long, rasping note, his shoulders swaying rhythmically against Luke's, his bandaged hand dangling between his legs. Luke regarded him with admiration and envy. The Negro represented, he thought, something splendid and heroic. Something that made life possible under any circumstances. A kind of impregnable simplicity. A completeness. An undividedness. The boxer sleeps, thought Luke. An exact statement. Said all that was necessary to say. Luke glanced at the Negro and seemed to see his life in graphic design. A strong black line pushing stubbornly forward without a curve. Beside it, his own life, a wavering thread of gray. Not even that anymore. The thread broken. Lost in space that stretched terrifyingly about him.

The bus lurched. The baby woke up and whined a little and the mother comforted it in a low voice.

Luke took another long drink and drifted back into sleep.

It seemed endless. He could stay neither asleep nor awake. Being completely wakeful would be better than this intermittent dozing, this constant jarring out of sleep and back into it. His brain felt stunned. He wanted to think. There were things that he needed to think out before the bus reached Memphis. But couldn't.

Then suddenly the lights flared up and he found that the bus had stopped moving. It was standing in the business section of a small city. The Negro pugilist had gotten up and was lifting his suitcase down from the rack. The woman with the baby had already disappeared.

"What's this place?" Luke inquired sleepily of the Negro grinning down at him.

"This here's Champaign," the Negro yelled jubilantly as he swung the suitcase to his shoulder. "Home for me, but for you, just a ten minute stop."

"Good luck," said Luke.

"Same to you, boy!" sang the Negro.

The dozing passengers stirred fretfully. Luke glanced at the now completely vacant back seat. All the boxes gone. He hardly dared to trust in the miracle of their removal.

Then he got to his feet and stumbled out of the bus.

On the street it seemed much cooler. There was a freshness in the air. Must have been raining lately. Yes, there were puddles of rainwater in the street and the lighted windows of the café were still streaming. Looked pretty from the outside, the lights and the moving forms diffused. He opened the screen door. Inside electric fans were droning. In the rear a Brunswick Selecter being played. Nasal tenor inquiring if it was true what they said about Dixie. Luke grinned to himself. Do they really flog women down there? But the tune was light and infectious. It shocked him a little out of his daze. The place was full of young fellows. In one corner they were playing a game, shooting marbles into little sockets. Others were seated about a porcelain-topped table drinking beer. Champaign was a college town. Champaign and Urbana. University of Illinois. These must be summer students. He remembered his own college days a few years back and felt a nostalgic pang. Grinned ironically to himself. Sat down at the counter but could think of nothing that he wanted. Just as well. Thirty cents and all the next day.

"Glass of milk," he ordered finally in a low voice. Perhaps it would help him to get some real sleep now that he had that whole back seat to himself.

When he'd finished drinking the milk he went back outside. Next to the café was a small open lot containing lighted billboards. He sat on a low wooden fence and stared at a poster advertising a coming show. Jane Barlow and Stark Navle in *Sacramento*. Navle's head glittered darkly like the back of a cockroach. Nevertheless it was a nice-looking sign. The colors were bright but not glaring. Like the dresses that girls wear to summer dances, it had an air of pleasing insouciance which said in effect the the world is like this—*very gay*!

Somewhere in the wet grass a cricket began chirping.

A young couple strolled by. He heard their low voices.

"You know I didn't mean it that way," murmured the young man.

"How did you mean it then?" she lisped babyishly. The words were like the movement of a body in the dark. A female body arching itself slowly upwards against the male pressure. He felt in his own loins the sweet answering thrill. Clenched his fist as he gazed after the girl's figure. White dress. Expanse of hips. The young man's arm slid carefully about the waist. Nothing hurried. Plenty of time. Movement of bodies in the dark. Now in light. Appeared distinctly for an instant in the yellow pool through the dripping café windows, their shadows flying out to prodigious lengths across the dim street and then their self-absorbed figures reswallowed by night.

He gulped and looked again at the movie poster. Jane Barlow had gorgeous breasts. In her pictures she alsways wore gowns cut down low at the neck. You could often see the little groove between the two delectable promontories of her bust. Her hips were ample, too. They swayed when she walked even better than those of April East, who was corseted a little too tightly, and she had a way of looking at a man with her lips parted and her eyes opened wide . . .

"Wouldn't kick her out of bed," he reflected dully.

Then ceased thinking about the poster. Listened to the cricket's chirping. What's he talking to himself about? Refined old ladies making conversation on the church lawn. Or Professor Abbott on Restoration Drama. Reading passages from *Venice Preserv'd* or *Cato* or *Conquest of Granada*. The long, heroic speeches of Almonzaro. Or Belvidera declaiming windily of love. Of love, of love. Luke grinned. Those were living people, too, those Restoration poets. Thomas Otway was alive once. So were Addison and Dryden. And they believed a great deal of what they wrote. Or thought that they believed it. Heroic tragedy and heroic love. And all the while in private people were doing and thinking what they were doing and thinking today. Exactly the same thing in the same way. The vicious intrigues. Constantly draining their passion like running sores on prostitute flesh. And toilets that didn't flush. And the dangers of bathing and fresh air in winter. And the rotting teeth. And horse dung all over the narrow streets. And the diseases and the deaths and the ignorance. And the masses suffering and dying ignominiously while the nobility wept for the plight of sweet Belvidera. Or applauded the wit of perfumed fops. Extremes of sentimentality and of cynicism. The life at Whitehall no less extravagant than a Wycherley farce. The king's mistress threatening to have a miscarriage if she didn't get the first ride in his new French calèche. Seventy thousand dying in London of the plague. Thirteen thousand homes destroyed by one fire. And all of that happened and was allowed to happen and the rich and the poor alike lived and died, the fawning poets, the lewd and elegant lords, the prudish lascivious ladies, the diseased and ignorant multitudes—all of these lived and died upon the earth and nothing was done about it. The pretty and dully saccharine poems were preserved. The heroic tragedies were sacredly kept for posterity. Discreetly all that was terrible and dark in the individual lives of the people was left unsaid and forgotten. Over and done long ago. Doesn't count anymore. New people to cover the earth these days. And the earth still merrily reeling through space. Throwing off gay sparks toward those problematical beings on Mars!

And I being here, thought Luke: that's the strangest of all. I somehow being a part of all this. Accidentally involved. A part of the general iridescence. A bit of spume in the flying tide. I being here. Somehow extraordinary beyond all measure. Sitting on the top rail of a low fence in the middle of night. Here in a strange town. Looking at a colored poster. Thinking about Restoration poets and the universe and social injustice. All without rhyme or reason. Listening to the chirping of a cricket in a field of wet grass. Astonishing, isn't it! Ten minute stop in a strange town—home for me, but for you—just a ten minute stop! I get you, thought Luke. I don't belong. I'm not one of the actors. That's why I'm able to sit here and look at the show. No, I'm not really a part of it. Not one of the *dramatis personae*. Not dark enough or not light enough. Not enough—what do they call it? Centrifugal force? Specific gravity? Let it go at that . . .

Here again his thoughts trailed off into nothing and he only heard the chirping of the cricket in the wet grass.

Katy-did, did-she-Katy, did-she-kid-kid-kid.

It seemed a sort of pointedly foolish commentary upon the fact of existence. Luke smiled to himself. It was pleasant, really, to be sitting here. Coolness of night air. Fresh smell of recent rain on the grass. Voices of unknown people and faint strains of music from a bright café. Quite pleasant. But what connection did it have with him? None whatsoever. These ten minutes had absolutely no bearing upon anything that had gone before or anything that might conceivably come after. Perhaps that was why he found this brief space of time so peculiarly agreeable. He seemed to be removed from the ordinary stream of life for this short interval and to be looking back or down upon himself with an air of quiet detachment. A kind of catharsis, it was, like being very drunk. *Was* he perhaps very drunk? Luke smiled to himself. Perhaps that was it. But not in the usual fashion. An intensifying of perceptions rather than the usual fantastic diffusion.

He smiled to himself and turned his face back toward the street with an increased alertness. Felt himself vividly alive and upon the verge of taking some kind of definite action.

At this moment the college boys were crowding out of the café door. Behind them the proprietor was shouting loud, outraged words. But the boys were jubilant, their voices shrill, their movements abrupt and erratic.

One of them approached the huge Blueflyer and stood directly in front of it with an air of pygmy defiance.

"Bush to Memphish!" he shouted. "Lesh all go to Memphish!"

"Aw, the hell with Memphis!" shouted another.

"No kiddin', I wanta go somewhere!" pleaded the first, his voice trailing off from its defiant pitch and sinking to a childlike whine. "I'm sick an' tired of school. I'm gonna quit school an' go to Memphish!"

The bus passengers were now streaming out of the café and returning to their seats in the bus. It was very late at night, an hour when no kind of behavior seems extraordinary, and the tired travellers only blinked their eyes and muttered sleepily as the drunk boy staggered among them, catching at their sleeves and shrilly enquiring:

"Who'sh going to Memphish? I wanta know about Memphish!"

Luke rose from the fence rail and went over to the boy swaying in the glare of the giant headlights.

"I'm going to Memphis," he said quietly. "What do you want to know about it?"

The boy caught Luke's sleeve and peered anxiously into his face.

"How ish it down there? Like they shay in shongs?"

Luke shook off his hand, fighting down an impulse to strike him.

"It's pretty hot this time of year," he replied, still quietly. "But otherwise a very nice town. On the river and the people are friendly. Southern provincialism's a rather good sort. People not constantly keyed up for competitive struggle, you know. Ideas of social justice rather blurred. But that's inevitable where there's two races that can't be mixed and each of them scared of the other. Take the Arabs and the Jews. We don't have things like that. Front Street and the levee, they're pretty swell in Memphis, especially on Saturday mornings when the country people come into town from all three states, Mississippi, Arkansas, and Tennessee. . . ."

The college boy laughed and caught again at Luke's sleeve.

"Who shaid I was intereshted in all that?"

"Nobody. I'm just trying to sell you a ticket."

"How'sh the night life down there?"

"Very beautiful at night," said Luke. "Five point standards with frosted globes all up and down Main Street. Gorgeous theatrical signs and . . . "

"Aw, no, I mean the night life, the dancing, the . . . "

"Dancing? They have dancing on the roofs of the Peabody and Claridge hotels. Also there's . . . "

"How'sh the mooshic?"

"Sounds swell over the radio. I've never . . ."

"And the girls, the girls, the *girls*?"

The motor of the bus had started roaring. The pavement beneath them shook with its thunder. Luke heard his voice rising in tone.

"Here! Here's my ticket!" he screamed.

Five or six of the college boys were now swarming around him. He extended toward the boy the torn white stub.

"Here's my ticket to Memphis! It's yours for two bucks! Understand? Paid seven for it myself. All yours for just two bucks . . . "

Now the bus driver was yelling something. So was the café proprietor. The motor's savage roar had infected them all, even the sleepy passengers. They leaned out of the windows and laughed and hooted and made angry gestures. The air thundered and shook. The very walls and pavements of the street seemed to be roused to fury. The college boys pressed in close around Luke, clutching him by the coat lapel and the sleeves. Their breaths were strong with beer, their eyes and their faces demonically inflamed. Some of them shoved him toward the bus door, others dragged him backwards. The ticket stub dropped from his fingers and was trampled underfoot. He felt terribly frightened and with a desperate effort broke away. He darted in front of the roaring engine. The street was a momentary plethora of sound and motion. Then faded behind him. He splashed through water that seemed knee-deep. Then darkness gathered about him. The other side of the street. An areaway between two buildings. This is madness. Lost my mind. But what do I care? Ha, ha! Leaned against dark wall and breathed. Bricks rough and damp to the back of his head. Cool wind playing upon his face. Smell of wet grass. Coolness. Cool darkness. The night after fever . . .

When he opened his eyes a few moments later the bus was gone. The confusion was over. Light glimmered faintly in the puddles scattered about the tarred street surface. Forms inside the brilliantly lighted café moved diffusely behind the rain blurred and beaded windows. Music drifted out faintly. An old tune. "Star Dust." Very pleasant to hear. The scene was attractive. Symphonic completeness that reality seldom achieves. A picture by Turner. "Rainy Nocturne" might be the title . . .

He went back across the street and advanced purposefully through wet grass, knee-high, toward the illuminated billboard. Stark Navle's glittering black head grew larger as he approached. The face was outlined with a single stroke of purple paint. The mustache looked like the whiskers of a cat.

Miaouuu, he purred mockingly as he drew closer.

Jane Barlow's hair was yellow. Her lips were crimson daubs. She was smiling at Navle with mouth open. Waiting to be kissed. The name of the picture was *Sacramento*. What was Sacramento? A city on the western coast . . .

"No kiddin', I wanta go somewhere!" That was what the drunk boy had said. What did it matter where? Memphis or Chicago or Sacramento. Or Champaign, Illinois. A strange town in the middle of night with a cricket chirping in wet grass and electric lights shining on the painted poster of a coming show. What did it matter what place? Any place that the night covered was all right for lying down and going to sleep.

He advanced still closer to the painted poster, leaned against it with both palms, kissed the purple brush stroke at the base of Jane Barlow's throat, gave Stark Navle a loud bird: then stretched himself out in the tall grass somewhere near the spot where the cricket was chirping and turned his face away from the lighted poster and fell into a sound, blissful sleep.

c. 1936 (Not previously published)

Gift of an Apple

For an hour since leaving the range of low hills he had walked with the sun very hot on the back of his neck. The rough canvas strap chafed his shoulders and the small of his back had grown sensitive to the pack's rhythmic thudding. He shifted it now and then but no position gave him more than momentary relief. Cars passed very seldom. They were nearly all transient families in dusty jalopies. The kids grinned and waved but the older folks pretended not to see him. Once a 1932 Ford came along and stopped. There were three drunk men and a woman and the woman leaned out and asked him how much money he had. Sixty-five cents, he told her. That won't do us much good, she said. We hocked our spare tire to buy this last tank of gas and now we got to take on a passenger that can buy us some more. You understand, don't you? The car lurched forward and she flopped back and he saw that what she had said was true, there was just the rim of the spare above the orange and black New Mexico license plates.

My God, he thought, suppose I had to walk all the way to Lexington, Kentucky. In California it was relatively easy to thumb a ride but as you went further east the people seemed to grow more suspicious. Maybe it was because your appearance deteriorated from the road, your clothes got dusty and out of condition and the series of disappointments made it hard to muster that gay, inviting smile which makes them stop. When you're fresh and in good spirits you can exercise a sort of mental compulsion over the drivers. You do it with your eyes mostly. You sort of project something out of your eyes that attracts their attention and if they're not sons of bitches they can't help stopping. But that's in the west. Further east they're all sons of bitches. Half of the time if one of them stops he's a queer and you have to be groped all over to pay for your ride. Or else he's a drunk who criticizes his wife and curses his boss and scares you shitless careening all over the road at seventy-five miles an hour. Or like that Ford back there, they're broke and they want you to help buy the gas.

He looked back. The sun was dropping down toward the hills behind him. The shape of it became more distinct with the fiery brilliance waning. It was perfectly round, a little bit fuzzy at the edges, like one of those red tennis balls. In the less intense light everything seemed to stand out plainly. Some while earlier the town he approached had been lost in a wavering glare. Now it acquired definition. He could see the late sun glinting on a steeple and a few pointed roofs that were perched just on this side of the second low range of hills. He wondered if he would get there before dark and began to consider dully the problem of getting a bed.

Suddenly he saw not far ahead of him an automobile with a trailer. It was a very old car, cream-colored with dust. The tires were off the trailer's back wheels. It must have been there a mighty long time. A little tin stove-pipe projected from the peaked roof and sent up a thin curl of smoke. All around were baskets and pottery which were apparently for sale and along the wall of the trailer facing the road were hung strings of velvety red coxcomb, bright orange bittersweet and pale yellow gourds. It was a roadside stand which had probably been there all summer long selling this stuff to tourists on their way back from vacations in the hill country.

The back of the trailer faced him and as he approached it he could see through canvas flaps the shape of a woman. She was huge and black-haired. He wondered for a moment how she could manage to live in such close quarters. He thought of a bottle that he had once pulled out of the Sunflower River. He had dived from a log and his hands, touching the sandy bottom, came on this five gallon jug. He fastened a rope to the handle and he and another boy lugged it out of the river. Inside was a large catfish. They all wondered how it had gotten in there for now it was much too large to get through the mouth of the bottle. It must have swum in when it was a minnow and somehow grown up inside. Too big to get out. He thought about that as he looked at the big foreign woman. The others had wanted to break the jug open and cook the catfish for supper but the idea of this had repelled him because there was something not normal about a catfish that had grown up inside a bottle.

He started to walk on by but caught the woman's dark eyes staring out at him through the canvas flaps. He stopped in the road and said "Hello" to the woman.

She came out on the small platform. He heard the boards groaning slightly beneath her weight. She stood above him blinking with the sun in her eyes. She had a face like the catfish. Dark and blunt-featured. Coarse hairs along her upper lips. Her arms were folded against the great loose bulge of her bosom. She was dressed in a cheap silk underslip. Her legs and arms were bare, loose-fleshed and brown. He was shocked to see there were even a few dark hairs in the middle of her chest where the neck of the underslip sagged down. He had never seen a woman before with hair on her chest. It made him think of that hermaphrodite in the sidewalk show at Dodge City. The barker pointing to the woman-man standing in the window, one side of her a fully developed female and the other a man, according to what he claimed. It didn't seem possible, though.

"Hello," said the woman. "You want to buy something, huh?"

"I don't have any money," he told her. "But I thought you might have something to eat you could give me."

The woman said nothing. She blinked her eyes at the sun in a good-humored silence.

He looked at the dried ropes of sage, dill, garlic and red pepper that curtained the upper part of the doorway. He thought of rich, oily foods—his mouth watered.

The woman backed into the trailer. He heard heavy movements inside like the catfish floundering in the bottle after the water had been poured out. A mean thing to do. They had crouched on the bank and watched it until it quit flopping.

The woman came back to the platform.

"I give you an apple," she said.

"Oh, thanks."

He stretched out his hand. Saw the palm of it glittering darkly with sweat. Drew it back and quickly wiped it on the side of his corduroy pants and then held it out once more to receive the apple. It was a dark wine red. He could tell the moment his fingers touched it how it would taste.

The woman seated herself on the top step of the trailer.

"Sit down," she said hoarsely.

"Thanks."

He seated himself on the bottom step, at the same time raising the apple to his mouth. The hard red skin popped open, the sweet juice squirted out and his teeth sank into the firm white meat of the apple. It is like the act of love, he thought, as he ground the skin and pulp between his jaw teeth. His tongue rolled around the front of his mouth and savored the sweet-tasting juice. He licked the outside of his lips and felt them curving into a sensuous smile. The pulp dissolved in his mouth. He tried not swallowing it. Make it last longer, he thought. But it melted like snow between his grinding teeth. It all turned to liquid and flowed on down his throat. He couldn't stop it. It is like the act of love, he thought again. You try to make it last longer. Draw out the sweet final moment. But it can't be held at that point. It has to go over and down, it has to be finished. And then you feel cheated somehow.

"That was good," he said to the woman. "I never tasted an apple as good as that!"

"Maybe it tasted good because you was hungry," she said.

"Yes. Maybe."

She went back inside. He saw her stoop over the basket again and take out another apple. Good. He removed his pocketknife from his pants and shaved the remaining bits of white meat off the core of the apple that he had already eaten to let her see that he was hungry all right.

She came out again but she didn't offer the second apple to him. She ate it herself. Opened her own huge jaws and munched like a horse. He looked away from her. He felt very tired, his legs ached. It was good to sit facing the sun, a round orange ball directly above the low purple line of the wooded hills. Wind came up across the fields now and stirred the tall seeding grass and made the willow leaves sigh.

He thought of the woman being here in this spot all summer. Sleeping at night on a cot by the side of the road with the moon looking down at her big dark female body and her arms thrown out to receive the cool wind like a lover, her flesh moist with sweat . . .

He looked at her again. He had to say something to keep his lips from spreading into a senseless grin.

"What time is it?"

The woman grunted vaguely.

He hitched at the belt of his trousers.

"Your man gone into town, has he?"

"Yeah. Him and my boy have gone into town to get drunk."

She laughed shortly.

"What are *you* going to do?" he asked her.

She blew out air through her nostrils and curled up her lips. Her eyes did not stop at his face. They went on down his body. He could almost feel them. He leaned back quickly in response to the suggested caress. His shoulders touched the round bulge of her knee. Soft as though without bone. He wondered what her age was. Forty-five? Forty? Might even be younger than that. She spoke of her boy going out to get drunk with his dad. He must be nearly my age, he thought. But dark races grew up early. For instance the little Greek girl that lived in his block at home. Back in the alley night after night behind her father's restaurant, between the ash pit and the three huge garbage pails. Mmmm. Panting for breath. With the hard concrete and all those cold wet smells. Potato peelings and cantaloupe rinds and damp coffee grounds. Bits of ash pressed into the palms of his hands. But the hardness around them making the comfort inside her sweeter. Only eleven years old she was. And the nervous spasms and groanings. Not normal perhaps.

"What are you going to do?" he asked her again.

"Me? I'm going to make supper."

"What have you got for supper?"

"Meat."

"A big piece?"

"Yes. A pretty big piece."

"Enough for two people?"

"Naw, I don't know," she said. "I ought to save some for my boy."

"He'll probably get some in town."

"Naw. I don't know."

He smiled and narrowed his eyes but she looked away. She fixed her eyes on the round orange ball of the sun. It was now sending up wide beams of pale orange light between the feathery masses of pale grey cloud. Very pretty. It made him think of a dress his sister had worn one Easter Sunday. Streets paved with gold. Oh, yes. The black rails. Fire escape? No. Tracks of the viaduct. And the train screaming by. His mother. How clear her voice!—Irma, don't stand by the window like that. The soot flying in. Confirmation. The five colored eggs in one corner. Pale blue and pink and yellow and green. Hardboiled eggs. He wondered if he had eaten them afterwards. Eggs were good hardboiled. The white coming loose from the yellow center. The yellow a round ball, rich and grainy, forming a paste in the mouth and sticking to the teeth so that the taste remained for a long time afterwards. Mmmm. He'd like to be eating some hardboiled eggs right now.

"I'm still kind of hungry," he told her.

She suddenly stirred. Lifted her hand from her lap and placed it on the back of his head. Ran the fingers down his neck and under the collar of his shirt.

Inwardly he recoiled from the touch but he kept his eyes on her face.

"You got nice skin like a girl's."

"Thanks."

"How old are you, huh?"

"Nineteen."

"Umph!"

She grunted as if she had just been stuck with a pin. Got up from the steps and gave him a slight, playful kick with the toe of her dusty slipper.

"Go on," she said. "You're too young!"

"How do you mean, too young?"

"Nineteen is just how old my own boy is! You better go 'way!"

He looked up at her and saw it was no use to argue. Big, heavy and dark she stood in the door of the trailer, her face set in a slight frown, looking out at the sun. An old dago slut she was. Such women make little rules for themselves, more sacred than Holy Law. If he had said twenty-one or even said twenty, it might have been okay with her, but not nineteen because that was the age of her boy . . .

Oh, well.

He rose easily from the bottom step of the trailer and brushed off the seat of his trousers. Swung the canvas pack over his shoulders again. It felt lighter now. He started off down the road. Chuckled a little and looked back over his shoulder. The car and trailer stood out distinct against the waning gold light. The fields were darkening. Grayish dusk closing in. Just the tip of the orange sun was left on top of the hills like a big conflagration up there. His eyes went down once more to the trailer's peaked roof. He saw a thin curl of smoke rising up from the tin stovepipe and heard the rattle of pans. The old woman was in there like a catfish caught in a bottle. She was making herself some supper. She would eat it alone. Fat elbows planted on either side of the tin plate and her shoulders crouched way over. Wheezing a little. Washing it down with scalding black coffee. The rich, oily meat. A big piece. The old bitch. Oh, well. She would die some day. Some ugly disease like cancer. It might be already started inside her dark flesh. Just as well. A stingy old bitch like that . . .

He went on down the road. The air was fresh. A wind was coming up. He saw ahead of him, dimly, white frame buildings spotted with faint yellow light.

He could still taste the apple that he had eaten. The inside of his mouth was fresh and sweet with that taste. Maybe it was better that way, just having that taste in his mouth, the clean white taste of the apple.

c. 1936 (Not previously published)

The Field of Blue Children

That final spring at the State University a restlessness came over Myra which she could not understand. It was not merely the restlessness of superabundant youth. There was something a little neurotic about it. Nothing that she did seemed quite satisfying or complete. Even when she returned from a late formal dance, where she had swung from partner to partner the whole evening through, she did not feel quite ready to tumble exhausted into bed. She felt as though there must be something still further to give the night its perfect fullness. Sometimes she had the almost panicky sensation of having lost or forgotten something very important. She would stand quite still for a moment with tightened forehead, trying to remember just what it was that had slipped from her fingers—been left behind in the rumble seat of Kirk's roommate's roadster or on the sofa in the dimly lighted fraternity lounge between dances.

"What's the matter?" Kirk or somebody else would ask and she would laugh rather sharply.

"Nothing. I just felt like I'd forgotten something!"

The feeling persisted even when every article was accounted for. She still felt as though something were missing. When she had returned to the sorority house she went from room to room, exchanging anecdotes of the evening, laughing at them far more than their humor warranted. And when finally everyone else had gone to bed, she stayed up alone in her room and sometimes she cried bitterly without knowing why, crushing the pillow against her mouth so that no one could hear—or else she sat in pajamas on the window seat and looked out across the small university town with all its buildings and trees and open fields a beautiful dusky blue in the spring night, the dome of the administration building like a snowy peak in the distance and the stars astonishingly large and close—she felt as though she would strangle with an emotion whose exact nature or meaning she could not understand.

When half-drunken groups of serenaders, also restless after late dances, paused beneath her house, she turned on the bed lamp and leaned above them, patting her hands together in a pantomime of delighted applause. When they left, she remained at the window, looking out with the light extinguished, and it was sad, unbearably sad, to hear their hoarse voices retreating down moon-splashed avenues of trees till they could not be heard any longer or else were drowned in the noise of a starting motor whose raucous gravel-kicking departure ebbed quickly to a soft, musical hum and was succeeded at length by the night's complete blue silence.

Still seated at the window, she waited with tight throat for the sobbing to commence. When it did, she felt better. When it did not, her vigil would sometimes continue till morning began and the restless aching had worn itself out.

That spring she took Kirk Abbott's fraternity pin. But this did not radically change her manner of living. She continued to accept dates with other men. She went out almost wherever she was asked with almost whoever asked her, and when Kirk protested she didn't try to explain the fever that made her behave in this way, she simply kissed him until he stopped talking and was in a mood to forgive her for almost anything that she might conceivably do.

From the beginning of adolescence, perhaps earlier, Myra had written a little verse. But this spring it became a regular practice. Whenever the rising well of unexplainable emotion became so full that its hurt was intolerable, she found that it helped her a little to scribble things down on paper. Single lines or couplets, sometimes whole stanzas, leapt into her mind with the instant completeness of slides flashed on the screen of a magic lantern. Their beauty startled her: sometimes it was like a moment of religious exaltation. She stood in a frozen attitude; her breath was released in a sigh. Each time she felt as though she were about to penetrate some new area of human thought. She had the sensation of standing upon the verge of a shadowy vastness which might momentarily flower into a marvelous crystal of light, like a ballroom that is dark one moment and in the next moment illuminated by the sunlike brilliance of a hundred glass chandeliers and reflecting mirrors and polished floors. At such times she would turn out the light in her bedroom and go quickly to the window. When she looked out across the purple-dark town and the snowy white dome above the quadrangle, or when she sat as in a spell, listening to the voices that floated down the quiet streets, singers of blues songs or laughing couples in roadsters, the beauty of it no longer tormented her, she felt instead a mysterious quietness as though some disturbing question had been answered and life had accordingly become a much simpler and more pleasurable experience.

"Words are a net to catch beauty!"

She wrote this in the back of a notebook toward the close of a lecture on the taxing powers of Congress. It was late in April when she wrote this—and from then on it seemed that she understood what she wanted and the hurt bewilderment in her grew less acute.

In the Poetry Club to which Myra belonged there was a boy named Homer Stallcup who had been in love with her for a year or more. She could tell this by the way that he looked at her during the club sessions, which were the only occasions on which they met. Homer never looked directly at her, his eyes slid quickly across her face, but something about his expression, even about the tense pose of his body as he sat gripping his knees, made her feel his awareness of her. He avoided sitting next to her or even directly across from her—the chairs were usually arranged in a circle—and because of this she had at first thought that he must dislike her, but she had come gradually to understand that his shyness toward her had an exactly opposite meaning.

Homer was not a fraternity member. He waited on tables at a campus restaurant, fired furnaces and did chores for his room and board. Nobody in Myra's social *milieu* knew him or paid him any attention. He was rather short, stocky and dark. Myra thought him good-looking, but certainly not in any usual way. He had intense black eyes, a straight nose with flaring nostrils, full, mobile lips that sometimes jerked nervously at the corners. All of his movements were overcharged. When he rose from a chair he would nearly upset it. When he lighted a cigarette his face would twist into a terrible scowl and he would fling the burnt match away like a lighted firecracker.

He went around a great deal with a girl of his own intellectual type, a girl named Hertha something or other, who was rather widely known on the campus because of her odd behavior. In classes she would be carried away by enthusiasm upon some subject, either literary or political, and she would talk so rapidly that nobody could understand what she was saying and she would splutter and gasp and make awkward gestures—as though she were trying to pluck some invisible object out of the air—till the room was in an uproar of amusement and the instructor had to turn his face to the blackboard to conceal his own laughter.

Hertha and this boy, Homer, made a queer picture together, she nearly a foot taller, often rushing along a foot or more in advance of him, clutching him by the coat sleeve as though afraid that he might escape from her, and every minute or so one or both of them bursting into violent laughter that could be heard for a block.

Homer wrote poetry of a difficult sort. It was uneven. Parts of it were reminiscent of Hart Crane, parts were almost as naively lucid as Sara Teasdale's. But there were lines and phrases which stabbed at you with their poignant imagery, their fresh observation. When he had given a reading at a symposium, Hertha would always leap out of her chair as though animated by an electric charge, her blinking, near-sighted eyes tensely sweeping the circle of superciliously smiling faces, first demanding, then begging that they concur in the extravagant praise which her moist lips babbled. Only Myra would say anything when Hertha was finished. The rest were too baffled or too indifferent or even too hostile. And Homer's face, darkly flushed, would be turned to his lap throughout the rest of the meeting. His fingers would fold down corners of the neat pages as though the poetry had been erased from them or had never been written on them, as though these pages were simply blank pieces of paper for his fingers to play with.

Myra always wanted to say something more, but her critical vocabularly was slight.

"I think that was lovely," she would say. Or "I liked that very much." And Homer would not lift his eyes, his face would turn even darker, and she would bite her tongue as though in remorse for an unkind speech. She wanted to put her hands over his fingers, to make them stop crumpling the neat pages, to make them be still.

It was not till the last meeting of the year, in early June, that Myra had the courage to approach him. After that meeting she saw him standing by the water fountain at the end of the corridor. She rushed impulsively up to him and told him, all in one breath, that his was the best unpublished verse she'd ever heard, that he should submit it to some of the good literary magazines, that she thought the other members of the club were absolute fools for not understanding.

Homer stood with his fists clenched in his pockets. He did not look at her face the whole time she was speaking. When she had stopped, his excitement burst through. He tore a sheaf of manuscripts from his brief case and thrust them into her hands.

"Please read them," he begged, "and let me know what you think."

They went downstairs together. On the bottom step he tripped or slid and she had to catch his arm to prevent him from falling. She was both touched and amused by this awkwardness and by his apparent delight in walking beside her. As they went out of the white stone building the late afternoon sun, yellow as lemon, met their faces in a beneficent flood. The air was filled with the ringing of five-thirty bells and the pliant voices of pigeons. A white feather from one of the stirring wings floated down and lighted upon Myra's hair. Homer lifted it off and thrust it in his hatband, and all the way home, after leaving him, Myra could feel that quick, light touch of his fingers. She wondered if he would keep the pigeon's feather; treasure it, possibly, for a long while afterward because it had once touched her person.

That night, when the sorority house was submerged in darkness, she took out the sheaf of poems and read them through without stopping. As she read she felt a rising excitement. She did not understand very much of what she was reading, but there was a cumulative effect, a growing intensity in the sequence. When she had finished she found herself trembling: trembling as when you step from warm water into chill air.

She dressed and went downstairs. She didn't know what she was planning to do. Her movements were without any conscious direction. And yet she had never moved with more certainty.

She opened the front door of the sorority house, ran down the brick-paved walk, turned to the left and continued swiftly through the moonlit streets till she had reached Homer's residence. It startled her to find herself there. There were cicadas burring in the large oaks—she had not heard them until this moment. And when she looked upward she saw a close group of stars above the western gable of the large frame house. The Seven Sisters. They were huddled together like virgin wanderers through a dark forest. She listened and there was not a voice anywhere, nothing except the chant of cicadas and the faint, faint rustling of her white skirt when she moved.

She went quickly around the side of the house to the door that she had seen Homer come out of in the mornings. She gave two short, distinct raps, then flattened herself against the brick wall. She was breathing rapidly. After waiting a while, she knocked again. Through the glass pane she could see down a flight of stairs into the basement. The door of a lamplit room was open. She saw first a moving shadow, then the boy himself, catching a heavy brown robe about his body and frowning up at the door as he mounted toward it.

As the door came open she gasped his name.

For a whole minute, it seemed, he said nothing. Then he caught her arm and pulled her inside the door.

"Myra, it's you."

"Yes, it's me," she laughed. "I don't know what came over me. I've been reading your poetry and I just felt like I had to see you at once and tell you . . ."

Her breath gave out. She leaned against the closed door. It was her eyes this time, and not his, that looked for concealment. She looked down at the bottom of his ugly brown bathrobe and she saw his bare feet beneath it, large and bony and white, and the sight of them frightened her. She remembered the intense, fleeting way of his eyes sliding over her face and body and the way he trembled that afternoon when she came up to him in the corridor, how those large feet had tripped on the bottom stair and she had been forced to catch him to keep him from falling.

"There was one thing in particular," she went on with a struggle. "There was something about a field of blue flowers . . ."

"Oh, yes," he whispered. "The blue children, you mean!"

"Yes, that was it!" Now she lifted her eyes, eagerly.

"Come down to my room, Myra."

"I couldn't!"

"You couldn't?"

"No, of course not! If anyone caught me . . ."

"They wouldn't!"

"I'd be expelled!"

There was a slight pause.

"Wait a minute!"

He ran down three steps and turned.

"Wait for me just one minute, Myra!"

She felt her head nodding. She heard his running down the rest of the steps and into the basement room where he lived. Through the door she saw his shadow moving about the floor and the walls. He was dressing. Once he stepped into the portion of the bedroom that she could see through the half-open door and he stood in her sight naked from the waist up, and she was startled and strangely moved by that brief glimpse of his full, powerful chest and arms, strikingly etched with shadows thrown by the lamp. In that moment he acquired in her mind a physical reality which he had never had before. A very great physical reality, greater than she had felt in Kirk Abbott or in any of the other young men that she had gone with on the campus.

A minute later he stepped out of the door and closed it and came quietly up the short flight of steps to where she was standing.

"I'm sorry I took so long."

"It wasn't long."

He took her arm and they went out of the door and around to the front of the house. The oak tree in the front lawn appeared gigantic. Everything was peculiarly sharpened or magnified; even the crunch of gravel under their two pairs of white shoes. She expected to see startled, balloon-like heads thrust out of all the upstairs windows, to hear voices calling a shrill alarm, her name shouted from roof-tops, the rushing of crowds in pursuit . . .

"Where are we going?" she asked as he led her south along the brick walk.

"I want to show you the field I describe in the poem."

It wasn't far. The walk soon ended and under their feet was the plushy coolness of earth. The moon flowed aqueously through the multitude of pointed oak leaves: the dirt road was also like moving water with its variations of light and shade. They came to a low wooden fence. The boy jumped over it. Then held out his arms. She stepped to the top rail and he lifted her down from it. On the other side his arms did not release her but held her closer.

"This is it," he told her, "the field of blue children."

She looked beyond his dark shoulder. And it was true. The whole field was covered with dancing blue flowers. There was a wind scudding through them and they broke before it in pale blue waves, sending up a soft whispering sound like the infinitely diminished crying of small children at play.

She thought of the view from her window at night, those nights when she cried bitterly without knowing why, the dome of the administration building like a white peak and the restless waves of moonlit branches and the stillness and the singing voices, mournfully remote, blocks away, coming closer, the tender, foolish ballads, and the smell of the white spirea at night, and the stars clear as lamps in the cloud-fretted sky, and she remembered the choking emotion that she didn't understand and the dread of all this coming to its sudden, final conclu-

sion in a few months or weeks more. And she tightened her arms
about the boy's shoulders. He was almost a stranger. She knew that
she had not even caught a first glimpse of him until this night, and yet
he was inexpressibly close to her now, closer than she had ever felt any
person before.

He led her out over the field where the flowers rose in pale blue
waves to her knees and she felt their soft petals against her bare flesh
and she lay down among them and stretched her arms through them
and pressed her lips against them and felt them all about her, accepting
her and embracing her, and a kind of drunkenness possessed her. The
boy knelt beside her and touched her cheek with his fingers and then
her lips and her hair. They were both kneeling in the blue flowers,
facing each other. He was smiling. The wind blew her loose hair into
his face. He raised both hands and brushed it back over her forehead
and as he did so his hands slipped down behind the back of her head
and fastened there and drew her head toward him until her mouth was
pressed against his, tighter and tighter, until her teeth pressed painfully against her upper lip and she tasted the salt taste of blood. She
gasped and let her mouth fall open and then she lay back against the
whispering blue flowers.

Afterward she had sense enough to see that it was impossible. She
sent the poems back to the boy with a short note. It was a curiously
stilted and formal note, perhaps because she was dreadfully afraid of
herself when she wrote it. She told him about the boy Kirk Abbott
whom she was going to marry that summer and she explained to
Homer how impossible it would have been for them to try and go on
with the beautiful but unfortunate thing that had happened to them
last night in the field.

She saw him only once after that. She saw him walking across the
campus with his friend Hertha, the tall, weedy girl who wore thick-
lensed glasses. Hertha was clinging to Homer's arm and shaking with
outlandishly shrill laughter; laughter that could be heard for blocks and
yet did not sound like real laughter.

Myra and Kirk were married in August of that year. Kirk got a job
with a telephone company in Poplar Falls and they lived in an efficiency
apartment and were reasonably happy together. Myra seldom felt restless any more. She did not write verse. Her life seemed to be perfectly
full without it. She wondered sometimes if Homer had kept on with his

writing but she never saw any of it in the literary magazines so she supposed it couldn't have amounted to very much after all.

One late spring evening a few years after their marriage Kirk Abbott came home tired from the office hungry for dinner and found a scribbled note under the sugar bowl on the drop-leaf table.

"Driven over to Carsville for just a few hours. Myra."

It was after dark: a soft, moony night.

Myra drove south from the town till she came to an open field. There she parked the car and climbed over the low wooden fence. The field was exactly as she had remembered it. She walked quickly out among the flowers; then suddenly fell to her knees among them, sobbing. She cried for a long time, for nearly an hour, and then she rose to her feet and carefully brushed off her skirt and stockings. Now she felt perfectly calm and in possession of herself once more. She went back to the car. She knew that she would never do such a ridiculous thing as this again, for now she had left the last of her troublesome youth behind her.

1937 (Published 1939)

In Memory of an Aristocrat

I went there the first time with a young Jew named Carl who called himself a musician with about as much justice as I have sometimes referred to myself as a writer, though it is true that he used to play light classics on the fiddle at the Court of the Two Sisters where I was employed as a waiter during the holiday season and he played rather well when drunk. At this time, however, both of us were out of regular work. We were both hungry and Carl said that Irene always had something cooking. It might be stew, he said, or vegetable soup or even scalloped oysters, but if it *is* oysters, he warned me, be sure to smell 'em first. The last time she had oysters they give me the runs, said Carl. I covered more distance that night, he said, in much less time than when those bloodhounds followed me out of Friarspoint, Mississippi!

While on the subject of oysters he also advised me against eating raw ones with whiskey. There's something about the chemical reaction, said Carl, that turns the oysters to rocks in your stomach and I have seen big men, he told me, drop dead in their shoes right here in New Orleans bars just because they was from out of town and nobody took the trouble to warn 'em, like I'm warning *you*—and here he jabbed me viciously with one finger—that whiskey turns oysters to *rocks* when the two get mixed in your belly!

Carl was a fountain of wisdom on a vast number of subjects. The way that he lived when he was out of work, which was usually because his fiddle music was fairly corn, is worthy of a narrative all by itself. This much I'll tell you now. His chief occupation was what he called "conking the queers." "Rolling" and "knocking over" are variations of the same expression which refers to the action of terminating an assignation with one of these gentlemen by the application of a loaded stick or blunt end of an ice cleaver to exactly the right portion of his skull at the unsuspecting moment of inclination, and then proceeding, before the victim woke up, to relieve him of whatever wealth was detachable from his person. So when Carl said that business was good and you hadn't seen alleycats picketing the Two Sisters lately, you understood right away what he referred to. Mardi Gras time was what he chiefly lived in expectation of. But Mardi Gras was still a month away. It was now the sad, sweet season of Lent with one day a slow, slow rain and the next a bright, misty sunlight with everything still wet and exuding a delicately, freshly rotten smell which is something you always remember about the old French Quarter and want to go back to sometime.

Irene was the name of the girl we were going to see. She had one of those little crib-like rooms on the further end of Bourbon, very deep in the Quarter, a room that opened directly onto the street with the usual green-shuttered window and door. Outside hung a shingle that stated simply IRENE'S—PUBLIC INVITED. She was a well-known member of the Quarter Rats which is not an official society of any kind but is roughly inclusive, I suppose, of all those persons, creative or otherwise, who have wandered into the Quarter and remained there more or less permanently because of the fact that it is the cheapest and most comfortable place in America for fugitives from economic struggle.

Irene was *chez elle*. The shutters were closed and the room was very dusky so the only thing that struck me forcibly when I first entered was the smell of something cooking on the stove. The only chair was occupied by a Negro woman whom Irene had called in off the street because she had an interesting-looking face. She did have that. She was black as tar with very large spatulate features. She was telling Irene's fortune when we came in and Irene motioned us to sit down and be still. We did this. We sat down on the bed with Irene and Carl immediately started groping Irene's legs under the wrapper and the Negress grinned and went on with her prophecies in a rich, fluent voice that was infinitely soothing to listen to.

Honey, she said, you're going to have an awful lot of success with these here pictures.

Am I? said Irene. Her voice was trembling with unaffected wistfulness.

You sure are, honey. Why, your art work is going to make you famous. You're going to have pictures for sale, honey, in the biggest stores on Royal Street. You know what I can see? I can see you drivin' along Canal in a great big high-powered car with a man in a full-dress suit!

Yes? interrupted Irene. What does he look like, honey?

Han'some as Jesus! grinned the Negro woman.

Honestly?

Yes, an' honey, he's got ten-dollar bills bulgin' out of his vest pockets an' his pants is stuffed with stocks an' bonds enough to choke a full-grown mule!

We all laughed at this and the Negress got up and started asking for things. She wanted Irene to give her the cherry-colored smock that hung by the washstand. Irene gave her that. Then she wanted the new bar of toilet soap and the box of sweet pea powder. She got both of those, and then Irene told her she'd better be going before she craved the bed we were sitting on.

I could use a bed like that, said the Negress.

Yes, and I'd let you have it, laughed Irene, except it's indispensable to me in my line of work!

So the Negro woman bundled her presents up neatly and took her good-humored departure.

I wonder if she was telling the truth, said Irene.

About what?

Me making good as an artist!

She lit a cigarette which she had rolled on a special little machine which she had for that purpose. A wide rubber band it was that worked on a couple of spools. A very handy little contraption for nervous people like Irene and myself whose hands shake when they're rolling so that most of the tobacco gets spilled out. Irene showed us how it worked and we rolled out several cigarettes. Carl would have kept on rolling till he'd filled his pockets if Irene hadn't stopped him. He was delighted with the machine and I remember that quite a little discussion went on about it.

It came out in the course of the conversation that Irene used to pose for night classes at the WPA in New York. She took off her wrapper and showed us her body which Carl said was unusually good. I didn't think so. She was one of those big, dark girls, everything about her on a monumental scale. Okay for Carl who was pretty good sized himself but sort of putting me in a protective shadow. Yes, I was reminded somehow of the goddamnedest poem I have ever read that was written by a boy from Cape Girardeau who said who said the shadows nestled under the big elm tree like puppies under the mother dog's belly. Whenever I notice a disparity in size I think about that image and I remember the boy who conceived it, a very small, timid-looking fresh-man at the University of Missouri who was—

Excuse me, that's something else that belongs in another story.

Irene was big all right, and the lower part of her body was disproportionately heavy. It was almost as though the camera had been placed at her feet. I mean everything seemed to be on a larger scale toward the bottom. But she was not in any way unpleasant to look at. You could look at her and imagine feelings of pleasure. She was capacious all right—built, as Carl said, for comfort. And her face was rather splendid. Also large but with something noble about it. She had been through a lot, you could tell, and had gone through it pretty bravely. The lines of humor were permanent lines in her face. There was nearly always an air of quiet laughter about her, together with something that was deeply, incurably hurt. You wanted to know what it was but it didn't come out very quickly. Her face seemed to have risen slowly out of some stifling black cloud and now to have come into sunlight that showed the scars but gave her clean air to breathe. What she made me think of as I looked at her standing there naked and smiling at me and Carl was the title of a book, or perhaps a phrase from a poem which I have seen somewhere. The tower beyond tragedy—that's what it was.

So Irene was beautiful if you took long enough to see it, and she was also a very lovable person if you were not too squeamish about certain inessential matters. She was the good kind of Bohemian, not the phony kind whose freedom is a ready-made accessory to a studio but the kind who has made her own freedom, forged it like a suit of armor with a desperate labor out of a very desperate need.

This is lyricism almost in a class with the boy's from Cape Girardeau, but thinking about Irene is compulsion to poetry even when you ordinarily stick to prose. Somebody should have loved her who was a good poet. Maybe somebody did and the poem will yet be written.

Carl enjoyed looking at her and she was pleased by his frank admiration. After a while she lay down there on the bed between us. You can play all you want to, she laughed, but don't try anything else.

We lay there on the bed and played with Irene and discussed our three vocations. Irene told us that she always saw abstract designs when she was love-making. One time she said she had to get up right in the middle of things and draw a sketch on the wallpaper.

I've never been able to decide, she said, which is more important, the thing itself or the quality of it that you reproduce in your work.

Emotion, I suggested, or emotion remembered in tranquillity?

Yeah, she said. Her face grew very thoughtful.

I knew another writer, she said, who warned me that I was abusing my emotions. Bitches, he told me, got so they couldn't feel anything at all. Do you suppose that's true?

Naw, said Carl.

I don't think so either, she said more cheerfully. From personal experience I would say it's just the other way round.

How do you mean? Carl asked.

Well, the more I feel, she said, the more I seem to be capable of feeling. It scares me a little because if I keep on, some day I'll feel so much that it will probably kill me!

I was reminded of an epigrammatic statement, whose I don't remember, but it seemed appropriate.

There is only one true aristocracy, I told her a little pontifically, and that is the aristocracy of passionate souls!

Irene turned and looked at me strangely. A slow, delighted smile appeared on her face.

Thanks, she said. Excuse me just a minute!

She got up from the bed and took a piece of charcoal and scribbled the statement which I had quoted on the wall space between two paintings.

Thanks, she repeated, I'm glad you gave me that, it's something I want to remember!

It was raining outside, one of those slow New Orleans rains, and the yellow spot on the ceiling got darker and it began to exude little cold drops of water which struck Irene each time in the close proximity of her navel. She seemed to take a masochistic pleasure in this mild torture. We'd watch the drop forming up there and speculate on the number of minutes that it would take to fall. Carl always made the closest guess. When the drop descended Irene would shriek and squirm on the bed and this seemed to get Carl excited. He kept throwing one of his legs over hers in spite of the warning she gave him, so finally she jumped up and slapped him sharply. The trouble with you is, she told him, you're always wanting something for nothing. Then Carl accused her of being anti-Semitic and she started bawling him out for his lack of social convictions.

During the heat of this quarrel I got up from the bed and helped myself to some stew. It was terribly thick and gummy, all of the constituents had gone to pieces so that nothing in it was distinguishable from anything else. It was one of those stews that remind you of nothing so much as that famous brook of Longfellow's that continues everlastingly with a magnificent disregard for the vital statistics of men. I wondered if this would be as bad as those scalloped oysters Carl had spoken about but nevertheless took a chance.

After a while the quarrel on the bed was patched up.

You stay over there, said Irene.

She meant me. And then with a surprising touch of modesty she flung the Japanese wrapper over the foot of the large brass bed so that it erected a little screen between us. I have no wish to titillate anyone's fancy but for the sake of the record I will have to pronounce the noises that Irene made in the next few minutes the most impressive that I have heard in a woman's bedroom. Gaspings, moans, smothered *darlings,* and at the climax a hoarse, rapid breathing which was so intense that it really alarmed me a little.

All that time I was eating out of the stew and I was so distracted by the noise that I forgot to notice how much of the stuff I was eating. When I looked down at last, the noise on the bed having now subsided a little, the pot of stew was almost entirely exhausted.

Irene got up. Her face was shining with sweat.

You'll have to go now, she said.

What for? said Carl.

You know what for, said Irene. I got to get busy now!

How can you paint in this light? I asked her, hoping she wouldn't notice the stew was all gone.

Paint! she snorted. I'm not going to paint!

What are you going to do then?

The answer was in one syllable, a word that you see not infrequently scrawled in white soap on windows in less desirable districts or printed in lavatories.

My God, I thought, is she really?

When we had left Carl told me the little he knew about her. She was from Brooklyn and had gotten her start in painting as a student in a night class at the WPA. During the day she worked in a garment shop. There was a strike and some bloody warfare with police and scabs in which she had been badly beaten and locked up in jail. She was very bitter about the treatment she had received from the Union. It seems they had let her down pretty badly, come to some sort of cowardly compromise with the garment shop employer and allowed him to discharge Irene and one or two others who had worked most actively in the strike.

By this time she had been painting for several years and had accumulated enough canvases to cover the walls of a room. She packed all her paintings and shipped them down to New Orleans where she heard an artist could subsist on practically nothing. She had hitch-hiked down there (last winter it was) and set up the studio and lived the life of an artist with that particular modification, if it is really a modification, which her desperate need of money had imposed.

As for her paintings, I thought they were really surprisingly good. They were very raw and terrific. Pictures of pregnant women in soiled cotton dresses and bums sleeping in doorways. Screaming strike-workers, hideous scabs and bosses. There was one that was quite indecent but powerful as hell: a policeman nude except for his cap and his badge, beating a woman striker with a club while his sex organ stood in complete erection. This sounds like very bad painting but surprisingly it wasn't. Each of the pictures packed a tremendous wallop, they hit you right smack between the eyes with the force and precision that only comes from the fury of a first-rate talent. Irene was a furious girl, she was possessed of a demon, but more than anything else I think, Irene was an artist . . .

Well—

A few days later Carl landed in the House of Detention for a five-week term. Mardi Gras came around, the time he had been waiting for, and there he was locked up. Irene felt terribly sorry for him. I didn't know that she liked him but apparently she did because now she visited the "house" every day or so with a tin of Union Leader and a pad of cigarette papers. They would sit on opposite sides of the bars and she would roll the cigarettes on the little machine she brought with her and lick them carefully and hand them through the grating and Carl would say *thanks,* morosely, and we would talk about painting and music and writing until an officer said the visiting period was over.

On the last day of Mardi Gras Irene and I went out together in costumes which she had devised in her studio. Hers was a grass skirt and a very scanty brassière. She was very drunk that day, as nearly everyone was, and we got separated in the terrible mob at the head of Royal Street. I heard her shrieking once or twice and then she disappeared as completely as though she'd gone down for the third and last time in the boiling human sea that swept around us.

I spent the rest of the day looking for her: found her at last, about ten o'clock in the evening, in a small bar on Dauphine. She was unconscious, in fact prostrate on the floor, but she had a death grip on her purse which was fairly bulging with money. The man at the bar said she had been working there (they had rooms in back) but had passed out cold just about half an hour ago. My God, he said as he looked at her, Jesus Christ! And he shook his head over and over and laughed way down deep in his throat . . .

I called a cab and took her home in it. She began to come to and she was very grateful. She wanted to give me half of the money she'd made. Stay here for the night, she said, I'm going to be sick later on.

I stayed. It is something great to remember because she talked continuously that night, lying in the dark on the big brass bed while the crowds went by on the walk in fantastic costumes, you heard them hawking and spitting and laughing and retching outside, you heard the electric victrola in the corner barroom playing "It Makes No Difference Now" and you heard the wagon go by, not once but time and again, and sometimes skyrockets lit the sky, you could hear them exploding softly, or nigger-devils spit excitedly across the narrow streets, the tamale vendors cried out and the pedestrians were fewer, they walked slower now, some of them dropped on the walk, fell in their fancy costumes and rolled out into the gutter, you heard them snoring, you knew the police would collect them about daybreak and jam them like baggage into the stuffy little cells adjoining night-court, you felt very sorry for them and wondered how much they had in their wallets and if it would be worth trying . . .

She talked all night. Lay there too exhausted to move except when she had to vomit, but kept on talking and talking. The whole of her former life passed before me in brilliant parade. I saw the mean-souled bosses and the gallant strike-workers, I saw the brutal policemen, I saw the shrewd, self-interested union organizers and the relief workers who kept their hearts in their notebooks. I saw stray, beautiful glimpses of fire and passion and tenderness. I felt the deep, hungry love as though the whole intolerable ache of humanity had somehow found its way into this twenty-six year old girl's heart.

I wanted, she said—(and this is something that I will always re-member)—I wanted, she said, to stretch out the long, sweet arms of my art and embrace the whole world!

She said this at the end of everything else and it was, I think, what she had been trying to say all the time and hadn't till then found the perfect utterance for. Now she was silent. I turned over and saw that now at last Irene had fallen asleep. And her face as she slept was white and lovely and tender, the face of a sleeping child.

This was Irene.

Two or three weeks after Mardi Gras there was held what was known as the Annual Spring Display of paintings by New Orleans artists. It was sponsored, of course, by a select private group of the more successful painters, the ones who if they lived in the Quarter lived there only because it had atmosphere and whose studios were sparsely furnished with very beautiful things, great oval gilt-framed mirrors and inch-thick Oriental carpets and the kind of vases that the tragic protagonist knocks over when sneaking home late at night in two-reel comedies.

That is how I imagine them to be without, I must admit, having entered more than a couple.

Irene had submitted ten of her best canvases and for some time before the display she went around white and excited in a new black crepe dress with a silver and rhinestone buckle. She shaved her heavy legs, now, and wore some neat black slippers and even affected an ivory cigarette holder. She had a quick, nervous smile for everyone in the Quarter. I would wake up some mornings and hear her voice on the street and think she was calling me but when I stepped out on the balcony I could see she was merely holding a casual conversation with the woman who sold perfume at Hové King's or a tangerine vendor or one of the prostitutes at the corner bar. The union organizers who had disappointed and betrayed her, the gallant workers in the garment shops, the mean-souled bosses and the sadistic policemen, all of these had receded from the surface of her mind. Art stood out above everything else, it bathed the landscape in a radiant, heavenly glow. Her eyes were lit with it, it trembled on her lips when she spoke, magnified her voice to a trumpet and filled the bigness of her body with a new kind of universal passion. She wanted to stretch out the long, sweet arms of her art—(I keep remembering that speech!)—and embrace the whole world . . .

Well—

I didn't see her for several days and then she suddenly burst into the restaurant one Sunday while I was clearing the tables after the midday meal.

Something has happened, she panted.

What?

I can't tell you! How long will you be?

About ten minutes.

Okay. I'll wait till you're through.

But Irene couldn't sit still. She paced tigerishly up and down the Bohemian dining room with its charcoal nudes on the walls.

I want a job, she said.

Doing what?

Painting this kind of stuff! she said. I want to decorate somebody's bathroom with scatalogical sketches, I want to draw obscene images on the ceilings of bedrooms!

Why?

Because I'm finished, she said, I'm all washed-up and I'm tired of being a whore!

It was sunny that day, terrifically bright on the streets, and Irene's face was like a wound that should have been wrapped up. The bandages were torn away, the gentle humor, the tolerance and the good will so that nothing was visible but the raw, bleeding hurt, the fury and the terrific frustrated bitterness.

Rejected! she said. Every one of them completely rejected!

As we approached the artists' salon I could see that something special was going on that afternoon. The curbs were lined with the kind of motors that the Negro woman had told Irene she would ride down Canal Street in with a man in a full-dress suit.

We'd better not go in there now, I advised.

I got to, said Irene, before they burn my pictures!

Burn them?

Yes, she said, they're planning to destroy my work!

It was the society crowd making a gracious bow to respectable art. Elegant people were standing around with little demitasse cups and frosted cakes and the air was pregnant with polite exclamations.

Irene was shaking terribly now and her face was chalk white. I could see that she was determined to make some kind of a scene and I began to make mental notes of ways to get out quickly.

What she did was to go in the back room where they had piled the rejected canvases like spare pieces of lumber after a house has been built. Their backs were outward, their faces were turned to the wall as though they stood there in shame. Irene, breathing heavily, stooping awkwardly, snatched among them until she had found her own. Then she lifted the largest and stalked with it into the bustling brightness of the little spring salon. As I looked at the persons and objects that she was moving amongst I had a warning sense of something desperately irreconcilable in the air. These delicate vases, these little china cups, these blossoms, these nicely chiseled bits of terra cotta, and also these people with their fastidious clothes and their reserved little voices, they were all too fragile and Irene was something too fierce. There could be no peace between them. I saw her moving straight forward, black and terrible as a thundercloud in all the pale spring brightness, I saw the people before her dividing politely, murmuring and giving way. I heard their nice exclamations, their Ohs and their Ahs. And I thought to myself, If one were conducting a tour of battlefields in action, one might say, *Here on the left is a gorgeous specimen of a twentieth-century man with the top of his skull blown off*, and that one, the stout dowager with the violets at her bosom, would point delicately with her littlest gloved finger and say, *How very nicely it's done!*

This was bitterness, not truth, but expressed my feelings.

Irene had moved over to the middle-aged man in frock coat and pince-nez standing beneath the leathery green fronds of a large potted palm. At first she seemed to be speaking without very much agitation. He was gently, politely warding off her objections. I could see him making fatherly little faces and touching her shoulder with the tip of one finger, just enough to establish contact without the risk of any contamination, while the saliva dribbled ever so slightly from the corner of his mouth.

Then Irene started raising her voice. There was a stir all around her. Coffee cups were set down with tiny click-clicks, a very faint spsss-spsss-spsss began to be heard under or above the ordinary chatter, eyebrows climbed higher, spruce little men craned their necks, rooster-wise, debutantes shimmered and giggled with little breathless spasms, large women waggled their bottoms the way that they do when a disturbance is pending.

Is this the floor show? someone asked.

The girl with the orchids giggled.

At this point Irene's voice rose abruptly to shouting proportions. Something like pandemonium was then beginning to be let loose at the Annual Spring Display, though it was still on a fairly small scale compared to later developments. You know how it is when a crowd of our best people discover all at once that something on the order of the Bubonic Plague has suddenly reared its hideous face amongst them.

The social pattern, which is everything, is suddenly disrupted. There is no longer any logical motion so that they swarm without reason. The head is cut off the chicken, as it were, and she is flying about the yard spouting blood in complete abandon while her frenzied companions cackle in useless sympathy and dismay. Why doesn't she put her head on? What can be done to stop it? The answer is nothing, nothing! On a stage you could ring down the curtain, in a bar you could summon the bouncers, but here amongst our nicest people there is no preparation for anything outrageous to happen. Suppose the police were called? The papers would be full of it tomorrow, a disorderly scene at the Annual Spring Display, it would completely crowd out the references to who served coffee and who was the chairman of what. It would constitute a regular scandal. But could this person be allowed to continue? No, she could not!

Who is she, anyhow? Does anyone know?

What? I can't hear you!

Oh!

Who?

Some Quarter Rat who paints disgusting pictures that couldn't be shown!

Of the actual altercation I could see very little. When I heard the loud impact, the sound of ripping canvas, I said to myself, Christ, she's busted that picture over somebody's head!

Hysteria broke loose at this point. Women who had been exclaiming in little pussycat voices abruptly learned how to scream the way that swimming is learned by suddenly falling in water. Something loud crashed, a window I think it was. I was alarmed, unable to see but full of the wildest conjectures.

Irene! I shouted. Could she have been thrown out?

There was a brief contortion among the tight group of people who now surrounded Irene. The white-haired official was frenziedly spewed from amongst them. He shot straight forward across the floor to the phone on the opposite wall and shouted into its mouth such words as Disturbance, Riot, Police!

But it was too late, this action too tardily taken. Irene was beyond restraint. As the wall of backs divided I had caught a glimpse of her face. My God, what a sight! Her face was no longer colorless, it was livid. Her dress had been torn loose in the struggle and one of her large white breasts was exposed. She was pinioned for that short moment by two stout gentlemen but they could not possibly hold her. She stamped on the toes of one and jabbed her knee into the other's groin so they both fell away with desperate looks of anguish.

Then she was out. Nothing on earth could stop her, not even the Maginot line. Like a human tornado she swept around the four walls, plucking the nice pictures down and tossing them onto the floor, hurling them at her pursuers or at the tea table. The glittering percolator went over, the cut-glass bowl full of pale green sherbet followed right after it. Millions of voices seemed to be shouting together, but over them all, all of the other voices, was always Irene's. Such words as she screamed the nicer ladies had never heard whispered before. Dykes she called them, bitches and son of bitches and—

Well—

As quickly as it had started, just that quickly the whole thing came to a finish. Irene was worn out, she collapsed. She sank down weakly onto the floor among the scattered canvases and frosted cookies and slithering balls of green sherbet. She started crying into a surprisingly small and dainty white handkerchief that she had miraculously produced from the torn bosom of her black crepe dress with the silver and rhinestone buckle. Her thick black hair had come loose and was hanging around her shoulders, she was such a *big* girl, so remarkably big and strong-looking, and now she was crumpled into a heap on the floor and sobbing like a tired child with nothing but havoc around her and people standing back, now, everyone waiting quietly, exhaustedly for the wagon which had been sent for to finally come and remove her. What had been done had been done, the disturbance was practically over . . .

It was exactly one day after this that I lost my job at the Bohemian eating place which resulted in such a crisis in my personal affairs that nothing else seemed to matter. A fellow named Parrott had a jalopy that he was hoping to get to Hollywood in. Between us we had sixteen dollars: with that and a ten-inch section of rubber tube we managed to reach the West Coast about three weeks later. I was going to write pictures for Parrott to star in, but both of us were shortly employed as pin boys at a bowling alley in Laguna Beach.

One Saturday night late that spring I dropped in Mona's for a glass of beer. There was a disturbance in progress. A gentleman had been knocked unconscious in the parking lot and divested of his wallet containing about eighty-six bucks. There was something nostalgic in the atmosphere of this crime so that I couldn't help smiling just a little in spite of the gentleman's hysterical condition. It all blew over in a few minutes, the gentleman said that it was so dark he couldn't possibly identify his assailant and he and the officer very quickly disappeared. They had hardly gone when the floor show started. I was seated at a remote table and could hear a great deal better than I could see. Somebody was playing "The Blue Danube" on a very corny fiddle. I didn't need two guesses. I moved up close to the mike and when his turn was finished I brought Carl over to my table and we had a drink together.

Listen, Carl, I said, You've got eighty-six bucks. You know what you ought to do with it?

Naw. What?

Send Irene a present!

Sure that would be swell, said Carl, except I wouldn't know where to send it to.

Isn't she still in the Quarter?

Hell, no, she took a powder right after that big blowup at the spring display. Somebody in the outfit got big-hearted and they dropped the charges against her. Me, I got sprung about the same time, too, but when I dropped around at her studio, it was empty, by Jesus, all the pictures down off the walls, everything gone except—

Except *what*, Carl?

He grinned.

Do you remember that thing you said to her one night that she liked so much that she wrote it down on the wall?

Uh-huh, sure I remember! There is only one aristocracy, I repeated, the aristocracy of passionate souls.

Yeah! said Carl. Well, *that* was still there.

Then he got up. I got to play another number, he said. What would you like?

Two bits, I told him. I want to cry in some beer.

                                        c. 1940 (*Not previously published*)

The Dark Room

"And your husband, Mrs. Lucca, how long has he been out of employment?"

"God knows how long."

"I've got to have a definite answer, please."

"It musta been since 1930. Maybe longer than that. My husband, he got laid off cause his head was no good. He couldn't remember no more."

"He hasn't worked since?"

"No. He been sick ever since. His head is no good."

"Your sons?"

"Sons? Frank and Tony went off. Frank went to Chicago I think. I don't know. Tony was never no good. The other two, Silva and Lucio still are in school."

"They're attending grammar school?"

"Still are in school."

Mrs. Lucca's broom delved with sudden vigor beneath the bare kitchen table. Brought out a lead spoon, some scraps of paper and a piece of twine. She picked up the spoon and placed it on the table.

"I see," said Miss Morgan. "And you have a daughter?"

"Yes. One girl."

"She is employed?"

"No. She don't work."

"Her name and age, please."

"Name Tina. How old she is? She come just before Silva. Silva fifteen."

"That would make her about sixteen, I suppose?"

"Sixteen."

"I see. I would like to talk to your daughter, Mrs. Lucca."

"Talk to her?"

"Yes, where is she?"

"In there," said Mrs. Lucca, pointing to a closed door.

The social worker got up.

"May I see her?"

"No, don't go in there. She don't like it."

Miss Morgan stiffened.

"Doesn't *like* it? Why not? Is she ill?"

"I dunno whatsamatter with her," said Mrs. Lucca. "She don't want nobody to go in the room with her and she don't want the light turned on."

The broom reached under the stove and extracted a broken cup handle. Mrs. Lucca grunted as she stooped to pick it up. She tossed it into the coal scuttle.

"What is the matter with her, Mrs. Lucca?"

"Who? Tina? I dunno."

"Really! How long has this been going on?"

"God knows how long."

"Please, Mrs. Lucca, try to give straight answers to my questions. Evading them won't improve matters any."

Mrs. Lucca seemed mildly puzzled.

"How long has she been in that room?" repeated Miss Morgan.

"How long? Maybe 'bout six monts."

"Six *months*? Are you *sure*?"

"She started actin' queer long about New Year's. He didn't come over that night. It was the first night he didn't come over in a long time and it was New Year's. She called up his place and his ma told her he was out and not to call him no more. She said he was going to marry some Jewish girl."

"*He*? Who is *he*?"

"The boy she went steady with a long time. A Jewish boy named Sol."

"Was that what made her start behaving like this?"

"Maybe it was. I dunno. She hung up the receiver and come in the kitchen and heated some water. She said she had pains in her stomach."

"Did she?"

"I dunno. Maybe she did. Anyway she went to bed with it and ain't been up since."

Mrs. Lucca's broom made timid excursions around the chair in which the social worker was seated. Miss Morgan drew her feet in quickly with the fastidious gesture of a cat avoiding spilled water. The grimy broom straws moved aimlessly off toward the other end of the room.

"You mean that she's been shut up in that room ever since?"

"Yeah."

"How long has that been?"

"Since last New Year's."

"Six months?"

"Yeah."

"Doesn't she ever come out?"

"She comes out when she got to go to bathroom. She comes out then but that's the only time she ever comes out."

"What does she do in there?"

"I dunno. She just lays in there in the dark and she won't come out. Sometimes she makes a lot of noise, crying and all. The folks upstairs complain sometimes. But mostly she don't say nothing. She just lays in there on the bed."

"Does she eat?"

"Yeah, she eats. Sometimes."

"Sometimes? You mean she doesn't take regular meals?"

"Not regular. Just what he brings her."

"*He*? Who do you mean, Mrs. Lucca?"

"Sol."

"Sol?"

"Yeah, Sol, the boy she went steady with such a long time."

"You mean he comes?"

"Yeah, he comes sometimes."

"I thought you said he got married to some Jewish girl?"

"He did. He married that Jewish girl his folks wanted him to."

"And still he comes to see your daughter?"

"Yeah, he comes to see her. He's the only one she lets in the room with her."

"He goes in there? In the room? With the girl?"

"Yeah."

"Does she know he's married to that other girl?"

"I dunno what she knows. I can't tell. She don't say nothing."

"And yet she lets him come in and talk to her?"

"She lets him come in but he don't talk to her none though."

"Doesn't talk to her? What *does* he do, Mrs. Lucca?"

"I dunno. It's dark in there. I can't tell. Nobody says nothing. He just goes in there and stays awhile and comes out."

"You mean, Mrs. Lucca, you let that man go into the room with her, your daughter, her being in such a condition as that?"

"Yeah. She likes him to go in there with her. It makes her quiet for a while. When he don't come around she takes on something awful. The folks upstairs complain about it sometimes. But when he comes she's better. She stops making noise. And he brings her something to eat every time and she eats whatever he brings her."

The broom made a wide, circular sweep, piling trash into one corner.

"It helps out that way," continued Mrs. Lucca. "We don't have much. Just what we can get from relief and that don't amount to so much. Sometimes we don't even . . ."

"Mama, can I have fifteen cents?"

It was one of the boys, Silva or Lucio, sticking his head through the open window off the fire escape. His nose was bloody.

"Give me fifteen cents, Mama. I bet Jeep he couldn't lick me and he did and he says he'll beat me up worse if I don't come across wit' the dough!"

"Shut up," said Mrs. Lucca.

The boy looked, startled, at Miss Morgan and went clattering back down the fire escape. Shrill cries were heard from the alley and the running of many feet.

Miss Morgan's gaze had not wavered. She was unaware of interruption.

"I suppose you know, Mrs. Lucca, that you can be held responsible!"

"For what?"

There was a blank, strained moment between them.

"Never mind. How long has this thing been going on?"

"What thing?"

"Between this man and your daughter?"

"Tina? Sol? I dunno! God knows how long!"

"That isn't an answer, Mrs. Lucca."

"You want to know how long she's been going with Sol? Almost since she started to school when she was eleven years old."

"I mean how long has this man been coming into her room like that?"

The broom shook itself petulantly and then continued its vague meanderings about the bare kitchen floor.

"Maybe five or six monts. I dunno."

"And you and your husband, Mrs. Lucca, neither of you made any effort to keep him away?"

Mrs. Lucca looked down at the shuffling straws in mute concentration.

"Your husband, Mrs. Lucca, did nothing to prevent this man's coming here?"

"My husband is been sick a long time."

Mrs. Lucca placed a tired forefinger against her forehead.

"He don't think good anymore. And me, I can't do nothing. I got to work all the time. We get along the best that we can. What happens it isn't our fault. It's God's will. That's all we can say, Miss Morgan."

"I see, Mrs. Lucca."

The voice seemed to draw a white chalk line through the air. Mrs. Lucca stopped sweeping and waited. She knew that a verdict was on the point of being delivered. She steeled herself for the words without visibly tensing.

"Mrs. Lucca, the girl will have to be taken away."

"Tina? She won't like that."

"I'm afraid we can't consult her wishes about the matter. Nor yours, Mrs. Lucca."

"I don't think she'll want to be going away nowhere. You don't know Tina. She's stubborn. She screams something awful whenever you try to make her do something she don't want to do. She screams and kicks and bites so you can't come near her."

"She'll have to go."

"I hope she will. I sure hope she will. It ain't decent for her to be laying in there in the dark all the time. It's bad for the boys."

"Boys?"

"Yeah, Silva and Lucio. It ain't decent for them, her layin' there naked like that."

"Naked!"

"Yeah. She won't keep a stitch of clothes on her."

The notebook slapped together with an exclamatory sound. Miss Morgan screwed the lid on her fountain pen.

"She'll have to be taken away in the morning and held for a long observation."

"I hope she'll go but I don't think she will unless he takes her."

"He? You mean?"

"Sol."

"Sol!"

"Yeah, the boy she went steady with such a long time."

"I see! I *see!*"

Mrs. Lucca's broom resumed its slow motion, backwards and forwards, without any obvious purpose. A dry skin of onion rattled under the grimy straws. Backwards and forwards. The damp boards creaked.

c. 1940 (Not previously published)

The Mysteries of the Joy Rio

I

Perhaps because he was a watch repairman, Mr. Gonzales had grown to be rather indifferent to time. A single watch or clock can be a powerful influence on a man, but when a man lives among as many watches and clocks as crowded the tiny, dim shop of Mr. Gonzales, some lagging behind, some skipping ahead, but all ticking monotonously on in their witless fashion, the multitude of them may be likely to deprive them of importance, as a gem loses its value when there are too many just like it which are too easily or cheaply obtainable. At any rate, Mr. Gonzales kept very irregular hours, if he could be said to keep any hours at all, and if he had not been where he was for such a long time, his trade would have suffered badly. But Mr. Gonzales had occupied his tiny shop for more than twenty years, since he had come to the city as a boy of nineteen to work as an apprentice to the original owner of the shop, a very strange and fat man of German descent named Kroger, Emiel Kroger, who had now been dead a long time. Emiel Kroger, being a romantically practical Teuton, had taken time, the commodity he worked with, with intense seriousness. In practically all his behavior he had imitated a perfectly adjusted fat silver watch. Mr. Gonzales, who was then young enough to be known as Pablo, had been his only sustained flirtation with the confusing, quicksilver world that exists outside of regularities. He had met Pablo during a watch-makers' convention in Dallas, Texas, where Pablo, who had illegally come into the country from Mexico a few days before, was drifting hungrily about the streets, and at that time Mr. Gonzales, Pablo, had not grown plump but had a lustrous dark grace which had completely bewitched Mr. Kroger. For as I have noted already, Mr. Kroger was a fat and strange man, subject to the kind of bewitchment that the graceful young Pablo could cast. The spell was so strong that it interrupted

99

the fleeting and furtive practices of a lifetime in Mr. Kroger and induced him to take the boy home with him, to his shop-residence, where Pablo, now grown to the mature and fleshy proportions of Mr. Gonzales, had lived ever since, for three years before the death of his protector and for more than seventeen years after that, as the inheritor of shop-residence, clocks, watches, and everything else that Mr. Kroger had owned except a few pieces of dining-room silver which Emiel Kroger had left as a token bequest to a married sister in Toledo.

Some of these facts are of dubious pertinence to the little history which is to be unfolded. The important one is the fact that Mr. Gonzales had managed to drift enviably apart from the regularities that rule most other lives. Some days he would not open his shop at all and some days he would open it only for an hour or two in the morning, or in the late evening when other shops had closed, and in spite of these caprices he managed to continue to get along fairly well, due to the excellence of his work, when he did it, the fact that he was so well established in his own quiet way, the advantage of his location in a neighborhood where nearly everybody had an old alarm clock which had to be kept in condition to order their lives (this community being one inhabited mostly by people with small-paying jobs), but it was also due in measurable part to the fact that the thrifty Mr. Kroger, when he finally succumbed to a chronic disease of the bowels, had left a tidy sum in government bonds, and this capital, bringing in about a hundred and seventy dollars a month, would have kept Mr. Gonzales going along in a commonplace but comfortable fashion even if he had declined to do anything whatsoever. It was a pity that the late, or rather long-ago, Mr. Kroger, had not understood what a fundamentally peaceable sort of young man he had taken under his wing. Too bad he couldn't have guessed how perfectly everything suited Pablo Gonzales. But youth does not betray its true nature as palpably as the later years do, and Mr. Kroger had taken the animated allure of his young protégé, the flickering lights in his eyes and his quick, nervous movements, his very grace and slimness, as meaning something difficult to keep hold of. And as the old gentleman declined in health, as he did quite steadily during the three years that Pablo lived with him, he was never certain that the incalculably precious bird flown into his nest was not one of sudden passage but rather the kind that prefers to keep a faithful commitment to a single place, the nest-building kind, and not only that, but the very-rare-indeed-kind that gives love back as generously as he takes it. The long-ago Mr. Kroger had paid little attention to his illness, even when it entered the stage of acute pain, so intense was his absorption in what he thought was the tricky business of holding Pablo close to him. If only he had known that for all this time after his decease the boy would still be in the watchshop, how it might have relieved him! But on the other hand, maybe this anxiety, mixed as it was with so much tenderness and sad delight, was actually a blessing, standing as it did between the dying old man and a concern with death.

Pablo had never flown. But the sweet bird of youth had flown from Pablo Gonzales, leaving him rather sad, with a soft yellow face that was just as round as the moon. Clocks and watches he fixed with marvelous delicacy and precision, but he paid no attention to them; he had grown as obliviously accustomed to their many small noises as someone grows to the sound of waves who has always lived by the sea. Although he wasn't aware of it, it was actually light by which he told time, and always in the afternoons when the light had begun to fail (through the narrow window and narrower, dusty skylight at the back of the shop), Mr. Gonzales automatically rose from his stooped position over littered table and gooseneck lamp, took off his close-seeing glasses with magnifying lenses, and took to the street. He did not go far and he always went in the same direction, across town toward the river where there was an old opera house, now converted into a third-rate cinema, which specialized in the showing of cowboy pictures and other films of the sort that have a special appeal to children and male adolescents. The name of this movie house was the Joy Rio, a name peculiar enough but nowhere nearly so peculiar as the place itself.

The old opera house was a miniature of all the great opera houses of the old world, which is to say its interior was faded gilt and incredibly old and abused red damask which extended upwards through at least three tiers and possibly five. The upper stairs, that is, the stairs beyond the first gallery, were roped off and unlighted and the top of the theater was so peculiarly dusky, even with the silver screen flickering far below it, that Mr. Gonzales, used as he was to close work, could not have made it out from below. Once he had been there when the lights came on in the Joy Rio, but the coming on of the lights had so enormously confused and embarrassed him, that looking up was the last thing in the world he felt like doing. He had buried his nose in the collar of his coat and had scuttled out as quickly as a cockroach makes for the nearest shadow when a kitchen light comes on.

I have already suggested that there was something a bit special and obscure about Mr. Gonzales' habitual attendance at the Joy Rio, and that was my intention. For Mr. Gonzales had inherited more than the material possessions of his dead benefactor: he had also come into custody of his old protector's fleeting and furtive practices in dark places, the practices which Emiel Kroger had given up only when Pablo had come into his fading existence. The old man had left Mr. Gonzales the full gift of his shame, and now Mr. Gonzales did the sad, lonely things that Mr. Kroger had done for such a long time before his one lasting love came to him. Mr. Kroger had even practiced those things in the same place in which they were practiced now by Mr. Gonzales, in the many mysterious recesses of the Joy Rio, and Mr. Gonzales knew about this. He knew about it because Mr. Kroger had told him. Emiel Kroger had confessed his whole life and soul to Pablo Gonzales. It was his theory, the theory of most immoralists, that the soul becomes intolerably burdened with lies that have to be told to the world in order to be permitted to live in the world, and that unless this burden is relieved by entire honesty with *some one* person, who is trusted and adored, the soul will finally collapse beneath its weight of falsity. Much of the final months of the life of Emiel Kroger, increasingly dimmed by morphia, were devoted to these whispered confessions to his adored apprentice, and it was as if he had breathed the guilty soul of his past into the ears and brain and blood of the youth who listened, and not long after the death of Mr. Kroger, Pablo, who had stayed slim until then, had begun to accumulate fat. He never became anywhere nearly so gross as Emiel Kroger had been, but his delicate frame disappeared sadly from view among the irrelevant curves of a sallow plumpness. One by one the perfections which he had owned were folded away as Pablo put on fat as a widow puts on black garments. For a year beauty lingered about him, ghostly, continually fading, and then it went out altogether, and at twenty-five he was already the nondescriptly plump and moonfaced little man that he now was at forty, and if in his waking hours somebody to whom he would have to give a true answer had enquired of him, Pablo Gonzales, how much do you think about the dead Mr. Kroger, he probably would have shrugged and said, *Not much now. It's such a long time ago.* But if the question were asked him while he slept, the guileless heart of the sleeper would have responded, *Always, always!*

II

Now across the great marble stairs, that rose above the first gallery of the Joy Rio to the uncertain number of galleries above it, there had been fastened a greasy and rotting length of old velvet rope at the center of which was hung a sign that said to *Keep Out*. But that rope had not always been there. It had been there about twenty years, but the late Mr. Kroger had known the Joy Rio in the days before the flight of stairs was roped off. In those days the mysterious upper galleries of the Joy Rio had been a sort of fiddler's green where practically every device and fashion of carnality had run riot in a gloom so thick that a chance partner could only be discovered by touch. There were not rows of benches (as there were now on the orchestra level and the one gallery still kept in use), but strings of tiny boxes, extending in semicircles from one side of the great proscenium to the other. In some of these boxes brokenlegged chairs might be found lying on their sides and shreds of old hangings still clung to the sliding brass loops at the entrances. According to Emiel Kroger, who is our only authority on these mysteries which share his remoteness in time, one lived up there, in the upper reaches of the Joy Rio, an almost sightless existence where the other senses, the senses of smell and touch and hearing, had to develop a preternatural keenness in order to spare one from making awkward mistakes, such as taking hold of the knee of a boy when it was a girl's knee one looked for, and where sometimes little scenes of panic occurred when a mistake of gender or of compatibility had been carried to a point where radical correction was called for. There had been many fights, there had even been rape and murder in those ancient boxes, till finally the obscure management of the Joy Rio had been compelled by the pressure of notoriety to shut down that part of the immense old building which had offered its principal enticement, and the Joy Rio, which had flourished until then, had then gone into sharp decline. It had been closed down and then reopened and closed down and reopened again. For several years it had opened and shut like a nervous lady's fan. Those were the years in which Mr. Kroger was dying. After his death the fitful era subsided, and now for about ten years the Joy Rio had been continually active as a third-rate cinema, closed only for one week during a threatened epidemic of poliomyelitis some years past and once for a few days when a small fire had damaged the projection booth. But nothing happened there now of a nature to provoke a disturbance. There were no complaints to the management or the police, and the dark glory of the upper galleries was a legend in such memories as that of the late Emiel Kroger and the present Pablo Gonzales, and one by one, of course, those memories died out and the legend died out with them. Places like the Joy Rio and the legends about them make one more than usually aware of the short bloom and the long fading out of things. The angel of such a place is a fat silver angel of sixty-three years in a shiny dark-blue alpaca jacket, with short, fat fingers that leave a damp mark where they touch, that sweat and tremble as they caress between whispers, an angel of such a kind as would be kicked out of heaven and laughed out of hell and admitted to earth only by grace of its habitual slyness, its gift for making itself a counterfeit being, and the connivance of those that a quarter tip and an old yellow smile can corrupt.

But the reformation of the Joy Rio was somewhat less than absolute. It had reformed only to the point of ostensible virtue, and in the back rows of the first gallery at certain hours in the afternoon and very late at night were things going on of the sort Mr. Gonzales sometimes looked for. At those hours the Joy Rio contained few patrons, and since the seats in the orchestra were in far better condition, those who had come to sit comfortably watching the picture would naturally remain downstairs; the few that elected to sit in the nearly deserted rows of the first gallery did so either because smoking was permitted in that section—or *because* . . .

There was a danger, of course, there always is a danger with places and things like that, but Mr. Gonzales was a tentative person not given to leaping before he looked. If a patron had entered the first gallery only in order to smoke, you could usually count on his occupying a seat along the aisle. If the patron had bothered to edge his way toward the center of a row of seats irregular as the jawbone of poor Yorick, one could assume as infallibly as one can assume anything in a universe where chance is the one invariable, that he had chosen his seat with something more than a cigarette in mind. Mr. Gonzales did not take many chances. This was a respect in which he paid due homage to the wise old spirit of the late Emiel Kroger, that romantically practical Teuton who used to murmur to Pablo, between sleeping and waking, a sort of incantation that went like this: Sometimes you will find it and other times you won't find it and the times you don't find it are the times when you have got to be careful. Those are the times when you have got to remember that other times you *will* find it, not *this* time but the *next* time, or the time *after* that, and then you've got to be able to go home without it, yes, those times are the times when you have got to be able to go home without it, go home *alone* without it . . .

Pablo didn't know, then, that he would ever have need of this practical wisdom that his benefactor had drawn from his almost life-long pursuit of a pleasure which was almost as unreal and basically unsatisfactory as an embrace in a dream. Pablo didn't know then that he would inherit so much from the old man who took care of him, and at that time, when Emiel Kroger, in the dimness of morphia and weakness following hemorrhage, had poured into the delicate ear of his apprentice, drop by slow, liquid drop, this distillation of all he had learned in the years before he found Pablo, the boy had felt for this whisper the same horror and pity that he felt for the mortal disease in the flesh of his benefactor, and only gradually, in the long years since the man and his whisper had ceased, had the singsong rigmarole begun to have sense for him, a practical wisdom that such a man as Pablo had turned into, a man such as Mr. Gonzales, could live by safely and quietly and still find pleasure . . .

III

Mr. Gonzales was careful, and for careful people life has a tendency to take on the character of an almost arid plain with only here and there, at wide intervals, the solitary palm tree and its shadow and the spring alongside it. Mr. Kroger's life had been much the same until he had come across Pablo at the watchmakers' convention in Dallas. But so far in Mr. Gonzales' life there had been no Pablo. In his life there had been only Mr. Kroger and the sort of things that Mr. Kroger had looked for and sometimes found but most times continued patiently to look for in the great expanse of arid country which his lifetime had been before the discovery of Pablo. And since it is not my intention to spin this story out any longer than its content seems to call for, I am not going to attempt to sustain your interest in it with a description of the few palm trees on the uneventful desert through which the successor to Emiel Kroger wandered after the death of the man who had been his life. But I am going to remove you rather precipitately to a summer afternoon which we will call *Now* when Mr. Gonzales learned that he was dying, and not only dying but dying of the same trouble that had put the period under the question mark of Emiel Kroger. The scene, if I can call it that, takes place in a doctor's office. After some hedging on the part of the doctor, the word malignant is uttered. The hand is placed on the shoulder, almost contemptuously comforting, and Mr. Gonzales is assured that surgery is unnecessary because the condition is not susceptible to any help but that of drugs to relax the afflicted organs. And after that the scene is abruptly blacked out . . .

Now it is a year later. Mr. Gonzales has recovered more or less from the shocking information that he received from his doctor. He has been repairing watches and clocks almost as well as ever, and there has been remarkably little alteration in his way of life. Only a little more frequently is the shop closed. It is apparent, now, that the disease from which he suffers does not intend to destroy him any more suddenly than it destroyed the man before him. It grows slowly, the growth, and in fact it has recently shown signs of what is called a remission. There is no pain, hardly any and hardly ever. The most palpable symptom is loss of appetite and, as a result of that, a steady decrease of weight. Now rather startlingly, after all this time, the graceful approximation of Pablo's delicate structure has come back out of the irrelevant contours which had engulfed it after the long-ago death of Emiel Kroger. The mirrors are not very good in the dim little residence-shop, where he lives in his long wait for death, and when he looks in them, Mr. Gonzales sees the boy that was loved by the man whom he loved. It is almost Pablo. Pablo has almost returned from Mr. Gonzales.

And then one afternoon . . .

IV

The new usher at the Joy Rio was a boy of seventeen and the little Jewish manager had told him that he must pay particular attention to the roped-off staircase to see to it that nobody slipped upstairs to the forbidden region of the upper galleries, but this boy was in love with a girl named Gladys who came to the Joy Rio every afternoon, now that school was let out for the summer, and loitered around the entrance where George, the usher, was stationed. She wore a thin, almost transparent, white blouse with nothing much underneath it. Her skirt was usually of sheer silken material that followed her heart-shaped loins as raptly as George's hand followed them when he embraced her in the dark ladies' room on the balcony level of the Joy Rio. Sensual delirium possessed him those afternoons when Gladys loitered near him. But the recently changed management of the Joy Rio was not a strict one, and in the summer vigilance was more than commonly relaxed. George stayed near the downstairs entrance, twitching restively in his tight, faded uniform till Gladys drifted in from the afternoon streets on a slow tide of lilac perfume. She would seem not to see him as she sauntered up the aisle he indicated with his flashlight and took a seat in the back of the orchestra section where he could find her easily when the "coast was clear," or if he kept her waiting too long and she was more than usually bored with the film, she would stroll back out to the lobby and inquire in her childish drawl, Where is the Ladies' Room, Please? Sometimes he would curse her fiercely under his breath because she hadn't waited. But he would have to direct her to the staircase, and she would go up there and wait for him, and the knowledge that she was up there waiting would finally overpower his prudence to the point where he would even abandon his station if the little manager, Mr. Katz, had his office door wide open. The ladies' room was otherwise not in use. Its light-switch was broken, or if it was repaired, the bulbs would be mysteriously missing. When ladies other than Gladys enquired about it, George would say gruffly, The ladies' room's out of order. It made an almost perfect retreat for the young lovers. The door left ajar gave warning of footsteps on the grand marble staircase in time for George to come out with his hands in his pockets before whoever was coming could catch him at it. But these interruptions would sometimes infuriate him, especially when a patron would insist on borrowing his flashlight to use the cabinet in the room where Gladys waited with her crumpled silk skirt gathered high about her flanks (leaning against the invisible dried-up washbasin) which were the blazing black heart of the insatiably concave summer.

In the old days Mr. Gonzales used to go to the Joy Rio in the late afternoons but since his illness he had been going earlier because the days tired him earlier, especially the steaming days of August which were now in progress. Mr. Gonzales knew about George and Gladys; he made it his business, of course, to know everything there was to be known about the Joy Rio, which was his earthly heaven, and, of course, George also knew about Mr. Gonzales; he knew why Mr. Gonzales gave him a fifty cent tip every time he inquired his way to the men's room upstairs, each time as if he had never gone upstairs before. Sometimes George muttered something under his breath, but the tributes collected from patrons like Mr. Gonzales had so far ensured his complicity in their venal practices. But then one day in August, on one of the very hottest and blindingly bright afternoons, George was so absorbed in the delights of Gladys that Mr. Gonzales had arrived at the top of the stairs to the balcony before George heard his footsteps. Then he heard them and he clamped a sweating palm over the mouth of Gladys which was full of stammerings of his name and the name of God. He waited, but Mr. Gonzales also waited. Mr. Gonzales was actually waiting at the top of the stairs to recover his breath from the climb, but George, who could see him, now, through the door kept slightly ajar, suspected that he was waiting to catch him coming out of his secret place. A fury burst in the boy. He thrust Gladys violently back against the washbasin and charged out of the room without even bothering to button his fly. He rushed up to the slight figure waiting near the stairs and began to shout a dreadful word at Mr. Gonzales, the word "morphodite." His voice was shrill as a jungle bird's, shouting this word "morphodite." Mr. Gonzales kept backing away from him, with the lightness and grace of his youth, he kept stepping backwards from the livid face and threatening fists of the usher, all the time murmuring, No, no, no, no, no. The youth stood between him and the stairs below so it was toward the upper staircase that Mr. Gonzales took flight. All at once, as quickly and lightly as ever Pablo had moved, he darted under the length of velvet rope with the sign "Keep Out." George's pursuit was interrupted by the manager of the theater, who seized his arm so fiercely that the shoulder seam of the uniform burst apart. This started another disturbance under the cover of which Mr. Gonzales fled farther and farther up the forbidden staircase into regions of deepening shadow. There were several points at which he might safely have stopped but his flight had now gathered an irresistible momentum and his legs moved like pistons bearing him up and up, and then—

At the very top of the staircase he was intercepted. He half turned back when he saw the dim figure waiting above, he almost turned and scrambled back down the grand marble staircase, when the name of his youth was called to him in a tone so commanding that he stopped and waited without daring to look up again.

Pablo, said Mr. Kroger, come up here, Pablo.

Mr. Gonzales obeyed, but now the false power that his terror had given him was drained out of his body and he climbed with effort. At the top of the stairs where Emiel Kroger waited, he would have sunk exhausted to his knees if the old man hadn't sustained him with a firm hand at his elbow.

Mr. Kroger said, This way, Pablo. He led him into the Stygian blackness of one of the little boxes in the once-golden horseshoe of the topmost tier. Now sit down, he commanded.

Pablo was too breathless to say anything except, Yes, and Mr. Kroger leaned over him and unbuttoned his collar for him, unfastened the clasp of his belt, all the while murmuring, There now, there now, Pablo.

The panic disappeared under those soothing old fingers and the breathing slowed down and stopped hurting the chest as if a fox was caught in it, and then at last Mr. Kroger began to lecture the boy as he used to, Pablo, he murmured, don't ever be so afraid of being lonely

that you forget to be careful. Don't forget that you will find it sometimes but other times you won't be lucky, and those are the times when
you have got to be patient, since patience is what you must have when
you don't have luck.

The lecture continued softly, reassuringly, familiar and repetitive as
the tick of a bedroom clock in his ear, and if his ancient protector and
instructor, Emiel Kroger, had not kept all the while soothing him with
the moist, hot touch of his tremulous fingers, the gradual, the very
gradual dimming out of things, his fading out of existence, would have
terrified Pablo. But the ancient voice and fingers, as if they had never
left him, kept on unbuttoning, touching, soothing, repeating the ancient lesson, saying it over and over like a penitent counting prayer
beads, Sometimes you will have it and sometimes you won't have it, so
don't be anxious about it. You must always be able to go home alone
without it. Those are the times when you have got to remember that
other times you will have it and it doesn't matter if sometimes you
don't have it and have to go home without it, go home alone without it,
go home alone without it. The gentle advice went on, and as it went on,
Mr. Gonzales drifted away from everything but the wise old voice in
his ear, even at last from that, but not till he was entirely comforted by
it.

1941 (Published 1954)

Portrait of a Girl in Glass

We lived in a third floor apartment on Maple Street in Saint Louis, on a block which also contained the Ever-ready Garage, a Chinese laundry, and a bookie shop disguised as a cigar store.

Mine was an anomalous character, one that appeared to be slated for radical change or disaster, for I was a poet who had a job in a warehouse. As for my sister Laura, she could be classified even less readily than I. She made no positive motion toward the world but stood at the edge of the water, so to speak, with feet that anticipated too much cold to move. She'd never have budged an inch, I'm pretty sure, if my mother who was a relatively aggressive sort of woman had not shoved her roughly forward, when Laura was twenty years old, by enrolling her as a student in a nearby business college. Out of her "magazine money" (she sold subscriptions to women's magazines), Mother had paid my sister's tuition for a term of six months. It did not work out. Laura tried to memorize the typewriter keyboard, she had a chart at home, she used to sit silently in front of it for hours, staring at it while she cleaned and polished her infinite number of little glass ornaments. She did this every evening after dinner. Mother would caution me to be very quiet. "Sister is looking at her typewriter chart!" I felt somehow that it would do her no good, and I was right. She would seem to know the positions of the keys until the weekly speed drill got underway, and then they would fly from her mind like a bunch of startled birds.

At last she couldn't bring herself to enter the school any more. She kept this failure a secret for a while. She left the house each morning as before and spent six hours walking around the park. This was in February, and all the walking outdoors regardless of weather brought on influenza. She was in bed for a couple of weeks with a curiously happy little smile on her face. Of course Mother phoned the business

110

college to let them know she was ill. Whoever was talking on the other end of the line had some trouble, it seems, in remembering who Laura was, which annoyed my mother and she spoke up pretty sharply. "Laura has been attending that school of yours for two months, you certainly ought to recognize her name!" Then came the stunning disclosure. The person sharply retorted, after a moment or two, that now she *did* remember the Wingfield girl, and that she had not been at the business college *once* in about a month. Mother's voice became strident. Another person was brought to the phone to verify the statement of the first. Mother hung up and went to Laura's bedroom where she lay with a tense and frightened look in place of the faint little smile. Yes, admitted my sister, what they said was true. "I couldn't go any longer, it scared me too much, it made me sick at the stomach!"

After this fiasco, my sister stayed at home and kept in her bedroom mostly. This was a narrow room that had two windows on a dusky areaway between two wings of the building. We called this areaway Death Valley for a reason that seems worth telling. There were a great many alley cats in the neighborhood and one particularly vicious dirty white Chow who stalked them continually. In the open or on the fire escapes they could usually elude him but now and again he cleverly contrived to run some youngster among them into the cul-de-sac of this narrow areaway at the far end of which, directly beneath my sister's bedroom windows, they made the blinding discovery that what had appeared to be an avenue of escape was really a locked arena, a gloomy vault of concrete and brick with walls too high for any cat to spring, in which they must suddenly turn to spit at their death until it was hurled upon them. Hardly a week went by without a repetition of this violent drama. The areaway had grown to be hateful to Laura because she could not look out on it without recalling the screams and the snarls of killing. She kept the shades drawn down, and as Mother would not permit the use of electric current except when needed, her days were spent almost in perpetual twilight. There were three pieces of dingy ivory furniture in the room, a bed, a bureau, a chair. Over the bed was a remarkably bad religious painting, a very effeminate head of Christ with teardrops visible just below the eyes. The charm of the room was produced by my sister's collection of glass. She loved colored glass and had covered the walls with shelves of little glass articles, all of them light and delicate in color. These she washed and polished with endless care. When you entered the room there was always this soft, transparent radiance in it which came from the glass absorbing whatever faint light came through the shades on Death Valley. I have no idea how many articles there were of this delicate glass. There must have been hundreds of them. But Laura could tell you exactly. She loved each one.

She lived in a world of glass and also a world of music. The music came from a 1920 victrola and a bunch of records that dated from about the same period, pieces such as "Whispering" or "The Love Nest" or "Dardanella." These records were souvenirs of our father, a man whom we barely remembered, whose name was spoken rarely. Before his sudden and unexplained disappearance from our lives, he had made this gift to the household, the phonograph and the records, whose music remained as a sort of apology for him. Once in a while, on payday at the warehouse, I would bring home a new record. But Laura seldom cared for these new records, maybe because they reminded her too much of the noisy tragedies in Death Valley or the speed drills at the business college. The tunes she loved were the ones she had always heard. Often she sang to herself at night in her bedroom. Her voice was thin, it usually wandered off-key. Yet it had a curious childlike sweetness. At eight o'clock in the evening I sat down to write in my own mousetrap of a room. Through the closed doors, through the walls, I would hear my sister singing to herself, a piece like "Whispering" or "I Love You" or "Sleepy Time Gal," losing the tune now and then but always preserving the minor atmosphere of the music. I think that was why I always wrote such strange and sorrowful poems in those days. Because I had in my ears the wispy sound of my sister serenading her pieces of colored glass, washing them while she sang or merely looking down at them with her vague blue eyes until the points of gem-like radiance in them gently drew the arching particles of reality from her mind and finally produced a state of hypnotic calm in which she even stopped singing or washing the glass and merely sat without motion until my mother knocked at the door and warned her against the waste of electric current.

I don't believe that my sister was actually foolish. I think the petals of her mind had simply closed through fear, and it's no telling how much they had closed upon in the way of secret wisdom. She never talked very much, not even to me, but once in a while she did pop out with something that took you by surprise.

After work at the warehouse or after I'd finished my writing in the evening, I'd drop in her room for a little visit because she had a restful and soothing effect on nerves that were worn rather thin from trying to ride two horses simultaneously in two opposite directions.

I usually found her seated in the straight-back ivory chair with a piece of glass cupped tenderly in her palm.

"What are you doing? Talking to it?" I asked.

"No," she answered gravely, "I was just looking at it."

On the bureau were two pieces of fiction which she had received as Christmas or birthday presents. One was a novel called the *Rose-Garden Husband* by someone whose name escapes me. The other was *Freckles* by Gene Stratton Porter. I never saw her reading the *Rose-Garden Husband*, but the other book was one that she actually lived with. It had probably never occurred to Laura that a book was something you read straight through and then laid aside as finished. The character Freckles, a one-armed orphan youth who worked in a lumber camp, was someone that she invited into her bedroom now and then for a friendly visit just as she did me. When I came in and found this novel open upon her lap, she would gravely remark that Freckles was having some trouble with the foreman of the lumber camp or that he had just received in injury to his spine when a tree fell on him. She frowned with genuine sorrow when she reported these misadventures of her story-book hero, possibly not recalling how successfully he came through them all, that the injury to the spine fortuitously resulted in the discovery of rich parents and that the bad-tempered foreman had a heart of gold at the end of the book. Freckles became involved in romance with a girl he called The Angel, but my sister usually stopped reading when this girl became too prominent in the story. She closed the book or turned back to the lonelier periods in the orphan's story. I only remember her making one reference to this heroine of the novel. "The Angel is nice," she said, "but seems to be kind of conceited about her looks."

Then one time at Christmas, while she was trimming the artificial tree, she picked up the Star of Bethlehem that went on the topmost branch and held it gravely toward the chandelier.

"Do stars have five points really?" she enquired.

This was the sort of thing that you didn't believe and that made you stare at Laura with sorrow and confusion.

"No," I told her, seeing she really meant it, "they're round like the earth and most of them much bigger."

She was gently surprised by this new information. She went to the window to look up at the sky which was, as usual during Saint Louis winters, completely shrouded by smoke.

"It's hard to tell," she said, and returned to the tree.

So time passed on till my sister was twenty-three. Old enough to be married, but the fact of the matter was she had never even had a date with a boy. I don't believe this seemed as awful to her as it did to Mother.

At breakfast one morning Mother said to me, "Why don't you cultivate ʋome nice young friends? How about down at the warehouse? Aren't there some young men down there you could ask to dinner?"

This suggestion surprised me because there was seldom quite enough food on her table to satisfy three people. My mother was a terribly stringent housekeeper, God knows we were poor enough in actuality, but my mother had an almost obsessive dread of becoming even poorer. A not unreasonable fear since the man of the house was a poet who worked in a warehouse, but one which I thought played too important a part in all her calculations.

Almost immediately Mother explained herself.

"I think it might be nice," she said, "for your sister."

I brought Jim home to dinner a few nights later. Jim was a big red-haired Irishman who had the scrubbed and polished look of well-kept chinaware. His big square hands seemed to have a direct and very innocent hunger for touching his friends. He was always clapping them on your arms or shoulders and they burned through the cloth of your shirt like plates taken out of an oven. He was the best-liked man in the warehouse and oddly enough he was the only one that I was on good terms with. He found me agreeably ridiculous I think. He knew of my secret practice of retiring to a cabinet in the lavatory and working on rhyme schemes when work was slack in the warehouse, and of sneaking up on the roof now and then to smoke my cigarette with a view across the river at the undulant open country of Illinois. No doubt I was classified as screwy in Jim's mind as much as in the others', but while their attitude was suspicious and hostile when they first knew me, Jim's was warmly tolerant from the beginning. He called me Slim, and gradually his cordial acceptance drew the others around, and while he remained the only one who actually had anything to do with me, the others had now begun to smile when they saw me as people smile at an oddly fashioned dog who crosses their path at some distance.

Nevertheless it took some courage for me to invite Jim to dinner. I thought about it all week and delayed the action till Friday noon, the last possible moment, as the dinner was set for that evening.

"What are you doing tonight?" I finally asked him.

"Not a God damn thing," said Jim. "I had a date but her Aunt took sick and she's hauled her freight to Centralia!"

"Well," I said, "why don't you come over for dinner?"

"Sure!" said Jim. He grinned with astonishing brightness.

I went outside to phone the news to Mother.

Her voice that was never tired responded with an energy that made the wires crackle.

"I suppose he's Catholic?" she said.

"Yes," I told her, remembering the tiny silver cross on his freckled chest.

"Good!" she said. "I'll bake a salmon loaf!"

And so we rode home together in his jalopy.

I had a curious feeling of guilt and apprehension as I led the lamb-like Irishman up three flights of cracked marble steps to the door of Apartment F, which was not thick enough to hold inside it the odor of baking salmon.

Never having a key, I pressed the bell.

"Laura!" came Mother's voice. "That's Tom and Mr. Delaney! Let them in!"

There was a long, long pause.

"Laura?" she called again. "I'm busy in the kitchen, you answer the door!"

Then at last I heard my sister's footsteps. They went right past the door at which we were standing and into the parlor. I heard the creaking noise of the phonograph crank. Music commenced. One of the oldest records, a march of Sousa's, put on to give her the courage to let in a stranger.

The door came timidly open and there she stood in a dress from Mother's wardrobe, a black chiffon ankle-length and high-heeled slippers on which she balanced uncertainly like a tipsy crane of melancholy plumage. Here eyes stared back at us with a glass brightness and her delicate wing-like shoulders were hunched with nervousness.

"Hello!" said Jim, before I could introduce him.

He stretched out his hand. My sister touched it only for a second.

"Excuse me!" she whispered, and turned with a breathless rustle back to her bedroom door, the sanctuary beyond it briefly revealing itself with the tinkling, muted radiance of glass before the door closed rapidly but gently on her wraithlike figure.

Jim seemed to be incapable of surprise.

"Your sister?" he asked.

"Yes, that was her," I admitted. "She's terribly shy with strangers."

"She looks like you," said Jim, "except she's pretty."

Laura did not reappear till called to dinner. Her place was next to Jim at the drop-leaf table and all through the meal her figure was slightly tilted away from his. Her face was feverishly bright and one eyelid, the one on the side toward Jim, had developed a nervous wink. Three times in the course of the dinner she dropped her fork on her plate with a terrible clatter and she was continually raising the water glass to her lips for hasty little gulps. She went on doing this even after the water was gone from the glass. And her handling of the silver became more awkward and hurried all the time.

I thought of nothing to say.

To Mother belonged the conversational honors, such as they were. She asked the caller about his home and family. She was delighted to learn that his father had a business of his own, a retail shoe store somewhere in Wyoming. The news that he went to night school to study accounting was still more edifying. What was his heart set on beside the warehouse? Radio-engineering? My, my, my! It was easy to see that here was a very up-and-coming young man who was certainly going to make his place in the world!

Then she started to talk about her children. Laura, she said, was not cut out for business. She was domestic, however, and making a home was really a girl's best bet.

Jim agreed with all this and seemed not to sense the ghost of an implication. I suffered through it dumbly, trying not to see Laura trembling more and more beneath the incredible unawareness of Mother.

And bad as it was, excruciating in fact, I thought with dread of the moment when dinner was going to be over, for then the diversion of food would be taken away, we would have to go into the little steam-heated parlor. I fancied the four of us having run out of talk, even Mother's seemingly endless store of questions about Jim's home and his job all used up finally—the four of us, then, just sitting there in the parlor, listening to the hiss of the radiator and nervously clearing our throats in the kind of self-consciousness that gets to be suffocating.

But when the blancmange was finished, a miracle happened.

Mother got up to clear the dishes away. Jim gave me a clap on the shoulders and said, "Hey, Slim, let's go have a look at those old records in there!"

He sauntered carelessly into the front room and flopped down on the floor beside the victrola. He began sorting through the collection of worn-out records and reading their titles aloud in a voice so hearty that it shot like beams of sunlight through the vapors of self-consciousness engulfing my sister and me.

He was sitting directly under the floor-lamp and all at once my sister jumped up and said to him, "Oh—you have freckles!"

Jim grinned. "Sure that's what my folks call me—Freckles!"

"Freckles?" Laura repeated. She looked toward me as if for the confirmation of some too wonderful hope. I looked away quickly, not knowing whether to feel relieved or alarmed at the turn that things were taking.

Jim had wound the victrola and put on *Dardanella*.

He grinned at Laura.

"How about you an' me cutting the rug a little?"

"What?" said Laura breathlessly, smiling and smiling.

"Dance!" he said, drawing her into his arms.

As far as I knew she had never danced in her life. But to my everlasting wonder she slipped quite naturally into those huge arms of Jim's, and they danced round and around the small steam-heated parlor, bumping against the sofa and chairs and laughing loudly and happily together. Something opened up in my sister's face. To say it was love is not too hasty a judgment, for after all he had freckles and that was what his folks called him. Yes, he had undoubtedly assumed the identity—for all practical purposes—of the one-armed orphan youth who lived in the Limberlost, that tall and misty region to which she retreated whenever the walls of Apartment F became too close to endure.

Mother came back in with some lemonade. She stopped short as she entered the portieres.

"Good heavens! Laura? Dancing?"

Her look was absurdly grateful as well as startled.

"But isn't she stepping all over you, Mr. Delaney?"

"What if she does?" said Jim, with bearish gallantry. "I'm not made of eggs!"

"Well, well, well!" said Mother, senselessly beaming.

"She's light as a feather!" said Jim. "With a little more practice she'd dance as good as Betty!"

There was a little pause of silence.

"Betty?" said Mother.

"The girl I go out with!" said Jim.

"Oh!" said Mother.

She set the pitcher of lemonade carefully down and with her back to the caller and her eyes on me, she asked him just how often he and the lucky young lady went out together.

"Steady!" said Jim.

Mother's look, remaining on my face, turned into a glare of fury.

"Tom didn't mention that you went out with a girl!"

"Nope," said Jim. "I didn't mean to let the cat out of the bag. The boys at the warehouse'll kid me to death when Slim gives the news away."

He laughed heartily but his laughter dropped heavily and awkwardly away as even his dull senses were gradually penetrated by the unpleasant sensation the news of Betty had made.

"Are you thinking of getting married?" said Mother.

"First of next month!" he told her.

It took her several moments to pull herself together. Then she said in a dismal tone, "How nice! If Tom had only told us we could have asked you *both*!"

Jim had picked up his coat.

"Must you be going?" said Mother.

"I hope it don't seem like I'm rushing off," said Jim, "but Betty's gonna get back on the eight o'clock train an' by the time I get my jalopy down to the Wabash depot—"

"Oh, then, we mustn't keep you."

Soon as he'd left, we all sat down, looking dazed.

Laura was the first to speak.

"Wasn't he nice?" she asked. "And all those freckles!"

"Yes," said Mother. Then she turned to me.

"You didn't mention that he was engaged to be married!"

"Well, how did I know that he was engaged to be married?"

"I thought you called him your best friend down at the warehouse?"

"Yes, but I didn't know he was going to be married!"

"How peculiar!" said Mother. "How very peculiar!"

"No," said Laura gently, getting up from the sofa. "There's nothing peculiar about it."

She picked up one of the records and blew on its surface a little as if it were dusty, then set it softly back down.

"People in love," she said, "take everything for granted."

What did she mean by that? I never knew.

She slipped quietly back to her room and closed the door.

Not very long after that I lost my job at the warehouse. I was fired for writing a poem on the lid of a shoe-box. I left Saint Louis and took to moving around. The cities swept about me like dead leaves, leaves that were brightly colored but torn away from the branches. My nature changed. I grew to be firm and sufficient.

In five years' time I had nearly forgotten home. I had to forget it, I couldn't carry it with me. But once in a while, usually in a strange town before I have found companions, the shell of deliberate hardness is broken through. A door comes softly and irresistibly open. I hear the tired old music my unknown father left in the place he abandoned as faithlessly as I. I see the faint and sorrowful radiance of the glass, hundreds of little transparent pieces of it in very delicate colors. I hold my breath, for if my sister's face appears among them—the night is hers!

June 1943 (Published 1948)

The Angel in the Alcove

Suspicion is the occupational disease of landladies and long association with them has left me with an obscure sense of guilt I will probably never be free of. The initial trauma in this category was inflicted by a landlady I had in the old French Quarter of New Orleans when I was barely twenty. She was the archetype of the suspicious landlady. She had a room of her own but preferred to sleep on a rattling cot in the downstairs hall so that none of her tenants could enter or leave the establishment during the night without her grudging permission. When finally I left there I fooled the old woman. I left by way of a balcony and a pair of sheets. I was miles out of town on the Old Spanish Trail to the West before the old woman found out I had gotten past her.

The downstairs hall of this rooming house on Bourbon Street was totally lightless. You had to grope your way through it with cautious revulsion, trailing your fingers along the damp, cracked plaster until you arrived at the door or the foot of the stairs. You never reached either without the old woman's challenge. Her ghostly figure would spring bolt upright on the rattling iron cot. She would utter one syllable—*Who?* If she were not satisfied with the identification given, or suspected that you were taking your luggage out in a stealthy departure or bringing somebody in for carnal enjoyment, a match would be struck on the floor and held toward you for several moments. In its weirdly flickering light she would squint her eyes at you until her doubts were dismissed. Then she would flop back down in a huddle of sour blankets and if you waited to listen you would hear mutterings vicious and coarse as any that drunks in Quarter barrooms ever gave voice to.

She was a woman of paranoidal suspicion and her suspicion of me was unbounded. Often she came in my room with the morning paper and read aloud some item concerning an act of crime in the Quarter. After the reading she would inspect me closely for any guilty change of countenance, and I would nearly always gratify her suspicion with a deep flush and inability to return her look. I am sure she had chalked up dozens of crimes against me and was only waiting for some more concrete betrayal to call the police, a captain of whom, she had warned me, was her first cousin.

The landlady was a victim of dead beats, that much should be admitted in her defense. None of her tenants were regular payers. Some of them clung to their rooms for months and months with only promises given of future payments. One of these was a widow named Mrs. Wayne. Mrs. Wayne was the most adroit sponger in the house. She even succeeded in finagling gratuities from the landlady. Her fortune was in her tongue. She was a wonderful raconteur of horribly morbid or salacious stories. Whenever she smelled food cooking her door would fly open and she would dart forth with a mottled blue and white saucepan held to her bosom coquettishly as a lace fan. Undoubtedly she was half starved and the odor of food set her off like a powerful drug, for there was an abnormal brilliance in her chatter. She tapped on the door from which the seductive smell came but entered before there could be any kind of response. Her tongue would be off before she was fairly inside and no amount of rudeness short of forcible ejection from the room would suffice to discourage her. There was something pitifully winning about the old lady. Even her bad-smelling breath became a component of her unwholesome appeal. To me it was the spectacle of so much heroic vitality in so wasted a vessel that warmed my heart toward the widow. I never did any cooking in my attic bedroom. I only met Mrs. Wayne in the landlady's kitchen on those occasions when I had earned my supper by some small job on the premises. The landlady herself was not entirely immune to Mrs. Wayne's charm and the stories unmistakably entranced her. As she put things on the stove she would always remark, If the bitch gets a sniff of this cookin' wild horses won't hold 'er!

In eight years' time such characters disappear, the earth swallows them up, the walls absorb them like moisture. Undoubtedly old Mrs. Wayne and her battered utensil have made their protesting departure and I am not at all sure that with them the world has not lost the greatest pathological genius since Baudelaire or Poe. Her favorite subject was the deaths of relatives and friends which she had attended with an eye and ear from which no agonizing detail escaped annotation.

Her memory served them up in the landlady's kitchen so graphically that I would find myself sick with horror and yet so fascinated that the risk of losing my appetite for a hard-earned supper would not prevail upon me to shut my ears. The landlady was equally spellbound. Gradually her gruff mumblings of disbelief and impatient gestures would give way to such morbid enjoyment that her jaws would slacken and dribble. A faraway mesmerized look would come into her usually pin-sharp eyes. All the while Mrs. Wayne with the saucepan held to her bosom would be executing a slow and oblique approach to the great kitchen stove. So powerful was her enchantment that even when she was actually removing the lid from the stewpot and ladling out some of its contents into her saucepan, although the landlady's look would follow her movements there would not appear to be any recognition. Not until the hapless protagonist of the story had endured his final conclusion—his eyeballs popped from their sockets and ghastly effluvia drenching his bedclothes—did the charm loosen enough to permit the narrator's listeners any clear knowledge of what went on outside the scene that was painted. By that time Mrs. Wayne had scraped her saucepan clean with wolfish relish and made her way so close to the door that if any unpleasantness attended the landlady's emergence from trance, the widow could be out of earshot before it achieved a momentum.

In this old house it was either deathly quiet or else the high plaster walls were ringing like fire bells with angry voices, with quarrels over the use of the lavatory or accusations of theft or threats of eviction. I had no door to my room which was in the attic, only a ragged curtain that couldn't exclude the barrage of human wretchedness often exploding. The walls of my room were pink and green stippled plaster and there was an alcove window. This alcove window shone faintly in the night. There was a low bench beneath it. Now and again when the room was otherwise lightless a misty grey figure would appear to be seated on this bench in the alcove. It was the tender and melancholy figure of an angel or some dim, elderly madonna. The apparition occurred in the alcove most often on those winter nights in New Orleans when slow rain is falling from a sky not clouded heavily enough to altogether separate the town from the moon. New Orleans and the moon have always seemed to me to have an understanding between them, an intimacy of sisters grown old together, no longer needing more than a speechless look to communicate their feelings to each other. This lunar atmosphere of the city draws me back whenever the waves of energy which removed me to more vital towns have spent themselves and a time of recession is called for. Each time I have felt some rather profound psychic wound, a loss or a failure, I have returned to this city. At such periods I would seem to belong there and no place else in the country.

During this first period in New Orleans none of the small encouragements in my life as a writer had yet come along and I had already accepted the terms of anonymity and failure. I had already learned to make a religion of endurance and a secret of my desperation. The nights were comforting. When the naked lightbulb had been turned off and everything visible gone except the misty alcove set deeply and narrowly into the wall above Bourbon, I would seem to slip into another state of being which had no trying associations with the world. For a while the alcove would remain empty, just a recess that light came faintly into: but after my thoughts had made some dreamy excursion or other and I turned again to look in that direction, the transparent figure would noiselessly have entered and seated herself on the bench below the window and begun that patient watching which put me to sleep. The hands of the figure were folded among the colorless draperies of her lap and her eyes were fixed up on me with a gentle, unquestioning look which I came to remember as having belonged to my grandmother during her sieges of illness when I used to go to her room and sit by her bed and want to say something or put my hand over hers but could not do either, knowing that if I did I would burst into tears that would trouble her more than her illness.

The appearance of this grey figure in the alcove never preceded the time of falling asleep by more than a few moments. When I saw her there I thought comfortably, Ah, now, I'm about to slip away, it will all be gone in a moment and won't come back until morning . . .

On one of those nights a more substantial visitor came to my room. I was jolted out of sleep by a warmth that was not my own, and I awoke to find that someone had entered my room and was crouching over the bed. I jumped up and nearly cried out, but the arms of the visitor passionately restrained me. He whispered his name which was that of a tubercular young artist who slept in the room adjoining. I want to, I want to, he whispered. So I lay back and let him do what he wanted until he was finished. Then without any speech he got up and left my room. For a while afterwards I heard him coughing and muttering to himself through the wall between us. Turbulent feelings were on both sides of the wall. But at last I was drowsy again. I cocked an eye toward the alcove. Yes, she was there. I wondered if she had witnessed the strange goings on and what her attitude was toward perversions of longing. But nothing gave any sign. The two weightless hands so loosely clasping each other among the colorless draperies of the lap, the cool and believing grey eyes in the faint pearly face, were immobile as statuary. I felt that she had permitted the act to occur and had neither blamed nor approved, and so I went off to sleep.

Not long after the episode in my room the artist was involved in a terrible scene with the landlady. His disease was entering the final stage, he coughed all the time but managed to go on working. He was a quicksketch artist at the Court of the Two Parrots which was around the corner on Toulouse. He did not trust anybody or anything. He lived in a world completely hostile to him, unrelentingly hostile, and no other being could enter the walls about him for more than the frantic moments desire drove him to. He would not give in to the mortal fever which licked all the time at his nerves. He invented all sorts of trivial complaints and grudges to hide from himself the knowledge that he was dying. One of these subterfuges to which he resorted was a nightly preoccupation with bedbugs. He claimed that his mattress was infested with them, and every morning he made an angry report to the landlady on the number that had bitten him during the night. These numbers grew and grew to appalling figures. The old woman wouldn't believe him. Finally one morning he did get her into the room to take a look at the bedclothes.

I heard him breathing hoarsely while the old woman shuffled and rattled about the corner his bed was in.

Well, she finally grunted, I ain't found nothin'.

Christ, said the artist, you're blind!

Okay! You show me! What is there on this bed?

Look at that! said the artist.

What?

That spot of blood on the pillow.

Well?

That's where I smashed a bedbug as big as my thumbnail!

Ho, ho, ho, said the landlady. That's where you spit up blood!

There was a pause in which his breathing grew hoarser. His speech when it burst out again was dreadfully altered.

How dare you, God damn you, say that!

Ho, ho, ho! I guess you claim you never spit up no blood?

No, no, never! he shouted.

Ho, ho, ho! You spit up blood all the time. I've seen you spit on the stairs and in the hall and on the floor of this bedroom. You leave a trail of it everywhere that you go, a bloody track like a chicken that runs with its head off. You hawk and you spit and you spread contamination. And that ain't all that you do by a long shot neither!

Now, yelled the artist—What kind of a dirty insinuation is *that*?

Ho, ho, ho! Insinuation of nothin' but what's known facts!

Get out! he shouted.

I'm in my own house and I'll say what I want where I please! I know all about you degenerates in the Quarter. I ain't let rooms ten years in the Quarter for nothin'. A bunch of rotten half-breeds and drunks an' degenerates, that's what I've had to cope with. But you're the worst of the bunch, barring none! And it's not just here but at the Two Parrots, too. Your awful condition's become the main topic of talk at the place where you work. You spit all around your easel in the courtyard. It's got to be mopped with a strong disinfectant each night. The management is disgusted. They wish you would fold up your easel and get to hell out. They only don't ask you because you're a pitiful case. Why, one of the waitresses told me some customers left without paying their bill because you was hawking and spitting right next to their table. That's how it is, and the management's fed up with it!

You're making up lies!

It's God's own truth! I got it from the cashier!

I ought to hit you!

Go on!

I ought to knock your ugly old lying face in!

Go on, go on, just try it! I got a nephew that's a captain on the police force! Hit me an you'll land smack in the House of Detention! A rubber hose on your back is what you'll git in there!

I ought to twist those dirty lies out of your neck!

Ho, ho, just try it! Even the effort would kill you!

You'll be punished, he gasped. One of these nights you'll get a knife stuck in you!

By you, I suppose? Ho, ho! You'll die on the street, you'll cough up your lungs in the gutter! You'll go to the morgue. Nobody will claim that skinny cadaver of yours. You'll go in a box and be dumped off a barge in the river. The sooner the better is how I look at it, too. A case like you is a public nuisance and danger. You've got no right to expose healthy people to you. You ought to go into the charity ward at Saint

Vincent's. That is the place for a person in dying condition who ain't got the sense to know what is really wrong with him but goes about raising a stink about bugs putting blood on his pillow. Huh! Bugs! You're the bugs that puts blood all over this linen! It's you, not bugs, that makes such a filthy mess at the Court of Two Parrots it's got to be scoured with lye when you leave ev'ry night! It's you, not bugs, that drives the customers off without paying their checks. The management's not disgusted with bugs, but with you! And if you don't leave of your own sweet accord pretty quick you'll be given y'ur notice. And I'm not keepin' yuh neither. Not after y'ur threats an' the scene that you've made this mawnin'. I want you to gather all of y'ur old junk up, all of y'ur dirty old handkerchiefs an' y'ur bottles, and get 'em all out of here by twelve o'clock noon, or by God, an' by Jesus, anything that's left here is going straight down to the incinerator! I'll gather it up on the end of a ten-foot pole and dump it into the fire, cause nothing you touch is safe for human contact!

He ran from the room, I heard him running downstairs and out of the building. I went to the alcove window and watched him spinning wildly around in the street. He was crazed with fury. A waiter from the Chinese restaurant came out and caught at his arm, a drunk from a bar reasoned with him. He sobbed and lamented and wandered from door to door of the ancient buildings until the drunk had maneuvered him into a bar.

The landlady and a fat old Negress who worked on the place removed the young man's mattress from his bed and lugged it into the courtyard. They stuffed it into the iron pit of the incinerator and set it afire and stood at respectful distance watching it burn. The landlady wasn't content with just the burning, she made a long speech at the top of her voice about it.

It's not bein' burned because of no bugs, she shouted. I'm burnin' this mattress because it's contaminated. A T.B. case has been on it, a filthy degenerate and a liar!

She went on and on until the mattress was fully consumed, and after.

Then the old Negress was sent upstairs to remove the young man's belongings. It had begun to rain and despite the landlady's objections the Negress put all of the things beneath the banana tree in the courtyard and covered them with a discarded sheet of linoleum weighted down with loose bricks.

At sundown the young man returned to the place. I heard him coughing and gasping in the rainy courtyard as he collected his things from under the fantastic green and yellow umbrella of the banana tree. He seemed to be talking about all the wrongs he had suffered since he had come into the world, but at last the complaints were centered upon the loss of a handsome comb. Oh, my God, he muttered, She's stolen my comb, I had a beautiful comb that I got from my mother, a tortoise-shell comb with a silver and pearl handle on it. That's gone, it's been stolen, the comb that belonged to my mother!

At last it was found, or the young man gave up the search, for his talk died out. A wet silver hush fell over the house on Bourbon as daylight and rain both ended their business there, and in my room the luminous dial of a clock and the misty gray of the alcove were all that remained for me of the visible world.

The episode put an end to my stay at the house. For several nights after that the transparent grey angel failed to appear in the alcove and sleep had to come without any motherly sanction. So I decided to give up my residence there. I felt that the delicate old lady angel had tacitly warned me to leave, and that if I ever was visited by her again, it would be at another time in another place—which still haven't come.

October 1943 (Published 1948)

Oriflamme

Immediately on waking that morning she felt the gravity of flesh which had virtually pinned her to her bed for weeks now mysteriously lifted away from her during the night. Some heavy sheath of air had unwound from her and had been replaced by atmosphere of an impalpable and electric kind. It could be the weather, changing from sullen to brilliant. All articles of glass in the room were pulsating with that brilliance as her body was with a renewed vitality.

Thoughtlessly she stretched her hand to the bedside phone, wanting to speak to someone: then the voices of the few people she knew rang dissonantly in her ears: there was not one voice among the babble of voices that she wanted to separate from the others, no, this morning's lightness couldn't be trusted to them. Which of them would be likely to say to her, Yes, I know what you mean, I understand what you're saying. The air is different this morning.

For there was a conspiracy of dullness in the world, a universal plan to shut out the resurgences of spirit which might interfere with clockwork. Better to keep your elevation unseen until it is higher than strangers' hands can reach to pull you down to their level.

She put the telephone down and sat on the edge of her bed. The little unsteadiness she felt in rising was not due to weakness but to this astonishing lack of gravity. Now here was a peculiar thing. Until this moment she had not understood the meaning of her illness. It was all the same thing, sickness and fatigue and all attritions of the body and spirit, it all came from the natural anarchy of a heart that was compelled to wear uniform.

She went to her closet. It was full of discreetly colored and fashioned garments which all appeared the same style and shade and appeared to be designed for camouflage, for protective concealment, of that anarchy of the heart. She had lived up till now a subterranean exis-

128

tence, not only because she had employment in the economy basement of Famous-Barr, under the forbidding scrutiny of Mr. Mason and countless strangers who pinned her to the counter as illness had lately pinned her to the bed, but because she had not trusted the whisper in her that said, The truth has not yet been spoken!

Could she speak it?

There is speech and there are verbal symbols. The telephone had warned her against the first, but as she looked at the closet with its garments for winter, so appropriately descended from the backs of sheep, it occurred to her that revolution begins in putting on bright colors.

She left the closet and returned to the wardrobe trunk where lighter clothes were preserved for lighter seasons. She tore it open, breathing heavily with excitement. Disappointment was there also. The clothes smelt of camphor and none of them had a really challenging air.

She slammed the closet door shut, having snatched from it the first dress that came to her reach.

Obviously it was necessary to get hold of something new . . .

She tore off her nightgown and stood shivering in front of the chilly closet mirror. How thin she was! No wonder she never looked really well in clothes. They could not express the mysterious delicacy of her body. It was white but not white. It was blue spilled delicately over white. And there were glints of silver and rose. Nobody knew about that. Only one person had ever seemed to suspect it. The high school dance in Grenada, Mississippi. That red-faced boy who beat the kettle-drum so loudly and not in tempo and his virtuosity with the percussion had made Miss Fitzgerald so mad she had dragged him off the platform and slapped him and he had grinned and started dancing alone. She herself had then edged out a little from the corner she sat in, watching the couples dance. She was shy and had not been well lately. He had spun over to where she was standing and had wordlessly seized her and spun her with him around the yellow gymnasium and though she had started coughing and tasted the hot, metallic flavor of blood in her mouth, he had not let her go: not till they had gone clear around the room to the Blue Danube and had come to the festooned entrance. Then he had taken her arm and led her out. She tried to conceal the red stain on the hand that she had coughed into as soon as he had released her. But it was dark in the hall, nearly dark, and the two or three out there were grinning toward the brilliant entrance of the gymnasium.

Still not speaking, he jerked her into another door. In there it was all dark completely and smelt of sweaty clothes. They banged against something that rang out like an ugly, toneless bell, the metal door of a locker. He backed her against it and pinioned her there while his hands explored her body. It was thrilling and shameful. Thrilling then and shameful afterward. Guy was the red boy's name. He had dropped out of school a week or two after this and had disappeared from Grenada. He was not heard of again until the following year when it became known that he had met with an accident on a freight train somewhere in the West. Had lost both legs. And later it became known that he was dead and that his widowed mother had said she was glad of it because he had broken her heart with his vagrant existence . . .

Thinking of him she had always thought of those beautiful paper lanterns and crepe-paper ribbons that hung defeated in the yellow gymnasium . . .

But that was so long ago now!

Outside!

It was indeed a new season if not a new world. The air had been given those shots which the doctor suggested. The blue was not only vivid but energetic. And there was white, too, the sort of white that her hidden body was made of. A mass of bonny white cloud stood over the Moolah Temple. It suddenly made up its mind and started moving. It moved now over the Langan & Taylor Storage. A nude young bather it was. An innocent white sky-lounger had taken off clothes and become a body that floats. And I shall, too. Or am already floating. Floating. The power of anarchy moves me. I have both legs. No accident has deprived me of forward motion. If chance is blind, it is still not set against me. And so I move. Past Langan & Taylor Storage and Hartwig's Beauty Salon. Past the doctor's suggestion, Go slowly and you'll go far. I am looking for something. But that means hesitation and I can't wait. He didn't and lost his legs. I still have mine and they're bearing me forward. I want, and will have, the banner that he let go of. The first that I see. Desire is. Wearing apparel. See and have on, that quickly. The white sky-lounger, capricious runner in heaven, has dropped a red dress somewhere. For me to put on and become her eternal sister. Oh, where? Not far off, Anna! The window is blazing with it already. Across the avenue, yes! In Paris Designs! The window is blazing with it. Correct as a go sign. Grab it!

She couldn't speak for a minute, her throat was too full of breathlessness—or breath.

I want that dress, she panted, the red one displayed in the window!
Very well, miss.
I haven't much time, please hurry!
I'm doing my best. It's a little bit difficult getting things out of the window.
Then let me do it!
That won't be necessary, the woman said coldly.
She now had the flag and was gingerly folding it up.
Her hands were gray. They were alien to the fabric as mice to roses. Their touch would wither it, dampen it, smother its flame.
Anna snatched the silk from her.
Don't wrap it up, madam! I want to put it on now!
The woman fell back as if cold water had drenched her.
But this is red silk, a dress for the evening, miss!
I realize that but I want to put it on now! Where is your dressing room?
Here, but—
Anna swept by her and plunged into the dim closet. The dress was all wine and roses flung onto her body.
Take by surprise and the world gives up resistance.
She paid the woman.
The blowing street took part in her celebration. She moved, she moved, in a glorious banner wrapped, the red part of a flag!

It flashed, it flashed. It billowed against her fingers. Her body surged forward. A capital ship with cannon. Boom. On the far horizon. Boom. White smoke is holy. Nobody understands it. It goes on, on, without the world's understanding. Red is holy. Nobody understands it. It goes on, on, without the world's understanding. Blue is holy. Blue goes on without the world's understanding. Flags are holy but nobody understands them. Flags go on without the world's understanding. Boom. Goes on without the world's understanding. The heart can't wait. Revolts without understanding. Boom. Goes on. Without the world's understanding. . .

The red silk raised and lowered beneath her with power, the effortless power of wings that bore her forward. Into the brilliant new morning. No plan. No waiting. She moved without a direction. Direction was unimportant. The world was lost. She felt it slipping behind her, a long way back. There was only Mr. Mason still in view. But even he was beginning to fall back now. Could not keep up his paunchy satyr pursuit. When young he could run. That season he first appeared at Famous-Barr, he was just out of college. He moved with a spring, was jaunty, inclined to jokes. The cloves on his breath were exciting. His manicured fingers were just removed from a fireplace. In locker-room blackness they might have been like Guy's, exploring, demanding, creating life in the blood. But the lights were never turned out in the bargain basement, and that one time they went to the Loew's State Theater, his fingers had not adventured beyond her knee. The bus going home had been so everlasting. They ran out of talk and a self-conscious coldness developed. Before they reached the place where she got off, they were strangers. Her throat was so tight that she had distrusted her voice. At the door he said, Well, this has been nice, Miss Kimball. And she, unable to open her mouth or her heart, had flung herself sobbing, not on the bed but on the floor—as soon as she heard his feet going down the steps. . . . The next day he had been jollier than ever. But with a difference. Why pretend? There is a failure with people. And that is why some people become so savage and tear at life and leave it in shreds and tatters. Because in gentleness there is failure so often. If you can't whisper, then it is wise to shout. Better to have it broken and violated but still in your clasp than never to have at all. In the end perhaps they understand more than you think and some remember and there is a fleshless reunion . . .

He'd worn not well in the five years that had followed. When things don't change, their sameness becomes an accretion. That is why all society puts on flesh. Succumbs to the cubicles and begins to fill them. The bargain basement had put fat on Mr. Mason. The change boxes took his youth and gave him quarters. Some other girl now was employed at counter seven. Well, let her have it, the Pepperel and percale, and Mr. Mason. And give her the scissors, give her the spool of tape. She would have assurance. A competent Miss she would be. She would cut through cloth with the long, sure stroke of an oarsman. As I cut now through the novel brilliance of morning! I, I am the red silk of a flag! Let nobody stop me till I have—

She had become a little disoriented. Before her stood a gigantic equestrian statue. Her chin just reached the top of the granite pediment. There were the hooves on the level with her eyes. It looked as though the horse was about to step on her. Her eyes traveled upward to study the towering figure. All green it had turned with an ancient, mossy greenness. It bore a shield and elevated a sword. The look was fierce and compelling. Who was this stranger, this menacing giant on horseback? Her eyes descended to gaze at the inscription. *Saint Louis* it said. Ah, yes, the name of the city. No wonder she felt so breathless. She had climbed to the highest point in the park, and now if she turned to look in the other direction, all of the city named for this ruthless horseman would stretch underneath, to the east as far as the river. She would not turn. The city had never pleased her. The terrible horseman over the heads of people was image enough of what she felt in the city. Her hope had died in a basement of this city. Her faith had died in one of its smug churches. Her love had not survived a journey across it. She would not turn to face the sprawling city. Instead she would move across to that public fountain. No longer swiftly. What am I dragging behind me? Twenty-eight years and all those institutions . . .

Now here is the fountain. But, no, it isn't a fountain. It is a shallow cement bowl for sparrows. But even the sparrows have found it a false invitation. The bowl is dry. It contains a few oak leaves disintegrating. And all this green. I wasn't prepared for green. The green has to be taken gently. Not swallowed but sipped the way birds do water if bowls aren't dry. But all at once in a gulf of green too quickly! All men have known, adventurers and pilgrims, that green is the stuff that sweeps you down and under. Cannot be trusted, is eager to overwhelm you. A butterfly boat that a child lets go in the dusk is safer than I in the middle of this green breaking. Go slowly now. The earth is still horizontal. But awfully windy. There's too much sky to let go of and too much to keep. But friendlier than this avalanche of green. Now, where has she gone, that amiable young sky pilgrim, that innocent nude without any avoirdupois? Oh, yes, I see her. A long way off to the left. She has made good progress! And I? I've come to the—

No. Sit down on that bench over there till my breath comes back. This pain reminds me of school inoculations . . .

Close to the one where the birds were disappointed, Anna herself was all at once a fountain. The foam of a scarlet ocean crossed her lips. Oh, oh. The ocean the butterfly boat is a voyager on . . .

The green of leaves, the scarlet ocean of blood, together they wash and break on the deathless blue. It makes a flag—but nobody understands it . . .

January 1944 (Published 1974)

The Vine

The woman's body beside him while he slept was something he felt with the faint and thoughtless sentience of plants to sunlight: when it was gone, when she had left the bed, he knew the same blind, formless want that plants must feel without that warmth about them. While they slept there was a continuity between their bodies that he had grown to depend upon. In winter he never had quite heat enough in his own flesh; he always had to borrow a little from hers—there was always some contact between them, his knees curved into hers, his arm wrapped vinelike across her shoulders. But even when the nights were excessively warm, as they now were in late summer, his hand or his foot must remain in touch with some part of the woman. This was essential to his feeling of security. When the contact was broken, though he didn't awake, the comfort of sleep was lost and he turned fretfully this way and that, sometimes muttering her name aloud—*Rachel—Rachel*. If she was still in the room, she would return to the bed and then, her temporary loss having stirred in him a sleepy desire, he would take her body almost as a child takes the breast of its mother, a sort of blind, instinctive, fumbling possession that hardly emerged from the state of sleep—the way that plants expand into sunlight with that sweet, thoughtless gratitude that living matter feels for what sustains its being.

And so for some time now, with Rachel gone, he had slept unquietly. The cumulative, unsatisfied want drew him gradually out of sleep. His eyelids opened. Above him stretched a ceiling with a network of fine silver threads and memorized patches of brown from pipes that leaked in the rented rooms above. The square window admitted a harsh brilliance which was like the insolent stare of someone he knew despised him but which he could not escape from.

134

He closed his eyelids: pouted.

"Jesus, I feel like I've got a mouthful of old chicken feathers!"

Rachel said nothing.

He turned and saw that her side of the bed was empty. The covers were neatly folded back, the pillow smoothed out as though she hadn't slept there at all that night. For a moment he wondered stupidly if she had. Of course. His body that had recorded like an exposed film while his mind was sleeping gave back to him now the long, sweet history of her presence near him. And then he remembered also her restless tossing which kept him awake until he complained, "Rachel, why don't you lie still?" and she had said, "Oh, my God!" and he had said, "What?" and she had said nothing more—and he had then fallen asleep.

"Rachel."

The emptiness of the room replied to him with the desultory drone of a large horsefly; its wings flashed blue against the shining copper screen, as though his wife had been transformed into an insect.

Slightly grinning at this fantastic notion, he pushed himself up on his elbows and squinted about.

The prankish spirit of earlier years recurred sometimes in little tricks they played on each other, which made him think now that she might be hiding to tease him. But there was really not a place in the one-room apartment where a woman, even as tiny as Rachel, might conceal herself. The closet door was open; the kitchen alcove made a full confession from this angle.

Grunting, he bent over—saw beneath his folding bed the pale-blue garters he had lost but not his wife.

Through a series of hesitant, half-hearted movements, he got himself out of bed and over to their single window. Beyond its proscenium arch the world was presenting another hot day's beginning. The street, which was a street in the Village, was narrow and vacant: you might almost suppose that during the night a plague had wiped out the entire population. No, there was a figure, a woman, yes, but not Rachel, coming out of an areaway. He watched her pad mincingly to the delicatessen whose windows bore a chaos of whitewashed signs and price quotations. That was very likely where Rachel had gone, an empty milk bottle in a paper bag—how much had she taken of their small cash under the Dresden doll on the bureau? He went immediately to see, recalling the precise amount there had been when they went to bed. A quarter was missing. A phone call? And a subway fare? . . .

He chuckled a little uneasily: and then there was no longer anything to postpone the dreaded approach to the mirror. In his crumpled purple pajamas with white frogs on them, he moved anxiously to that soap-splashed glass over the sink to make the morning analysis of his looks. In his youth he had been very handsome indeed, an ideal juvenile type, and even at forty-three, not having permitted himself to exceed a ten-pound concession to middle years, he still had a fairly comfortable sense of being attractive. Ah, but his hair, they said it stopped thinning at forty and if you got it that far you had it for keeps. How true was this notion? He inclined his head as low as he could and still see into the glass. The crown was becoming more visible every day, yes, blooming forth pink as a rose. Ah, well. It was also said that thinning hair was a sign of superior male vigor. That could be; it cost him nothing to think so.

Automatically he began to rotate his scalp beneath the close grip of ten fingers, halting at the count of sixty with a breathless grunt of relief.

That completed, he went back to the window. He reached it just in time to see the spinsterish woman who had gone into the delicatessen coming back out of it bearing her package clasped tight against her flat bosom as though afraid that someone would snatch it from her. Have you ever noticed, he inquired of himself, how tightly anxious people hold onto things such as hatbrims while waiting in managers' offices? Huh! Yesterday when he walked out of McClintic's, his panama was so dented it had to be reblocked! Oh, yes. Now he knew what he had to do this morning. Call Edie Van Cleve about that part in the road company of *Violets Are Blue*! He took a dime and descended in his bathrobe to the downstairs hall. "Your reading was fine," she told him, "but Mr. David-son feels you're a shade too young for the part." Going back up the stairs his heart jolted strangely. A palpitation. He had them off and on. The doctor had told him there was nothing organically wrong, no pathological lesion. "If you took your heart out," said the doctor, "you would find that it looked exactly like a normal heart, only a little overdeveloped because of the strenuous life that you've been leading." This statement was meant to be reassuring, more so than Donald had found it. What strenuous life? He had never overextended himself at work or at play. Rehearsals could be a strain. But he always felt fine while working. It was only during the last two or three years, that held these long periods of unwanted inaction, that he had begun to decline from the pink of condition.

Steps in the hall—*Rachel*? No, they contined upstairs . . .

He began to curse her, teasingly, as though she could hear him, his eyes fixed on the framed photograph of the Glow Worm Ballet, girls in shimmering tutus going through some intricate dance routine. They had held tiny flashlights that winked off and on in the stage's rosy dusk. At the end of the line was Rachel, a shade smaller, quicker, and more graceful than the others. His act had followed hers. He was the straight man in a vulgar dialogue with a comedian now dead of heart disease. Tommy Watson. Huh. There was Tommy's picture. Kind of nice not having to compare it with the way he looked now. And there was his own picture in a straw hat and a bow tie. Not much older than his son would now be. But they had not had any children, he and Rachel. They had scrupulously avoided the chance of any for about ten years. And then one summer, about three years ago, Rachel had grown pensive. He couldn't snap her out of it. They were playing in summer stock. All at once Rachel had started looking her age, and the manager said, "I'm sorry but we can't light her anymore for ingénue parts, and we've got all the character women that we can use." That was a *horrible* thing. Rachel went around looking half conscious for a number of days. And then one night she said, "I want a baby." He demurred a little, but she was persistent. "We've got to have a baby." They stopped the preventive devices, and waited six months. And when it still didn't happen, they went to a doctor. Both were thoroughly examined, and at the end, the doctor talked to Rachel. Donald waited nervously outside. When she came out she looked at him sort of oddly.

"What did he say?"

"He says we can't have children."

"There's something wrong with you, honey?"

"Not with me," she told him. "He says *you're sterile* . . ."

This had struck Donald a nasty blow where it hurts a man most. The many flattering attentions which he had received in his youth had inflated his sexual vanity and it had never retracted to normal size.

On the way home from the doctor's he had been flushed and silent. At last he said huskily:

"Rachel?"

"Yes?"

"Don't let anyone know."

"Don't be silly, Donald. It's nothing to be ashamed of. But why advertise it?"

"Exactly . . ."

But their relations had been altered by the discovery. They laughed to think what trouble they had taken all those years to avoid something that couldn't have happened. But the joke was on Donald, really, and it was hard to accept for that reason. For a while the psychic trauma was so acute that he found it difficult to make love to Rachel. But Rachel understood it better than he. She won him tenderly back and gradually the humiliation faded from his mind and things became almost the same as they had been before. Donald was not inclined to keep old hurts alive, and if Rachel was still brooding about her disappointment, she wore no outward sign of it. Donald got a fairly good part in a show that ran nine months in New York, and they saved a bit of mony. When it went on the road, it perished under Claudia Cassidy's incorruptible justice in Chicago. Since that engagement Donald had had nothing but TV and not much of that.

Donald had once read somewhere that the way to combat a feeling of depression was to take unusual pains with your appearance. "Dress Your Blues Away" was the stimulating title of this column of advice; he remembered having read it aloud to Rachel during a time when she seemed to be giving in to her moods. It had been addressed to female readers, but there was nothing about the theory that was not adaptable to a youngish middle-aged man who took a better than normal pride in presenting a good appearance, and so he took out Rachel's manicure set and cleaned and trimmed and polished his nails; he powered his plumpish body with lilac talcum and applied cologne to his armpits, donned a fresh pair of faintly pink-tinted nylon boxer's shorts, and removed from its laundryman's sheath one of a pair of snow-white linen suits that he had been husbanding all summer against some days of importance that hadn't arrived. "I've never known a man that looks as good as you in white linen," someone had said to him once. But that was in another country and the wench was dead, for when he actually caught a full-length view of himself, outside, on the dazzlingly unreal streets, in one of those sudden mirrors sandwiched between shopwindows, he saw that the tightness which he felt in the linen and which he thought might be attributable only to its laundered crispness was indisputably owing to the expansion about his middle. He tried unbuttoning the jacket: this felt better, but when he passed another sidewalk mirror, he noticed that the starched jacket now flared behind him in a way that made him look like a bantam rooster strutting along the street in snowy feathers. It took no more than this to undo all he had done to "dress away his blues," and he continued aimlessly through noonday brilliance, through crowds that all seemed to have appointments to keep, definite places to go, he noticed that no one seemed to be looking at him and this was something that he had never noticed before and he tried deliberately to catch the eyes of people moving in the opposite stream on the walk. He slowed his walk and stared hard into faces looming toward him, not only the faces of pretty girls tripping out for lunch hour, but faces of women of his own generation, and with mounting dismay a feeling close to a beginning of panic, he failed to hold their attention for more than a second and one girl, as she passed him, uttered a startled laugh, not necessarily at him, but if not at him, at what? She was walking alone . . .

He turned, directly after this experience, into a drugstore and ordered a bicarbonate of soda which he seized the instant the boy at the counter released it and drained it down without pause. Ah, that did relieve the gaseous compression which he felt under his heart, and that irritable organ seemed to beat more evenly than it had on the street. The city is full, he said to himself, of people that talk and laugh to themselves on the street, it is full of completely self-centered people capable only of seeing themselves in mirrors, and even if strangers don't gaze at you on the sidewalk as they once did, a summer or two gone by, that means only—that means only—*what?*—he failed to complete the reflection, having observed that the stool next to his at the soda fountain was now occupied by a girl whom he judged to be a young stenographer having her midday coke; she was probably dieting to keep her hips down, yes, they lapped somewhat over the chromium periphery of the stool, somewhat overhanging it like the hood of a mushroom, yes, he murmured encouragingly to himself as he met her eyes in the mirror at the moment when his fingers, the knuckles of his right hand, came gently into contact with her left buttock and gave it a couple of slight nudges. Her eyes blinked in the mirror but she continued to sip her coke without smiling or turning toward him. The blink and the unchanged expression were an equivocal reaction and so he tried it once more.

The woman did not turn toward him, there was still no change in her expression, but she began to speak to him in a low, rapid voice like the buzz of a swarm of stinging insects.

He preferred not to hear what she was saying to him, and he got up with a rapidity that made his head swim and charged out the door.

He consoled himself, or tried to console himself, with the observation that the Village now was overrun with women who hated men.

He knew not where he was going, but he was headed toward Washington Square.

Whew!!

He stopped.

He was in front of the Whitney Museum . . .

Boom, boom, boom, boom, boom, went that abused organ, his heart! Abused by what? "Tensions of his profession," said the doctor . . .

Boom, boom, boom . . .

In front of the museum was a cheerfully colored poster advertising a showing of nonobjective patintings . . .

Rachel . . .

What she had probably left somewhere in their room was a little note explaining that she had gone to spend the day with one of her girl friends, perhaps with Jane Austin, the one that lived uptown, on Columbus Circle, one that was equally friendly to them both. Well—

A pair of youngsters, a boy and a girl of the longhaired Village crowd, came up alongside him and also stared at the poster, and he moved over a little, respectfully to hear their comments. He recognized the name Mondrian as one he had heard before, but the reproduction was still meaningless to him as a strip of linoleum in a clean, bright kitchen. There was a whole world of such things to which he had no entrance, and though he was vain, he was humble at heart, and never sucked at enthusiasms to which he was an outsider. He stood there respectfully listening to the young couple's comments and then, God help him, the bicarb erupted in a belch so loud that the kids turned and burst into giggles!

He wasn't yet recovered from his lightheaded spell but had to move on . . .

Arrived at the Square, he caught a Fifth Avenue bus to Jane Austin's apartment, but there was no upper deck and it seemed to him, with disturbing vagueness, that maybe it had been a long time since there had been opendeck buses on Fifth Avenue; he couldn't remember if they still had them or not, and—

Thoughts trailed off without distinct ends or beginnings.

Jane was at home with a white cloth tied about her somewhat large-featured head, which look startled at him when she opened the door. Her greeting was an odd one; she said, "Get you!" and though he supposed it was an allusion to the white linen suit and mermaid-figured pale-blue and white silk tie, it wasn't as pleasant and warm a greeting as a caller might hope for.

"Rachel here?" he demanded heartily.

"Why, no! Should she be here?"

"Well, I thought maybe—"

"I haven't seen you or Rachel since that party in June."

He thought there was something a little too clipped and short-winded in her speech, and she didn't even apologize for her appearance. Evidently she had not suffered from depression that morning, or if she had, she had certainly no faith in the "Dress Your Blues Away" theory, but to give the devil her due, she was at least making some efforts to clean up the mess and disorder remaining from what must have been a very large party last night, to which, for some reason, she had omitted to ask them. But then New York is a place where everybody knows too many people . . .

He waited a moment for Jane to say, Sit down, and since she didn't, he walked casually past her and settled himself on the sofa.

He thought about the party last month, wondering if it contained some clue to Jane's altered attitude toward him. There had been a good deal of indiscriminate lechery, the sort of thing that Rachel never took part in but which he sometimes did, no more seriously than a man might join a bunch of kids playing baseball. Rachel had left early with a married couple, but he had stayed on. He remembered now that he and Jane and some other person had drifted into the bedroom and there had been some rather involved goings-on, in the course of which someone had gotten sore at someone and made a scene, he didn't remember about what or how it turned out except that he left soon after and stayed in a bar till it closed. Maybe the fight had been more serious than he recalled its having been. That would explain why Jane was behaving so coldly.

"Rachel has disappeared," he said to Jane.

"When?"

"This morning."

"Did she?"

Her manner expressed no interest. The room was filled with the musty flavor of dust and heat and liquor and stale tobacco. He waited for Jane to offer him a drink. He saw at least one bottle of Haig & Haig which had several fingers of liquor still left in it. But Jane was being obtuse. She leaned on the handle of the vacuum with a slight frown and a faraway look. She lived by herself in this unpleasantly bright apartment. Donald could never quite imagine people living alone. It seemed less conceivable, somehow, than life on the moon. How did they get up in the morning? How did they know when to eat, or where or how did they make up their minds about any of the little problems of existence? When you came home alone after being alone on the street, how was it bearable not having someone to tell all the little things you had on your mind? When you really thought about it, when you got down to it, what was there to live for outside of all-encompassing and protecting intimacy of marriage? And yet a great many women like Jane Austin got on without it. There were also men who got on without it. But he, he could not think of it! Going to bed alone, the wall on one side of you, empty space on the other, no warmth but your own, no flesh in contact with yours! Such loneliness was indecent! No wonder people who lived those obscenely solitary lives did things while sober that *you* only did when drunk . . .

He looked at Jane and felt kind of sorry for her, although she was certainly not being very nice to him today.

Well, she probably felt a little neglected. He should have called her or made some further advances after those blurred goings-on in the bedroom that night.

His ears were abruptly assailed by the renewed whine of the vacuum cleaner.

"Jane!"

"Excuse me just a few minutes. I'm expecting company and I've got things to redd up a little."

She gave him a quick, hard smile as she pushed the infernal apparatus across the floor. The odor became more and more nauseating. He raised his legs from the floor and stretched full-length on the sofa.

This sort of treatment he certainly would not put up with!

"Jane—*Jane!*"

She turned off the cleaner.

"What *is* it?"

"I'm feeling lonesome," he said.

"Are you?"

"Jane, don't you ever feel lonesome?"

"Never."

"Why don't you settle down, Jane?"

"What do you mean?"

"Get married!"

"Hanh!"

She started to turn on the vacuum. He grabbed it from her and rested his chin on the handle.

She put her hands on her hips and stared at him so uncordially that he was almost intimidated.

"Where do you think Rachel is?"

"Worried about her?"

"Oh, no," he laughed, "I'm not optimistic enough to think she's gone for good!"

Jane did not smile nor even glance at him again. She pushed the cleaner into a closet and began pounding the silk pillows into shape. She tugged at the corner of the one on which he was resting.

This was intolerable!

He grabbed her by both shoulders and jerked her down on top of him and squashed his mouth against hers. He tried to force her lips open, at the same time pushing his hands down her back. All at once he felt a terrific blow on the side of his head. It stunned him. Green light flashed in his eyes and there was a sickening spasm in his stomach. He leaned over the edge of the sofa and that bicarbonate of soda he had had at the drugstore spilled into the inadequate cup of his hands.

He wiped them stupidly on his handkerchief.

"What did you hit me with?"

It was an unnecessary question. On the floor were shattered bits of blue pottery which he remembered seeing in the shape of a vase that contained a pair of sunflowers.

"You might have killed me with that," he said to her sadly.

She was standing over him, panting, and the disgust on her face was completely unfeigned.

"You make me sick!" she said. "Now please get out!"

The room had not changed in his absence, only the light shone through a different window. The light was different. While he was gone upon his unhappy excursion about the city, the light in the room had performed the circuit of a lifetime, from violence to exhaustion. Now it did not stare at him nor make any harsh demands. It stayed near the window in a golden blur. The horsefly had also moved to that other window and showed a recession of power. Against the exterior light its delicate wings still glinted as points of blue flame, but the furious dives at the screen were now interspersed with periods of reflection which seemed to admit that failure was not any longer the least imaginable of all eventualities. Donald crossed immediately to the screen and gently unlatched it to let the fly out. He did this rather silly thing unconsciously, just as he opened doors for cats or children. He was a very kind man. There was something soft and passive about his mind which made it unusually responsive to the problems of creatures smaller or even weaker than himself. He stood awhile at the window. What was it this moment was trying to make him remember? Oh, my God, yes, that long-ago play he was in. That was his first acting job; he played the part of an adolescent coal miner who was killed in the collapse of a shaft. His mother was played by that old bitch Florence Kerwin. At the last curtain she slowly advanced to a window flooded with yellow gelatine and said in a tremulous whisper, "All sunsets are remembrance." There was a count of five and a very slow curtain. Before the curtain was down the seats were banging up and the little patter of applause was drowned in the shuffle of feet. The mysterious little Alabama spinster who wrote the play was standing breathlessly beside him in the wings as old Florence Kerwin came off.

The actress glanced at them both and shouted. "The play's a turkey!"

The manager was standing there, too, and the spinster author turned to him uncomprehendingly.

"What is a turkey?" she asked.

"A bird with feathers!" he told her.

Donald had put his arms about her shoulders as she began to cry those tears that innocence is bathed in when it blunders trustfully into the glittering microcosm of Broadway, and over the quivering shoulders of Miss Charlotte Something or Other, who never was heard of again, he could see the coldly furious little manager tacking the closing notice upon the board.

Now Donald began to look around for the note Rachel must have left to explain her very long absence. He looked everywhere that a note might conceivably be left, even under the bed and the stove in case it had blown to the floor. At last he opened the closet where Rachel kept her clothes. Then for the second time that afternoon he received a blow that all but cracked his skull. Her clothes were gone from the closet. Her suitcase was also gone. Almost nothing remained but empty hangers.

Rachel is not coming back!

Until his blurred sight focused he moved toward the wall where against her protests he kept the picture of Rachel as a Glow Worm. On her lips was the gay, artificial smile of show business, the spangled tutu was lifted to show her bare thighs. Her bosom was visible through the sheer band of chiffon, no one had ever had such a lovely bosom as Rachel still had, but then . . .

In just a few moments the curtain of the finale would be coming down and they would go out to eat and then home to bed. In the hotel room a shade would be lowered for the beginning of something instead of the end. Oh, God, what pleasure those early nights had contained, things that couldn't even be said with music! Wasn't it natural to be vain in those days? It wasn't ridiculous to be vain in those days, both of them young and both of them lovely, then, coming together with such a crazed abandon that daylight would crowd the windows before their hands and arms and mouths would begin to let go of each other. Then they would go out to breakfast without having slept, no stockings on Rachel, he without socks or tie, and gorge themselves, hungry as wolves, on bowls of steaming cereal and cups of sweet black coffee and platters of bacon and eggs. What did they say to each other? It didn't seem that they ever talked to each other; he couldn't remember conversations between them. It was all longing and satisfaction of longing. They helped each other undress when they had returned from breakfast, gently each took the other's shoes off, and they fell on the bed like a pair of rag dolls a child dropped there, their bodies athwart each other in silly positions, so much light in the room for people to sleep in but not enough to keep them awake much longer . . .

Oh, Rachel, where have you gone?

No other refuge was thinkable but sleep, so he went to the bed and lifelessly took off his clothes. Under the covers he doubled his body up in a round, embryonic position. He closed his teeth on a corner of the pillow, the one that was hers, and began to release his tears.

Rachel, Rachel! Oh, Rachel!

Then all at once he heard her returning footsteps.

All in a rush of calling and sobbing she entered. Before he could lift his shoulders from the bed she had fallen upon him. She tore back the covers and scalded his face with her tears. Her cheekbones were awfully sharp. There was so little flesh on her arms, they were actually skinny, and yet they embraced him so fiercely he couldn't breathe.

"Oh, Rachel," he sobbed, and she moaned, "Donald, Donald!"

The name of a person you love is more than language—but after a while, when their sobbing had quieted a little, he held her fiery head in the crook of his arm and began to recite the litany of his sorrows. He told her about his misfortunes, the ones of this day and the probable ones of tomorrow. He told her about his illness, his palpitations, his possible death before long. He told her his beauty was lost, his time was now past. He had not been given that part he had counted upon. Strangers had laughed at him on the street. And Jane had misunderstood him; she had struck him over the head with a piece of blue pottery that might have killed him—

And Rachel whose sorrows were scarcely less than his own, said nothing about them but set her lips on his throat and answered with infinite softness to everything that he told her, "I know, I know!"

1944 (Published 1954)

The Malediction

When a panicky little man looks for a place to stay in an unknown town, the counter-magic of learning abruptly deserts him. The demon spirits that haunted a primitive world are called back out of exile. Slyly, triumphantly, then, they creep once more through the secret pores of rocks and veins of wood that knowledge had forced them out of. The lonely stranger, scared of his shadow and shocked by the sound of his footsteps, marches through watchful ranks of lesser deities with dark intentions. He does not look at houses as much as they look at him. Streets have an attitude toward him. Signposts, windows, doorways all have eyes and mouths that observe him and whisper about him. The tension in him coils up tighter and tighter. If someone smiles to offer a sudden welcome, this simple act may set off a kind of explosion. The skin of his body, as cramped as a new kid glove, may seem to be split down the seams, releasing his spirit to kiss stone walls and dance over distant roof-tops. The demons are once more dispersed, thrust back into limbo; the earth is quiet and docile and mindless again, a dull-witted ox that moves in a circular furrow, to plow up sections of time for man's convenience.

This was, in fact, the way that Lucio felt when he first encountered his future companion, the cat. She was the first living creature in all of the strange northern city that seemed to answer the asking look in his eyes. She looked back at him with cordial recognition. Almost he could hear the cat pronouncing his name. "Oh, so it's *you, Lucio*!" she seemed to be saying, "I've sat here waiting for you a long, long time!"

Lucio smiled in return and went on up to the steps on which she was seated. The cat did not move. Instead she purred very faintly. It was a sound that was scarcely a sound. It was a barely distinguishable vibration in the pale afternoon air. Her amber eyes did not blink but they narrowed slightly—anticipating his touch which followed at once. His fingers met the soft crown of her head and moved down over the bony furred ridge of her back: under his fingers he felt the faint, faint quiver of her body as she purred. She raised her head slightly to gaze up at him. It was a feminine gesture: the gesture of a woman who glances up at her lover's face as he embraces her, a rapt, sightless glance, undeliberate as the act of breathing.

"Do you like cats?"

The voice was directly above him. It belonged to a large blonde woman in a gingham dress.

Lucio flushed guiltily and the woman laughed.

"Her name is Nitchevo," said the woman.

He repeated the name haltingly.

"Yes, it's peculiar," she said. "One of our roomers give her that name Nitchevo. He was a Russian or something. Stayed here before he took sick. He found that cat in an alley and brought her home an' fed her an' took care of her an' let her sleep in his bed, an' now we can't get rid of th' dog-gone thing. Twice already today I thrown cold water on her and still she sits!—I guess she's waitin' for him to come back home. But he won't, though. I was havin' a conversation the other day with some boys he used to work with down at the plant. It's too bad now. They tell me he's right on the verge of kickin' the bucket out west where he went for his lungs when he started to spit up blood.—Tough luck is what I call it.—He wasn't a bad sort of a fellow as them Polacks go."

Her voice trailed off and she turned away, smiling vaguely, as if to go back inside.

"Do you keep boarders?" he asked.

"No," said the woman. "Everybody along here does but us. My husband is not a very well man anymore. Got hurt in an accident down at the plant and now he's not good for nothing except being tooken care of. So me—" she sighed, "I got to work out at that bakery down on James Street."

She laughed and held up her palms, the sweating lines of which were traced with a chalky whiteness.

"That's how I got all this flour. My next-door-neighbor, Mizz Jacoby, tells me I smell like a fresh loaf of bread. Well—I don't have time to keep boarders, all I can keep is roomers. I got rooms I could show you—if you would be interested."

She paused in good-humored reflection—stroked her hips and allowed her gaze to slide off on a gentle excursion among the barren treetops.

"As a matter of fack," she continued, "I guess I could show you that room the Russian vacated. If you ain't superstitious about occupying the room that a man took sick in as bad as that. They say that it ain't contagious but I don't know."

She turned and went into the house and Lucio followed.

She showed him the room that the Russian had lately moved out of. It had two windows, one that faced the brick wall of a laundry that smelled of naphtha, another that opened upon a narrow back-yard where greenish-blue cabbage heads were scattered about like static fountains of sea-water among the casual clumps of unweeded grass.

As he looked out that back window and the woman stood behind him, breathing warmly upon the nape of his neck and smelling of flour, he saw Nitchevo, the cat, picking her way with slow grace among the giant cabbage heads.

"Nitchevo," remarked the woman.

"What does it mean?" he asked her.

"Oh, I don't know. I guess something crazy in Russian.—He told me but I forgotten."

"I'll take the room if I can do like the Russian and keep the cat here with me."

"Oh!" laughed the woman. "You want to do like the *Russian!*"

"Yes," said Lucio.

"Him an' me were pretty good friends," she told him. "He helped me out with things my husband ain't good for now that he's had that accident down at the plant."

"Yes?—Well, how about it?"

"Well—" she sat down on the bed. "I never take nobody in without talking a little. There's some things I like to be sure of before I make final arrangements—You understand that."

"Oh, yes."

"For instance, I don't like fairies."

"What?"

"Fairies!—I had one once that used to go out on the street in a red silk scarf and bring men back to the room.—I don't like that."

"I wouldn't do that."

"Well, I just wanted to know. You looked kind of strange."

"I'm foreign."

"What kind of foreigner are you?"

"My folks were Sicilians."

"What?"

"An island near Italy."

"Oh.—I guess that's all right."

She looked at him—winked and grinned.

"Musso!" she said. "That's what I'll call you—*Musso!*"

Ponderously coquettish, she rose from the bed and poked him in the stomach with her thumb.

"Well—how about it?" he asked her.

"Okay.—Have you got a job yet?"

"Not yet."

"Go down to the plant and ask for Oliver Woodson. Tell him Mizz Hutcheson sent yuh.—He'll give you a job all right with my recommendation."

"Thank you—*thank* you!"

She grinned and chuckled and sighed and turned slowiy away. "My husband has got the war-news on the radio all of the time.—It gives me a pain in the place that I sit down on.—But a sick man's got to be humored.—That's how it is."

But Lucio wasn't listening. He had turned back to the window to look at the cat. She was still down there in the yard, patiently waiting between two large cabbageheads to receive the verdict that settled her future existence. Oh, what a passion of longing there was in her look. But dignity, too.

Quickly he moved past the woman and down the front stairs.

"Where are you going?" she called.

"Out! In back!—For the cat!"

Lucio got a job at the plant through the man named Woodson. The work that he did was what he had always done, a thing that you did with your fingers without much thought. A chain clanked beneath you, you made some little adjustment, the chain moved on. But each time it moved beyond your place in the line it took a part of you with it. The energy in your fingers was drained out slowly. It was replaced by energy further back in your body. Then this was drained out also. When the day ended you were left feeling empty. What had gone out of you? Where had it gone to? *Why?*—You bought the evening papers the yelling boys poked toward you. Maybe here was a clue to all of these questions. Perhaps the latest edition would tell you what you lived for and why you labored. But no! The papers avoided that subject. Instead they announced the total amount of tonnage now lost at sea. The number of planes brought down in aerial combat. Cities captured, towns bombarded.—The facts were confusing, the paper fell out of your fingers, your head ached dully . . .

Oh, my God, and when you got up in the morning, there was the sun in the same position you saw it the day before—beginning to rise from the graveyard back of the street, as though its nightly custodians were the fleshless dead—seen through the town's invariable smoke haze, it was a ruddy biscuit, round and red, when it might just as well have been square or shaped like a worm—anything might have been anything else and had as much meaning to it . . .

The foreman seemed to dislike him, or maybe suspect him of something. Often he stopped directly behind Lucio's back and watched him working—stood there an unnecessarily long time and before he moved off always grunted a little and in a way that suggested any number of menacing possibilities.

Lucio thought to himself: I will not be able to keep this job very long.

He wrote his brother a letter.—This brother named Silva was serving a ten-year sentence in a Texas prison. He was Lucio's twin but their natures were not alike. Yet they were close to each other. Silva had been the rebel, a boy who loved music and whiskey, whose life was nocturnal as the life of a cat, a sleek young man he had been, with always the delicate scent of women about him. His clothes flung carelessly about the flat, which they had shared in the town further south, were faintly dusted with powder from women's bodies. Small trinkets tumbled out of his pockets, testimonials of intimacy with Gladys or Mabel or Ruth. When he awoke he always wound up the victrola and when he wanted to sleep, he switched the radio off.—Lucio rarely saw him either awake or asleep. They very seldom discussed their lives with each other but once Lucio found a revolver in his brother's coat pocket. He left the revolver on the bed which they used at opposite hours—under it he placed a pencilled note. This is your death, said the note. When he came home the revolver had disappeared. In its place on the bed was a pair of workman's gloves that Lucio used at the foundry. Pinned to it was a note in Silva's irregular hand. Here is *yours*, said the note.—Shortly thereafter Silva had gone to Texas and there was arrested and given a ten-year term on a holdup charge. Lucio started the letters which now had gone on for eight years. Each time he wrote he informed his brother of some purely fanciful advancement in his career. He told him that he had become a foreman and a stockholder in the corporation. That he belonged to a country club and drove a Cadillac car—that recently he had moved north to assume a much better position with several times as much pay. These lies were further and further elaborated: they began to comprise a sort of dream existence. His face flushed while he wrote them—his hand shook so that toward the end of the letter the writing would be illegible almost. It was not that he wanted to arouse his unfortunate brother's envy, it was not that at all.—But he had loved the brother intensely and Silva had always been so contemptuous of him in a kind sort of way.—Silva apparently believed the news in the letters. How well you are doing! he wrote. You could see he was startled and proud—so that Lucio thought with dread of the time when the truth must be known, when his brother got out of the prison . . .

Lucio's feeling that he could not long hold the job became an obsession with him: a certain knowledge that clung to his brain all the time. In the evenings, with Nitchevo the cat, he could shut it partly away. Nitchevo's presence was a denial of all the many threatening elements of chance. You could see that Nitchevo did not take stock in chance. She believed that everything progressed according to a natural, predestined order and that there was nothing to be apprehensive about. All of her movements were slow and without agitation. They were accomplished with a consummate grace. Her amber eyes regarded each object with unblinking serenity. Even about her food she made no haste. Each evening Lucio brought home a pint of milk for her supper and breakfast: Nitchevo sat quietly waiting on her haunches while he poured it into the cracked saucer borrowed from the landlady and set it on the floor beside the bed. Then he lay down on the bed, expectantly watching, while Nitchevo came slowly forward to the pale blue saucer. She looked up at him once—slowly—with her unflickering yellow eyes before she started to eat, and then she gracefully lowered her small chin to the saucer's edge, the red satin tip of tongue protruded and the room was filled with the sweet, faint music of her gentle lapping. He watched her and as he watched her his mind smoothed out. The tight knots of anxiety loosened and were absorbed. The compressed and gaseous feeling inside his body was forgotten and his heart beat more quietly. He began to feel sleepy as he watched the cat—sleepy and entranced. Her form grew in size and the rest of the room dwindled and receded. It seemed to him, then, that they were of equal dimensions. He was a cat like Nitchevo—they lay side by side on the floor, lapping milk in the comfortable, secure warmth of a locked room beyond which no factories or foremen existed, nor large blonde landladies with hauntingly full-fleshed bosoms.

Nitchevo took a long time about drinking her milk. Often he was asleep before she had finished. He would awake later on and find her small warmth against him—he would sleepily raise his hand to caress her and he would feel the faint, faint vibration of the vertebral ridges along her back as she purred. She was getting fatter. Her sides filled out.—Of course there had been no spoken declaration of love between the two of them, but each understood that a contract existed between them to last their whole lives. Lucio talked to the cat in drowsy whispers—he never fabricated such stories as those that he wrote to his brother but merely denials of worries that plagued him most. He told her that he was not going to lose his job, that he would always be able to give her the saucer of milk night and morning and let her sleep on his bed; he told her that nothing disastrous was going to happen to them, that there was nothing to be afraid of between heaven and earth. Not even the sun, that rose newly burnished each day from the heart of the cemetery, would break the enchantment which they had established between them.

One evening Lucio fell asleep with the light in his room still burning. The landlady, who was sleepless that night, saw it shining under the crack of his door and she came to the door and knocked and getting no response, she pushed it open. She found the strange little man asleep on the bed with the cat curled against his bare chest. His face was sharp and prematurely aged and his eyes, when they were open, made it look older still, but now they were closed, and his body was thin and white and underdeveloped like that of a spindly boy. He did not look like very much of a man, she observed. But she wanted to test his manhood. The Russian had also been thin, cadaverous almost, and always coughing as though an army of vandals were tearing him down from inside. Nevertheless, there had been a great fire in his nature which magnified him as a lover, made him assume almost a great physical stature. So she remembered the Russian who occupied that room before and she came to the side of the bed and threw the cat down to the floor and placed her hand on the sleeping little man's shoulder. Lucio woke and found her seated beside him, smiling, still smelling of the bed's warmth and faintly of flour. Her face was double in his unfocussed vision. Two large beaming moons that swam in the room's amber glow. Her hand on his shoulder burnt him, stung him painfully as the hide of a steaming horse had once stung his fingers when he touched it as a child. Her mouth was wet, the heat of her bosom engulfed him. The roses upon the wallpaper—how large they were!—And then they sank back into shadow . . .

When the landlady had gone he went back to sleep again, scarcely aware of what had happened between them—except that now he felt more completely rested and quiet and the bed, it seemed to have risen

to a great height over the dark, huddled roofs and bristling stacks of
the factory town—and to be floating loose among stars that were not
as chill as they looked, but warm with a human warmth that was
scented with flour . . .

The life in the house grew sweet and familiar to him.

Sometimes when he entered the downstairs hall at fifteen after five
on a wintry evening, he called out loudly and bravely, Heigho, Everybody, heigho! The blonde landlady moved out from the radio noise as
though she was drugged, with a body stuffed full of honey-sweet
popular songs—moons, roses, blue skies, rainbows after showers, cottages, sunsets, gardens, loves lasting forever!—She smiled with so
much of it in her and touched her broad forehead and let her hand slide
down her body, pressing herself here and there and enjoying the
knowledge of so much sweet flesh on her and willing to share it. . . .
Yes, yes, moons, lovers, roses—followed him up the hallstairs and into
his bedroom and spilled themselves over the bed in a great, wild heap of
"I love you!"—"Remember me always" and "Meet me tonight by the
moonlight!"—the radio filled her up like a ten-gallon jug which the dark
little man unstoppered upstairs before supper.

But the work-a-day life in the plant was more and more strained.
Lucio went at this work with a feverish haste, his anxiety coiling up
tight whenever the foreman stopped at his place in the line. The grunt
which he uttered, somewhat louder each time, was like a knife thrust
into the center of Lucio's back: all his blood flowed out through the
wound so that he scarcely had strength to remain on his feet. His hands
went faster and faster until they lost their rhythm and the metal strips
jammed and the machine cried in a loud and furious voice, which ended
abruptly the man's illusion as master.

"God damn!" said the foreman," Why dontcha watch whatcha doin'?
I'm tired a the way yuh bung up things all a time with yuh jittery
fingers!"

He wrote to his brother that night that he had received another
considerable boost in salary: he enclosed three dollars for candy and
cigarettes and said that he was planning to engage another great
lawyer to reopen Silva's case and take it, if necessary, to the United
States Supreme Court.

"In the meantime," he ended, "sit tight!—There is nothing to worry
about—absolutely."

This was the same type of statement he made every night to the cat.

But only a few days later there came a letter from the warden of the Texas prison, a man with the curious name of Mortimer J. Stallcup, returning the money and tersely announcing the convict brother, Silva, had recently been shot dead in an attempted jail-break.

Lucio showed this letter to his friend the cat. At first she seemed to observe it without much feeling. Then she became interested—she poked it with one white, tentative paw, mewed and set her teeth into a corner of the crisp paper. Lucio dropped it to the floor and she pushed it gently across the rug with her nose and her paws.

After a while he got up and poured out her milk which had grown rather warm in the steam-heated room. The radiators hissed. Her tongue lapped gently.—The roses on the wallpaper shimmered through tears that drained all the tension out of the little man's body.

Returning from the plant one evening that winter he had a rather curious adventure. There was a place a few blocks from the plant called the Bright Spot Cafe. Out of it on this particular evening stumbled a man who looked like a plain street beggar. He caught at Lucio's sleeve and after a long, steady glance with eyes as enflamed as the cemetery-horizon before daybreak, he made a remarkable statement:

"Don't be afraid of these stinking sons-of-bitches. They grow like weeds and like stinkweeds are cut down. They run away from their conscience and can't be still a minute.—Watch for the sun!—It comes up out of their graveyard every morning!"

The speech rambled on for some time in prophetic vein—when at last he let go of Lucio's arm, to which he clung for support, he headed back to the swinging door he emerged from. Just before going inside he made a final statement which struck home profoundly.

"*Do you know who I am?*" he shouted. "*I'm God Almighty!*"

"What?" said Lucio.

The old man nodded and grinned—waved in farewell and passed back into the brightly lighted cafe.

Lucio knew that the old man was probably drunk and a liar but like most people he sometimes had the ability to believe what he wanted to believe in despite of all logic. And so there were nights that harsh, northern winter when he comforted himself and the cat with the recollection of the old man's statement. God was perhaps, he remembered, a resident of this strangely devitiated city whose gray-brown houses were like the dried skins of locusts. God was, like Lucio, a lonely and bewildered man Who felt that something was wrong but could not correct it, a man Who sensed the blundering sleepwalk of time and hostilities of chance and wanted to hide Himself from them in places of brilliance and warmth.

Nitchevo the cat did not need to be told that God had taken up his residence in the factory town. She had already discovered his presence twice: first in the Russian, then in Lucio. It is doubtful that she really distinguished between them. They both represented the same quality of infinite mercy. They made her life safe and pleasant. From the alley they had brought her to the house. The house was warm, the rugs and the pillows were soft. She rested in perfect content, a content which was not, like Lucio's, merely nocturnal but stayed with her all through the days as well as the nights—which was never broken. (If He the Creator did not order all things well, He conferred one inestimable benefit in the animal kingdom when He deprived all but man of the disquieting faculty of examining the future.) Nitchevo, being a cat, existed in only one sliding moment of time: that moment was good. It did not occur to the cat that convicts might be attempting escapes from Texas prisons and being shot down (which accident terminated escape through dream), that wardens were writing terse letters announcing such facts, that foremen grunted contemptuously when they stood behind men whose fingers trembled with fear of doing things badly. That wheels cried out and cracked the whip as the master. That men were blind who thought they saw things plainly, that God had been driven to drink—Nitchevo did not know that this curious accident of matter, the earth, was whirling dangerously fast and some day, unexpectedly, it would fly apart from its own excessive momentum and shatter itself into little bits of disaster.

Nitchevo purred under Lucio's fingers in absolute contradiction of all circumstances that threatened their common existence—and that was perhaps why Lucio loved her so much.

It was now mid-January and every morning the wind with a tireless impatience would grab at the smoke of the plant and thrust it southeast of the town where it hung in a restless bank above the graveyard: the sun rose through it at seven o'clock in the morning, red as the eyeball of a drunken beggar, and stared accusingly till it sank again on the opposite side, across the turgid river: the river kept running away, polluted, ashamed, looking neither to the right nor to the left, but steadily running and running. The final week of the month the stockholders came in town for a crucial meeting. Glittering black and rushing close to the earth as beetles on desperate errands, the limousines sped toward the plant: disgorged their corpulent contents at private doorways and waited uneasily, like a nest of roaches, in cinder-covered parkways back of the plant.

What was hatching inside the conference chambers no one who actually worked at the plant could tell. It took some time for the eggs to incubate: secret and black and laid in coagulate clusters, they ripened slowly.

This was the problem: there was a slump at the plant. The stockholders had to decide what action to take, whether to cheapen the product and make it available thus to a wider market or else cut down on production. The answer was obvious: they would cut down on production, preserving the margin of profit, and wait for the need of the people to make more demand. This was promptly arranged. The wheels got their orders and stopped: the workers were stopped by the wheels. One third of the plant shut down and the men were laid off: the black roach-nest dispersed from the cinder parkway: the problem was solved.

Lucio—yes—was among them.

There were sixty-eight of them given their notices that morning. There was no protest, there was no demonstration, no angry voices were lifted. It was almost as though these sixty-eight factory workers had known from the beginning that this was in store. Perhaps in the wombs of their mothers the veins that had fed them had sung in their ears this song: Thou shalt lose thy job, thou shalt be turned away from the wheels and the bread taken from thee!

It was a glittering wasteland, the town that morning. All week the snow had fallen, lightless and thick. But now the sun shone upon it. Each separate crystal was radiant and alive. The roofs were exclamatory. The steep, narrow streets were ruthlessly brilliant as arrows.

Cold, cold, cold is the merciless blood of thy father!

In Lucio two things competed. One was the need to find his companion the cat. The other and equal need was that of his body to loosen its agonized tension, to fall, to let go, to be swept on like a river.

He managed to keep on walking as far as the Bright Spot Cafe.

There he was met by the man he had met once before, the beggarly stranger, the man who had called himself God.

Out of the lively, rotating glass door of this building, the stranger emerged with an armful of empty beer bottles the management had rejected because they were not purchased there.

"Like weeds," he repeated glumly, "like noxious weeds!"

He pointed southeast of the town with the arms not burdened with bottles.

"Watch for the sun. It comes from the cemetery."

His spittle gleamed in the terrible glare of the morning.

"I clench my fist and this is the fist of God."

Then he noticed the discharged worker before him.

"Where do you come from?" he asked.

"The plant," said Lucio faintly.

The angry glow in the bloodshot eyes waxed brighter.

"The plant, *the plant!*" groaned the stranger.

His small black shoe, bound up with adhesive tape and wads of paper, spattered the snow as it stamped.

He shook his fist in the bristling stacks' direction.

"Cupidity and stupidity!" he shouted. "That is the two-armed cross on which they have nailed me!"

An iron-loaded truck came by with a sloshing thunder.

The old man's face convulsed with rage as it passed.

"Lies, lies, lies, lies!" he shouted. "They've covered their bodies with lies and they won't stand washing! They want to be scabbed all over, they want no skin but the crust of their greediness on them! Okay, okay, let 'em have it! But let 'em have *more* and *more!* Maggots as well as lice! Yeah, pile th' friggin' dirt of their friggin' graveyard on 'em, shovel 'em under *deep*—till I can't *smell* 'em!"

The sound of this malediction was drowned in another truck's thunder, but Lucio heard the man's words. He stopped on the walk beside him. The stranger's vehemence was so great he had dropped his bottles. Together they crouched to the walk and picked them up with the grave and voiceless preoccupation of children gathering flowers. When they were finished and he, the stranger, had spat out the phlegm that choked him, he caught hold of Lucio's arm and peered at him wildly.

"Where are you going?" he asked.

"Home," the little man told him, "I'm going home."

"Yes, go home," said the stranger. "Back to the bowels of earth. But not forever. The humble cannot be destroyed, they keep on going!"

"Going?" asked Lucio. "*Where?*"

"Where?" said the prophet, "*Where?*—I don't know *where!*" He began to sob—his sobbing shook him so that he dropped the bottles once more. And this time when Lucio crouched to assist in the gathering up, his strength went from him suddenly in a wave that swept far out and left him stranded, empty and flat and very nearly lifeless, upon the walk in the rapidly blackening snow outside the cafe.

"Drunk," said the burly policeman.

The man who had called himself God protested but he could do nothing.

The wagon was called and Lucio thrust inside it.

"Nitchevo, Nitchevo," was all he could say when they asked him where his home was.—So they bore him away.

For nearly an hour the man who called himself God remained on the corner outside of the Bright Spot Cafe. He appeared to be puzzled by something.

At last he shrugged and moved on down the street to the next beer parlor.

What is your name? What did your mother die of? Do you have dreams at night?

No, no, no, no. No name, no mother, no dreams. Please leave me alone.

He was a very bad patient. Refuses to co-operate, the doctors decided.

Finally after a week they turned him away.

He went directly back to the rooming house. The door was unlocked. The hall was frosty and silent.

Where was the cat? Not there, he could tell without asking. If she had been there he would have been able to feel her breath in the stillness. There would have been something liquid and warm in the air like the womb of the mother remembered a long way off.

Mrs. Hutcheson heard him and came from the rear of the house where the radio blared a ceaseless popular dream.

"I heard that you'd been laid off," was all that she said.

It was easy to see that the Swanee and roses and moonlight had been turned off to meet a stricter occasion. Her amplitude now was hostile. It blocked his way.

He started to go upstairs but she blocked the staircase.

"The room has been taken," she told him.

"Oh."

"I can't afford to let my rooms be vacant."

"No."

"I got to be practical, don't I?"

"Yes."

"Everyone's got to be practical. That's how it is."

"I see.—Where is the cat?"

"The cat?—I turned her out Wednesday."

Now for the last time vehemence stirred inside him. Energy. Anger. Protest.

"No, no, no!" he shouted.

"Be still!" said the woman. "What do you think I am? The nerve of some people—expect me to play nursemaid to a sick alley cat!"

"Sick?" said Lucio—he was suddenly quiet.

"Yes," said the woman.

"What was the matter with her?"

"How should I know?—She cried all night and created an awful disturbance.—I turned her out."

"Where did she go?"

The woman laughed harshly. "Where did she go! How on earth should I know where that dirty cat went! She might have gone to the devil for all I know!"

Her great bulk turned and she climbed back up the stairs. The door of Lucio's former room stood open. The woman entered. A male voice spoke her name and the door was closed.

Lucio went back out of the enemy's house.

Dimly, remotely, and without any definite feeling, he knew that the game was up. Yes, he could see behind him the whole of his time on earth. Mad pilgrimage of the flesh. Its twistings and turnings, its seemingly empty excursions. He saw how the lines, delusively parallel-seeming, had now converged and had made all forward motion impossible from now on.

He was not conscious of fear nor self-pity nor even regret anymore.

He walked to the corner and turned instinctively down.

Then there occurred once more and for the last time in his life a great and a merciful thing: an act of God.

At the entrance of an alley just beyond where he stood he saw abruptly the limping and oddly misshapen figure of his lost companion.—The *cat*! Yes! Nitchevo!

He stood quite still and let his friend approach him. This she did, but with great difficulty. Their eyes were ropes that drew them slowly together in spite of the body's resistance. For she was hurt very badly, she could hardly move . . .

The consummation was gradual. Still it progressed. And all of the time the eyes of the cat stayed on him.

Her amber eyes regarded him with their usual dignified, unquestioning devotion as though he had only returned from a few minutes' absence and not after days and days of hunger, calamity, cold.

Lucio reached down and gathered her into his arms. He observed now the cause of her limping. One of her legs had been crushed. It must have been for several days in that condition. It had festered and turned black and was very ill-smelling. Her body in his arms felt like a tiny bundle of bones and the sound that she made to greet him was less than a sound.

How had it happened, this injury? Nitchevo could not tell him. Neither could he tell her what had happened to him. He could not describe the foreman who watched and grunted, the calm superiority of doctors, nor the landlady, blond and dirty, in whom desire could be satisfied as well by one man as another.

Silence and physical closeness spoke for them both.

He knew she could not go on living. She knew it, too. Her eyes were tired and dark: eclipsed in them now was that small, sturdy flame which means a desire to go on and which is the secret of life's heroic survival. No. The eyes were eclipsed. They were full to the amber brims with all of the secrets and sorrows the world can answer our ceaseless questioning with. Loneliness—yes. Hunger. Bewilderment. Pain. All of these things were in them. They wanted now to be closed on what they had gathered and not have to hold any more.

He carried her down the steep, cobbled street toward the river. It was an easy direction. The whole town slanted that way.

The air had grown dark, no longer containing the terrible brilliance of sunlight reflected on snow. The wind took the smoke up quickly and sent it scudding across low roofs in sheep-like surrender. There was cold in the air and a sooty gathering darkness. The wind whined a little as thin metal wires drawn taut.

High up on the bank, on the levee, a truck rumbled past. It was loaded with ingots of metal. Iron from the forge of the plant that was soaring away into darkness as the earth averted this side of its face from the stinging slap of the sun and gradually gave it the other.

Lucio spoke to the cat as the stream climbed about them.

"Soon," he whispered. "Soon, soon, very soon."

Only a single instant she struggled against him: clawed his shoulder and arm in a moment of doubt. *My God, My God, why hast Thou forsaken me?* Then the ecstasy passed and her faith returned, they went away with the river. Away from the town, away and away from the town, as the smoke, the wind took from the chimneys—

Completely away.

(*Published 1945*)

The Important Thing

They met at the spring dance by the Baptist Female College which Flora was attending that year. The college was in the same town as the State University at which John was completing his sophomore year. He knew only one girl at the college and wasn't able to find her in the ballroom. It was hot and crowded in there and had that feverish, glaring effect which usually prevails at a spring dance given by a sectarian girls' school. The room was lighted by four or five blazing chandeliers and the walls were covered with long mirrors. Between dances the couples stood about stiffly in their unaccustomed formal dress and glanced uneasily at their reflections in the highly polished glass, shifted their weight from foot to foot, nervously twisted or flipped their program cards. None of them seemed to know each other very well. They talked in loud, unnatural voices, shrieked with laughter or stood sullenly quiet. The teachers flitted among them with bird-like alacrity, intently frowning or beaming, introducing, prompting, encouraging. It was not like a social affair. It was more like an important military maneuver.

John walked around the edge of the floor several times and was rather relieved at not finding the one girl he knew. When he arrived at the palm-flanked entrance he turned to go out, but just then his arm was violently plucked by one of the teachers, a middle-aged woman with frowzy gray hair, sharp nose and large yellow teeth. She looked so wild and Harpy-like that John involuntarily squirmed aside from her grasp.

"Are you alone?" she shrieked in his ear.

The band was thumping out a terrifically loud fox trot. John rubbed his ear and pointed vaguely toward the door. She tightened her grasp on his arm and propelled him across the floor by a series of jerks that careened him from one dancing couple to another till they reached a

163

corner where stood an apparently stranded group of young Baptist Females beneath the protective fronds of an enormous boxed palm.

The Harpy gave his arm a final twist and John found himself facing a tall, thin girl in a pink taffeta dress who stood slightly apart from her fellow refugees. He caught the name Flora shrieked through the increasing din. He didn't notice the girl's face. He was too furious at being roped in like this to even look at her. They advanced awkwardly toward each other. John slid his arm around her unbelievably slender waist. Through the silk he could feel the hard ridge of her spine. There was no weight in her body. She floated before him so lightly that it was almost like dancing by himself, except that the cord of bone kept moving beneath his warm, sweating fingers and her fine, loose hair plastered itself against his damp cheek.

The fox trot had reached a crescendo. Cymbals were clashing and drums beating out double time. The girl's lips moved against his throat. Her breath tickled his skin but he couldn't hear a word she was saying. He looked helplessly down at her. Suddenly she broke away from him. She stood slightly off from him, her eyes crinkling with laughter and one hand clutched to her mouth. The music stopped.

"What're you laughing at?" John asked.

"The whole situation," said Flora. "You no more wanted to dance than I did!"

"Didn't you want to?"

"Of course not. When I think of dancing I think of Isadora Duncan who said she wanted to teach the whole world how to dance, but this wasn't what she meant—do you think it was?"

She had a way of looking up that made her face very brilliant and for a few moments obscured the fact that she was by no means pretty. But there was something about her, something which already excited him a little, and so he said:

"Let's go outside."

They spent practically all the rest of the evening in the oak grove between the gymnasium and the chapel, strolling around and smoking his cigarettes. While smoking the girl would flatten herself against a tree trunk for smoking was forbidden on the campus.

"This is the advantage of being a fence-pole," she told him. "You can hide behind anything with the slightest diameter."

Everything that she said had a wry, humorous twist and even when it wasn't humorous she would laugh slightly and John had the impression that she was unusually clever. They went into the empty chapel for a while and sat in a back pew and talked about religion.

"It is all so archaic," Flora said. "It is all a museum piece!"

John had recently become an agnostic himself. They agreed that Christian religion and Hebrew, in fact nearly all religions were based on a concept of guilt.

"*Mea culpa!*" said John, thinking that she would say, "What's that?" But she didn't. She nodded her head. And he was excited to discover that she, too, was interested in writing. She had won a literary prize in high-school and she was now editor of the college literary magazine. The teacher who had brought them together was Flora's English instructor.

"She thinks I'm very talented," said Flora. "She wants me to send one of my stories to Harper's."

"Why don't you?" asked John.

"Oh, I don't know," said Flora. "I think the main thing is just expressing yourself as honestly as you can. I am not interested in style," she went on, "it's such a waste of time to do things over and get the right cadence and always just the right word. I'd rather just scramble through one thing and then rush into another, until I have said everything I have to say!"

How extraordinary it was that she and John should feel exactly the same way about this! He confessed that he was himself a writer and that two or three of his stories were coming out in the University's literary magazine—and when Flora heard this she was almost absurdly moved.

"I'd love to see them, I've got to see them!" she cried.

"I'll bring them over," he promised.

"When?"

"As soon as they come out!"

"I don't care how the style is as long as they're honest. They've got to be honest!" she pleaded. "Are they?"

"I hope so," he answered uneasily.

She had taken his arm and was squeezing it in a grip that was almost as tight as a wrestler's and with every excited inflection in her speech she squeezed it tighter. There was no relaxation in Flora, none of the softness and languor which he found physically interesting in girls. He could not imagine her lying passively still and quietly submitting the way he thought a girl should to a man's embraces.

"What do you think about human relations?" she asked him just at the moment when this disturbing image was in his mind.

"That's a large subject," said John.

"Oh, what a large, large subject! And it is the one I will never be able to cope with!"

"Why?" asked John.

"I'm equal to anything else, but not human relations! I'll always be moving when other people are still, and still when they're moving," said Flora, "and it will be a terrible mess and a mix-up from start to finish!"

"You shouldn't feel that way about it," he told her lamely, astonished at the way her words fitted exactly what he had been thinking.

She looked up at John. "You'll have the same trouble!" she told him. "We'll never be happy but we'll have lots of excitement and if we hold on to our personal integrity everything won't be lost!"

He wasn't quite sure what Flora was talking about, and personal integrity seemed the vaguest of terms. Was it something like what she meant by "honest" writing?

"Yes, something," said Flora, "but ever so much more difficult, because writing is ideal reality and living is not ideal . . ."

At the window of the gymnasium they stood for a while and watched the dancers who had reached what appeared to be nearly the point of exhaustion. Faces that had been flushed and perspiring when they had left the room were now quite desperate-looking and the men in the jazz band seemed to be playing now out of sheer inability to break an old habit. Some of the paper streamers had come unfastened and fallen upon the floor, others hung limply from the ceiling and in one corner a small crowd, mostly teachers, were clustered about a girl who had fainted.

"Don't they look silly!" said Flora.

"Who?"

"Dancers—everybody!"

"What isn't silly, in your opinion?" asked John.

"Give me a little while to answer that question!"

"How long shall I give you?"

"I'll tell you right now—The Important Thing isn't silly!"

"What Important Thing?" John asked.

"I don't know yet," said Flora. "Why do you think I'm living, except to discover what The Important Thing is?"

John didn't see her again that spring. Final examinations came soon after the dance, and besides he was not altogether sure that she was the sort he would get along with. She was not good-looking and her intensity which was so charming while he was with her seemed afterwards a little—fantastic!

Very soon after he returned to school that fall he ran into her on the campus. She was now enrolled as a sophomore in the State University. He barely recognized her. It had been so dark in the oak grove, where they spent most of their time at the spring dance, that he hadn't gotten a very clear impression of her face. She was at once homelier and more attractive than he remembered. Her face was very wide at the top and narrow at the bottom: almost an inverted pyramid. Her eyes were large and rather oblique, hazel brown with startling flecks of blue or green in them. Her nose was long and pointed and the tip covered with freckles. She had a way of smiling and blinking her eyes very rapidly as she talked. She talked so fast and shrilly that he felt a little embarrassed. He noticed a group of girls staring at her and giggling. Fools! he thought, and was angry at himself for having felt embarrassed.

It was noon when they met and she was on her way to the boarding house where she was staying. She hadn't pledged a sorority. She announced the fact with an air of proud defiance that John liked.

"I could see that I wouldn't fit into any of them," she said. "I'd rather be independent, wouldn't you? The trouble with this world is that everybody has to compromise and conform. Oh, I'm sick of it! I won't do it! I shall live my own life just the way that I please!"

John had felt the same way about joining a fraternity and he told her so.

"Ah, we're a couple of Barbs!" she shrieked. "Isn't that marvelous? The other girls at the boarding house simple detest being called Barbs—but I adore it! I think it's really thrilling to be called a barbarian! It makes you feel like you could strip off your clothes and dance naked in the streets if you felt like doing it!"

John felt a warm glow as though he'd been drinking. It was the way he'd felt in the oak grove, talking to her last spring. It seemed suddenly that he had a great deal to say. He became excited and started talking rapidly about a one-act play that he was writing. It was full of involved symbolism and hard to explain. But Flora nodded her head with quick, eager jerks and supplied words wherever he stumbled. She seemed to know intuitively what he was trying to say.

"Oh, I think that's marvelous, marvelous!" she kept repeating.

He was thinking of submitting it to the one-act play contest. His roommate had urged him to do so.

"My goodness, why don't you!" exclaimed Flora.

"Oh, I don't know," John said. "I think the main thing is just express-ing one's self, don't you?"

Immediately afterwards they both laughed, remembering that Flora had said the same thing about the story her English teacher had wanted her to send to Harper's. "Was it accepted?" John asked.

"No, it came back with a printed card," she admitted ruefully. "But I don't care. I'm writing poetry now. They say that you should write poetry while you're young and feel things keenly."

She laughed and caught John's arm.

"I feel things very keenly, don't you?"

They sat down on the front steps of the boarding house and talked until the bell tolled for one o'clock classes. Both of them had missed their lunch.

They saw a great deal of each other after that. They had many interests in common. They were both on the staff of the University's literary magazine and belonged to the Poetry and French Clubs. It was the year of the national election and John became twenty-one just in time to vote. Flora spent hours arguing with him about politics and finally convinced him that he must vote for Norman Thomas. Later they both joined the Young Communists' League. John became a very enthusiastic radical. He helped operate a secret printing press and distribute pamphlets about the campus attacking fraternities, political control of the University, academic conservatism, and so forth. He was once called before the Dean of Men and threatened with expulsion. Flora thought this was terribly thrilling.

"If you get expelled," she promised, "I'll quit school too!"

But it all blew over and they both remained in the University.

All of these things served to draw them closer together. But for some reason they were not altogether at ease with each other. John always had the feeling that something very important was going to happen between them. He could not have explained why he felt that way. Perhaps it was the contagion of Flora's intensity. When he was with her he felt the kind of suppressed excitement a scientist might feel upon the verge of an important discovery. A constant expectation or suspense. Was Flora conscious of the same thing? Sometimes he felt sure that she was. But her enthusiasm was so diffuse that he could never be sure. One thing after another caught her interest. She was like a precocious child just discovering the world, taking nothing in it for granted, receiving each impression with the fresh wonder of a child but an adult's mature understanding. About most things she talked very frankly. But once in a while she would become oddly reticent.

Once he asked her where she came from.

"Kansas," she told him.

"I know, but what place in Kansas?"

He was surprised to see her face coloring. They were in the reference room of the library that evening, studying together at one of the yellow oak tables. She opened her notebook and ignored his question.

"What place?" he insisted, wondering why she flushed.

Abruptly she slammed the notebook shut and faced him with a laugh.

"What does it matter what place?"

"I just wanted to know."

"Well, I won't tell you!"

"Why not?"

"Because it doesn't matter where you come from. It only matters where you're going!"

"Where are you going, then?"

"I don't know!"

She leaned back in the straight yellow oak chair and shook with laughter.

"How on earth should I know where I'm going?"

The librarian approached them with a warning frown.

"Please not so loud. This room's for study."

"Where are you going?" John repeated under his breath.

Flora hid her face in the notebook and continued laughing.

"Where are you going, where are you going, where are you going!" John whispered. He did it to tease her. She looked so funny with the black leather notebook covering her face, only her braided hair showing and her throat flushed Turkey red.

All at once she jumped up from the table and he saw that her face was contorted with crying. She rushed out of the room and he couldn't get her to speak a word to him all the way back to her boarding house.

Some time later he found the name of her home town on the envelope of a letter which she'd forgotten to remove from a book of poems she'd loaned him. The envelope was postmarked from Hardwood, Kansas. John grinned. It was a hick town in the northwestern part of the state and probably the deadest spot on earth. . . .

Despising himself for doing so, he opened the letter and read it. It was from Flora's mother and was a classic of its kind. It complained of the money Flora was having to spend on board and books, urged her to spend less time writing nonsense and buckle down to hard work so that she could get a teaching job when she got through with her schooling because times were getting to be very bad . . .

"The ground and the people and the business and everything else is dried up around here," wrote the mother. "I don't know what things are coming to. It must be God's judgment, I guess. Three solid years of drought. Looks like this time God is planning to dry the wickedness out of the world instead of drowning it out!"

That spring John bought a used car for thirty-five dollars and every free afternoon he and Flora drove around the lovely country roads and had picnic lunches which Flora prepared. He was getting used to Flora's odd appearance and her absurd animation, but other people weren't. She had become something of a "character" on the campus. John was at this time being rushed by a professional fraternity and he was told that some of the fellows thought that Flora was a very queer person for him to be seen around with. Now and again his mind would go back to their first conversation in the oak grove of the Baptist Female College, the talk about human relations and her inability to cope with them, and it appeared to him that she was not even going half way in attempting to. There was no reason for her to talk so loudly on such eclectic subjects whenever they passed along a crowded corridor of a university building, there was surely no reason for her to be so rude to people she wasn't interested in, walking abruptly away without an excuse when talk turned to things she classified as inane—which was almost everything John's other friends talked about.

Other girls on the campus, he could look at and imagine in the future, settled down into average middle-class life, becoming teachers or entering other professions. But when he looked at Flora he could not see her future, he could not imagine her becoming or doing any known thing, or going back to Hardwood, Kansas, or going anywhere else. She did not fit happily or comfortably into the university cosmos but in what other place or circumstances—he asked himself—could she have found any refuge whatsoever? Perhaps he was no more like other people than she was, but his case was different. He was more adaptable, he demanded a good deal less of people and things. Come up against a barrier, he was of a nature to look for a way around it. But Flora—

Flora had decided that the English department of the University was hopelessly reactionary and the only course she took an interest in, now, was geology. Their favorite spot, that spring, was an abandoned rock quarry where Flora searched for fossils. She danced around the quarry like a bright, attractive little monkey on a wire, her green smock fluttering in the wind and her voice constantly flowing up to him, sometimes shrill with excitement and sometimes muted with intense absorption.

"Don't you ever want to be still?" John asked her.

"Never till I have to!"

John would get tired of waiting and would open the lunch-box. She would finally join him on the hilltop, too tired to eat, and would spread her fossils around her and pore delightedly over them while John munched sandwiches of peanut butter and jelly or swiss cheese on rye. The rest of the afternoon they would spend talking about literature and life, art and civilization. They both had tremendous admiration for the ancient Greeks and the modern Russians. Greece is the world's past, said Flora, and Russia is the future—which John thought a brilliant statement, though it sounded a little familiar as if he had come across it somewhere before in a book.

Their discussions would continue unflaggingly till sundown, but as dusk began to settle they would become a little nervous and constrained, for some reason, and there would be long pauses in their talk, during which it was curiously difficult for them to look at each other. After a while, when it was getting really dark, Flora would abruptly jump up from the grass and brush off her smock.

"I guess we'd better be going," she would say. Her voice would sound with the dull, defeated tone of someone who has argued a long time about something very important without making any impression upon the other's mind. John would feel strangely miserable as he followed her down the hill to where they had parked the old roadster. He would also feel that something had been left unsaid or undone, a feeling of incompletion . . .

It was the last Saturday before the end of the spring term. They were going to spend the whole day out in the country, studying for a final examination in a French course which they were taking together. Flora had prepared sandwiches and deviled eggs. And John, with some trepidation, had purchased a quart of red wine. He put the bottle in the side pocket of the roadster and didn't mention it until after they'd finished eating because he knew Flora didn't like drinking. She had no moral objections, she said, but thought it was a senseless, wasteful practice. She refused to drink any of the wine. "But you may, if you wish," she added with a primness that made John laugh.

They were seated as usual on the grassy hill above the rock quarry. It was called Lover's Leap. Flora held the notebook which they had prepared together and was quizzing John. She was leaning against one of the large white boulders scattered about the hilltop and John was stretched at her feet. He held the wine bottle between his knees and drank out of the thermos cup. Flora's constraint at first sight of the bottle wore off. She called him Bacchus.

"I wish I had time to make you a wreath," she said. "You'd look too adorable with a wreath of green leaves!"

"Why don't you be a nymph?" John asked. "Take off your clothes and be a wood nymph! I'll chase you through the birch trees!"

The idea pleased John very much. He laughed loudly. But Flora was embarrassed. She cleared her throat and held the notebook in front of her face, but he could see by the base of her throat that she was blushing. He stopped laughing, feeling somewhat embarrassed himself. He knew what she was thinking. She was thinking what might happen if he should catch her among the birch trees with all her clothes off . . .

John drank another cupful of wine. He felt very good. He had removed his jacket and unbuttoned the collar of his shirt and rolled up the sleeves. The sun shone dazzlingly in his eyes, made rainbows in his eyelashes, warmed the bare flesh of his throat and arms. A comfortable glow passed through him. He was newly conscious of the life in his body; flexed his legs, rubbed his stomach and arched his thighs. He no longer listened to the questions that Flora was asking him out of the notebook. She had to repeat them two or three times before they were clear.

At last she became disgusted and tossed the notebook aside.

"I believe you're getting intoxicated!" she told him sharply.

He looked indolently up at her.

"Maybe I am! What of it?"

He noticed that she was not very pretty. Especially not when she drew her brows together and squinted her eyes like that. Her face was irregular and bony-looking. Rather outlandish. So broad at the top and narrow at the bottom. Long pointed nose, and eyes, flecked with different colors, which were too large for the rest of her and always so filled with superfluous brightness. Reminded him of an undersized child he once knew in grammar school. For some reason they called him Peekie and threw rocks at him after school. A timid, ridiculous creature with a high, squeaky voice that everyone mocked. The large boys caught him after school and asked him the meaning of obscene words or pulled the buttons off his knickers. She was like that. A queer person. But there was something exciting about her just as there'd been something exciting about Peekie that made the larger boys want to amuse themselves with him. There was something about her that he wanted to set his hands on in a rough way—twist and pull and tease! Her skin was the most attractive thing about her. It was very fine and smooth and white . . .

John's eyes traveled down her body. She wore a black sweater and a black and white checked shirt. As he looked at her legs a brisk wind tossed the skirt up and he could see the bare flesh above where the stockings ended. He rolled over on his stomach and placed both hands on her thighs. He'd never touched her so intimately before but somehow it seemed a perfectly natural thing to do. She made a startled movement away from him. Suddenly he thought he knew what the important thing was that was going to happen between them. He caught her by the shoulders and tried to pull her down in the grass, but she fought against him wildly. Neither of them said anything. They just fought together like two wild animals, rolling in the grass and clawing at each other. Flora clawed at John's face and John clawed at Flora's body. They accepted this thing, this desperate battle between them, as though they'd known all along it was coming, as though it had been inevitable from the start. Neither of them spoke a word until they were at last exhausted and lay still on the grass, breathing heavily and looking up at the slowly darkening sky.

John's face was scratched and bleeding in several places. Flora pressed her hands against her stomach and groaned. He had kicked her with his knee trying to make her lie still.

"It's all over now," he said. "I'm not going to hurt you." But she continued moaning.

The sun had gone down and dusk gathered. There was a big purplish red blotch in the western sky that looked like a bruised place.

John got up to his feet and stood silently staring at the angry afterglow. A way off to the left was the university town, beginning to emerge through its leafy clouds with the sparkling animation of a Saturday night in late spring. There would be many gay parties and dances that night. Girls in dresses that seemed to be woven of flowers would whirl about polished dance floors and couples would whisper and laugh behind clumps of ghostly spirea. These were the natural celebrations of youth. He and this girl had been searching for something else. What was it? Again and again later on the search would be made, the effort to find something outside of common experience, digging and rooting among the formless rubble of things for the one lost thing that was altogether lovely—and perhaps every time a repetition of this, violence and ugliness of desire turned to rage . . .

He spoke aloud to himself. "We didn't have anything—we were fooling ourselves."

He turned from the dark, haunting beauty of the town and looked down at Flora. She blinked her eyes and drew her breath sharply. She looked almost ugly, her face covered with sweat and grass stain. She was not like a girl. He wondered that he had never noticed before how anonymous was her gender, for this was the very central fact of her nature. She belonged nowhere, she fitted in no place at all, she had no home, no shell, no place of comfort or refuge, she was a fugitive with no place to run to. Others in her position might make some adjustment. The best of whatever is offered, however not right. But Flora would not accept it, none of the ways and means. The most imperfect part of her was the most pure. And that meant—

"Flora . . ."

He held out his hand and put his heart in his eyes. She felt the sudden turning of understanding and took his hand and he pulled her gently to her feet.

For the first time they stood together in the dark without any fear of each other, their hands loosely clasped and returning each other's look with sorrowful understanding, unable to help each other except through knowing, each completely separate and alone—but no longer strangers . . .

(Published 1945)

One Arm

In New Orleans in the winter of '39 there were three male hustlers usually to be found hanging out on a certain corner of Canal Street and one of those streets that dive narrowly into the ancient part of the city. Two of them were just kids of about seventeen and worth only passing attention, but the oldest of the three was an unforgettable youth. His name was Oliver Winemiller and he had been the light heavyweight champion boxer of the Pacific fleet before he lost an arm. Now he looked like a broken statue of Apollo, and he had also the coolness and impassivity of a stone figure.

While the two younger boys exhibited the anxious energy of sparrows, darting in and out of bars, flitting across streets and around corners in pursuit of some likely quarry, Oliver would remain in one spot and wait to be spoken to. He never spoke first, nor solicited with a look. He seemed to be staring above the heads of passers-by with an indifference which was not put on, or surly and vain, but had its root in a genuine lack of concern. He paid almost no attention to weather. When the cold rains swept in from the Gulf the two younger boys stood hunched and shuddering in shabby coats that effaced them altogether. But Oliver remained in his skivvy shirt and his dungarees which had faded nearly white from long wear and much washing, and held to his body as smooth as the clothes of sculpture.

Conversations like this would occur on the corner.

"Aren't you afraid of catching cold, young fellow?"

"No, I don't catch cold."

"Well, there's a first time for everything."

"Sure is."

"You ought to go in somewhere and get warmed up."

"Where?"

"I have an apartment."

"Which way is it?"

"A few blocks down in the Quarter. We'll take a cab."

"Let's walk and you give me the cab-fare."

Oliver had been in his crippled condition for just two years. The injury had been suffered in the seaport of San Diego when he and a group of shipmates had collided with the wall of an underpass while driving a rented car at seventy-five miles an hour. Two of the sailors in the car had been killed outright, a third had received a spinal injury that would keep him in a wheel chair for the rest of his life. Oliver got off lightest with just the loss of an arm. He was eighteen then and his experience had been limited. He came from the cotton fields of Arkansas, where he had known only hard work in the sun and such emotional adventures as farm boys have on Saturday nights and Sunday afternoons, a tentative knowledge of girls that suddenly exploded into a coarse and startling affair with a married woman whose husband he had hauled lumber for. She was the first to make him aware of the uncommon excitement he was able to stir. It was to break off this affair that he left home and entered the navy at a base in Texas. During his period of training he had taken up boxing and while he was still a "boot" he became an outstanding contender for the navy championship. The life was good fun and no thinking. All that he had to deal with was the flesh and its feelings. But then the arm had been lost, and with it he was abruptly cut off from his development as an athlete and a young man wholly adequate to the physical world he grew into.

Oliver couldn't have put into words the psychic change which came with his mutilation. He knew that he had lost his right arm, but didn't consciously know that with it had gone the center of his being. But the self that doesn't form words nor even thoughts had come to a realization that whirled darkly up from its hidden laboratory and changed him altogether in less time than it took new skin to cover the stump of the arm he had lost. He never said to himself, I'm lost. But the speechless self knew it and in submission to its unthinking control the youth had begun as soon as he left the hospital to look about for destruction.

He took to knocking about the country, going first to New York. It was there that Oliver learned the ropes of what became his calling. He fell in with another young vagrant who wised him up to his commodity value and how to cash in on it. Within a week the one-armed youth was fully inured to the practices and the culture of the underworld that seethed around Times Square and the Broadway bars and the bench-lined walks of the park, and foreign as it was, the shock that it gave him was slight. The loss of the arm had apparently dulled his senses. With it had gone the wholesome propriety that had made him leave home when the coarse older woman had introduced him to acts of unnatural ardor. Now he could feel no shame that green soap and water did not remove well enough to satisfy him.

When summer had passed, he joined the southern migration. He lived in Miami a while. He struck it rich down there. He made the acquaintance of some wealthy sportsmen and all that season he passed from one to another with money that piled up faster than he could spend it on clothes and amusement. Then one night he got drunk on a broker's yacht in the harbor at Palm Beach and, for no reason that was afterward sure to him, he struck the man's inclined head eight times with a copper book end, the final stroke splitting the skull. He swam to shore, collected his things and beat it out of the state. This ended the more affluent chapter of Oliver's existence. From that time on he moved for protection in less conspicuous channels, losing himself in the swarm of his fugitive kind wherever a town was large enough for such traffic to pass without too much attention.

Then, one evening during this winter in New Orleans, shortly after the Mardi Gras season and when he was beginning to think of heading back North, Oliver was picked up by a plain-clothes man and driven to jail, not on an ordinary charge of lewd vagrancy, but for questioning in connection with the murder of the wealthy broker in the harbor at Palm Beach. They got a full confession from him in fifteen minutes.

He hardly made any effort to dodge their questions.

They gave him half a tumbler of whiskey to loosen his tongue and he gave them a lurid account of the party the broker had given on his yacht. Oliver and a girl prostitute had been given a hundred dollars each to perform in what is called a blue movie, that is, a privately made film of licentious behavior among two or more persons, usually with some crude sort of narrative sequence. He and the girl had undressed by drunken stages before the camera and the yacht party, and had gone through a sequence of such embraces and intimacies as only four walls and a locked door usually witness. The film was not finished. To his own astonishment, Oliver had suddenly revolted, struck the girl and kicked the camera over and fled to the upper deck. Up there he had guessed that if he remained on the yacht he would do something still more violent. But when the others finally went ashore in a launch, Oliver had remained because the host had wheedled him with money and the promise of more.

"I knew when they left him alone with me that he would be sorry," Oliver said in his statement to the police. It was this admission which the prosecutor used to establish premeditation in the case.

Everything went against him at the trial. His testimony was ineffectual against the prestige of the other witnesses, all of whom swore that nothing irregular had occurred on the yacht. [No one remembered anything about the blue movie except Oliver, the girl prostitute was equally unheard of.] And the fact that Oliver had removed from the victim's body a diamond ring and a wallet assured the youth's conviction and doomed him to the chair.

The arrest of the broker's killer was given space in papers all over the country. The face of the one-armed youth was shot from newspapers into the startled eyes of men who had known him in all those places Oliver had passed through in his aimless travels. None of these men who had known him had found his image one that faded readily out of mind. The great blond youth who had been a boxer until he had lost an arm had stood as a planet among the moons of their longing, fixed in his orbit while they circled about him. Now he was caught somewhere, he had crashed into ruin. And in a sense this ruin had returned him to them. He was no longer on highways or tracks going further, but penned in a corner and waiting only for death.

He began to receive letters from them. Each morning the jailor thrust more envelopes through the bars of his cell. The letters were usually signed by fictitious names and if they requested an answer, the address given would be general delivery in one of those larger cities where Oliver's calling was plied. They were written on fine white paper, some of them were faintly scented, and some enclosed paper money. The messages were similarly phrased. All of them spoke of their shock at his dilemma, they couldn't believe it was true, it was like a bad dream, and so forth. They made allusions to the nights which he had spent with them, or the few hours which they almost invariably pronounced to be the richest of their entire experience. There was something about him, they wrote, not only the physical thing, important as that was, which had made him haunt their minds since.

What they were alluding to was the charm of the defeated which Oliver had possessed, a quality which acts as a poultice upon the inflamed nerves of those who are still in active contention. This quality is seldom linked with youth and physical charm, but in Oliver's case it had been, and it was this rare combination which had made him a person impossible to forget. And because he was sentenced to death,

Oliver had for these correspondents the curtained and abstract quality of the priest who listens without being visible to confessions of guilt. The usual restraints upon the unconscious were accordingly lifted and the dark joys of *mea culpa* were freely indulged in. The litanies of their sorrows were poured onto paper like water from broken dams. To some he became the archetype of the Savior Upon The Cross who had taken upon himself the sins of their world to be washed and purified in his blood and passion. Letters of this sort enraged the imprisoned boy and he clamped them under one foot and tore them to pieces and tossed the pieces in his slop bucket.

With the mechanical cruelty of the law, the execution of Oliver's sentence had given him several months in which to expect it and they were the months of summer. In his stifling cubicle there was very little to do while waiting for death and time enough with the impetus of disaster for the boy's malleable nature to be remolded still again, and the instrument of this process became the letters.

He sat on a folding chair or sprawled on his cot those first few weeks in the death house in a way that was not unlike the way in which he had stood against a brick-wall in rain-soaked dungarees and skivvy shirt on the New Orleans corner till someone had asked him for the time or a light. He was given a deck of cards with stains of candy bars on them and tattered books of comic and adventure cartoons to pass away time with. And there was a radio at the end of the corridor. But Oliver was cut off from the world that blared through the mouth of the radio and from that world of one-dimensional clownery and hero-ism in the raw colors of childhood's spectrum which the cartoon strips celebrated. All of these rushed by him instead of with him, and only the letters remained in connection with him.

After a while he not only read all of the letters, but folded them back in their envelopes and began to accumulate them in rubber bands on a shelf. One night without thinking he took them down from the shelf and placed them beneath his pillow, and he went to sleep with his one hand resting on them.

A few weeks before the time for his execution Oliver began to write out replies to those men who had begged to hear from him. He used a soft lead pencil that dwindled rapidly to a stub beneath his awkward pressure. He wrote on manila paper and mailed the replies in govern-ment stamped envelopes to all of those cities that he had formerly haunted.

Having had no surviving family to write to, this was Oliver's first attempt at writing letters. He wrote at first with a laborious stiffness. The composition of the simplest sentence would knot up the muscles in his one powerful arm, but as the writing went on a greater laxity developed in a wonderfully short time. Soon the sentences gathered momentum as springs that clear out a channel and they began to flow out almost expressively after a while and to ring with the crudely eloquent backwoods speech of the South, to which had been added salty idioms of the underworld he had moved in, and the road, and the sea. Into them went the warm and vivid talk that liquor and generous dealing had brought from his lips on certain occasions, the *chansons de geste* which American tongues throw away so casually in bars and hotel bedrooms. The cartoon symbol of laughter was often employed, that heavily drawn HA-HA with its tail of exclamatory punctuation, its stars and spirals, and setting that down on paper was what gave him most relief, for it had the feel of the boiling intensity in him. He would often include a rough illustration, a sketch of the chair that he was condemned to sit in.

The letters would go like this.

"Yes, I remember you plainly. I met you in the park in back of the public library, or was it in the men's room in the Greyhound depot. I met so many they sometimes get mixed up. However you stand out plainly. You asked for the time or a light and we got to talking and first thing I knew we was in your apartment drinking. And how is Chicago now that it's summer again? I sure would appreciate feeling those cool lake breezes or pouring down shots of that wonderful Five Star Connyack where we shacked up that day. I tell you it's hot in this cooler. Cooler is good. Ha-ha! One thing I can sure count on is it's going to get hotter before it gets cooler again. If you get what I mean. I mean the chair on the wire that is patiently waiting for me to sit down in it. The date is the tenth of August and you are invited except that you could not get in. It is very exclusive. I guess you would like to know if I am afraid. The answer is Yes. I do not look forward to it. I was a boxer until I lost my arm and after that happened I seemed to go through a change which I cannot account for except I was very disgusted with all of the world. I guess I stopped caring about what happened to me. That is to say I had lost my self-respect.

"I went all over the country without any plans except to keep on moving. I picked up strangers in every city I went to. I had experience with them which only meant money to me and a place to shack up for the night and liquor and food. I never thought it could mean very much to them. Now all of these letters like yours have proven it did. I meant something very important to hundreds of people whose faces and names had slipped clean out of my mind as soon as I left them. I feel as if I had run up a debt of some kind. Not money but feelings. I treated some of them badly. Went off without even so much as saying good-bye in spite of all their generosity to me and even took things which hadn't been given to me. I cannot imagine how some of these men could forgive me. If I had known then, I mean when I was outside, that such true feelings could even be found in strangers, I mean of the kind that I picked up for a living, I guess I might have felt there was more to live for. Anyhow now the situation is hopeless. All will be over for me in a very short while. Ha-ha!

"You probably didn't know that I was an artist as well as being a one-armed champion boxer and therefore I'm going to draw you a wonderful picture!"

This writing of letters became his one occupation, and as a stone gathers heat when lain among coals, the doomed man's brain grew warmer and warmer with a sense of communion. Coming prior to disaster, this change might have been a salvation. It might have offered a center for personal integration which the boy had not had since the mandala dream of the prize ring had gone with the arm. A personality without a center throws up a wall and lives in a state of siege. So Oliver had cultivated his cold and absolute insularity behind which had lain the ruined city of the crippled champion. Within those battlements had been little or nothing to put up a fight for survival. Now something was stirring within.

But this coming to life was unmerciful, coming so late. The indifference had passed off when it should have remained to make death easier for him. And time passed quicker. In the changeless enclosure of his cell the time that stood between the youth and his death wore away like the soft lead pencil that he wrote with, until only a stub too small for his grasp was left him.

But how alive he still was!

Before imprisonment he had thought of his maimed body as something that, being broken, was only fit for abuse. You God-damned cripple, he used to groan to himself. The excitement he stirred in others had been incomprehensible and disgusting to him. But lately the torrent of letters from men whom he had forgotten who couldn't stop thinking of him had begun to revive his self-interest. Autoerotic sensations began to flower in him. He felt the sorrowful pleasure that stirred his groin in response to manipulation. Lying nude on the cot in the southern July, his one large hand made joyless love to his body, exploring all of those erogenous zones that the fingers of others, hundreds of strangers' fingers, had clasped with a hunger that now was beginning to be understandable to him. Too late, this resurrection. Better for all those rainbows of the flesh to have stayed with the arm cut off in San Diego.

During the earlier period of his confinement Oliver had not particularly noticed or cared about the spatial limitations of his cell. Then he had been satisfied to sit on the edge of his cot and move no more than was necessary for bodily functions. That had been merciful. However, it was now gone and every morning he seemed to wake up in a space that had mysteriously diminished while he slept. The inner repressions took this way of screaming for their release. The restlessness became a phobia and the phobia was turning into panic.

He could not remain still for a moment. His heavy foot pads sounded from the end of the hall like an ape's, for he walked barefooted with rapid, shuffling strides around and around the little space of his cage. He talked to himself in a monotonous undertone that grew louder, as the days passed, until it began to compete with the endless chatter and blare of the guards' radio. At first he would hush up when he was ordered to, but later his panic deafened him to the guards' voices, until they shouted threats at him. Then he would grip the bars of his cage door and shout back at them names and curses more violent than their own. The doomed boy's behavior cut off whatever acts of humanity these hard men might have shown him as he drew close to his death. Finally, on the third day before his execution, they punished one of his tantrums by turning the fire-hose on him, until he was crushed to the floor in a strangling heap. He lay there and sobbed and cursed with his brain spinning through a dizzy spiral of nightmares.

By this time, the writing of letters was altogether cut off, but during his quieter intervals he drew wild pictures in his manila tablet and printed out the violent comic-strip symbols, especially the immense HA-HA with its screaming punctuation. Sedatives were put in his food in the last few days, but the drugs were burned up in the furnace of his nerves and the little sleep they gave him would plunge him in worse nightmares than the ones of waking.

The day before he would die Oliver received a visitor in the death cell.

The visitor was a young Lutheran minister who had just come out of the seminary and had not yet received an appointment to a church. Oliver had refused to see the prison chaplain. This had been mentioned in the local newspapers with a picture of Oliver and a caption, Condemned Youth Refuses Consolation of Faith. It had spoken also of the hard and unrepentant nature of the boy who was to die very soon and of his violent behavior in the prison. But the picture was incongruous to these facts, the face of the blond youth having a virile but tender beauty of the sort that some painter of the Renaissance might have slyly attributed to a juvenile saint, a look which had sometimes inspired commentators to call him "the baby-faced killer."

From the moment that he had seen this photograph the Lutheran minister had been following out a series of compulsions so strong that he appeared to himself to be surrendering to an outside power. His earnestness was so apparent that he had no trouble convincing the warden that his mission to the youth was divinely inspired, but by the time the pass was issued, the force of his compulsions had so exhausted the young minister that he fell into a state of nervous panic and would have fled from the building if he had not been attended by a guard.

He found Oliver seated on the edge of his cot senselessly rubbing the sole of a bare foot. He wore only a pair of shorts and his sweating body radiated a warmth that struck the visitor like a powerful spotlight. The appearance of the boy had not been falsely reported. At his first swift glance the minister's mind shot back to an obsession of his childhood when he had gone all of one summer daily to the zoo to look at a golden panther. The animal was supposed to be particularly savage and a sign on its cage had admonished visitors to keep their distance. But the look in the animal's eyes was so radiant with innocence that the child, who was very timid and harassed by reasonless anxieties, had found a mysterious comfort in meeting their gaze and had come to see them staring benignly out of the darkness when his own eyes were closed before sleeping. Then he would cry himself to sleep for pity of the animal's imprisonment and an unfathomable longing that moved through all of his body.

But one night he dreamed of the panther in a shameful way. The immense clear eyes had appeared to him in a forest and he had thought, if I lie down very quietly the panther will come near me and I am not afraid of him because of our long communions through the bars. He took off his clothes before lying down in the forest. A chill wind began to stir and he felt himself shivering. Then a little fear started in his nerves. He began to doubt his security with the panther and he was afraid to open his eyes again, but he reached out and slowly and noiselessly as possible gathered some leaves about his shuddering nudity and lay under them in a tightly curled position trying to breathe as softly as possible and hoping that now the panther would not discover him. But the chill little wind grew stronger and the leaves blew away. Then all at once he was warm in spite of the windy darkness about him and he realized that the warmth was that of the golden panther coming near him. It was no longer any use trying to conceal himself and it was too late to make an attempt at flight, and so with a sigh the dreamer uncurled his body from its tight position and lay outstretched and spread-eagled in an attitude of absolute trust and submission. Something began to stroke him and presently because of its liquid heat he realized that it was the tongue of the beast bathing him as such animals bathe their young, starting at his feet but progressing slowly up the length of his legs until the narcotic touch arrived at his loins, and then the dream had taken the shameful turn and he had awakened burning with shame beneath the damp and aching initial of Eros.

He had visited the golden panther only once after that and had found himself unable to meet the radiant scrutiny of the beast without mortification. And so the idyl had ended, or had seemed to end. But here was the look of the golden panther again, the innocence in the danger, an exact parallel so unmistakably clear that the minister knew it and felt the childish instinct to curl into a protective circle and cover his body with leaves.

Instead, he reached into his pocket and took out a box of tablets.

The very clear gaze of the boy was now fixed on him, but neither of them had spoken and the guard had closed the door of the cell and withdrawn to his station at the end of the corridor, which was out of their sight.

"What is that?" asked the boy.

"Barbital tablets. I am not very well," the minister whispered.

"What is the matter with you?"

"A little functional trouble of the heart."

He had put the tablet on his tongue, but the tongue was utterly dry. He could not swallow.

"Water?" he whispered.

Oliver got up and went to the tap. He filled an enamelled tin cup with tepid water and handed it to his caller.

"What have you come here for?" he asked the young man.

"Just for a talk."

"I have got nothing to say but the deal is rigged."

"Then let me read something to you?"

"What's something?"

"The twenty-first Psalm."

"I told them I didn't want no chaplain in here."

"I am not the chaplain, I am just—"

"Just what?"

"A stranger with sympathy for the misunderstood."

Oliver shrugged and went on rubbing the sole of his foot. The minister sighed and coughed.

"Are you prepared," he whispered.

"I'm not prepared for the hot seat, if that's what you mean. But the seat is prepared for me, so what is the difference?"

"I am talking about Eternity," said the minister. "This world of ours, this transitory existence, is just a threshold to something Immense beyond."

"Bull," said Oliver.

"You don't believe me?"

"Why should I?"

"Because you are face to face with the last adventure!"

This answer had shot from his tongue with a sort of exultant power. He was embarrassed by the boy's steady look. He turned away from it as he finally had from the golden panther's the last time he had gone to him.

"Ha-ha!" said Oliver.

"I'm only trying to help you realize—"

Oliver cut in.

"I was a boxer. I lost my arm. Why was that?"

"Because you persisted in error."

"Bull," said Oliver. "I was not the driver of the car. I yelled at the son of a bitch, slow down, you fucker. Then came the crash. A boxer, my arm comes off. Explain that to me."

"It gave you the chance of a lifetime."

"A chance for what?"

"To grow your spiritual arms and reach for God." He leaned toward Oliver and gripped the prisoner's knees. "Don't think of me as a man, but as a connection!"

"Huh?"

"A wire that is plugged in your heart and charged with a message from God."

The curiously ambient look of the condemned youth was fixed on his visitor's face for several seconds.

Then he said, "Wet that towel."

"What towel?"

"The one that is over the chair you're sitting in."

"It's not very clean."

"I guess it is clean enough to use on Ollie."

"What do you want to do with it?"

"Rub the sweat off my back."

The minister dampened the crumpled and stiffened cloth and handed it to the boy.

"You do it for me."

"Do what?"

"Rub the sweat off my back."

He rolled on his stomach with a long-drawn sigh, an exhalation that brought again to his frightened visitor's mind the golden panther of fifteen years ago. The rubbing went on for a minute.

"Do I smell?" asked Oliver.

"No. Why?"

"I am clean," said the boy. "I took a bath after breakfast."

"Yes."

"I have always been careful to keep myself clean. I was a very clean fighter—and a very clean whore!"

He said, "Ha-ha! Did you know that I was a whore?"

"No," said the other.

"Well, that's what I was all right. That was my second profession."

The rubbing continued for another minute, during which an invisible drummer had seemed to the minister to be advancing from the end of the corridor to the door of the cell and then to come through the bars and stand directly above them.

It was his heartbeat. Now it was becoming irregular and his breath whistled. He dropped the towel and dug in his white shirt pocket for the box of sedatives, but when he removed it he found that the cardboard was pulpy with sweat and the tablets had oozed together in a white paste.

"Go on," said Oliver. "It feels good."

He arched his body and pulled his shorts further down. The narrow and sculptural flanks of the youth were exposed.

"Now," said Oliver softly, "rub with your hands."

The Lutheran sprang from the cot.

"No!"

"Don't be a fool. There's a door at the end of the hall. It makes a noise when anybody comes in it."

The minister retreated.

The boy reached out and caught him by the wrist.

"You see that pile of letters on the shelf? They're bills from people I owe. Not money, but feelings. For three whole years I went all over the country stirring up feelings without feeling nothing myself. Now that's all changed and I have feelings, too. I am lonely and bottled up the same as you are. I know your type. Everything is artistic or else it's religious, but that's all a bunch of bullshit and I don't buy it. All that you need's to be given a push on the head!"

He moved toward the man as if he would give him the push.

The caller cried out. The guard came running to let him out of the cell. He had to be lifted and half carried down the corridor and before he had reached the end of it, he started to retch as if his whole insides were being torn out.

Oliver heard him.

"Maybe he'll come back tonight," the doomed boy thought. But he didn't come back and then Oliver died with all his debts unpaid. However, he died with a good deal more dignity than he had given his jailors to expect of him.

During the last few hours his attention returned to the letters. He read them over and over, whispering them aloud. And when the warden came to conduct him to the death chamber, he said, "I would like to take these here along with me." He carried them into the death chamber with him as a child takes a doll or a toy into a dentist's office to give the protection of the familiar and loved.

The letters were resting companionably in the fork of his thighs when he sat down in the chair. At the last moment a guard reached out to remove them. But Oliver's thighs closed on them in a desperate vise that could not have been easily broken. The warden gave a signal to let them remain. Then the moment came, the atmosphere hummed and darkened. Bolts from across the frontiers of the unknown, the practically named and employed but illimitably mysterious power that first invested a static infinitude of space with heat and brilliance and motion, were channeled through Oliver's nerve cells for an instant and then shot back across those immense frontiers, having claimed and withdrawn whatever was theirs in the boy whose lost right arm had been known as "lightning in leather."

The body, unclaimed after death, was turned over to a medical college to be used in a classroom laboratory. The men who performed the dissection were somewhat abashed by the body under their knives. It seemed intended for some more august purpose, to stand in a gallery of antique sculpture, touched only by light through stillness and contemplation, for it had the nobility of some broken Apollo that no one was likely to carve so purely again.

But death has never been much in the way of completion.

1945 (Published 1948)

The Interval

Gretchen had allowed a fellow teacher at the Iowa City grade school to talk her into taking a summer trip to California in the friend's old Ford and the trip had been a disappointment all the way around, so that by the first week of August she felt that she had thrown her vacation away. Gretchen was a submissive German type of girl and her friend had made all the plans and arrangements for the trip but it turned out that Gretchen had to pay more than her share of the expenses. Whenever they stopped for gas the girlfriend's pocketbook was inconveniently located at the moment, it was under a pile of luggage on the back seat, and the same thing held true when they started off in the mornings. The girlfriend, Augusta, would hop in the Ford sedan first and would have a terrible time getting the engine to turn over, so she would holler out to Gretchen, "Honey you settle with the man for the cabin and I'll square it with you later." But it was always later, later, and poor Gretchen who had been brought up to respect even small coins was made wretched by the continual depletions of her year's savings which had been converted into traveler's checks in twenty-five and ten dollar denominations. It turned out that Augusta had not saved much for the trip. She had apparently expected to take it on a shoestring, and one not even on her own shoe. So by the time they got to the West Coast, Gretchen and Augusta were still on speaking terms, but just barely, and it was creditable more to Gretchen's German patience than to anything Augusta said or did to give her companion some pleasure out of the trip. In fact when they arrived in Hollywood and started taking those tours of the stars' palatial residences, poor Gretchen was so dispirited that all the houses looked alike to her. She kept saying to herself, This is where dear little Shirley or beautiful Gloria lives, and she would try to pump up her enthusiasm about it, but it was just another big house, imposing as a prosperous

189

funeral parlor, and even the glimpse of a white-coated domestic who presumably helped a star off with her wraps and brought her breakfast up on a silver service, could not lift Gretchen's heart with more than the most perfunctory of thrills. Augusta did not allow this unresponsive condition to pass without comment. "Honey," she said, "you depress me. Perk up, smile, say something! You act like there's just been a death in the family, honey!" She only intensified Gretchen's gloom in this way, making her girlfriend feel a social burden in spite of the fact that it was continually she who engaged and paid for the guide while Augusta was outside taking a look at the weather. And every time they went out on one of those tours, to Beverly Hills or Santa Monica, the girlfriend Augusta would give her short, piercing glances that made Gretchen blush, and follow it up with some little critical comment such as, "Honey, have you ever tried an astringent lotion on your throat at night?" It made Gretchen feel that she was literally falling to pieces, though actually she was not quite twenty-seven, a healthy girl, with a solid, durable figure.

Gretchen had begun to plot ways of escaping from Augusta, some of them quite dramatic, such as secretly packing and slipping away at midnight. But Augusta was a skillful manipulator of many strings. Whenever it had come to the point when Gretchen might actually have executed some such plan, Augusta would suddenly turn on a great deal of charm, she would bubble with enthusiasm for some new plan, she would remember the name and address of some young professor at Southern Cal whom she was certain that Gretchen would adore, and Gretchen would hopefully wait around for this to fizzle out also. She had just about come to the end of the rope with Augusta when they finally made the move to Laguna Beach. "Honey, we're going to hobnob with the stars," she screamed at Gretchen when she came in one night from a round of The Strip with a newly-annexed boyfriend whom Gretchen had not even been introduced to. Gretchen had been interrupted in the middle of secretly packing up for about the fourth time, but if Augusta noticed, she pretended not to. "Carl knows Cary Grant and the crowd he runs around with, honey, it's all arranged! We're driving up to Laguna tomorrow morning! Isn't it dreamy? I can't believe it is true!" So off they went to Laguna. Now Gretchen had always somewhat prided herself, in private, on having a really nice figure and she hoped that this advantage would turn the tables a little. However it didn't seem to work out that way. They got to Laguna Beach all prepared for a plunge into glamor but one of those vague upsets of plans had occurred, the wonderful beach house that some-body said Carl could use had just burned down or blown up and been washed out by the tide. Anyway there was no place to go but another small tourist cabin with twin beds touching each other. And the first thing Augusta did when they got there was yell at Gretchen, "Honey, you pay the first week and I'll pay the second!" And before Gretchen could deliver the answer she had framed in her mind, Augusta had dashed off to pick up Carl at a club.

It was only Augusta who made the plunge into glamor, for her newly-acquired sweetheart, who was named Carl Zerbst, had some-how come into the possession of a convertible Buick roadster which was all scarlet and chromium, it was the brightest thing possible to imagine, and had six horns each of which made a different musical sound. Some days he had this car and some days he didn't, and when he had it, he and Augusta would be in hysterically gay spirits and when he didn't have it, when somebody named Sam had it, a person who was vaguely much older and vaguely pretty terrible in some way, he and Augusta would look as if the whole domestic and foreign situation had gone to pieces. However it made no difference to Gretchen whether they had it or not because she never got in it. There was always some excuse why she could not come along, but someone was going to come down from L.A. pretty soon. Carl had invited him down for Gretchen's sake. But there was a limit to what Gretchen could take in the way of such vague reassurances. Whenever the four-wheeled phenomenon flashed by, she got a lump in her throat, even got one when she heard the distant music of its horns, not because she really cared to be in it. She had begun to think it was hideous, it struck her like a blow in the face when she saw it. But she was miserably lonesome, not only in the little tourist cabin but on the beach. The lump stayed in her throat all the time, and when she had to speak to Augusta about something, during the infrequent times that they were in the tourist cabin to-gether, she would have such a choking sensation words wouldn't come out. As for the advantage of her nice figure, even this seemed to be totally discounted. The first time she got into her new bathing-suit, Augusta gave her one of those critical glances and said to her, "Honey, you have been sitting down too much this year. Your hips are spread-ing." This may not have been true but it completed the ruin of Gret-chen's faith in herself. She felt herself heavy and awkward. She blushed when people glanced at her on the beach. On the beach she was as lonely as she was in the tourist cabin. Nothing and no place was any good for her now, and Augusta was evidently having the time of her life with the boy named Carl and his several movie connections.

So that was about the way things stood when Jimmie entered the picture at Laguna.

Jimmie was one of those somewhat talented boys who, from the age of fifteen on, are perpetually right on the verge of accomplishing something of a glamorous nature, getting a part in a hit show or going into the movies or on the air, but it was always just on the verge and not over. His friends' belief and enthusiasm were sustained for quite a while on such an airy diet but it began to wear out. The eagerness died gradually out of their voices when they said, Jimmie has talent, just got a letter from Jimmie on the West Coast and, what do you know, he is going to be signed to play opposite Hedy Lamarr in her next picture. But time enough had passed for him to arrive somewhere, to have made a dozen pictures with great stars, but he hadn't arrived anywhere but Laguna Beach and you'd have to look quickly and closely to discern his prettily boyish features in one of the crowd scene appearances he had made on the screen.

He was twenty-seven the summer that Gretchen met him, which was a rather advanced age for a boy of his type. He couldn't afford to get much older than that, for his hair was the sort that is gone soon after thirty and the boyish fullness of his face was soon to take on an omen of obesity. It may seem odd to harp on Jimmie's looks so, but his looks were just about all that he had to go on. He was loosely connected with the same crowd that Carl Zerbst was, only he never had even the loan of such a flashy conveyance as Carl Zerbst had. Nevertheless he seemed to be well-enough liked, he cut quite a figure at Mona's, which was the place outside of Laguna where fun-lovers went when the sun had withdrawn from the beach. He could be counted on for the quick and right answer and he fitted in quite acceptably with both crowds.

There were two crowds that he and Carl Zerbst moved around in, not mutually exclusive but different enough for it to be something of a trick to operate with an equally fair degree of success in each. In the afternoons you could always find Jimmie playing volleyball on the beach with a number of other bright and anonymous young fellows of the sort that abounded on Southern California beaches before the war started and during the years there was so much unemployment. Jimmie had on sky-blue trunks of a satiny finish that sparkled in the sun when he leapt and shouted. He cut fantastic capers, asserting himself all over whatever place he was in, giving nobody a moment's chance to ignore him.

The trouble was that nearly all of the others did the same thing so that sometimes it was as if each was performing in a separate ring, possibly in a translucent glass sphere of some kind. The rule of the game was to seem to be part of the others, but each was translucently walled away from the rest by his self-absorbed brightness. Nearly each one had his talent and his good looks, the act that he could put on, the gaiety and the good times that his youth called for. But these were not stable commodities. They were not to be counted on for more than five summers or three summers or even two. And having a thing in your grasp that dissolves without ceasing makes for an acid brewed at the roots of the heart. This acid is kept down there for a certain time only, and then it begins to rise and appear on the surface. It changes the prettiest face in a frightening manner, showing up in the eyes and around the mouth, affecting even the voice. A shocking anomaly when the wolf's eyes begin to peer out of the lamb's soft face!—ridiculous and too awful to think about . . .

The meeting with Jimmie came about in this way. Jimmie was worried about his scalp condition. He had been warned that saltwater dried the scalp and contributed to baldness, so he did not go in the water in the presence of others. He had bought a rubber swimming cap which he carried up the beach with him to a secluded spot where he could put it on unobserved and take a swim by himself, for he felt that a man wearing a swimming cap was somewhat ludicrous-looking and not in the bright tradition. Now on this afternoon that he met Gretchen the volleyball game had broken up a little before sundown and he had started up the beach for his solitary swim when he noticed that the girl who had been watching him all afternoon with lonely eyes was a little way up ahead of him, walking disconsolately in the same direction as he. He was not a boy who wasted much thought on others, but those who said that Jimmie had a good heart were right about it. It pleased him to think that his charm was something that could be used to bring sunlight to dark places. So when he noticed this lonely girl ahead of him on the beach, he overtook her and started a conversation.

Gretchen was so grateful she made no effort to hide it. The desire for real companionship had been thwarted for two months, since the California trip started, and this was the first release. She found herself chattering as freely as Augusta and all at once the conviction that she had a nice figure returned. Her simplicity and his boyish high spirits got them along quite easily together. He wasn't ashamed to put on the swimming cap in Gretchen's presence. He put it on and they went in swimming together. The big waves knocked them over each other, against and around each other, and Gretchen's excitement gave her a glow that more than made up for the imperfections of her form and features, and if Jimmie had declined somewhat from the meridian of his beauty, it was not in Gretchen's eyes enough to notice.

Jimmie was the type that cuts up with girls but doesn't make many passes. There had been a few embarrassed chapters in his life of the sort that a sophisticated person would guess from something barely visible about him. He would never be definite about such a thing as that. It was like his talent and his thinning blond hair and everything else in his ephemeral makeup. He was well-liked by girls and got along with them fine in the presence of others but when alone with a girl he was less at ease, it was usually something that he tried to avoid. And so he was somewhat surprised and pleased with himself when at the suggestion of a particularly big wave he found himself and the girl in a juxtaposition more definite than he had planned. And he didn't get up and she didn't try to either. It was a lovely sunset, exactly the sort of the pulp romance illustrations, and somebody's portable radio on the other side of the rocks played all the most melting tunes, such as "Melancholy Baby," "Kiss Me Again," and "It's Only a Paper Moon."

The first year of their marriage they stayed in California and the brief spurt of manly assurance that being married gave Jimmie served him well for a while. He got a little extra work in the movies and she gave private instruction to movie people's kids in Beverly Hills. Jimmie met a young fellow who was supposed to be a rising star on the lot, their lives were briefly lit by his terrible glamour. But it turned out to be a disadvantage for the rising young star was suddenly disgraced somehow or other and Jimmie was included in the dismissal. There was no more extra work to be had and the manly assurance petered out of Jimmie and he began to lie around the apartment in shorts or his pale blue bathrobe not even much caring to go to the beach anymore. She was so in love with him by this time, for hers was the sort of devotion that can't stop growing, that nothing he did caused her anything worse than perplexity or sorrow. That is to say that she never flew into rages or hit him over the head with the kitchen stove as she would have been thoroughly justified in doing, particularly after the ex-rising star of the studio began to use their apartment as social and business headquarters and even took to sleeping there when he got put out of the Beverly Wilshire Hotel. She was so in love with Jimmie that he could almost convince her that Bobby was a nice boy. She only felt sorrow and perplexity when Bobby, stinking with liquor, fell in their bedroom at

three in the morning and had to be put to bed on the other side of
Jimmie because you couldn't just leave him lying there on the floor in
his stupefied condition.

So the California interval petered out and they returned disconsolately to Dubuque, the war having started and Jimmie involved with his
draft board. But Jimmie had a talk with the doctors and it was mutually
and amicably agreed that his temperament was not just right for the
army, and he got out of it. He went into one of the local defense plants
and by this time the fact that Jimmie had talent, or had had talent, was
universally forgotten and ignored, it was now a living faith only to
Jimmie and Gretchen. To Gretchen the living faith was Jimmie himself
who could do nothing wrong but who could make little mistakes. Who
could be misled by wrong people, because of his trusting nature, and
who was just too naturally sweet to be safe in a world of people who
have no respect for the finer things anymore.

He was twenty-nine and he hadn't changed much from the summer
that she met him in Laguna, but just enough to make all the difference
in the world with somebody of his pretty-boy, baby-face type. He was a
pretty boy who wasn't very pretty anymore and although he only
weighed about 165 pounds which wasn't too much for his five feet and
seven inches, he nevertheless looked rather pudgy in clothes that
weren't carefully tailored. Somebody down at the defense plant had
mortified him to death by calling him Piggy for a nickname. It wasn't
fair to call him that. He did have a very short turned up nose and a
round face so that he looked like one of those pretty little pigs in the
colored cartoons, but the sobriquet was unkind to a boy who had
hobnobbed with the near-royalty of Hollywood and Broadway and who
everybody with any perception should know had a brilliant future as
soon as the war was over.

As the spring of their first year in Dubuque rolled around Gretchen's
sorrow and perplexity had grown to alarming dimensions which was
not improved when a telegram arrived from New York signed Bobby
and saying COME QUICK CHANCE OF A LIFETIME WILL EX-
PLAIN WHEN I SEE YOU. Gretchen could see nothing to be very
joyful about in this message but Jimmie let out a wild whoop of joy and
rushed to the bureau and started throwing shirts, socks and neckties
into his suitcase. "Baby, this is the break that we've lived for!" he kept
saying.

"But what is it, Jimmie?" she pleaded.

"I'm sure it's about the Repertory deal."

"What deal is that," she enquired of him sweetly and gently.

But he didn't stop to tell her, in case he knew, and at six o'clock in the evening of the same day he had hopped on a plane with somebody's cancelled reservation and two hundred fifty dollars from their savings account which left them all but cleaned out. It has not been mentioned, though perhaps understood, that he had already gotten his release from the defense plant. A sort of occupational neurosis had taken care of that. His hands had started shaking uncontrollably at work so that he was too much of a nuisance and the doctor at the plant had agreed with him that further routine employment for a man of his talent might lead to a serious crack-up.

So he was off to Broadway. And about a week after his departure came a brief wire, which said, JUST ARRIVED EVERYTHING TOO WONDERFUL FOR WORDS THINGS HAVE NEVER LOOKED BRIGHTER FOR YOU AND ME DEAREST BABY WITH ALL MY LOVE JIMMIE.

At first she thought it was only the excitement of this wire that affected her stomach and put her to bed for a day, but the doctor informed her the manifestations were of a less psychic order. She didn't even know where to reach Jimmie to let him know that they were going to have it. Someone suggested wiring him in care of Actor's Equity which she did, but evidently the wire was not delivered to him. Three weeks had passed since his flight to whatever wonderful thing it was that Bobby had lured him off to. Then came one of those big Jumbo postcards, covered all over with his feverish childish scrawl in pale green ink and the face of it bearing a picture of "The Great White Way." "In the left-hand corner," wrote Jimmie, "you will see the house that we open in after the Boston try-out." That was the only allusion he made to the wonderful thing he had gone to. In the left-hand corner was an indiscriminate welter of lighted marquees announcing everything from Betty Grable to Ruby Foo's. Which one was he going to open in after the Boston try-out? It didn't matter. She packed her things and made ready to join Jimmie in his long-delayed but seemingly imminent and astonishing plunge to glory. Then came one of those vague let-downs their life had been so full of. UNION DIFFICULTY HAD TIED UP OUR PLANS BUT BOBBY IS IN CLOSE TOUCH WITH THE RICHEST ANGEL ON BROADWAY. DO NOT COME HERE UNTIL I ADVISE YOU FURTHER. WITH ALL DEAREST LOVE TO YOU, JIMMIE.

She managed to conceal this wire from her folks and proceeded with her departure. She wired Jimmie: GOT YOUR MESSAGE BUT CANNOT ALTER PLANS FOR REASONS THAT I WILL EXPLAIN TO YOU WHEN I SEE YOU. She then liquidated the remainder of their savings account on a train ticket and a two-piece suit with an adjustable waist-line.

He met her at the train all smiles and she instantly burst into tears and told him her story. Jimmie cried, too, in the cab that took them to Bobby's. Why didn't you let me know, he kept repeating. Wire? Actor's Equity? No, of course he didn't get it! How would they know where he was? Oh, well, anyhow—

Bobby was wonderful to them and again, in spite of past history, she was almost persuaded that he was a very sweet guy as Jimmie insisted. Certainly his apartment was a dream! And he gave it to them, lock, stock and sunlamp. He stayed next door with a bachelor friend of his who was also in show business. And the first few days were wonderfully bright and cheerful with everybody talking and acting like characters in a drawing room comedy of the smartest description. Unmistakably Jimmie had gotten in with a really up-and-coming set of people. She could see that he was just dizzy with it. He was even more exhilarated than he had seemed that first summer at Laguna Beach when vague studio prospects had tossed him among the clouds. However the exact thing which all of this exuberance was leading up to was still a bit too obscure for Gretchen's comfort. She dared not show her anxiety to Jimmie but she would certainly have appreciated plainer speech on the subject of the big deal that seemed to be cooking.

Nobody seemed to have time to sit down and discuss it with her and when she brought it up when they were, finally, alone in bed together, he would say, Baby, this repertory idea would only make sense to somebody who was born in a wardrobe trunk!

Exactly what that meant was no more certain than anything else had been.

Along toward the end of her second week at Bobby's there was a curious and distressing scene. The bachelor friend that Bobby was staying with burst into the apartment at about four in the morning and shouted her name in the living room. She was alone in bed, for Bobby and Jimmie had gone off somewhere in connection with something about the repertory deal. She hastily slipped on her robe and went to the living room but by the time she had got there Bobby and Jimmie

himself had entered the apartment and a fierce struggle was in progress. Bobby who was much the biggest and huskiest of the three had
pinioned the arms of his hysterical friend, and the friend was screaming things that made only the vaguest but most horrible sense to her.
They got him out of the apartment, but by the time they did so,
Gretchen felt she could not remain there any longer. They all sat down
and talked things over quietly. "You don't believe it?" Jimmie kept
pleading. And she said, "No, I don't, of course I don't, I couldn't!" But
she could not look at him, all she could do was sit there stupidly crying
and clinging on to his hand and letting him kiss her and squeeze her
shoulders spasmodically against him. Bobby made coffee and they sat
up all night and by the time morning came it had all been settled that
she should go back to Dubuque till the union difficulty and so forth had
blown over. And as for those things the hysterical friend had shouted,
forget them altogether and just go on as if nothing at all had happened—and have the baby.

    She had the baby that summer in Dubuque, and when fall came she
went back to teaching again and she and the baby lived in the home of
her parents. It was very much like the life before she knew Jimmie, for
she had not been a popular girl and had lived at home very quietly.
There was a difference in that the interval with Jimmie had left her
with hunger for more than a routine comfort. But she didn't complain
of the fox-teeth in her heart. She felt as if she had done something
wrong and foolish for which she was now enduring a necessary pen-
ance. She was patient at teaching and studied at night and thought that
maybe that summer she'd be with Jimmie somewhere, in the East or at
home, and being somewhat enlightened, a bit less confused, it might be
possible to continue their life on a more realistic basis. Having the son
had meant very little at first because she was still so absorbed in the
lack of Jimmie. It was perhaps foolish of her to want the child to be like
him. But she did, and was pleased that its eyes stayed blue and its hair
showed no sign of getting any darker. It seemed to have a light nature
the same as Jimmie and she was certain that it was exhibiting signs of
Jimmie's talent. It laughed before it could talk and the laugh was like
Jimmie's, sudden and unimaginably charming as his was or had been
when they had first met at Laguna. The truth of it was that the
wayward Jimmie the First was undergoing a very wonderful metamor-
phosis in the mind of his wife. He was becoming a pearl in the shell of
her recollection. She was seeing him more and more as he was on the
beach that summer at Laguna, in the wonderful sparkling blue trunks,

leaping into the air with bursts of laughter among those anonymous bright young men who ignored her. It seemed as if he had gone right up in one of those skyward leaps and never come back to the earth, which was in a sense precisely what Jimmie had done.

On a descending scale of enthusiasm the messages about the repertory deal that was cooking in New York continued to reach her. But they became vaguer than ever and the lapses between them were longer. And then one day came an ordinary government-stamped postcard, not even graced with a picture of lighted marquees. It was not at all like Jimmie. She thought wildly for a moment that Bobby must have written it, or one of those others whom she had never trusted in spite of Jimmie's insistence that they were so nice. Certainly one thing after another had blown up and they had witnessed and experienced and tacitly admitted the blowing up of them. But here was the message purportedly from Jimmie. "The repertory deal has gone up in smoke like everything else in my life. I have disappointed you and disappointed myself and everyone else who ever had any faith in me. There is nothing left to believe in and nothing to hope for except that you will forget me. With all my love, Jimmie."

Surely it was a forged document or something that Bobby dictated and forced him to write with a revolver pressed to his temple. The ink was pale green and the handwriting, childishly crooked, could only be Jimmie's. In a few days some word would come to refute it, some jubilant contradiction would surely follow. She waited and while she waited went patiently on with her untheatrical life. But no more messages came from the wayward Jimmie, and the hope he expressed in the last one was slow to come true.

October 1945 (Not previously published)

Tent Worms

Billy Foxworth had been grumbling for days about the tent worms that were building great, sagging canopies of transparent gray tissue among the thickly grown berry trees that surrounded their summer cottage on the Cape. His wife, Clara, had dreams and preoccupations of her own, and had listened without attention to these grumblings. Once in a while she had looked at him darkly and thought, If he but knew! He has more to worry about than those tent worms! "Tent worms? What are tent worms?" she once murmured dreamily but her mind wandered off while he defined them to her. He must have gone on talking about them for quite a while, for her mind described a wide orbit among her private reflections before he brought her back to momentary attention by slamming his coffee cup down on the saucer and exclaiming irritably, "Stop saying 'Yes, yes, yes' when you're not listening to a goddamn word I say!"

"I heard you," she protested crossly. "You were maundering like an old woman about those worms! Am I supposed to sit here starry-eyed with excitement while you—"

"All right," he said. "You asked me what they were and I was trying to tell you."

"I don't care what they are," she said. "Maybe they bother you but they don't bother me."

"Stop being childish!" he snapped.

They had a sun terrace on the back of their cottage where Clara reclined in a deck chair all afternoon, enjoying her private reflections while Billy worked at his typewriter on the screened porch just within. For five years Clara had not thought about the future. She was thinking about it now. It had become a tangible thing once more, owing to the information she had, to which Billy did not have access, in spite of the fact that it concerned Billy even more than herself, because it

200

concerned what was happening to Billy that Billy did not or was not supposed to know about. No, he did not know about it, she was practically sure that he didn't, or if he did, it was only in his unconscious, kept back there because he refused to accept it or didn't even dare to suspect it. That was why he had become so childish this summer, maundering like an idiot about those worms when it was August and they would be leaving here soon, going back to New York, and certainly Billy would never come back here again and she, God knows—let the worms eat the whole place up, let them eat the trees and the house and the beach and the ocean itself as far as she was concerned!

But about three o'clock one afternoon she smelled smoke. She looked around and there was Billy with a torch of old newspapers, setting fire to the tent worms' canopies of webby gray stuff. There he was in his khaki shorts holding up a flaming torch of newspapers to the topmost branches of the little stunted trees where the tent worms had built their houses.

He was burning them out, childishly, senselessly, in spite of the fact that there were thousands of them. Yes, looking over the trees from the sun terrace she could see that the tent worms had spread their dominion from tree to tree till now, finally, near the end of the summer, there was hardly a tree that did not support one or more of the gray tissue canopies that devoured their leaves. Still Billy was attempting to combat them single-handed with his silly torches of paper.

Clara got up and let out a loud cry of derision.

"What in hell do you think you are doing!"

"I am burning out the tent worms," he answered gravely.

"Are you out of your mind? There are millions of them!"

"That's all right, I'm going to burn them all out before we leave here!"

She gave up. Turned away and sank back in her deck chair.

All that afternoon the burning continued. It was no good protesting, although the smoke and odor were quite irritating. The best that Clara could do was drink, and so she did. She made herself a thermos of Tom Collinses and she drank them all afternoon while her husband attacked the insects with his paper torches. Along about five o'clock Clara Foxworth began to feel happy and carefree. Her dreams took a sanguine turn. She saw herself that winter in expensive mourning, in handsomely tailored black suits with a little severe jewelry and a cape of black furs, and she saw herself with various escorts, whose features were still indistinguishable, in limousines that purred comfortably through icy streets from a restaurant to a theater, from a theater to an apartment, not yet going to nightclubs so soon after—

Ah! Her attitude was healthy, she was not being insincere and pretending to feel what she didn't. Pity? Yes, she felt sorry for him but when love had ceased being five or six years ago, why make an effort to think it would be a loss?

Toward sundown the phone rang.

It rang so rarely now that the sound surprised her. Not only she but their whole intimate circle—of friends?—had drawn back from them into their own concerns, as actors disperse to their offstage lives when a curtain had fallen and they're released from performance.

She took her time about answering, having already surmised that the caller would be their doctor, and it was.

Professional cheer is uncheering.

"How's it going, sweetie?"

"How's what going?"

"Your escape from the poisonous vapors of the metropolis?"

"If that's a serious question, Doc, I'll give you a serious answer. Your patient is nostalgic for the poisonous vapors and so is creating some here."

"What, what?"

"Is the connection bad?"

"No, just wondered what you meant."

"I will enlighten you gladly. Billy, your patient, is polluting the air of our summer retreat by burning out something called tent worms. The smoke is suffocating, worse than carbon monoxide in a traffic jam in a tunnel. I'm coughing and choking and still he keeps at it."

"Well, at least he's still active."

"Oh, that he is. Would you like me to call him to the phone?"

"No, just tell him I—no, don't tell him I called, he might wonder why."

"Why in hell didn't you tell him so he'd know and—"

She didn't know how to complete her protestation so she cried into the phone: "I can't bear it, it's more than I can bear. My mind is full of awful, awful thought, speculations about how long I'll have to endure it, when will it be finished."

"Easy, sweetie."

"Easy for you, not me. And don't call me sweetie, I'm not a sweetie, there's nothing sweet about me, I've turned savage. Unless he stops burning those tent worms, I'm going to go, alone, back to the city, at least no diseased vegetation and paper torches, and him staggering out there. Got to hang up. He's coming toward the house."

"Clara, it's hard to be human, but for God's sake try."

"Can you tell me how to? Write me a prescription so that I can?"

She glanced out the picture window between the phone and the slow, exhausted return of Billy toward the sun deck, which the sun was deserting.

"Clara, love takes disguises. Your mind is probably full of fantasies that you'll dismiss with shame when this ordeal is over."

"You scored a point there. I'm full of fantasies of a bit of a future."

"You mentioned a prescription."

"Yes. What?"

"Recollection of how it was before."

"Seems totally unreal."

"Right now, yes, but try to."

"Thanks. I'll try to breathe. If only the sea wind would blow the smoke away . . ."

When she returned to the sun deck he had completed his exhausted return. He had a defeated look and he had burned himself in several places and applied poultices of wet baking soda, which smelled disagreeably. He took the other sun chair and pulled it a little away from where his wife was reclining and turned it so that she wouldn't look at his face.

"Giving it up?" she murmured.

"Ran out of paper and matches," he answered faintly.

There was no more talk between them. The tide was returning shoreward and now the smooth water was lapping quietly near them.

Tent worms, she said to herself.

Then she said it out loud: "Tent worms!"

"Why are you shouting about it, it's nothing to shout about. A blight on vegetation is like a blight on your body."

"This is just a place rented for summer and we'll never come back."

"A man in his youth is like a summer place," he said in such a soft, exhausted voice that she didn't catch it.

"What was that?"

He repeated it to her a little louder.

Then she knew that he knew. Their chairs remained apart on the sun deck as the sun disappeared altogether.

As dark falls, a pair of long companions respond to the instinct of drawing closer together.

Unsteadily she rose from her deck chair and hauled it closer to his. His scorched hand rested on his chair arm. After a while, the sentimental moon risen from the horizon to replace the sun's vigil, she placed her hand over his.

A chill wind of shared apprehension swept over the moonlit sun deck and their fingers wound together. She thought of their early passion for each other and how time had burned it down as he attempted to burn the tent worms away from their summer place to which they, no, would never return, separately or together.

c. 1945 (Published 1980)

Desire and the Black Masseur

From his very beginning this person, Anthony Burns, had betrayed an instinct for being included in things that swallowed him up. In his family there had been fifteen children and he the one given least notice, and when he went to work, after graduating from high school in the largest class on the records of that institution, he secured his job in the largest wholesale company of the city. Everything absorbed him and swallowed him up, and still he did not feel secure. He felt more secure at the movies than anywhere else. He loved to sit in the back rows of the movies where the darkness absorbed him gently so that he was like a particle of food dissolving in a big hot mouth. The cinema licked at his mind with a tender, flickering tongue that all but lulled him to sleep. Yes, a big motherly Nannie of a dog could not have licked him better or given him sweeter repose than the cinema did when he went there after work. His mouth would fall open at the movies and saliva would accumulate in it and dribble out the sides of it and all his being would relax so utterly that all the prickles and tightenings of a whole day's anxiety would be lifted away. He didn't follow the story on the screen but watched the figures. What they said or did was immaterial to him, he cared about only the figures who warmed him as if they were cuddled right next to him in the dark picture house and he loved every one of them but the ones with shrill voices.

The timidest kind of a person was Anthony Burns, always scuttling from one kind of protection to another but none of them ever being durable enough to suit him.

Now at the age of thirty, by virtue of so much protection, he still had in his face and body the unformed look of a child and he moved like a child in the presence of critical elders. In every move of his body and every inflection of speech and cast of expression there was a timid apology going out to the world for the little space that he had been

205

somehow elected to occupy in it. His was not an inquiring type of mind. He only learned what he was required to learn and about himself he learned nothing. He had no idea of what his real desires were. Desire is something that is made to occupy a larger space than that which is afforded by the individual being, and this was especially true in the case of Anthony Burns. His desires, or rather his basic desire, was so much too big for him that it swallowed him up as a coat that should have been cut into ten smaller sizes, or rather there should have been that much more of Burns to make it fit him.

For the sins of the world are really only its partialities, its incompletions, and these are what sufferings must atone for. A wall that has been omitted from a house because the stones were exhausted, a room in a house left unfurnished because the householder's funds were not sufficient—these sorts of incompletions are usually covered up or glossed over by some kind of makeshift arrangement. The nature of man is full of such makeshift arrangements, devised by himself to cover his incompletion. He feels a part of himself to be like a missing wall or a room left unfurnished and he tries as well as he can to make up for it. The use of imagination, resorting to dreams or the loftier purpose of art, is a mask he devises to cover his incompletion. Or violence such as a war, between two men or among a number of nations, is also a blind and senseless compensation for that which is not yet formed in human nature. Then there is still another compensation. This one is found in the principle of atonement, the surrender of self to violent treatment by others with the idea of thereby clearing one's self of his guilt. This last way was the one that Anthony Burns unconsciously had elected.

Now at the age of thirty he was about to discover the instrument of his atonement. Like all other happenings in his life, it came about without intention or effort.

One afternoon, which was a Saturday afternoon in November, he went from his work in the huge wholesale corporation to a place with a red neon sign that said "Turkish Baths and Massage." He had been suffering lately from a vague sort of ache near the base of his spine and somebody else employed at the wholesale corporation had told him that he would be relieved by massage. You would suppose that the mere suggestion of such a thing would frighten him out of his wits, but when desire lives constantly with fear, and no partition between them, desire must become very tricky; it has to become as sly as the adversary, and this was one of those times when desire outwitted the enemy under the roof. At the very mention of the word "massage," the desire woke up and exuded a sort of anesthetizing vapor all through Burns' nerves, catching fear off guard and allowing Burns to slip by it. Almost without knowing that he was really going, he went to the baths that Saturday afternoon.

The baths were situated in the basement of a hotel, right at the center of the keyed-up mercantile nerves of the downtown section, and yet the baths were a tiny world of their own. Secrecy was the atmosphere of the place and seemed to be its purpose. The entrance door had an oval of milky glass through which you could only detect a glimmer of light. And even when a patron had been admitted, he found himself standing in labyrinths of partitions, of corridors and cubicles curtained off from each other, of chambers with opaque doors and milky globes over lights and sheathings of vapor. Everywhere were agencies of concealment. The bodies of patrons, divested of their clothing, were swatched in billowing tent-like sheets of white fabric. They trailed barefooted along the moist white tiles, as white and noiseless as ghosts except for their breathing, and their faces all wore a nearly vacant expression. They drifted as if they had no thought to conduct them.

But now and again, across the central hallway, would step a masseur. The masseurs were Negroes. They seemed very dark and positive against the loose white hangings of the baths. They wore no sheets, they had on loose cotton drawers, and they moved about with force and resolution. They alone seemed to have an authority here. Their voices rang out boldly, never whispering in the sort of apologetic way that the patrons had in asking directions of them. This was their own rightful province, and they swept the white hangings aside with great black palms that you felt might just as easily have seized bolts of lightning and thrown them back at the clouds.

Anthony Burns stood more uncertainly than most near the entrance of the bathhouse. Once he had gotten through the milky-paned door his fate was decided and no more action or will on his part was called for. He paid two-fifty, which was the price of a bath and massage, and from that moment forward had only to follow directions and submit to care. Within a few moments a Negro masseur came to Burns and propelled him onward and then around a corner where he was led into one of the curtained compartments.

Take off your clothes, said the Negro.

The Negro had already sensed an unusual something about his latest patron and so he did not go out of the canvas-draped cubicle but remained leaning against a wall while Burns obeyed and undressed. The white man turned his face to the wall away from the Negro and fumbled awkwardly with his dark winter clothes. It took him a long time to get the clothes off his body, not because he wilfully lingered about it but because of a dream-like state in which he was deeply falling. A faraway feeling engulfed him and his hands and fingers did not seem to be his own, they were numb and hot as if they were caught in the clasp of someone standing behind him, manipulating their motions. But at last he stood naked, and when he turned slowly about to face the Negro masseur, the black giant's eyes appeared not to see him at all and yet they had a glitter not present before, a liquid brightness suggesting bits of wet coal.

Put this on, he directed and held out to Burns a white sheet.

Gratefully the little man enveloped himself in the enormous coarse fabric and, holding it delicately up from his small-boned, womanish feet, he followed the Negro masseur through another corridor of rustling white curtains to the entrance of an opaque glass enclosure which was the steam-room. There his conductor left him. The blank walls heaved and sighed as steam issued from them. It swirled about Burns' naked figure, enveloping him in a heat and moisture such as the inside of a tremendous mouth, to be drugged and all but dissolved in this burning white vapor which hissed out of unseen walls.

After a time the black masseur returned. With a mumbled command, he led the trembling Burns back into the cubicle where he had left his clothes. A bare white table had been wheeled into the chamber during Burns' absence.

Lie on this, said the Negro.

Burns obeyed. The black masseur poured alcohol on Burns' body, first on his chest and then on his belly and thighs. It ran all over him, biting at him like insects. He gasped a little and crossed his legs over the wild complaint of his groin. Then without any warning the Negro raised up his black palm and brought it down with a terrific whack on the middle of Burns' soft belly. The little man's breath flew out of his mouth in a gasp and for two or three moments he couldn't inhale another.

Immediately after the passing of the first shock, a feeling of pleasure went through him. It swept as a liquid from either end of his body and into the tingling hollow of his groin. He dared not look, but he knew what the Negro must see. The black giant was grinning.

I hope I didn't hit you too hard, he murmured.

No, said Burns.

Turn over, said the Negro.

Burns tried vainly to move but the luxurious tiredness made him unable to. The Negro laughed and gripped the small of his waist and flopped him over as easily as he might have turned a pillow. Then he began to belabor his shoulders and buttocks with blows that increased in violence, and as the violence and the pain increased, the little man grew more and more fiercely hot with his first true satisfaction, until all at once a knot came loose in his loins and released a warm flow.

So by surprise is a man's desire discovered, and once discovered, the only need is surrender, to take what comes and ask no questions about it: and this was something that Burns was expressly made for.

Time and again the white-collar clerk went back to the Negro masseur. The knowledge grew quickly between them of what Burns wanted, that he was in search of atonement, and the black masseur was the natural instrument of it. He hated white-skinned bodies because they abused his pride. He loved to have their white skin prone beneath him, to bring his fist or the palm of his hand down hard on its passive surface. He had barely been able to hold this love in restraint, to control the wish that he felt to pound more fiercely and use the full of his power. But now at long last the suitable person had entered his orbit of passion. In the white-collar clerk he had located all that he longed for.

Those times when the black giant relaxed, when he sat at the rear of the baths and smoked cigarettes or devoured a bar of candy, the image of Burns would loom before his mind, a nude white body with angry red marks on it. The bar of chocolate would stop just short of his lips and the lips would slacken into a dreamy smile. The giant loved Burns, and Burns adored the giant.

Burns had become absent-minded about his work. Right in the middle of typing a factory order, he would lean back at his desk and the giant would swim in the atmosphere before him. Then he would smile and his work-stiffened fingers would loosen and flop on the desk. Sometimes the boss would stop near him and call his name crossly. Burns! Burns! What are you dreaming about?

Throughout the winter the violence of the massage increased by fairly reasonable degrees, but when March came it was suddenly stepped up.

Burns left the baths one day with two broken ribs.

Every morning he hobbled to work more slowly and painfully but the state of his body could still be explained by saying he had rheumatism.

One day his boss asked him what he was doing for it. He told his boss that he was taking massage.

It don't seem to do you any good, said the boss.

Oh, yes, said Burns, I am showing lots of improvement!

That evening came his last visit to the baths.

His right leg was fractured. The blow which had broken the limb was so terrific that Burns had been unable to stifle an outcry. The manager of the bath establishment heard it and came into the compartment.

Burns was vomiting over the edge of the table.

Christ, said the manager, what's been going on here?

The black giant shrugged.

He asked me to hit him harder.

The manager looked over Burns and discovered his many bruises.

What do you think this is? A jungle? he asked the masseur.

Again the black giant shrugged.

Get the hell out of my place! the manager shouted. Take this perverted little monster with you, and neither of you had better show up here again!

The black giant tenderly lifted his drowsy partner and bore him away to a room in the town's Negro section.

There for a week the passion between them continued.

This interval was toward the end of the Lenten season. Across from the room where Burns and the Negro were staying there was a church whose open windows spilled out the mounting exhortations of a preacher. Each afternoon the fiery poem of death on the cross was repeated. The preacher was not fully conscious of what he wanted nor were the listeners, groaning and writhing before him. All of them were involved in a massive atonement.

Now and again some manifestation occurred, a woman stood up to expose a wound in her breast. Another had slashed an artery at her wrist.

Suffer, suffer, suffer! the preacher shouted. Our Lord was nailed on a cross for the sins of the world! They led him above the town to the place of the skull, they moistened his lips with vinegar on a sponge, they drove five nails through his body, and He was The Rose of the World as He bled on the cross!

The congregation could not remain in the building but tumbled out on the street in a crazed procession with clothes torn open.

The sins of the world are all forgiven! they shouted.

All during this celebration of human atonement, the Negro masseur was completing his purpose with Burns.

All the windows were open in the death chamber.

The curtains blew out like thirsty little white tongues to lick at the street which seemed to reek with an overpowering honey. A house had caught fire on the block in back of the church. The walls collapsed and the cinders floated about in the gold atmosphere. The scarlet engines, the ladders and powerful hoses were useless against the purity of the flame.

The Negro masseur leaned over his still breathing victim.

Burns was whispering something.

The black giant nodded.

You know what you have to do now? the victim asked him. The black giant nodded.

He picked up the body, which barely held together, and placed it gently on a clean-swept table.

The giant began to devour the body of Burns.

It took him twenty-four hours to eat the splintered bones clean.

When he had finished, the sky was serenely blue, the passionate services at the church were finished, the ashes had settled, the scarlet engines had gone and the reek of honey was blown from the atmosphere.

Quiet had returned and there was an air of completion.

Those bare white bones, left over from Burns' atonement, were placed in a sack and borne to the end of a car line.

There the masseur walked out on a lonely pier and dropped his burden under the lake's quiet surface.

As the giant turned homeward, he mused on his satisfaction.

Yes, it is perfect, he thought, it is now completed!

Then in the sack, in which he had carried the bones, he dropped his belongings, a neat blue suit to conceal his dangerous body, some buttons of pearl and a picture of Anthony Burns as a child of seven.

He moved to another city, obtained employment once more as an expert masseur. And there in a white-curtained place, serenely conscious of fate bringing toward him another, to suffer atonement as it had been suffered by Burns, he stood impassively waiting inside a milky white door for the next to arrive.

And meantime, slowly, with barely a thought of so doing, the earth's whole population twisted and writhed beneath the manipulation of night's black fingers and the white ones of day with skeletons splintered and flesh reduced to pulp, as out of this unlikely problem, the answer, perfection, was slowly evolved through torture.

April 1946 (Published 1948)

Something about Him

There was something about him, something they didn't like, they didn't know what. Mrs. Archie Henderson made a further analysis than most when she said that he was "too oily." He acted like a new preacher on his first Sunday, you know, trying to please everybody but so dreadfully afraid that he wouldn't that his politeness was almost gruesomely excessive, ducking jerkily up and down at the front door and wringing hands so fiercely that the married ladies' rings cut into their fingers and they whispered afterward among themselves, "What a strong personality!" But Haskell wasn't a preacher, he was just an ordinary dime-a-dozen grocery clerk. There were Haskells in Grenada and also a family of Haskells down near Biloxi. However, none of these were related to him, not even remotely it seemed. He had no family connections whatsoever. This might have been forgiven the way things are nowadays, but . . .

Well, for instance, one Monday morning Mrs. Archie Henderson came into the store with her ten-year-old daughter Lucinda. Fat runs in the Henderson family, and Lucinda was right in the family tradition. She was very, very plump and buck-toothed and had committed the indiscretion, that Monday morning, of hanging a necklace of purple clover about her scarcely visible neck.

Mrs. Henderson was extremely self-conscious about the child's appearance—or lack of it—and people who knew her tactfully mentioned nothing about Lucinda except her reported skill at domestic science. But Haskell didn't know this and so he decided to compliment Lucinda on her chain of purple clover. He touched it delicately with his finger tips and exclaimed: "How pretty! How awfully pretty that is!"

Mrs. Henderson glared at him suspiciously.

"Yes. Pretty. Give me two bars of Waltke's Extra Family soap."

213

When he had fetched her the soap she jerked Lucinda's arm roughly and marched straight out of the store.

Mr. Olliphant Owens, the boss, came over to Haskell's counter.

"What did she get sore about?"

"Why, nothing, not a thing!" said Haskell. "Of course not!"

Mr. Owens gave him the same look that customers gave him, puzzled, uneasy, a little bit hostile.

There is something about him, thought Mr. Owens, something that I don't like. But he couldn't decide what it was . . .

On Saturday afternoons Haskell was off and he went to the public library. He sat down in a secluded corner and polished his glasses meticulously for several minutes and then opened a volume of modern verse. He would alter his position frequently without ever removing his eyes from the book. It was like he was steering around hazardous turns in an auto race—you know, his body bent stiffly forward, his neck extended so that the cords stood out, and little crystal beads of sweat coming forth on his forehead and even his fingers clenched on the sides of the book. Yes, it was *ludicrous*-looking. Not because Haskell himself was homely. He wasn't. His features were quite regular and his figure was nicer than most of the nonathletic type. Except for these eccentric manners of his he might have been called good-looking.

"What is it about him?" asked Miss Rose, who was the Assistant Librarian. "Nobody seems to like him, but I think he's nice."

Her superior, Miss Jamison, glanced at Haskell sharply.

"I don't like the way he rubs his glasses and blows on 'em and then puts cotton under the bridge so it won't chafe his nose."

"Oh, I wouldn't hold that against him," said Miss Rose. "I think it's refreshing to see a man who is careful about little things, and heaven knows those red marks on your nose that you get from wearing glasses do look pretty awful!"

Miss Jamison's animosity became more defined as Miss Rose warmed in his defense.

"If glasses are properly adjusted," she snapped, "they don't make ridges. I take mine to the optician's whenever I go to Memphis and have them refitted—free of charge!"

"He reads good books," said Miss Rose.

"I think his taste in poetry is extremely queer."

"Well, it's unusual," said Miss Rose, "for anybody to read modern verse, least of all a clerk in a grocery store."

"A clerk in a grocery store is unusual as a subject for conversation," said Miss Jamison. "I personally am not interested!"

However, Miss Rose was. She concluded that she liked Haskell and, only through saying it once or twice to herself, the idea became firmly fixed in her mind, so that now when he entered the library Saturday mornings she gave him her pleasantest slightly worn smile and made some little remark about the weather which, however unimportant, was always given an accent of sprightly concern.

"Such brilliant sunlight this morning!"

"Yes, *isn't* it, though!"

Or else she would say: "It's terribly cloudy! I should have brought my umbrella!"

And Haskell agreed: "Yes, it *is* cloudy! I guess I should have brought *mine!*"

One Sunday morning she saw him go into the First Presbyterian Church. She made plans all that week, and the following Sunday she went there herself, wearing a brown tweed jacket with a little corsage of rosebuds and lilies of the valley fastened on the lapel. She glanced about her discreetly as the service commenced. But he wasn't there. She felt quite terribly let down. Miserable, in fact. She fastened her eyes on the stained glass picture of the Shepherd Jesus and composed her face with marvelous fortitude as she began to feel once more, gnawing voraciously under the tweed and crisp linen, under the charming corsage of pink and white flowers, that fox-toothed loneliness which always plagued her when she was not occupied with books and rubber stamps and ink pads and yellow library cards . . .

The following Saturday something miraculous happened.

Haskell sneezed violently as he stepped in the library door.

"You have a bad cold," said Miss Rose.

"Yes, my room is so drafty," said Haskell. "I have had one continual cold all winter."

"Oh, goodness, you ought to *move!*"

"I've thought of moving," he said, "but I can't find a place near the store."

"Oh! Now I *wonder!*"

"Yes?"

"Mrs. Stovall's got a vacant room on her third floor, and it's just exactly one block from where you stay now!"

"Is that right? How fortunate! I wonder if you could give me this lady's address?"

"Of *course!*" She laughed breathlessly. "It's where *I* stay!"

"Oh! In*deed!*"

His voice assumed an almost girlish falsetto.

"Now that makes it very, very nice in*deed!*"

She wrote the address on a slip of paper—her fingers trembled so it was scarcely legible.

"You'd better see Mrs. Stovall right away," she advised.

"Oh, I shall, I *shall!*—I'll make inquiries at *once!*"

He went away from the desk—then had to return for his book. In her confusion she dropped it, and Haskell said: "Pardon! I *beg* your pardon!"

She whispered: "Not at all."

Her voice died away very oddly. She cleared her throat.

She learned from Mrs. Stovall that evening that Haskell had paid five dollars down on the room and would move in the first of the month.

Soon afterward and without acknowledging to herself any special reason, she went to the Delta Gift Shoppe and purchased an exquisite French negligee of shell-pink crepe de chine with a froth of ivory lace at the throat and sleeves.

That night when she was alone in her room she slipped it on and stood in front of the long oval mirror. It created a new Miss Rose, not one who was employed at the Blue Hill Public Library, but one who danced all night in open pavilions, laughed recklessly in Mediterranean moonlight and won huge sums, they said, at roulette in the gambling casino . . .

It was the first of March when Haskell moved in.

They were very constrained, at first, when they met in the hall or on the stairs. They both laughed nervously and edged unnecessarily close to the wall to prevent their clothes from touching.

Miss Rose went on with her dreams and her speculations.

One morning she stood just on the inside of her door till she heard him descending the stairs from the third floor. Then she caught the creamy lace about her throat and stepped out of her bedroom. She stood there in his full gaze for three ecstatic moments before she scurried into the bathroom with a slight hysterical giggle and locked the door—while Haskell proceeded unsteadily down the rest of the stairs.

Already in early March the Mississippi spring was well advanced. The trees were in leaf, there was a great deal of wind and rain which caused talk of high water and possible floods on the river.

The mornings had an exceptional quality when it had rained all night and stopped at daybreak, the clouds having thinned like smoke until they were gone altogether, except for some milky white threads which still clung like bits of shattered web to the pointed church steeples or tallest treetops. It was as though in the course of the night some radiant white cloth, like a bridal veil, had been drawn swiftly over the sky and fragments of it had caught on these sharp projections and been torn loose and held there . . .

"It must have been on a morning like this," said Haskell, "that Robert Browning wrote that poem of his—"

" 'God's in his heaven,' you mean? 'All's right with the world'?"

"Yes!" said Haskell. There was a pause and then he asked:

"Do you agree about that?"

Miss Rose's heart leaped.

"I do *sometimes*," she murmured. "I *certainly* do this *morning!*"

"Occasionally," said Haskell. "I have my doubts. The lark and the snail and the dew are not always convincing. Not always *completely* convincing. You know what I mean?"

He looked down at her very slyly and something new came out of his eyes. It was almost palpable. It seemed to touch her cheek with little, tentative fingers. A palpable though very timid caress.

"Yes, I know what you mean," she breathed.

He caught her elbow as she stepped over the curb. His touch, his slight upward pressure, seemed to release her from all effect of gravity so that she felt as though she were floating with feathery lightness over the street. The laughter bubbled out of her lips irrepressibly like water gone down the wrong way. At the opposite curb his pressure was resumed. She caught her breath. She was lifted up and blown forward, a thin tissue kite that was suddenly caught in a rising wind.

"My goodness, what weather!" she cried.

"Isn't it marvelous, though?"

And then instead of turning at his usual corner he walked up another block to the library steps and said good-bye to her there and they both looked back at the same time and smiled as she entered the Public Library door. That heavy oak door with its foolish brass knocker and elaborate molding had never admitted her with so little resistance. It seemed to swing open from someone pushing inside. She stepped away to avoid a collision. But there was nobody but her, it was her own frail grasp that had drawn it so easily open!

The room inside was wonderfully light and spacious. Brilliance was refracted from every surface, from the yellow oak tables and chairs, from ink pads and pencils, even from old Miss Jamison's knobby cheekbones.

What alacrity, what spontaneous good humor she displayed all that morning to the library patrons!

Miss Jamison watched her sourly and suffered from gas on the stomach.

"I tell you he deliberately overcharged me three cents on the grits and four on the canned asparagus!" shrieked Mrs. Austin. She drummed the grocery counter with her blue knuckles. "Seven cents isn't much but it just irritates me beyond all bearing to have somebody try to put something over on me like that, just as though I didn't know simple arithmetic when I've been keeping house and watching accounts for going on thirty years!"

When Haskell returned to the counter he showed them conclusively that the mistake was not his, the mistake was in Mrs. Austin's own computations, but this only whetted her fury, so that when he had gone to the back of the store again she leaned over the counter and whispered stridently to Mr. Owens:

"There is something about him that I don't like anyhow. I never *did* and I'm not the only one that *don't!* I've heard others say the same thing. There's something about him that's just *irritating* to people. I just can't say what it is, but if I was you, Mr. Owens, I wouldn't truck with him in this store, I'd have him out of here so fast it would make his head swim!"

"Hmmm," said Mr. Owens. The young man was neat and courteous and he was very reliable—but nobody seemed to like him.

Haskell was given his notice that very next morning, while he was standing behind the butcher's huge white refrigerator tying about his lean waist the immaculate strings of an apron with fingers that were as delicate in their precision as the fingers of a young woman.

"Sorry I have to let you go," said Mr. Owens. "You've done your work well but you haven't made a good impression on the customers, you just haven't pleased 'em somehow—I've had sev'ral complaints."

Haskell looked at him dumbly: "What?"

"You heard me," said Mr. Owens. "I can't keep you here."

He started to move away. Haskell followed.

"Why don't they like me, Mr. Owens? What have they got against me?"

Mr. Owens made an impatient gesture: "How should I know? It's something *about* you, I guess!"

He felt a curious relief when Haskell was gone—shouted good morning to all his customers with a heartiness that fairly rattled the canned goods off the shelves.

Haskell went home at once and packed his valise. On his way to the station he dropped in at the library to return a volume of Emerson's *Essays* that Miss Rose had taken out for him the night before.

"Sorry I won't get to read them," he said. "I'm leaving town."

"You're taking a trip?" she asked, trembling.

"No, I'm leaving for good," he told her. "I've lost my job."

"Why? Why?"

"I don't know why," he said. "Mr. Owens says it's something *about* me."

A stranger came up to the counter and asked for a book of Edna Ferber's about pioneers.

"Haskell!" she called.

But he had already gone out the library door. She saw his oddly-shaped hat bobbing across the window. She would have pursued him except for the stranger's presence, his eyes fixed on her, pinioning her attention coldly like a blade thrust down on quivering, agonized wings . . .

About noon Miss Jamison came in and asked her what was the matter and she said she guessed that she had caught a spring cold.

She didn't confess what had actually happened till about a week later when Miss Jamison noticed Haskell's absence from his usual place on Saturday afternoon.

"He's gone," said Miss Rose. "He got fired from the store and left town."

Miss Jamison whinnied exultantly. "Gracious! Not even able to hold a *clerical* job!"

"It wasn't his fault," said Miss Rose.

"Well, maybe it wasn't his fault. But there was something about him that I didn't like. I don't know what it was, but I guess Mr. Owens must have felt the same way."

"What was it?" demanded Miss Rose.

"Well, it must have been partly the way that he looked at you and smiled all the time and said how nice everything was and you knew that he didn't mean a word of it!"

"Oh, but he did, he was sincerely anxious to please *every*one!"

"Anxious, yes, that's the word!"

"That's nothing *against* him!"

"It's nothing *for* him, either."

"People are just malicious!" said Miss Rose. "I can't understand them, they're all so *mean* and *malicious!*"

She gave her colleague a look that included her so definitely in this general indictment that Miss Jamison moved nervously to the other end of the counter and hummed a Scottish ballad off-key.

During the night it had rained and all morning it had cleared till now at the sun's meridian, or shortly thereafter, the air was as keen and brilliant as a polished blade is. There was not much warmth in it yet but it was replete with sound and motion: boxcars shunting about the freight yards, whistles screaming urgently, sparrows restlessly crossing the windows, dropping lime on the damp gray stone, at intersections the traffic signals changing and cars moving onward or halting . . .

At one forty-five Miss Rose put on her tweed jacket, which she now wore every day, and walked to the corner drugstore for milk and a sandwich. In windows she caught her image, angular, tall, her wrists too long for the sleeves of the brown tweed jacket, the hem of the skirt—yes!—uneven.

"*Oh, God,*" she whispered.

"Milk and a cream cheese sandwich."

(*Published 1946*)

The Yellow Bird

Alma was the daughter of a Protestant minister named Increase Tutwiler, the last of a string of Increase Tutwilers who had occupied pulpits since the Reformation came to England. The first American progenitor had settled in Salem, and around him and his wife, Goody Tutwiler, née Woodson, had revolved one of the most sensational of the Salem witch trials. Goody Tutwiler was cried out against by the Circle Girls, a group of hysterical young ladies of Salem who were thrown into fits whenever a witch came near them. They claimed that Goody Tutwiler afflicted them with pins and needles and made them sign their names in the devil's book quite against their wishes. Also one of them declared that Goody Tutwiler had appeared to them with a yellow bird which she called by the name of Bobo and which served as interlocutor between herself and the devil to whom she was sworn. The Reverend Tutwiler was so impressed by these accusations, as well as by the fits of the Circle Girls when his wife entered their presence in court, that he himself finally cried out against her and testified that the yellow bird named Bobo had flown into his church one Sabbath and, visible only to himself, had perched on his pulpit and whispered indecent things to him about several younger women in the congregation. Goody Tutwiler was accordingly condemned and hanged, but this was by no means the last of the yellow bird named Bobo. It had manifested itself in one form or another, and its continual nagging had left the Puritan spirit fiercely aglow, from Salem to Hobbs, Arkansas, where the Increase Tutwiler of this story was preaching.

Increase Tutwiler was a long-winded preacher. His wife sat in the front pew of the church with a palm-leaf fan which she would agitate violently when her husband had preached too long for anybody's endurance. But it was not always easy to catch his attention, and Alma, the daughter, would finally have to break into the offertory hymn in order to turn him off. Alma played the organ, the primitive kind of organ that had to be supplied with air by an old Negro operating a pump in a stifling cubicle behind the wall. On one occasion the old Negro had fallen asleep, and no amount of discreet rapping availed to wake him up. The minister's wife had plucked nervously at the strings of her palm-leaf fan till it began to fall to pieces, but without the organ to stop him, Increase Tutwiler ranted on and on, exceeding the two hour mark. It was by no means a cool summer day, and the interior of the church was yellow oak, a material that made you feel as if you were sitting in the middle of a fried egg.

At last Alma despaired of reviving the Negro and got to her feet. "Papa," she said. But the old man didn't look at her. "Papa," she repeated, but he went right on. The whole congregation was whispering and murmuring. One stout old lady seemed to have collapsed, because two people were fanning her from either side and holding a small bottle to her nostrils. Alma and her mother exchanged desperate glances. The mother half got out of her seat. Alma gave her a signal to remain seated. She picked up the hymnbook and brought it down with such terrific force on the bench that dust and fiber spurted in all directions. The minister stopped short. He turned a dazed look in Alma's direction. "Papa," she said, "it's fifteen minutes after twelve and Henry's asleep and these folks have got to get to dinner, so for the love of God, quit preaching."

Now Alma had the reputation of being a very quiet and shy girl, so this speech was nothing short of sensational. The news of it spread throughout the Delta, for Mr. Tutwiler's sermons had achieved a sort of unhappy fame for many miles about. Perhaps Alma was somewhat pleased and impressed by this little celebration that she was accordingly given on people's tongues the next few months, for she was never quite the same shy girl afterwards. She had not had very much fun out of being a minister's daughter. The boys had steered clear of the rectory, because when they got around there they were exposed to Mr. Tutwiler's inquisitions. A boy and Alma would have no chance to talk in the Tutwiler porch or parlor while the old man was around. He was obsessed with the idea that Alma might get to smoking, which he thought was the initial and, once taken, irretrievable step toward perdition. "If Alma gets to smoking," he told his wife, "I'm going to denounce her from the pulpit and put her out of the house." Every time he said this Alma's mother would scream and go into a faint, as she knew that every girl who is driven out of her father's house goes right into a good-time house. She was unable to conceive of anything in between.

Now Alma was pushing thirty and still unmarried, but about six months after the episode in the church, things really started popping around the minister's house. Alma had gotten to smoking in the attic, and her mother knew about it. Mrs. Tutwiler's hair had been turning slowly gray for a number of years, but after Alma took to smoking in the attic, it turned snow-white almost overnight. Mrs. Tutwiler concealed the terrible knowledge that Alma was smoking in the attic from her husband, and she didn't even dare raise her voice to Alma about it because the old man might hear. All she could do was stuff the attic door around with newspapers. Alma *would* smoke; she claimed it had gotten a hold on her and she couldn't stop it now. At first she only smoked twice a day, but she began to smoke more as the habit grew on her. Several times the old man had said he smelled smoke in the house, but so far he hadn't dreamed that his daughter would dare take up smoking. But his wife knew he would soon find out about it, and Alma knew he would too. The question was whether Alma cared. Once she came downstairs with a cigarette in her mouth, smoking it, and her mother barely snatched it out of her mouth before the old man saw her. Mrs. Tutwiler went into a faint, but Alma paid no attention to her, just went on out of the house, lit another cigarette, and walked down the street to the drugstore.

It was unavoidable that sooner or later people who had seen Alma smoking outside the house, which she now began to do pretty regularly, would carry the news back to the preacher. There were plenty of old women who were ready and able to do it. They had seen her smoking in the White Star drugstore while she was having her afternoon Coke, puffing on the cigarette between sips of the Coke and carrying on a conversation with the soda jerk, just like anyone from that set of notorious high school girls that the whole town had been talking about for several generations. So one day the minister came into his wife's bedroom and said to her, "I have been told that Alma has taken to smoking."

His manner was deceptively calm. The wife sensed that this was not an occasion for her to go into a faint, so she didn't. She had to keep her wits about her this time—that is, if she had any left after all she had been through with Alma's smoking.

"Well," she said, "I don't know what to do about it. It's true."

"You know what I've always said," her husband replied. "If Alma gets to smoking, out she goes."

"Do you want her to go into a good-time house?" inquired Mrs. Tutwiler.

"If that's where she's going, she can go," said the preacher, "but not until I've given her something that she'll always remember."

He was waiting for Alma when she came in from her afternoon smoke and Coke at the White Star drugstore. Soon as she walked into the door he gave her a good, hard slap, with the palm of his hand on her mouth, so that her front teeth bit into her lip and it started bleeding. Alma didn't blink an eye, she just drew back her right arm and returned the slap with good measure. She had bought a bottle of something at the drugstore, and while her father stood there, stupefied, watching her, she went upstairs with the mysterious bottle in brown wrapping paper. And when she came back down they saw that she had peroxided her hair and put on lipstick. Alma's mother screamed and went into one of her faints, because it was evident to her that Alma was going right over to one of the good-time houses on Front Street. But all the iron had gone out of the minister's character then. He clung to Alma's arm. He begged and pleaded with her not to go there. Alma lit up a cigarette right there in front of him and said, "Listen here, I'm going to do as I please around here from now on, and I don't want any more interference from you!"

Before this conversation was finished the mother came out of her faint. It was the worst faint she had ever gone into, particularly since nobody had bothered to pick her up off the floor. "Alma," she said weakly, "Alma!" Then she said her husband's name several times, but neither of them paid any attention to her, so she got up without any assistance and began to take a part in the conversation. "Alma," she said, "you can't go out of this house until that hair of yours grows in dark again."

"That's what you think," said Alma.

She put the cigarette back in her mouth and went out the screen door, puffing and drawing on it and breathing smoke out of her nostrils all the way down the front walk and down to the White Star drugstore, where she had another Coke and resumed her conversation with the boy at the soda counter. His name was Stuff—that was what people called him—and it was he who had suggested to Alma that she would look good as a blonde. He was ten years younger than Alma but he had more girls than pimples.

It was astonishing the way Alma came up fast on the outside in Stuff's affections. With the new blond hair you could hardly call her a dark horse, but she was certainly running away with the field. In two weeks' time after the peroxide she was going steady with Stuff; for Alma was smart enough to know there were plenty of good times to be had outside the good-time houses on Front Street, and Stuff knew that, too. Stuff was not to be in sole possession of her heart. There were other contenders, and Alma could choose among them. She started going out nights as rapidly as she had taken up smoking. She stole the keys to her father's Ford sedan and drove to such nearby towns as Lakewater, Sunset, and Lyons. She picked up men on the highway and went out "juking" with them, making the rounds of the highway drinking places; never got home till three or four in the morning. It was impossible to see how one human constitution could stand up under the strain of so much running around to night places, but Alma had all the vigor that comes from generations of firm believers. It could have gone into anything and made a sensation. Well, that's how it was. There was no stopping her once she got started.

The home situation was indescribably bad. It was generally stated that Alma's mother had suffered a collapse and that her father was spending all his time praying, and there was some degree of truth in both reports. Very little sympathy for Alma came from the older residents of the community. Certain little perfunctory steps were taken to curb the girl's behavior. The father got the car key out of her pocket one night when she came in drunk and fell asleep on the sofa, but Alma had already had some duplicates of it made. He locked the garage one night. Alma climbed through the window and drove the car straight through the closed door.

"She's lost her mind," said the mother. "It's that hair bleaching that's done it. It went right through her scalp and now it's affecting her brain."

They sat up all that night waiting for her, but she didn't come home. She had run her course in that town, and the next thing they heard from Alma was a card from New Orleans. She had got all the way down there. "Don't sit up," she wrote. "I'm gone for good. I'm never coming back."

Six years later Alma was a character in the old French Quarter of New Orleans. She hung out mostly on "Monkey Wrench Corner" and picked up men around there. It was certainly not necessary to go into a good-time house to have a good time in the Quarter, and it hadn't taken her long to find that out. It might have seemed to some people that Alma was living a wasteful and profligate existence, but if the penalty for it was death, well, she was a long time dying. In fact she seemed to prosper on her new life. It apparently did not have a dissipating effect on her. She took pretty good care of herself so that it wouldn't, eating well and drinking just enough to be happy. Her face had a bright and innocent look in the mornings, and even when she was alone in her room it sometimes seemed as if she weren't alone—as if someone were with her, a disembodied someone, perhaps a remote ancestor of liberal tendencies who had been displeased by the channel his blood had taken till Alma kicked over the traces and jumped right back to the plumed-hat cavaliers.

Of course, her parents never came near her again, but once they dispatched as emissary a young married woman they trusted.

The woman called on Alma in her miserable little furnished room— or crib, as it actually was—on the shabbiest block of Bourbon Street in the Quarter.

"How do you live?" asked the woman.

"What?" said Alma, innocently.

"I mean how do you get along?"

"Oh," said Alma, "people give me things."

"You mean you accept gifts from them?"

"Yes, on a give-and-take basis," Alma told her.

The woman looked around her. The bed was unmade and looked as if it had been that way for weeks. The two-burner stove was loaded with unwashed pots in some of which grew a pale fungus. Tickets from pawnshops were stuck round the edge of the mirror along with many, many photographs of young men, some splitting their faces with enormous grins while others stared softly at space.

"These photographs," said the woman, "are these—are these your friends?"

"Yes," said Alma, with a happy smile. "Friends and acquaintances, strangers that pass in the night!"

"Well, I'm not going to mention this to your father!"

"Oh, go on and tell the old stick-in-the-mud," said Alma. She lit a cigarette and blew the smoke at her caller.

The woman looked around once more and noticed that the doors of the big armoire hung open on white summer dresses that were covered with grass stains.

"You go on picnics?" she asked.

"Yes, but not church ones," said Alma.

The woman tried to think of something more to ask but she was not gifted with an agile mind, and Alma's attitude was not encouraging.

"Well," she said finally, "I had better be going."

"Hurry back," said Alma, without getting up or looking in the woman's direction.

Shortly thereafter Alma discovered that she was becoming a mother.

She bore a child, a male one, and not knowing who was the father, she named it John after the lover that she had liked best, a man now dead. The son was perfect, very blond and glowing, a lusty infant.

Now from this point on the story takes a strange turn that may be highly disagreeable to some readers, if any still hoped it was going to avoid the fantastic.

This child of Alma's would have been hanged in Salem. If the Circle Girls had not cried out against Alma (which they certainly would have done), they would have gone into fifty screaming fits over Alma's boy.

He was thoroughly bewitched. At half past six every morning he crawled out of the house and late in the evening he returned with fists full of gold and jewels that smelled of the sea.

Alma grew very rich indeed. She and the child went North. The child grew up in a perfectly normal way to youth and to young manhood, and then he no longer crawled out and brought back riches. In fact that old habit seemed to have slipped his mind somehow, and no mention was ever made of it. Though he and his mother did not pay much attention to each other, there was a great and silent respect between them while each went about his business.

When Alma's time came to die, she lay on the bed and wished her son would come home, for lately the son had gone on a long sea voyage for unexplained reasons. And while she was waiting, while she lay there dying, the bed began to rock like a ship on the ocean, and all at once not John the Second, but John the First appeared, like Neptune out of the ocean. He bore a cornucopia that was dripping with seaweed and his bare chest and legs had acquired a greenish patina such as a bronze statue comes to be covered with. Over the bed he emptied his horn of plenty which had been stuffed with treasure from wrecked Spanish galleons: rubies, emeralds, diamonds, rings, and necklaces of rare gold, and great loops of pearls with the slime of the sea clinging to them.

"Some people," he said, "don't even die empty-handed."

And off he went, and Alma went off with him.

228   TENNESSEE WILLIAMS: COLLECTED STORIES

The fortune was left to The Home for Reckless Spenders. And in due time the son, the sailor, came home, and a monument was put up. It was a curious thing, this monument. It showed three figures of indeterminate gender astride a leaping dolphin. One bore a crucifix, one a cornucopia, and one a Grecian lyre. On the side of the plunging fish, the arrogant dolphin, was a name inscribed, the odd name of Bobo, which was the name of the small yellow bird that the devil and Goody Tutwiler had used as a go-between in their machinations.

(*Published 1947*)

The Night of the Iguana

Opening onto the long South verandah of the Costa Verde hotel near Acapulco were ten sleeping rooms, each with a hammock slung outside its screen door. Only three of these rooms were occupied at the present time, for it was between the seasons at Acapulco. The winter season when the resort was more popular with the cosmopolitan type of foreign tourists had been over for a couple of months and the summer season when ordinary Mexican and American vacationists thronged there had not yet started. The three remaining guests of the Costa Verde were from the States, and they included two men who were writers and a Miss Edith Jelkes who had been an instructor in art at an Episcopalian girls' school in Mississippi until she had suffered a sort of nervous breakdown and had given up her teaching position for a life of refined vagrancy, made possible by an inherited income of about two hundred dollars a month.

Miss Jelkes was a spinster of thirty with a wistful blond prettiness and a somewhat archaic quality of refinement. She belonged to an historical Southern family of great but now moribund vitality whose latter generations had tended to split into two antithetical types, one in which the libido was pathologically distended and another in which it would seem to be all but dried up. The households were turbulently split and so, fairly often, were the personalities of their inmates. There had been an efflorescence among them of nervous talents and sickness, of drunkards and poets, gifted artists and sexual degenerates, together with fanatically proper and squeamish old ladies of both sexes who were condemned to live beneath the same roof with relatives whom they could only regard as monsters. Edith Jelkes was not strictly one or the other of the two basic types, which made it all the more difficult for her to cultivate any interior poise. She had been lucky enough to channel her somewhat morbid energy into a gift for painting. She painted canvases of an originality that might some day be noted, and in the meantime, since her retirement from teaching, she was combining her painting with travel and trying to evade her neurasthenia through the distraction of making new friends in new places. Perhaps some day she would come out on a kind of triumphant plateau as an artist or as a person or even perhaps as both. There might be a period of five or ten years in her life when she would serenely climb over the lightning-shot clouds of her immaturity and the waiting murk of decline. But perhaps is the right word to use. It would all depend on the next two years or so. For this reason she was particularly needful of sympathetic companionship, and the growing lack of it at the Costa Verde was really dangerous for her.

Miss Jelkes was outwardly such a dainty teapot that no one would guess that she could actually boil. She was so delicately made that rings and bracelets were never quite small enough originally to fit her but sections would have to be removed and the bands welded smaller. With her great translucent gray eyes and cloudy blond hair and perpetual look of slightly hurt confusion, she could not pass unnoticed through any group of strangers, and she knew how to dress in accord with her unearthly type. The cloudy blond hair was never without its flower and the throat of her cool white dresses would be set off by some vivid brooch of esoteric design. She loved the dramatic contrast of hot and cold color, the splash of scarlet on snow, which was like a flag of her own unsettled components. Whenever she came into a restaurant or theatre or exhibition gallery, she could hear or imagine that she could hear a little murmurous wave of appreciation. This was important to her, it had come to be one of her necessary comforts. But now that the guests of the Costa Verde had dwindled to herself and the two young writers—no matter how cool and yet vivid her appearance, there was little to comfort her in the way of murmured appreciation. The two young writers were bafflingly indifferent to Miss Jelkes. They barely turned their heads when she strolled onto the front or back verandah where they were lying in hammocks or seated at a table always carrying on a curiously intimate sounding conversation in tones never loud enough to be satisfactorily overheard by Miss Jelkes, and their responses to her friendly nods and Spanish phrases of greeting were barely distinct enough to pass for politeness.

Miss Jelkes was not at all inured to such offhand treatment. What had made travel so agreeable to her was the remarkable facility with which she had struck up acquaintances wherever she had gone. She was a good talker, she had a fresh and witty way of observing things. The many places she had been in the last six years had supplied her with a great reservoir of descriptive comment and humorous anecdote, and of course there was always the endless and epic chronicle of the Jelkeses to regale people with. Since she had just about the right amount of income to take her to the sort of hotels and *pensions* that are frequented by professional people such as painters and writers or professors on sabbatical leave, she had never before felt the lack of an appreciative audience. Things being as they were, she realized that the sensible action would be to simply withdraw to the Mexican capital where she had formed so many casual but nice connections among the American colony. Why she did not do this but remained on at the Costa Verde was not altogether clear to herself. Besides the lack of society there were other drawbacks to a continued stay. The food had begun to disagree with her, the Patrona of the hotel was becoming insolent and the service slovenly and her painting was showing signs of nervous distraction. There was every reason to leave, and yet she stayed on.

Miss Jelkes could not help knowing that she was actually conducting a siege of the two young writers, even though the reason for it was still entirely obscure.

She had set up her painting studio on the South verandah of the hotel where the writers worked in the mornings at their portable typewriters with their portable radio going off and on during pauses in their labor, but the comradeship of creation which she had hoped to establish was not forthcoming. Her eyes formed a habit of darting toward the two men as frequently as they did toward what she was painting, but her glances were not returned and her painting went into an irritating decline. She took to using her fingers more than her brushes, smearing and slapping on pigment with an impatient energy that defeated itself. Once in a while she would get up and wander as if absentmindedly down toward the writers' end of the long verandah, but when she did so, they would stop writing and stare blankly at their papers or into space until she had removed herself from their proximity, and once the younger writer had been so rude as to snatch his paper from the typewriter and turn it face down on the table as if he suspected her of trying to read it over his shoulder.

She had retaliated that evening by complaining to the Patrona that their portable radio was being played too loudly and too long, that it was keeping her awake at night, which she partially believed to be true, but the transmission of this complaint was not evidenced by any reduction in the volume or duration of the annoyance but by the writers' choice of a table at breakfast, the next morning, at the furthest possible distance from her own.

That day Miss Jelkes packed her luggage, thinking that she would surely withdraw the next morning, but her curiosity about the two writers, especially the older of the two, had now become so obsessive that not only her good sense but her strong natural dignity was being discarded.

Directly below the cliff on which the Costa Verde was planted there was a small private beach for the hotel guests. Because of her extremely fair skin it had been Miss Jelkes' practice to bathe only in the early morning or late afternoon when the glare was diminished. These hours did not coincide with those of the writers who usually swam and sunbathed between two and six in the afternoon. Miss Jelkes now began to go down to the beach much earlier without admitting to herself that it was for the purpose of espionage. She would now go down to the beach about four o'clock in the afternoon and she would situate herself as close to the two young men as she could manage without being downright brazen. Bits of their background and history had begun to filter through this unsatisfactory contact. It became apparent that the younger of the men, who was about twenty-five, had been married and recently separated from a wife he called Kitty. More from the inflection of voices than the fragmentary sentences that she caught, Miss Jelkes received the impression that he was terribly concerned over some problem which the older man was trying to iron out for him. The younger one's voice would sometimes rise in agitation loudly enough to be overheard quite plainly. He would cry out phrases such as *For God's sake* or *What the Hell are you talking about!* Sometimes his language was so strong that Miss Jelkes winced with embarrassment and he would sometimes pound the wet sand with his palm and hammer it with his heels like a child in a tantrum. The older man's voice would also be lifted briefly. Don't be a fool, he would shout. Then his voice would drop to a low and placating tone. The conversation would fall below the level of audibility once more. It seemed that some argument was going on almost interminably between them. Once Miss Jelkes was astonished to see the younger one jump to his feet with an incoherent outcry and start kicking sand directly into the face of his older companion. He did it quite violently and hatefully, but the older man only laughed and grabbed the younger one's feet and restrained them until the youth dropped back beside him, and then they had surprised Miss Jelkes even further by locking their hands together and lying in silence until the incoming tide was lapping over their bodies. Then they had both jumped up, apparently in good humor, and made racing dives in the water.

Because of this troubled youth and wise counsellor air of their conversations it had at first struck Miss Jelkes, in the beginning of her preoccupation with them, that the younger man might be a war veteran suffering from shock and that the older one might be a doctor who had brought him down to the Pacific resort while conducting a psychiatric treatment. This was before she discovered the name of the older man, on mail addressed to him. She had instantly recognized the name as one that she had seen time and again on the covers of literary magazines and as the author of a novel that had caused a good deal of controversy a few years ago. It was a novel that dealt with some sensational subject. She had not read it and could not remember what the subject was but the name was associated in her mind with a strongly social kind of writing which had been more in vogue about five years past than it was since the beginning of the war. However the writer was still not more than thirty. He was not good-looking but his face had distinction. There was something a little monkey-like in his face as there frequently is in the faces of serious young writers, a look that reminded Miss Jelkes of a small chimpanzee she had once seen in the corner of his cage at a zoo, just sitting there staring between the bars, while all his fellows were hopping and spinning about on their noisy iron trapeze. She remembered how she had been touched by his solitary position and lackluster eyes. She had wanted to give him some peanuts but the elephants had devoured all she had. She had returned to the vendor to buy some more but when she brought them to the chimpanzee's cage, he had evidently succumbed to the general impulse, for now every man Jack of them was hopping and spinning about on the clanking trapeze and not a one of them seemed a bit different from the others. Looking at this writer she felt almost an identical urge to share something with him, but the wish was thwarted again, in this instance by a studious will to ignore her. It was not accidental, the way that he kept his eyes off her. It was the same on the beach as it was on the hotel verandahs.

On the beach he wore next to nothing, a sort of brilliant diaper of printed cotton, twisted about his loins in a fashion that sometimes failed to even approximate decency, but he had a slight and graceful physique and an unconscious ease of movement which made the immodesty less offensive to Miss Jelkes than it was in the case of his friend. The younger man had been an athlete at college and he was massively constructed. His torso was burned the color of an old penny and its emphatic gender still further exclaimed by luxuriant patterns of hair, sunbleached till it shone like masses of crisped and frizzed golden wire. Moreover his regard for propriety was so slight that he would get in and out of his colorful napkin as if he were standing in a private cabana. Miss Jelkes had to acknowledge that he owned a certain sculptural grandeur but the spinsterish side of her nature was still too strong to permit her to feel anything but a squeamish distaste. This reaction of Miss Jelkes was so strong on one occasion that when she had returned to the hotel she went directly to the Patrona to enquire if the younger gentleman could not be persuaded to change clothes in his room or, if this was too much to ask of him, that he might at least keep the dorsal side of his nudity toward the beach. The Patrona was very much interested in the complaint but not in a way that Miss Jelkes had hoped she would be. She laughed immoderately, translating phrases of Miss Jelkes' complaint into idiomatic Spanish, shouted to the waiters and the cook. All of them joined in the laughter and the noise was still going on when Miss Jelkes standing confused and indignant saw the two young men climbing up the hill. She retired quickly to her room on the hammock-verandah but she knew by the reverberating merriment on the other side that the writers were being told, and that all of the Costa Verde was holding her up to undisguised ridicule. She started packing at once, this time not even bothering to fold things neatly into her steamer trunk, and she was badly frightened, so much disturbed that it affected her stomach and the following day she was not well enough to undertake a journey.

It was this following day that the Iguana was caught.

The Iguana is a lizard, two or three feet in length, which the Mexicans regard as suitable for the table. They are not always eaten right after they are caught but being creatures that can survive for quite a while without food or drink, they are often held in captivity for some time before execution. Miss Jelkes had been told that they tasted rather like chicken, which opinion she ascribed to a typically Mexican way of glossing over an unappetizing fact. What bothered her about the Iguana was the inhumanity of its treatment during its interval of captivity. She had seen them outside the huts of villagers, usually hitched to a short pole near the doorway and continually and hopelessly clawing at the dry earth within the orbit of the rope-length, while naked children squatted around it, poking it with sticks in the eyes and mouth.

Now the Patrona's adolescent son had captured one of these Iguanas and had fastened it to the base of a column under the hammock-verandah. Miss Jelkes was not aware of its presence until late the night of the capture. Then she had been disturbed by the scuffling sound it made and had slipped on her dressing gown and had gone out in the bright moonlight to discover what the sound was caused by. She looked over the rail of the verandah and she saw the Iguana hitched to the base of the column nearest her doorway and making the most pitiful effort to scramble into the bushes just beyond the taut length of its rope. She uttered a little cry of horror as she made this discovery.

The two young writers were lying in hammocks at the other end of the verandah and as usual were carrying on a desultory conversation in tones not loud enough to carry to her bedroom.

Without stopping to think, and with a curious thrill of exultation, Miss Jelkes rushed down to their end of the verandah. As she drew near them she discovered that the two writers were engaged in drinking rum-coco, which is a drink prepared in the shell of a cocoanut by knocking a cap off it with a machete and pouring into the nut a mixture of rum, lemon, sugar and cracked ice. The drinking had been going on since supper and the floor beneath their two hammocks was littered with bits of white pulp and hairy brown fibre and was so slippery that Miss Jelkes barely kept her footing. The liquid had spilt over their faces, bare throats and chests, giving them an oily lustre, and about their hammocks was hanging a cloud of moist and heavy sweetness. Each had a leg thrown over the edge of the hammock with which he pushed himself lazily back and forth. If Miss Jelkes had been seeing them for the first time, the gross details of the spectacle would have been more than association with a few dissolute members of the Jelkes family had prepared her to stomach, and she would have scrupulously avoided a second glance at them. But Miss Jelkes had been changing more than she was aware of during this period of preoccupation with the two writers, her scruples were more undermined than she suspected, so that if the word *pigs* flashed through her mind for a moment, it failed to distract her even momentarily from what she was bent on doing. It was a form of hysteria that had taken hold of her, her action and her speech were without volition.

"Do you know what has happened!" she gasped as she came toward them. She came nearer than she would have consciously dared, so that she was standing directly over the young writer's prone figure. "That horrible boy, the son of the Patrona, has tied up an Iguana beneath my bedroom. I heard him tying it up but I didn't know what it was. I've been listening to it for hours, ever since supper, and didn't know what it was. Just now I got up to investigate, I looked over the edge of the verandah and there it was, scuffling around at the end of its little rope!"

Neither of the writers said anything for a moment, but the older one had propped himself up a little to stare at Miss Jelkes.

"There *what* was?" he enquired.

"She is talked about the Iguana," said the younger.

"Oh! Well, what about it?"

"How can I sleep?" cried Miss Jelkes. "How could anyone sleep with that example of Indian savagery right underneath my door!"

"You have an aversion to lizards?" suggested the older writer.

"I have an aversion to brutality!" corrected Miss Jelkes.

"But the lizard is a very low grade of animal life. Isn't it a very low grade of animal life?" he asked his companion.

"Not as low as some," said the younger writer. He was grinning maliciously at Miss Jelkes, but she did not notice him at all, her attention was fixed upon the older writer.

"At any rate," said the writer, "I don't believe it is capable of feeling half as badly over its misfortune as you seem to be feeling for it."

"I don't agree with you," said Miss Jelkes. "I don't agree with you at all! We like to think that we are the only ones that are capable of suffering but that is just human conceit. We are not the only ones that are capable of suffering. Why, even plants have sensory impressions. I have seen some that closed their leaves when you touched them!"

She held out her hand and drew her slender fingers into a chalice that closed. As she did this she drew a deep, tortured breath with her lips pursed and nostrils flaring and her eyes rolled heavenwards so that she looked like a female Saint on the rack.

The younger man chuckled but the older one continued to stare at her gravely.

"I am sure," she went on, "that the Iguana has very definite feelings, and you would be, too, if you had been listening to it, scuffling around out there in that awful dry dust, trying to reach the bushes with that rope twisted about its neck, making it almost impossible for it to breathe!"

She clutched her throat as she spoke and with the other hand made a clawing gesture in the air. The younger writer broke into a laugh, the older one smiled at Miss Jelkes.

"You have a real gift," he said, "for vicarious experience."

"Well, I just can't stand to witness suffering," said Miss Jelkes. "I can endure it myself but I just can't stand to witness it in others, no matter whether it's human suffering or animal suffering. And there is so much suffering in the world, so much that is necessary suffering, such as illnesses and accidents which cannot be avoided. But there is so much unnecessary suffering, too, so much that is inflicted simply because some people have a callous disregard for the feelings of others. Sometimes it almost seems as if the universe was designed by the Marquis de Sade!"

She threw back her head with an hysterical laugh.

"And I do not believe in the principle of atonement," she went on. "Isn't it awful, isn't it really preposterous that practically all our religions should be based on the principle of atonement when there is really and truly no such thing as guilt?"

"I am sorry," said the older writer. He rubbed his forehead. "I am not in any condition to talk about God."

"Oh, I'm not talking about God," said Miss Jelkes. "I'm talking about the Iguana!"

"She's trying to say that the Iguana is one of God's creatures," said the younger writer.

"But that one of God's creatures," said the older, "is now in the possession of the Patrona's son!"

"That one of God's creatures," Miss Jelkes exclaimed, "is now hitched to a post right underneath my door, and late as it is I have a very good notion to go and wake up the Patrona and tell her that they have got to turn it loose or at least to remove it some place where I can't hear it!"

The younger writer was now laughing with drunken vehemence. "What are you bellowing over?" the older one asked him.

"If she goes and wakes up the Patrona, anything can happen!"

"What?" asked Miss Jelkes. She glanced uncertainly at both of them.

"That's quite true," said the older. "One thing these Mexicans will not tolerate is the interruption of sleep!"

"But what can she do but apologize and remove it!" demanded Miss Jelkes. "Because after all, it's a pretty outrageous thing to hitch a lizard beneath a woman's door and expect her to sleep with that noise going on all night!"

"It might not go on all night," said the older writer.

"What's going to stop it?" asked Miss Jelkes.

"The Iguana might go to sleep."

"Never!" said Miss Jelkes. "The creature is frantic and what it is going through must be a nightmare!"

"You're bothered a good deal by noises?" asked the older writer. This was, of course, a dig at Miss Jelkes for her complaint about the radio. She recognized it as such and welcomed the chance it gave to defend and explain. In fact this struck her as being the golden moment for breaking all barriers down.

"That's true, I am!" she admitted breathlessly. "You see, I had a nervous breakdown a few years ago, and while I'm ever so much better than I was, sleep is more necessary to me than it is to people who haven't gone through a terrible thing like that. Why, for months and months I wasn't able to sleep without a sedative tablet, sometimes two of them a night! Now I hate like anything to be a nuisance to people, to make unreasonable demands, because I am always so anxious to get along well with people, not only peaceably, but really *cordially* with them—even with strangers that I barely *speak* to—However it some-times happens . . ."

She paused for a moment. A wonderful thought had struck her.

"I know what I'll do!" she cried out. She gave the older writer a radiant smile.

"What's that?" asked the younger. His tone was full of suspicion but Miss Jelkes smiled at him, too.

"Why, I'll just move!" she said.

"Out of Costa Verde?" suggested the younger.

"Oh, no, no, no! No, indeed! It's the nicest resort hotel I've ever stopped at! I mean that I'll change my room."

"Where will you change it to?"

"Down here," said Miss Jelkes, "to this end of the verandah! I won't even wait till morning. I'll move right now. All these vacant rooms, there couldn't be any objection, and if there is, why, I'll just explain how totally impossible it was for me to sleep with that lizard's commotion all night!"

She turned quickly about on her heels, so quickly that she nearly toppled over on the slippery floor, caught her breath laughingly and rushed back to her bedroom. Blindly she swept up a few of her belong-ings in her arms and rushed back to the writers' end of the verandah where they were holding a whispered consultation.

"Which is your room?" she asked.

"We have two rooms," said the younger writer coldly.

"Yes, one each," said the older.

"Oh, of course!" said Miss Jelkes. "But I don't want to make the embarrassing error of confiscating one of you gentlemen's beds!"

She laughed gaily at this. It was the sort of remark she would make to show new acquaintances how far from being formal and prudish she was. But the writers were not inclined to laugh with her, so she cleared her throat and started blindly toward the nearest door, dropping a comb and a mirror as she did so.

"Seven years bad luck!" said the younger man.

"It isn't broken!" she gasped.

"Will you help me?" she asked the older writer.

He got up unsteadily and put the dropped articles back on the disorderly pile in her arms.

"I'm sorry to be so much trouble!" she gasped pathetically. Then she turned again to the nearest doorway.

"Is this one vacant?"

"No, that's mine," said the younger.

"Then how about *this* one?"

"That one is mine," said the older.

"Sounds like the Three Bears and Goldilocks!" laughed Miss Jelkes. "Well, oh, dear—I guess I'll just have to take *this* one!"

She rushed to the screen door on the other side of the younger writer's room, excitingly aware as she did so that this would put her within close range of their nightly conversations, the mystery of which had tantalized her for weeks. Now she would be able to hear every word that passed between them unless they actually whispered in each other's ear!

She rushed into the bedroom and let the screen door slam.

She switched on the suspended light bulb and hastily plunged the articles borne with her about a room that was identical with the one that she had left and then plopped herself down upon an identical white iron bed.

There was silence on the verandah.

Without rising she reached above her to pull the cord of the light bulb. Its watery yellow glow was replaced by the crisp white flood of moonlight through the gauze-netted window and through the screen of the door.

She lay flat on her back with her arms lying rigidly along her sides and every nerve tingling with excitement over the spontaneous execution of a piece of strategy carried out more expertly than it would have been after days of preparation.

For a while the silence outside her new room continued.

Then the voice of the younger writer pronounced the word "Goldilocks!"

Two shouts of laughter rose from the verandah. It continued without restraint till Miss Jelkes could feel her ears burning in the dark as if rays of intense light were concentrated on them.

There was no more talk that evening, but she heard their feet scraping as they got off the hammocks and walked across the verandah to the further steps and down them.

Miss Jelkes was badly hurt, worse than she had been hurt the previous afternoon, when she had complained about the young man's immodesty on the beach. As she lay there upon the severe white bed that smelled of ammonia, she could feel coming toward her one of those annihilating spells of neurasthenia which had led to her breakdown six years ago. She was too weak to cope with it, it would have its way with her and bring her God knows how close to the verge of lunacy and even possibly over! What an intolerable burden, and why did she have to bear it, she who was so humane and gentle by nature that even the sufferings of a lizard could hurt her! She turned her face to the cold white pillow and wept. She wished that she were a writer. If she were a writer it would be possible to say things that only Picasso had ever put into paint. But if she said them, would anybody believe them? Was her sense of the enormous grotesquerie of the world communicable to any other person? And why should it be told if it could be? And why, most of all, did she make such a fool of herself in her frantic need to find some comfort in people!

She felt that the morning was going to be pitilessly hot and bright and she turned over in her mind the list of neuroses that might fasten upon her. Everything that is thoughtless and automatic in healthy organisms might take on for her an air of preposterous novelty. The act of breathing and the beat of her heart and the very process of thinking would be self-conscious if this worst-of-all neuroses should take hold of her—and take hold of her it would, because she was so afraid of it! The precarious balance of her nerves would be all overthrown. Her entire being would turn into a feverish little machine for the production of fears, fears that could not be put into words because of their all-encompassing immensity, and even supposing that they could be put into language and so be susceptible to the comfort of telling—who was there at the Costa Verde, this shadowless rock by the ocean, that she could turn to except the two young writers who seemed to despise her? How awful to be at the mercy of merciless people!

Now I'm indulging in self-pity, she thought.

She turned on her side and fished among articles on the bed table for the little cardboard box of sedative tablets. They would get her through the night, but tomorrow—oh, tomorrow! She lay there senselessly crying, hearing even at this distance the efforts of the captive Iguana to break from its rope and scramble into the bushes . . .

II

When Miss Jelkes awoke it was still a while before morning. The moon, however, had disappeared from the sky and she was lying in blackness that would have been total except for tiny cracks of light that came through the wall of the adjoining bedroom, the one that was occupied by the younger writer.

It did not take her long to discover that the younger writer was not alone in his room. There was no speech but the quality of sounds that came at intervals though the partition made her certain the room had two people in it.

If she could have risen from bed and peered through one of the cracks without betraying herself she might have done so, but knowing that any move would be overheard, she remained on the bed and her mind was now alert with suspicions which had before been only a formless wonder.

At least she heard someone speak.

"You'd better turn out the light," said the voice of the younger writer.

"Why?"

"There are cracks in the wall."

"So much the better. I'm sure that's why she moved down here."

The younger one raised his voice.

"You don't think she moved because of the Iguana?"

"Hell, no, that was just an excuse. Didn't you notice how pleased she was with herself, as if she had pulled off something downright brilliant?"

"I bet she's eavesdropping on us right this minute," said the younger.

"Undoubtedly she is. But what can she do about it?"

"Go to the Patrona."

Both of them laughed.

"The Patrona wants to get rid of her," said the younger.

"Does she?"

"Yep. She's crazy to have her move out. She's even given the cook instructions to put too much salt in her food."

They both laughed.

Miss Jelkes discovered that she had risen from the bed. She was standing uncertainly on the cold floor for a moment and then she was rushing out of the screen door and up to the door of the younger writer's bedroom.

She knocked on the door, carefully keeping her eyes away from the lighted interior.

"Come in," said a voice.

"I'd rather not," said Miss Jelkes. "Will you come here for a minute?"

"Sure," said the younger writer. He stepped to the door, wearing only the trousers to his pyjamas.

"Oh," he said. "It's you!"

She stared at him without any idea of what she had come to say or had hoped to accomplish.

"Well?" he demanded brutally.

"I—I heard you!" she stammered.

"So?"

"I don't understand it!"

"What?"

"Cruelty! I never could understand it!"

"But you do understand spying, don't you?"

"I wasn't spying!" she cried.

He muttered a shocking word and shoved past her onto the porch.

The older writer called his name: "Mike!" But he only repeated the shocking word more loudly and walked away from them. Miss Jelkes and the older writer faced each other. The violence just past had calmed Miss Jelkes a little. She found herself uncoiling inside and comforting tears beginning to moisten her eyes. Outside the night was changing. A wind had sprung up and the surf that broke on the other side of the landlocked bay called Coleta could now be heard.

"It's going to storm," said the writer.

"Is it? I'm glad!" said Miss Jelkes.

"Won't you come in?"

"I'm not at all properly dressed."

"I'm not either."

"Oh, well—"

She came in. Under the naked light bulb and without the dark glasses his face looked older and the eyes, which she had not seen before, had a look that often goes with incurable illness.

She noticed that he was looking about for something.

"Tablets," he muttered.

She caught sight of them first, among a litter of papers.

She handed them to him.

"Thank you. Will you have one?"

"I've had one already."

"What kind are yours?"

"Seconal. Yours?"

"Barbital. Are yours good?"

"Wonderful."

"How do they make you feel? Like a water-lily?"

"Yes, like a water lily on a Chinese lagoon!"

Miss Jelkes laughed with real gaiety but the writer responded only with a faint smile. His attention was drifting away from her again. He stood at the screen door like a worried child awaiting the return of a parent.

"Perhaps I should—"

Her voice faltered. She did not want to leave. She wanted to stay there. She felt herself upon the verge of saying incommunicable things to this man whose singularity was so like her own in many essential respects, but his turned back did not invite her to stay. He shouted the name of his friend. There was no response. The writer turned back from the door with a worried muttering but his attention did not return to Miss Jelkes.

"Your friend—" she faltered.

"Mike?"

"Is he the—right person for you?"

"Mike is helpless and I am always attracted by helpless people."

"But you," she said awkwardly. "How about you? Don't you need somebody's help?"

"The help of God!" said the writer. "Failing that, I have to depend on myself."

"But isn't it possible that with somebody else, somebody with more understanding, more like *yourself*—!"

"You mean *you?*" he asked bluntly.

Miss Jelkes was spared the necessity of answering one way or another, for at that moment a great violence was unleashed outside the screen door. The storm that had hovered uncertainly on the horizon was now plunging toward them. Not continually but in sudden thrusts and withdrawals, like a giant bird lunging up and down on its terrestrial quarry, a bird with immense white wings and beak of godlike fury, the attack was delivered against the jut of rock on which the Costa Verde was planted. Time and again the whole night blanched and trembled, but there was something frustrate in the attack of the storm. It seemed to be one that came from a thwarted will. Otherwise surely the frame structure would have been smashed. But the giant white bird did not know where it was striking. Its beak of fury was blind, or perhaps the beak—

It may have been that Miss Jelkes was right on the verge of divining more about God than a mortal ought to—when suddenly the writer leaned forward and thrust his knees between hers. She noticed that he had removed the towel about him and now was quite naked. She did not have time to wonder nor even to feel much surprise for in the next few moments, and for the first time in her thirty years of preordained spinsterhood, she was enacting a fierce little comedy of defense. He thrust at her like the bird of blind white fury. His one hand attempted to draw up the skirt of her robe while his other tore at the flimsy goods at her bosom. The upper cloth tore. She cried out with pain as the predatory fingers dug into her flesh. But she did not give in. Not she herself resisted but some demon of virginity that occupied her flesh fought off the assailant more furiously than he attacked her. And her demon won, for all at once the man let go of her gown and his fingers released her bruised bosom. A sobbing sound in his throat, he collapsed against her. She felt a wing-like throbbing against her belly, and then a scalding wetness. Then he let go of her altogether. She sank back into her chair which had remained demurely upright throughout the struggle, as unsuitably, as ridiculously, as she herself had maintained her upright position. The man was sobbing. And then the screen door opened and the younger writer came in. Automatically Miss Jelkes freed herself from the damp embrace of her unsuccessful assailant.

"What is it?" asked the younger writer.

He repeated his question several times, senselessly but angrily, while he shook his older friend who could not stop crying.

I don't belong here, thought Miss Jelkes, and suiting action to thought, she slipped quietly out the screen door. She did not turn back into the room immediately adjoining but ran down the verandah to the room she had occupied before. She threw herself onto the bed which was now as cool as if she had never lain on it. She was grateful for that and for the abrupt cessation of fury outside. The white bird had gone away and the Costa Verde had survived its assault. There was nothing but the rain now, pattering without much energy, and the far away sound of the ocean only a little more distinct than it had been before the giant bird struck. She remembered the Iguana.

Oh, yes, the Iguana! She lay there with ears pricked for the painful sound of its scuffling, but there was no sound but the effortless flowing of water. Miss Jelkes could not contain her curiosity so at last she got out of bed and looked over the edge of the verandah. She saw the rope. She saw the whole length of the rope lying there in a relaxed coil, but not the Iguana. Somehow or other the creature tied by the rope had gotten away. Was it an act of God that effected this deliverance? Or was it not more reasonable to suppose that only Mike, the beautiful and helpless and cruel, had cut the Iguana loose? No matter. No matter who did it, the Iguana was gone, had scrambled back into its native bushes and, oh, how gratefully it must be breathing now! And she was grateful, too, for in some equally mysterious way the strangling rope of her loneliness had also been severed by what had happened tonight on this barren rock above the moaning waters.

Now she was sleepy. But just before falling asleep she remembered and felt again the spot of dampness, now turning cool but still adhering to the flesh of her belly as a light but persistent kiss. Her fingers approached it timidly. They expected to draw back with revulsion but were not so affected. They touched it curiously and even pityingly and did not draw back for a while. *Ah, Life,* she thought to herself and was about to smile at the originality of this thought when darkness lapped over the outward gaze of her mind.

1948 (Published 1948)

The Poet

The poet distilled his own liquor and had become so accomplished in this art that he could produce a fermented drink from almost any kind of organic matter. He carried it in a flask strapped about his waist, and whenever fatigue overtook him he would stop at some lonely point and raise the flask to his lips. Then the world would change color as a soap bubble penetrated by a ray of light and a great vitality would surge and break as a limitless ocean through him. The usual superfluity of impressions would fall away so that his senses would combine in a single vast ray of perception which blinded him to lesser phenomena and experience as candles might be eclipsed in a chamber of glass exposed to a cloudless meridian of the sun.

His existence was one of benevolent anarchy, for no one of his time was more immune to the influence of states and organizations. In populated sections he might subsist as a scavenger on the refuse of others, but in the open country he lived as a ruminant beast on whatever green things were acceptable to his stomach.

A tall and angular man with eyes of turquoise and skin of clear amber, he had the cleanliness and beauty of sculpture. Such beauty is not allowed to pass unnoticed. He had never sought out any contact with people except the ideal one of audience and poet, but it sometimes happened that the sexual hunger of strangers would be visited on him. This would occur when bodily exhaustion had overtaken him after some great expansion of vision and when he had crept for refuge into an areaway. While he was resting there some anonymous passer-by, who prowled the alleys at night, might happen to notice the poet and enter beside him with hotly exploring fingers and ravenous lips. In daylight the poet would waken to find his clothing torn open and

246

sometimes not only a dampness of mouths on his flesh but painful bruises, and sometimes also a coin or a ring or some other grateful token thrust in a pocket or in the palm of his hand, but he would straighten his clothes and continue upon his way without any shame or resentment, and the briefly lingering dampness of such embraces would outlast his memory of them.

Mercifully it so happened that scratching about for existence had grown to be automatic. It occupied none of his thought and did not intrude on the inner life of the man. His poems were not written down, for his was a genius of speech. An earlier period of his life had been spent in a singular kind of evangelism. Then he had gone into places of public resort and delivered speeches of exhortation. Hardly a day had gone by without some violence being used upon him. He was often imprisoned and still more often was beaten. But gradually rage was purified out of his nature. He saw the childishness of it. Then he fell into silence for a time. He entered the places and looked about him and left them, addressing no one. For several years this retreat into silence continued. When it was broken, the character of his speech had changed entirely. The moral anger had given place to the telling of marvelous stories which he told in the open. His audience, then, was found among adolescents, boys and girls who were poised for that brief and hesitant spell between the coming of wisdom and its willful rejection which is the condition on which the young are admitted to pockets of social states based on nothing pure in their natures. The poet had learned that his audience could only be found in this particular age-group. Now wherever he went he would gather about him the young and beautiful listeners to stories. He would pick them up at the entrances to schools and parks and playgrounds. His very appearance would magnetize the young people. Instinctively they would know him as a man who had dared to resist the will of the organizations which they would be forced to succumb to. Adults would judge him to be a worthless crank of some kind, but the young were drawn to him with a mysterious yearning and hung on his syllables as bees cluster on the inexhaustible chalice of a flower.

Whoever loves the young loves also the sea. It was therefore natural that the latter phase of the poet's life should be spent on the seacoast. For ten months, now, he had lived on a tropical coast whose tremendous scape of open water and sky provided his stories with an ideal *mise*

en scène. He had occupied a little driftwood shack. He could not remember if he had built it himself or found it already erected. It was
situated at a point where the beach curved gently and smoothly inland
and rose in a fanlike sweep of golden dunes. In a large iron drum, cast
up from a wreck at sea, he had distilled his liquor of fiery potency and
he kept this reservoir buried in sand behind his driftwood lodging.

Whenever he gave them a signal, his youthful audience would as-
semble about him and each time more would come and each time from
villages which were further removed. For a long time, now, the poet
had felt that his stories so far had been little more than preliminary
exercises to some really great outpouring which might be more of a
plastic than verbal creation. He felt that this culmination was now close
at hand. The imminence grew in him with the warnings of fever. His
body burned and thinned and his gold hair whitened. His heart had
swollen. The arteries were distended. At times he would seem to be
holding an incubus in his bosom, whose fierce little purplish knot of a
head was butting against his ribs and whose limbs were kicking and
squirming with convulsions. Now and again arterial blood would spurt
from his mouth and nostrils. He noticed these warnings of death's
unspeakable outrage encroaching upon him, but felt he had power
enough to hold it in check until the event that he lived for had come to
pass. It came that summer, late in the crazed month of August. The
night preceding its coming the poet had wandered along the beach in a
state of delirium in which he seemed to be making a steep ascent
without any effort of breathlessness of climbing and at the height of
this progress he could see below him as a picture puzzle with all its
pieces fitted precisely together the whole of his time on earth. He noted
triumphantly that the scattered instances had closed in a design and
that the design could be closed into a vision. When morning came, it
dropped him down the whole way, but he knew for what purpose. It
was to call the children. A signal fire must be lit to summon the
children. He started immediately to prepare it. But for the first time the
inflammable stuff was difficult to gather. The fragments of dried wood
seemed to be miles separated. He probed for them in the dunes and
among the scrubby bushes until his knuckles were bleeding and the
incubus in his breast had all but broken through the crumbling cage of
his ribs. When finally there was enough to light the signal, a wind
sprang up and he had to oppose the wind. He had to crouch over the
flames till they blackened the skin of his chest and he had to embrace
the fiery sticks with his arms to hold them together. Then all at once

the opposition was over. The ocean took back the wind. The air was motionless and the ocean appeared to be struck like a statue in a blaze of calm, and now the pillar of smoke rose thin and straight as a tree without any branches. The poet withdrew from the point of fiendish trial, dragging himself on hands and knees to the merciful restoration held in the drum. A single taste of it lifted him to his feet. Once more and for the last time, the limitless ocean surged and broke in his veins, that ocean of scarlet the butterfly boat rocks on, which is being alive.

The pillar of smoke soon caught the children's attention. With faces barely washed for the early morning, they rose like birds from the villages to surge up the hillsides and tumble crazily down them, past the fenced in fields where their parents labored the soil, past doorways where old women crouched in dull astonishment at their windy passage, past everything stationary, incensed as they were by the demon of rushing forward, responding as only the ones of their age could respond to anything thin as smoke but promising vision.

A long way off the poet could hear their cries and knew they were coming. He rose from beside the drum and walked erect and powerful to the end of the beach where the children would appear. With clothing cast off along the course of their journey and nude bodies shining with wetness, the children swept over the last separating dune and enveloped the waiting figure of the poet.

In front of his driftwood lodging he brought them to rest. There he stood in their midst and began his story. The scaffolding of the heavens remained very high and he proceeded to build a stairs for the children. They let their playthings go. The puppets of painted wreckage which he had carved for the children fell from their clasp as they began to take part in the narrative's action. They chased each other among the scarves of foam. Their leaps were prodigious, their shouts were everlasting, and always he called them back for another lesson, stretching his wasted arms like the crossbars of a ship on a drunken ocean. He compelled them to understand the rapture of vision and how it could let a man break out of his body. Before the slanting wall of the driftwood house, his eyes shot arrows of pale blue lightning at them, he leaned and gestured and imitated the ocean. A huge blue rocking horse seemed to be loose among them whose plumes were smoky blue ones the sky could not hold and so let grandly go of.

The story continued till dusk, and at that time the children's parents came for them. The men of the villages had become suspicious of the poet. They now surrounded his lodging and called him out. The poet came out and stood exhausted among them, peering almost blindly into their faces, now that the poetry had forsaken his body and left him old and wasted and shrunken gray. Without any explanation they told him to leave. The poet nodded agreement to their command, and frowned with sorrow, seeing the children far away on the beach and moving further among the shepherding mothers.

When all the dispersing crowd had gone from sight, the poet returned to his house. He wrapped in a piece of sailcloth his small collection of things, mementos of distances walked along the ocean. He said good-bye to the ocean. He waved to it gravely with one of his hands that were like the arrowy skeletons of birds. He turned back inland after his ten months' stay on the shore of the ocean. When he had climbed with an effort that took his breath to the highest dune and had turned and looked behind him where his residence of driftwood appeared even smaller than it actually was as it huddled in growing night and in emptiness now at the edge of the plunging surf, he felt that finally all of his gold was spent and that what remained was only the clink of copper. Suddenly he resisted the thought of exile. He was bound to this place by more than ten months' custom. This was the place where he had finally told his greatest story, and if he would be remembered at all, it could only be here, by the children of this coastal region.

Staggering with exhaustion the poet retraced his steps. Still for a moment as he approached the ocean his brain could hold it. His vision still contained it. Then it rocked and split and the dark showed through it, tremendous and rushing toward him. He fell on the beach. His body remained at that spot for a long, long time. The sun and the sand and the water washed it continually and swept away all but the bones and the stiff white garments.

The children, scattering further than usual from their homes without the signal to draw them, happened at dusk on the skeleton of the poet. They had grown older but had not yet discarded their tender feelings. They circled about the skeleton of the poet, bewildered and sorrowful, aware of a loss they could not express to each other. One of them finally went to the great iron drum containing the poet's liquor. Having once seen the poet drink of it, he cupped his palm in the liquor and drank a portion. The others followed suit. It coursed as flame through their bodies and made them reel. They became very drunk and suddenly, of a single accord, they lay in the sand beside the huge iron drum and back of the driftwood shack, and thrust and plunged their bodies against each other.

Not far off shore two vessels engaged in battle. One of them was sunk, and as night fell, the bodies of drowned sailors washed onto the beach. The children, by that time exhausted, wandered along the beach and gazed at the bodies which were beginning already to wear the look of corruption. Alone among them the skeleton of the poet appeared immune to decay. And for the last time of all, for now they were old enough to be conscripted into the service of states and organizations, the children remotely sensed the presence of something outside the province of matter. Then they turned homewards. The wind blew about them odors of smoke and death as they returned to their villages, never again to rise from them as swallows when distant smoke announced to them, Here is vision!

(*Published 1948*)

Chronicle of a Demise

The many letters which have come into my hands from provincial members of the Order requesting some information about our Saint's disappearance were left unanswered till now because among us at the Center some hope still persisted that we would be given a sign on which we could premise some faith in her transfiguration. That hope having lately been formally abandoned, there seems no longer to be any valid excuse for further withholding the facts set down hereunder.

Our Saint's admired exaltation, during the swift last summer of her life, the two months spent on a cot on the roof of her cousin's East Side apartment building, was due not so much to any profound resurgence of faith in the Order as it was to the coffee drunk black without sugar, two or three times a day on an empty stomach. This coffee was all that the Saint was willing to take from her cousin's table and this she only accepted because we had been assured that if she did not accept it, it would be poured down the kitchen drain.

The coffee was brought up to her not by the cousin himself but by his orphan nephew, a child of ten who was crippled and had some difficulty in climbing the stairs. On one occasion the crippled child stumbled as he was approaching the Saint with the pot of coffee and a small amount of the coffee was splashed on her forehead. Now I was a witness to this slight misadventure from which a rumor derived that the cousin's party had plotted to blind the Saint, and while I am not an apologist for the cousin's behavior, I consider it my duty to report that a bit of loose tar-paper on the roof and not any plot downstairs was responsible for the spilling of the coffee.

The coffee was always brought up in the battered aluminum percolator that it was prepared in. The Saint drank it from the percolator's

spout, supporting herself on her elbows and looking out over the roof-
tops toward the East River, where she believed she would see the ship
returning if it returned that summer.

Under the cot was the scarlet heart-shaped box, once a container of
Valentine's Day candies, in which were kept the articles of our faith.
There appears no longer to be the slightest reason for holding back
knowledge of how these things were collected. They were collected at
random, in subway stations and under the seats of trains, in gutters
and alleys of many different towns, even by theft from persons whose
homes she visited while the Saint and myself were engaged in the
membership drive.

The charge which was made by some members of the Left that the
Saint had begun to entertain doubts in regard to the articles is based on
the entrance for August first in my journal. Upon that date I had come
to see her about the nomination of something that Agatha Doyle had
placed in the "Possible Box." This article was a piece of purple tinfoil
which Agatha had picked up on Father Duffy's Square. The Saint
looked it over but seemed to be unimpressed. I put the article back in
the "Possible Box." There was an interval of silence between us, and
then the Saint, who had raised herself on her elbows to look at the
article Agatha had proposed, dropped suddenly back on her pillow and
made the remark which those on the Left construed as a disavowal.

The articles in the box are destructible matter.

That was all that she said, and it was said in a tone of no particular
bitterness. It was somewhat unexpected, however, and I turned my
face to the chimney in order to hide a momentary embarrassment
while I transcribed the statement. The Saint reached out and took hold
of my tablet and pencil and under the statement which I had just copied
down, she wrote this highly significant addition.

Matter is not what matters! And then she smilingly handed back the
journal.

I am sure you must see how far this actually was from a disavowal.
The fact it was so misconstrued is evidence of the extremes to which
the Left was now carried in its determined effort to create a schism.

By the close of July the apostasy of the Saint's cousin had grown too
apparent for anyone to ignore. His dwindling attendance had now
fallen off to the point that he ceased to appear at the Saturday rear-
rangements. Once when a thunderstorm came from across the East
River and made it advisable to take the collection downstairs, as the
iron cot itself appeared to be in some danger of blowing away, the

Cousin refused to have the articles placed in his apartment. He claimed that his wife had developed a strong nervous dread of the things in the box and that having them near her was likely to give her convulsions. The child with his leg in a brace delivered this message to us just as we were grouping about the box, preparatory to taking it downstairs. The Saint, supported on one side by Agatha Doyle and by myself on the other, was having a manifestation and seemed not to catch a single word of the message. The child, as he read it aloud from the typewritten sheet of coarse manila paper, was rubbing a bruise on his forearm, a purplish discoloration, which led me to feel that the mission had been forced upon him. The attitude of the child is not important, but extremists of both parties have attributed to him a sort of precocious Machiavellianism which fairness compels me to say was not borne out by anything I observed. He was innocent of design as a carrier pigeon.

The child had already slipped back down the stairs before any of us who were attending the Saint had time to absorb the import of the message. Agatha Doyle let go of the Saint's right arm. The Saint bounded up like a paper kite on a string. I shouted, Agatha, what on earth are you doing? It took three others besides myself and Miss Doyle to haul the Saint back down. Of course by this time the manifestation had passed. She seemed to be stunned and we thought it best not to mention our reason for not removing the box from the roof. The storm had already passed over, at least the worst of it had. Agatha Doyle was securing the Saint to the cot with the belt of her dress, when, not five minutes after he gave us the message, the child reappeared and was bearing the percolator. I noted he had a second bruise on his arm, the same arm, but lower, close to the wrist and his eyes were inflamed as if the child had been weeping. He thrust the coffeepot toward the recumbent Saint. Agatha took it first. She gave me a startled glance and passed it to me. I looked in the percolator and found it was empty. It had been thoroughly scoured. Not even an odor of coffee remained about it.

To all of us on the Right, and even to most of the so-called Liberal group, it was plainly evident that things could not go on as they had been going and that some sort of culmination was close at hand.

It came in the last week of August.

A record number of seven new articles had been placed in the Possible Box the night before, and a meeting had been called to consider the sanctification of a wad of spearmint gum that Hannibal Weems had picked up on the steps of an escalator in Gimbel's department store the previous Tuesday. The rites of induction had been already concluded. The Saint, supported on one hand by Doster Parker and on the other by me, was delivering such an enraptured incantation that she appeared unaware of her cousin's tardy arrival on the roof. He had come out on the roof in ceremonial dress, complete with the one and rather shocking exception of worn canvas sneakers which had an offensive odor. He leaned against the chimney, looking on sullenly as the sanctified articles were installed in the Box. The seven new articles had been placed at the bottom. This was, of course, an arbitrary disposal. Under more usual circumstances, degrees of sanctity would have been determined and the articles put in strictly graded positions. This would have called for a twenty-four hour session which at the time not even the indefatigable Mr. Parker was in a condition to undertake without recess. All but four or five of us had gone downstairs to partake of a buffet supper, prepared and served by girls of the Junior Committee. A few of the party in power remained on the roof, near the Saint who had fallen silent and seemed to be exhausted. The party of Opposition was all withdrawn from the roof except for the Cousin. The Cousin began to mutter. He circled about the chimney several times, in widening orbits which bore him continually closer to the cot.

It was darkening in the East. On the other side of the river the great power plant was already lighted up for the summer evening.

The Cousin at last spoke out, addressing the Saint.

I know what has happened, he said. The expedition has returned and you are stalling for time because it came back empty-handed!

At this remark the Misses Doyle and La Mantia scrambled away from the cot like a pair of frightened hens and rushed pell-mell down the stairs. The Saint and her cousin and I were all that remained on the roof.

To my astonishment, then, the Saint replied, Yes, the expedition returned last week empty-handed.

What are your plans? asked the Cousin.

The Saint replied that the ship had already sailed on another voyage.

Secretly? asked the Cousin.

Of course, said the Saint.

The Cousin appeared to receive this answer calmly. Then all at once his arm shot out and grabbed hold of the box. It will have to end now! he shouted.

He flung the box with all his force from the roof.

There was a brief confusion.

The Saint drew open her gown and opened her chest. Her heart divided as leaves of thin tissue paper. The leaves blew out, they blew in the face of the Cousin who sputtered and coughed as though he had sniffed red pepper. I made an attempt to hold the leaves from dispersion. I caught a few of them and thrust the few I had caught back into the cleft of her bosom. But it was too late. The clock-spring was making a little rasping noise. Then this stopped, too. Her two clenched hands came open. Her eyeballs, hard and beautifully blue as marbles, sprung straight out on their glittering coiled attachments.

Let her go, said the Cousin.

We both released the limbs we were holding down. A fine cool spray was dashed back into our faces as all her tissues divided and lifted away. In half a minute she had gone altogether. The Cousin said nothing but stared at the empty cot. His wife could now be heard at the foot of the stairs calling him down to supper. He went without speaking and as there was obviously nothing more to be done, I followed him down from the roof, picked up my hat and silently left the building.

This is all that I have to report of the matter.

Now as for instructions, I really have none to give you. The Center has now disbanded and ceased to exist as an organizational unit. The future course of individual members is now a matter of individual choice. As for myself, I am intending to travel, but where I shall go and the purpose of my going are matters I feel at liberty not to divulge.

(Published 1948)

Rubio y Morena

The writer Kamrowski had many acquaintances, especially now that his name had begun to acquire some public luster, and he also had a few friends which he had kept over the years the way that you keep a few books you have read several times but are not willing to part with. He was essentially a lonely man, not self-sufficient but living as though he were. He had never been able to believe that anybody sincerely cared much about him and perhaps no one did. When women treated him tenderly, which sometimes happened in spite of his reserve, he suspected them of trying to pull the wool over his eyes. He was not at ease with them. It even embarrassed him to sit across from a woman at a restaurant table. He could not return her look across the table nor keep his mind on the bright things she was saying. If she happened to wear an ornament at her throat or on the lapel of her jacket, he would keep his eyes on this pin and stare at it so intently that finally she would interrupt her talk to ask him why he found it so fascinating or might even unfasten it from her dress and hand it across the table for closer inspection. When going to bed with a woman, desire would often desert his body as soon as he put off his clothes and exposed his nakedness to her. He felt her eyes on him, watching, knowing, involving, and the desire ran out of him like water, leaving him motionless as a dead body on the bed beside her, impervious to her caresses and burning with shame, repulsing her almost roughly if she persisted in trying to waken his passion. But when she had given up trying, when she had finally turned away from his unresponsive body and fallen asleep, then he would turn slowly, warm with desire, not shame, and begin to approach the woman until with a moan of longing, greater than even his fear of her had been, he would rouse her from sleep with the brutal haste of a bull in loveless coupling.

It was not the kind of lovemaking that women respond to with much understanding. There was no tenderness in it, neither before nor after the act was completed, with the frigid embarrassment first and the satiety afterwards, both making him rough and coarse and nearly speechless. He thought of himself as being no good with women, and for that reason his relations with them had been infrequent and fleeting. It was a kind of psychic impotence of which he was bitterly ashamed. He felt it could not be explained, so he never tried to explain it. And so he was lonely and unsatisfied outside of his work. He was uniformly kind to everybody just because he found it easier to be that way, but he forgot nearly all of his social engagements, or if he happened to remember one while he was working, he would sigh, not very deeply, and go on working without even stopping to call on the phone and say, Excuse me, I'm working. His attachment to his work was really somewhat absurd, for he was not an especially good writer. In fact, he was nearly as awkward in his writing as he had been in his relations with women. He wrote the way that he had always made love, with a feeling of apprehension, rushing through it blindly and feverishly as if he were fearful of being unable to complete the act.

You may be wondering why you are presented with these unpleasantly clinical details in advance of the story. It is in order to make more understandable the relationship which the story deals with, a rather singular relationship between the writer Kamrowski and a Mexican girl, Amada, which began in the Mexican border town of Laredo, one summer during the war when Kamrowski was returning from a trip through the Mexican interior.

Because of his suspiciously foreign name and appearance and a nervous habit of speech that easily gave the impression of an accent, Kamrowski had been detained at the border by customs and immigration officials. They had confiscated his papers for an examination by experts in code, and Kamrowski had been forced to remain in Laredo while this examination was in progress. He had taken a room at the Texas Star Hotel. It was intensely hot, the night he spent there. He lay on the huge sagging deck of the bed and smoked cigarettes. Because it was such a hot night, he lay there naked with the windows open and the door open, too, hoping to make a draft of air on his body. The room was quite dark except for his cigarette and the corridor of the hotel was almost lightless. About three A.M. a figure appeared in the doorway. It was so tall that he took it to be a man. He said nothing but went on smoking and the figure in the doorway appeared to be staring at him.

He had heard things about the deportment of guests at the Texas Star Hotel and so he was not surprised when the door pushed farther open and the figure came in and advanced to the edge of the bed. It was only when the head inclined over him and the heavy black hair came tumbling over his bare flesh that he realized the figure to be a woman's. No, he said, but the caller paid no attention and, after a while, Kamrowski was reconciled to it. Then pleased and, at last, delighted. The meeting had been so successful that in the morning Kamrowski had kept her with him. He asked her no questions. She asked him none. They simply went off together, and seemingly it did not matter where they went . . .

For a few months Kamrowski and the Mexican girl named Amada had traveled around the southern states in a rattletrap car held together by spit and a prayer, and most of that time the girl sat mutely beside him while he thought his own thoughts. What her thoughts were he had not the least idea and not much concern. He only saw her turn her head once and that was when they were passing down the main street of a little town in Louisiana. He turned to see what she looked at. A gaudily dressed Negro girl stood on a streetcorner in a cluster of roughly dressed white men. Amada smiled faintly and nodded. *Puta*, she said, only that; but the faint smile of recognition remained on her face for quite a while after the corner had slipped out of sight. She did not often smile and that was why the occurrence had stuck in his mind.

Companionship was not a familiar or easy thing for Kamrowski, not even the companionship of men. The girl was the first he had lived with at all continuously, and to his content he found it possible to forget her presence except as some almost abstract comfort like that of warmth or of sleep. Sometimes he would feel a little astonished, a little incredulous over this sudden alliance of theirs, this accidental coming together of their two so different lives. Sometimes he wondered just why he had taken her with him and he could not explain this thing to himself and yet he did not regret it. He had not realized, at first, what a curious-looking person she was, not until other people had noticed it for him. Sometimes when they stopped at a filling station or entered a restaurant at night, he would notice the way strangers looked at her with a sort of amused surprise, and then he would look at her too, and he, too, would be amused and surprised at the strangeness of her appearance. She was tall and narrow shouldered and most of the flesh of her body was centered about the hips which were as large as the rump of a horse. Her hands were large as a man's but not capable. Their movements were too nervous and her feet clopped awkwardly around. She was forever stumbling or getting caught on something because of her ungainly size and motions. Once the sleeve of her jacket got caught in the slammed car door, and instead of quietly opening the door and disengaging the caught sleeve, she began to utter short, whimpering cries and to tug at the caught sleeve till the material gave way and a piece of sleeve tore loose. Afterwards he noticed that her whole body was shaking as if she had just passed through some nervous ordeal and throughout their supper at the hotel café she would keep lifting up the torn sleeve and frowning at it with a mystified expression as if she did not understand how it got that way, then glancing at him with her head slightly tilted in a look of inquiry as if to ask him if he understood what had happened to the torn sleeve. After the supper, when they had gone upstairs, she took out a pair of scissors and cut the sleeve neatly across to give it an edge. He pointed out to her that this made a disparity between the lengths of the two sleeves. Ha ha, said the girl. She held the jacket up to the light. She saw the disparity herself and began to laugh at it. Finally she threw the jacket into the wastepaper basket and she lay down on the bed with a copy of a movie magazine. She thumbed through it rapidly till she came to a picture of a young male star on a beach. She stopped at that page. She drew the magazine close to her eyes and stared at it with her large mouth hanging open for half an hour, while Kamrowski lay on the bed beside her, only comfortably, warmly half-conscious of her until before sleep, as peacefully as he would sleep, he turned to embrace her.

Kamrowski had grown to love her. Unfortunately, he was even less articulate in speaking about such things than he would have been in trying to write about them. He could not make the girl understand the tenderness he felt toward her. He was not a man who could even say, I love you. The words would not come off his tongue, not even in the intimacies of the night. He could only speak with his body and his hands. With her childlike mind, the girl must have found him altogether baffling. She could not have been able to believe that he loved her, but she must have been equally unable to fathom his reason for staying with her if he did not. Kamrowski would never know how she explained these things to herself or if she tried to explain them or if she was really as mindless as she had seemed—not looking for reasons for things but only accepting that which happens to be as simply being. No. He would never know how. The dark figure in the doorway of the hotel, even mistaken at first for that of a man, did not come into the light. It remained in shadow. *Morena.* She called him *Rubio* sometimes when she touched him. *Rubio* meant blond one. Sometimes he would answer *Morena* which means dark. *Morena.* That's all she was. Something dark. Dark of skin, dark of hair, dark of eyes. But mystery can be loved as well as knowledge and there could be little doubt that Kamrowski loved her.

Nevertheless, a change became evident after they had lived together for less than a year, which may not seem a long time but was actually a relationship of unprecedented duration in the life of Kamrowski. This change seemed to have several reasons, but perhaps the real one was none of those apparent. For one thing, the presence of women had ceased to disturb him so greatly. That nervous block described in the beginning was now so thoroughly dissolved by virtue of the effortless association with Amada, that his libido had now begun to ask for an extended field of play. The mind of a woman no longer emasculated him. The simple half-Indian girl had restored his male dominance. In his heart he knew this and was grateful, but one does not always return a gift with an outward show of devoir. He paid her back very badly. That winter season, which they spent in a southern city, he began to go out in society for the first time in his life, for he had lately become what is called a Name and received a good deal of attention. It was possible, now, to ignore the ornament at the throat of the woman and return, at least now and again, the look of her eyes without too much mortification. It was also possible to make amatory advances before she had gone to sleep.

That winter Kamrowski began to form other attachments of more than a night's duration, one in particular with a young woman who was also a writer and a member of the urban intelligentsia. She had, also, one defect. She wore contact lenses which she used to remove before going to bed and Kamrowski had to ask her not to put them on the table beside the bed but in the little drawer of the table. But this was an unimportant item in the affair which went along smoothly. He began to make love to this girl, Ida, more regularly than he made love to Amada. Now when Amada would turn to him on the bed, he would often avert himself from her and pretend to be sleeping. He would hear her beginning to cry beside him. Her hand would move inquiringly down his body, and once he seized her hand and slammed it roughly away from him. Then she got out of bed. He got up, too, and went into the kitchen and sat there with a pitcher of ice water. He heard her packing her things as she had done often before. Her trunk was a military locker. The bottom of it was filled with random keepsakes, such as restaurant menus, pictures of actors torn from movie magazines, postcards from all the places they had visited in their travels. Sometimes, while she was packing, she would stalk into the kitchen, holding up some article, such as a towel that she had filched from a hotel bathroom. Is this yours or mine? she would ask. He would shrug. She would make a terrible face at him and return to the bedroom to continue her packing. He knew that she would unpack everything in the morning. In the morning she would restore the souvenir menus and postcards to their places about the mirror and the mantel because without him there was no place for her to go and no one to go with. He did not want to feel sorry for her. He was enjoying himself too much to allow a shadow of contrition to weigh upon him too heavily, and so he would think to himself, for self-exoneration, during such scenes: She was only a whore in a third-class hotel where I found her. Why isn't she happy? Well, I don't give a damn!

And yet he was very glad, when he had finished drinking the pitcher of ice water, to find that she was no longer packing but had gone back to bed. Then he would make love to her more tenderly than he had for many weeks past.

It was a morning after an incident such as this that Kamrowski first discovered that the girl had begun to steal from him. Thereafter, whenever he put on his clothes in the morning, he would find his pockets lighter of money than they had been before. At first she took only silver, but as the earnings of his novel increased, she began to increase the amounts of her thefts, taking one dollar bills, then five and ten dollar bills. Finally, Kamrowski had to accuse her of it. She wailed miserably but she did not deny it. For about a week the practice was suspended. Then it started again, first with the silver, increasing again to bills of larger denomination. He tried to thwart her by taking the money out of his pockets and hiding it somewhere about the apartment. But when he did this, she would waken him in the night by her slow and systematic search for it. What are you looking for? he would ask the girl. I am looking for matches, she'd tell him. So at last he humored her in it. He only cashed small checks and let her steal what she wanted. It remained a mystery to him what she did with the money. She apparently bought nothing with it and yet it did not seem to linger in her possession. What did she want with it? She had everything that she needed or seemed to wish. Perhaps it was simply her way of paying him back for the infidelities which he was now practicing all the time.

It was later that winter of their residence in the large southern city that the ill health of Amada became apparent. She did not speak of her suffering, but she would sometimes get up in the night and light a holy candle in a transparent red glass cup. She would crouch beside it mumbling Spanish prayers with a hand pressed to her side where some pain was located. It made her furious when he got up or questioned her about it. She behaved as if she were suffering from some disgraceful secret. Mind your own business, she would snarl back at him if he asked, What is it? Hours later she would waken him again, crawling back into bed with an exhausted sigh which told him that the attack of pain had subsided. Then, moved by pity, he would turn to her slowly and press her to him as gently as possible so that his pressure wouldn't renew the pain. She would not go to a doctor. She said she had been to a doctor a long time ago and that he had told her she had a disease of the kidneys the same as her father had had and that there was nothing to do but try to forget it. It doesn't matter, she said, I am going to forget it.

She made an elaborate effort to conceal the attacks as they became more frequent and more severe, thinking perhaps that her illness would disgust him and he might forsake her completely. She would steal out of bed so cautiously that it would take her five or ten minutes to disengage herself from the covers and creep to the chair in the corner, and if she lit the prayer candle, she would crouch over it with cupped hands to conceal the flame. It was evident to Kamrowski that the infection in her body, whatever it was, was now passing from a chronic into an acute stage. He would have been more concerned if he had not just then started to work on another novel. The girl Amada began to exist for him on the other side of a center which was his writing. Everything outside of that existed in a penumbra as shadowy forms on the further side of a flame. Days and events were uncertain. The ringing of the doorbell and the telephone was ignored. Eating became irregular. He slept with his clothes on, sometimes in the chair where he worked. His hair grew long as a hermit's. He grew a beard and mustache. A lunatic brightness appeared in his eyes while his ordinarily smooth face acquired hollows and promontories and his hands shook. He had fits of coughing and palpitations of the heart which sometimes made him think he was dying and greatly speeded up his already furious tempo of composition.

Afterwards he could not remember clearly how things had been between himself and Amada during this feverish time. He ceased to make love to her, he ceased that altogether, and he was only dimly aware of her presence in the apartment. He gave her commands as if she were a servant and she obeyed them quickly and wordlessly with an air of fright. Get me coffee! he would suddenly yell at her. Play that record again, he would say, with a jerk of his thumb at the Victrola. But he was not conscious of her except as a creature to carry out such commissions.

During this interval she had quit stealing his money. Most of the day she would sit at the opposite end of the wide front room in which he was working. As long as she stayed at that end of the room, her presence did not distract him from his work, but if she entered unbidden his half of the room or if she asked him some question, he would yell at her furiously or even hurl a book at her. She became very quiet. When she went to the kitchen or bathroom, she would move one foot at a time, slowly and stealthily, gazing back at him to make sure he had no objection. Her face had changed, too, in the same way that his had changed. The long equine face had become even bonier than before and dreadfully sallow and the eyes now glittered as if they looked into a room where a great light was. She moved about with an odd stateliness which must have come from the suffering caused by the movement. One hand was now always pressed to the side that hurt her and she moved with exaggerated uprightness in defiance of the temptation to ease her discomfort by crouching. These details of her appearance he could not have noticed at the time, not consciously, and yet they came to him vividly in recollection. It was only afterwards, too, that he troubled himself to wonder how she might have interpreted this disastrous change in their way of living together. She must have thought that all affectionate feeling for her was gone and that he was now enduring her company out of pity only. She stopped stealing his money at night. For a month she sat in the corner and watched him, watched him with the dumb, wanting look of an animal in pain. Occasionally she would dare to cross the room. When he seemed to be resting from his labor, she would come to his side and run her fingers inquiringly down his body to see if he desired her, and finding out that he didn't, she would retire again speechlessly to her side of the room.

Then all at once she left him. He had spent a night out with his new blond mistress and returned to find that Amada had packed her locker-trunk and removed it from the apartment, this time in grim earnest.

He made no attempt to find her. He believed that she would necessarily return of her own accord, for he could not imagine her being able to do otherwise. But she did not return to him, as the days passed, nor did any word of her reach him. He was not certain how he felt about this. He thought for a while that he might even be somewhat relieved by the resulting simplification of his life and the absence of that faint odor of disease which had lately hung sadly over the bed they had slept in. There was still always the book, sometimes loosening its grip now that the first draft was finished, but still making him insensible as a paranoiac to everyday life. During the intervals when the work dropped off, when there was discouragement or a stop for reflection, Kamrowski would take to the streets and follow strange women. He glutted his appetite with a succession of women and continually widened the latitude of his experience, till, all at once, he was filled with disgust at himself and the circus-trapeze of longing on which he had kicked himself senselessly back and forth since the flight of the girl he had lived with. He didn't want any more of that now or ever.

And so one night, about five months after their separation, the image of Amada stalked with a sound of trumpets through the midnight walls of his apartment. She stood like some apparition of flame at the foot of his bed, all luminous from within as an X-ray picture. He saw the tall white bones of her standing there, and he sat bolt upright in the sweat-dampened covers and gave a loud cry; then he fell back on his face to weep uncontrollably till the coming of morning. When daylight was coming, even before the windows had turned really white, he rose to pack his valise and arrange for the trip to Laredo, to find the lost girl and bring her back into the empty room in his heart. He assumed without thinking that Laredo was where she would be, because it was where he had found her.

He was not wrong about that. She had returned to Laredo five months ago but not to the Texas Star where he had found her. The manager of the hotel pretended to have no knowledge of the girl, but the Mexican porter told him that he would find her in the home of her family on the outskirts of town, in a house without number on a street without name, at the bottom of a steep hill on which stood an ice plant.

When Kamrowski arrived at the door of the gray wooden house to which these directions took him—a building no more than a shack which leaned exhaustedly on the edge of a steep and irregular road of gray dust—all of the female family came to the door and talked excitedly among themselves, brushing him avidly up and down with their eyes, half smiling and half snarling at him like a pack of wild dogs. They seemed to be arguing almost hysterically among themselves as to whether or not this stranger should be admitted. He was so sick with longing to see the lost girl that he could not bring out the little Spanish he knew. All he could say was Amada, more and more loudly. And then all at once, from some recess of the building, a loud, hoarse voice was lifted like the crow of a cock. It had a ring of anger but the word called out was the affectionate name she used to call him. Rubio, which meant blond. He swept past the women, brushing them aside with both arms, and made for the direction from which the fierce call had come. He fairly hurled himself against the warped door and broke into a room which was all dark except for a vigil light in a red glass cup. He looked that way where the light in the glass cup was. There he saw her. She was lying upon a pallet arranged upon the bare floor.

It was impossible to judge her appearance in the windowless room, a sort of storage closet, with that one candle burning, especially since he had just come in from the glare of a desert sunset. He made out, gradually, that she was wearing a man's undershirt and he noticed how big her hands and her elbows were now that the arms were so emaciated, and her head seemed almost as big as the head of a horse and the familiar, coarse hair was hanging like a horse's mane about her scrawny neck and shoulders. His first emotion was fury as well as pity. What does this mean, what are you doing in here? he cried out fiercely. Mind your own business, she yelled back at him, exactly as if they had never been separated. Then he swallowed his rage at her family, still going on with their high-pitched argument beyond the door he had slammed shut. He crouched on his haunches beside the pallet and took hold of her hand. She tugged away from his grasp but not quite strongly enough to break it. She seemed to be trying to seem more alive than she was. She did not let herself entirely back down on the pallet, although he could see it was an effort for her to remain propped up on her elbow. And she did not allow her voice to drop but kept it at the same loud and harsh pitch. She did not remove her eyes from his face which she seemed to be straining to examine, but she did not return his look directly. She seemed to be staring at his nose or his mouth. There was a great bewilderment in her look, a wonder at his being there, at his coming to see her. She asked him several times, What are you doing here in Laredo? And his answer, I came here to see you, did not seem to satisfy her. At last he leaned over and touched her shoulder and said, You ought to lie back. She glared at him fiercely. I am all right, she said. Her dark eyes were now immense. All of the light that came from the ruby glass cup was absorbed in those eyes and magnified into a beam that shot into his heart and deprived that moonlike organ of all its shadows, exposing in brutal relief the barrenness of it the way that the moon's landscape, with the sun full on it, turns into a hard and flat disk whose light is borrowed. He could not endure it. He sprang from beside the pallet. He dug in his pocket and pulled out a handful of bills. Take these, he whispered hoarsely. He tried to stuff them into her hands. I don't want your money, she answered. Then after a slight pause she muttered, Give it to them. She jerked her head toward the door beyond which the family were now preparing noisily for supper. He felt defeated altogether. He sighed and looked down at his hands. Her own hands lifted, then, and reached falteringly toward his head. Rubio, she whispered, the word for blond. Tiredly one of her hands dropped down his body to see if he desired her, and discovering that he did not, she smiled at him sadly and let her eyes fall shut. She seemed to be falling asleep; so then he leaned over and kissed her gently at the edge of her large mouth. Morena, he whispered, which was the word for dark one. Instantly the long bony arms flung about him an embrace which took his breath. She pressed their faces painfully together, her Indian cheekbones bruising his softer flesh. Scalding tears and the pressure of those gaunt arms broke finally all the way through the encrusted shell of his ego, which had never before been broken all the way through, and he was released. He was let out of the small but apparently rather light and comfortable room of his known self into a space that lacked the comfort of limits. He entered a space of bewildering dark and immensity, and yet not dark, of which light is really the darker side of the sphere. He was not at home in it. It gave him unbearable fright, and so he crawled back.

He crawled back out of the gaunt embrace of the girl. I will come back in the morning, he said to the girl as he rose from beside the pallet and crawled back into the small room he was secure in . . .

When he returned in the morning, the atmosphere of his reception was different. There was an air of excitement in the place that he could not fathom, and all of the women seemed to have on their best clothes. He thought perhaps it was because of the money that he had left in the sickroom. He started to cross to that room, but the old woman plucked his sleeve and pointed toward another. She led him into the parlor of the house and he was astonished to find that they had moved the girl there. Because he did not understand their speech, he could not realize at first that she had died in the night; this he did not realize until he had picked up her hand, nearly as dark as a Negro's, and found it cool and stiffened. They had dressed her in white, a nightgown of clean white linen that shone with starch, and when he released the hand, the oldest woman advanced and placed it carefully back in its former position on the flat bosom.

He noticed also that the odor of sickness was gone, or possibly lost in the odor of burning wax, for a great many candles had been brought into the room and set in ruby glass cups on the window ledges. The blinds had been lowered against the meridian glare of the flat desert country, but the glare filtered through pinpoint perforations in the old fabric so that each blind was like a square of green sky with stars shining in it. The mourners assembled there were mostly neighbors' children, the smallest ones naked, the larger dressed in gray rags. One little girl was holding a homemade doll, roughly cut out of wood and painted into a grotesque semblance of human infancy. Coarse black hair had been attached to the head. It seemed somehow like an effigy of the dead girl. Unable to look upon the actual face and its now intolerable mystery, Kamrowski stole to the side of the half-naked child and gently and timidly thrust his hand toward the doll. He touched the coarse black hair of the doll with a finger. The child complained faintly and hugged the doll closer to her. Kamrowski began to tremble. He felt that his hand must keep in touch with the doll. He must not let the child move away with her precious possession, and so with one hand he stroked the head of the child while with the other hand's finger he kept in touch with the familiar black hair. But still the child edged away, withdrawing from his caress and regarding him with huge distrustful brown eyes.

Meanwhile a whispered consultation seemed to be going on among the women. It grew louder with excitement and finally the grandmother, with an abrupt decision, separated herself from the group and approached Kamrowski and cried out to him in English, Where is Amada's money, where is her money?

He stared at the old woman stupidly. What money? She made a fierce spitting noise as she thrust toward him a handful of yellow papers. He looked down at them. They seemed to be telegraph forms. Yes, they were all money orders, sent from the city in which he had lived with Amada. The sums were those she had stolen at night from his pockets.

Kamrowski looked wildly about for a way to escape. The women were closing about him like a wolf pack, now all jabbering at once. He made for the outer door. Beside the door the little girl with the doll appeared to him dimly. Impulsively he reached out and snatched the doll from the child as he ran past her into the dusty brilliance of the road. He ran as fast as he could up the steep and irregular dirt road with the wailing child running behind him, feeling only a need of hanging onto the child's grotesque plaything till he was alone somewhere and able to cry.

(Published 1948)

The Resemblance between a Violin Case and a Coffin

Inscribed to the memory of Isabel Sevier Williams

With her advantage of more than two years and the earlier maturity of girls, my sister moved before me into that country of mysterious differences where children grow up. And although we naturally continued to live in the same house, she seemed to have gone on a journey while she remained in sight. The difference came about more abruptly than you would think possible, and it was vast, it was like the two sides of the Sunflower River that ran through the town where we lived. On one side was a wilderness where giant cypresses seemed to engage in mute rites of reverence at the edge of the river, and the blurred pallor of the Dobyne place that used to be a plantation, now vacant and seemingly ravaged by some impalpable violence fiercer than flames, and back of this dusky curtain, the immense cotton fields that absorbed the whole visible distance in one sweeping gesture. But on the other side, avenues, commerce, pavements and homes of people: those two, separated by only a yellowish, languorous stream that you could throw a rock over. The rumbling wooden bridge that divided, or joined, those banks was hardly shorter than the interval in which my sister moved away from me. Her look was startled, mine was bewildered and hurt. Either there was no explanation or none was permitted between the one departing and the one left behind. The earliest beginning of it that I can remember was one day when my sister got up later than usual with an odd look, not as if she had been crying, although perhaps she had, but as though she had received some painful or frightening surprise, and I observed an equally odd difference in the manner toward her of my mother and grandmother. She was escorted to the kitchen table for breakfast as though she were in danger of toppling over on either side, and everything was handed to her as though she could not reach for it. She was addressed in hushed and solicitous voices, almost the way that docile servants speak to an employer. I was baffled and a little disgusted. I received no attention at all, and the one or two glances given me by my sister had a peculiar look of resentment in them. It was as if I had struck her the night before and given her a bloody nose or a black eye, except that she wore no bruise, no visible injury, and there had been no altercation between us in recent days. I spoke to her several times, but for some reason she ignored my remarks, and when I became irritated and yelled at her, my grandmother suddenly reached over and twisted my ear, which was one of the few times that I can remember when she ever offered me more than the gentlest reproach. It was a Saturday morning, I remember, of a hot yellow day and it was the hour when my sister and I would ordinarily take to the streets on our wheels. But the custom was now disregarded. After breakfast my sister appeared somewhat strengthened but still alarmingly pale and as silent as ever. She was then escorted to the parlor and encouraged to sit down at the piano. She spoke in a low whimpering tone to my grandmother who adjusted the piano stool very carefully and placed a cushion on it and even turned the pages of sheet music for her as if she were incapable of finding the place for herself. She was working on a simple piece called "The Aeolian Harp," and my grandmother sat beside her while she played, counting out the tempo in a barely audible voice, now and then reaching out to touch the wrists of my sister in order to remind her to keep them arched. Upstairs my mother began to sing to herself which was something she only did when my father had just left on a long trip with his samples and would not be likely to return for quite a while, and my grandfather, up since daybreak, was mumbling a sermon to himself in the study. All was peaceful except my sister's face. I did not know whether to go outside or stay in. I hung around the parlor a little while, and finally I said to Grand, Why can't she practice later? As if I had made some really brutal remark, my sister jumped up in tears and fled to her upstairs bedroom. What was the matter with her? My grandmother said, Your sister is not well today. She said it gently and gravely, and then she started to follow my sister upstairs, and I was deserted. I was left alone in the very uninteresting parlor. The idea of riding alone on my wheel did not please me for often when I did that, I was set upon by the rougher boys of the town who called me Preacher and took a peculiar delight in asking me obscene questions that would embarrass me to the point of nausea . . .

In this way was instituted the time of estrangement that I could not understand. From that time on the division between us was ever more clearly established. It seemed that my mother and grandmother were approving and conspiring to increase it. They had never before bothered over the fact that I had depended so much on the companionship of my sister but now they were continually asking me why I did not make friends with other children. I was ashamed to tell them that other children frightened me nor was I willing to admit that my sister's wild imagination and inexhaustible spirits made all other substitute companions seem like the shadows of shades, for now that she had abandoned me, mysteriously and willfully withdrawn her enchanting intimacy, I felt too resentful even to acknowledge secretly, to myself, how much had been lost through what she had taken away . . .

Sometimes I think she might have fled back into the more familiar country of childhood if she had been allowed to, but the grown-up ladies of the house, and even the colored girl, Ozzie, were continually telling her that such and such a thing was not proper for her to do. It was not proper for my sister not to wear stockings or to crouch in the yard at a place where the earth was worn bare to bounce a rubber ball and scoop up starry-pointed bits of black metal called jacks. It was not even proper for me to come into her room without knocking. All of these proprieties struck me as mean and silly and perverse, and the wound of them turned me inward.

My sister had been magically suited to the wild country of childhood but it remained to be seen how she would adapt herself to the uniform and yet more complex world that grown girls enter. I suspect that I have defined that world incorrectly with the word uniform; later, yes, it becomes uniform, it straightens out into an all too regular pattern. But between childhood and adulthood there is a broken terrain which is possibly even wilder than childhood was. The wilderness is interior. The vines and the brambles seem to have been left behind but actually they are thicker and more confusing, although they are not so noticeable from the outside. Those few years of dangerous passage are an ascent into unknown hills. They take the breath sometimes and bewilder the vision. My mother and maternal grandmother came of a calmer blood than my sister and I. They were unable to suspect the hazards that we were faced with, having in us the turbulent blood of our father. Irreconcilables fought for supremacy in us; peace could never be made: at best a smoldering sort of armistice might be reached after many battles. Childhood had held those clashes in abeyance. They were somehow timed to explode at adolescence, silently, shaking the earth where we were standing. My sister now felt those tremors under her feet. It seemed to me that a shadow had fallen on her. Or had it fallen on me, with her light at a distance? Yes, it was as if someone had carried a lamp into another room that I could not enter. I watched her from a distance and under a shadow. And looking back on it now, I see that those two or three years when the fatal dice were still in the tilted box, were the years of her beauty. The long copperish curls which had swung below her shoulders, bobbing almost constantly with excitement, were unexpectedly removed one day, an afternoon of a day soon after the one when she had fled from the piano in reasonless tears. Mother took her downtown. I was not allowed to go with them but was told once more to find someone else to play with. And my sister returned without her long copper curls. It was like a formal acknowledgment of the sorrowful differences and division which had haunted the house for some time. I noted as she came in the front door that she had now begun to imitate the walk of grown ladies, the graceful and quick and decorous steps of my mother, and that she kept her arms at her sides instead of flung out as if brushing curtains aside as she sprang forward in the abruptly lost days. But there was much more than that. When she entered the parlor, at the fading hour of the afternoon, it was as momentous as if brass horns had sounded, she wore such beauty. Mother came after her looking flushed with excitement and my grandmother descended the stairs with unusual lightness. They spoke in hushed voices. Astonishing, said my mother. She's like Isabel. This was the name of a sister of my father's who was a famed beauty in Knoxville. She was probably the one woman in the world of whom my mother was intimidated, and our occasional summer journeys to Knoxville from the Delta of Mississippi were like priestly tributes to a seat of holiness, for though my mother would certainly never make verbal acknowledgment of my aunt's superiority in matters of taste and definitions of quality, it was nevertheless apparent that she approached Knoxville and my father's younger sister in something very close to fear and trembling. Isabel had a flame, there was no doubt about it, a lambency which, once felt, would not fade from the eyes. It had an awful quality, as though it shone outward while it burned inward. And not long after the time of these recollections she was to die, quite abruptly and irrelevantly, as the result of the removal of an infected wisdom tooth, with her legend entrusted to various bewildered eyes and hearts and memories she had stamped, including mine, which have sometimes confused her with very dissimilar ladies. She is like Isabel, said my mother in a hushed voice. My grandmother did not admit that this was so. She also admired Isabel but thought her too interfering and was unable to separate her altogether from the excessively close blood-connection with my father, whom I should say, in passage, was a devilish man, possibly not understood but certainly hard to live with . . .

What I saw was not Isabel in my sister but a grown stranger whose beauty sharpened my sense of being alone. I saw that it was all over, put away in a box like a doll no longer cared for, the magical intimacy of our childhood together, the soap-bubble afternoons and the games with paper dolls cut out of dress catalogues and the breathless races here and there on our wheels. For the first time, yes, I saw her beauty. I consciously avowed it to myself, although it seems to me that I turned away from it, averted my look from the pride with which she strolled into the parlor and stood by the mantel mirror to be admired. And it was then, about that time, that I began to find life unsatisfactory as an explanation of itself and was forced to adopt the method of the artist of not explaining but putting the blocks together in some other way that seems more significant to him. Which is a rather fancy way of saying I started writing . . .

My sister also had a separate occupation which was her study of music, at first conducted under my grandmother's instruction but now entrusted to a professional teacher whose name was Miss Aehle, an almost typical spinster, who lived in a small frame house with a porch covered by moonvines and a fence covered by honeysuckle. Her name was pronounced *Ail*-ly. She supported herself and a paralyzed father by giving lessons in violin and piano, neither of which she played very well herself but for which she had great gifts as a teacher. If not great gifts, at least great enthusiasm. She was a true romanticist. She talked so excitedly that she got ahead of herself and looked bewildered and cried out, What was I saying? She was one of the innocents of the world, appreciated only by her pupils and a few persons a generation older than herself. Her pupils nearly always came to adore her, she gave them a feeling that playing little pieces on the piano or scratching out little tunes on a fiddle made up for everything that was ostensibly wrong in a world made by God but disarrayed by the devil. She was religious and ecstatic. She never admitted that anyone of her pupils, even the ones that were unmistakably tone-deaf, were deficient in musical talent. And the few that could perform tolerably well she was certain had genius. She had two real star pupils, my sister, on the piano, and a boy named Richard Miles who studied the violin. Her enthusiasm for these two was unbounded. It is true that my sister had a nice touch and that Richard Miles had a pure tone on the fiddle, but Miss Aehle dreamed of them in terms of playing duets to great ovations in the world's capital cities.

Richard Miles, I think of him now as a boy, for he was about seventeen, but at that time he seemed a complete adult to me, even immeasurably older than my sister who was fourteen. I resented him fiercely even though I began, almost immediately after learning of his existence, to dream about him as I had formerly dreamed of storybook heroes. His name began to inhabit the rectory. It was almost constantly on the lips of my sister, this strange young lady who had come to live with us. It had a curious lightness, that name, in the way that she spoke it. It did not seem to fall from her lips but to be released from them. The moment spoken, it rose into the air and shimmered and floated and took on gorgeous colors the way that soap bubbles did that we used to blow from the sunny back steps in the summer. Those bubbles lifted and floated and they eventually broke but never until other bubbles had floated beside them. Golden they were, and the name of Richard had a golden sound, too. The second name, being Miles, gave a suggestion of distance, so Richard was something both radiant and far away.

My sister's obsession with Richard may have been even more intense than mine. Since mine was copied from hers, it was probably hers that was greater in the beginning. But while mine was of a shy and sorrowful kind, involved with my sense of abandonment, hers at first seemed to be joyous. She had fallen in love. As always, I followed suit. But while love made her brilliant, at first, it made me laggard and dull. It filled me with sad confusion. It tied my tongue or made it stammer and it flashed so unbearably in my eyes that I had to turn them away. These are the intensities that one cannot live with, that he has to outgrow if he wants to survive. But who can help grieving for them? If the blood vessels could hold them, how much better to keep those early loves with us? But if we did, the veins would break and the passion explode into darkness long before the necessary time for it.

I remember one afternoon in fall when my sister and I were walking along a street when Richard Miles appeared suddenly before us from somewhere with a startling cry. I see him bounding, probably down the steps of Miss Aehle's white cottage, emerging unexpectedly from the vines. Probably Miss Aehle's because he bore his violin case, and I remember thinking how closely it resembled a little coffin, a coffin made for a small child or a doll. About people you knew in your childhood it is rarely possible to remember their appearance except as ugly or beautiful or light or dark. Richard was light and he was probably more beautiful than any boy I have seen since. I do not even remember if he was light in the sense of being blond or if the lightness came from a quality in him deeper than hair or skin. Yes, probably both, for he was one of those people who move in light, provided by practically everything about them. This detail I do remember. He wore a white shirt, and through its cloth could be seen the fair skin of his shoulders. And for the first time, prematurely, I was aware of skin as an attraction. A thing that might be desirable to touch. This awareness entered my mind, my senses, like the sudden streak of flame that follows a comet. And my undoing, already started by Richard's mere coming toward us, was now completed. When he turned to me and held his enormous hand out, I did a thing so grotesque that I could never afterwards be near him without a blistering sense of shame. Instead of taking the hand I ducked away from him. I made a mumbling sound that could have had very little resemblance to speech, and then brushed past their two figures, his and my beaming sister's, and fled into a drugstore just beyond.

That same fall the pupils of Miss Aehle performed in a concert. This concert was held in the parish house of my grandfather's church. And for weeks preceding it the pupils made preparation for the occasion which seemed as important as Christmas. My sister and Richard Miles were to play a duet, she on the piano, of course, and he on the violin. They practiced separately and they practiced together. Separately my sister played the piece very well, but for some reason, more portentous than it seemed at the time, she had great difficulty in playing to Richard's accompaniment. Suddenly her fingers would turn to thumbs, her wrists would flatten out and become cramped, her whole figure would hunch rigidly toward the piano and her beauty and grace would vanish. It was strange, but Miss Aehle was certain that it would be overcome with repeated practice. And Richard was patient, he was incredibly patient, he seemed to be far more concerned for my sister's sake than his own. Extra hours of practice were necessary. Sometimes when they had left Miss Aehle's, at the arrival of other pupils, they would continue at our house. The afternoons were consequently unsafe. I never knew when the front door might open on Richard's dreadful beauty and his greeting which I could not respond to, could not endure, must fly grotesquely away from. But the house was so arranged that although I hid in my bedroom at these hours of practice, I was still able to watch them at the piano. My bedroom looked out upon the staircase which descended into the parlor where they practiced. The piano was directly within my line of vision. It was in the parlor's lightest corner, with lace-curtained windows on either side of it, the sunlight only fretted by patterns of lace and ferns.

During the final week before the concert—or was it recital they called it?—Richard Miles came over almost invariably at four in the afternoon, which was the last hour of really good sunlight in late October. And always a little before that time I would lower the green blind in my bedroom and with a fantastic stealth, as if a sound would betray a disgusting action, I would open the door two inches, an aperture just enough to enclose the piano corner as by the lateral boundaries of a stage. When I heard them enter the front door, or even before, when I saw their shadows thrown against the oval glass and curtain the door surrounded or heard their voices as they climbed to the porch, I would flatten myself on my belly on the cold floor and remain in that position as long as they stayed, no matter how my knees or elbows ached, and I was so fearful of betraying this watch that I kept over them while they practiced that I hardly dared to breathe.

The transference of my interest to Richard now seemed complete. I would barely notice my sister at the piano, groan at her repeated blunders only in sympathy for him. When I recall what a little puritan I was in those days, there must have been a shocking ambivalence in my thoughts and sensations as I gazed down upon him through the crack of the door. How on earth did I explain to myself, at that time, the fascination of his physical being without, at the same time, confessing to myself that I was a little monster of sensuality? Or was that actually before I had begun to associate the sensual with the impure, an error that tortured me during and after pubescence, or did I, and this seems most likely, now, say to myself, Yes, Tom, you're a monster! But that's how it is and there's nothing to be done about it. And so continued to feast my eyes on his beauty. This much is certain. Whatever resistance there may have been from the "legion of decency" in my soul was exhausted in the first skirmish, not exterminated but thoroughly trounced, and its subsequent complaints were in the form of unseen blushes. Not that there was really anything to be ashamed of in adoring the beauty of Richard. It was surely made for that purpose, and boys of my age made to be stirred by such ideals of grace. The sheer white cloth in which I had originally seen his upper body was always worn by it, and now, in those afternoons, because of the position of the piano between two windows that cast their beams at cross angles, the white material became diaphanous with light, the torso shone through it, faintly pink and silver, the nipples on the chest and the armpits a little darker, and the diaphragm visibly pulsing as he breathed. It is possible that I have seen more graceful bodies, but I am not sure that I have, and his remains, I believe, a subconscious standard. And looking back upon him now, and upon the devout little mystic of carnality that I was as I crouched on a chill bedroom floor, I think of Camilla Rucellai, that highstrung mystic of Florence who is supposed to have seen Pico della Mirandola entering the streets of that city on a milkwhite horse in a storm of sunlight and flowers, and to have fainted at the spectacle of him, and murmured, as she revived, *He will pass in the time of lilies!* meaning that he would die early, since nothing so fair could decline by common degrees in a faded season. The light was certainly there in all its fullness, and even a kind of flowers, at least shadows of them, for there were flowers of lace in the window curtains and actual branches of fern which the light projected across him; no storm of flowers but the shadows of flowers which are perhaps more fitting.

The way that he lifted and handled his violin! First he would roll up the sleeves of his white shirt and remove his necktie and loosen his collar as though he were making preparations for love. Then there was a metallic snap as he released the lock on the case of the violin. Then the upper lid was pushed back and the sunlight fell on the dazzling interior of the case. It was plush-lined and the plush was emerald. The violin itself was somewhat darker than blood and even more lustrous. To Richard I think it must have seemed more precious. His hands and his arms as he lifted it from the case, they said the word love more sweetly than speech could say it, and, oh, what precocious fantasies their grace and tenderness would excite in me. I was a wounded soldier, the youngest of the regiment and he, Richard, was my young officer, jeopardizing his life to lift me from the field where I had fallen and carry me back to safety in the same cradle of arms that supported his violin now. The dreams, perhaps, went further, but I have already dwelt sufficiently upon the sudden triumph of unchastity back of my burning eyes; that needs no more annotation . . .

I now feel some anxiety that this story will seem to be losing itself like a path that has climbed a hill and then lost itself in an overgrowth of brambles. For I have now told you all but one of the things that stand out very clearly, and yet I have not approached any sort of conclusion. There is, of course, a conclusion. However indefinite, there always is some point which serves that need of remembrances and stories.

The remaining very clear thing is the evening of the recital in mid-November, but before an account of that, I should tell more of my sister in this troubled state of hers. It might be possible to willfully thrust myself into her mind, her emotions, but I question the wisdom of it: for at that time I was an almost hostile onlooker where she was concerned. Hurt feelings and jealous feelings were too thickly involved in my view of her at that time. As though she were being punished for a betrayal of our childhood companionship, I felt a gratification tinged with contempt at her difficulties in the duet with Richard. One evening I overheard a telephone call which mother received from Miss Aehle. Miss Aehle was first perplexed and now genuinely alarmed and totally mystified by the sudden decline of my sister's vaunted aptitude for the piano. She had been singing her praises for months. Now it appeared that my sister was about to disgrace her publicly, for she was not only unable, suddenly, to learn new pieces but was forgetting the old ones. It had been planned, originally, for her to play several solo numbers at the recital before and leading up to the duet with Richard. The solos now had to be canceled from the program, and Miss Aehle was even fearful that my sister would not be able to perform in the duet. She wondered if my mother could think of some reason why my sister had undergone this very inopportune and painful decline? Was she sleeping badly, how was her appetite, was she very moody? Mother came away from the telephone in a very cross humor with the teacher. She repeated all the complaints and apprehensions and questions to my grandmother who said nothing but pursed her lips and shook her head while she sewed like one of those venerable women who understand and govern the fates of mortals, but she had nothing to offer in the way of a practical solution except to say that perhaps it was a mistake for brilliant children to be pushed into things like this so early . . .

Richard stayed patient with her most of the time, and there were occasional periods of revival, when she would attack the piano with an explosion of confidence and the melodies would surge beneath her fingers like birds out of cages. Such a resurgence would never last till the end of a piece. There would be a stumble, and then another collapse. Once Richard himself was unstrung. He pushed his violin high into the air like a broom sweeping cobwebs off the ceiling. He strode around the parlor brandishing it like that and uttering groans that were both sincere and comic; when he returned to the piano, where she crouched in dismay, he took hold of her shoulders and gave them a shake. She burst into tears and would have fled upstairs but he caught hold of her by the newel post of the staircase. He would not let go of her. He detained her with murmurs I couldn't quite hear, and drew her gently back to the piano corner. And then he sat down on the piano stool with his great hands gripping each side of her narrow waist while she sobbed with her face averted and her fingers knotting together. And while I watched them from my cave of darkness, my body learned, at least three years too early, the fierceness and fire of the will of life to transcend the single body, and so to continue to follow light's curve and time's . . .

The evening of the recital my sister complained at supper that her hands were stiff, and she kept rubbing them together and even held them over the spout of the teapot to warm them with the steam. She looked very pretty, I remember, when she was dressed. Her color was higher than I had ever seen it, but there were tiny beads of sweat at her temples and she ordered me angrily out of her room when I appeared in the doorway before she was ready to pass the family's inspection. She wore silver slippers and a very grownup-looking dress that was the greenish sea-color of her eyes. It had the low waist that was fashionable at that time and there were silver beads on it in loops and fringes. Her bedroom was steaming from the adjoining bath. She opened the window. Grandmother slammed it down, declaring that she would catch cold. Oh, leave me alone, she answered. The muscles in her throat were curiously prominent as she stared in the glass. Stop powdering, said my grandmother, you're caking your face with powder. Well, it's my face, she retorted. And then came near to flying into a tantrum at some small critical comment offered by Mother. I have no talent, she said, I have no talent for music! Why do I have to do it, why do you make me, why was I forced into this? Even my grandmother finally gave up and retired from the room. But when it came time to leave for the parish house, my sister came downstairs looking fairly collected and said not another word as we made our departure. Once in the automobile she whispered something about her hair being mussed. She kept her stiff hands knotted in her lap. We drove first to Miss Aehle's and found her in a state of hysteria because Richard had fallen off a bicycle that afternoon and skinned his fingers. She was sure it would hinder his playing. But when we arrived at the parish house,

Richard was already there as calm as a duckpond, playing delicately with the mute on the strings and no apparent disability. We left them, teacher and performers, in the cloakroom and went to take our seats in the auditorium which was beginning to fill, and I remember noticing a half-erased inscription on a blackboard which had something to do with a Sunday School lesson.

No, it did not go off well. They played without sheet music, and my sister made all the mistakes she had made in practicing and several new ones. She could not seem to remember the composition beyond the first few pages; it was a fairly long one, and those pages she repeated twice, possibly even three times. But Richard was heroic. He seemed to anticipate every wrong note that she struck and to bring down his bow on the strings with an extra strength to cover and rectify it. When she began to lose control altogether, I saw him edging up closer to her position, so that his radiant figure shielded her partly from view, and I saw him, at a crucial moment, when it seemed that the duet might collapse altogether, raise his bow high in the air, at the same time catching his breath in a sort of "Hah!" a sound I heard much later from bullfighters daring a charge, and lower it to the strings in a masterful sweep that took the lead from my sister and plunged them into the passage that she had forgotten in her panic. . . . For a bar or two, I think, she stopped playing, sat there motionless, stunned. And then, finally, when he turned his back to the audience and murmured something to her, she started again. She started playing again but Richard played so brilliantly and so richly that the piano was barely noticeable underneath him. And so they got through it, and when it was finished they received an ovation. My sister started to rush for the cloakroom. But Richard seized her wrist and held her back. Then something odd happened. Instead of bowing she suddenly turned and pressed her forehead against him, pressed it against the lapel of his blue serge suit. He blushed and bowed and touched her waist with his fingers, gently, his eyes glancing down . . .

We drove home in silence, almost. There was a conspiracy to ignore that anything unfortunate had happened. My sister said nothing. She sat with her hands knotted in her lap exactly as she had been before the recital, and when I looked at her I noticed that her shoulders were too narrow and her mouth a little too wide for real beauty, and that her recent habit of hunching made her seem a little bit like an old lady being imitated by a child.

At that point Richard Miles faded out of our lives for my sister refused to continue to study music, and not long afterwards my father received an advancement, an office job as a minor executive in a northern shoe company, and we moved from the South. No, I am not putting all of these things in their exact chronological order, I may as well confess it, but if I did I would violate my honor as a teller of stories . . .

As for Richard, the truth is exactly congruous to the poem. A year or so later we learned, in that northern city to which we had moved, that he had died of pneumonia. And then I remembered the case of his violin, and how it resembled so much a little black coffin made for a child or a doll . . .

October 1949 (Published 1950)

Two on a Party

He couldn't really guess the age of the woman, Cora, but she was certainly not any younger than he, and he was almost thirty-five. There were some mornings when he thought she looked, if he wasn't flattering himself, almost old enough to be his mother, but there were evenings when the liquor was hitting her right, when her eyes were lustrous and her face becomingly flushed, and then she looked younger than he. As you get to know people, if you grow to like them, they begin to seem younger to you. The cruelty or damaging candor of the first impression is washed away like the lines in a doctored photograph, and Billy no longer remembered that the first night he met her he had thought of her as "an old bag." Of course, that night when he first met her she was not looking her best. It was in a Broadway bar; she was occupying the stool next to Billy and she had lost a diamond ear-clip and was complaining excitedly about it to the barman. She kept ducking down like a diving seal to look for it among the disgusting refuse under the brass rail, bobbing up and down and grunting and complaining, her face inflamed and swollen by the exertion, her rather heavy figure doubled into ludicrous positions. Billy had the uncomfortable feeling that she suspected him of stealing the diamond ear-clip. Each time she glanced at him his face turned hot. He always had that guilty feeling when anything valuable was lost, and it made him angry; he thought of her as an irritating old bag. Actually she wasn't accusing anybody of stealing the diamond ear-clip; in fact she kept assuring the barman that the clasp on the ear-clip was loose and she was a goddam fool to put it on.

Then Billy found the thing for her, just as he was about to leave the bar, embarrassed and annoyed beyond endurance; he noticed the sparkle of it almost under his shoe, the one on the opposite side from the ducking and puffing "old bag." With the sort of schoolteacherish austerity that he assumed when annoyed, when righteously indignant over something, an air that he had picked up during his short, much earlier, career as an English instructor at a midwestern university, he picked up the clip and slammed it wordlessly down on the bar in front of her and started to walk away. Two things happened to detain him. Three sailors off a Norwegian vessel came one, two, three through the revolving door of the bar and headed straight for the vacant stools just beyond where he had been sitting, and at the same instant, the woman, Cora, grabbed hold of his arm, shouting, Oh, don't go, don't go, the least you can do is let me buy you a drink! And so he had turned right around, as quickly and precisely as the revolving door through which the glittering trio of Norsemen had entered. Okay, why not? He resumed his seat beside her, she bought him a drink, he bought her a drink, inside of five minutes they were buying beer for the sailors and it was just as if the place was suddenly lit up by a dozen big chandeliers.

Quickly she looked different to him, not an old bag at all but really sort of attractive and obviously more to the taste of the dazzling Norsemen than Billy could be. Observing the two of them in the long bar mirror, himself and Cora, he saw that they looked good together, they made a good pair, they were mutually advantageous as a team for cruising the Broadway bars. She was a good deal darker than he and more heavily built. Billy was slight and he had very blond skin that the sun turned pink. Unfortunately for Billy, the pink also showed through the silky, thin yellow hair on the crown of his head where the baldness, so fiercely but impotently resisted, was now becoming a fact that he couldn't disown. Of course, the crown of the head doesn't show in the mirror unless you bow to your image in the glass, but there is no denying that the top of a queen's head is a conspicuous area on certain occasions which are not unimportant. That was how he put it, laughing about it to Cora. She said, Honey, I swear to Jesus I think you're more self-conscious about your looks and your age than I am! She said it kindly, in fact, she said everything kindly. Cora was a kind person. She was the kindest person that Billy had ever met. She said and meant everything kindly, literally everything; she hadn't a single malicious bone in her body, not a particle of jealousy or suspicion or evil in her nature, and that was what made it so sad that Cora was a lush. Yes, after he stopped thinking of her as "an old bag," which was almost immediately after they got acquainted, he started thinking of Cora as a lush, kindly, yes, but not as kindly as Cora thought about him, for Billy was not, by nature, as kind as Cora. Nobody else could be. Her kindness was monumental, the sort that simply doesn't exist any more, at least not in the queen world.

Fortunately for Billy, Billy was fairly tall. He had formed the defensive habit of holding his head rather high so that the crown of it wouldn't be so noticeable in bars, but unfortunately for Billy, he had what doctors had told him was a calcium deposit in the ears which made him hard of hearing and which could only be corrected by a delicate and expensive operation—boring a hole in the bone. He didn't have much money; he had just saved enough to live, not frugally but carefully, for two or three more years before he would have to go back to work at something. If he had the ear operation, he would have to go back to work right away and so abandon his sybaritic existence which suited him better than the dubious glory of being a somewhat better than hack writer of Hollywood film scenarios and so forth. Yes, and so forth!

Being hard of hearing, in fact, progressively so, he would have to crouch over and bend sidewise a little to hold a conversation in a bar, that is, if he wanted to understand what the other party was saying. In a bar it's dangerous not to listen to the other party, because the way of speaking is just as important as the look of the face in distinguishing between good trade and dirt, and Billy did not at all enjoy being beaten as some queens do. So he would have to bend sidewise and expose the almost baldness on the crown of his blond head, and he would cringe and turn red instead of pink with embarrassment as he did so. He knew that it was ridiculous of him to be that sensitive about it. But as he said to Cora, age does worse things to a queen than it does to a woman.

She disagreed about that and they had great arguments about it. But it was a subject on which Billy could hold forth as eloquently as a southern Senator making a filibuster against the repeal of the poll tax, and Cora would lose the argument by default, simply not able to continue it any longer, for Cora did not like gloomy topics of conversation so much as Billy liked them.

About her own defects of appearance, however, Cora was equally distressed and humble.

You see, she would tell him, I'm really a queen myself. I mean it's the same difference, honey, I like and do the same things, sometimes I think in bed if they're drunk enough they don't even know I'm a woman, at least they don't act like they do, and I don't blame them.

Look at me, I'm a mess. I'm getting so heavy in the hips and I've got these big udders on me!

Nonsense, Billy would protest, you have a healthy and beautiful female body, and you mustn't low-rate yourself all the time that way, I won't allow it!

And he would place his arm about her warm and Florida-sun-browned shoulders, exposed by her backless white gown (the little woolly-looking canary yellow jacket being deposited on a vacant bar stool beside her), for it was usually quite late, almost time for the bars to close, when they began to discuss what the years had done to them, the attritions of time. Beside Billy, too, there would be a vacant bar stool on which he had placed the hat that concealed his thinning hair from the streets. It would be one of those evenings that gradually wear out the exhilaration you start with. It would be one of those evenings when lady luck showed the bitchy streak in her nature. They would have had one or two promising encounters which had fizzled out, coming to a big fat zero at three A.M. In the game they played, the true refinement of torture is to almost pull in a catch and then the line breaks, and when that happens, each not pitying himself as much as he did the other, they would sit out the final hour before closing, talking about the wicked things time had done to them, the gradual loss of his hearing and his hair, the fatty expansion of her breasts and buttocks, forgetting that they were still fairly attractive people and still not old.

Actually, in the long run their luck broke about fifty-fifty. Just about every other night one or the other of them would be successful in the pursuit of what Billy called "the lyric quarry." One or the other or both might be successful on the good nights, and if it was a really good night, then both would be. Good nights, that is, really good nights, were by no means as rare as hen's teeth, nor were they as frequent as streetcars, but they knew very well, both of them, that they did better together than they had done separately in the past. They set off something warm and good in each other that strangers responded to with something warm and good in themselves. Loneliness dissolved any reserve and suspicion, the night was a great warm comfortable meeting of people, it shone, it radiated, it had the effect of a dozen big chandeliers, oh, it was great, it was grand, you simply couldn't describe it, you got the colored lights going, and there it all was, the final pattern of it and the original pattern, all put together, made to fit exactly, no, there were simply no words good enough to describe it. And if the worst happened, if someone who looked like a Botticelli angel drew a knife, or if the law descended suddenly on you, and those were eventualities the possibility of which a queen must always consider, you still could say you'd had a good run for your money.

Like everyone whose life is conditioned by luck, they had some brilliant streaks of it and some that were dismal. For instance, that first week they operated together in Manhattan. That was really a freak; you couldn't expect a thing like that to happen twice in a lifetime. The trade was running as thick as spawning salmon up those narrow cataracts in the Rockies. Head to tail, tail to head, crowding, swarming together, seemingly driven along by some immoderate instinct. It was not a question of catching; it was simply a question of deciding which ones to keep and which to throw back in the stream, all glittering, all swift, all flowing one way which was toward you!

That week was in Manhattan, where they teamed up. It was, to be exact, in Emerald Joe's at the corner of Forty-second and Broadway that they had met each other the night of the lost diamond clip that Billy had found. It was the week of the big blizzard and the big Chinese Red offensive in North Korea. The combination seemed to make for a wildness in the air, and trade is always best when the atmosphere of a city is excited whether it be over a national election or New Year's or a championship prizefight or the World Series baseball games; anything that stirs up the whole population makes it better for cruising.

Yes, it was a lucky combination of circumstances, and that first week together had been brilliant. It was before they started actually living together. At that time, she had a room at the Hotel Pennsylvania and he had one at the Astor. But at the end of that week, the one of their first acquaintance, they gave up separate establishments and took a place together at a small East Side hotel in the Fifties, because of the fact that Cora had an old friend from her hometown in Louisiana employed there as the night clerk. This one was a gay one that she had known long ago and innocently expected to be still the same. Cora did not understand how some people turn bitter. She had never turned bitchy and it was not understandable to her that others might. She said this friend on the desk was a perfect setup; he'd be delighted to see them bringing in trade. But that was the way in which it failed to work out . . .

That second week in New York was not a good one. Cora had been exceeding her usual quota of double ryes on the rocks and it began all at once to tell on her appearance. Her system couldn't absorb any more; she had reached the saturation point, and it was no longer possible for her to pick herself up in the evenings. Her face had a bloated look and her eyes remained bloodshot all the time. They looked, as she said, like a couple of poached eggs in a sea of blood, and Billy had to agree with her that they did. She started looking her oldest and she had the shakes.

Then about Friday of that week the gay one at the desk turned bitchy on them. Billy had expected him to turn, but Cora hadn't. Sooner or later, Billy knew, that frustrated queen was bound to get a severe attack of jaundice over the fairly continual coming and going of so much close-fitting blue wool, and Billy was not mistaken. When they brought their trade in, he would slam down the key without looking at them or speaking a word of greeting. Then one night they brought in a perfectly divine-looking pharmacist's mate of Italian extraction and his almost equally attractive buddy. The old friend of Cora's exploded, went off like a spit-devil.

I'm sorry, he hissed, but this is *not* a flea-bag! You should have stayed on Times Square where you started.

There was a scene. He refused to give them their room key unless the two sailors withdrew from the lobby. Cora said, Fuck you, Mary, and reached across the desk and grabbed the key from the hook. The old friend seized her wrist and tried to make her let go.

Put that key down, he shrieked, or you'll be sorry!

He started twisting her wrist; then Billy hit him; he vaulted right over the desk and knocked the son-of-a-bitch into the switchboard.

Call the police, call the police, the clerk screamed to the porter.

Drunk as she was, Cora suddenly pulled herself together. She took as much command of the situation as could be taken.

You boys wait outside, she said to the sailors, there's no use in you all getting into S.P. trouble.

One of them, the Italian, wanted to stay and join in the roughhouse, but his buddy, who was the bigger one, forcibly removed him to the sidewalk. (Cora and Billy never saw them again.) By that time, Billy had the night clerk by the collar and was giving him slaps that bobbed his head right and left like something rubber, as if that night clerk was everything that he loathed in a hostile world. Cora stopped him. She had that wonderful, that really invaluable faculty of sobering up in a crisis. She pulled Billy off her old friend and tipped the colored porter ten dollars not to call in the law. She turned on all her southern charm and sweetness, trying to straighten things out. You darling, she said, you poor darling, to the bruised night clerk. The law was not called, but the outcome of the situation was far from pleasant. They had to check out, of course, and the hysterical old friend said he was going to write Cora's family in Alexandria, Louisiana, and give them a factual report on how she was living here in New York and how he supposed she was living anywhere else since she'd left home and he knew her.

At that time Billy knew almost nothing about Cora's background and former life, and he was surprised at her being so upset over this hysterical threat, which seemed unimportant to him. But all the next day Cora kept alluding to it, speculating whether or not the bitch would really do it, and it was probably on account of this threat that Cora made up her mind to leave New York. It was the only time, while they were living together, that Cora ever made a decision, at least about places to go and when to go to them. She had none of that desire to manage and dominate which is a typically American perversion of the female nature. As Billy said to himself, with that curious harshness of his toward things he loved, she was like a big piece of seaweed. Sometimes he said it irritably to himself, just like a big piece of seaweed washing this way and that way. It isn't healthy or normal to be so passive, Billy thought.

Where do you want to eat?

I don't care.

No, tell me, Cora, what place would you prefer?

I really don't care, she'd insist, it makes no difference to me.

Sometimes out of exasperation he would say, All right, let's eat at the Automat.

Only then would Cora demur.

Of course, if you want to, honey, but couldn't we eat some place with a liquor license?

She was agreeable to anything and everything; she seemed to be grateful for any decision made for her, but this one time, when they left New York, when they made their first trip together, it was Cora's decision to go. This was before Billy began to be terribly fond of Cora, and at first, when Cora said, Honey, I've got to leave this town or Hugo (the hotel queen) will bring up Bobo (her brother who was a lawyer in Alexandria and who had played some very unbrotherly legal trick on her when a certain inheritance was settled) and there will be hell to pay, he will freeze up my income—then, at this point, Billy assumed that they would go separate ways. But at the last moment Billy discovered that he didn't want to go back to a stag existence. He discovered that solitary cruising had been lonely, that there were spiritual comforts as well as material advantages in their double arrangement. No matter how bad luck was, there was no longer such a thing as going home by himself to the horrors of a second- or third-class hotel bedroom. Then there *were* the material advantages, the fact they actually did better operating together, and the fact that it was more economical. Billy had to be somewhat mean about money since he was living on savings that he wanted to stretch as far as he could, and Cora more than carried her own weight in the expense department. She was only too eager to pick up a check and Billy was all too willing to let her do it. She spoke of her income but she was vague about what it was or came from. Sometimes looking into her handbag she had a fleeting expression of worry that made Billy wonder uncomfortably if her finances, like his, might not be continually dwindling toward an eventual point of eclipse. But neither of them had a provident nature or dared to stop and consider much of the future.

Billy was a light traveler, all he carried with him was a three-suiter, a single piece of hand luggage and his portable typewriter. When difficulties developed at a hotel, he could clear out in five minutes or less. He rubbed his chin for a minute, then he said, Cora, how about me going with you?

They shared a compartment on the Sunshine Special to Florida. Why to Florida? One of Cora's very few pretensions was a little command of French; she was fond of using little French phrases which she pronounced badly. Honey, she said, I have a little *pied-à-terre* in Florida.

Pied-à-terre was one of those little French phrases that she was proud of using, and she kept talking about it, her little *pied-à-terre* in the Sunshine State.

Whereabouts is it, Billy asked her.

No place fashionable, she told him, but just you wait and see and you might be surprised and like it.

That night in the shared compartment of the Pullman was the first time they had sex together. It happened casually, it was not important and it was not very satisfactory, perhaps because they were each too anxious to please the other, each too afraid the other would be disappointed. Sex has to be slightly selfish to have real excitement. Start worrying about the other party's reactions and the big charge just isn't there, and you've got to do it a number of times together before it becomes natural enough to be a completely satisfactory thing. The first time between strangers can be like a blaze of light, but when it happens between people who know each other well and have an established affection, it's likely to be self-conscious and even a little embarrassing, most of all afterwards.

Afterwards they talked about it with a slight sense of strain. They felt they had gotten that sort of thing squared away and would not have to think about it between them again. But perhaps, in a way, it did add a little something to the intimacy of their living together; at least it had, as they put it, squared things away a bit. And they talked about it shyly, each one trying too hard to flatter the other.

Gee, honey, said Cora, you're a wonderful lay, you've got wonderful skin, smooth as a baby's, gee, it sure was wonderful, honey, I enjoyed it so much, I wish you had. But I know you didn't like it and it was selfish of me to start it with you.

You didn't like it, he said.

I swear I *loved* it, she said, but I knew that *you* didn't like it, so we won't do it again.

He told Cora that she was a wonderful lay and that he had loved it every bit as much as she did and maybe more, but he agreed they'd better not do it again.

Friends can't be lovers, he said.

No, they can't, she agreed with a note of sadness.

Then jealousy enters in.

Yes, they get jealous and bitchy . . .

They never did it again, at least not that completely, not any time during the year and two months since they started living together. Of course, there were some very drunk, *blind* drunk nights when they weren't quite sure what happened between them after they fell into bed, but you could be pretty certain it wasn't a sixty-six in that condition. Sixty-six was Cora's own slightly inexact term for a normal lay, that is, a lay that occurred in the ordinary position.

What happened? Billy would ask when she'd had a party.

Oh, it was wonderful, she would exclaim, a sixty-six!

Good Jesus, drunk as he was?

Oh, I sobered him up, she'd laugh.

And what did you do, Billy? Take the sheets? Ha ha, you'll have to leave this town with a board nailed over your ass!

Sometimes they had a serious conversation, though most of the time they tried to keep the talk on a frivolous plane. It troubled Cora to talk about serious matters, probably because matters were too serious to be talked about with comfort. And for the first month or so neither of them knew that the other one actually had a mind that you could talk to. Gradually they discovered about each other the other things, and although it was always their mutual pursuit, endless and indefatigable, of "the lyric quarry" that was the mainstay of their relationship, at least upon its surface, the other things, the timid and tender values that can exist between people, began to come shyly out and they had a respect for each other, not merely to like and enjoy, as neither had ever respected another person.

It was a rare sort of moral anarchy, doubtless, that held them together, a really fearful shared hatred of everything that was restrictive and which they felt to be false in the society they lived in and against the grain of which they continually operated. They did not dislike what they called "squares." They loathed and despised them, and for the best of reasons. Their existence was a never-ending contest with the squares of the world, the squares who have such a virulent rage at everything not in their book. Getting around the squares, evading, defying the phony rules of convention, that was maybe responsible for half their pleasure in their outlaw existence. They were a pair of kids playing cops and robbers; except for that element, the thrill of something lawless, they probably would have gotten bored with cruising. Maybe not, maybe so. Who can tell? But hotel clerks and house dicks and people in adjoining hotel bedrooms, the specter of Cora's family in Alexandria, Louisiana, the specter of Billy's family in Montgomery, Alabama, the various people involved in the niggardly control of funds, almost everybody that you passed when you were drunk and hilariously gay on the street, especially all those bull-like middle-aged couples that stood off sharply and glared at you as you swept through a hotel lobby with your blushing trade—all, all, all of those were natural enemies to them, as well as the one great terrible, worst of all enemies, which is the fork-tailed, cloven-hoofed, pitchfork-bearing devil of Time!

Time, of course, was the greatest enemy of all, and they knew that each day and each night was cutting down a little on the distance between the two of them running together and that demon pursuer. And knowing it, knowing that nightmarish fact, gave a wild sort of sweetness of despair to their two-ring circus.

And then, of course, there was also the fact that Billy was, or had been at one time, a sort of artist *manqué* and still had a touch of homesickness for what that was.

Sometime, said Cora, you're going to get off the party.

Why should I get off the party?

Because you're a serious person. You are fundamentally a serious sort of a person.

I'm not a serious person any more than you are. I'm a goddam remittance man and you know it.

No, I don't know it, said Cora. Remittance men get letters enclosing checks, but you don't even get letters.

Billy rubbed his chin.

Then how do you think I live?

Ha ha, she said.

What does 'Ha Ha' mean?

It means I know what I know!

Balls, said Billy, you know no more about me than I do about you.

I know, said Cora, that you used to write for a living, and that for two years you haven't been writing but you're still living on the money you made as a writer, and sooner or later, you're going to get off the party and go back to working again and being a serious person. What do you imagine I think of that portable typewriter you drag around with you everywhere we go, and that big fat portfolio full of papers you tote underneath your shirts in your three-suiter? I wasn't born yesterday or the day before yesterday, baby, and I know that you're going to get off the party some day and leave me on it.

If I get off the party, we'll get off it together, said Billy.

And me do *what?* she'd ask him, realistically.

And he would not be able to answer that question. For she knew and he knew, both of them knew it together, that they would remain together only so long as they stayed on the party, and not any longer than that. And in his heart he knew, much as he might deny it, that it would be pretty much as Cora predicted in her Cassandra moods. One of those days or nights it was bound to happen. He would get off the party, yes, he would certainly be the one of them to get off it, because there was really nothing for Cora to do but stay on it. Of course, if she broke down, that would take her off it. Usually or almost always it's only a breakdown that takes you off a party. A party is like a fast-moving train—you can't jump off it, it thunders past the stations you might get off at, very few people have the courage to leap from a thing that is moving that fast, they have to stay with it no matter where it takes them. It only stops when it crashes, the ticker wears out, a blood vessel bursts, the liver or kidneys quit working. But Cora was tough. Her system had absorbed a lot of punishment, but from present appearances it was going to absorb a lot more. She was too tough to crack up any time soon, but she was not tough enough to make the clean break, the daring jump off, that Billy knew, or felt that he knew, that he was still able to make when he was ready to make it. Cora was five or maybe even ten years older than Billy. She rarely looked it, but she was that much older and time is one of the biggest differences between two people.

I've got news for you, baby, and you had better believe it.

What news?

This news, Cora would say. You're going to get off the party and leave me on it!

Well, it was probably true, as true as anything is, and what a pity it was that Cora was such a grand person. If she had not been such a nice person, so nice that at first you thought it must be phony and only gradually came to see it was real, it wouldn't matter so much. For usually queens fall out like a couple of thieves quarreling over the split of the loot. Billy remembered the one in Baton Rouge who was so annoyed when he confiscated a piece she had a lech for that she made of Billy an effigy of candle wax and stuck pins in it with dreadful imprecations, kept the candle-wax effigy on her mantel and performed black rites before it. But Cora was not like that. She didn't have a jealous bone in her body. She took as much pleasure in Billy's luck as her own. Sometimes he suspected she was more interested in Billy having good luck than having it herself.

Sometimes Billy would wonder. Why do we do it?

We're lonely people, she said, I guess it's as simple as that . . .

But nothing is ever quite so simple as it appears when you are comfortably loaded.

Take this occasion, for instance.

Billy and Cora are traveling by motor. The automobile is a joint possession which they acquired from a used car dealer in Galveston. It is a '47 Buick convertible with a brilliant new scarlet paint job. Cora and Billy are outfitted with corresponding brilliance; she has on a pair of black and white checked slacks, a cowboy shirt with a bucking broncho over one large breast and a roped steer over the other, and she has on harlequin sun-glasses with false diamonds encrusting the rims. Her freshly peroxided hair is bound girlishly on top of her head with a diaphanous scarf of magenta chiffon; she has on her diamond ear-clips and her multiple slave bracelets, three of them real gold and two of them only gold-plated, and hundreds of little tinkling gold attachments, such as tiny footballs, liberty bells, hearts, mandolins, choo-choos, sleds, tennis rackets, and so forth. Billy thinks she has overdone it a little. It must be admitted, however, that she is a noticeable person, especially at the wheel of this glittering scarlet Roadmaster. They have swept down the Camino Real, the Old Spanish Trail, from El Paso eastward instead of westward, having decided at the last moment to resist the allure of Southern California on the other side of the Rockies and the desert, since it appears that the Buick has a little tendency to overheat and Cora notices that the oil pressure is not what it should be. So they have turned eastward instead of westward, with a little side trip to Corpus Christi to investigate the fact or fancy of those legendary seven connecting glory-holes in a certain tearoom there. It turned out to be fancy or could not be located. Says Cora: You queens know places but never know where places are!

A blowout going into New Orleans. That's to be expected, said Cora, they never give you good rubber. The spare is no good either. Two new tires had to be bought in New Orleans and Cora paid for them by hocking some of her baubles. There was some money left over and she buys Billy a pair of cowboy boots. They are still on the Wild West kick. Billy also presents a colorful appearance in a pair of blue jeans that fit as if they had been painted on him, the fancily embossed cowboy boots and a sport shirt that is covered with leaping dolphins, Ha Ha! They have never had so much fun in their life together, the colored lights are going like pinwheels on the Fourth of July, everything is big and very bright celebration. The Buick appears to be a fairly solid investment, once it has good rubber on it and they get those automatic devices to working again . . .

It is a mechanical age that we live in, they keep saying.

They did Mobile, Pensacola, West Palm Beach and Miami in one continual happy breeze! The scoreboard is brilliant! Fifteen lays, all hitching rides on the highway, since they got the convertible. It's all we ever needed to hit the jackpot, Billy exults . . .

Then comes the badman into the picture!

They are on the Florida keys, just about midway between the objective, Key West, and the tip of the peninsula. Nothing is visible about them but sky and mangrove swamp. Then all of a sudden that used car dealer in Galveston pulls the grinning joker out of his sleeve. Under the hood of the car comes a loud metallic noise as if steel blades are scraping. The fancy heap will not take the gas. It staggers gradually to a stop, and trying to start it again succeeds only in running the battery down. Moreover, the automatic top has ceased to function; it is the meridian of a day in early spring which is as hot as midsummer on the Florida keys . . .

Cora would prefer to make light of the situation, if Billy would let her do so. The compartment of the dashboard is filled with roadmaps, a flashlight and a thermos of dry martinis. The car has barely uttered its expiring rattle and gasp when Cora's intensely ornamented arm reaches out for this unfailing simplification of the human dilemma. For the first time in their life together, Billy interferes with her drinking, and out of pure meanness. He grabs her wrist and restrains her. He is suddenly conscious of how disgusted he is with what he calls her Oriental attitude toward life. The purchase of this hoax was her idea. Two thirds of the investment was also her money. Moreover she had professed to be a pretty good judge of motors. Billy himself had frankly confessed that he couldn't tell a spark plug from a carburetor. So it was Cora who had examined and appraised the possible buys on the used car lots of Galveston and come upon this 'bargain'! She had looked under the hoods and shimmied fatly under the chassis of dozens of cars before she arrived at this remarkably misguided choice. The car had been suspiciously cheap for a '47 Roadmaster with such a brilliantly smart appearance, but Cora said it was just as sound as the American dollar! She put a thousand dollars into the deal and Billy put in five hundred which had come in from the resale to pocket editions of a lurid potboiler he had written under a pseudonym a number of years ago when he was still an active member of the literary profession.

Now Cora was reaching into the dashboard compartment for a thermos of martinis because the car whose purchase was her responsibility had collapsed in the middle of nowhere . . .

Billy seizes her wrist and twists it.

Let go of that goddam thermos, you're not gonna get drunk!

She struggles with him a little, but soon she gives up and suddenly goes feminine and starts to cry.

After that a good while passes in which they sit side by side in silence in the leather-lined crematorium of the convertible.

A humming sound begins to be heard in the distance. Perhaps it's a motorboat on the other side of the mangroves, perhaps something on the highway . . .

Cora begins to jingle and jangle as she twists her ornamented person this way and that way with nervous henlike motions of the head and shoulder and torso, peering about on both sides and half rising and flopping awkwardly back down again, and finally grunting eagerly and piling out of the car, losing her balance, sprawling into a ditch, ha ha, scrambling up again, taking the middle of the road and making great frantic circles with her arms as a motorcycle approaches. If the cyclist had desired to pass them it would have been hardly possible. Later Billy will remind her that it was *she* who stopped it. But right now Billy is enchanted, not merely at the prospect of a rescue but much more by the looks of the potential instrument of rescue. The motorcyclist is surely something dispatched from a sympathetic region back of the sun. He has one of those blond and block-shaped heads set upon a throat which is as broad as the head itself and has the smooth and supple muscularity of the male organ in its early stage of tumescence. This bare throat and the blond head above it have never been in a country where the sun is distant. The hands are enormous square knobs to the golden doors of Paradise. And the legs that straddle the quiescent fury of the cycle (called Indian) could not have been better designed by the appreciative eyes and fingers of Michelangelo or Phidias or Rodin. It is in the direct and pure line of those who have witnessed and testified in stone what they have seen of a simple physical glory in mankind! The eyes are behind sunglasses. Cora is a good judge of eyes but she has to see them to judge them. Sometimes she will say to a young man wearing sunglasses, Will you kindly uncover the windows of your soul? She considers herself to be a better judge of good and bad trade than is Billy whose record contains a number of memorable errors. Later Cora will remember that from the moment she saw this youth on the motorcycle something whispered *Watch Out* in her ear. Honey, she will say, later, he had more Stop signs on him than you meet when you've got five minutes to get to the station! Perhaps this will be an exaggerated statement, but it is true that Cora had misgivings in exact proportion to Billy's undisguised enchantment.

As for right now, the kid seems fairly obliging. He swings his great legs off the cycle which he rests upon a metal support. He hardly says anything. He throws back the hood of the car and crouches into it for a couple of minutes, hardly more than that, then the expressionless blond cube comes back into view and announces without inflection, Bearings gone out.

What does that mean, asks Cora.

That means you been screwed, he says.

What can we do about it?

Not a goddam thing. You better junk it.

What did he say, inquires Billy.

He said, Cora tells him, that the bearings have gone out.

What are bearings?

The cyclist utters a short barking laugh. He is back astraddle the frankly shaped leather seat of his Indian, but Cora has once more descended from the Buick and she has resorted to the type of flirtation that even most queens would think common. She has fastened her bejeweled right hand over the elevated and narrow front section of the saddle which the boy sits astride. There is not only proximity but contact between their two parties, and all at once the boy's blond look is both contemptuous and attentive, and his attitude toward their situation has undergone a drastic alteration. He is now engaged in it again.

There's a garage on Boca Raton, he tells them. I'll see if they got a tow truck. I think they got one.

Off he roars down the Keys!

One hour and forty-five minutes later the abdicated Roadmaster is towed into a garage on Boca Raton, and Cora and Billy plus their new-found acquaintance are checking, all three, into a tourist cabin at a camp called The Idle-wild, which is across the highway from the garage.

Cora has thought to remove her thermos of martinis from the dashboard compartment, and this time Billy has not offered any objection. Billy is restored to good spirits. Cora still feels guilty, profoundly and abjectly guilty, about the purchase of the glittering fraud, but she is putting up a good front. She knows, however, that Billy will never quite forgive and forget and she does not understand why she made that silly profession of knowing so much about motors. It was, of course, to impress her beloved companion. He knows so much more than she about so many things, she has to pretend, now and then, to know *something* about *something*, even when she knows in her heart that she is a comprehensive and unabridged dictionary of human ignorance on nearly all things of importance. She sighs in her heart because she's become a pretender, and once you have pretended, is it ever possible to stop pretending?

Pretending to be a competent judge of a motor has placed her in the sad and embarrassing position of having cheated Billy out of five hundred dollars. How can she make it up to him?

A whisper in the heart of Cora: *I love him!*

Whom does she love?

There are three persons in the cabin, herself, and Billy and the young man from the highway.

Cora despises herself and she has never been much attracted to men of an altogether physical type.

So there is the dreadful answer! She is in love with Billy!

I am in love with Billy, she whispers to herself.

That acknowledgment seems to call for a drink.

She gets up and pours herself another martini. Unfortunately someone, probably Cora herself, has forgotten to screw the cap back on the thermos bottle and the drinks are now tepid. No drink is better than an ice-cold martini, but no drink is worse than a martini getting warm. However, be that as it may, the discovery just made, the one about loving Billy, well, after *that* one the temperature of a drink is not so important so long as the stuff is still liquor!

She says to herself: I have admitted a fact! Well, the only thing to do with a fact is admit it, but once admitted, you don't have to keep harping on it.

Never again, so long as she stays on the party with her companion, will she put into words her feelings for him, not even in the privacy of her heart . . .

Le coeur a ses raisons que la raison ne connaît pas!

That is one of those little French sayings that Cora is proud of knowing and often repeats to herself as well as to others.

Sometimes she will translate it, to those who don't know the French language, as follows:

The heart knows the scoop when the brain is ignorant of it!

Ha ha!

Well, now she is back in the cabin after a mental excursion that must have lasted at least a half an hour.

Things have progressed thus far.

Billy has stripped down to his shorts and he has persuaded the square-headed blond to do likewise.

Cora herself discovers that she has made concessions to the unseasonable warmth of the little frame building.

All she is wearing is her panties and bra.

She looks across without real interest at the square-headed stranger. Yes. A magnificent torso, as meaningless, now, to Cora as a jigsaw puzzle which put together exhibits a cow munching grass in a typical one tree pasture . . .

Excuse me, people, she remarks to Billy. I just remembered I promised to make a long-distance call to Atlanta.

A long-distance call to Atlanta is a code message between herself and Billy.

What it means is this: The field is yours to conquer!

Cora goes out, having thrown on a jacket and pulled on her checkerboard slacks.

Where does Cora go? Not far, not far at all.

She is leaning against a palm tree not more than five yards distant from the cabin. She is smoking a cigarette in a shadow.

Inside the cabin the field is Billy's to conquer.

Billy says to the cyclist: How do you like me?

Huh . . .

(That is the dubious answer to his question!)

Billy gives him a drink, another one, thinking that this may evoke a less equivocal type of response.

How do you like me, now?

You want to know how I like you?

Yes!

I like you the way that a cattleman loves a sheepherder!

I am not acquainted, says Billy, with the likes and dislikes of men who deal in cattle.

Well, says the square-headed blond, if you keep messing around I'm going to give you a demonstration of it!

A minute is a microscope view of eternity.

It is less than a minute before Cora hears a loud sound.

She knew what it was before she even heard it, and almost before she heard it, that thud of a body not falling but thrown to a floor, she is back at the door of the cabin and pushing it open and returning inside.

Hello! is what she says with apparent good humor.

She does not seem to notice Billy's position and bloody mouth on the floor . . .

Well, she says, I got my call through to Atlanta!

While she is saying this, she is getting out of her jacket and checkerboard slacks, and she is not stopping there.

Instant diversion is the doctor's order.

She is stripped bare in ten seconds, and on the bed.

Billy has gotten outside and she is enduring the most undesired embrace that she can remember in all her long history of desired and undesired and sometimes only patiently borne embraces . . .

Why do we do it?

We're lonely people. I guess it's simple as that . . .

But nothing is ever that simple! Don't you know it?

And so the story continues where it didn't leave off . . .

Trade ceased to have much distinction. One piece was fundamentally the same as another, and the nights were like waves rolling in and breaking and retreating again and leaving you washed up on the wet sands of morning.

Something continual and something changeless.

The sweetness of their living together persisted.

We're friends! said Cora.

She meant a lot more than that, but Billy is satisfied with this spoken definition, and there's no other that can safely be framed in language.

Sometimes they look about them, privately and together, and what they see is something like what you see through a powerful telescope trained upon the moon, flatly illuminated craters and treeless plains and a vacancy of light—much light, but an emptiness in it.

Calcium is the element of this world.

Each has held some private notion of death. Billy thinks his death is going to be violent. Cora thinks hers will be ungraciously slow. Something will surrender by painful inches . . .

Meanwhile they are together.

To Cora that's the one important thing left.

Cities!

You queens know places, but never know where places are!

No Mayor has ever handed them a gold key, nor have they entered under a silken banner of welcome, but they have gone to them all in the northern half of the western hemisphere, this side of the Arctic Circle! Ha ha, just about all . . .

Many cities!

Sometimes they wake up early to hear the awakening tumult of a city and to reflect upon it.

They're two on a party which has made a departure and a rather wide one.

Into brutality? No. It's not that simple.

Into vice? No. It isn't nearly that simple.

Into what, then?

Into something unlawful? Yes, of course!

But in the night, hands clasping and no questions asked.

In the morning, a sense of being together no matter what comes, and the knowledge of not having struck nor lied nor stolen.

A female lush and a fairy who travel together, who are two on a party, and the rush continues.

They wake up early, sometimes, and hear the city coming awake, the increase of traffic, the murmurous shuffle of crowds on their way to their work, the ordinary resumption of daytime life in a city, and they reflect upon it a little from their, shall we say, bird's-eye situation.

There's the radio and the newspaper and there is TV, which Billy says means "Tired Vaudeville," and everything that is known is known very fully and very fully stated.

But after all, when you reflect upon it at the only time that is suitable for reflection, what can you do but turn your other cheek to the pillow?

Two queens sleeping together with sometimes a stranger between them . . .

One morning a phone will ring.

Cora will answer, being the lighter sleeper and the quicker to rise.

Bad news!

Clapping a hand over the shrill mouthpiece, instinctive gesture of secrecy, she will cry to Billy.

Billy, Billy, wake up! They've raided the Flamingo! The heat is on! Get packed!

Almost gaily this message is delivered and the packing performed, for it's fun to fly away from a threat of danger.

(Most dreams are about it, one form of it or another, in which man remembers the distant mother with wings . . .)

Off they go, from Miami to Jacksonville, from Jacksonville to Savannah or Norfolk, all winter shuttling about the Dixie circuit, in spring going back to Manhattan, two birds flying together against the wind, nothing real but the party, and even that sort of dreamy.

In the morning, always Cora's voice addressing room service, huskily, softly, not to disturb his sleep before the coffee arrives, and then saying gently, Billy, Billy, your coffee . . .

Cup and teaspoon rattling like castanets as she hands it to him, often spilling a little on the bedclothes and saying, Oh, honey, excuse me, ha ha!

1951–52 (Published 1954)

Three Players of a Summer Game

I

Croquet is a summer game that seems, in a curious way, to be composed of images the way that a painter's abstraction of summer or one of its games would be built of them. The delicate wire wickets set in a lawn of smooth emerald that flickers fierily at some points and rests under violet shadow in others, the wooden poles gaudily painted as moments that stand out in a season that was a struggle for something of unspeakable importance to someone passing through it, the clean and hard wooden spheres of different colors and the strong rigid shape of the mallets that drive the balls through the wickets, the formal design of those wickets and poles upon the croquet lawn—all of these are like a painter's abstraction of a summer and a game played in it. And I cannot think of croquet without hearing a sound like the faraway boom of a cannon fired to announce a white ship coming into a harbor which had expected it anxiously for a long while. The faraway booming sound is that of a green-and-white striped awning coming down over a gallery of a white frame house. The house is of Victorian design carried to an extreme of improvisation, an almost grotesque pile of galleries and turrets and cupolas and eaves, all freshly painted white, so white and so fresh that it has the blue-white glitter of a block of ice in the sun. The house is like a new resolution not yet tainted by any defection from it. And I associate the summer game with players coming out of this house, out of the mysteries of a walled place, with the buoyant air of persons just released from a suffocating enclosure, as if they had spent the fierce day bound in a closet, were breathing freely at last in fresh atmosphere and able to move without hindrance. Their clothes are as light in weight and color as the flattering clothes of dancers. There are three players—a woman, a man, and a child.

303

The voice of the woman player is not at all a loud one; yet it has a pleasantly resonant quality that carries it farther than most voices go and it is interspersed with peals of treble laughter, pitched much higher than the voice itself, which are cool-sounding as particles of ice in a tall shaken glass. This woman player, even more than her male opponent in the game, has the grateful quickness of motion of someone let out of a suffocating enclosure; her motion has the quickness of breath released just after a moment of terror, of fingers unclenched when panic is suddenly past or of a cry that subsides into laughter. She seems unable to speak or move about moderately; she moves in convulsive rushes, whipping her skirts with long strides that quicken to running. The whipped skirts are white ones. They make a faint crackling sound as her pumping thighs whip them open, the sound that comes to you, greatly diminished by distance, when fitful fair-weather gusts belly out and slacken the faraway sails of a yawl. That agreeably cool summer sound is accompanied by another which is even cooler, the ceaseless tiny chatter of beads hung in long loops from her throat. They are not pearls but they have a milky lustre, they are small faintly speckled white ovals, polished bird's eggs turned solid and strung upon glittery filaments of silver. This woman player is never still for a moment; sometimes she exhausts herself and collapses on the grass in the conscious attitudes of a dancer. She is a thin woman with long bones and skin of a silky lustre and her eyes are only a shade or two darker than the blue-tinted bird's-egg beads about her long throat. She is never still, not even when she has fallen in exhaustion on the grass. The neighbors think she's gone mad but they feel no pity for her, and that, of course, is because of her male opponent in the game.

This player is Brick Pollitt, a man so tall with such a fiery thatch of hair on top of him that I never see a flagpole on an expanse of green lawn or even a particularly brilliant cross or weather vane on a steeple without thinking suddenly of that long ago summer and Brick Pollitt and begin to assort again the baffling bits and pieces that make his legend. These bits and pieces, these assorted images, they are like the paraphernalia for a game of croquet, gathered up from the lawn when the game is over and packed carefully into an oblong wooden box which they just exactly fit and fill. There they all are, the bits and pieces, the images, the apparently incongruous paraphernalia of a summer that was the last one of my childhood, and now I take them out of the oblong box and arrange them once more in the formal design on the lawn. It would be absurd to pretend that this is altogether the way it was, and yet it may be closer than a literal history could be to the hidden truth of it. Brick Pollitt is the male player of this summer game, and he is a drinker who has not yet completely fallen beneath the savage axe blows of his liquor. He is not so young any more but he has not yet lost the slim grace of his youth. He is a head taller than the tall woman player of the game. He is such a tall man that, even in those sections of the lawn dimmed under violet shadow, his head continues to catch fiery rays of the descending sun, the way that the heavenward pointing index finger of that huge gilded hand atop a Protestant steeple in Meridian goes on drawing the sun's flame for a good while after the lower surfaces of the town have sunk into lingering dusk.

The third player of the summer game is the daughter of the woman, a plump twelve-year-old child named Mary Louise. This little girl had made herself distinctly unpopular among the children of the neighborhood by imitating too perfectly the elegant manners and cultivated eastern voice of her mother. She sat in the electric automobile on the sort of a fat silk pillow that expensive lap dogs sit on, uttering treble peals of ladylike laughter, tossing her curls, using grown-up expressions such as, "Oh, how delightful" and "Isn't that just lovely." She would sit in the electric automobile sometimes all afternoon by herself as if she were on display in a glass box, only now and then raising a plaintive voice to call her mother and ask if it was all right for her to come in now or if she could drive the electric around the block, which she was sometimes then permitted to do.

I was her only close friend and she was mine. Sometimes she called me over to play croquet with her but that was only when her mother and Brick Pollitt had disappeared into the house too early to play the game. Mary Louise had a passion for croquet; she played it for itself, without any more shadowy and important connotations.

What the game meant to Brick Pollitt calls for some further account of Brick's life before that summer. He was a young Delta planter who had been a celebrated athlete at Sewanee, who had married a New Orleans debutante who was a Mardi Gras queen and whose father owned a fleet of banana boats. It had seemed a brilliant marriage, with lots of wealth and prestige on both sides, but only two years later Brick had started falling in love with his liquor and Margaret, his wife, began to be praised for her patience and loyalty to him. Brick seemed to be throwing his life away as if it were something disgusting that he had suddenly found in his hands. This self-disgust came upon him with the abruptness and violence of a crash on a highway. But what had Brick crashed into? Nothing that anybody was able to surmise, for he seemed to have everything that young men like Brick might hope or desire to have. What else is there? There must have been something else that he wanted and lacked, or what reason was there for dropping his life and taking hold of a glass which he never let go of for more than one waking hour? His wife, Margaret, took hold of Brick's ten-thousand-acre plantation as firmly and surely as if she had always existed for that and no other purpose. She had Brick's power of attorney and she managed all of his business affairs with celebrated astuteness. "He'll come out of it," she said. "Brick is passing through something that he'll come out of." She always said the right thing; she took the conventionally right attitude and expressed it to the world that admired her for it. She had never committed any apostasy from the social faith she was born to and everybody admired her as a remarkably fine and brave little woman who had too much to put up with. Two sections of an hourglass could not drain and fill more evenly than Brick and Margeret changed places after he took to drink. It was as though she had her lips fastened to some invisible wound in his body through which drained out of him and flowed into her the assurance and vitality that he had owned before marriage. Margaret Pollitt lost her pale, feminine prettiness and assumed in its place something more impressive—a firm and rough-textured sort of handsomeness that came out of her indefinite chrysalis as mysteriously as one of those metamorphoses that occur in insect life. Once very pretty but indistinct, a graceful sketch that was done with a very light pencil, she became vivid as Brick disappeared behind the veil of his liquor. She came out of a mist. She rose into clarity as Brick descended. She abruptly stopped being quiet and dainty. She was now apt to have dirty fingernails which she covered with scarlet enamel. When the enamel chipped off, the gray showed underneath. Her hair was now cut short so that she didn't have to "mess with it." It was wind-blown and full of sparkle; she jerked a comb through it to make it crackle. She had white teeth that were a little too large for her thin lips, and when she threw her head back in laughter, strong cords of muscle stood out in her smooth brown throat. She had a booming laugh that she might have stolen from Brick while he was drunk or asleep beside her at night. She had a practice of releasing the clutch on a car and shooting off in high gear at the exact instant that her laughter boomed out, not calling good-bye but thrusting out one bare strong arm, straight out as a piston with fingers clenched into a fist, as the car whipped up and disappeared into a cloud of yellow dust. She didn't drive her own little runabout nowadays so much as she did Brick's Pierce Arrow touring car, for Brick's driver's license had been revoked. She frequently broke the speed limit on the highway. The patrolmen would stop her, but she had such an affability, such a disarming way with her, that they would have a good laugh together, she and the highway patrolman, and he would tear up the ticket.

Somebody in her family died in Memphis that spring, and she went there to attend the funeral and collect her inheritance, and while she was gone on that profitable journey, Brick Pollitt slipped out from under her thumb a bit. Another death occurred during her absence. That nice young doctor who took care of Brick when he had to be carried to the hospital, he suddenly took sick in a shocking way. An awful flower grew in his brain like a fierce geranium that shattered its pot. All of a sudden the wrong words came out of his mouth; he seemed to be speaking in an unknown tongue; he couldn't find things with his hands; he made troubled signs over his forehead. His wife led him about the house by one hand, yet he stumbled and fell flat; the breath was knocked out of him, and he had to be put to bed by his wife and the Negro yardman; and he lay there laughing weakly, incredulously, trying to find his wife's hand with both of his while she looked at him with eyes that she couldn't keep from blazing with terror. He stayed under drugs for a week, and it was during that time that Brick Pollitt came to see her. Brick came and sat with Isabel Grey by her dying husband's bed and she couldn't speak, she could only shake her head, incessantly as a metronome, with no lips visible in her white face, but two pressed narrow bands of a dimmer whiteness that shook as if some white liquid flowed beneath them with an incredible rapidity and violence which made them quiver . . .

God was the only word she was able to say; but Brick Pollitt somehow understood what she meant by that word, as if it were in a language that she and he, alone of all people, could speak and understand; and when the dying man's eyes forcibly opened on something they couldn't bear to look at, it was Brick, his hands suddenly quite sure and steady, who filled the hypodermic needle for her and pumped its contents fiercely into her husband's hard young arm. And it was over. There was another bed at the back of the house and he and Isabel lay beside each other on that bed for a couple of hours before they let the town know that her husband's agony was completed, and the only movement between them was the intermittent, spasmodic digging of their fingernails into each other's clenched palm while their bodies lay stiffly separate, deliberately not touching at any other points as if they ab-horred any other contact with each other, while this intolerable thing was ringing like an iron bell through them.

And so you see what the summer game on the violet-shadowed lawn was—it was a running together out of something unbearably hot and bright into something obscure and cool . . .

The young widow was left with nothing in the way of material posses-sions except the house and an electric automobile, but by the time Brick's wife, Margaret, had returned from her profitable journey to Memphis, Brick had taken over the post-catastrophic details of the widow's life. For a week or two, people thought it was very kind of him, and then all at once public opinion changed and they decided that Brick's reason for kindness was by no means noble. It appeared to observers that the widow was now his mistress, and this was true. It was true in the limited way that most such opinions are true. It is only the outside of one person's world that is visible to others, and all opinions are false ones, especially public opinions of individual cases. She was his mistress, but that was not Brick's reason. His reason had something to do with that chaste interlocking of hands their first time together, after the hypodermic; it had to do with those hours, now receding and fading behind them as all such hours must, but neither of them could have said what it was aside from that. Neither of them was able to think very clearly about the matter. But Brick was able to pull himself together for a while and take command of those post-cata-strophic details in the young widow's life and her daughter's.

The daughter, Mary Louise, was a plump child of twelve. She was my friend that summer. Mary Louise and I caught lightning bugs and put them in Mason jars to make flickering lanterns, and we played the game of croquet when her mother and Brick Pollitt were not inclined to play it. It was Mary Louise that summer who taught me how to deal with mosquito bites. She was plagued by mosquitoes and so was I. She warned me that scratching the bites would leave scars on my skin, which was as tender as hers. I said that I didn't care. "Someday you will," she told me. She carried with her constantly that summer a lump of ice in a handkerchief. Whenever a mosquito bit her, instead of scratching the bite she rubbed it gently with the handkerchief-wrapped lump of ice until the sting was frozen to numbness. Of course, in five minutes it would come back and have to be frozen again, but eventually it would disappear and leave no scar. Mary Louise's skin, where it was not temporarily mutilated by a mosquito bite or a slight rash that sometimes appeared after eating strawberry ice cream, was ravishingly smooth and tender. The association is not at all a proper one, but how can you recall a summer in childhood without some touches of impropriety? I can't remember Mary Louise's plump bare legs and arms, fragrant with sweet pea powder, without also thinking of an afternoon drive we took in the electric automobile to the little art museum that had recently been established in the town. We went there just before the five o'clock closing time, and straight as a bee, Mary Louise led me into a room that was devoted to replicas of famous antique sculptures. There was a reclining male nude (the "Dying Gaul," I believe) and it was straight to this statue that she led me. I began to blush before we arrived there. It was naked except for a fig leaf, which was of a different colored metal from the bronze of the prostrate figure, and to my astonished horror, that afternoon, Mary Louise, after a quick, sly look in all directions, picked the fig leaf up, removed it from what it covered, and then turned her totally unembarrassed and innocent eyes upon mine and inquired, smiling very brightly, "Is yours like that?"

My answer was idiotic; I said, "I don't know!" and I think I was blushing long after we left the museum . . .

The Greys' house in the spring when the doctor died of brain cancer was very run down. But soon after Brick Pollitt started coming over to see the young widow, the house was painted; it was painted so white that it was almost a very pale blue; it had the blue-white glitter of a block of ice in the sun. Coolness of appearance seemed to be the most desired of all things that summer. In spite of his red hair, Brick Pollitt had a cool appearance because he was still young and thin, as thin as the widow, and he dressed as she did in clothes of light weight and color. His white shirts looked faintly pink because of his skin underneath them. Once, I saw him through an upstairs window of the widow's house just a moment before he pulled the shade down. I was in an upstairs room of my house and I saw that Brick Pollitt was divided into two colors as distinct as two stripes of a flag, the upper part of him, which had been exposed to the sun, almost crimson and the lower part of him white as this piece of paper.

While the widow's house was being repainted (at Brick Pollitt's expense), she and her daughter lived at the Alcazar Hotel, also at Brick's expense. Brick supervised the renovation of the widow's house. He drove in from his plantation every morning to watch the house painters and gardeners at work. Brick's driving license had been restored to him, and it was an important step forward in his personal renovation—being able to drive his own car again. He drove it with elaborate caution and formality, coming to a dead stop at every cross street in the town, sounding the silver trumpet at every corner, inviting pedestrians to precede him, with smiles and bows and great circular gestures of his hands. But observers did not approve of what Brick Pollitt was doing. They sympathized with his wife, Margaret, that brave little woman who had to put up with so much. As for Dr. Grey's widow, she had not been very long in the town; the doctor had married her while he was an intern at a big hospital in Baltimore. Nobody had formed a definite opinion of her before the doctor died, so it was no effort, now, to simply condemn her, without any qualification, as a strumpet, common in everything but her "affectations."

Brick Pollitt, when he talked to the house painters, shouted to them as if they were deaf, so that all the neighbors could hear what he had to say. He was explaining things to the world, especially the matter of his drinking.

"It's something," he shouted, "that you can't cut out completely right away. That's the big mistake that most drinkers make—they try to cut it out completely, and you can't do that. You can do it for maybe a month or two months, but all at once you go back on it worse than before you went off it, and then the discouragement is awful—you lose all faith in yourself and just give up. The thing to do, the way to handle the problem, is like a bullfighter handles a bull in a ring. Wear it down little by little, get control of it gradually. That's how I'm handling this thing! Yep. Now, let's say that you get up wanting a drink in the morning. Say it's ten o'clock, maybe. Well, you say to yourself, 'Just wait half an hour, old boy, and then you can have one.' Well, at half past ten you still want that drink, and you want it a little bit worse than you did at ten, but you say to yourself, 'Boy, you could do without it half an hour ago so you can do without it now.' You see, that's how you got to argue about it with yourself, because a drinking man is not one person—a man that drinks is two people, one grabbing the bottle, the other one fighting him off it, not one but two people fighting each other to get control of a bottle. Well, sir, if you can talk yourself out of a drink at ten, you can still talk yourself out of a drink at *half past* ten! But at *eleven* o'clock the need for the drink is greater. Now *here's* the important thing to remember about this struggle. You got to watch those scales, and when they tip too far against your power to resist, you got to give in a little. That's not weakness. *That's strategy!* Because don't forget what I told you. A drinking man is not one person but two, and it's a battle of wits going on between them. And so I say at eleven, 'Well, *have* your drink at that hour, *go on*, and *have* it! One drink at eleven won't hurt you!'

"What time is it, now? Yep! Eleven . . . All right, I'm going to have me that one drink. I could do without it, I don't crave it, but the important thing is . . ."

His voice would trail off as he entered the widow's house. He would stay in there longer than it took to have one drink, and when he came out, there was a change in his voice as definite as a change of weather or season, the strong and vigorous tone would be a bit filmed over.

Then he would usually talk about his wife. "I don't say my wife Margaret's not an intelligent woman. She is, and both of us know it, but she don't have a good head for property values. Now, you know Dr. Grey, who used to live here before that brain thing killed him. Well, he was my physician, he pulled me through some bad times when I had that liquor problem. I felt I owed him a lot. Now, that was a terrible thing the way he went, but it was terrible for his widow, too; she was left with this house and that electric automobile and that's all, and this house was put up for sale to pay off her debts, and—well, I bought it. I bought it, and now I'm giving it back to her. Now, my wife Margaret, she. And a lot of other folks, too. Don't understand about this . . .

"What time is it? Twelve? High noon! . . . This ice is melted . . ."

He'd drift back into the house and stay there half an hour, and when he came back out, it was rather shyly with a sad and uncertain creaking of the screen door pushed by the hand not holding the tall glass, but after resting a little while on the steps, he would resume his talk to the house painters.

"Yes," he would say, as if he had only paused a moment before, "it's the most precious thing that a woman can give to a man—his lost respect for himself—and the meanest thing one human being can do to another human being is take his respect for himself away from him. I. I had it took away from me . . ."

The glass would tilt slowly up and jerkily down, and he'd have to wipe his chin dry.

"I had it took away from me! I won't tell you how, but maybe, being men about my age, you're able to guess it. That was how. Some of them don't want it. They cut it off. They cut it right off a man, and half the time he don't even know when they cut it off him. Well, I knew it all right. I could feel it being cut off me. Do you know what I mean? . . . That's right . . .

"But once in a while there's one—and they don't come often—that wants for a man to keep it, and those are the women that God made and put on this earth. The other kind come out of hell, or out of . . . I don't know what. I'm talking too much. Sure. I know I'm talking too much about private matters. But that's all right. This property is mine. I'm talking on my own property and I don't give a s—— who hears me! I'm not shouting about it, but I'm not sneaking around about it neither. Whatever I do, I do it without any shame, and I've got a right to do it. I've been through a hell of a lot that nobody knows. But I'm coming out of it now. God damn it, yes, I am! I can't take all the credit. And yet I'm proud. I'm goddam proud of myself, because I was in a pitiful condition with that liquor problem of mine, but now the worst is over. I've got it just about licked. That's my car out there and I drove it up here myself. It's no short drive, it's almost a hundred miles, and I drive it each morning and drive it back each night. I've got back my driver's license, and I fired the man that was working for my wife, looking after our place. I fired that man and not only fired him but give him a kick in the britches that'll make him eat standing up for the next week or two. It wasn't because I thought he was fooling around. It wasn't that. But him and her both took about the same attitude toward me, and I didn't like the attitude they took. They would talk about me right in front of me, as if I wasn't there. 'Is it time for his medicine?' Yes, they were giving me dope! So one day I played possum. I was lying out there on the sofa and she said to him, 'I guess he's passed out now.' And he said, 'Jesus, dead drunk at half past one in the afternoon!' Well. I got up slowly. I wasn't drunk at that hour, I wasn't even half drunk. I stood up straight and walked slowly toward him. I walked straight up to them both, and you should of seen the eyes of them both bug out! 'Yes, Jesus,' I said, 'at half past one!' And I grabbed him by his collar and by the seat of his britches and turkey-trotted him right on out of the house and pitched him on his face in a big mud puddle at the foot of the steps to the front verandah. And as far as I know or care, maybe he's still laying there and she's still screaming, 'Stop, Brick!' But I believe I did hit her. Yes, I did. I did hit her. There's times when you got to hit them, and that was one of those times. I ain't been to the house since. I moved in the little place we lived in before the big one was built, on the other side of the bayou, and ain't crossed over there since . . .

"Well, sir, that's all over with now. I got back my power of attorney which I'd give to that woman and I got back my driver's license and I bought this piece of property in town and signed my own check for it and I'm having it completely done over to make it as handsome a piece of residential property as you can find in this town, and I'm having that lawn out there prepared for the game of croquet."

Then he'd look at the glass in his hands as if he had just then noticed that he was holding it; he'd give it a look of slightly pained surprise, as if he had cut his hand and just now noticed that it was cut and bleeding. Then he would sigh like an old-time actor in a tragic role. He would put the tall glass down on the balustrade with great, great care, look back at it to make sure that it wasn't going to fall over, and walk very straight and steady to the porch steps and just as steady but with more concentration down them. When he arrived at the foot of the steps, he would laugh as if someone had made a comical remark; he would duck his head genially and shout to the house painters something like this: "Well, I'm not making any predictions because I'm no fortuneteller, but I've got a strong idea that I'm going to lick my liquor problem this summer, ha ha, I'm going to lick it this summer! I'm not going to take no cure and I'm not going to take no pledge, I'm just going to prove I'm a man with his balls back on him! I'm going to do it step by little step, the way that people play the game of croquet. You know how you play that game. You hit the ball through the wicket and then you drive it through the next one. You hit it through that wicket and then you drive on to another. You go from wicket to wicket, and it's a game of precision—it's a game that takes concentration and precision, and that's what makes it a wonderful game for a drinker. It takes a sober man to play a game of precision. It's better than shooting pool, because a pool hall is always next door to a gin mill, and you never see a pool player that don't have his liquor glass on the edge of the table or somewhere pretty near it, and croquet is also a better game than golf, because in golf you've always got that nineteenth hole waiting for you. Nope, for a man with a liquor problem, croquet is a summer game and it may seem a little bit sissy, but let me tell you, it's a game of precision. You go from wicket to wicket until you arrive at that big final pole, and then, bang, you've hit it, the game is finished, you're there! And then, and not until then, you can go up here to the porch and have you a cool gin drink, a buck or a Collins— Hey! Where did I leave that glass? Aw! Yeah, hand it down to me, will you? Ha ha—thanks."

He would take a birdlike sip, make a fiercely wry face, and shake his head violently as if somebody had drenched it with scalding water.

"This God damn stuff!" He would look around to find a safe place to set the glass down again. He would select a bare spot of earth between the hydrangea bushes, deposit the glass there as carefully as if he were planting a memorial tree, and then he would straighten up with a great air of relief and expand his chest and flex his arms. "Ha, ha, yep, croquet is a summer game for widows and drinkers, ha ha!"

For a few moments, standing there in the sun, he would seem as sure and powerful as the sun itself; but then some little shadow of uncertainty would touch him again, get through the wall of his liquor, some tricky little shadow of a thought, as sly as a mouse, quick, dark, too sly to be caught, and without his moving enough for it to be noticed, his still fine body would fall as violently as a giant tree crashes down beneath a final axe stroke, taking with it all the wheeling seasons of sun and stars, whole centuries of them, crashing suddenly into oblivion and rot. He would make this enormous fall without a perceptible movement of his body. At the most, it would show in the faint flicker of something across his face, whose color gave him the name people knew him by. Something flickered across his flame-colored face. Possibly one knee sagged a little forward. Then slowly, slowly, the way a bull trots back from its first wild, challenging plunge into the ring, he would fasten one hand over his belt and raise the other one hesitantly to his head, feeling the scalp and the hard round bowl of the skull underneath it, as if he dimly imagined that by feeling that dome he might be able to guess what was hidden inside it, the dark and wondering stuff beneath that dome of calcium, facing, now, the intricate wickets of the summer to come . . .

II

For one reason or another, Mary Louise Grey was locked out of the house a great deal of the time that summer, and since she was a lonely child with little or no imagination, apparently unable to amuse herself with solitary games—except the endless one of copying her mother—the afternoons that she was excluded from the house "because Mother has a headache" were periods of great affliction. There were several galleries with outside stairs between them, and she patrolled the galleries and wandered forlornly about the lawn, and from time to time, she went down the front walk and sat in the glass box of the electric. She would vary her steps, sometimes walking sedately, sometimes skipping, sometimes hopping and humming, one plump hand always clutching the handkerchief that contained the lump of ice. This lump of ice to rub her mosquito bites had to be replaced at frequent intervals. "Oh, iceman," the widow would call sweetly from an upstairs window, "don't forget to leave some extra pieces for little Mary Louise to rub her mosquito bites with!"

Each time a new bite was suffered Mary Louise would utter a soft cry in a voice that had her mother's trick of carrying a great distance without being loud.

"Oh, Mother," she would moan, "I'm simply being devoured by mosquitoes!"

"Darling," her mother would answer, "that's dreadful, but you know that Mother can't help it; she didn't create the mosquitoes and she can't destroy them for you!"

"You could let me come in the house, Mama."

"No, I can't let you come in, precious. Not yet."

"Why not, Mother?"

"Because Mother has a sick headache."

"I will be quiet."

"You say that you will, but you won't. You must learn to amuse yourself, precious; you mustn't depend on Mother to amuse you. Nobody can depend on anyone else forever. I'll tell you what you can do till Mother's headache is better. You can drive the electric out of the garage. You can drive it around the block, but don't go into the business district with it, and then you can stop in the shady part of the drive and sit there perfectly comfortably till Mother feels better and can get dressed and come out. And then I think Mr. Pollitt may come over for a game of croquet. Won't that be lovely?"

"Do you think he will get here in time to play?"

"I hope so, precious. It does him so much good to play croquet."

"Oh, I think it does all of us good to play croquet," said Mary Louise in a voice that trembled just at the vision of it.

Before Brick Pollitt arrived—sometimes half an hour before his coming, as though she could hear his automobile on the highway thirty miles from the house—Mary Louise would bound plumply off the gallery and begin setting up the poles and wickets of the longed-for game. While she was doing this, her plump little buttocks and her beginning breasts and her shoulder-length copper curls would all bob up and down in perfect unison.

I would watch her from the steps of my house on the diagonally opposite corner of the street. She worked feverishly against time, for experience had taught her the sooner she completed the preparations for the game the greater would be the chance of getting her mother and Mr. Pollitt to play it. Frequently she was not fast enough, or they were too fast for her. By the time she had finished her perspiring job, the verandah was often deserted. Her wailing cries would begin, punctuating the dusk at intervals only a little less frequent than the passing of cars of people going out for evening drives to cool off.

"Mama! Mama! The croquet set is ready!"

Usually there would be a long, long wait for any response to come from the upstairs window toward which the calls were directed. But one time there wasn't. Almost immediately after the wailing voice was lifted, begging for the commencement of the game, Mary Louise's thin pretty mother showed herself at the window. She same to the window like a white bird flying into some unnoticed obstruction. That was the time when I saw, between the dividing gauze of the bedroom curtains, her naked breasts, small and beautiful, shaken like two angry fists by her violent motion. She leaned between the curtains to answer Mary Louise not in her usual tone of gentle remonstrance but in a shocking cry of rage: "Oh, be still, for God's sake, you fat little monster!"

Mary Louise was shocked into petrified silence that must have lasted for a quarter of an hour. It was probably the word "fat" that struck her so overwhelmingly, for Mary Louise had once told me, when we were circling the block in the electric, that her mother had told her that she was *not* fat, that she was only plump, and that these cushions of flesh were going to dissolve in two or three more years and then she would be just as thin and pretty as her mother.

Sometimes Mary Louise would call me over to play croquet with her, but she was not at all satisfied with my game. I had had so little practice and she so much, and besides, more importantly, it was the company of the grown-up people she wanted. She would call me over only when they had disappeared irretrievably into the lightless house or when the game had collapsed owing to Mr. Brick Pollitt's refusal to take it seriously. When he played seriously, he was even better at it than Mary Louise, who practiced her strokes sometimes all afternoon in preparation for a game. But there were evenings when he would not leave his drink on the porch but would carry it down onto the lawn with him and would play with one hand, more and more capriciously, while in the other hand he carried the tall glass. Then the lawn would become a great stage on which he performed all the immemorial antics of the clown, to the exasperation of Mary Louise and her thin, pretty mother, both of whom would become very severe and dignified on these occasions. They would retire from the croquet lawn and stand off at a little distance, calling softly, "Brick, Brick" and "Mr. Pollitt," like a pair of complaining doves, both in the same ladylike tones of remonstrance. He was not a middle-aged-looking man—that is, he was not at all big around the middle—and he could leap and run like a boy. He could turn cartwheels and walk on his hands, and sometimes he would grunt and lunge like a wrestler or make long crouching runs like a football player, weaving in and out among the wickets and gaudily painted poles of the croquet lawn. The acrobatics and sports of his youth seemed to haunt him. He called out hoarsely to invisible teammates and adversaries— muffled shouts of defiance and anger and triumph, to which an incongruous counterpoint was continually provided by the faint, cooing voice of the widow, "Brick, Brick, stop now, please stop. The child is crying. People will think you've gone crazy." For Mary Louise's mother, despite the extreme ambiguity of her station in life, was a woman with a keener than ordinary sense of propriety. She knew why the lights had gone out on all the screened summer porches and why the automobiles drove past the house at the speed of a funeral procession while Mr. Brick Pollitt was making a circus ring of the croquet lawn.

Late one evening when he was making one of his crazy dashes across the lawn with an imaginary football hugged against his belly, he tripped over a wicket and sprawled on the lawn, and he pretended to be too gravely injured to get back on his feet. His loud groans brought Mary Louise and her mother running from behind the vine-screened end of the verandah and out upon the lawn to assist him. They took him by each hand and tried to haul him up, but with a sudden shout of laughter he pulled them both down on top of him and held them there till both of them were sobbing. He got up, finally, that evening, but it was only to replenish his glass of iced gin, and then returned to the lawn. That evening was a fearfully hot one, and Brick decided to cool and refresh himself with the sprinkler hose while he enjoyed his drink. He turned it on and pulled it out to the center of the lawn. There he rolled about the grass under its leisurely revolving arch of water, and as he rolled about, he began to wriggle out of his clothes. He kicked off his white shoes and one of his pale green socks, tore off his drenched white shirt and grass-stained linen pants, but he never succeeded in getting off his necktie. Finally, he was sprawled, like some grotesque fountain figure, in underwear and necktie and the one remaining pale green sock, while the revolving arch of water moved with cool whispers about him. The arch of water had a faint crystalline iridescence, a mist of delicate colors, as it wheeled under the moon, for the moon had by that time begun to poke with an air of slow astonishment over the roof of the little building that housed the electric. And still the complaining doves of the widow and her daughter cooed at him from various windows of the house, and you could tell their voices apart only by the fact that the mother murmured "Brick, Brick" and Mary Louise still called him Mr. Pollitt. "Oh, Mr. Pollitt, Mother is so unhappy, Mother is crying!"

That night he talked to himself or to invisible figures on the lawn. One of them was his wife, Margaret. He kept saying, "I'm sorry, Margaret, I'm sorry, Margaret, I'm so sorry, so sorry, Margaret. I'm sorry I'm no good, I'm sorry, Margaret, I'm so sorry, so sorry I'm no good, sorry I'm drunk, sorry I'm no good, I'm so sorry it all had to turn out like this . . ."

Later on, much later, after the remarkably slow procession of touring cars stopped passing the house, a little black sedan that belonged to the police came rushing up to the front walk and sat there for a while. In it was the chief of police himself. He called "Brick, Brick," almost as gently and softly as Mary Louise's mother had called him from the lightless windows. "Brick, Brick, old boy. Brick, fellow," till finally the inert fountain figure in underwear and green sock and unremovable necktie staggered out from under the rotating arch of water and stumbled down to the walk and stood there negligently and quietly conversing with the chief of police under the no longer at all astonished, now quite large and indifferent great yellow stare of the August moon. They began to laugh softly together, Mr. Brick Pollitt and the chief of police, and finally the door of the little black car opened and Mr. Brick Pollitt got in beside the chief of police while the common officer got out to collect the clothes, flabby as drenched towels, on the croquet lawn. Then they drove away, and the summer night's show was over . . .

It was not quite over for me, for I had been watching it all that time with unabated interest. And about an hour after the little black car of the very polite officers had driven away, I saw the mother of Mary Louise come out into the lawn; she stood there with an air of desolation for quite a while. Then she went into the small building in back of the house and drove out the electric. The electric went sedately out into the summer night, with its buzzing no louder than a summer insect's, and perhaps an hour later, for this was a very long night, it came back again containing in its glass show box not only the young and thin and pretty widow but a quiet and chastened Mr. Pollitt. She curved an arm about his immensely tall figure as they went up the front walk, and I heard him say only one word distinctly. It was the name of his wife.

Early that autumn, which was different from summer in nothing except the quicker coming of dusk, the visits of Mr. Brick Pollitt began to have the spasmodic irregularity of a stricken heart muscle. That faraway boom of a cannon at five o'clock was now the announcement that two ladies in white dresses were waiting on a white gallery for someone who was each time a little more likely to disappoint them than the time before. But disappointment was not a thing that Mary Louise was inured to; it was a country that she was passing through not as an old inhabitant but as a bewildered explorer, and each afternoon she removed the oblong yellow wood box, lugged it out of the little building in which it lived with the electric, ceremoniously opened it upon the center of the silken green lawn, and began to arrange the wickets in their formal pattern between the two gaudily painted poles that meant beginning, middle and end. And the widow, her mother, talked to her from the gallery, under the awning, as if there had been no important alteration in their lives or their prospects. Their almost duplicate voices as they talked back and forth between gallery and lawn rang out as clearly as if the enormous corner lot were enclosed at this hour by a still more enormous and perfectly translucent glass bell which picked up and carried through space whatever was uttered beneath it, and this was true not only when they were talking across the lawn but when they were seated side by side in the white wicker chairs on the gallery. Phrases from these conversations became catchwords, repeated and mocked by the neighbors, for whom the widow and her daughter and Mr. Brick Pollitt had been three players in a sensational drama which had shocked and angered them for two acts but which now, as it approached a conclusion, was declining into unintentional farce, which they could laugh at. It was not difficult to find something ludicrous in the talks between the two ladies or the high-pitched elegance of their voices.

Mary Louise would ask, "Will Mr. Pollitt get here in time for croquet?"

"I hope so, precious. It does him so much good."

"He'll have to come soon or it will be too dark to see the wickets."

"That's true, precious."

"Mother, why is it dark so early now?"

"Honey, you know why. The sun goes south."

"But why does it go south?"

"Precious, Mother cannot explain the movements of the heavenly bodies, you know that as well as Mother knows it. Those things are controlled by certain mysterious laws that people on earth don't know or understand."

"Mother, are we going east?"

"When, precious?"

"Before school starts."

"Honey, you know it's impossible for Mother to make any definite plans."

"I hope we do. I don't want to go to school here."

"Why not, precious? Are you afraid of the children?"

"No, Mother, but they don't like me, they make fun of me."

"How do they make fun of you?"

"They mimic the way I talk and they walk in front of me with their stomachs pushed out and giggle."

"That's because they're children and children are cruel."

"Will they stop being cruel when they grow up?"

"Why, I suppose some of them will and some of them won't."

"Well, I hope we go east before school opens."

"Mother can't make any plans or promises, honey."

"No, but Mr. Brick Pollitt—"

"Honey, lower your voice! Ladies talk softly."

"Oh, my goodness!"

"What is it, precious?"

"A mosquito just bit me!"

"That's too bad, but don't scratch it. Scratching can leave a permanent scar on the skin."

"I'm not scratching it. I'm just sucking it, Mother."

"Honey, Mother has told you time and again that the thing to do when you have a mosquito bite is to get a small piece of ice and wrap it up in a handkerchief and rub the bite gently with it until the sting is removed."

"That's what I do, but my lump of ice is melted!"

"Get you another piece, honey. You know where the icebox is!"

"There's not much left. You put so much in the ice bag for your headache."

"There must be some left, honey."

"There's just enough left for Mr. Pollitt's drinks."

"Never mind that . . ."

"He needs it for his drinks, Mother."

"Yes, Mother knows what he wants the ice for, precious."

"There's only a little piece left. It's hardly enough to rub a mosquito bite with."

"Well, use it for that purpose, that purpose is better, and anyhow when Mr. Pollitt comes over as late as this, he doesn't deserve to have any ice saved for him."

"Mother?"

"Yes, precious?"

"I love ice and sugar!"

"What did you say, precious?"

"I said I loved ice and sugar!"

"Ice and sugar, precious?"

"Yes, I love the ice and sugar in the bottom of Mr. Pollitt's glass when he's through with it."

"Honey, you mustn't eat the ice in the bottom of Mr. Pollitt's glass!"

"Why not, Mother?"

"Because it's got liquor in it!"

"Oh, no, Mother, it's just ice and sugar when Mr. Pollitt's through with it."

"Honey, there's always a little liquor left in it."

"Oh, no, not a drop's left when Mr. Pollitt's through with it!"

"But you say there's sugar left in it, and, honey, you know that sugar is very absorbent."

"It's what, Mummy?"

"It absorbs some liquor and that's a good way to cultivate a taste for it, and, honey, you know what dreadful consequences a taste for liquor can have. It's bad enough for a man, but for a woman it's fatal. So when you want ice and sugar, let Mother know and she'll prepare some for you, but don't ever let me catch you eating what's left in Mr. Pollitt's glass!"

"Mama?"

"Yes, precious?"

"It's almost completely dark now. Everybody is turning on their lights or driving out on the river road to cool off. Can't we go out riding in the electric?"

"No, honey, we can't till we know Mr. Pollitt's not—"

"Do you still think he will come?"

"Precious, how can I say? Is Mother a fortuneteller?"

"Oh, here comes the Pierce, Mummy, here comes the Pierce!"

"Is it? Is it the Pierce?"

"Oh, no. No, it isn't. It's a Hudson Super Six. Mummy, I'm going to pull up the wickets, now, and water the lawn, because if Mr. Pollitt does come, he'll have people with him or won't be in a condition to play croquet. And when I've finished, I want to drive the electric around the block."

"Drive it around the block, honey, but don't go into the business district with it."

"Are you going with me, Mummy?"

"No, precious, I'm going to sit here."

"It's cooler in the electric."

"I don't think so. The electric goes too slowly to make much breeze."

If Mr. Pollitt did finally arrive those evenings, it was likely to be with a caravan of cars that came from Memphis, and then Mrs. Grey would have to receive a raffish assortment of strangers as if she herself had invited them to a party. The party would not confine itself to the downstairs rooms and galleries but would explode quickly and brilliantly as a rocket in all directions, overflowing both floors of the house, spilling out upon the lawn and sometimes even penetrating the little building that housed the electric automobile and the oblong box that held the packed-away croquet set. On those party nights, the fantastically balustraded and gabled and turreted white building would glitter all over, like one of those huge night excursion boats that came downriver from Memphis, and it would be full of ragtime music and laughter. But at some point in the evening there would be, almost invariably, a startling disturbance. Some male guest would utter a savage roar, a woman would scream, you would hear a shattering of glass. Almost immediately afterward, the lights would go out in the house, as if it really were a boat that had collided fatally with a shoal underwater. From all the doors and galleries and stairs, people would come rushing forth, and the dispersion would be more rapid than the arrival had been. A little while later, the police car would pull up in front of the house. The thin, pretty widow would come out on the front gallery to receive the chief of police, and you could hear her light voice tinkling like glass chimes, "Why, it was nothing, it was nothing at all, just somebody who drank a little too much and lost his temper. You know how that Memphis crowd is, Mr. Duggan, there's always one gentleman in it who can't hold his liquor. I know it's late, but we have such a huge lawn—it occupies half the block—that I shouldn't think anybody who wasn't overcome with curiosity would have to know that a party had been going on!"

And then something must have happened that made no sound at all.

It wasn't an actual death, but it had nearly all the external evidence of one. When death occurs in a house, the house is unnaturally quiet for a day or two before the occurrence is finished. During that interval, the enormous, translucent glass bell that seems to enclose and separate one house from those that surround it does not transmit any noise to those who are watching but seems to have thickened invisibly so that very little can be heard through it. That was the way it had been five months ago, when the pleasant young doctor had died of that fierce flower grown in his skull. It had been unnaturally quiet for several days, and then a peculiar grey car with frosted windows had crashed through the bell of silence and the young doctor had emerged from the house in a very curious way, as if he were giving a public demonstration of how to go to sleep on a narrow bed in atmosphere blazing with light and while in motion.

That was five months ago, and it was now early October.

The summer had spelled out a word that had no meaning, and the word was now spelled out and, with or without any meaning, there it was, inscribed with as heavy a touch as the signature of a miser on a check or a boy with chalk on a fence.

One afternoon, a fat and pleasantly smiling man, whom I had seen times without number loitering around in front of the used car lot which adjoined the Paramount movie, came up the front walk of the Greys' with the excessive nonchalance of a man who is about to commit a robbery. He pushed the bell, waited awhile, pushed it again for a longer moment, and then was admitted through an opening that seemed to be hardly wide enough for his fingers. He came back out almost immediately with something caught in his fist. It was the key to the little building that contained the croquet set and the electric automobile. He entered that building and drew its folding doors all the way open to disclose the ladylike electric sitting there with its usual manner of a lady putting on or taking off her gloves at the entrance to a reception. He stared at it a moment, as if its elegance were momentarily baffling. But then he got in it and he drove it out of the garage, holding the polished black pilot stick with a look on his round face that was like the look of an adult who is a little embarrassed to find himself being amused by a game that was meant for children. He drove it serenely out into the wide, shady street and at an upstairs window of the house there was some kind of quick movement, as if a figure looking out had been startled by something it watched and then had retreated in haste . . .

Later, after the Greys had left town, I saw the elegant square vehicle, which appeared to be made out of glass and patent leather, standing with an air of haughty self-consciousness among a dozen or so other cars for sale in a lot called "Hi-Class Values" next door to the town's best movie, and as far as I know, it may be still sitting there, but many degrees less glittering by now.

The Greys were gone from Meridian all in one quick season: the young doctor whom everyone had liked in a hesitant, early way and had said would do well in the town with his understanding eyes and quiet voice; the thin, pretty woman, whom no one had really known except Brick Pollitt; and the plump little girl, who might someday be as pretty and slender as her mother. They had come and gone in one season, yes, like one of those tent shows that suddenly appear in a vacant lot in a southern town and cross the sky at night with mysteriously wheeling lights and unearthly music, and then are gone, and the summer goes on without them, as if they had never come there.

As for Mr. Brick Pollitt, I can remember seeing him only once after the Greys left town, for my time there was also of brief duration. This last time that I saw him was a brilliant fall morning. It was a Saturday morning in October. Brick's driver's license had been revoked again for some misadventure on the highway due to insufficient control of the wheel, and it was his legal wife, Margaret, who sat in the driver's seat of the Pierce Arrow touring car. Brick did not sit beside her. He was on the back seat of the car, pitching this way and that way with the car's jolting motion, like a loosely wrapped package being delivered somewhere. Margaret Pollitt handled the car with a wonderful male assurance, her bare arms brown and muscular as a Negro field hand's, and the car's canvas top had been lowered the better to expose on its back seat the sheepishly grinning and nodding figure of Brick Pollitt. He was clothed and barbered with his usual immaculacy, so that he looked from some distance like the president of a good social fraternity in a gentleman's college of the South. The knot of his polka dot tie was drawn as tight as strong and eager fingers could knot a tie for an important occasion. One of his large red hands protruded, clasping over the outside of the door to steady his motion, and on it glittered two bands of gold, a small one about a finger, a large one about the wrist. His cream-colored coat was neatly folded on the seat beside him and he wore a shirt of thin white material that was tinted faintly pink by his skin beneath it. He was a man who had been, and even at that time still was, the handsomest you were likely to remember, physical beauty being of all human attributes the most incontinently used and wasted, as if whoever made it despised it, since it is made so often only to be disgraced by painful degrees and drawn through the streets in chains.

Margaret blew the car's silver trumpet at every intersection. She leaned this way and that way, elevating or thrusting out an arm as she shouted gay greetings to people on porches, merchants beside store entrances, people she barely knew along the walks, calling them all by their familiar names, as if she were running for office in the town, while Brick nodded and grinned with senseless amiability behind her. It was exactly the way that some ancient conqueror, such as Caesar or Alexander the Great or Hannibal, might have led in chains through a capital city the prince of a state newly conquered.

1951–52 (Published 1952)

The Coming of Something to the Widow Holly

The widow Isabel Holly was a rooming house owner. How she had come to be one she hardly knew. It had crept up on her the same as everything else. She had an impression, however, that this was the house where she had lived as a bride. There had been, she also believed, a series of more or less tragic disappointments, the least of which had been Mr. Holly's decease. In spite of the fact that the late Mr. Holly, whose first name she could no longer remember, had left her with an adequate trust fund, she had somehow felt compelled at one time or another to open her house on Bourbon Street in New Orleans to persons regarding themselves as "paying guests." In times more recent the payments had dwindled away and now it seemed that the guests were really dependents. They had also dwindled in number. She had an idea that there had once been many, but now there were only three, two middle-aged spinsters and a bachelor in his eighties. They got along not well together. Whenever they met on the stairs or in the hall or at the door of the bathroom, there was invariably some kind of dispute. The bolt on the bathroom door was continually broken, repaired, and broken again. It was impossible to keep any glassware about the place. Mrs. Holly had finally resorted to the use of nothing but aluminum in the way of portable fixtures. And while objects of this material withstood shocks better themselves, they also inflicted considerably more damage on whatever they struck. Time and again one of the terrible three tenants would appear in the morning with a bloodstained bandage about the head, a bruised and swollen mouth or a blackened eye. In view of the circumstances it was reasonable to suppose that they would, at least one of them, move out of the premises. Nothing, however, seemed further from their intention. They clung as

326

leeches to their damp-smelling rooms. All were collectors of things, bottle caps or matchboxes or tin-foil wrappings, and the length of their tenancy was eloquently witnessed by the vast store of such articles stacked about the moldy walls of their bedrooms. It would be hard to say which of the three was the least desirable tenant, but the bachelor in his eighties was certainly the one most embarrassing to a woman of gentle birth and breeding as Isabel Holly unquestionably had been and was.

This octogenarian recluse had run up a great many debts. The last few years he had seemed to be holding an almost continual audience with his creditors. They stamped in and out of the house, in and out, not only during the day but sometimes at the most unlikely hours of the night. The widow Holly's establishment was located in that part of the old French Quarter given over mostly to honky-tonks and bars. The old man's creditors were heavy drinkers, most of them, and when the bars closed against them at night, the liquor having inflamed their tempers, they would stop off at Mrs. Holly's to renew their relentless siege of her tenant, and if he declined to answer the loud ringing and banging at the door, missiles of various kinds were thrown through the panes of the windows wherever the shutters were fallen off or unfastened. In New Orleans the weather is sometimes remarkably good. When this was the case, the creditors of the old man were less obnoxious, at times merely presenting their bills at the door and marching quietly away. But when it was bad outside, when the weather was nasty, the language the creditors used in making demands was indescribably awful. Poor Mrs. Holly had formed the habit of holding her hands to her ears on days when the sun wasn't out. There was one particular tradesman, a man named Cobb who represented some mortician's establishment, who had the habit of using the worst epithet in the English language at the top of his voice, over and over again with increasing frenzy. Only the middle-aged women, Florence and Susie, could cope with the tradesman Cobb. When they acted together, he could be driven away, but only at the sacrifice of broken banisters.

The widow Holly had only once made any allusion to these painful scenes between the tradesman Cobb and her bachelor tenant. On that occasion, after a particularly disagreeable session in the downstairs hall, she had timidly inquired of the old man if some kind of settlement couldn't be reached with his friend from the undertakers.

Not till I'm dead, he told her.

And then he went on to explain, while bandaging his head, that he had ordered a casket, the finest casket procurable, that it had been especially designed and built for him—now the unreasonable Mr. Cobb wished him to pay for it, even before his decease.

This son of an illegitimate child, said the roomer, suspects me of being immortal! I wish it were true, he sighed, but my doctor assures me that my life expectancy is barely another eighty-seven years!

Oh, said poor Mrs. Holly.

Mild as her nature was, she was nearly ready to ask him if he expected to stay in the rooming house all that time—but just at this moment, one of the two indistinguishable female tenants, Florence or Susie, opened the door of her bedroom and stuck her head out.

This awful disturbance has got to stop! she yelled.

To emphasize her demand, she tossed an aluminum washbasin in their direction. It glanced off the head of the man who had ordered his casket and struck Mrs. Holly a terrible blow in the bosom. The octo-generian's head was bandaged with flannel, several layers of it, and padded with damp cardboard, so the blow did not hurt him nor even catch him off guard. But as Isabel Holly fled in pain down the stairs to the cellar—her usual sanctuary—she glanced behind her to see the powerful old gentleman yanking a wooden post from the balustrade and shouting at Florence or Susie the very same unrepeatable word that the undertaker had used.

FOR PROBLEMS CONFER WITH
A. ROSE, METAPHYSICIAN!

This was the legend which Isabel Holly found on a business card stuck under her door facing Bourbon.

She went at once to the address of the consultant and found him seemingly waiting to receive her.

My dear Mrs. Holly, he said, you seem to be troubled.

Troubled? she said, Oh, yes, I'm terribly troubled. There seems to be something important left out of the picture.

What picture? he asked her gently.

My life, she told him.

And what is the element which appears to be missing?

An explanation.

Oh—an explanation! Not many people ask for *that* anymore.

Why? Why don't they? she asked.

Well, you see— Ah, but it's useless to tell you!

Then why did you wish me to come here?

The old man took off his glasses and closed a ledger.

My dear Mrs. Holly, he said, the fact of the matter is that you have a very unusual destiny in store. You are the first of your kind and character ever to be transplanted to this earth from a certain star in another universe!

And what is that going to result in?

Be patient, my dear. Endure your present trials as well as you can. A change is coming, a very momentous change, not only for you but for practically all others confined to this lunatic sphere!

Mrs. Holly went home and, before long, this interview, like everything else in the past, had faded almost completely out of her mind. The days behind her were like an unclear, fuzzy negative of a film that faded when exposed to the present. They were like a dull piece of thread she would like to cut and be done with. Yes, to be done with forever, like a thread from a raveled hem that catches on things when you walk. But where had she put the scissors? Where had she put away everything sharp in her life, everything which was capable of incision? Sometimes she searched about her for something that had an edge that she could cut with. But everything about her was rounded or soft.

The trouble in the house went on and on.

Florence Domingo and Susie Patten had quarreled. Jealousy was the reason.

Florence Domingo had an aged female relative who came to pay her a call about once a month, bringing an empty paper bag in the usually vain hope that Florence would give her something of relative value to take away in it. This indigent old cousin was extremely deaf, as deaf, you might say, as a fence pole, and consequently her conversations with Florence Domingo had to be carried on at the top of both their lungs, and since these conversations were almost entirely concerned with the other roomers at Mrs. Holly's, whatever degree of peace had prevailed under the roof before one of these visits was very drastically reduced right after one took place and sometimes even during its progress. Now Susie Patten never received a visitor and this comparative unpopularity of Susie's was not allowed to pass without comment by Florence and her caller.

How is old Susie Patten? the cousin would shriek.

Terrible. Same as ever, Florence would shout back.

Does she ever go out anywhere to pay a call? the cousin would yell.

Never, never! Florence would reply at the top of her lungs, and nobody comes to see her! She is a friendless soul, completely alone in the world.

Nobody comes to her?

Nobody!

Never?

Never! Absolutely *never!*

When the cousin got up to go, Florence Domingo would say to her, Now close your eyes and hold out your paper bag and see what you find in it when you get downstairs. This was her playful fashion of making a gift, and the old cousin was forbidden to look in the bag till she had left the house, and so great was her curiosity and her greed that she'd nearly break her neck in her rush to get out after the gift was presented. Usually it turned out to be a remnant of food of some kind, such as a half-eaten apple with the bitten places turned brown and withered about the edges where Florence had left her tooth marks, but once when the conversation had not gone to suit Miss Domingo, it was the corpse of a rat that she had dropped in the held-out paper bag and the visits had been suspended for three months. But now the visits were going on again and the vexation of Susie Patten was well-nigh indescribable. Then an idea came to her. She launched a counteroffensive and a very clever one, too. Susie invented a caller of her own. Susie was very good at speaking in two voices: that is, she would speak in her own voice and then she would answer in a different one as if she were carrying on a conversation with someone. This invented caller of Susie's, moreover, was not an old woman. It was a gentleman who addressed her as Madam.

Madam, the invented caller would say, You are wearing your beautiful dotted Swiss today!

Oh, do you like it? Susie would cry out.

Yes, it goes with your eyes, the caller would tell her.

Then Susie would make kissing sounds with her mouth, first soft ones, then very loud ones, and then she would rock back and forth rapidly in her rocking chair and go, Huff, huff, huff! And after a suitable interval she would cry out to herself, *Oh, no!* Then she would rock some more and go, Huff, huff, again, and presently, after another suitable pause, the conversation would be resumed and in due course it would turn to the subject of Florence Domingo. Disparaging comments would be made on the subject and also upon the subject of the Domingo collection of tin-foil wrappings and the Domingo's female relative with the paper bag held out for a gift when she left.

Madam, cried Susie's caller, that woman is not fit to live in a respectable house!

No, indeed, she is not, Susie would agree with him loudly, and all this while Florence Domingo would be listening to every word that was spoken and every sound produced in the course of the long social call. Florence was only half sure that the caller existed, but she could not be completely sure that he didn't, and her doubt and uncertainty on this subject was extremely nerve-racking, and something really had to be done about it.

Something was done about it.

Isabel Holly, the widow who owned the building and suffered this— what shall we call it?—knew there was going to be trouble in the house when she saw Miss Domingo come in the front door one evening with a medium-sized box labeled EXPLOSIVES.

The widow Holly did not wait for eventualities that night. She went right out on the street, dressed as she was, in a pair of rayon bloomers and a brassière. She had hardly gotten around the corner when the whole block shook with a terrible detonation. She kept on running, shuddering in the cold, till she came to the park, the one beside the Cabildo, and there she knelt and prayed for several hours before she dared to turn back toward her home.

When Isabel Holly crept back to the house on Bourbon, she found it a shambles. The rooms were silent. But as she tiptoed past them, she saw here and there the bloody, inert, and hoarsely panting figures of easily twenty tradesmen including the ruffian Cobb. All over the floors and the treads of the stairs were little glittering objects which first she mistook for fragments of glass, but when she picked one up she found it to be coin. Apparently money had been forthcoming from some quarter of the establishment, it had been cast around everywhere, but the creditors of the old man were still in no condition to gather it up. There must have been a great deal of violence preceding the money's disbursal.

Isabel Holly tried to think about this, but her brain was like a cracked vessel that won't hold water, and she was staggering with weariness. So she gave it up and dragged herself to her bedroom. In an envelope half thrust under the door she found a message which only increased the widow's mystification.

The message went as follows:

"My dear Mrs. Holly, I think that with my persuasion the ghastly disturbance has stopped. I am sorry I cannot wait till you return home as I am sure that you must feel a good deal of sorrow and confusion over conditions here. However I shall see you personally soon, and stay a good deal longer. Sincerely, Christopher D. Cosmos."

The weeks that followed were remarkably tranquil. All three of the incorrigible tenants remained locked in their rooms apparently in a state of intimidation. The violently paid-off creditors called at the house no more. The carpenters came and patched things up in silence. Telegraph messengers tiptoed up the stairs and rapped discreetly at the roomers' doors. Boxes began to be carried in and out— It soon appeared to Mrs. Holly's hardly believing mind that general preparations were being made by the terrible two and one to move from the premises.

As a matter of fact a bulletin corroborating this hopeful suspicion appeared in the downstairs hall not very long afterwards.

"We have decided," said this bulletin, "in view of your cousin's behavior, not to maintain our residence here any longer. This decision is absolutely unalterable and we would prefer not to discuss it. Signed: Florence Domingo, Susie Patten, Regis de Winter." (The signatures of the roomers.)

After her roomers' departure, Isabel Holly found it harder than ever to concentrate on things. Often during the day she would sit down worriedly at the kitchen table or on her unmade bed and clasp her forehead and murmur to herself, I've got to think, I've simply *got* to think! But it did no good, it did no good at all. Oh, yes, for a while she would *seem* to be thinking of something. But in the end it was always pretty much like a lump of sugar making strenuous efforts to preserve its integrity in a steamingly warm cup of tea. The cubic shape of a thought would not keep. It relaxed and dissolved and spread out flat on the bottom or drifted away.

At last one day she paid another visit to the house of the metaphysician. On his door was nailed a notice: "I've gone to Florida to stay young forever. Dear Love to all my enemies. Good-bye." She stared at it hopelessly for a moment and started to turn away. But just in the nick of time, a small white rodent squeezed from beneath the door and dropped at her feet an envelope sealed as the one that Christopher Cosmos had left at her house the time of the last disturbance. She tore it open and read the following message: "I have returned and am sleeping in your bedroom. Do not wake me up till after seven o'clock. We've had a long hard trip around the cape of the sun and need much rest before we start back again. Sincerely, Christopher D. Cosmos."

When Isabel Holly returned, there was, indeed, a sleeping man in her bedroom. She stood in the door and nearly stopped breathing with wonder. Oh, how handsome he was! He had on the uniform of a naval commander. The cloth was crisp and lustrous as deeply banked winter snow: The shoulders of the coat were braided; the braids were clasped to the garment with ruby studs. The buttons were aquamarine. And the chest of the man, exposed by the unbuttoned jacket, was burnished as fine, pale gold with diamond-like beads of perspiration on it.

He opened one eye and winked and murmured 'hello' and lazily rolled on his stomach and went back to sleep.

She couldn't decide what action she ought to take. She wandered vaguely about the house for a while, observing the changes which had occurred in her absence.

Everything now was put straight. It was all spick and span as if a regiment of servants had worked industriously for days, scrubbing and polishing, exacting a radiance from the dullest objects. Kitchen utensils worn away with rust and various other truck which could not be renovated had been thrown into or heaped beside an incinerator. GET RID OF THIS NONSENSE was scrawled on a laundry cardboard in the Commander's handwriting. Also among the stuff which her marvelous visitor had ordained for destruction were various relics of the late Mr. Holly, his stomach pump, the formidable bearded photograph of his mother in her daredevil outfit, the bucket of mutton tallow he greased himself with thrice weekly in lieu of bathing, the 970-page musical composition called *Punitive Measures* which he had striven tirelessly to master upon a brass instrument of his own invention—all of this reliquary truck was now heaped inside or beside the giant incinerator.

Wonders will never cease! the widow murmured as she returned upstairs.

A state of irresolution was not unfamiliar to the widow Holly, but this was the first time that it had made her light-footed as well as lightheaded. She rose to the chambers above with no effort of climbing, as a vapor rises from water into first morning light. There was not much light, not even in the parlor that fronted Bourbon Street, there was hardly more light than might have emanated from the uncovered chest of the slumbering young Commander in her bedroom. There was just light enough to show the face of the clock if she leaned toward it as if to invite a kiss. It was seven o'clock—so soon!

The widow did not have a cold, but as she folded some garments over a nest of pine cones in the parlor fireplace, she began to sniff. She sniffed again and again; all of the muscles under the surface of her chilly young skin began to quiver, for somewhere in the house, tremulous with moments coming and going as almost bodiless creatures might rush through a room made of nothing but doors, someone was surely holding a sugar-coated apple on a forked metal stick above a flame's rapid tongue, until the skin of it hissed and crackled and finally split open, spilling out sweet juices, spitting them into the flame and filling the whole house, now, all of the chill and dim chambers, upstairs and down, with an odor of celebration in the season of Advent.

(Published 1953)

Hard Candy

Once upon a time in a southern seaport of America there was a seventy-year-old retired merchant named Mr. Krupper, a man of gross and unattractive appearance and with no close family connections. He had been the owner of a small sweetshop, which he had sold out years before to a distant and much younger cousin with whose parents, no longer living, he had emigrated to America fifty-some years ago. But Mr. Krupper had not altogether relinquished his hold on the shop and this was a matter of grave dissatisfaction to the distant cousin and his wife and their twelve-year-old daughter, whom Mr. Krupper, with an old man's interminable affection for a worn-out joke, still invariably addressed and referred to as "The Complete Little Citizen of the World," a title invented for her by the cousin himself when she was a child of five and when her trend to obesity was not so serious a matter as it now appeared. Now it sounded like a malicious jibe to the cousins, although Mr. Krupper always said it with a benevolent air, "How is the complete little citizen of the world today?" as he gave her a quick little pat on the cheek or the shoulder, and the child would answer, "Drop dead!" which the old man never heard, for his high blood pressure gave him a continual singing in the ears which drowned out all remarks that were not shouted at him. At least he seemed not to hear it, but one could not be sure about Mr. Krupper. The degree of his simplicity was hard to determine.

Sick old people live at varying distances from the world. Sometimes they seem to be a thousand miles out on some invisible sea with the sails set in an opposite direction, and nothing on shore seems to reach them, but then, at another time, the slightest gesture or faintest whisper will reach them. But dislike and even hatred seems to be something to which they develop a lack of sensibility with age. It seems to come as naturally as the coarsening of the skin itself. And Mr. Krupper showed no sign of being aware of how deeply his cousins detested his morning calls at the shop. The family of three would retire to the rooms behind the shop when they saw him coming, unless they happened to be detained by customers, but the old man would wait patiently until one of them was forced to reappear. "Don't hurry, I have got nothing but time," he used to say. He never left without scooping up a fistful of hard candies which he kept in a paper bag in his pocket. This was the little custom which the cousins found most exasperating of all, but they could do nothing about it.

It was this way: the little shop had maintained itself so poorly since the cousins took over that they had never been able to produce more than the interest on the final payment that was due to Mr. Krupper. So they were forced to permit his depredations. Once the cousin, the male one, sourly remarked that Mr. Krupper must have a very fine set of teeth for a man of his years if he could eat so much hard candy, and the old man had replied that he didn't eat it himself. "Who does?" inquired the cousin, and the old man said, with a yellow-toothed grin, "The birds!" The cousins had never seen the old man eat a piece of the candy. Sometimes it accumulated in the paper bag till it swelled out of his pocket like a great tumor, and then other times it would be mysteriously depleted, flattened out, barely visible under the shiny blue flap of the pocket, and then the cousin would say to his wife or daughter, "It looks like the birds were hungry." These ominous and angry little jests had been continuing almost without variation over a very long time. The magnitude of the cousins' dislike for the old man was as difficult to determine as the degree of the old man's insensibility to it. After all, it was based on nothing important, two or three cents' worth of hard candies a day and a few little apparently innocent exchanges of words among them, but it had been going on so long, for so many years. The cousins were not imaginative people, not even sufficiently so to complain to themselves about the tepid and colorless regularity of their lives and the heartbreaking fruitlessness of their dull will to go on and do well and keep going, and the little girl blowing up like a rubber toy, continually, senselessly and sadly popping the sweets in her mouth, not even knowing that she was doing it, crying sadly when told that she had to stop it, insisting quite truthfully that she didn't know she had done it, and five minutes later, doing it again, getting her fat hands slapped and crying again but not remembering later, already fatter than either of her fat parents and developing gross, unladylike habits, such as belching and waiting on customers with a running nose and being called Fatty at school and coming home crying about it. All of these things could easily be associated in some way with the inescapable morning calls of old Mr. Krupper, and all of these little sorrows and resentments could conveniently adopt the old man as their incarnate image, which they did . . .

In the course of this story, and very soon now, it will be necessary to make some disclosures about Mr. Krupper of a nature too coarse to be dealt with very directly in a work of such brevity. The grossly naturalistic details of a life, contained in the enormously wide context of that life, are softened and qualified by it, but when you attempt to set those details down in a tale, some measure of obscurity or indirection is called for to provide the same, or even approximate, softening effect that existence in time gives to those gross elements in the life itself. When I say that there was a certain mystery in the life of Mr. Krupper, I am beginning to approach those things in the only way possible without a head-on violence that would disgust and destroy and which would actually falsify the story.

To have hatred and contempt for a person, as the cousins had for old Mr. Krupper, calls for the assumption that you know practically everything of any significance about him. If you admit that he is a mystery, you admit that the hostility may be unjust. So the cousins failed to see anything mysterious about the old man and his existence. Sometimes the male cousin or his wife would follow him to the door when he went out of the shop, they would stand at the door and stare after him as he shuffled along the block, usually with one hand clasped over the pocket containing the bag of hard candies as if it were a bird that might spring out again, but it was not curiosity about him, it was not interested speculation concerning the old man's goings and comings that motivated their stares at his departing back, it was only the sort of look that you turn to give a rock on which you have stubbed your toe, a senselessly vicious look turned upon an insensibly malign object. There was not room in the doorway for both of the grown cousins, fat as they were, to stare after him at once. The one that got there first was the one that stared after him and the one that uttered the "faugh" of disgust as he finally disappeared from view, a "faugh" as disgusted as if they had penetrated to the very core of those mysteries about him which we are approaching by cautious indirection. The other one of the cousins, the one that had failed to achieve first place at the door, would be standing close behind but with a blocked vision, and the old man's progress down the street and his eventual turning would be a vicarious spectacle enjoyed, or rather detested, only through the commentary provided by the cousin in the favored position. Naturally there was not much to comment upon. An old man's progress down a city block is not eventful. Sometimes the one in the door would say, *He has picked up something on the sidewalk.* The other one would answer, *Faugh! What?*— momentarily alarmed that it might have been something of value, gratified to learn that the old man had dropped it again some paces beyond. Or the reporter would say, *He is looking into a window! Which one? The haberdashery window! Faugh! He'll never buy nothing . . .* But the comments would always end with the announcement that he had crossed the street to the small public square in which Mr. Krupper seemed to spend all his mornings after the call at the sweetshop. The comments and the stares and the faughs of disgust betrayed no real interest or curiosity or speculation about him, only the fiercely senseless attention given to something acknowledged to have no mysteries whatsoever . . .

For that matter, it would be hard for anybody to discover, from outside observation not carried to the point of actual sleuthing, what it was that gave Mr. Krupper the certain air he had of being engaged in something far more momentous than the ordinary meanderings of an old man retired from business and without close family ties. To notice something you would have to be looking for something, and even then a morning might pass or part of an afternoon or even sometimes a whole day without anything meeting your observation that would strike you as a notable difference. Yes, he was like almost any other old man of the sort that you see stooping painfully over to collect the scattering pages of an abandoned newspaper or shuffling out of a public lavatory with fingers fumbling at buttons or loitering upon a corner as if for a while undecided which way to turn. Unattached and aimless, these old men are always infatuated with little certainties and regularities such as those that ordered the life of Mr. Krupper as seen from outside. Habit is living. Anything unexpected reminds them of death. They will stand for half an hour staring fiercely at an occupied bench rather than take one which is empty but which is not familiar and therefore seems insecure to them, the sort of a cold bench on which the heart might flutter and stop or the bowels suddenly loosen a hot flow of blood. These old men are always picking little things up and are very hesitant about putting anything down, even if it is something quite worthless which they had picked up only a moment before out of simple lack of attention. They usually have on a hat, and in the South, it is usually a very old white one turned yellow as their teeth or gray as their cracked fingernails and stubbly beards. And they have a way of removing this hat now and then with a gesture that looks like a deferential salute, as if some great invisible lady had passed before them and given them a slight bow of recognition; and then, a few moments later, when the faint breeze has tickled and tousled their scalps a bit, the hat goes back on, more slowly and carefully than it had been removed; and then they gently change their position on the bench, always first curving their fingers tenderly under the ransacked home of their gender. Sighs and grunts are their language with themselves, speaking always of a weariness and a dull confusion, either alleviated by some little change or momentarily aggravated by it. Ordinarily there is no more mystery in their lives than there is in a gray dollar-watch which is almost consumed by the moments that it has ticked off. They are the nice old men, the sweet old men and the clean old men of the world. But our old man, Mr. Krupper, is a bird of a different feather, and it is now time, in fact it is probably already past time, to follow him further than the public square into which he turned when the cousins no longer could watch him. It is necessary to advance the hour of the day, to skip past the morning and the early afternoon, spent in the public square and the streets of that vicinity, and it is necessary to follow Mr. Krupper by streetcar into another section of the city.

No sooner has he got upon this streetcar than Mr. Krupper undergoes a certain alteration, not too subtle to betray some outward signals: for he sits in the streetcar with an air of alertness that he did not have on the bench in the public square, he sits more erect and his various little gestures, fishing in his pocket for something, shifting about on the dirty blond straw bench, changing the level of the window shade, are all executed with greater liveliness and precision, as if they were the motions of a much younger man. Anticipation does that, and we would notice that about him, that mysterious attitude of expectancy, very slightly but noticeably increasing as the car whines along to the other part of the city. And we might even notice him beginning to color faintly as he prepares to ring the bell and rise from his seat a block in advance of the stop at which he descends. When he descends it is with all the painful, wheezing concentration of an inexpert climber following a rope down the side of an Alp, and his muttered *thanks* is too low to be audible as he sets foot to pavement. This he does, finally, with a vast sigh, an almost cosmic respiration, and he lifts his eyes well above the level of the roof-tops without appearing to look into the sky, a purely mechanical elevation that might once have had meaning, a salute to rational Providence which is supposed to be situated somewhere above the level of the roof-tops, if anywhere at all. And now Mr. Krupper has arrived within a block of where he is actually going and which is the place where the mysteries of his nature are to be made unpleasantly manifest to us. For some reason, a silly, squeamish kind of dissimulation, Mr. Krupper prefers to walk the last block to his destination rather than descend from the streetcar immediately before it. As he walks, and still a little before we know where he is going, we notice him making various anxious little preparations and adjustments. First he pats the bag of hard candies. Then he reaches into the opposite pocket of his jacket and pulls out a handful of quarters, counts them, makes sure there are exactly eight, and drops them back in the pocket. He then removes from the breast pocket of the jacket, from behind a protruding white handkerchief, always the whitest thing in his possession, a pair of dark-lensed glasses, lenses so dark that the eyes are not visible behind them. He puts these on. And now for the first time he seemingly dares to look directly toward the place that attracts him, and if we follow his glance we see that it is nothing less apparently innocent than an old theater building called the Joy Rio.

So that much of the mystery is dissolved, and it is nothing more ostensibly remarkable than the little clocklike regularity of going three times a week, on Monday, Thursday and Saturday afternoons at about half past four, to a certain third-rate cinema situated near the water front and known as the Joy Rio. And if we followed Mr. Krupper only as far as the door of that cinema, nothing of an esoteric nature would be noticeable, unless you thought it peculiar that he should go three times a week to a program changed only on Mondays or that he never paused to inspect the outside posters in that gradual, reflective manner of most old men who make a habit of going to the movies but went directly up to the ticket window, or that even before he crossed the street to the block on which the cinema was located, he not only put on the secretive-looking glasses but accelerated his pace as if he were urged along by a bitter wind that nipped particularly at the back of the old man's neck. But naturally we are not going to follow him only that far, we are going to follow him past the ticket window and into the interior of the theater. And right away, as soon as we have made that entrance, a premonition of something out of the ordinary is forced upon us. For the Joy Rio is not, by any means, an ordinary theater. It is the ghost of a once elegant house where plays and operas were performed long ago. But the building does not exist within the geographic limits of that part of the city which is regarded as having an historical value. Its decline into squalor, its conversion into a third-rate cinema, has not been particularly annotated by a sentimental press or public. Actually it is only when the lights are brought on, for a brief interval between shows or at their conclusion, that the place is distinguishable from any other cheap movie house. And then it is only distinguishable by looking upwards. Looking upwards you see that it contains not only the usual orchestra and balcony sections but two tiers of boxes extending in horseshoe design from one side of the proscenium to the other, but the faded gilt, the terribly abused red damask of these upper reaches of the Joy Rio never bloom into sufficient light to make a strong impression from the downstairs. You have to follow Mr. Krupper up the great marble staircase that still rises beyond the balcony level before you really begin to explore the physical mysteries of the place. And that, of course, is what we are going to do.

That is what we are going to do, but first we are going to orientate ourselves a little more specifically in time, for although these visits of Mr. Krupper to the Joy Rio are events of almost timeless repetition, our story is the narrative of one particular time and involving another individual, both of which must first be established, together, before we resume the company of Mr. Krupper.

We come, then, to a certain afternoon when a shadowy youth who may as well remain nameless has come into the Joy Rio without any knowledge of its peculiar character and for no other reason than to catch a few hours' sleep, for he is a stranger in the city who does not have the price of a hotel bedroom and who is in terror of being picked up for vagrancy and set to work for the city at no pay and a poor diet. He is very sleepy, so sleepy that his motions are more instinctive than conscious. The film showing that afternoon at the Joy Rio is an epic of the western ranges, full of loud voices and gunplay, so the boy turns as far away from the noisy and brilliant screen as the geography of the Joy Rio will allow him. He climbs the stairs to the first gallery. It is dark up there, but still noisy; so he continues his ascent, only faintly surprised to find that it is possible to do so. The darkness increases as he approaches the second level and the clamor of the screen is more than correspondingly reduced. In the gloom, as he makes a turn of the stairs, he passes what seems for a moment to be, almost believably, a naked female figure. He pauses there long enough to find out that it is only a piece of life-size statuary, cold to the fingers, and disappointingly hard in the places where he fondly touches it, a nymph made of cobwebbed stone in a niche at the turn of the stairs. He goes on up, and sleep is already descending on him, a black, fuzzy blanket, by the time he has wandered blindly into that one of the row of boxes which is to be occupied also, in a few minutes, by the old man whose mysteries are the sad ones of the Joy Rio . . .

By the time that Mr. Krupper arrives at the box and assures the usher's neutrality with a liberal tip, the boy has plummeted like a stone to the depths of sleep, all the way down to the velvety bottom of it, without a ripple to mark where he has fallen. Head lolls forward and thighs move apart and fingers almost brush the floor. The wet lips have fallen apart and the breath whistles faintly but not enough to be heard by Mr. Krupper. It is so dim in the box that the fat old man nearly sits down in the boy's lap before he discovers that his usual seat has been taken. At first Mr. Krupper thinks this nearly invisible companion may be a certain Italian youth of his acquaintance who sometimes shares the box with him for a few minutes, at rare intervals, five or six weeks apart, and he whispers inquiringly the name of this youth, which is Bruno, but he gets no answer, and he decides, no, it could not be Bruno. The slight odor that made him think it might be, an odor made up of sweat and tobacco and the prodigality of certain youthful glands, is not at all unfamiliar to the old man's nose, and while he is now convinced that it is not Bruno, this time, it nevertheless makes him feel a stir of anticipatory happiness in his bosom, which also heaves from the exertion of having just climbed two flights of the grand staircase. In a crouched position he locates the other chair and carefully sets it where he wants it to be, at a nicely calculated space from the one that is occupied by the sleeper, and then Mr. Krupper deposits himself on the seat with the stiff-kneed elaboration of an old camel. It sets the blood charging through him at breakneck speed. Ah, well. That much is completed.

A few minutes pass in which Mr. Krupper's eyesight adjusts itself to the almost pitch-black condition of light in the box, but even then it is impossible to make out the figure beside him in any detail. Yes, it is young, it is slender. The hair is dark and lustrous, the odor is captivating. But the head of the sleeper has lolled a bit to one side, the side away from Mr. Krupper, and sometimes it is possible, in the dark, to make very dangerous mistakes. There are certain pursuits in which even the most cautious man must depart from absolute caution if he intends at all to enjoy them. Mr. Krupper knew that. He had known it for a great many years, and that was why he had observed such elaborate caution in nearly every other department of his life, to compensate for those necessary breaches of caution that were the sad concomitant of his kind of pleasure. And so as a measure of caution, Mr. Krupper digs into his pocket for a box of matches which he carries with him only for this purpose, to secure that one relatively clear glance at a fellow-occupant of the dark box. He strikes the match and leans a little bit forward. And then his heart, aged seventy and already strained from the recent exertion of the stairs, undergoes an alarming spasm, for never in this secret life of his, never in thirty years' attendance of matinees at the Joy Rio, has old Mr. Krupper discovered beside him, even now within contact, inspiring the dark with its warm animal fragrance, any dark youth of remotely equivalent beauty.

The match burns his fingers, he lets it fall to the floor. His vest is half unbuttoned, but he unbuttons it further to draw a deep breath. Something is hurting in him, first in his chest, then lower, a nervous contraction of his unhealthy intestines. He whispers to himself the German word for calmness. He leans back in the uncomfortable small chair and attempts to look at the faraway flickering square of the motion picture. The excitement in his body will not subside. The respiration will not stabilize. The contraction of his intestinal nerves and muscles gives him sharp pain, and he is wondering, for a moment, if it will not be necessary for him to return hastily downstairs to move his bowels. But then, all at once, the sleeper beside him stirs and half sits up in the gloom. The lolling head suddenly jerks erect and cries a sharp word in Spanish. "Excuse me," says Mr. Krupper, softly, involuntarily. "I didn't know you were there." The youth gives a grunting laugh and seems to relax once more. He makes a sad, sighing sound as he slouches down once more in the chair beside Mr. Krupper. Mr. Krupper feels somewhat calmer now. It is hard to say why but the almost unbearable acuteness of the proximity, the discovery, now has passed, and Mr. Krupper himself assumes a more relaxed position in his hard chair. The muscular spasm and the tachycardia now are gently eased off and the bowels appear to be settled. Minutes pass in the box. Mr. Krupper has the impression that the youth beside him, that vision, has not yet returned to slumber, although the head has lolled again to one side, this time the side that is toward him, and the limbs fallen apart with the former relaxation. Slowly, as if secretively, Mr. Krupper digs in his jacket pocket for the hard candies. One he unwraps and places in his own mouth which is burning and dry. Then he extracts another which he extends on the palm of his hand, which shakes a little, toward the youthful stranger. He clears his throat which feels as if it would be difficult to produce a sound, and manages to say, "A piece of candy?" "Huh," says the youth. The syllable has the sound of being startled. For a moment it seems that he is bewildered or angry. He makes no immediate move to take or reject the candy, he only sits up and stares. Then all at once he grunts. His fingers snatch at the candy and pop it directly into his mouth, paper wrapping and all. Mr. Krupper hastens to warn him that the candy is wrapped up. He grunts again and removes it from his mouth, and Mr. Krupper hears him plucking the rather brittle wrapping paper away, and afterwards he hears the candy crunching noisily between the jaws of the youth. Before the jaws have stopped crunching, Mr. Krupper has dug the whole bag out of his pocket and now he says, "Take some more, take several pieces, there's lots." Again the youth hesitates slightly. Again he grunts. Then he digs his hand into the bag and Mr. Krupper feels it lighter by half when the hand has been removed. "Hungry?" he whispers with a questioning note. The youth grunts again, affirmatively and in a way that seems friendly. Don't hurry, thinks Mr. Krupper. Don't hurry, there's plenty of time, he's not going to go up in smoke like the dream that he looks! So he puts the remains of the candy in his pocket, and makes a low humming sound as of gratification as he looks back toward the flickering screen where the cowboy hero is galloping into a sunset. In a moment the picture will end and the lights will go up for an interval of a minute before the program commences all over again. There is, of course, some danger that the youth will leave. That possibility has got to be considered, but the affirmative answer to the question "Hungry?" has already given some basis, not quite a pledge, of continuing association between them.

Now just before the lights go up, Mr. Krupper makes a bold move. He reaches into the pocket opposite to the one containing the bag of hard candy and scoops out all that remain of the quarters, about six altogether, and jostles them ever so slightly together in his fist so they tinkle a bit. This is all that he does. And the lights come gradually on, like daybreak only a little accelerated; the once elegant theater blooms dully as a winter rose beneath him as he leans forward in order to seem to be interested in the downstairs. He is a little panicky but he knows that the period of light will be very short, not more than a minute or two. But he also knows that he is fat and ugly. Mr. Krupper knows that he is a terrible old man, shameful and despicable even to those who tolerate his caresses, perhaps even more so to those than to the others who only see him. He does not deceive himself at all about that, and that is why he took the six quarters out and shook them together a little before the lights were brought on. Yes, now. Now the lights are beginning to darken again, and the youth is still there. If he is now alert to the unpleasant character of Mr. Krupper's appearance, he is nevertheless still beside him. And he is still unwrapping the bits of hard candy and crunching them between his powerful young jaws, steadily, with the automatic, invariable rhythm of a horse masticating his food.

The lights are now down again and the panic has passed. Mr. Krupper abandons the pretense of staring downstairs and leans back once more in the unsteady chair. Now something rises in him, something heroic, determined, and he leans toward the youth, turning around a little, and with his left hand he finds the right hand of the youth and offers the coins. At first the hand of the youth will not change its position, will not respond to the human and metallic pressure. Mr. Krupper is about to fly once more into panic, but then, at the very moment when his hand is about to withdraw from contact with the hand of the youth, that hand turns about, revolves to bring the palm upward. The coins descend, softly, with a slight tinkle, and Mr. Krupper knows that the contract is sealed between them.

When around midnight the lights of the Joy Rio were brought up for the last time that evening, the body of Mr. Krupper was discovered in his remote box of the theater with his knees on the floor and his ponderous torso wedged between two wobbly gilt chairs as if he had expired in an attitude of prayer. The notice of the old man's death was given unusual prominence for the obituary of someone who had no public character and whose private character was so peculiarly low. But evidently the private character of Mr. Krupper was to remain anonymous in the memories of those anonymous persons who had enjoyed or profited from his company in the tiny box at the Joy Rio, for the notice contained no mention of anything of such a special nature. It was composed by a spinsterly reporter who had been impressed by the sentimental values of a seventy-year-old retired merchant dying of thrombosis at a cowboy thriller with a split bag of hard candies in his pocket and the floor about him littered with sticky wrappers, some of which even adhered to the shoulders and sleeves of his jacket.

It was, among the cousins, the Complete Little Citizen of the World who first caught sight of this astonishingly agreeable item in the paper and who announced the tidings in a voice as shrill as a steam whistle announcing the meridian of the day, and it was she that exclaimed hours later, while the little family was still boiling with the excitement and glory of it, *Just think, Papa, the old man choked to death on our hard candy!*

March 1953 (Published 1954)

Man Bring This Up Road

Mrs. Flora Goforth had three Easter-egg-colored villas perched on a sea cliff a little north of Amalfi, and being one of those enormously wealthy old ladies who come to be known as art patrons, often only because they have served, now and then, as honorary sponsor or hostess at some of those social functions, balls or banquets which take place on the fashionable periphery of the art world, she was diligently sought after by that flock of young people who fly to Europe in summer with one large suitcase and a small one, a portable typewriter or a paintbox, and a book of traveler's checks that hardly amount to a hundred dollars by the time they have passed through Paris; and for this reason, because she was pursued and besieged by this flock of gifted, improvident young wanderers of summer, she had found it advisable not to improve the landward approaches to her siege on the Divina Costiera of Italy but to leave them as they were left by the hand of God, a mortal hazard to any creature less agile than a mountain goat.

However, Mrs. Goforth was now edging timorously into her seventies. Other rich old ladies of her acquaintance were popping off, here and there, with the jazzy rhythm of fireworks on the Fourth of July. She had to have bright young people around her at times, that summer, to forget those reports on mortality that kept appearing in the Paris *Herald Tribune* or cables from the States, so she would send out her motor launch now and again to pick up a select group of them from such nearby resorts as Capri or Positano, sometimes even from Naples.

But Jimmy Dobyne was not called for or recently invited by Mrs. Goforth; he reached her by the goat path up the landward approach to her domain that summer, and it was the gardener's boy, Giulio, who warned her of his arrival by handing her a thin volume that had the shocking word "Poems" on its cover, passing it to her through the crack of her bedroom door and stammering in his pidgin English: Man bring this up road!

For several days her great old sunflower head had been drooping on its stem with incipient boredom and so Mrs. Goforth thought twice before she knew what to do, and then she said, also in pidgin English: Bring man out on terrace so can see.

When Giulio had vanished she picked up her German field glasses and crouched at her bedroom window in the white villa to inspect the Trojan horse guest. Presently he appeared, a young man wearing only a pair of *lederhosen* and bearing slung from his shoulders in a rucksack all that he owned, including four more copies of that volume of verse which he had offered as a visiting card to his hoped-for hostess. Giulio led him out upon the terrace and then drew back and Jimmy Dobyne stood blinking anxiously in the fierce noonday sun, looking here and there for his hoped-for hostess but seeing only an aviary full of small bright-plumaged birds, a fishpool of colorful fish and a chattering monkey that was chained to a pillar and everywhere cascades of violent purplish-red bougainvillea vines.

Mrs. Goforth? he called.

There was no response to his call except the loud chattering of the monkey chained to a corner post of the low balustrade that enclosed the terrace. Having not much to look at or consider, Jimmy looked at the monkey; its enchainment, he thought, could hardly be anything but a punitive measure. Near it was a bowl containing remnants of fruit but there was no water bowl and the length of the chain did not permit the monkey to get into shade. Not far from the reach of the chain was the fishpool and the monkey had stretched its chain as far toward the pool as it could, which was not far enough to reach it. Without any thought about it, just as a reflex, Jimmy scooped up some water from the pool in the food bowl and placed it within the monkey's reach on the terrace. The monkey sprang to the bowl and started drinking from it with such incontinent thirst that Jimmy laughed out loud.

Signor!

The gardener's boy had come back to the terrace. He jerked his head toward the far end of the terrace and said: Come!

He led Jimmy to a bedroom in the pink villa.

Jimmy Dobyne was at least temporarily "in." As soon as Giulio left him alone in his guest room in the pink villa, Jimmy flung himself, all dusty and sweaty as he was, on the bed and blinked up at the painted cupids on the celestial blue ceiling.

His fatigue was so great that it even eclipsed his hunger and within a minute or two he fell into a sleep that lasted all that day and the night that followed and half the day after that.

After her siesta the day of Jimmy's arrival, Mrs. Goforth went over to the pink villa to steal a look at her uninvited guest. She found him still in his *lederhosen*, his rucksack on the floor beside the bed.

She opened the canvas bag and, like an experienced thief, she rooted thoroughly but quietly through it till she discovered what she was looking for, his passport, wrapped up in a bunch of washed but not ironed shirts. She checked the date of his birth. It was in September, 1922, which confirmed her impression that he was a good bit older than he appeared. She said "Hello" several times, tonelessly as a parrot, to test the depth of his sleep, and, since he remained as dead asleep as ever, she turned on a bedside lamp so she could look at him better. She bent over him, brought her nose within a few inches of his parted lips to see if he smelled of liquor or tooth decay as young poets sometimes do when they're not so young any more. His breath was odorless, but Mrs. Goforth could see that it was more than the fatigue of traveling by foot in rough country that had cast a color on his lower eyelids as if a bougainvillea petal had been rubbed on them.

Mrs. Goforth was not displeased, on the whole, by her close inspection of her self-invited guest but she made a telephone call to check on his past history and present reputation.

There was a lady on Capri who had known Jimmy well in his heyday, which was in the forties, and this lady gave her some information about him. She told her that he had been discovered at a ski lodge in Nevada in 1940 by one of those ladies of Mrs. Goforth's generation and social set who had "popped off" lately. This lady had brought him to New York and made him a shining star in the world of Connecticut and Long Island weekends, of ballet balls and so forth. He'd been the odd combination of ski instructor and poet, and this lady who launched him had brought out his book of poems through the sort of small publishing house called a vanity press. However, the book had created a sensation. He had been taken seriously as a poet, but after that the poems stopped for some reason. He'd coasted on his early celebrity all through the forties, but lately things had gone against him. It started with his "sleeping trick" a couple of summers ago. Mrs. Goforth naturally didn't understand what that was but her friend on Capri gave a vivid account of it. It seemed that he had worn out his welcome at a rich lady's villa on Capri, he had been asked to give up his room for another guest expected and had tried to avoid this eviction by playing this sleeping trick on his hostess. He had taken a large dose of sleeping tablets but had also left an early-morning call so that they'd find him early enough to revive him.

As soon as he was able to leave he was told to do so. It was after that that he started "constructing mobiles."

Oh, he's constructing mobiles?

That's what he's been doing since he dried up as a poet. You know what mobiles are?

Of course I know what they are!

Well, he constructed mobiles but they didn't move, he didn't construct them right, he made them too heavy or something and they just don't move.

He gave that up?

No, as far as I know, he's still constructing mobiles. Hasn't he got any with him?

Oh! Mrs. Goforth remembered some odd metal objects among the stuff in the rucksack.

What?

Yes, I believe he still is, I think he's brought some with him.

Is he still *there*?

Yes. Sleeping in the pink villa, for hours and hours, completely dead to the world there!

Well . . .

What?

Good luck with him, Flora. Watch out for the sleeping trick, though . . .

As Jimmy Dobyne came up to the breakfast table on the terrace of the white villa the next morning, he said to Mrs. Goforth: I think you must be the kindest person I've ever known in my life!

Then I'm afraid you haven't known many kind people in your life, said his hostess.

She nodded slightly in a way that could be interpreted as a permission to sit at the table and Jimmy sat down.

Coffee?

Thank you, said Jimmy.

He was ravenously hungry, the hungriest he could remember ever being in a life that had contained more than one prolonged fast for secular reasons. He tried to look about for something to eat without appearing to take his eyes from his hostess, but there seemed to be nothing on the chaste white serving table but the silver urn and the china; there apparently wasn't even cream and sugar.

As if she read his mind or the almost panicky tightening of his stomach muscles, her smile turned brighter and she said: For breakfast I have nothing but black coffee. I find that anything solid takes the edge off my energies, and it's the time after breakfast when I do my best work.

He smiled back at her, thinking that in the next breath she'd surely say, But of course you order anything that you like. How about eggs and bacon, or would you like to begin with a honeydew melon?

But the long minute stretched even longer and the words that finally followed her ruminative look made no sense to him: Man bring this up road, huh?

What, Mrs. Goforth?

That's what the little boy said when he gave me your book. I haven't read it but I heard it talked about when it first came out.

You asked me to give you a copy last winter at the Ballet Ball, but you were never in when I called.

Well, well, that's how it goes. When did it first come out?

In 1946.

Hmm, a long time ago. How old are you?

He thought a moment and said rather softly, as if he were asking for confirmation of the statement: Thirty.

Thirty-four, she said promptly.

How do you know?

I took a look at your passport while you were having that record-smashing siesta.

He made an effort to look playfully reproachful. Why did you do that?

Because I've been plagued by imposters. I wanted to be sure that you were the true Jimmy Dobyne, since last summer I had the false Paul Bowles and the year before that I had the false Truman Capote and the false Eudora Welty, and as far as I know they're still down there in that little grass hut on the beach, where undesirables are transferred when the villas are overcrowded. I call it the Oubliette. Y'know what that is, don't you? An oubliette? It's a medieval institution that I think, personally, was discarded too soon. It was a dungeon where people were put for keeps, to be forgotten. So that's what I call my little grass house on the beach, I call it the Oubliette. From the French verb *oublier*—that means to forget. And I do really forget them. Maybe you think I'm joking but it's the truth. Y'see, I've been through a lot of unpleasant experiences with free-loaders and I have developed a sort of complex about it. I don't want to be taken, I can't stand to be made a patsy. Understand what I mean? This is nothing personal. You come with your book with a photograph of you on it which still looks like you, just, well, ten years younger, but still unmistakably you. You're not the false Jimmy Dobyne, I'm sure about that.

Thank you, said Jimmy. He didn't know what else to say.

Of course some people have got an oubliette in their minds. That's also a good institution, a mental oubliette, but I am afflicted with perfect memory, almost total recall, as the psychologists call it. Faces, names, everything, everything, everything!—comes back to me . . .

She smiled at him so genially that he smiled back, although her rapid flow of speech made him flinch as if a pistol were aimed at him in the hand of a madman.

However, she went on, I don't keep up with the new personalities in the world of art. Of course you're not a new personality in it, you're almost a veteran, aren't you? I said a veteran, I didn't say a has-been. Ha, ha, I didn't call you a has-been, I said a veteran, baby! Ho ho ho . . .

Jimmy increased his smile because she was laughing, but he knew that it had turned to a tortured grimace.

There was an involuntary lapse in his attention to what she was saying while he said to himself: Don't give up! The road goes on from here. He wasn't certain that he was sure of it, though. Between him and anything coming after there was Naples again, and yesterday— there was Naples . . .

He had walked along the long, long row of hotels facing Santa Lucia, the bay, and in front of almost every hotel there had been sidewalk tables where he had encountered people he used to know well. And even when they didn't appear to see him, although he knew that they did, he had stopped and talked a bit with them, as charmingly as he knew how. Not one of them, no, not a single one, had asked him to sit down with them at their sidewalk table! *Frightening? my God, yes!* Something must be visible in his face that let them know he had crossed over a certain frontier of . . .

He didn't want to identify that frontier, to give it a name.

To his surprise, he was standing on his feet and shading his eyes to peer down at the beach. Oh, yes, I see it! he said.

What?

Your oubliette, I think it looks very attractive.

Well, she told him, it's not in use this summer.

Why is it out of use now? It seems like a perfect solution, Mrs. Goforth.

Well, she said, it's still on my property and some people hold me responsible for the ones that I put there. I don't want to know, I never let myself know, what happened to them. As far as I know, or want to, they're all washed out by the tide, all phonies and free-loaders and so forth that think I owe them a living! What do you do? You don't write poetry any more, that much I know, but what do you do now?

Oh, now? I construct mobiles.

Oh, you mean those metal things that you hang from a ceiling to turn around in the wind.

Yes, that's right, said Jimmy, they're poetry in metal. I've got one for you.

Her geniality vanished. Her straight look at him drifted away from his face.

I don't accept presents, she said, except from old friends at Christmas, and as for mobiles, no, baby! I wouldn't know what to do with them. I think it would get on my nerves to watch them turning . . .

I'm sorry, he said, I wanted to give one to you.

What's wrong with you? she asked him with sudden sharpness.

Wrong? With me?

Yes, there's something wrong with you. What are you worried about?

I'm disappointed that you don't want a mobile.

I don't want or need anything at all in the world!

She made this pronouncement with such force that Jimmy felt compelled to try to disguise his fright with a smile that he knew was no more a smile than the response to a dentist's order to "Open wide."

You've got good teeth. Young man, you're blessed with a very fine set of teeth, said Mrs. Goforth.

She leaned toward him a little, squinting, and then said: Are they real?

Oh yes, said Jimmy, except for one molar back here.

Well, I have good teeth, too. In fact my teeth are so good people think they are false. But look!

She took her large incisors between her thumb and forefinger to demonstrate the firmness of their attachment. See, not even a bridge, and I'll be seventy-two years old in October. In my whole mouth I've had exactly three fillings, which are still there. You see them?

She pulled back her jowls, dropping her lower jaw till the morning sun lit three bits of gold in the purplish cavern.

This tooth here, she continued, was slightly chipped when my daughter's third baby hit me in the mouth with the butt of a water pistol at Murray Bay, Canada. I told my daughter that child would grow into a monster and it sure as hell did—

Might I have some sugar? Jimmy interposed gently.

Oh, no thank you, she muttered rather crossly, I never take it because they once found a small trace of sugar in my urine . . .

A slightly frightened look clouded her gaze for a moment. All at once she sneezed. The sneeze was not at all violent but it seemed to throw her into a regular frenzy.

Angelina, Angelina! she bellowed. *Subito, subito,* Kleenex!

She sat crouched over, awaiting another sneeze, but all that happened was a couple of sniffs. She sat up slowly and fixed her angry glare on his face again. I'm allergic to something that grows around here. I haven't found out what it is, but when I do—

The sentence was no less forceful for remaining unfinished.

I hope it is not the bougainvillea vines, said Jimmy. I have never seen such wonderful bougainvillea vines in my life, or so many of them, either!

No, it isn't the bougainvillea, she said in her warning whisper, but I'm having an allergy specialist flown down here from Paris to check me with every goddammed plant on the place, and every animal, too!

She brooded a moment more, her slow gaze wandering among the two cocker spaniels, the aviary, the chained monkey, a kitten gazing Narcissus-like into the fishpool. That's right, she growled. He's going to check me with every plant and animal on the place. . . . Then she got up and left him sitting there, as if she were blown from her chair by her third faint sneeze. She went, crouched over, halfway down the terrace on little tottering steps, then stood stock-still and sneezed for a fourth time.

What a shame! called Jimmy. Can I do something?

Her answer was incoherent or inaudible or both and a moment or two later she was gone from the terrace.

Angelina burst out of the white villa with a box of Kleenex, the excited butler screaming: *Giù, giù, giù!* The maid said something in terror, mixed with fury, and started in several directions before the butler seized her by her long skinny elbows and shot her in the right one.

The sun on Jimmy was beginning to daze and blind him. He got up and moved into shadow.

On the small serving table he suddenly noticed a fine white napkin covering something that made a slight mound on a plate. With guilty haste he picked it up to look under it and felt like crying when he saw that it was only a heap of crested silver teaspoons.

He had turned and started slowly away from the painfully brilliant white table when Mrs. Goforth's voice, a little muffled by a bundle of disposable tissues held to her mouth and nostrils, called to him from the foot of the stairs to a lower terrace of the white villa: Come down here. We can talk in the library.

Jimmy had been about to vomit up his cup of black coffee. He held it down forcibly as he descended the stairs.

Mrs. Goforth was waiting on the lower terrace, and for the first time he observed her appearance and costume, being no longer distracted by the hope of a breakfast.

The upper part of her costume, a halter strap, seemed to be made of fish net dyed magenta with very wide interstices through which could be seen her terra cotta breasts, only the nipples being covered by little patches of magenta satin. This fish-net "bra" was tied behind her shoulders in a flirtatious bow knot with two long dangling tails. Her middle was bare and her Amazonian hips were confined by skin-tight shorts exactly the shade of the bougainvillea blossoms that overhung all the walls of Tre Amanti.

Come into the library, do hurry up! she called from the end of the terrace, and he tried hard to walk briskly but it seemed to take him an endless amount of time and he thanked God that she turned away just a second before he felt himself sway, so close to fainting that he had to rest the palm of his hand for a moment against the white stucco wall, bringing it away stained with the pink of bougainvillea that dripped everywhere.

The library seemed almost black as he felt his way in it.

Cool, huh? she called to him.

Oh, yes, very . . .

I love to move from a hot place to a cool place, she continued. It's the great pleasure of summer . . .

He still waited for the room to come clear, however dimly, till she called him once more and then he started forward. His vision was just beginning to recover, when—

He seemed to trip over something, halfway across the room, but afterward he was not sure if he had actually tripped over something or had stumbled in terror.

Standing there all naked terra cotta in the deep gloom, quite motionless for the moment he caught sight of her, she seemed like one of those immense fountain figures in plazas of far northern countries, but travestied by a sculptor with evil wit.

I am, she said, a completely informal person. How about you?

I—

What?

I—

What's the matter with you?

I—

Oh, for God's sake, she blustered, are you going to pretend you're shocked or something?

No, of—*course* not, but—

Silence followed, and continued.

She suddenly stooped to snatch up a small pink garment. The bus to Naples passes in half an hour, she snapped as she retreated behind a great table.

Mrs. Goforth?

Yes? What!

I—don't have a penny . . .

Naturally not! But I pay for as far as Naples and never farther! Also I'd like you to know that I—

Mrs. Goforth!

What?

Don't say anything more.

He covered his face with his hands.

The man was sobbing, my God, yes, he was bawling like a child!

Mrs. Goforth came back around the table. Some other person seemed to move into her body and take possession of her and she went to the sobbing young man and took him somewhat gingerly in her arms and pressed his head somewhat carefully to her bosom, as if it might break against her like a bird's egg.

You made me angry, she murmured, when you made that sarcastic remark about kindness on the breakfast terrace.

Why do you think it was a sarcastic remark?

Because everybody who knows me knows that I am colder-hearted than the gods of old Egypt!

Why?

I have no choice.

Why?

I've never had any choice . . .

Give me a job, said Jimmy.

Doing what?

Proving that you are kinder than you think.

I know what you mean, she said.

I mean what I say, he pleaded.

Well, she murmured. Maybe if you stay here for dinner tonight—

I'd be delighted! he said, a little too quickly and loudly.

O.K., she murmured.

She had gotten back into her scanty garments. The interview was abruptly finished by the running approach of the maid, crying out before she came in: *Telefono!* Long deestance!

Then she threw the door open and Mrs. Goforth swept past her, marching out, and Jimmy said to the maid: Please bring some bread and cheese to my room, I'm in the pink villa.

The maid's face showed no comprehension but it was at least an hour later, in his room in the pink villa, that he despaired of his request being honored.

At five o'clock the bedside phone tinkled and he lifted it to his ear and heard Mrs. Goforth saying all in one breath, My friend is coming back with a very large party, I'm very much afraid that every bed will be taken for the next week or two, it's such a pity, we would have loved to keep you!

It was the voice of a young girl and the click interrupted it so abruptly he thought he ought to call back—at least for a moment he wondered if he could. He held the white enameled receiver weakly in his hand for a minute before it sank into him that he must move on again even though there was nowhere to move on to.

He rang the little electric bell by the bed but no one came, so after a while, giving up finally the idea of getting a bite to eat before his departure, he picked up his packed rucksack and went out of the pink villa into the sun, which was as hot and yellow as it had been at "breakfast," perhaps even hotter and yellower, and started back down the same almost impassably steep path by which he had come.

In the white villa the gardener's boy delivered a message to the chatelaine of Tre Amanti.

Man gone back down road.

Oh good, I hope so, she murmured, it being her habit or fate never quite to believe a piece of good news until her own observation had proved it true, and sometimes not even then.

1953 (Published 1959)

The Mattress by the Tomato Patch

My landlady, Olga Kedrova, has given me a bowl of ripe tomatoes from the patch that she lies next to, sunning herself in the great white and blue afternoons of California. These tomatoes are big as my fist, bloody red of color, and firm to the touch as a young swimmer's pectoral muscles.

I said, Why, Olga, my God, it would take me a month to eat that many tomatoes, but she said, Don't be a fool, you'll eat them like grapes, and that was almost how I ate them. It is now five o'clock of this resurrected day in the summer of 1943, a day which I am recording in the present tense although it is ten years past. Now there are only a couple of the big ripe tomatoes left in the pale-blue china bowl, but their sweetness and pride are undimmed, for their heart is not in the bowl which is their graveyard but in the patch that Olga lies next to, and the patch seems to be inexhaustible. It remains out there in the sun and the loam and in the consanguine presence of big Olga Kedrova. She rests beside the patch all afternoon on a raggedy mattress retired from service in one of her hotel bedrooms.

This resurrected day is a Saturday and all afternoon pairs of young lovers have wandered the streets of Santa Monica, searching for rooms to make love in. Each uniformed boy holds a small zipper bag and the sun-pinked-or-gilded arm of a pretty girl, and they seem to be moving in pools of translucent water. The girl waits at the foot of steps which the boy bounds up, at first eagerly, then anxiously, then with desperation, for Santa Monica is literally flooded with licensed and unlicensed couples in this summer of 1943. The couples are endless and their search is unflagging. By sundown and long after, even as late as two or three in the morning, the boy will bound up steps and the girl wait below, sometimes primly pretending not to hear the four-letter word he mutters after each disappointment, sometimes saying it for him when he resumes his dogged hold on her arm. Even as daybreak comes they'll still be searching and praying and cursing with bodies that ache from pent-up longing more than fatigue.

Terrible separations occur at daybreak. The docile girl finally loses faith or patience; she twists violently free of the hand that bruises her arm and dashes sobbing into an all-night café to phone for a cab. The boy hovers outside, gazing fiercely through fog and window, his now empty fist opening and closing on itself. She sits between two strangers, crouches over coffee, sobbing, sniffing, and maybe after a minute she goes back out to forgive him and rests in his arms without hope of anything private, or maybe she is relentless and waits for the cab to remove her from him forever, pretending not to see him outside the fogged window until he wanders away, drunk now, to look for more liquor, turning back now and then to glare at the hot yellow pane that shielded her from his fury. Son-of-a-bitch of a four-letter word for a part of her woman's body is muttered again and again as he stumbles across the car tracks into Palisades Park, under royal palm trees as tall as five-story buildings and over the boom of white breakers and into mist. Long pencils of light still weave back and forth through the sky in search of enemy planes that never come over and nothing else seems to move. But you never can tell. Even at this white hour he might run into something that's better than nothing before the paddy wagon picks him up or he falls onto one of those cots for service men only at some place like the Elks' Lodge.

Olga knows all this, but what can she do about it? Build more rooms single-handed? To look at Olga you'd almost believe that she could. She is the kind of woman whose weight should be computed not in pounds but in stones, for she has the look of a massive primitive sculpture. Her origin is the Middle East of Europe. She subscribes to the *Daily Worker*, copies of which she sometimes thrusts under my door with paragraphs boxed in red pencil, and she keeps hopefully handing me works by Engels and Veblen and Marx which I hold for a respectful interval and then hand back to her with the sort of vague comment that doesn't fool her a bit. She has now set me down as a hopelessly unregenerate prostitute of the capitalist class, but she calls me "Tennie" or "Villyums" with undiminished good humor and there is nothing at all that she doesn't tell me about herself and nothing about myself that she doesn't expect me to tell . . . When I first came to stay here, late in the spring, and it came out in our conversation that I was a writer at Metro's, she said, Ha ha, I know you studio people! She says things like this with an air of genial complicity which a lingering reserve in my nature at first inclined me to pretend not to understand. But as the summer wore on, my reserve dropped off, and at present I don't suppose we have one secret between us. Sometimes while we are talking, she will go in my bathroom and continue the conversation with the door wide open and her seated figure in full view, looking out at me with the cloudlessly candid eyes of a child who has not yet learned that some things are meant to be private.

This is a house full of beds and I strongly suspect that big Olga has lain in them all. These big old-fashioned brass or white iron beds are like the keyboard of a concert grand piano on which she is running up and down in a sort of continual arpeggio of lighthearted intrigues, and I can't much blame her when I look at her husband. It is sentimental to think that all sick people deserve our sympathy. Ernie is sick but I can't feel sorry for him. He is a thin, sour man whose chronic intestinal trouble was diagnosed eight years ago as a cancer, but whose condition today is neither much worse nor better than when the diagnosis was made, a fact that confirms the landlady's contempt for all opinions that don't come through "The Party."

Ernie does the woman's work around the apartment-hotel, while Olga soaks up the sun on the high front steps or from the mattress by the tomato patch out back. From those front steps her lively but unastonished look can comprehend the whole fantasy of Santa Monica Beach, as far north as the "Gone with the Wind" mansion of former film star Molly Delancey and as far south as the equally idiotic but somewhat gayer design of the roller coasters at Venice, California.

Somehow it seems to me, because I like to think so, that this is the summer hotel, magically transplanted from the Crimean seacoast, where Chekhov's melancholy writer, Trigorin, first made the acquaintance of Madame Arcadina, and where they spent their first weekend together, sadly and wisely within the quiet sound of the sea, a pair of middle-aged lovers who turn the lights off before they undress together, who read plays aloud to each other on heaps of cool pillows and sometimes find that the pressure of a hand before falling asleep is all that they really need to be sure they are resting together.

The Palisades is a big white wooden structure with galleries and gables and plenty of space around it. It stands directly over a municipal playground known as "Muscle Beach." It is here that the acrobats and tumblers work out in the afternoons, great powerful Narcissans who handle their weightless girls and daintier male partners with a sort of tender unconsciousness under the blare and activity of our wartime heavens.

While I am working at home, during my six-week lay-off-without-pay from the studio (a punishment for intransigence that presages a short term of employment and forces me to push my play anxiously forward), it is a comfort now and then to notice Big Olga dreaming on the front steps or sprawled on that old mattress in back of the building.

I like to imagine how the mattress got out there . . .

This is how I see it.

On one of those diamond-bright mornings of early summer, Big Olga looms into an upstairs bedroom a soldier and his girl-friend have occupied for the weekend which has just passed. With nonchalant grunts, she looks at the cigarette stains and sniffs at the glasses on the bedside table. With only at token wrinkle or two of something too mild to be defined as disgust, she picks up the used contraceptives tossed under the bed, counts them and murmurs "My God" as she drops them into the toilet and comes back out of the bathroom without having bothered to wash her hands at the sink. The boy and the girl have plainly enjoyed themselves and Olga is not the kind to resent their pleasure and she is philosophical about little damages to beds and tables incurred in a storm of love-making. Some day one of them will fall asleep or pass out in bed with a lighted cigarette and her summer hotel will burn down. She knows this will happen some day but till it happens, oh, well, why worry about it.

She goes back to the bed and jerks off the crumpled sheets to expose the mattress.

My God, she cries out, the condition this mattress is in!

Bad? says Ernie.

Completely ruined, she tells him.

Pigs, says Ernie.

But Olga is not unhappy.

Pigs, pigs, pigs, says Ernie with almost squealing repugnance, but Olga says, Aw, shut up! A bed is meant to make love on, so why blow your stack about it?

This shuts Ernie up, but inwardly he boils and becomes short-winded.

Ernie, says Olga, you take that end of the mattress.

She picks up the other.

Where does it go? asks Ernie.

The little man backs toward the door but Olga thinks differently of it. She gives an emphatic tug toward the gallery entrance. This way, she says roughly, and Ernie, who rarely presumes anymore to ask her a question, tags along with his end of the mattress dragging the carpet. She kicks the screen door open and with a joyous gasp she steps out into the morning above the ocean and beach. The white clocktower of downtown Santa Monica is looking out of the mist, and everything glistens. She sniffs like a dog at the morning, grins connivingly at it, and shouts, Around this way!

The mattress is lugged to the inland side of the gallery, and Ernie is still not aware of what she is up to.

Now let go, says Olga.

Ernie releases his end and staggers back to the scalloped white frame wall. He is broken and breathless, he sees pinwheels in the sky. But Olga is chuckling a little. While the pinwheels blinded him, Olga has somehow managed to gather both ends of the mattress into her arms and has rolled them together to make a great cylinder. Hmmm, she says to herself. She likes the feel of the mattress, exults in the weight of it on her. She stands there embracing the big inert thing in her arms and with the grip of her thighs. It leans against her, a big exhausted lover, a lover that she has pressed upon his back and straddled and belabored and richly survived. She leans back with the exhausted weight of the mattress resting on her, and she is chuckling and breathing deeply now that she feels her power no longer contested. Fifteen, twenty, twenty-five years are in her of life still, not depleted more than enough to make her calm and easy. Time is no problem to her. Hugging the mattress, she thinks of a wrestler named "Tiger" who comes and goes all summer, remembers a sailor named Ed who has spent some liberties with her, thinks of a Marine Sergeant, brought up in a Kansas orphanage, who calls her Mama, feels all the weight of them resting lightly on her as the weight of one bird with various hurrying wings, staying just long enough to satisfy her and not a moment longer. And so she grips the big mattress and loves the weight of it on her. Ah, she says to herself, ah, hmmm . . .

She sees royal palm trees and the white clocktower of downtown Santa Monica, and possibly says to herself, Well, I guess I'll have a hot barbecue and a cold beer for lunch at the Wop's stand on Muscle Beach and I'll see if Tiger is there, and if he isn't, I'll catch the five o'clock bus to L.A. and take in a good movie, and after that I'll walk over to Olivera

Street and have some tamales with chili and two or three bottles of Carta Blanca and come back out to the beach on the nine o'clock bus. That will be after sundown, and three miles east of the beach, they turn the lights out in the bus (because of the wartime blackout), and Olga will have chosen a good seat-companion near the back of the bus, a sailor who's done two hitches and knows the scoop, so when the lights go out, her knees will divide and his will follow suit and the traveling dusk will hum with the gossamer wings of Eros. She'll nudge him when the bus slows toward the corner of Wilshire and Ocean. They'll get off there and wander hand-in-hand into the booming shadows of Palisades Park, which Olga knows like a favorite book never tired of. All along that enormously tall cliff, under royal palms and over the Pacific, are little summer houses and trellised arbors with beaches where sudden acquaintances burst into prodigal flower.

All of these things, these prospects, too vivid to need any thought, are in her nerves as she feels the weight of the mattress between her breasts and thighs, and now she is ready to show the extent of her power. She tightens the grip of her arms on the soft-hard bulk and raises the mattress to the height of her shoulders.

Watch out, my God, says Ernie, you'll rupture yourself!

Not I! says Olga, I'll not rupture myself!

Ha ha, look here! she orders.

Her black eyes flash as she coils up her muscles.

One for the money, two for the show, three to get ready, and four to GO!

Christ Almighty, says Ernie without much breath or conviction, as the mattress sails, yes, almost literally sails above the rail of the gallery and out into the glistening air of morning. Fountains of delicate cotton fiber spurt out of at least a thousand ruptures in its cover the moment the wornout mattress plops to the ground.

Hmmm, says Olga.

The act has been richly completed. She grips the rail of the gallery with her hands that have never yet been fastened on anything they could not overwhelm if they chose to. The big brass bangles she has attached to her ears are jingling with silly but rapturous applause, and Ernie is thinking again, as he has thought so often, since death so thoughtlessly planted a slow seed in his body: How is it possible that I ever lay with this woman, even so long ago as that now is!

With an animal's sense of what goes on behind it, Olga knows what her invalid husband feels when she exhibits her power, and her back to him is neither friendly nor hostile. And if tonight he has a cramp in the bowels that doubles him up, she'll help him to the bathroom and sit yawning on the edge of the tub with a cigarette and a Hollywood fan magazine, while he sweats and groans on the stool. She'll utter good-humored "phews" and wave her cigarette at the stench of his anguish, sometimes extending a hand to cup his forehead. And if he bleeds and collapses, as he sometimes does, she'll pick him up and carry him back to bed and fall asleep with his hot fingers twitching in hers, doing it all as if God had told her to do it. There are two reasons: He is a mean and sick little beast that once mated with her and would have been left and forgotten a long time ago except for the now implausible circumstance that she bore two offspring by him—a daughter employed as "executive secretary to a big wheel at Warner's." (She has to stay at his place because he's a lush and needs her constant attention.) And this one, "My God, look at him." A blown up Kodachrome snapshot of a glistening wet golden youth on some unidentified beach that borders a jungle. He makes his nakedness decent by holding a mass of red flowers before his groin. Olga lifts the picture and gives it five kisses as fast as machine gun fire, which leave rouge stains on the glass, as bright as the blossoms the grinning boy covers his sex with.

So those are the circumstances she feels behind her in Ernie, and yet they cast no shadow over the present moment. What she is doing is what is usual with her, she's thinking in terms of comfort and satisfaction as she looks down at the prostrate bulk of the mattress. Her eyes are soaking up the possibilities of it. The past of the mattress was good. Olga would be the last to deny its goodness. It has lain beneath many summers of fornications in Olga's summer hotel. But the future of the mattress is going to be good, too. It is going to lie under Olga on afternoons of leisure and under the wonderful rocking-horse weather of Southern California.

That is what the veteran mattress has done for the past few summers. The rain and the sun have had their influence on it. Unable to dissolve and absorb it into themselves, the elements have invested it with their own traits. It is now all softness and odors of ocean and earth, and it is still lying next to the prodigal patch of tomatoes that make me think of a deck of green-backed cards in which everything but diamonds and hearts have been thrown into discard.

(What do you bid? demands the queen of hearts. But that is Olga, and Olga is bidding *forever*!)

On afternoons of leisure she lies out there on this overblown mattress of hers and her slow-breathing body is steamed and relaxed in a one-piece sarong-type garment that a Hollywood pin-up girl would hardly dare to appear in. The cocker spaniel named Freckles is resting his chin on her belly. He looks like a butterscotch pudding with whipped cream on it. And these two indolent creatures drift in and out of attention to what takes place in Olga's summer hotel. The quarrels, the music, the wailing receipt of bad news, the joyful shouting, everything that goes on is known and accepted. Without even feeling anything so strong as contempt, their glances take in the activities of the husband having words with a tenant about a torn window shade or sand in a bathtub or wet tracks on the stairs. Nobody pays much attention to poor little Ernie. The Ernies of the world are treated that way. They butt their heads against the walls of their indignation until their dry little brains are shaken to bits. There he goes now, I can see him out this window, trotting along the upstairs gallery of the projecting back wing of the building with some linen to air, some bedclothes on which young bodies have taken their pleasure, for which he hates them. Ernie treats everyone with the polite fury of the impotent cuckold, and they treat Ernie in such an offhand manner it turns him around like a top till he runs down and stops. Sometimes while he complains, they walk right past him dripping the brine of the ocean along the stairs, which Ernie must get down on his hands and knees to wipe up. Pigs, pigs, is what he calls them, and of course he is right, but his fury is too indiscriminate to be useful. Olga is also capable of fury, but she reserves it for the true beast which she knows by sight, sound, and smell, and although she has no name for it, she knows it is the beast of mendacity in us, the beast that tells mean lies, and Olga is not to be confused and thrown off guard by smaller adversaries. Perhaps all adversaries are smaller than Olga, for she is almost as large as the afternoons she lies under.

And so it goes and no one resists the going.

The wonderful rocking-horse weather of California goes rocking over our heads and over the galleries of Olga's summer hotel. It goes rocking over the acrobats and their slim-bodied partners, over the young cadets at the school for flyers, over the ocean that catches the blaze of the moment, over the pier at Venice, over the roller coasters and over the vast beach homes of the world's most successful kept women—not only over those persons and paraphernalia, but over all that is shared in the commonwealth of existence. It has rocked over me all summer, and over my afternoons at this green and white checkered table in the yellow gelatine flood of a burlesque show. It has gone rocking over accomplishments and defeats; it has covered it all and absorbed the wounds with the pleasures and made no discrimination. For nothing is quite so cavalier as this horse. The giant blue rocking-horse weather of Southern California is rocking and rocking with all the signs pointing forward. Its plumes are smoky blue ones the sky can't hold and so lets grandly go of . . .

And now I am through with another of these afternoons so I push the chair back from the table, littered with paper, and stretch my cramped spine till it crackles and rub my fingers gently over a dull pain in my chest, and think what a cheap little package this is that we have been given to live in, some rubbery kind of machine not meant to wear long, but somewhere in it is a mysterious tenant who knows and describes its being. Who is he and what is he up to? Shadow him, tap his wires, check his intimate associates, if he has any, for there is some occult purpose in his coming to stay here and all the time watching so anxiously out of the windows . . .

Now I am looking out of a window at Olga who has been sunning herself on that smoking-car joke of a mattress the whole livelong afternoon, while she ages at leisure and laps up life with the tongue of a female bull. The wrestler Tiger has taken the room next to mine, that's why she keeps looking this way, placidly alert for the gleam of a purple silk robe through his window curtains, letting her know of his return from the beach, and before he has hung the robe on a hook on the door, the door will open and close as softly as an eyelid and Olga will have disappeared from her mattress by the tomato patch. Once the cocker spaniel had the impudence to sniff and bark outside Tiger's door and he was let in and tossed right out the back window, and another time I heard Tiger muttering, Jesus, you fat old cow, but only a few moments later the noises that came through the wall made me think of the dying confessions of a walrus.

And so it goes and no one resists the going.

The perishability of the package she comes in has cast on Olga no shadow she can't laugh off. I look at her now, before the return of Tiger from Muscle Beach, and if no thought, no knowledge has yet taken form in the protean jelly-world of brain and nerves, if I am patient enough to wait a few moments longer, this landlady by Picasso may spring up from her mattress and come running into this room with a milky-blue china bowl full of reasons and explanations for all that exists.

1953 (Published 1954)

The Kingdom of Earth

Talking about Salvation I think there's a great deal of truth in the statement that either you're saved or you ain't and the best thing to do is find out which and stick to it. What counts most is personal satisfaction, at least with most people, and God knows you'll never get that by straining and struggling for something which you are just not cut out for.

Now I passed through a period in my life in which I struggled. It grew out of all that talk which the Gallaway girl had spread through the county about me having a mother with part nigger blood. There wasn't a word of truth in it but as long as there is such a thing as jealousy in human nature, and that will be a long time, there are bound to be certain people who will give ears to slander. I was what is called a wood's colt. Daddy got me offen a woman with Cherokee blood in Alabama. I am one eight Cherokee and the rest is white. But the Gallaway girl had spread them rumors about me all through the county. People turned against me. Everyone acted suspicious. I went around by myself, having too much pride or character or something to try and force my company where I wasn't wanted. I was hurt bad by the way that the Gallaway girl had acted when we broke up. I was lonesome as a lost dog and didn't know which way to turn.

And then one evening while Gypsy Smith was preaching around this section, I dropped in there and heard this wonderful sermon on spiritual struggle. It started me thinking about the lustful body and how I ought to put up a struggle against it. And struggle I did for quite a while after that. The chances are it might of still been going on if Lot hadn't brought that woman back with him from Memphis which showed me just how useless the whole thing was, as far as I personally was concerned anyhow.

Lot come home from Memphis one Saturday morning last summer and brought this woman back with him. I was working out in the south field, spraying the damned army worms, when I seen the Chevy come turning in off the highway onto the drive. The car was yellow all over with dust and the spare tire was off. I guessed he had hocked it to pay for gas on the road.

I went to the house to meet them and Lot was drunk.

This is my wife, he said. Her name is Myrtle.

I didn't say a word to them. I just stood and looked her over. She had on a two-piece thing, the skirt part white and the top of it blue polka-dotted. It was made out of two big dotted bandannas, which she had hitched together. It hung on crooked, and showed a part of her tits, the biggest that I ever seen on a young woman's body, sunburned the color of sorghum halfway down to her nipples and underneath that pure white and pearly-looking.

Well, she said, hello, Brother, and made like she would kiss me, but I turned away in disgust because I wanted her to know how I felt about it. It was a real bitch trick to marry a dying man which she must have known Lot was. Lot was a TB case and he had it so bad they let the air out of one of his lungs in Memphis. I guess she must have known what the setup was, that the place was Lot's and not mine although I did all the work on it. But Lot was a son by marriage and so, when Dad died, it was Lot that he left the place to. After Dad died and I learned how I had been fucked, I quit the place and went to Meridian to work in a stave mill there but I got these pitiful letters from Lot, saying please come back and I did with the understanding that when Lot died, which was bound to be pretty soon, the place would be mine.

Well, I thought to myself after meeting this woman, the sensible thing to do is just lay low and see how things work out, at least for a while. So I went back out to the field and continued my spraying. I didn't come in for supper. I told the nigger girl, Clara, to bring my supper out to me. She brung it out in a bucket, and after I ate it, I went to the Crossroads Inn to drink me some beer. Luther Peabody was there. He offered me to a liquor and while he was drinking he said to me, What's this I hear about Lot bringing home a wife. Who said wife, I asked him. Well, said Luther, that's what somebody told me, that Lot had brung home a woman about as big as a house. A house and Lot, said Scotty, who works at the bar, and all of them hollered. He's brung home a woman for practical nursing, I told them. And that was all that I had to say about it.

It must of been half past ten when I come back to the house. The lamp was on in the kitchen and she was in there heating up something or other on the stove. I didn't let on like I even noticed her presence. I walked right past her and on up to the attic. I pushed my cot in the gable to get the breeze but there wasn't a breath of it stirring.

I thought things over but didn't decide nothing yet. Along toward morning I started to hear some noise. I went downstairs barefooted. The bedroom door was open and they was in there panting like two hound-dogs.

I went outside and wandered around in the fields till it was sunup. I then went back to the house. The nigger was there to fix breakfast and after a while the woman came into the kitchen. She had on a light-blue satin kimono which she didn't bother to fasten around her even. The black girl, Clara, kept looking at me and giggling and when she set my plate down she said, What are you looking at? I said, Nothing much. And then she let out a laugh like a horse. I couldn't blame her. Me saying nothing much about them two huge knockers!

When breakfast was over I called Lot out on the porch for a little talk. Look here, I said, I overheard you last night in the room with that woman at half past five in the morning. How long do you think you'll last in your condition? Inside of a month that lovely Miss Myrtle of yourn'll fuck the last breath from your body and go on back to the Memphis cathouse you must of got her out of as fresh as a daisy!

That speech of mine made him sore and he acted like he was going to take a sock at me but I got mine in first. I knocked him off the back steps. Then she come out. She called me a dirty prick and lots of other nice things like that and then she started to crying. You don't understand, she bawled. I love him and he loves me. I laughed in her face. Last winter, I told her, he took the sheets himself. What do you mean? she asked me. Ask Lot, I told her, and then I walked off and left them to chew that over.

I went off laughing. The sun was up good, then, and hot as blazes. I had my jug of liquor stashed in a clump of snow-on-the-mountain. I went out to it and took a pretty good drink. It made me drunk right off because I had drunk a good deal the night before. The ground kept tilting up and down like a steamboat. I'd run a ways forward and then stagger back a little and laughing my head off at what I'd said to the woman. It was a hell of a thing to tell a woman. It wasn't exactly nice to tell anybody. But I was mad as blazes at what he'd done, come swaggering back with a whore he called his wife for no other reason than just to put on a show of independence.

I went back out to where I'd left the sprayer. The niggers was setting around it swapping stories. They got on up in a sort of half-hearted way. I said, Look here, if you all don't want to work, clear off the place. Otherwise hop to it! Well, they hopped. And by time to quit we had sprayed the whole north field from the road to the river. (You got to keep after them buggers or, Jesus, they sure will ruin you!)

When dark had come down I parked the sprayer under a big cotton-wood and went back to the house. The lights was out so I turned on a lamp in the kitchen and warmed up supper. I had what was left of the greens and some corn and some sweet potatoes. There was some coffee left in a pot on the stove. I drunk it black, against my better judgment. It keeps me from sleeping in summer, especially when I am horny from not getting much and it had been six weeks since I'd laid a woman. I thought to myself, I am twenty-five and strong. I ought to quit fooling around and get me a girl to go steady with. The reason I hadn't till now was them false stories the Gallaway girl had started. The Gallaway girl was not in town this summer. She'd gone up North, knocked up and not by me neither, but not till after she'd spread them lies about me all through Two River County. The girl who worked at the hamburger joint on the highway told me she'd heard it but wouldn't say who from. I figured it must of been Lot that done the first talking. I called him on it. Of course, he swore that he never. I give him a licking within one inch of his life, because nobody else would have a reason to do it except he was jealous, and Lot was so fucking jealous he barely could breathe.

But never mind that, for that was all in the past.

The air in the kitchen was hot and it seemed to be humming. I guess my blood was kind of overheated. My hand fell down in my lap between my legs. My head was tired, and almost before I known what I was doing, I had it out and had started playing with it. I don't want that, I said. So I got up quick and went around to the big rain barrel out back and thrown water in my face and over my body. But the water only seemed to make it stiffer. It showed no signs of going back down neither. I put my two hands on it and jerked a little. It was a real big thing. Two hands just barely covered it. And so I set down there beside the rain barrel and jerked my peter. The moon was out and as white as a blond girl's head. I thought about Alice, but that didn't do much good, and jerking wasn't much fun so I quit and just set there and groaned and slapped at mosquitoes. There was no wind. There wasn't a breath of air stirring. I looked upstairs. The lamp was on in their bedroom. I listened awhile and I could hear them grunting. Yes, they was at it again. (I could hear them grunting together like a pair of pigs in a sty in a dusty place in the sun when the spring's getting warm.) I thought of her legs, just as soft as silk without a dark hair on them, and of her titties, the biggest that I ever seen on a young woman's body, the color of sorghum molasses halfway down and the rest pure white with little sweat beads on them. Then of her belly. Round and bulging out. And it would sure be good to press up against it or get her body turned over and up on the knees a little and then climb on and stick it up and under. Jesus, all the way in, right on up to the hilt, and then start working it in and out and feel it getting hotter until she started to pant and all of that hot, wet stuff come off between you. Good, good, good. The best thing in the world, that burning sensation and then the running over, the sweet relaxing and letting all of it go, shot off inside her, leaving you weak and satisfied completely and ready for sleep. Yes, there was nothing like it in all the world, nothing able to compare with it even. Just that thing and nothing more is perfect. The rest is shit. All of the rest is nothing hardly but shit. But that thing's good, and if you never had nothing else but that, no money, no property, no success in the world, and still had that, why, that would make it still worth living for you. Yes, you could come on home to a house with a tin roof on it in blazing heat and look for water and not find a drop to drink and look for food and not find a single crumb of it. But if on the bed you had you a naked woman, maybe not even terribly young and good-looking, and she looked up and said, I want it, Daddy. . . . why, then I say you got a square deal out of life and anybody that don't think so has just not fucked the right woman.

But that sort of thinking was doing me no good at all so I went back in the kitchen and filled and lit my pipe. I looked at the sink with the dishes piled up in it. A lot of improvement this Myrtle had made on the place. But then she wasn't a woman. A woman's a woman but a cunt is just a cunt, and that's what this Myrtle was, she was just a cheap piece of tail. I could use one, there wasn't no doubt about that. But if I brought one home to live with me, by God it would have to be one that I was able to feel a little respect for.

I went to the screen door to pee and waited several minutes before I could. A long way off I heard a hound-dog baying. It sounded sad. In spite of myself, I went right back to my old train of thoughts. I thought of the Gallaway girl and the nights we spent out there at Moon Lake, dancing and drinking and carrying on in a boathouse. She used to French me as well as everything else. If I had wanted to talk, I could of told people how she used to French me. No clean woman would do it. An old whore told me its what they call a snake-fuck, that tongue-wiggling business, but I've got to admit it sure feels good to have that thing done to you, and she was an expert.

Of course, I known it was doing no good whatsoever to run over all those memories in my mind, like shuffling through a worn-out deck of cards, but it just seemed like my mind was set on that subject and nothing would stop it. It's like the preacher says, the gates of the soul is got to close on the body and keep the body out or the body will break them down and overrun the soul and everything else decent in you. The fact of the matter is, though, I never did seem to have any gates to close. I was made without them. Some people are, I guess. Just made without them, and that was sure enough the case with me. I'd say to myself, This sort of thing is dirty, and I'd remember what the preacher had said and make a struggle to close the gates on the body. I'd reach for the gates to close them and find I hadn't a thing to catch hold of. I thought to myself, as I stood there on the steps, You freak of nature, you're letting in mosquitoes and not accomplishing anything but that. So I turned around and went back in the kitchen. One place was as hot as another. At least in there I had a chair to set on. So I seated myself in a chair at the kitchen table. I propped my feet up on the edge of the table. Between my legs that big old thing was throbbing. Yep, just burning and throbbing like a bee had stung it, and not a gate did I have to close against it.

I guess my trouble was partly a lack of schooling. I never think of anything much to do but drinking and screwing and trying my damnest to make something out of the place and not having much luck at it. I guess if a fellow could pick up a book at night, that ought to make a good deal of difference with him. Oh, I could read, I could make out most of the words, but dogged if reading would close them gates on the body. I tried it awhile and then I would close the book and throw it down in disgust. Made-up stuff was not satisfying to me. They's not one word of truth in all this writing, I used to think, and the fellow that wrote it is trying to fool the public. So I'd come back to what I was struggling against. Poker, I like to play that but always seem to come out at the little end of the horn. I like to go in town and look at a movie or go to a carnival show, but only ever so often, not all the time the way some people do it. Looking at them screen stars don't close the gates on the body and don't ever think that it does. I've seen young boys that would play with themselves at the movies, and I don't blame them. They's nothing that makes a fellow quite so horny as setting there in the dark and looking up at one of them beautiful actresses messing around in a little pair of lace step-ins or a fancy wrapper. The screen industry is run by Jews with hot pants and that's why they put on all of these sexy pictures. You come back out and there ain't one inch of the soul that ain't overrun by the longings of the body.

Well, I was still in the kitchen while the night wore away, but I had a feeling that something was going to happen before the night ended and I was not mistaken.

It must have been about half past twelve when all of a sudden a big commotion begins. I heard him coughing and then her running and shouting my name in the hall.

I just set tight on the chair and waited to see what would happen.

After a while she come on down to the kitchen to fill up the water pitcher.

Didn't you hear me calling you, Chicken? she says.

I just set there and looked at her. The way she was dressed in only her silk underwear brought into my mind a thing somebody had wrote on the wall of a Memphis bus depot. Girls sure wear some real cute little French panties, and the fellow that wrote it must of been thinking of somebody built like Myrtle.

She filled up the water pitcher and clumped it down on the table.

Lot's took sick, she told me.

I didn't say nothing.

He seems to be awful sick. I wanted to call a doctor but he said no, he'd be all right in the morning.

I still didn't say a thing to her.

What's wrong with him? she asked me after a while.

He's got TB, I told her.

She put on a shocked expression. How bad is it? she asked me.

I told her they'd let the air out of one of his lungs at the Memphis hospital because the X-rays had showed it was all eaten up with disease.

Why didn't somebody tell me? she asked.

She set there and whimpered a little and I said nothing but just kept looking at her.

I've had a bad time, she told me. You don't understand how it is with a woman like me. I used to work in a dry-goods store in Biloxi.

What are you planning to give me, I said, your life story?

No, she said. I just wanted to tell you something. Then I was thin and I hadn't dyed my hair and I looked real pretty. I was fifteen then and I didn't go out with the boys. I was just as nice as any girl you could think of. But you can imagine what happened. The man that managed the store kept walking by me and every time that he did he would touch my body. First on my arm, he would just pinch my arm a little, and then on my shoulders and finally on my hips. I told my girl friend about it. Honey, she said, pretend like you don't notice, just try and ignore it and maybe he'll quit after while. But she didn't know Charlie. He pinched me harder and hung around me longer all the time. What could I do? Pretend like I didn't notice? I told my friend and she said, Honey, just take him aside and have a sincere conversation. Tell him that you're not used to that sort of treatment. So that's what I done. I went in his office to the back of the store. It was late one Saturday in the middle of summer. I said, Mr. Porter, I don't think you're playing exactly fair and square. What do you mean? he asked me. Well, I said, you seem to be taking advantage of the fact you're my boss to take some liberties with me which I don't like because of my decent upbringing. But Charlie just grinned. He walked up to me and put his hands on my hips. Is this what you mean? he said. And then he kissed me. Then it was all over with me. I tried to walk one way and Charlie pushed me the other. He kicked the office door shut and backed me up against a big roller-top desk and took me by force right there. He had my cherry right there on that roller-top desk. He was a man about forty with sandy red hair. You know the sort that I mean, like a great big bull, and I fell in love with him. I got to admit that he made me happy that summer and my memories of it are still the best that I've got. They say that you always lose your heart with your cherry. I don't know about that. Some girls don't like it at first but I got to admit that from the beginning I loved it.

She wiped her eyes on the edge of the tablecloth.

Is that the end of the story? I asked her.

No, she said, the end was only beginning. He got tired of me. He said his wife had found us out and he had to let me go. Some girls would have made him trouble. I could of because I was only fifteen at the time. But I had too much pride so I just packed up and moved to Pensacola. Then to New Orleans. I finally come to Memphis. It wasn't till then I ever worked in a house and then it was only to pay for an operation I'd had to have.

I picked up Lot on a street. He looked like a kid. Sort of thin and pitiful-looking. It touched me the way that he laid on me like a baby. He seemed so lonesome, and it's the truth that I loved him. He slept in my arms just like a baby would and when he woke up he said would I come home with him and we'd be married. At first I laughed. It seemed ridiculous to me. But then I thought, Oh, well, as the fellow says, they's a hell of a lot more to it, this business of sex, than a couple of people jumping up and down on each other's eggs. So I said yes, and we set out the very next morning . . .

Now what shall I do? she asked.

Do about what? I asked her.

You, she said. The minute I laid eyes on you, the first glance I look at that big powerful body, I said to myself, Oh, oh, your goose is cooked, Myrtle!

So what shall I do about it?

Well, I said, when somebody's goose is cooked the best way to have it is cooked with plenty of gravy.

I picked up the lamp off the table and started up the stairs. She followed behind me. At the door of Lot's room she stopped but I kept going on. I known she would follow. I went on up to the attic and dropped my clothes on the floor beside the cot and set down on it and waited for her to come up which I known she would do. I don't think I ever in all my life looked forward to anything so much as I did to that woman coming up to bed with me. Of course, I was horny and crazy to get my gun off, but it wasn't just that. It was partly the fact that she was Lot's wife and the place had gone to Lot and he was the son by marriage and I was just a wood's colt that people accused of having some nigger blood. All that was mixed up in it. But anyhow I had never in all my life wanted anything so bad as I did for that woman to come up and go to bed with me. It wasn't five minutes before I heard her footsteps on the stairs coming up to the attic. And then I realized that I had been praying. I had been setting there praying to God to send that woman up to me. What do you make of that? Why would God have answered a prayer like that? What sort of God would pay attention to a prayer like that coming from someone like me who is sold to the Devil when thousands of good people's prayers, such as prayers for the sick and suffering and dying, are given no mind, no more than so many crickets buzzing outdoors in the summer. It just goes to show how little sense there is in all this religion and all this talk of Salvation. One fool is as big as another on this earth and they're all big enough.

But that is beside the point now. The point is Lot's wife was coming up to bed with me. And when I heard her coming, it stood straight up so you could hang a hat on it. I spread my legs and she came toward me and stooped beside the cot and stroked it and kissed it like it was something holy. She giggled and crooned and carried on something outlandish. I just lay back and looked at the sky and enjoyed it. Finally she wiggled up and got on the cot beside me. I felt of her body. So big and hot like a mountain that had a furnace inside it. I wanted to get inside that wonderful mountain. I ripped the drawers off her bottom. She pushed it up off the cot. Then I climbed on. She put the head of it in. I give a push and she yelled out, God Almighty. I drew it back and gave it another shove and she said, Oh, Blessed Mary. She said her prayers, at least that's how it sounded, all of the time that I was giving it to her. And when I come, and she did at the same time, I swear that her yelling nearly took the roof off. Oh, Blessed Mary, Mother of God, she shouted. I had to laugh. I thought the roof would blow off. And he must have heard her downstairs because it was just about that time that he started bawling our names.

Even before I come downstairs in the morning I known Lot was dead. And sure enough he was. I found his body laying across the doorsill. He'd gotten down out of bed and crawled on the floor as far as the door to the bedroom. He'd pushed the door half open. His body was stretched out halfway over the sill, and the blood that now was dried in the hot yellow sunlight had made a stream, or what was a stream till it dried, from the foot of the bed to the spot where his head was resting. The bed was just like a hog had been kilt on it. I wasn't surprised, because all of that livelong night we'd heard him bawling out, Myrtle, Myrtle, Myrtle. And later on he yelled my name out, Chicken, Chicken, Chicken. And once or twice she said in a half-hearted way, I reckon I better go down and make him hush that Godforsaken bawling. But I said, No, the bawling is good for his lungs. So we kept right on having our fun in the attic. The bawling quit by and by, a little while after sunup, and then it was quiet and I thought to myself, Lot's dead.

I called to Myrtle and she come downstairs too. We stood together in front of the door and looked at him.

Poor little kid, said Myrtle. She started to cry. But not very much or for long.

It's all for the best, I told her, and after a while she said she guessed it was, too.

We got hitched up that winter. I think she had already made up her mind to do it but stalled around for a while, pretending she couldn't decide if she wanted to go on back to the sporting house in Memphis or stay on here. I made out like I didn't care much which she did, so she come around and said, Yes, I'll stay here.

So we two got hitched up on the first of December. We have our troubles but get on pretty good, as good as most young couples do in the country. We're expecting a baby about the end of the summer. If it's a boy we aim to call him Lot, in memory of my brother, and if it's a girl I guess we will call her Lottie.

And now it seems like everything in my life is straightened out. I don't ever worry about them spiritual gates the preacher said to keep shut. Not having no gates can save you a lot of trouble. And after all, what does anyone know about the Kingdom of Heaven? It's earth I'm after and now I am honest about it and don't pretend I'm nothing but what I am, a lustful creature determined on satisfaction and likely as not to get my full share of it.

(Published 1954)

"Grand"

My grandmother formed quiet but deeply emotional attachments to places and people and would have been happy to stay forever and ever in one rectory, once her bedroom was papered in lemon yellow and the white curtains were hung there, once she had acquired a few pupils in violin and piano, but my grandfather always dreamed of movement and change, a dream from which he has not yet wakened in this ninety-sixth spring of his life.

Although he was married to a living poem, and must have known it, my grandfather's sole complaints against his wife were that she had no appreciation of poetry and not much sense of humor. "When we were quite young," he said, "I used to spend evenings reading poetry to her and she would fall asleep while I read"—which has sometimes made me wonder if her addiction to staying and his to going was the only difference which her infinite understanding had settled between them. My grandfather still is, and doubtless always has been, an unconsciously and childishly selfish man. He is humble and affectionate but incurably set upon satisfying his own impulses whatever they may be, and it was not until the last two or three years of their lives together that my grandmother began to rebel against it, and then it was for a reason that she couldn't tell him, the reason of death being in her, no longer possible to fly in front of but making it necessary, at last, to insist on staying when he wanted to leave.

When she married him she had not expected him to enter the ministry. He was then a schoolteacher and doing well at that vocation. He was a natural teacher, and soon after their marriage he was made head of a private girls' school in East Tennessee and my grandmother taught music there. At one time she had as many as fifty pupils in violin

379

and piano. Their combined incomes made them quite well off for those days.

Then all at once he told her that he had made up his mind to enter the Church, and from that time till the end of her days my grandmother never again knew what it was to live without personal privation. During that interval the reverend and charmingly selfish gentleman would conduct parties of Episcopalian ladies through Europe, deck himself out in the finest clerical vestments from New York and London, go summers to Chautauqua and takes courses at Sewanee, while my grandmother would lose teeth to save dental expenses, choose her eyeglasses from a counter at Woolworth's, wear at the age of sixty dresses which were made over from relics of her bridal trousseau, disguise illness to avoid the expense of doctors. She took eighteen-hour trips sitting up in a day coach whenever summertime or another crisis in her daughter's household called her to St. Louis, did all her own housework and laundry, sometimes kept two or three roomers, taught violin, taught piano, made dresses for my mother when my mother was a young lady, and afterwards for my sister, took an active part in all the women's guilds and auxiliaries, listened patiently and silently through fifty-five years of Southern Episcopalian ladies' guff and gossip, smiled beautifully but not widely in order not to show missing teeth, spoke softly, sometimes laughed like a shy girl although my grandfather often said that she wouldn't know a joke if she bumped into one in the middle of the road, skimped all year long—doing all these things without the aid of a servant, so that once a year, in the summer, she could take the long daycoach trip to St. Louis to visit her only child, my mother, and her three grandchildren which included myself and my sister and our little brother. She always came with a remarkable sum of money sewed up in her corset. I don't know just how much, but probably several hundred dollars—in spite of the fact that my grandfather's salary as a minister never exceeded a hundred and fifty dollars a month.

We called her "Grand." Her coming meant nickels for ice cream, quarters for movies, picnics in Forest Park. It meant soft and gay laughter like the laughter of girls between our mother and her mother, voices that ran up and down like finger exercises on the piano. It meant a return of grace from exile in the South and it meant the propitiation of my desperate father's wrath at life and the world which he, unhappy man, could never help taking out upon his children—except when the presence, like music, of my grandmother in the furiously close little city apartment cast a curious unworldly spell of peace over all there confined.

And so it was through the years, almost without any change at all, as we grew older. "Grand" was all that we knew of God in our lives! Providence was money sewed in her corset!

My grandmother never really needed a corset and why she wore one I don't quite know. She was never anything but straight and slender, and she bore herself with the erect, simple pride of a queen or a peasant. Her family were German—her maiden name was Rosina Maria Francesca Otte. Her parents had emigrated to America from Hamburg, I suppose sometime in the first half of the past century. They were Lutherans but my grandmother was educated in a Catholic convent and at the Cincinnati Conservatory of Music. I never saw my grandmother's father but he looks in pictures like Bismarck. I barely remember her mother, in fact I only remember that she was a spry little old lady who referred to scissors as "shears." About my great-grandfather Otto I remember only that it was said of him that he declined to eat salads because he said that grass was only for cows, and that he had come to America in order to avoid military service. He made a large fortune as a merchant and then he lost it all. The last bit of it was exchanged for a farm in East Tennessee, and his farm had an almost legendary character in my grandmother's life.

My grandmother Rose was one of four children who scattered like blown leaves when the family fortune was gone. One of the two brothers disappeared and was never heard of again, and the other, Clemence, still lives in Mobile, Alabama, and must be near ninety. My grandmother had a sister named Estelle who married twice, first to a Tennessee youth named Preston Faller who died young and then to an older man named Ralston, a judge who had the dubious distinction of presiding over the famous Scopes trial in East Tennessee, which was known as the "Monkey trial." Once or twice, in the summer, "Grand" took us to South Pittsburgh, Tennessee, to visit "the Ralstons," about which I remember honey kept in a barrel on the back porch, hot sun on pine needles, and the wildness and beauty of my grandmother's nephew, young Preston Faller Jr., whistling as he dressed for a dance in a room that contains in my memory only a glittering brass bed and roses on the wallpaper and dusk turning violet at the open windows. But I was a child of seven and it is really only the honey in the barrel on the back porch that I remember very clearly, and the watermelons set to cool in the spring water and the well water that tasted of iron, and the mornings being such mornings! I do remember that Preston Faller Jr. would drive his stepfather's car without permission to other towns and stay nights and I remember that once he took me to a minstrel show and that there was an accordion played in this show, and that the keys or buttons of the accordion are remembered as diamonds and emeralds and rubies set in mother-of-pearl. Preston Faller Jr. now lives in Seattle and is doing well there and has sent us pictures of his house and his Cadillac car. And to think that he was such a ne'er-do-well boy! But he was the son of the sister of my grandmother—how time flies!—he's over fifty now . . .

I spoke a while back of my grandmother's inherited farm which her bankrupt parents had retired to in East Tennessee. Actually it was only about two hundred acres of rocky, hilly soil—well, maybe three or four hundred acres—but it was divided by inheritance among the two sisters, my grandmother and Estelle, and their only known living brother, Clemence. Estelle died early of asthma and an overdose of morphine administered by a confused country doctor, and so this legendary farm belonged to my grandmother and her brother and the children of her sister. It was administered by Judge Ralston, the widower of Estelle. I remember only two things about it, or three. One, that my great-aunt Estelle had to live on it prior to her first marriage and that she told my grandmother that she was so lonely that she used to shout hello on the front porch in order to hear an echo from an opposite mountain. Then I remember that some of the timber was sold for several hundred dollars and that the proceeds were passed out among all the inheritors like holy wafers at Communion. And then I remember, finally, that one time, probably after the death of Judge Ralston, my grandmother paid a valedictory visit to this farm, which she had always dreamed might someday prove to contain a valuable deposit of mineral or oil or something, and found that the old homestead had been reduced to a single room which contained an old female squatter. This ancient squatter could not satisfactorily explain how she came to be there on my grandmother's property. "We came by and stayed" was about all she could say. My grandmother inquired what had become of the large porch and the stone chimney and the other rooms and the female squatter said that her husband and sons had had to burn the logs for fire in winter, and that was what had become of the porch and other rooms, that they had disposed financially of the stones in the chimney, too. My grandmother then inquired where they were, these male members of the squatter household, and the finger-thin old lady informed her that the husband had died and that the sons had gone in town a year ago with a big load of lumber and had never returned and she was still sitting there waiting for them to return or some word of them . . .

That was the end of the story of the farm, which had meant to my grandmother an assurance against a future in which she thought maybe all of us might have need of a bit of land to retire to . . .

The one thing that my grandmother dreaded most in the world was the spectre of that dependence which overtakes so many aged people at the end of their days, of having to be supported and cared for by relatives. In my grandmother's case there were no relatives who had ever stopped being at least emotionally dependent on her, but nevertheless this dread hung over her and that was why she continued to keep house in Memphis long after she was physically able to bear it and only gave up and came to St. Louis a few months before her death.

Some years earlier than that, when she and Grandfather were living in Memphis on his retirement pension of eighty-five dollars a month, I took refuge with them once more, after suffering a nervous collapse at my job in a St. Louis wholesale shoe company. As soon as I was able to travel, I took flight to their tiny cottage in Memphis and slept on the cot in the parlor. That summer I had a closer brush with lunacy than I had had any time since the shattering storms of my earliest adolescence, but gradually once again, as it had in those early crises, my grandmother's mysteriously peace-giving presence drew me back to at least a passable proximation of sanity. And when fall came I set out upon that long upward haul as a professional writer, that desperate, stumbling climb which brought me at last, exhausted but still breathing, out upon the supposedly sunny plateau of "fame and fortune." It began that Memphis summer of 1934. Also that summer, a turning point in my life, something of an opposite nature occurred to "Grand." Through the years, through her miracles of providence, her kitchen drudgery, her privations and music pupils and so forth, she had managed to save out of their tiny income enough to purchase what finally amounted to $7500 in government bonds.

One morning that memorable summer a pair of nameless con men came to call upon my fantastically unworldly grandfather. They talked to him for a while on the porch in excited undertones. He was already getting deaf, although he was then a relatively spry youth of eighty, and I saw him leaning toward them cupping an ear and giving quick nods of mysterious excitement. After a while they disappeared from the porch and he was gone from the house nearly all of that fierce yellow day. He came home in the evening, looking white and shaken, and said to my grandmother, "Rose, come out on the porch, I have something to tell you."

What he had to tell her was that for some unfathomable reason he had sold their bonds and transferred five thousand in cash to this pair of carrion birds who had called upon him that morning and addressed him as "Reverend" in voices of sinisterly purring witchery.

I see my grandmother now, looking off into dimming twilight space from a wicker chair on the porch in Memphis and saying only, "*Why, Walter?*"

She said, "Why, Walter," again and again, till finally he said, "Rose, don't question me any more because if you do, I will go away by myself and you'll never hear of me again!"

At that point she moved from the wicker chair to the porch swing and for a while I heard nothing, from my discreet position in the parlor, but the rasping voice of metal chain-links rubbed together as my grandmother swung gently back and forth and evening closed about them in their spent silence, which was, I felt without quite understanding, something that all their lives had been approaching, even half knowingly, a slow and terrible facing of something between them.

"*Why, Walter?*"

The following morning my grandfather was very busy and my grandmother was totally silent.

He went into the tiny attic of the bungalow and took out of a metal filing case a great, great, great pile of cardboard folders containing all his old sermons. He went into the back yard of the bungalow with this load, taking several trips, heaping all of the folders into the ashpit, and then he started a fire and fifty-five years of hand-written sermons went up in smoke. The blaze was incontinent. It rose far above the rim of the concrete incinerator, but what I most remember, more than that blaze, was the silent white blaze of my grandmother's face as she stood over the washtub, the stove, the kitchen table, performing the menial duties of the house and not once even glancing out of the window where the old gentleman, past eighty, was performing this auto-da-fé as an act of purification.

"*Why, Walter?*"

Nobody knows!

Nobody but my grandfather who has kept the secret into this his ninety-sixth spring on earth, and those rusty-feathered birds of prey who have gone wherever they came from—which I hope to be hell, and believe so . . .

I think the keenest regret of my life is one that doesn't concern myself, not even the failure of any work of mine nor the decline of creative energy that I am aware of lately. It is the fact that my grandmother died only a single year before the time when I could have given her some return for all she had given me, something material in partial recompense for that immeasurable gift of the spirit that she had so persistently and unsparingly of herself pressed into my hands when I came to her in need.

My grandfather likes to recall that she was born on All Souls' Day and that she died on the Feast of Epiphany, which is the sixth day of January.

The death occurred under merciless circumstances. Her health had been failing for the last five years till finally the thing she had always dreaded came to pass. She had to abandon and sell the home in Memphis and accept the shelter of my father's house in St. Louis because she was literally dying on her feet. Somehow she got through the process of pulling up stakes in Memphis, packing away possessions that had accumulated through sixty years of housekeeping and then that final eighteen-hour day-coach trip to St. Louis. But soon as she arrived there, with a temperature of 104, she collapsed and had to go, for the first time in her life, to a hospital. I was not anywhere near home at this time, the fall of 1943. I was doing a stint for a film studio in California. I got a letter from my mother giving me this news, that my grandmother was fatally ill with a malignant condition of long standing which had now affected her liver and lungs and placed a very brief limit to her remnant of life.

"Your grandmother," she wrote me, "has dropped down to eighty pounds but she won't give up. It's impossible to make her stay in bed. She insists on helping with the housework and this morning she did a week's laundry!"

I came home. It was a week before Christmas and there was a holly wreath on the door and somebody's next-door radio was singing "White Christmas" as I lugged my two suitcases up the front walk. I stopped halfway to the door. Through the frothy white curtains at the parlor windows I saw my grandmother moving alone through the lighted parlor like a stalking crane, so straight and tall for an old lady and so unbelievably thin!

It was a while before I could raise the brass knocker from which the

Christmas wreath was suspended. I waited and prayed that some other member of the family, even my father, would become visible through those white gauze curtains, but no other figure but the slowly stalking figure of my grandmother, who seemed to be moving about quite aimlessly to a soundless and terribly slow march tune, a ghostly brass band that was playing a death march, came into view!

The family, I learned later, had gone out to that monthly business banquet of my father's world called the Progress Club.

My grandfather was in bed. "Grand" was waiting up alone to receive me at whatever hour—I had not wired precisely when—I might appear at the family door for this last homecoming of mine that she would take part in.

As my grandmother drew the door open in response to my knock, I remember how she laughed like a shy girl, a girl caught sentimentalizing over something like a sweetheart's photograph, and cried out, in her young voice, "Oh, Tom, oh, Tom!" And as I embraced her, I felt with terror almost nothing but the material of her dress and her own arms burning with fever through that cloth.

She died about two weeks later, after a spurious, totally self-willed period of seeming recuperation.

I left the house right after dinner that evening. She had washed the dishes, refusing my mother's assistance or my grandfather's or mine, and was at the piano playing Chopin when I went out the door.

When I returned only two or three hours later, the whole two-story house which we now occupied was filled with the sound of her last struggle for breath.

On the stairs was a stranger who had heard me knock before I discovered that I did have the key.

He said, with no expression, "Your mother wants you upstairs."

I went upstairs. At the top of the steps, where my grandmother's hemorrhage had begun, was a pool of still fresh blood. There was a trail of dark wet blood into the bathroom and the toilet bowl still unflushed was deep crimson and there were clotted bits of voided lung tissue in the bowl and on the tiles of the bathroom floor. Later I learned that this incontinent giving up of her lifeblood had occurred almost immediately after I had left the house, three hours ago, and still in her bedroom my grandmother was continuing, fiercely, wildly, unyieldingly, her battle with death, which had already won that battle halfway up the stairs . . .

I didn't dare enter the room where the terrible struggle was going on. I stood across the hall in the dark room which had been my brother's before he entered the army. I stood in the dark room, possibly praying, possibly only sobbing, possibly only listening, I don't know which, and across the hall I heard my mother's voice saying over and over again, "Mother, what is it, Mother, what is it, what are you trying to tell me?"

I only dared to look in. My mother was crouched over the figure of my grandmother on the bed, mercifully obscuring her from me. My grandfather was kneeling in prayer beside his armchair. The doctor was hovering helplessly over all three with a hypodermic needle and a bowl of steaming water and this or that bit of useless paraphernalia.

Then all at once the terrible noise was still.

I went into the room.

My mother was gently closing my grandmother's jaws and eyes.

Some hours later neighbors began to arrive. My grandfather went downstairs to let them in, and standing at the top of the stairs, I heard him say to them, "My wife is very weak, she seems to be very weak now."

"Walter will never face the facts about things," was one of my grandmother's sayings about him.

Then a year or so ago my mother happened to tell me that she had finally found out what my grandmother was trying to tell her as she died, but hadn't the strength to. "Your grandmother kept pointing at the bureau, and later I found out that she had her corset in there with several hundred dollars sewed up in it!"

(Published 1964)

Mama's Old Stucco House

Mr. Jimmy Krenning wandered into the noon blaze of the kitchen for his breakfast coffee just wearing the shorts he had slept in. He'd lost so much weight that summer that the shorts barely hung on his narrow hipbones and thin belly. At first the colored girl, Brinda, who had lately taken the place of her bedridden mother at the Krennings', had been offended as well as embarrassed by this way he had of walking around in front of her as if she were not a young girl and not even human, as if she were a dog in there waiting on him. She was a shy, pretty girl, brought up with more gentility than most white girls in the town of Macon, Georgia. At first she thought he acted with this kind of impropriety around her because she was colored. That was when it offended her. Now she'd come to understand that Mr. Jimmy would have acted the same way with a white girl, with anybody of any race or any age or upbringing—he really and truly was so unconscious of being with anybody when he entered the kitchen for his coffee that it was a wonder he smiled or spoke when he entered. It was Mr. Jimmy's nights that made him behave that way. They left him as dazed as a survivor of a plane crash in which everyone but Mr. Jimmy had died, and now that she understood this, Brinda was no longer offended, but she was still embarrassed. She kept her eyes carefully away from him, but this was hard to do because he sat on the edge of the kitchen table, directly in the streak of noon blaze through the door, drinking coffee out of the Silex instead of the cup she'd put on the kitchen table.

She asked him if the coffee was hot enough for him. It had been off the stove since she heard him get out of bed half an hour ago. But Mr. Jimmy was so inattentive this morning he thought she was making a reference to the weather and said, God yes, this heat is breaking my balls.

This was the kind of talk that Brinda's mother had advised her to pretend not to hear. He don't mean nothing by it, her mother had explained to her. He's just acting smart or been drinking too much when he talks that way, and the best way to stop it is to pretend you don't hear it. When I get back to the Krennings', I'll straighten that boy out.

Brinda's Mama still expected, or pretended to expect, to return to work at the Krennings', but Brinda knew that her Mama was on her deathbed. It was a strange thing that Brinda's Mama and Mr. Jimmy's Mama had both took mortally sick the same summer, Mr. Jimmy's with a paralytic stroke and Brinda's with chronic liver trouble which had now reached a stage where she wasn't likely to ever get back on her feet. Even so, Brinda's Mama was better off than Mr. Jimmy's, who lay up there in that big old brass bed of hers absolutely speechless and motionless so that nobody knew if she was conscious or not, and had been like that since the first week of June which was three months ago. Although Brinda's Mama didn't know that it was the end for herself, she knew it was the end for old Mrs. Krenning and she sorrowed for her, asking Brinda each evening if Mrs. Krenning had shown any sign of consciousness during the day. Sometimes there were little things to report, some days it seemed that Mrs. Krenning was more alive in her eyes than other days, and a few times she had seemed to be making an effort to speak. She had to be spoon-fed by Brinda or the nurse and some days she'd reject the spoon with her teeth and other days accept it and swallow about half what she was given before beginning to let the soft food spill out her sunken gray jaw.

Brinda also cooked for Mr. Jimmy, she prepared his lunch and dinner, but he rarely would eat. She told her Mama it was a waste of food and time to cook for him, but her Mama said she had to keep on preparing the meals anyway and set the dining-room table for him whether he came down to it or not when she rang the dinner bell for him. Now Brinda only made cold things, such as thin-sliced sandwiches which she could wrap in glazed paper and leave in the icebox for him. The icebox was packed full of Mr. Jimmy's uneaten lunches and dinners, saucers and little bowls were stacked on top of each other, and then some mornings she would come in to find that during the night the big supply was suddenly cut down as if a gang of hungry guests had raided the icebox, and the kitchen table would be littered with remnants in dishes, and Brinda knew that that was exactly what had happened, that Mr. Jimmy had brought a crowd home the night before and they'd raided the icebox and devoured its store of meals for Mr. Jimmy that he had ignored. But Brinda no longer told her Mama how things were going at the Krennings' because one day her Mama had struggled out of bed and come over to the house to make an effort to straighten out Mr. Jimmy. But when she got there she was too weak and breathless to talk. All she could do was look at him and shake her head and shed tears and she couldn't get up the stairs to see Mrs. Krenning, so Mr. Jimmy had to support her out to his car and drive her back home. In the car she panted like an old dog and was only able to say, Oh, Mr. Jimmy, why are you doing like this?

So this morning Brinda waited outside long enough for Mr. Jimmy to finish his breakfast coffee. Sometimes after his coffee he would come blinking and squinting out the back screen door and cross to his "studio," a little whitewashed building with a skylight, which no one but he ever entered. Its walls had no windows to peek in, but once when he drove into town he'd left the door open, and Brinda went out to close it and saw inside a scene of terrible violence as if a storm, or a demon, had been caged in it, but now it was very quiet, only a fly buzzed in it, as if the storm or the demon that had smashed and turned everything over beneath the skylight's huge blue eye had fallen exhausted or died. Brinda had considered going in to try to straighten it up, but there was something about the disorder, something unnatural about it, that made it seem dangerous to enter, and so she just closed the door and returned to the comforting business of making up beds in the house. In the house there was always more than one bed to make up, not counting Mrs. Krenning's. The old woman's bed was made up by her night nurse and the soiled sheets put in the hall for Brinda to wash. There had been five night nurses for Mrs. Krenning since Brinda had taken her Mama's place at the house, and each of them had left with the same complaint, that the nights in the house were too outrageous to cope with. Now there was a male nurse taking care of the old lady at night, a repulsively coarse young man, redheaded, with arms as big as hams, covered with a fuzz of white hair. Brinda was too scandalized by this change to even speak of it to her Mama. She was afraid to go upstairs at the Krennings' until the day nurse came on at eleven. Once, when she had to go up to rouse Mr. Jimmy for a long-distance telephone call from New York, the male nurse had blocked her way on the back stairs, crouching, grinning and sticking his tongue out at her. She said, Excuse me, please, and tried to duck past him, and he had reached up after her and snatched her back down with one arm, like a red ham come to life, while the hand of the other made rough, breath-taking grabs at her breasts and belly, so that she screamed and screamed till Mr. Jimmy and his guest for the night ran naked out of his bedroom and the nurse had to let her go, pretending that he was just kidding. He called Mr. Jimmy "Cookie" and Mrs. Krenning "Old Faithful,"and filled the sickroom with candy-bar wrappings and empty pint bottles and books of colored comics, and ever since he had gone on duty at night Brinda felt she could see a look that was like an outcry of horror in the paralyzed woman's eyes when she would come up with her soft-boiled eggs in the mornings.

This morning it was the male nurse, not Jimmy, who stumbled out, blinking and squinting, onto the little porch off the kitchen. Hey, Snow White, he hollered, come in here, Cookie wants you!

Brinda had taken out some of Mrs. Krenning's washed bedclothes to dry in the yard and had deliberately stretched out, as long as she could, the process of hanging the heavy wet sheets on the clothesline to give the male nurse time to leave before she returned to the house, but he had hung around, this morning, a whole hour longer than usual when he came out to holler at her. Brinda returned to the kitchen to find that Mr. Jimmy was still sitting in there, although he had switched from coffee to whiskey and from the edge of the table to a kitchen chair.

Miss Brinda, he said, blinking and squinting at her as if at the noon-day sun, that son-of-a-bitch night nurse says Mama's just gone . . .

Brinda began to cry, automatically but sincerely, standing before Mr. Jimmy. He took her hand gently in his, and then, to her shame and dismay, Brinda moved a step forward and took his bare white shoulders into her arms, enfolded them like a lost child's in her dark honey-colored bare arms, and his head dropped down to her shoulder, rested on it lightly for a moment, and to her still greater dismay, Miss Brinda felt her hand seize the close-cropped back of his head and pull it tighter against her as if she wanted to bruise her shoulder with it. He let her do it for a moment or two, saying nothing, making no motion, before he pushed her gently away by his two hands on her waist, and said, Miss Brinda, you better go up and clean the room up a little before they come for Mama . . .

Brinda waited at the foot of the back stairs till she was certain the male nurse wasn't up there, then she went up and entered old Mrs. Krenning's bedroom. One glance told her that the old lady was gone. She caught her breath and ran about the room making a quick collection of sticky candy-bar wrappings, pint bottles and chocolate-smeared comic books, the litter in which Mrs. Krenning had flown from the world, still speechless, unable to cry, and then Brinda ran back down to the kitchen. She found herself shouting orders at Mr. Jimmy.

Mr. Jimmy, go upstairs and take a cold shower and shave and put on some clean white clothes because your Mama has gone!

Mr. Jimmy grunted in a vague sort of agreement, drew a long breath and went back upstairs while Brinda phoned the white people's under-taker, whose name and number, at her mother's instruction, she had penciled on the back leaf of Mr. Jimmy's little black book of telephone numbers. From the upstairs she could hear Mr. Jimmy's voice on the downstairs phone, speaking very low and unexcitedly to someone about what had happened, and presently the front doorbell started ringing and various young friends of Mr. Jimmy's began coming into the house, all seeming sober and talking in unusually quiet voices. Brinda put on her simple, clean white hat and ran to her Mama's. She knew that her Mama would make another effort to get out of bed and come over, but it seemed justified, this time, by the occasion. She was right about it. Her Mama wept a little and then said, Help me get up, Brinda, I got to go over there and see that it's handled right.

This time she seemed much firmer, although the effort to rise was probably even greater. Brinda got a cab for her. Holding her Mama's waist she could feel how thin the old dying woman had gotten, skin and bones now, but she walked with a slow, steady stride to the cab and sat up very straight in it. Presently they arrived at the Krennings' big house of worn-out stucco, now full of the friends of Mr. Jimmy with only two or three older people who were, or had been at some time, close friends of old Mrs. Krenning's. The atmosphere in the house was appropriately subdued, shades drawn, and everyone looking politely sympathetic, not putting on a false show, but observing the conven-tional attitude toward a death. There were a good many young men from the local air base present, but they were being nice too, talking softly and acting with suitable decorum. They all had drinks in their hands, but they were all keeping sober, and when the undertaker's assistants carried old Mrs. Krenning downstairs and out of the house on a sheet-covered stretcher, they kept a perfect silence except for one sobbing girl, who had risen abruptly and clutched Mr. Jimmy's shoulders, enjoying her burst of emotion.

Mr. Jimmy's glaze of detachment fell off him the very moment the door closed behind the men removing his mother from the house.

Okay, she's gone! And now I'm going to tell about my Mama! She was hard as my fist!

Oh, Jimmy, the sobbing girl pleaded. He pushed her away and struck his fist on a little chair-side table so hard that his drink bounced off it.

She was harder than my fist on this table! And she never let up on me once in my whole life, never! She was hard as my fist, she was harder than my goddam fist on this table, and that's the truth about her. But now she's gone from this house and she's not going to come back to it, so the house is mine now. Well, she owned me, she used to own me, like she owned this house, and she was hard as my fist and she was tight as my fist, she set on her goddam money like an old hen on a glass egg, she was tight and hard as my fist. I just got away once, that's all, just once in my life did I ever get away from her—an old faggot took me to New York with him and got tired of me there and told me to hit the street, and that's what I did, oh brother!

You want to know something? Even after I came back to this place, I never got a key to it, I never had my own door key. Not until after her stroke did I even have my own door key.

She'd lock up the house after supper, and if I'd gone out, she'd sit here waiting for me in this here chair. And you know what gave her the stroke? One night I came home and saw her through a front window sitting here waiting for me, to let me in when I rung the friggin' front doorbell, but I didn't ring it, I didn't knock or call, I just kicked the goddam door in. I kicked it in and she let out with a cry like a pig being slaughtered. And when I entered, when I come in the kicked-open door, she was lyin' here paralyzed on this here livin'-room floor, and never spoke or moved since, that was the way the old woman got her stroke. Well now, look here! Look at what I'm keepin' now in my pocket. See? Ev'ry goddam key to Mama's old stucco house!

He took out of his pants pocket and raised up and jangled a big bunch of keys on a brass ring ornamented by a pair of red dice.

Then a soft voice stopped him by calling, Mr. Jimmy!

It was Brinda's Mama, in the shadowy next room. He nodded slightly, his outburst over as suddenly as it burst out. He threw the keys in the air and caught them and thrust them back in his pocket and sank back down in a chair, all in one movement it seemed, and just at that moment, luckily no sooner, the minister and his wife arrived at the door and the former decorum fell back over the parlor as if it had only lifted to the ceiling and hung up there until the outburst was over and then had settled back down again undamaged.

Brinda was amazed by the strength of her Mama. It seemed to come back like a miracle to the old woman. She set to work in the kitchen preparing a large platter of thin-cut sandwiches, boiled two Silexes of coffee and emptied them into the big silver percolator, and set the dining-room table as nicely as if for a party, knowing where everything was that would make the best show, the best linen and silver, the five-branched candelabra and even a set of finger bowls and lace napkins.

Mr. Jimmy stayed in the parlor, though, and drank his liquor till late in the afternoon, ignoring the buffet lunch that Brinda's Mama set for condolence callers. Only the minister and a few other old ladies drifted into the living room and ate a little bit of it. Then sundown came, the company dispersed and Mr. Jimmy went out. Brinda's Mama lay down on a cot in the basement, her hand on the side that pained her but her face, which was only slightly darker than Brinda's, looking composed and solemn. Brinda sat with her awhile and they talked in a desultory fashion as the light faded through the small high windows in the basement walls.

The talk had run out completely and the light was all but gone when Mr. Jimmy was heard coming back in the house. Brinda's Mama had seemed to be dozing but now her dark eyes opened and she cleared her throat and, turning her head to Brinda still seated beside her, directed her to ask Mr. Jimmy to come downstairs for a minute so she could talk to him before they went back home.

Brinda delivered this message to Mr. Jimmy who said, in reply, Bring your Mama upstairs and I'll drive you all back in the car.

Brinda's Mama's strength had all gone again and it was a struggle getting her up from the basement. She sat down, panting, by the kitchen table while Mr. Jimmy took a shower upstairs. Several times her head jerked forward and Brinda caught at her to hold her in the chair. But when Mr. Jimmy came down, she summoned her force back again and rose from the chair. They rode through the town in silence, to the section for Negroes, and not till Mr. Jimmy was about to pull up at their door did Brinda's Mama speak to him. Then she said:

Mr. Jimmy, what in the name of the Lord has happened to you? What kind of life are you leading here nowadays!

He answered her gently: Well, y'know, I did no good in New York . . .

That's the truth, said Brinda's Mama, with sad conviction. You just got mixed with bad people and caught their bad ways. . . . And how come you give up your painting?

Brinda was scared when her Mama asked that question because, soon after she'd taken her Mama's place at the Krennings', she'd said to Mr. Jimmy one morning, when she was giving him coffee, Mr. Jimmy, Mama keeps askin' me if you work in your studio after breakfast an' when I tell her you don't, it seems to upset her so much that now I tell her you do, but I hate to lie to Mama, 'cause I think she knows when I'm lyin' . . .

That morning was the one time that Jimmy had been unkind to Brinda, not just unkind but violent. He had picked up a Silex of coffee and thrown it at the wall in the kitchen, and the kitchen wall was still brown-stained where the glass coffeepot had smashed on it. He had followed this action with a four-letter word, and then he had dropped his head in his shaking hands.

So Brinda expected something awful to happen at this moment, in response to her Mama's bold question, but all Mr. Jimmy did was to drive right through a red light at a street intersection.

Brinda's Mama said, You went through a stoplight, and Mr. Jimmy answered, Did I? Well, that's O.K. . . .

It was a fair distance from the Krennings' house to Brinda's and her Mama's, and a few blocks after Mr. Jimmy had driven through the stoplight, Mr. Jimmy slowed the car down again and the talk was continued.

Mr. Jimmy said, If I don't know, who knows?

Well, said Brinda's Mama, even if you quit workin', you can't do nothin', just nothin', you got to do somethin', don't you?

I do something, said Mr. Jimmy.

What do you do?

Well, about this time of evening, I drive out by the air base, I go a little bit past it, and then I turn around and drive back, and, here and there, along the road back into town, I pass young fliers thumbing a ride into town, and I pick out one to pick up, and I pick him up and we go to the house and we drink and discuss ourselves with each other and drink and, after a while, well, maybe we get to be friends or maybe we don't, and that's what I do now, you see . . .

He slowed the car down toward the house, stopped it right in front of the walk to the porch, with a deep sighing intake of breath, and released the wheel and his head fell back as if his neck was broken.

Brinda's Mama sighed too, and her head not only fell back against the car cushion but lolled to the side a little. They were like two broken-necked people, and with the uncomprehending patience of a dog, Brinda just sat and waited for them both to revive.

Then, at last, Mr. Jimmy sighed again, with a long intake of breath, and lurched out of the car and came around to the back seat to open the door for them as if they were two white ladies.

He not only assisted Brinda's Mama out of the car, but he kept a tight hold on her up to the porch. Perhaps if he hadn't she would have fallen down, but Brinda could sense that it was something more than one person giving another a necessary physical support for a little distance, and when they had got up the front steps, Mr. Jimmy still stayed. He took in his breath very loudly again with the same sighing sound as he had done twice before, and there was a prolonged hesitation, which Brinda found awkward and tense, though it did not seem to bother either her Mama or Mr. Jimmy. It was like something they were used to, or had always expected. They stood there at the top of the steps to the porch, and it was uncertain whether they were going to part at this point or going to remain together for a while longer.

They seemed like a pair of people who had quarreled and come to an understanding, not because of any agreement between them, but because of a mutual recognition of a sad, inescapable thing that gave them a closeness even through disappointment in trying to settle their quarrel.

Brinda's Mama said, Mr. Jimmy, sit down with us a little, and he did.

Both of the two chairs on the front porch were rockers. Brinda sat on the steps. Mr. Jimmy rocked, but her Mama sat still in her chair.

After a little while Brinda's Mama said, Mr. Jimmy, what are you going to do now?

I make no plans, I just go along, go along.

How long you plan to do that?

Long as I can, till something stops me, I guess.

Brinda's Mama nodded and then was silent as if inwardly calculating the length of time that might take. The silence continued as long as it might have taken her to arrive at a conclusion to this problem, and then she got up and said, I am going to die now, as quietly as if she had only said she was going in the dark house. Mr. Jimmy stood up as if a white lady had risen and held the screen door open while she unlocked the wooden one.

Brinda started in after her, but her Mama blocked her way in.

You go stay at the Krennings', you go on back there tonight an' clean up that mess in the place and you two stay there together and you look after each other, and, Brinda, don't let them white boys interfere with you. When you hear them come in, go down to the basement and lock the basement door an' you stay down there till daylight, unless Mr. Jimmy calls for you, and if he calls for you, go up an' see what he wants.

Then she turned to Mr. Jimmy and said, I thought a white boy like you was born with a chance in the world!

She then shut the door and locked it. Brinda couldn't believe that her Mama had locked her out, but that's what she'd done. She would have stayed there senselessly waiting before that locked door, but Mr. Jimmy gently took hold of her arm and led her out to his car. He opened the back door for her as if she were a white lady. She got in the car and going home, to the Krennings', Mr. Jimmy serenely drove through the stoplights as if he were color-blind. He drove home straight and fast, and when they arrived at the Krennings' Brinda observed that a soft light was burning downstairs, in the downstairs hall, and it seemed to say something that no one had said all day in so many words, that God, like other people, has two kinds of hands, one hand with which to strike and another to soothe and caress with.

(*Published 1965*)

The Knightly Quest

When Gewinner Pearce returned home after years of travel with a tutor-companion, the late Dr. Horace Greaves, everything visible from the airport, including the airport itself, was so unrecognizable to him that he thought the plane must have made an unscheduled stop. He was about to hurry back up the steps to the plane's cabin when he heard the voice of a woman calling his name. He gazed out toward the direction from which the call issued and what he saw was a young woman approaching him with the velocity of a football tackler and with a mink coat flapping about her. For a couple of moments she was intercepted and restrained in her approach by a pair of armed guards.

Hands off, hands off me! Don't you know who I am? I am Mrs. Braden Pearce, out here to meet the brother of my husband! His name's Gewinner—the same as the name of the town.

The steel-helmeted guards fell back from her with awkward little deferential salutes, and then she continued her rush toward Gewinner, who defended and braced himself as best he could by placing vertically before him his furled black silk umbrella and tensing his slight body to withstand the moment of impact. But he was surprised and relieved that this young wife of his brother, never seen before, slackened her pace just before she reached him, and instead of colliding with him, she introduced herself to him in a manner that was fast and vigorous but reasonably coherent.

Oh, Gewinner, she cried out to him as if he were in a far corner of the airfield, I bet you don't know who I am, I am Braden's wife, Violet, and Mother Pearce, God love her, was dying to meet you herself but she just couldn't make it because today is the day she's placing a wreath on the memorial to our boys in Kwat Sing How, and so, God love her, she appointed me in her place to welcome you home here.

Oh. Good, said Gewinner.

They were now moving toward the airport building, Violet still holding up her end of the unilateral conversation. How was your flight, was it nice? I recognized you the moment you started down the steps from the plane, not because you look like your brother, Braden, you don't a bit in the world, but you did look exactly like the way I expected you to look, I swear you did, and you do!

How did you expect me to look? asked Gewinner with unaffected interest in what her answer might be. He had a touch of the Narcissan in his nature and was always somewhat curious about the way he might appear to persons unaccustomed to his appearance.

Why, I know the family called you Prince, they did and still do, and if anybody ever looked like a prince out of a fairy-tale book, it's you, God love you, you do!

Then, without pause, she cried out, Oh, my God, they're playing "Babe's Stomp" again!

Playing what? asked Gewinner.

Baby, Babe, Babe, the President's daughter, you know!

No, I don't know, said Gewinner.

Well, first there was "Babe's Hop," and now there's "Babe's Stomp," and I want you to know that as much as I detested the hop, this stomp of hers makes the hop seem like a lovely thing to look back on, it actually does, no fooling!

Violet was referring to rhythm-band music that was coming thunderously from a sound apparatus atop the terminal building. It made the airport sound like a big discothèque, and several incoming passengers and persons there to receive them were going into spastic, stamping gyrations.

Gewinner shouted over this hullabaloo:

What's wrong with the air? he shouted; it has a peculiar smell to it.

Oh, that, shouted Violet, that's just the fumes from The Project.

What's The Project? Gewinner shouted back at her.

Shouting was unnecessary now, for "Babe's Stomp" had quit as abruptly as it had started. Gewinner's shouted question drew undesired attention in the sudden, comparative silence. People glanced at him with expressions of curiosity or incredulity or both.

Out of the side of her mouth, Violet said, No talk about it right now.

Then she called out the name William, William!

A dead-pan, uniformed man, presumably employed by the family, emerged from the airport crowd to take Gewinner's baggage-claim checks.

Now then, said Violet, we'll go wait in the car and get acquainted, unless you could use a wee drink at the bar. Frankly, I hope you can. I could sure in hell use a stinger under my belt. Whenever I rush about, it makes me thirsty. So come along, Prince, right up these steps here, to the Sky-lite Lounge. You know, we're all so excited that you've come home from your travels. Let's sit at the bar, it's quicker. Now where were you last in your travels?

In the Land of the Midnight Sun, said Gewinner, knowing from the wild but glazed look in her eyes that she'd pay no attention to this answer, which was made up. Where he'd last been in his travels was actually in Manhattan where his tutor-companion, Dr. Greaves, had fallen fatally prey to an overdosage of a drug he'd taken to expand his perceptions. This drug had not only expanded the perceptions of Dr. Greaves but had deranged them somewhat, so that the good, gray philosopher and doctor of humanities had walked right off the roof of a five-story brownstone in the Turtle Bay section of Manhattan as if he were responding to a call from outer space, which may have been exactly what he was doing . . .

In the cocktail lounge of the airport, Gewinner asked for a campari and soda but didn't get it, the drink being unknown to the barman. Violet showed a somewhat assertive streak in her nature by telling the barman to give them both stingers. She tossed down hers as fast as if she were putting out a fire in her stomach, and then she said to Gewinner, Why, Prince, you didn't drink enough of that stinger to keep a bird alive! Oh well, I'll finish it for you. So she tossed down Gewinner's stinger too. Now then, she said, that's what the doctor ordered and I obeyed the order, so let's make a run for the car before the family fink suspects we've been up here, Gewinner.

In the car on the way home, if home you could call it, Gewinner continued to observe almost nothing he had once known in the town which had now grown to a city. The sylvan park whose trees had been mostly willows had turned into a concrete playground full of monkeys disguised as children, at least that was the impression made upon Gewinner.

To himself more than to Violet he observed, I remember it being like a romantic ballet setting. I mean swans drifted about on a lake and there were cranes, herons, flamingos and even a peacock with several peahens around him, but now there's not a willow and not a swan or a lake for a swan to drift in.

Aw now, said Violet, you mustn't philosophize gloomily about it.

I wasn't philosophizing, I was simply remembering and observing, said Gewinner.

He gave Violet a rather sharp glance, wondering where she had gotten her education, if any.

I reckon you don't realize it, said Violet, pressing his arm as if to comfort him, but all these changes you notice are because of The Project.

And what exactly is that? asked Gewinner again.

Prince, you're not serious, are you!

Perfectly. I've never heard of The Project.

Well, now you have, said Violet, and furthermore you're just about to see it, the outside of it! There! Here! Look at it!

The limousine was now going by what appeared to be an enormous penitentiary for criminals of the most dangerous nature. Its grounds were enclosed by a tall metal fence on which, at intervals, were signs that said DANGER, ELECTRICALLY CHARGED, and just inside this enclosure, patrolling the grounds, were uniformed men with dogs. The dogs seemed to want to go faster than the men, they kept tugging at their leads and glancing back crossly at the men. Then the dogs would look ahead again with expressions that could be described as fiercely glaring. The men's and dogs' heads would pivot slightly from right to left and left to right as if the men and dogs had gone to the same training school and come out equally proficient at the art of patrolling, and it would be hard to say, if you had to, which glared more fiercely, the human guards or the dogs.

Why, here, said Gewinner, almost exclaiming about it, was my father's business, the Red Devil Battery Plant.

Yes, isn't it wonderful? said Violet with a certain sibilance in her speech. Your father's, God love your father, his Red Devil Battery Plant has been converted into The Project, and I want you to know that your brother, Braden Pearce, is the top man on the totem pole here, and it's not just great, it's the greatest!

What does The Project make or do? asked Gewinner.

Oh, I do love you, Prince, cried out Violet. To think you honestly don't know what The Project is for! Why, Prince, it's for the development of a thing to blow them all off the map of the world, for good and all and forever!

Who is them?

Why, *them* is *them*, who else! Are you serious, Prince, or are you just putting me on about it?

He heard a quick scratching sound and saw that she had snatched a little appointment book from her purse and was scribbling down something. She tore the page out and pressed it into his hand.

The message was: Change the subject, I think this car is bugged.

Gewinner had hardly read this peculiar message when Violet snatched the paper back from him, crumpled it, thrust it into her mouth, ground it between her teeth, swallowed, gagged, coughed, pressed a button that turned the radio on, clutched her throat and swallowed again, this time successfully.

Immediately after this curious series of actions, or compulsive syndrome, she began to chatter again.

Prince? Gewinner? I wish you could have seen the delighted expressions on their faces, Mama's and Braden's, when they heard you were on your way back here all of a sudden! It was a sight to behold, that I can tell you. Oh, here we are! Recognize it?

The car had turned into the drive of a gray stone building that had a resemblance, probably more deliberate than accidental, to something in the nature of an ancient Saracen castle brought up to date.

It's all that I've recognized since I got off the plane, said Gewinner, telling almost the truth.

Without asking questions, just by listening to and piecing together scraps of conversation, Gewinner came to know, in the following days, a number of things that accounted for the town's changes, such as the fact that his late father's Red Devil Battery Plant had sure enough been converted into a thing called The Project, and that The Project was engaged all day and all night in the development of some marvelously mysterious weapon of annihilation. The number of its personnel was greater than had been the town's population at the time when Gewinner had set out on his travels. Hordes of scientists, technicians, brass hats of degree high and low, intelligence officers, highly skilled workmen and ordinary workmen, all the way up and down the totem pole of importance, were involved in The Project's operations. As Violet put it, it was not only great but the greatest, not a bit of exaggeration about it.

The Project's personnel and their families were housed in new little concrete-block structures called Sunshine Houses, and a lot of new businesses, big and little, had sprung up to accommodate their needs and wholesome pleasures, most of them also named something very cheerful such as "Sweetheart," "Rainbow," and "Blue Bird."

One of these new businesses, between big and little, was the Laughing Boy Drive-in, situated on a corner diagonally across from the Pearce family mansion, and this drive-in provoked Gewinner Pearce's sense of personal outrage more strongly than any other vulgarity which had appeared in his home town during his absence. The drive-in was built on property that belonged to the Pearces. Gewinner's younger brother, Braden, had leased it for ninety-nine years to a boyhood chum whose portrait in golden neon smiled and laughed out loud with a big haw-haw, at ten-second intervals, from early dusk till midnight. And this, mind you, was on the finest residential boulevard in the city and the haw-hawing neon portrait of its owner was almost directly facing the Pearce mansion. Gewinner, of course, had no misapprehensions about the elegance and dignity of the Pearce place, but the fact remained that Gewinner was a Pearce, and the Laughing Boy in neon seemed a personal affront. It laughed so loudly that it punctuated all but the loudest passages of the symphonic music he played on his hi-fi at night to calm his nerves, and in addition to the haw-haw at the drive-in there was the honking of cars from morn to midnight, appealing for immediate servings of such items as King-burgers, barbecued ribs, malts, cokes, coffee and so forth. The carhops were girls and sometimes they'd lose control of their nerves under the constant pressure of their jobs and would have screaming fits; then, more than likely, there'd be the siren wail of an ambulance or a squad car or both. When the hysterical carhop had been rushed off to the Sunshine Emergency Center, the Laughing Boy would seem to be splitting his sides over the whole bit, and though Gewinner could understand how it all might seem ludicrous, in a ghastly way, the mechanical haw-haw somehow would kill the joke, at least for the prince of the Pearces.

Now for a little digression in the nature of turning back time.

While Gewinner had been on his travels he received from his mother exactly two communications a year, a cablegram at Christmas and a cablegram at Easter, both addressed to him care of American Express in London, a capital that Gewinner visited from time to time to refurbish his wardrobe. These cablegrams were very much to the point. The Christmas one said, Christ is born, Love, Mother, and the Easter one said, Christ is risen, Love, Mother. And once, between Christmas and Easter, Gewinner dispatched a cablegram to Mother Pearce that was utterly meaningless to her: it said, Dear Mother, What is He up to now? Love, Gewinner.

However, actually Mother Pearce's correspondence was far and away more loquacious than these twice yearly announcements to her traveling son would suggest, and "loquacious" is the *mot juste* for it, since all her outgoing letters and wires were shouted to a personal secretary, little Miss Genevieve Goodleigh. And "shouted" is the correct way to put it, as this correspondence was dictated while Mother Pearce was receiving her Vibra-Wonder treatment, a very loud, three-hour treatment that kept her from looking her age by a comfortable margin of give or take a few hours.

Now on this particular morning to which time has been reversed, a wire had come in from Gewinner, but Mother Pearce ignored all incoming letters and messages till after she'd shouted out, to the phenomenal Miss Goodleigh, her outgoing correspondence, and "phenomenal" is the precise term for Miss Goodleigh since she caught every word of this correspondence even when the Vibra-Wonder was operating in the highest of its five gears.

At this time, on this particular morning, Mother Pearce was shouting out a letter to the most prominent hostess in the nation's capital.

Darling Boo, she shouted, I am telling you no news that is news to you when I tell you the President and the First Lady with their divine daughter, Babe, were house guests of mine last weekend, and, oh my soul and body, what fun we girls had together while the menfolks were holding their top-level consultations on the crisis in Ghu-Ghok-Shu. Of course I already knew from previous get-togethers that the First Lady is more fun than a barrel or a boatload of monkeys, but this last visit was one continual howl. The climax of it was a jamboree at the Club Diamond Brite. I said to Mag, The ship of state is in responsible hands so we don't have to worry about it, and I want you to know we didn't, why, honey, while the Chief and my precious boy Braden were deciding where to strike next and what to strike with, you would never have guessed from our fun and frolic that anything more serious than a possum hunt was going on anywhere in the world. We had a couple of jazz bands to spell each other, we had the Wildcat Five which you know are the latest craze, we had a nigger you threw baseballs at and if you hit him he fell in a tank of cold water, and we had a couple of boxing kangaroos with a dog referee. So! What suddenly happened but this! The doors bang open at the height of the frolic and in comes my precious boy Braden pushing the Chief in a red, white and blue wheelbarrow, the Chief firing blanks out of two pistols. They were like two kids who have just burnt down the schoolhouse, and I tell you, honey, the photographers and newspaper boys had a field day, they went absolutely hog-wild, and the commotion and pandemonium was way, way out of control till all of a sudden the band struck up "Babe's Stomp," in honor of Babe, and Babe shot like a cannon ball over to my boy Braden and caught him in such a bear hug that I was scared for a second she'd crack his ribs. Do my stomp with me, honey, I heard her holler, and off they stomped together. It was a sight to be seen when they accidentally stomped into the honorary co-hostess and knocked her into the pastry end of the buffet table. Then Babe hollered to the band to play a slow number called "The Clinch," and, well, you know, Boo, I don't embarrass easy and it would be hard to find a First Lady as up-do-date as Mag is. This is what Mag said to me, Boo, she leaned over to me and said, Do you see what I see, Nelly? Our two children are dancing so tight together you couldn't paste a postage stamp between them, and look at the look in their eyes, I could cry like I do at a wedding!

Now what do you make of that, Boo? I'm sure you must see the tragic irony of it. Poor Violet was never and never could be cut out for her present position in life, I mean she was suddenly escalated way up beyond her natural limitations and would be a happier girl if she had recognized and never overstepped her personal potential. However, what I feel, Boo, is that here is a tragedy that can still be corrected in life. If Braden and Babe have been drawn together by such a powerful attraction to each other and a little propinquity like this, I think it's the will of God and we ought to feel morally obliged to do everything we can to bring them together more often. I'm writing you this because you're in a perfect position to throw them together up there and I can throw them together down here, and believe you me, it would be much harder to hold Babe and Braden apart than it is to get them together. Boo, do you see my point? I know that question is unnecessary because if you don't see my point you'd have to be blind as ten bats in a belfry, which isn't the case with you, Boo. Your vision and your thinking apparatus have always been up to snuff and a good deal higher. I think just a bit more propinquity at banquets up there and at cookouts and frolics down here will salvage the lives of a pair of fine young people that providence meant for each other. Now, Boo, keep this under your hat but if you think my suggestion is as wonderful as I do, get back to me on the teletype right away with one word, "wonderful," but if you have any reservations or questions about it, get back to me with the word "fog," and—

Oh, cried out Miss Goodleigh, my pencil point's broke!

Well hell, exclaimed Mother Pearce, what's going on here this morning?

Having never heard her employer speak with such violence before, Miss Goodleigh rushed sobbing into the bathroom to pull herself together.

While she was in there, Mother Pearce completed her Vibra-Wonder treatment and, having nothing else to do at the moment, idly picked up a wire which had come in that morning. This wire happened to be from Gewinner. It went as follows: Dear Mother, I was shocked and sorry to hear that father has gone to his heavenly mansion. I feel that I ought to be with you in this time of grief and remain as long as necessary to straighten out the unexpected curtailment of my travel expenses. Kill no fatted calf but expect my homecoming within the next few days. Will wire the precise time later. Fondest love, Gewinner.

God have mercy upon us, cried out Mother Pearce. She had observed that the wire contained no phone number she could call, no address to which she could wire to let the Prince know how little she needed his presence to console her in her newly widowed condition.

Now to turn back time more than a little bit further, Gewinner had been on the go since the spring of his sixteenth year, since a morning in that spring when his tutor-companion, the late Dr. Horace Greaves, had convinced Father and Mother Pearce so quickly and easily that their first-born son, the Prince in the tower, could be better instructed in the humanities while traveling here and there among foreign lands and seas. The late Dr. Horace Greaves had hardly begun to address the parents on this topic when the late Mr. Pearce had boomed out, *Fine, wonderful, great, for God's sake get going*, and Mother Pearce had almost simultaneously buzzed the chauffeur to whisk her son and his tutor as fast as a streak of blue lightning out to the airport and not let them out of his sight till they'd boarded a plane and the plane was off the ground.

So began the travels of Gewinner with his tutor-companion.

Gewinner thrived on these travels but the tutor-companion developed a nervous condition, complicated by insomnia, which culminated in a collapse that was followed by several relapses, and he finally wound up in a Bavarian spa that specialized in the ice cure for nervous disorders. So poor Dr. Greaves was packed in ice for three months, his temperature kept at the temperature level of the fish and the lizard, and during that chilly period in the doctor's stoical experience on earth,

Gewinner somehow managed to enlist in the navy. His hitch in the navy was remarkably short, it lasted for just ten days, give or take a few minutes. Then Gewinner was returned to civilian status and his name and all else pertinent to him was expunged from all records of the naval branch of the armed services, as if he, Gewinner, had never so much as existed.

Gewinner then wired Dr. Greaves: Get off the ice and let's get cracking again. And it just so happened that Dr. Greaves had, that very day the wire reached him, been taken out of the ice, and though the distinguished scholar and educator in the humanities had not yet had time to completely thaw out, he was at least as eager as Gewinner to get cracking again, especially toward the equator.

Two things occurred in close sequence to delay the resumption of their travels, and this delay was really more in the nature of a cancellation. One of these occurrences has been mentioned already, the fatal misadventure of Dr. Greaves in the Turtle Bay section of Manhattan, ironically at a farewell banquet on the roof of a five-story town house, a banquet at which the main course and the only course was a species of fungus related to the mushroom, under the influence of which the good doctor took off like a parachute jumper and ended his earthly travels on the inexorable pavement below. However, the second occurrence has yet to be mentioned. It was a bit of information that Gewinner received from a bank official, the information that his father had recently been planted in the family plot and that the estate had passed into the custody of Mother Pearce and the younger son, Braden. This circumstance affected Gewinner gravely, since it meant that his remittances would no longer be adequate to support his former high style of life and travel here and there on the earth's surface.

Gewinner suspected, sensibly, that if he went home for a while, it might not take him too long to convince Mother Pearce and his brother that he, Gewinner, had better be allowed to go on with his travels in the opulent style to which he was accustomed.

Though Gewinner's brother was a year younger than Gewinner, Braden Pearce had the maturity of a family man while Gewinner kept about him a graceful, adolescent look, thanks to his slimness and the quality of his skin, so smooth that it seemed to be made without pores, the way that the finest silk shows no sign of being woven.

Gewinner stayed in the tower of the gray stone mansion which had been designed to have a sort of pop-art resemblance to a medieval castle. He had moved into the tower while he was in his early teens in order to remove himself as far from the Pearce family life as the geography of the mansion permitted, and he had had an iron fire escape, almost as steep as a stepladder, put up between the lawn and a window of the tower so that his restless comings and goings at night would not disturb the family. They had called him the Prince as much in awe as in mockery of his refinements.

Braden Pearce had the look that football players get when they have been in business and married for several years: coarsening, thickening, getting flushed in the face, turning into one of those bullish men who shatter all opposition by the sheer weight and energy of their drive until drink softens them up at forty-five or fifty and the heart quits on them at sixty.

Right now Braden was at the peak of his male power. His wife, Violet, had a pale, dampish look in the mornings as if she had spent the night in a steam bath. Their bedroom, unfortunately for Gewinner, was directly under his room in the tower and they made noises like beasts of the jungle when they had sex, which was about every night. At his climax, Braden would howl and curse, and at hers, Violet would cry out like a yard full of peacocks. Apparently they would also roll and thrash about in their ecstasies, knocking things off their bedside tables. Some nights Mrs. Pearce would come to their door and call out, Is something wrong in there? Son, Violet, is something wrong in there? Neither would answer at once. Violet would be sobbing and making sounds as if she were dying of strangulation and Braden would be cursing and huffing for a minute or so after Mother Pearce's anxious call at the door. Then, at last, they both would answer together in hoarse voices, No, no, Mother, no, Mother, everything's fine, go on back to bed, Mother.

One night a widowed lady and her bachelor son, the Fishers, residents of the house next door, came over for a bridge game that went on after Violet and Braden had gone up to bed. Gewinner was in the game because he loved to outwit his mother at bridge, and they were playing away when the howling, cursing and religious and profane exclamations began to reverberate through the castle. Mrs. Pearce kept clearing her throat and then she asked Gewinner to turn the hi-fi on, but Gewinner, grinning wickedly, said, Oh Mother, I can't concentrate on my game with music playing. I think, said Mrs. Pearce—but she never completed the statement, for just then some very heavy object, probably Braden, fell to the floor and there was a shower of plaster from the ceiling over the bridge game and the chandelier swung like a pendulum, to exaggerate only slightly. The neighbor lady, Gewinner's partner in the bridge game, made repeated coughing sounds, explaining that she had a frog in her throat, while brushing plaster dust off her clothes.

Hmmm, said Mrs. Pearce with a tight-lipped attempt at a smile, partner, I have to pass.

Then, being dummy, she got up from the table, murmuring, Excuse me a moment, and went clattering upstairs to knock at the young couple's door.

Son? Violet? she could be heard calling, and before she could ask if anything was wrong, Braden's voice boomed through the house, bellowing out, For Chrissake, will you keep your ass on the bed? And Violet cried out shrilly, You're killing me, honey, I'm dying, let's stay on the floor!

Mrs. Pearce's partner, a nervous bachelor in his late forties, was quite flurried and flushed, since scenes of this nature are particularly embarrassing to Southern boys in the presence of their mothers. He forgot what was trumps, he almost seemed to be putting down cards at random. Nobody said anything after the neighbor lady's announcement that she had a frog in her throat but she and her son took turns at coughing. Then Gewinner began talking out loud but as if to himself, selecting a subject that seemed to have no relevance to the games upstairs and down. The speech unwound itself evenly from his lips which wore a smile like Hamlet's or the Mona Lisa's, or rather a bit on the sly side and also a bit on the side of the quietly savage. What he said in this curiously elliptical monologue, under the swaying chandelier and the continuing shower of dust, would never pass the scrutiny of a logician, if it were put on paper—where it is now being put, as if it came from a tape recorder that had picked up the very free associations of a hallucinated romantic.

Mrs. Fisher, he said, as if he were talking to her, the course of history changed when a troop of mercenary foot soldiers, equipped with a new weapon called the long bow, plopped to their knees among the little wildflowers that sprinkled the morning-dew-spangled grass on a certain field, in Normandy I believe, which became known to history as the Field of Agincourt. . . .

Mama, was the bid five spades?

No, son, it was six diamonds, doubled and redoubled, before the—

Oh.

Gewinner went on serenely and illogically as he played a brilliant game. Yes, he went on, the common foot soldiers didn't pick the wildflowers, probably didn't notice the wildflowers there, but set their arrows to the strings of their bows and let them fly at a charge of plumed knights in armor, and then something snapped in the clear morning air and was going to stay snapped for the rest of human time. The long bows' arrows struck with appalling accuracy, the charge of the knights was routed, the mercenary foot soldiers rose from the dew-sparkling field, rushed forward and knelt again upon the little wildflowers and let their arrows go twanging again at the white and silver foe on the field at Agincourt. I suppose it was a little bit like suddenly switching from a game of chess to a game of checkers. I mean the big game of sides against each other in the world. Am I making any sense? I doubt it. But since you're not listening to me, it doesn't make much difference. I used to feel that there was a sort of demented romanticism in this house being designed to suggest a medieval castle, but the absurdity went too far with the construction of the Laughing Boy Drive-in, catty-cornered across from the fake castle. The last time I was home for a visit, the castle had a banner flying from its tower, a bifurcated triangle of white silk emblazoned with a coat of arms and a motto, *Carpe Diem*, which means seize the day. All of which makes me suspect that back of the sun and way deep under our feet, at the earth's center, are not a couple of noble mysteries but a couple of joke books. However, as for myself, I still go out alone at night, and feel something back of the visible stars and something deep under my feet. I don't know what it is. Maybe it's just the pleasure of getting a little away from the fake medieval castle and the Laughing Boy Drive-in.

Pardon me, said Mrs. Fisher, did you say something?

I was just saying, said Gewinner, that every time the earth turns on its axis, a clerk in heaven, some badly paid little clerk, jots down another minus sign after whatever symbol they use for the Quixote syndrome, or whatever the hell they call it in heaven, and I don't know whether the angels burst into weeping or song every time.

The neighbor's son spoke up and said, What were you saying, Gewinner? I didn't catch it, either.

Oh, I was making no more sense than an agnostic priest mumbling Mass, but someone had to say something, and so I said that across the street, diagonally across from Pearce's Folly, there is a perfect little gem of neo-Colonial architecture that's famous for its barbecued ribs and chicken-in-a-basket and chocolate malts as thick as fresh cement and piping-hot ever-fresh coffee. And I'm not a liar when I tell you it makes as much noise, well, nearly as much, as Violet and Braden in bed, at least it's that noisy, or nearly, when one shift at The Project has sallied forth to make way for the next shift, let's see now, doubled, redoubled and you've lost seven tricks, what a blow for Mama when she comes back down.

The thumping on the floor above was still going on, and the son and mother, the Fishers, had turned from rose red to paper white, but the Widow Fisher produced her voice to ask Gewinner again what he was saying while she'd been preoccupied with her cards.

Oh, just babbling, he said, just to hear myself babbling, it helps my concentration to babble away playing cards. But when Mother Pearce comes down from her luckless effort to clip the wings of Eros, I'm going to make a suggestion, I'm going to suggest to her that she install a pipe organ in Violet's and Braden's bedroom behind a screen or tapestry. The organist could come in by way of a secret staircase and a sliding panel, and whenever Violet and Braden retire before guests have left the castle, the organist could play the "Hallelujah Chorus" from Handel's *Messiah* or Wagner's "Ride of the Valkyries."

Oh, there goes Violet like a yard full of peacocks, and now Braden's howling like a villain wrestler with his foot being twisted. Marvelous, yes. When I was in the navy for several days, I made the acquaintance of another recruit who showed me a photo of his baby and said, I made that baby the night I pushed the wall with both feet, man.

Now it seems like they've withdrawn to reorganize their forces, and Mother Pearce's coming back downstairs. Whose deal is it? Oh, mine, and I've already dealt while you all were paying no attention to my wandering reflections.

Mother Pearce came back into the room, saying, Well, well, well, in a loud cheerful tone at total variance with the sharpshooter blaze in her eyes.

What was going on, Mother? asked Gewinner.

Why, nothing at all to speak of, they were just romping and cutting up like a couple of kids when school lets out.

Oh, now, isn't that sweet, said the widow from next door, in a toneless voice.

Partner, have we finished a rubber? Yes? inquired Mother Pearce. Well, why don't we settle the score and have a round of nightcaps for the road.

Mother, suggested Gewinner, why don't we all trot over to the drive-in for a basket of chicken and French fries, since it's so close, so handy?

Now, Gewinner, said Mother Pearce, you'll have to get used to the drive-in when you're home from your travels. It's going to be on that corner for ninety-nine years, at least.

You mean barring a premature blast at The Project, Gewinner murmured. Then he added, louder: Mama, we beat you again, so before you make those nightcaps, shell out eighty-six in greenbacks, and forty-seven in quarters, dimes, nickels and pennies, since my partner and I will not accept your check or an I O U.

He had already risen from the card table and tossed about his shoulders a white silk scarf that was almost the size of a bed sheet and as flawlessly smooth as his skin, and now he was putting on a black topcoat which his bridge partner, the next-door widow, touched with incredulous fingers, and said, Why, that coat is—

She was going to say "moiré" when there came a call at the door, a voice calling out, Delivery from the Drive-in!

Gewinner said, Speak of the devil.

This delivery from the drive-in was, as always, two orders of chicken-in-the-basket with French fries. That's what Braden always called for when he and Violet had chalked up one more vigorous assault on the huge and dark siege of inertia that can be said to hang about the dynamics of existence—to put it in a somewhat or more than somewhat rhetorical fashion. Just what Braden felt when he had completed one of these furious assaults on the siege of inertia is a question that would have to be put to Braden, and it is doubtful that he would come up with a coherent answer if he tried to give one. The likeliest guess is that he felt like a rooster on a back fence at the sign of daybreak. Anyway one thing is certain. While Braden was still panting from his orgasm, he would pick up the bedroom phone and call the drive-in. Hey, Billy, the same, he would say. Violet would always say, No French fries for me, but Braden would ignore this interjection since a double portion of French fries had never fazed him. At his end of the line, Billy would say, Right over, man, right over!

This delivery from the drive-in was always delivered personally by the proprietor himself. The Laughing Boy, Billy, would carry the two piping-hot baskets straight up to the Braden Pearces' bedroom and he would often stay up there about an hour, having nightcaps with Violet and Braden and reminiscing with Braden about the spectacular tricks and pranks of their boyhood days and nights, such as the Halloween they went in the colored graveyard and dug up a preacher buried the day before and put him and his coffin side by side on the steps of his church along with a big printed sign nailed onto the coffin which said

THEY WOULDN'T LET ME IN HEAVEN SO I COME BACK TO PREACH SOME MORE
ABOUT HELL TO YOU SINFUL NIGGERS NEXT SUNDAY!

Oh, those were real fun days and nights in their boyhood, and
Braden and Billy would assure each other that they were not over yet,
no sir, not by a long shot, you could bet on that.

One time Braden said to Billy, I'll tell you something, Buddy, but you
forget I told you. Buddy, there's a big Halloween yet to be, but the
pranks and the jokes are such classified information, as they call it, that
I wouldn't dare even talk about 'em to you, and that's no shit. But this I
can say. We've got color TV and on this color TV, Buddy, the blacks and
the yellows are coming in so loud and clear that they're burning our
eyeballs over at The Project. That much I can tell you because you're
not a heavy drinker that repeats whatever he hears like a goddam
parrot. I can tell you this big Halloween's coming up, it's necessary like
breathing, and after this Halloween, what we're dreaming of at The
Project, man, is a white Christmas, and that white-hot snow is gonna
fall out of heaven and be as hot as all hell. That much I can tell you and I
tell you no lie, and I want you to remember I told you something I
wouldn't tell my wife unless she was lying there sleeping dead to the
world. Do you dig me?

On that particular night, when the privileged boyhood chum of
Braden's went back to close up the drive-in, he had a religious feeling.
He felt like he'd been to church and God had delivered the sermon . . .

This boyhood chum of Braden's, who was still such a chum despite
the widely different positions to which fate had assigned them, was
named Spangler, Billy Spangler, a lively-sounding name which suited
the bearer.

It was just a couple of weeks after Gewinner's return to the bosom of
his family, so to speak, that he had his first encounter with Billy. It
came about in this way. Gewinner did not have wheels of his own at
this time but Violet had graciously turned over to him her Caddy
convertible which was violet-colored to go with her name, and one fine
autumn morning Gewinner impulsively entered the drive of the drive-
in for which he had an almost obsessive distaste. He drove into the
drive-in without any conscious purpose. He didn't acknowledge to
himself that he was intensely curious about Braden's boyhood chum
who had that optimistic ninety-nine-year lease on a corner practically
facing the Pearce castle.

Gewinner nearly always came on like a cool one despite having a nervous system that kept spitting off hot sparks under his skin as though constantly celebrating a Chinese festival. The late Dr. Horace Greaves had taught Gewinner the secret of outward serenity but his pupil had surpassed the good doctor who would have to go into a state of samadhi when passing through customs in foreign air- or sea-ports. The good doctor's samadhi (a trancelike condition known to Hindu mystics and their disciples) was probably only synthetic since he could enter a customs shed with apparent, dreamlike composure but was apt to go to pieces if a customs officer inquired into the nature of certain pills and vials that were tucked away in his luggage. Then he would come out of samadhi and go directly into something close to hysteria, but Gewinner would lean across the customs counter and say to the officer, My uncle is a saintly man not long for this world, so please don't excite him.

No, Gewinner was not a cool one and yet he could do things that were very disturbing to him and do them with apparent serenity, and so he was able to drive directly up to the entrance of the Laughing Boy Drive-in as smoothly as if he lived there. Violet's Caddy convertible had three silver trumpets for announcing itself in traffic, the trumpets had three different musical notes. Gewinner blew them and Billy Spangler heard them. He recognized the car at once as Violet Pearce's violet-colored Caddy and noticed at once that there was, at the wheel, a young man he had not seen before. He thought he ought to step out of the drive-in to have a closer look at this young man who looked like a boy. He no sooner had this thought than he put it into action and stepped out a pace or two from the door. Then Gewinner had a look at Billy while Billy had a look at him. What Gewinner saw was a young fellow more than ordinarily good-looking with a figure that was lean except for the shoulders which were so heavily muscled that they seemed cramped by the mess jacket of his snowy white uniform. It was a fair-weather day and Billy Spangler seemed to be matching part of the weather. His eyes, looking at Gewinner, had a totally open, above-board and straightforward look. He looked like a young man who had never had an *arrière-pensée* in all his life, a young man who started performing an act a second or two before it consciously occurred to him, a young man whose appearance seemed still to reflect, joyfully, the tricks and pranks of his boyhood.

Gewinner was not disarmed by the glowing fair-weather artlessness of Billy's appearance, no, not at all. In fact there was something in the way Billy looked and smiled at him that set off sparklers and spit devils in Gewinner's nervous system, a scorching reminder of various irreconcilables in his nature. And just then the screen door sprang open and out rushed a girl carhop with such momentum that she collided with the back of Billy, let out a screeching laugh and stumbled back against the screen door, exclaiming, Well, I'll be! Excuse me!

Gewinner paid no attention to that little accident, but leaned a bit out of Violet's car and said to Billy, as slowly and precisely as if he were speaking to a retarded child, I would like to have a cup of black coffee, please, just black, no cream and no sugar and no toast or pastry with it.

O.K., said Billy. Then he turned to the girl who was still against the screen door as if impaled there, and said, Did you get that, honey. She gasped, Yes, and scrambled back into the drive-in.

Billy looked up and about him and shouted, Fine day!

Gewinner made no comment on it.

Then the girl exploded back out of the drive-in with an aluminum tray on which were a cup of piping-hot coffee, a china creamer, two little fluted-paper sugar containers and a glass of ice water. As she brushed past Billy on her way to the car, she let out another little hysterical cry. Billy followed behind her toward the car, walking behind her leisurely and observing her hips in her skintight gabardine slacks, the color of "white coffee." She got to the car and couldn't attach the tray to the door because her fingers shook so, but Billy came up tolerantly beside her and fastened the tray himself. And then he looked down into Gewinner's face and smilingly inquired, Ain't that Mrs. Braden Pearce's new Caddy you're driving there, son?

He did not say it exactly as though he were accusing Gewinner of stealing the car but it was apparent that he was one of the many people who sucked up to Braden. Gewinner's first dislike of the drive-in owner was a reflection of his dislike of his brother, and he ignored the question, coolly disregarded the amiably inquiring eyes and said to the girl, How long has this place been here?

The girl answered nervously, feeling his hostile vibration. She answered in the heavy drawl of the back country. She was freckled, all her features were too small and she had on too much eye pencil and lipstick but her breasts, under the cream-colored silk blouse, and the plushiness of her bottom made it disgustingly plain to Gewinner why this new young buck who owned the drive-in had hired her.

She said, About six months, I think, and her hand shook as she set the ice-water glass down again after removing the napkin underneath it and giving it to Gewinner.

Well, said Gewinner, it's really a shame to put up a thing like this in a residential district!

He said this in a voice that shook like the girl's hand as she set the water glass down. She didn't answer. She made a small noise in her throat and turned quickly away and started back to the little Colonial-style building. But Billy Spangler heard the remark as clearly as Gewinner had intended him to hear it, and he did not follow the girl back into the drive-in but stood leaning easily on the front fender of the new Caddy, glancing lazily back at the girl's hips again as she entered the shiny copper screen door, but then returning his steady gaze to the reddening face of Gewinner. He took his time about responding to Gewinner's attack on his place and the response that he made was quite moderate.

What, he said, is your objection to this drive-in?

It belongs on the highway, said Gewinner.

I thought about the highway, said Billy Spangler, but this is a lot more convenient for the people that work down there at The Project.

He nodded down the street which the Pearce residence was facing and which led directly up to The Project.

One of Gewinner's great regrets was that intense anger always clouded his mind so that he seldom could think of an immediate and effectually cutting reply to a remark that angered him. Also at such times his voice was always unsteady. Sometimes he even stammered, and so he often had to hold his tongue, and boil inside while he held it. This anger was so intense that at times he felt as though he were on the verge of an epileptic seizure. Now he could not return the look of Billy Spangler nor answer his calm speech nor even lift the coffee cup from the saucer. He was altogether immobilized for possibly half a minute or more while Billy Spangler stared at him and leaned on the Caddy's front fender. All he could do was boil and look down at the coffee while Spangler leisurely went on talking in the same unruffled voice about the advantages of the drive-in's location.

You know, he said, they're doing a mighty big and important job down there at The Project. I don't pretend to know exactly what and I guess it ain't a good thing to be too curious about it unless you're actually in it. But I know from the little I've seen or heard that the whole future security of this country is mixed up with it. Naturally there's got to be some changes in this town that don't suit everybody, like business places cropping up where there used to be private houses and smoke in the air and crowded housing conditions and so many people at the movies you have to stand in line to buy a ticket and then wait again to get to a seat. But all in all, this here's a fast-moving town with business booming. Like Mr. Pearce over there. He's got more different jobs than you can shake a stick at, and not just jobs but the top executive positions. The most important is being in charge of personnel at the plant, but he's sitting on practically every other board or organization in this town. And he's a guy that anybody can talk to. Drops by here every day even if it's just to smile and wave to somebody. And I know *he* don't have no objection at all to this here drive-in, in fact I know that he likes it. I know he likes it because he told me so himself and he leased me the piece of land that the drive-in's built on!

It was then, at this point, that Gewinner flew into action. He came unknotted all at once and he threw the car into gear and started it off before Billy Spangler could even remove his elbow from the fender, so that Spangler was almost knocked off balance and his shoulder was struck by the aluminum tray that was still attached to the rolled-down window of the convertible. He shouted, *Hey!* And Gewinner heard him running along the gravel as if he thought he might overtake the car, but Gewinner did not glance back, he did not even pause to properly remove the tray and its contents, just pushed them off the side of the car as he raced it around the corner on two wheels.

There were, of course, repercussions to the incident at the Laughing Boy Drive-in.

That evening Braden came storming up to Gewinner's little apartment in the tower.

Billy Spangler just come over with some fried chicken for me and Violet and he told me his shoulder was sore. I asked him what was wrong with his shoulder and he said he didn't want to tell me but he finally did. He said you went over there today to complain about the drive-in, you hit his shoulder with the tray when you drove out and pitched the tray and the crockery in the street. Now I'd like you to tell me what the shit is the meaning of a thing like this?

Oh, said Gewinner coolly, I believe that the Laughing Boy gave a reasonably accurate report on the incident at the drive-in this morning, but as for the meaning of it, perhaps it just means that Mother and you should not have reduced my travel allowance but kept it at the same level or even increased it.

Gewinner had his back turned to his brother and was ostensibly engaged in cataloguing his big collection of phonograph records, most of which were rare collector's items.

Now look here, Prince!

Yes?

Listen to what I'm telling you for your own good. Nobody comes in this town, not even my brother, without being known and observed and classified by the security counsel at The Project. I mean all unfamiliar persons and types coming here are classified by the new automation system under three headings, "good," "doubtful" or "bad" as security risks. The automation system and the intelligence office check and double-check and triple-check on every newcomer here or anywhere near here. And here's something else for you to know for your own good. New legislation is being pushed through at high speed for the isolation of all you don't-fit-inners, and that word "isolation" can mean several things, none of which things is pleasant for the isolated individual, Prince. There is too much at stake, too much pending, on a world-wide scale for the toleration of temperamental flare-ups and artistic hoopla, so here's what you do tomorrow. When I go to The Project I'll drop you by the drive-in. You go in there and offer an apology to my friend Billy Spangler, you apologize to him and shake hands with him and pay him for the crockery you broke up, that's what you do in the morning, and face the fact right now that there's got to be some of you don't-fit-inners for a while only, just for a little while till they can be weeded out of society-in-progress, but you are overdoing that privilege which is pro tem only. Understand what I'm saying?

Perfectly, said Gewinner, still coolly, but I would suggest that you save yourself the possible embarrassment of having a brother named Gewinner in isolation, whatever, wherever that is, by arranging with Mother for the restoration of my traveling allowance to its former level or a little higher to meet the inflation problem.

Braden's answer to that was a remark in the nature of obscenity, and the conversation between the brothers was over, it was permanently finished.

Alone in his tower that night, Gewinner opened a window and stood there listening to the faint, perpetual hum of activity at The Project. It moved through the air like the purring of some giant cat that never slept nor changed its menacingly crouched position.

For the first time in his life, as best he could remember, Gewinner thought about good and evil. It seemed to him that he knew, coldly, abstractly, which of the two was which, and also knew which of the two it would suit him better to serve in whatever way it was possible for him to serve it.

He felt a vibration in himself like a countervibration to the one that came from The Project.

I'm being silly, he thought. All I'm here for is to blackmail Mother and Braden into giving me back my travel expenses. What has good and evil got to do with that?

But he stayed at the window and the feeling of two dueling vibrations continued. Hmmm went The Project. Hmmm went Gewinner. And it seemed like an equal conflict, it gave him the sort of strength that a barefooted Hopi, treading bare ground in a dance, is said to draw up out of the blazing dark core of the earth.

Billy Spangler was a very moral guy and he would not have enjoyed his work or gotten nearly so much satisfaction out of the success of the drive-in if he had not been able to think of it as being in its own humble way a part of The Project. It really was in a way. Certainly most of its trade, by far the preponderance of it, came from people directly employed at The Project, and then, of course, virtually everybody and everything else in the town of Gewinner was at least obliquely associated with the Great New Thing. Spangler ran the drive-in as though he was operating a part of The Project, which was not difficult since he was close enough to the outer periphery of The Project's intricate bell system to be apprised of all the changes of shifts the moment that they were effected. When the night shift came on at eight thirty Spangler sent two of his girls home and kept only one on the job, at time and a half, one girl and a colored delivery boy with a bicycle who could carry the occasional calls for hot coffee up to guards who were posted at various points about the key entrances to the grounds. The commissary of the main plant remained open all night so that employees within the buildings did not need to call the drive-in for coffee but the guards could not leave their posts and they preferred their coffee brought in from Billy Spangler's drive-in because the coffee in the commissary was a chronic joke. That's commissary coffee, people would say to Billy when they wanted to tease him, and Billy was very proud of his own coffee. It pleased him to let people know that he lost money on his coffee, he made it so good. A fresh brew of it every hour regardless of how much was still left in the big old electric urns. I throw out more coffee than them drive-ins on the highway make, he would say. I guess it costs me money to serve coffee here, but that's O.K. The best is none too good for the boys down there at The Project.

All this was said so heartily and believed so genuinely that the boastfulness was as lovable as a small boy's. Everybody loved Billy, they thought he was full of fun and a really good Joe. But don't shit around with him, though, especially not any nigger, because ole Billy has got a load of TNT in that left arm of his, and his wiry build is a hell of a lot more powerful than it looks with clothes on.

Billy had done some amateur wrestling on the Monday night shows that the veterans' organization used to put on at the old Armory building, now torn down and being rebuilt much bigger, and those that had seen Billy wrestle those nights would never forget how he whipped off that purple silk robe with "Billy's Drive-in" inscribed on it and, *Wow*, what a build, holy Jesus, you felt like *shouting* the instant it was uncovered!

This evening Billy Spangler was alone at the drive-in with a new girl whom he had nicknamed Big Edna, not because she was really big but because it happened that one of the other two girls was also named Edna and was so petite that she barely missed being a midget.

This Big Edna, as Billy called her, was the country girl who had served the coffee to Gewinner Pearce that morning, and she had been shaking with nervousness ever since the awful scene had occurred. Every once in a while her eyes would turn red, and she would slip back into the powder room and come out a minute later looking pale and determined. Billy treated her gently. He wondered if this was her time of the month because otherwise he didn't understand why she took the little occurrence so damn serious. It didn't really have anything to do with her, it was just something that happened between him and Mr. Pearce's eccentric brother which was going to be all straightened out tomorrow. Mr. Pearce had told him it would be, and had reaffirmed his approval of the drive-in and of Billy Spangler and everything else about it so warmly that the two men had fawned on each other like a pair of lovers. And Billy Spangler had repeatedly assured Mr. Braden Pearce that he wasn't really injured and that it didn't matter a bit and he wanted him to just forget the whole thing and he was mad at himself, now, for mentioning a little occurrence like that to him. It was just that he hated to think there might ever be any source of misunderstanding between the drive-in and those wonderful folks that had leased the property to him. And Billy knew by the way that Braden Pearce's car swarmed into the grounds of the Pearce estate that he was going to raise holy hell with the eccentric brother who lived in the gray stone tower of the residence. That was all taken care of.

But the new girl, Big Edna, continued to shake over it. Now she was still shaking. Perhaps he should not have kept her on tonight. He worked the girls in rotation. That is, he worked them overtime in rotation, and this night it was Big Edna's turn to work overtime but he should have considered her sensitive feelings and let her go home. He wondered why he didn't send her home now. It would be surprising if there were as many as two more customers at the drive-in between now and closing time at midnight. Gewinner was a town where serious people (except for a freak or two like Braden's brother, who sometimes patrolled the streets, empty and dimly lit, in the convertible Caddy till three or four in the morning as if he were looking for a pickup) went to bed early and got up with the chickens. Those were the sort of hours The Project encouraged its employees and families of employees to keep, and sometimes a man would be quietly dropped from the rolls for no other reason than that he was known to be around town on week nights or late hours. The Project deserved and got from its men that kind of complete dedication, Billy Spangler knew that, and nobody respected it more than he did.

Billy Spangler was conscious of the great social changes that were now in the air. He felt the glorious warm wave of the new religiousness and he had made a bigger contribution than he could afford to the erection of a new Methodist church which was to have a swimming pool and badminton courts in the basement and an auditorium that looked like a somewhat glorified economics classroom. Reform was a mighty good thing and had been a long time coming. It had taken The Project to give everybody in town that serious, dedicated feeling that made them all like so many cells of one great uplifted being. This was a swell way to be and it was no doubt the way toward which the whole progress of mankind had always pointed. It was certainly the ultimate goal of The Project that all the world population of friendly Caucasians were going to have churches like that under the benignly paternal sponsorship of The Center. "The Center" was the new word, rather like a code word, for the immediate locality of The Project. Yes, there were going to be churches like that all over the world, once the great new principle was established and by God and by Jesus everybody was going to have to pitch in and do his bit like Billy Spangler was doing. No more fuck-offs like the sissy Pearce brother. Not here in this country or anywhere in any other country. It's all right to talk about tolerance and individual rights and all of that sort of business but you got to draw a line somewhere. If you give a man too much rope he will hang himself and it was the business of a Christian community dedicated to a Great New Thing to make sure that everybody had just enough rope to keep from being too conscious of confinement and at the same time not enough to tempt the weak ones or the ones that were a little unsettled to self-indulgent excesses of any description.

So Billy Spangler sat on the end of the counter and watched the new girl, Big Edna, putting the apple pie slices, left over from the day's business, back into paper cartons so that they could be picked up by the bakery and resold at a discount and Spangler get credit on them. This required a little bending over and each time the girl bent over she flushed a little. She had a brassiere on but not a tight one and her breasts were a good deal bigger than her age and maidenhood seemed to call for. Although Spangler did not talk dirty, sometimes the phrases of his rough boyhood would come into his mind, such as "a pair of ripe boobies." A pair of ripe boobies, he said to himself as he watched her, and the girl cleared her throat and flushed before she spoke to him as if the words in his mind had been spoken aloud.

Now what do I do with these here boxes? she asked him.

He told her just to leave them there on the counter. The bakery boy would pick them up at opening time in the morning.

And then she said, Will that be all, Mr. Spangler?

Yeah, said Billy, you can change out of your uniform now if you want to, honey.

She flushed deeper than ever and nodded her head a little. Then she turned her back to him and self-consciously rooted in her purse for the key to the girl's washroom where the girls left their clothes when they changed. Each of the girls had a key and there were only three of them. Big Edna could not seem to find hers in the purse and he could see her getting sort of panicky about it as she rooted around and still did not locate it. The trouble was that she had too much junk in the pocketbook. She was piling it all on the counter and Billy Spangler had to laugh at her back as he saw all the stuff she had in it, almost the whole cosmetic counter of a five-and-ten, right down to the little two-bit bottle of scent with a colored sweet pea on it. Billy laughed at her back but kept his eyes on her ass most of the time while she was continuing the frantic search for the key. If those gabardine slacks had been a half size smaller, by God, Big Edna could not have gotten into them with a shoehorn, and that was no lie. Billy got up off the counter, slid down off it, rather, and crossed gently over to Big Edna and laid his big hand on her shoulder, for he now perceived that the girl had started crying again, and he said to her gently, Now, honey, you got to stop getting so upset over nothing. That key is in there and if you wasn't so nervous you could find it. Now look here, now. Put all that stuff back in. Yep, that's the ticket, honey. Now give it to me and you go in the gents' room and wash your pretty little face and have a smoke and when you come back I'll have that little door key in the palm of my hand. You want to bet me?

Billy did not mean to let his hand slide down the girl's back, but sometimes a hand does something like that without any plan to. It did. It slid right down her back and onto the curve of her hips and underneath was a softness and a heat that seemed to transfer itself directly from that locality on her body to the frontal equator of his. And now Billy Spangler was the one who felt embarrassed and ill at ease. He flushed and turned his back on Big Edna and returned to the end of the counter with the now tightly packed pocketbook in his hand while she stood there as if she had struck roots in the position she had been in when his rebellious hand had made the inadmissible breach of consideration. For the hand of Billy Spangler had just now violated one of his firmest principles of conduct, which was never to take advantage of any opportunity that seemed to be offered by a female employee.

In Billy's defense it ought to be noted that he was a twenty-seven-year-old bachelor and had not been to bed with a girl since weeks ago when the Public Relations Committee at The Project had given little Eula Mayberry her train fare home. Eula had been the last survivor of the once thriving industry of prostitution which was one of the things that The Project had cleaned up in its drive to make the community worthy in every respect of the Great New Thing of which it was now The Center. Billy was planning to marry as soon as he found the right girl but in the meantime he didn't want to run the risk of getting mixed up with a wrong one because there is nothing that can bitch up a man's whole life worse than an unwise marriage can. There was ample evidence in Billy's life of the appeal that he had for bad women, and Billy believed that there were just two kinds of women, the good and the bad kind, and somehow it seemed like it was the bad kind that took the biggest interest in Billy. It seemed like he couldn't come near one of them kind of women without their reaching a hand out or trying to make him do it.

Well, it just wouldn't do. Billy had ambitions and matrimony was a definite part of his ambitions. He was going to find him a good little girl on a social level that was distinctly higher than his own had been. Maybe he'd have to wait four or five years for that to happen. Maybe it would not happen until after he had opened two or three more drive-ins and was an absolutely unmistakably up-and-coming young potentate of the commercial and social scene. But it was going to happen, it was bound to come. Patience and Spartan fortitude were required in the meantime, and incidentally it was necessary to allow himself to jerk off once a week in order to keep himself from going around all the time with a half-erection in those white pants to make the customers snicker. Tonight was the night for him to practice that melancholy little act of abasement and it made him sort of sweetly sad inside just thinking about it, knowing how much sweeter and better-feeling it was to do the other thing, which there were so many wonderful chances to do. But The Project called for men with characters of rock. And Billy thought of himself as being a part of The Project, still a humble part of it, but one that was on the right track to arrive someday, through humility and obedience and Spartan control of himself, at a position of far greater eminence and much closer to The Center than he now was.

Billy Spangler could not keep his mind on what he was supposed to be doing with the girl's pocketbook, which was looking for the lost key. Piece by piece and very, very slowly he removed the contents from the pocketbook but even if he had come across the key it is doubtful that he would have noticed it. All the while he was listening. He heard the girl undressing in the gents' washroom which was right back of where he was standing, and then he heard her put the toilet seat down and then he heard the flow of her urination and he wondered, if she had the rag on, if she were going to change it in there. But of course she wasn't going to. How could she? In the girls' washroom they had a Kotex dispenser but there was nothing but paper towels and toilet tissue in the men's. He wondered if she would have forgotten about that and have to try to put the old one back on or pad herself down there with toilet paper or coarse paper towels. But of course if she was that absent-minded she would probably have flushed the old one down the toilet when she finished peeing. Now he heard her finish and the toilet flush and if she had actually made that mistake she would now be about to realize it. Billy Spangler listened. He just couldn't help it. He stood there waiting and listening with her dusty, sweet-smelling pocketbook in his hand and even the pocketbook seemed to smell of the young girl's darkly crimson incubative condition.

And then Billy Spangler moved to the gents' room door. A great flow of air or water seemed to have swept him toward it—and the door, too—it pushed the door open, and there she was in the very condition in which his vivid intuition had shown her, naked from the waist down, a hand containing a wad of tissue paper clapped over the blond-haired groin and her face contorted with the beginning of tears. Billy heard himself saying out loud to her, but very softly, There, there, there, don't cry, you mustn't cry, baby! And the hand that he now put on her was made out of steel. His knees felt a thud as they hit on the concrete floor but after that he didn't feel anything that wasn't the plushy feel and heat and smell and taste of the sobbing girl's body.

The following morning Billy Spangler fired her. It was very, very clear to him now that Big Edna was the bad kind of girl. He did not believe that she had lost the key. He wasn't took in by that story. She was a country girl but she knew what she was up to when she pretended to be so scared and nervous, and not if he lived to be a thousand years old would he ever get over the dreadful degradation of what she had got him to do. He was not mean to her. This was not his way of doing a thing. He gave her a full week's pay, although she had only worked three days and a night, and he asked her if that was enough to get her back home to the hill town that she had come from the week before. He said good-bye to her nicely, even shook hands with her and said, Honey, what you should do is go and have a talk with the minister of your church. Tell him your problem. Always go to a man with the light of God in him when you get tempted by your animal nature. He said that to her in all sincerity and kindness because it was now completely apparent to Billy Spangler that it had been the animal nature of the girl, her devil, that had perpetrated the terrible misdeed, not his, not any part of his nature, for Billy knew that he had been brought to Jesus six years ago by an army chaplain in the jungles of Wangtsee.

When Billy turned around from the telephone over which he had just inserted an advertisement for a new girl in the *Courier-Times*, he saw that the tall young man who had entered behind his back and taken a seat at the counter was the Pearce boy, Gewinner, the one that had been responsible for yesterday's trouble.

The two men looked at each other. Billy felt his own face turning as cold and set as the face of the man sitting down, and he did not try to prevent himself from assuming a hard expression because he felt it was called for. Nevertheless he had to remember that this fellow was at least nominally a member of the Pearce family that had leased him the land on which the drive-in was built. Outside Billy saw the car of Braden Pearce waiting and the fine younger brother himself at the wheel of it, with an escort of two motorcycle cops standing by. Billy knew what had happened. Braden Pearce had compelled his brother to come here and make an apology to him for what had happened. Braden had literally dragged him over to make the apology and the restitution now coming up. So then Billy Spangler relaxed himself a little. He let the hard expression slip down from his face and he took a seat beside Gewinner and told the girl at the counter to give him some coffee.

Then he turned around and said to the other man, Well, son, I hope you like our coffee better today than you did yesterday morning. Leisurely he removed his jacket, rolled up his white poplin sleeve and showed the purplish bruise on his biceps where the tray had struck him as the car drove off. He just showed it and looked down at the other man's face which still had not spoken or altered its set expression.

Well, said Billy, there is no hard feelings between me and any member of the family you belong to and never will be as long as your brother, Braden, and I have got anything to do or say about it. I reckon you come in here to make an apology to me. But I want you to know you don't have to make it. All you have to do is set there and drink your coffee and leave the girl a dime tip!

With this benevolent speech still on his lips, Billy Spangler elevated his hips from the white porcelain stool and started out toward the sunshiny exterior to shake hands with Braden Pearce. But before he had completed the beginning of his easy movement, he heard a spitting sound. He did not quite turn around but he knew what had happened. Gewinner Pearce had spit in his cup of coffee. Billy had seen the quick snakelike jerking forward of the head of Gewinner and the startled look on the face of Little Edna and heard the sound of the spitting all at once. Billy was motionless. He stayed in a frozen position, half looking out toward the car of Braden Pearce and half regarding the crouched figure of Braden's brother. While he stayed immobilized that way, Gewinner had taken out his wallet. He set on the counter a hundred-dollar bill and then he said quietly, I am not the type that leaves a dime tip!

Almost immediately after he made that speech, in fact with the words still on his lips, he swept past Billy Spangler. The smooth, plushy sleeve of his light-tan overcoat brushed against Billy's bare arm as Gewinner swept past him, and Billy saw him go on out of the drive-in and cut rapidly across the street, not even turning to look at his brother's car.

Apparently only two people, besides Gewinner, knew that Gewinner Pearce had not apologized but had spit in his cup of coffee. Little Edna knew it and Billy Spangler knew it. They glanced at each other. Little Edna had a tight, scared face as she seized a wet dishcloth and wiped the counter, and Billy Spangler, for the first time in his adult life, had a feeling of fear, of anxiety cold and deep, way down in his warm young bowels, making them cold, and with it was also a touch of awe and revulsion.

Hey, Prince, called Braden to Gewinner, but Gewinner ignored him and stalked out to the street. Then Braden called out, Hey, Billy.

Billy came out of the drive-in like a man stumbling out of a bomb-shattered building, in a state of shock or concussion; he came out with his jaws a little ajar and a sightless look in his baby-blue eyes.

Well, what happened, did the prick apologize to you? I want to know the truth, now.

Somehow Billy couldn't report the truth of the weird thing that had happened inside, all he could do was jerk his head affirmatively and raise a hand as if saluting or bestowing a blessing.

O.K., that's that, shouted Braden and his bullet-proof limousine shot forward, preceded by two motorcycle cops with screaming sirens, reaching The Project before Gewinner reached the imitation drawbridge of the Pearce castle.

Gewinner assumed that there was bound to be another confrontation scene with his brother that evening and he thought he would show his boldness by coming downstairs for it. However, it so happened that Braden and Mother Pearce had hopped off by helicopter to the State Capital in order to appear at the deathbed of the Governor who had been shot down unexpectedly while laying the cornerstone of the Trust in God Mission Building.

Gewinner got this information from the butler in the great downstairs hall.

Then nobody's in, he reflected aloud.

Yes, me, in the gameroom, called out Violet.

He found her in there with a tall crystal shaker and a long silver spoon, stirring a considerable number of cocktails, apparently for one person which was herself.

I didn't go along with Braden and Mother Pearce, she told him somewhat unnecessarily.

Oh? Why not?

Because the whirlybird makes me so dizzy that I can't walk a straight line when I get off it. I guess it's just not my type of locomotion. Will you have a martin?

Is that some variation on a martini?

It's a boatload of martinis laced with a dash of absinthe, which is illegal in this country, but dear old Senator Connor got it through customs by putting a rum label on the bottle when he came back from his talks with General Amados in Rio, just a few days before he had his last stroke in Vegas.

She said all this so quickly and brightly that you might have thought she was making plans for Christmas, and Gewinner found himself feeling more at home with her than ever.

Do you mind if I take off my dinner jacket? he asked her.

I don't care if you take off everything you've got on.

I won't go as far as that, said Gewinner, removing only his jacket.

While she was chilling the martinis, he commented on the unseasonable warmth of the castle. He said: You know the castle is always overheated because Mother Pearce has anemia and control of the thermostat.

Oh, do I know! said Violet. Isn't she the cutest little thing? She goes around in her little Angora wool sweater as if she was always chilly in the castle and she keeps on turning the thermostat up a notch higher.

Maybe she wants to sweat us out.

That's a thought, agreed Violet.

Her next remark was something in the nature of a *non sequitur*.

This room, she said, isn't bugged. The library is bugged and so are the dining room and the conservatory. This room used to be bugged but something went wrong with the bugging apparatus just a few minutes after Braden and Mother Pearce went out of the castle *ce soir*.

Are you sure about that?

I'm as sure about that as if I'd broke it myself, so you and I can talk on any subject we choose.

Is there something in particular you wanted to discuss with me? asked Gewinner.

Excuse me for a moment, she said.

She went to a window and opened it to admit a pigeon that had a piece of paper attached with a rubber band to one leg. She removed the paper and scanned it hastily while the pigeon waited, either nervously or restlessly, on the billiard table.

Intuitively Gewinner decided that this was an occurrence which it was best to pretend not to notice.

Hmmm, said Violet.

Then she rolled the piece of paper into a ball which she dropped in her cocktail and swallowed. She then tore off a sheet of paper from a memo pad on the bar and scribbled rapidly on it. That done, she whistled to the pigeon which flapped over to the bar and held a leg out for the return message and the rubber band.

All this went off quite smoothly and in less than a minute the pigeon was flapping back out the window.

Violet looked more amused than bemused.

I don't know how Mother Pearce can possibly imagine that I could be so stupid as not to realize that she is promoting a match between your brother and Babe. I'd be so willing to surrender Braden to Babe that if I was a licensed justice of the peace or an ordained minister of the church I would be delighted to bind them together in holy matrimony. However, it's necessary for me to remain in the castle a little bit longer because of my appointment.

Violet, said Gewinner, you are a very unusual girl.

Thank you, she said, so are you. Oh, excuse me, I don't mean a girl, I mean unusual, honey.

Where are you from?

Oh, from a long time ago, was her somewhat mysterious answer.

Then she went on talking.

The calisthenics at night, she said, are making the skin of my body look like a boatload of orchids and I have a funny feeling that when Braden succumbs to the attractions of Babe, he's going to look like a boatload of orchids himself, because I think Babe, with her stomp and all, is a personality like a whole football team condensed into one single being. Why do I feel I can talk to you so freely?

Because the room isn't bugged?

Oh, that isn't it. I think what it is, is you are some kind of a changeling, something else, not of this world, you know.

Thank you, said Gewinner. May I ask you about the pigeon bit?

Of course you can. I have an old school chum named Gladys who thinks that the most obvious and discreet method of exchanging messages is by carrier pigeons. Would you like her to send you a little message that way?

What kind of message?

Oh, she'd think of something.

At this moment there was a terrific clatter in the hall that built to a climax when an unusually fat little girl bounced or bounded, or both, into the gameroom, and immediately began to heckle Violet.

Mommy Violet drinks too much, Mommy Violet drinks too much!

That's Mommy Violet's business, not yours, precious.

The child stuck out her tongue at her mother and at Gewinner in very rapid succession, and then rushed over to the slot machine that paid off in gumdrops. She hit the jackpot at the first try and howled with insane delight.

What is the name of this strange child? asked Gewinner.

Why, I don't remember, all I remember about her is that after the first look at her I got myself what they call a diaphragm and regard it as my dearest earthly possession.

Child, said Gewinner, if you like candy, run up to the tower and look around for a great big box up there. It's full of marshmallows and chocolate cherries and marzipan and divinity flavored with strychnine.

Oh goody good, screamed the child and clattered off to the tower without even asking what the strange words meant, having understood "candy."

Violet talked to Gewinner about The Project.

It seemed that Braden had gotten carried away by a mood of boastfulness one night and had bragged to Violet that it would soon be possible to possess and control the whole planet by pressing a button connected with a wire. You just pressed the button connected with the wire and the whole fucking thing would either be blown to bits or fall under the absolute dominion of The Project, and he, said Braden, was the one who would press the button when the delicacies and intricacies of the contraption were completely mastered.

Yes, but suppose, said Gewinner, reflectively, Braden did push the button but somebody else had cut the little wire?

I love you, said Violet, and I see that you love Braden as much as I do.

Yes, I would love to be there when he pressed the little button and it dawned on his sensitive mind that someone had cut the little wire . . .

There was not such a thing as a periodic spy scare in the town of Gewinner, now grown to a city. The scare was not periodic, it was constant. The Project and the town-city were haunted by it the way old people are haunted by dread of disease. Nobody came into The Project without going through an exhaustive screening process. It is not likely that anybody came into the town without being investigated or secretly watched. Everybody knew that there were a lot of plain-clothes detectives around the town. They called them the PeeCees, and whenever you saw somebody you didn't know standing around on a corner with an air of elaborate unconcern you could be pretty damn sure it was one of those PeeCees, and if he gave you a glance it was likely to loosen your bowels.

Anxiety was the occupational disease of The Project employees. There was a neurological hospital on the grounds and a whole staff of psychiatrists. Of course, as soon as a man showed signs of severe nervous unbalance he had to be let out, but God knows how many of the men were concealing little foxes of terror under their radiation-proof uniforms and helmets, anxieties growing into psychoses which they dared not speak of. The staff of doctors walked around with their hands clasped behind them, waiting for patients who were afraid to come in. Not till somebody actually broke down with the screaming meemies was the cat out of the bag, and then of course it was too late. He was hustled out of The Project and out of the town and sent to what they called Camp Tranquillity, which was supposedly a place of readjustment. The place did not have a very savory reputation among The Project employees. There were ugly rumors about it, rumors of people who went there and never were heard of again, at least not after the first hysterically gay postcard saying, *This place is heaven!* The rumors were never completely authenticated. But you must remember that even the mail coming into the town of Gewinner was screened by a special staff of postal employees. It was not opened. It was examined by a sort of fluoroscope machine, every letter or package that came into the town was examined this way. All that anyone knew for certain was that the first postcard (from the worker sent to Camp Tranquillity) was also the last. If inquiries were addressed to the camp by former friends of the worker, a form letter would be delivered in precisely five days, saying that So-and-so had made a remarkably rapid recovery and had graduated to Rancho Allegro, which was located somewhere in the Southwest—for some reason nobody ever found out exactly where.

It must be remembered about all this that the workers at The Project were extremely busy people, they had practically no time for contemplation and had been chosen for their jobs because they were not introverts, and if they developed introspective tendencies it was certainly not to their advantage to make a public show of them or even a private one. They were better off than any other skilled workers or unskilled workers in the country, especially since the dissolution of the major unions by a recent Act of Congress. They occupied model houses for which they paid a nominal rent and they were retired at the age of forty-five on a comfortable pension to certain segregated communities called Rainbow Lands and Bluebird Hills and Valleys where everybody was about the same age and everyone from the barber to the mortician was a state employee and all the bills were sent to Mr. Whiskers.

Nothing to worry about in Gewinner! That was the cry. No reason for any grouches. No reason for anybody to wear anything but a radiation-proof outfit and a happy smile. In fact, there was a ban on blues music in the town, and the government had established a Happy Song Center where a staff of composers devoted themselves to the composition of light-hearted ballads. There was never a lyric that didn't mention silver linings, blue birds, sunshine and smiles. These records were on all the café Wurlitzers and the disk jockeys played nothing else. But as I said already, one thing that wasn't mentioned, but that everybody thought about in secret, was the ever-menacing idea of *"the spy."* It interfered with really close and warm relationships among members of The Project community. You never knew, did you? No matter how simple and good a guy might seem to be, who knows but what he was a counterspy, taking notes on you all the time and the notes going into the files of the office that had the big wide-open blue eye painted on the opaque glass of its entrance, and nothing more.

Nobody could be more conscious of the spy threat than was Billy Spangler, and whenever he was screening a possible new employee at the drive-in, he turned on his intuitive powers with terrific concentration. Billy thought that he had singular powers along that line, he thought he was someone who had a real, native instinct about the characters of people, oh, not based on anything scientific but just, well, just a matter of natural sensibility, of aptitude for that sort of thing.

Now this particular morning, which was the morning after Gewinner Pearce had spit in his coffee at the drive-in, and a classified ad for a new waitress had gone into the papers, Billy Spangler was interviewing a number of teen-age girls for the vacancy. Billy knew that, for business reasons, the girl had to be a good-looker as well as efficient and sprightly. "Personable" was the word he used in the ad: Vacancy for lively, personable girl-waiter. Experience less important than background and character.

You may wonder why he used "girl-waiter" instead of "waitress" in the ad. Billy's use of that less usual term was because the word "girl" was a word that was almost continually in the simple heart of Billy. Girl, girl, girl. The word haunted him even more persistently than the idea of spies and counterspies in the town and The Project.

Sometimes when he was not thinking at all—and such times were not infrequent, Billy Spangler not being primarily a man of intellectual nature—at those times the word would hop into his thought without any apparent chain of associations, just the word, Girl, girl! And he would whisper it to himself and saliva would fill his mouth as he whispered it. Then he would watch himself. He would look around quickly and swallow. And he would glance self-consciously down the front of his trousers and edge behind the counter of the drive-in or the cashier's box until his emotion had subsided a little. So the request for a girl-waiter had gone into the papers and there were at least a dozen applicants for the job, mostly girls of high school age or a little older who were daughters of men in The Project.

There were two key questions in Billy Spangler's method of screening a possible new employee at the drive-in. Number one: What is your opinion of Gloria Butterfield? That was the name of a famous spy at The Project who had been caught by The Eye as she was on her way to deliver a set of blueprints into the hands of enemy agents in a nearby town, two old women and a man, who were posing as relatives of hers, one of whom pretended to be ill. The whole bunch was apprehended, of course. It was a very hush-hush affair, no public trial, only the barest comment in the newspapers, but of course word about it was whispered in conversation and it had never been officially denied that Gloria Butterfield and her associates had come to a particularly unhappy end which was something a little more colorful than capital punishment.

They didn't shoot no gun, they didn't cut no string. But one thing you can be sure of. Nobody's ever going to see the face of Gloria Butterfield again on *this* earth.

That was the slow and sententious way that Billy Spangler spoke of it. He gave the impression of knowing more about it than anybody else. When Gloria Butterfield was discussed, there was always some allusion to what Billy Spangler said. He was the unofficial expert on the case. He knows a whole lot about it that he's not saying, was the popular opinion. And this Gloria Butterfield case, and his pretentiously cryptic utterances about it, had vastly enhanced the prestige of Billy Spangler as a sort of oracle upon the subject of spies.

So much for screening question number one. If the girl passed it, that is, if she expressed a suitably adverse opinion on Gloria Butterfield and a sufficiently enthusiastic endorsement of the unknown but radical manner in which Gloria had been (allegedly) disposed of, Billy Spangler would then come up with his number-two inquiry which was very simple indeed: How do you feel about love? Usually the girls would relax a little and so would Billy when he asked this question. He would smile and expose his white teeth, teeth so perfect that they looked like a set of beautiful dentures except that you saw quite clearly that they were fitted into his healthy pink gums by nature. He would not only expose his beautiful teeth and gums when he asked this question but he would open his mouth sufficiently to expose the whole interior of his coral-pink mouth, glittering with spit like the interior of some little coral cave on the seashore that was filled and emptied to the rhythm of the tides. You saw his rather small pink tongue, the pink of which was a little darker than the pink of the gums, the tip of which was actually crimson and so smooth that the taste buds on it were almost invisible. It was like an artificial tongue of pink and crimson it was so perfect. And so when Billy Spangler opened his mouth and smiled and let his mouth hang a bit open after that foxy question, the girls would laugh with a little burst of pure joy, feeling that the really serious part of the interview was over. But actually Billy Spangler was still screening the girls at this point. Although the question appeared to be a light one and was asked in a playful manner, a wrong answer to it could terminate the whole interview on a very quick and negative note indeed. It was a serious question with Billy Spangler what the girls thought about love. He did not want a girl who thought too much about it nor did he want a girl who showed a neurotic antipathy to the idea of it. He wanted a girl to show a wholesomely light and joyous attitude toward it, as an abstract value, the sort of attitude that a boy has learned to expect from his mother, for instance. A clean-minded, openhearted attitude toward love in the abstract was what he looked for. And if, when he asked that question, the girl dummied up, he would know that something was amiss and he would say, Sorry, next girl!

Now on this particular morning Billy Spangler was upset about things. He had not felt really well since the incident with Gewinner Pearce, and the thing that had happened that night with Big Edna had been a severe psychic jolt although it had ended in a moral victory on his part. That is, he had shown the firmness of character to give her the sack the next day. But this morning the interviews had not gone well.

The girls were an indifferent-looking bunch for one thing, only one of them being what you would call a real looker. There was a sameness about them, a blank kind of neatness and trimness which made you feel a bit let down somehow. Sexiness was what they lacked, although Billy Spangler would hesitate to put it quite that way.

This applied to all of the girls but one. One of them it did not apply to, not even slightly. That girl was a regular looker, a really outstanding good-looker, she was personable *plus*, and Billy had interviewed her first of the lot. But there was something not quite right in her reaction to the number-one question about Gloria Butterfield. She had betrayed no nervousness. Without a ghost of a hesitation she had said right off that she thought that Gloria Butterfield was a thoroughly contemptible person, not only ignoble but stupid, stupid because she had allowed herself to be caught at her ignoble action. And she certainly deserved what she got. Any girl who would be that treacherous and that stupid deserved to be torn to pieces by wild dogs.

Now what bothered Billy Spangler was how this girl happened to make the remark about Gloria Butterfield being torn to pieces by wild dogs. Billy had never spoken of this bit of information. He knew of it from Braden Pearce, but under oath of secrecy, and only because of the extremely close buddy-relationship that he enjoyed with the great man across the road. He had never breathed a word of it to anybody and he was pretty goddamn certain that Braden would never have passed the information along to anyone else not in the inner circle of The Project. The fact that the girl betrayed her knowledge of it gave him quite a turn. He was noticeably startled when she came out with that remark. He thought he covered up his surprise pretty well but he could feel his face burning as he went quickly on to the next question. What do you think about love? The pretty girl's answer to that one was also just a little bit offbeat.

She looked Billy Spangler right straight in the eyes without the flicker of an eyelash and she said to him, Well, frankly, I have not had much experience with it but I think the idea is great!

No, that wasn't quite the way for a girl to answer the second question, but it was not seriously wrong. It was the answer to the Gloria Butterfield question that disturbed him, and yet Billy Spangler somehow could not bring himself to dismiss the girl immediately. He knew that he *should* but he *didn't*.

What he said to the girl—to quote him exactly—was, Stick around a little.

Where? she asked him, and he told her to sit down at the end of the counter and have a cup of coffee and a sandwich.

The girl smiled brightly and obeyed his instructions and Billy's eyes followed her body as it moved away from him. She had on a checkered wool skirt that fitted her real close across the hips and the hips were the shape that he had liked in Big Edna so fatally well, except that they were just a little bit smaller and possibly firmer. The breasts were even superior to Big Edna's. "Ripe boobies" was not exactly the word for her breasts in that shameful secret vocabulary of Billy's. No, a perfect phrase for them was "A nice handful!"

Well, the interviews went along pretty briskly but Billy found something wrong with each one of the other applicants, and inside of half an hour the girl who gave the wrong Gloria Butterfield answer was the only one left of the bunch. She had finished her coffee and she had also ordered a piece of butterscotch graham pie, which is a pie that is very rich and gooey with a crust of graham crackers, certainly not a dessert that a girl would order if she had any apprehensions about her figure. This girl obviously had none. What a trim little figure she had on her, and the breasts were a nice little handful and that was for sure. She had now pivoted around on the counter stool and was smiling expectantly the length of the drive-in at Billy Spangler who had planted himself self-consciously behind the cash register now that he found himself alone with her. It was the slow part of the morning now, the part between ten and twelve, and the two girls already working were sitting outside on the bench in front of the drive-in, looking fresh and inviting as Billy always expected his girls to do. So now there was plenty of time to give this applicant a really close screening. She had so much to recommend her, and the odd surprise that she had handed him on the Gloria Butterfield question might be very simply and easily explained.

Now, honey, he said—always treating his girls with that sort of comfortable affectionate familiarity like a big brother's—you said one thing that bothered me a little and I guess you know what it was. Now how did you happen to mention the "wild dogs" thing?

The girl stopped smiling. Oh, she said. She got up from the counter and started toward the door, her face looking flushed and her movements rather jerky.

Where are you going, asked Billy.

Home, said the girl. I don't think I want a job bad enough to work for a man who might be suspicious of me!

Now hold your horses, said Billy. You are going off half-cocked. Just because I was a little surprised because you knew of something that is known of by only a few people very closely connected with The Project is no good reason for you to blow up and say I am being unduly suspicious of you.

He had crossed to the door. The girl was trying to open it but Billy Spangler was leaning against it so that she couldn't.

Again the girl looked him straight in the eyes. Do you or do you not think I can be trusted? she demanded in a sharp tone.

Trusted? Why, honey, I'd bank every cent in my possession on that smile of yours, said Billy, that wonderful frank and open smile of yours and that pair of baby-blue eyes! Now you let go of that door and sit back down and—*Henry!*—he called in to the Negro cook in the kitchen.

Henry, he called, how about that fresh coffee? Bring two cups out here, and bring me out a piece of that fresh apple pie!

Billy Spangler was all smiles, he was wreathed in cherubic smiles that made him look like a butch and tender angel of honest-to-goodness young, sweet, pure-hearted manhood.

The girl responded. Who wouldn't? She sat back down again and opened her mouth so that Billy could look right into the coral pink interior of it, as wet and smooth as his own. Consciously at that moment he caught himself thinking about a French kiss, and as the coffee and apple pie were set in front of him, Billy Spangler had to cross his legs. But the girl did not stop smiling and she did not shut her mouth till Billy asked her what size shoes and uniform she took. Then she shut her mouth for a moment in order to speak.

Oh, she said, then I have got the job?

Yes indeed, she had it. . . .

All at once, in early February, there was an outbreak of crime in the town of Gewinner, interrupting a long period of such extreme orderliness that during the preceding year no misdemeanor has been committed of a nature more serious than the theft of an artichoke from a chain grocery. The first evidence of the crime wave was the discovery of a billfold that had been ripped apart and dropped at the entrance of an alley. This was like the first eruption of some epidemic pox, for within a few nights the ripped-up billfolds had increased to a score. Then to a hundred. The crimes were flawlessly executed. At least half of the victims were solitary patrolmen, assaulted upon their midnight rounds of the deserted downtown streets, and none of them could give a really satisfactory account of what had happened. They had seen or heard nothing to arouse suspicion or even particular attention prior to the knockout blow, delivered invariably to the back of the head, in some cases with such violence that the skull was fractured. It was like a big black cat had jumped on me, one of them asserted, and from this statement was derived the name "Black Cat Gang" that was fastened on the criminals. The victims who were not patrolmen were workers returning home from the nocturnal shifts at The Project. At first, workers in vehicles enjoyed immunity from the attacks and consequently an order was issued that no pedestrians would be permitted on the streets of Gewinner after 8 P.M. But almost immediately after this edict, a number of workers were found unconscious at the wheels of their cars, everything of value stripped from them, along the curbs of the residential sections. It was then ordered that no private vehicle should be operated at night containing less than two passengers; the police force was multiplied by ten and the streets were illuminated by giant lamps that gave a ghastly greenish hue to everything that they shone upon. Crime experts flooded into the city. Great banners were hung in the streets listing the precautions that were to be taken by the night workers of The Project: Drive well to the center of the street . . . slow down but do not stop at street intersections . . . maintain a uniform speed of twenty-five miles an hour in the business section and forty miles an hour in the residential sections . . . keep to the main thoroughfares wherever it is possible . . . do not pick up strangers under any circumstances, etc. Then during the last week of February a council meeting was held at which the investigating committee disclosed that the leader of the Black Cat Gang was none other than the Chief of Police. This encouraging bit of information was not released to the press but rumors of it leaked out and the effect on the civil population was rather demoralizing. Nocturnal life in the town got to be like one big continual wild West movie until the whole police force was sent to Camp Tranquillity and was replaced by government agents in armored cars. Then, at least on the surface, the town and The Project fell back into the former well-ordered pattern of existence. A record number of religious converts were made by all the churches and optimists in the pulpits referred to the crime wave, now under control, as "the Devil's Last Stand."

Gewinner Pearce loved most the hours between midnight and dawn, when only the graveyard shift at The Project was still awake. From his tower windows, with lights extinguished, he would watch until he saw the drive-in closed and Billy Spangler driving home in his neat little green coupe. Then Gewinner would prepare to go out. He did not dress warmly. He liked a feeling of chill which made him more conscious of the self-contained life in his body. Chill air about his limbs made them move more lightly, more buoyantly, and so he went out thinly clad. He wore no undergarments. All that he wore on his nocturnal prowlings was a midnight-blue tuxedo made of silk gabardine. Before getting into this garment Gewinner would bathe and anoint himself like a bride, standing among a maze of indirectly lighted mirrors in his shower room. His whole body would be sprayed with pine-scented eau de Cologne and lightly dusted with powder. Gossamer silk were his socks, nylons of the sheerest ply, and his shoes weighed hardly more than a pair of gloves. Crystalline drops cleared his eyes of fatigue, brushes polished the impeccable enamel of his teeth and an astringent solution assured his mouth and throat of an odorless freshness. Often this ritual of preparation would include internal bathing with a syringe, a warm enema followed by a cold one, for Gewinner detested the idea of harboring fecal matter in his lower intestines. He wore a single metal ornament which was a Persian coin, very ancient, that hung on a fine silver chain. He enjoyed the cold feeling of it as it swung pendulumlike across his ribs and bare nipples. It was carrying a secret, and that was something that Gewinner liked better than almost anything in the world, to have and to keep a secret. He also had the romantic idea that someday, some galactic night, he would find the right person to whom to make a gift of the coin. That person had not been found, never quite, and there was the sad but endurable possibility that the discovery would be postponed forever, but in the meantime the Persian coin was a delicately exciting reminder of the fact that night is a quest.

Once or twice when he had only recently resumed his residence in the town, Gewinner was accosted by patrolmen and asked for identification. Now the patrolmen knew him, they knew Gewinner and they knew Violet's Caddy. They might theorize about the mystery of his prowlings but no interference was offered, such was the power of the name that he bore and the curiously intimidating aura of his person.

Gewinner's night prowling followed a certain pattern. At a leisurely pace, always five miles less than the official speed limit for the confines of the municipality, he would pass down the main thoroughfare of the town, appearing, whenever he paused at a crossing, to look around for somebody. All the windows and doorways were locked and lightless. Every three or four blocks he would pass a patrolman who gave him a single, quick glance, full of alarm and discretion, which Gewinner boldly returned with a very slight nod, as though he were an inspector signifying a routine approval of their presence upon the sidewalks. When he arrived at the end of the main avenue, he would turn Violet's Caddy (now always at his disposal) to the right and proceed along a street of new and completely uniform cottages which had been put up by The Project. This street terminated at the athletic stadium of the high school, and there Gewinner would always stop for a while. Sometimes he would remain in the parked car, close to the main gate of the open stadium, and take a few puffs of a ciagarette which he would extinguish as soon as the car started off once more. But sometimes he would get out of the car and stroll to the water fountain inside the stadium. He would appear to drink though he never allowed the water to touch his lips. Then he would stand beside the fountain a minute or two, looking about the dark stands which were seldom quite empty. His eyes would sweep along the whole oblong of the open-air structure until the glow of a cigarette at some point would betray another visitor's presence. Gewinner would then remove from the pocket of the topcoat, never worn but carried across his arm, a white silk scarf which he would unfold and spread over a concrete bench that was close to the water fountain. Then he would sit down and wait. This was not in keeping with the convention of the place—for all such places have their peculiar conventions—and more often than not Gewinner would wait in vain. If he grew impatient but was still hopeful, he would take out a silver lighter and a cigarette. He would hold the flame of the lighter before his face for a count of ten, not lighting the cigarette, just holding the flame a little away from the tip. Then he would wait a while longer, and sometimes, reluctantly, fearfully, the one who had made the firefly glow in the distance would emerge from the stands and approach the fountain. When this stranger had arrived within a few feet of the fountain and Gewinner had obtained some impression of his general aspect, Gewinner would either rise abruptly and make a rapid exit from the stadium or else he would cross to the fountain just as the stranger arrived there and murmur a word or two as the stranger bent to drink. When this was the procedure, the following step was invariable. Side by side and moving rapidly, Gewinner and the stranger, now his companion, would cross wordlessly out of the stadium and to the parked car. The car would then abandon its former pretense of languor and would shoot rapidly through the sleeping community, out to a certain road that Gewinner had known in his boyhood, a road that terminated for his purposes in the Negro cemetery about two miles out of town, and there among the humble mossy tablets and weather-paled crosses of wood, in a certain covert among them, surrounded by winter rose-bushes, Gewinner would unfold the silk scarf again to its full length and width which gave it the dimensions of a bed sheet. Silently, never speaking, he would unclothe himself, standing immediately before the trembling stranger and staring directly and fiercely into the stranger's eyes, breathing upon his face his fragrant breath and dropping his clothes at his feet till he was quite naked; then, finally, not quite smiling, but lowering his eyes and turning half in profile as though he, too, were suddenly abashed by the strange occurrence, then he would murmur, *Well?* Am I too *ugly?*

Certainly Billy Spangler did not reconsider the hiring of the new girl, Gladys, but the night after he hired her was a restless night for him. He could not seem to get in the right position on his bed. The only position that seemed comfortable to him was on his belly but that position brought the wrong sort of thoughts, sensations and images into his mind and body, especially his body. At one point he even found himself pushing his pelvis rhythmically up and down at the luxuriously yielding mattress, and this undeliberate action made it plain to Billy that his experience with Big Edna had weakened, temporarily, the Spartan control which he prided himself on having over his healthy young urges. He turned at once on his back and began to say the Lord's Prayer. Usually when he had a touch of insomnia, he wouldn't get past the first few lines of the prayer before he started drifting into dream-land, but this night he got all the way through it and was as wakeful as before. Finally, he realized what he had on his mind. He had maybe put himself into a morally vulnerable situation by hiring a new girl who was not just a good-looker but a spectacular beauty. With this realiza-tion, he turned back onto his belly and seemed to go right to sleep.

When the new girl showed up for work the following morning, Billy was very careful to show her no special attention, no sign of favoritism. He put her right to work as if she'd been employed at the drive-in as long as the other two girls. Of course he kept an eye on her without letting her see it. He had to see how quickly she would catch on, and it was amazing how quickly she did. You'd think she'd been a carhop at a drive-in since her first day out of a crib or playpen, she moved around so briskly in response to orders. She kept her eyes and her mind on her work and showed absolutely no sign of any kind of emotional instabil-ity whatsoever.

By midafternoon, Billy was convinced that this new girl, Gladys, was one out of a million, at a conservative estimate. She was not only taking orders briskly and cheerily, but she was shouting the orders to the colored man in the kitchen with an authority of tone in her voice that made the orders come out double quick, quicker than they would come out when shouted by Billy himself.

My God, she is a goddess!

That's what he said to himself about this new girl at the drive-in, and now that she had so brilliantly proven herself as the best imaginable drive-in employee, Billy felt free to express his pleasure with her.

Goddess, he would say to her, how are things going? Are they wearing you down?

And she would smile and say, No, sir, I feel fine, just fine!

Fine? he would say.

And she would say, Yes, sir, fine.

It was the sort of a conversation that has no purpose except to express good will. And Billy felt that good will was the keystone of their relations. Oddly enough, he did not feel uncomfortable over the beauty of the new girl. Perhaps his experience with Big Edna had purified him. It had been like an eruption and perhaps a great deal of violence in him had found a way out and left him a whole lot quieter and cleaner inside. He felt as though he had taken a purgative, one that removed all the waste matter in the body and left it sweet and clean as a newborn baby's.

How are things going for you, honey? he would ask the new girl every time she went past him and she would say, Just fine, Mr. Spangler. I'm not tired a bit.

She had not yet put on the uniform of the drive-in. Big Edna's uniform did not fit her and it had been sent over to the tailor for alterations. It would be back at a quarter after five and then the new girl would change into it. Billy Spangler was anxious to see how the uniform would fit her and he imagined that it would look extremely good on her. Her shape was young and perfect and the way that she moved her body, sinuously and briskly, spoke of good health and clean living.

Promptly at five fifteen the uniform came back from the tailor shop and Billy said to the new girl, Gladys, your uniform has come, honey.

Oh, good, said Gladys. Her tone was very excited. You could tell that she regarded the uniform as a privilege and was eager to get into it, the way that a proud young soldier exults in putting on the uniform of his army. But something had gone wrong, either in the measurements or in the alterations, for when the new girl came out of the girls' lavatory there was a frown of dismay on her beautiful goddesslike face.

Oh, Mr. Spangler, she said, the pants are too tight on me! The top won't button!

What? said Billy in a tone of chagrin.

Look, she said to him.

Billy could see it was true. The pants had been made too narrow across the hips or the waist and the top button of the fly could not be fastened. The fly gaped open exposing the sheer pink undergarments of the girl with the flesh showing through it the color of a fresh young rose, and all at once Billy was intensely embarrassed.

Shall I take them back off? asked the girl. Billy thought for a moment with his face to the window, gazing distractedly out and his hands in his pockets while he stood there reflecting.

No, he said, finally. Just leave them on for the present and tomorrow we can have them adjusted again or maybe even buy you a brand-new pair.

From then on Billy was acutely uncomfortable in the drive-in, and his discomfort seemed to affect the three girls. One thing went wrong after another, little things not worth mentioning, really, but the accumulated annoyance and strain was very heavy indeed by the time the drive-in closed up.

The new girl bore herself with irreproachable dignity. Billy had to give her credit for that. Even when another button popped off the gaping fly she did not lose her poise. I lost another button, was all that she said. She had already fastened a clean blue dish towel about her waist like a sash to cover the exposed pink drawers.

For a couple of hours before closing time Billy had been saying to himself, I better send her home first. But somehow it slipped his mind and when it came time to close up he was startled to discover that he had dismissed the other two girls and had told the new one to stay.

Well, he said to himself, I guess that I felt she needed a little more briefing on how things are done around here.

It may be that a touch of paranoia is necessary to individual felicity in this world. A man does not necessarily have to have a messianic complex but on the other hand, little good is derived from a continually and totally iconoclastic point of view in regard to himself and his relative position. Gewinner was a romantic. We have already found that out about him. The mere fact of his ascent to the tower of the

Pearce residence offered us more than a clue to this dominant trait of his character. Of course, America, and particularly the Southern states, is the embodiment of an originally romantic gesture. It was discovered and established by the eternal Don Quixote in the human flux. Then, of course, the businessmen took over and Don Quixote was an exile at home: at least he became one when the frontiers had been exhausted. But exile does not extinguish his lambent spirit. His castles are immaterial and his ways are endless and you do not have to look into many American eyes to suddenly meet somewhere the beautiful grave lunacy of his gaze or to observe his hands making some constrained but limitless gesture, if only in the act of passing a salt shaker to an adjacent stranger in some nondescript beanery along Skid Row. He can talk to you with quiet wisdom about the ways of the world which he has traveled in his knightly quest. He can tell you where to get an excellent piece of nookie in a city two thousand miles removed from the place where you meet him or he can conduct you to one around the corner. Or perhaps his pocketknife has just carved a romantically large glory hole in the wooden partitions of the depot lavatory. He is not a good worker though he is sometimes brilliant. His jobs are not large enough for his knees and elbows and he detests the accumulation of fat on his body that comes with sedentary employment. He gets along badly with policemen. He is much too American for them. Our police force only gets along with false and dispirited people, broken upon the ancient wheel of Europe. Quixote de la Mancha has never been broken. The long skeleton of him is too elastic and springy. Our hope lies in the fact that our public instinctively loves him and that he makes an excellent politician. Our danger lies in the fact that he becomes impatient. But who can doubt, meeting him, returning the impulsive vigor of his handshake and meeting the lunatic honesty of his gaze, that he is the *one*, the *man*, the finally *elected*? And what does his madness matter?

America was built of paranoia by men who thought themselves superior to the common lot, who overlooked the ignominy of death, who observed the mysteries but did not feel belittled by them, who never paused to consider the vanity of their dreams and who consequently translated them into actions. So perpetually Quixote travels along his steep and windy roads, encumbered by rusty armor and mounted upon a steed whose ribs are as protuberant as his own. Behind him totters Sancho Panza bearing the overflow of knightly equipment and possibly a shade madder, by this time, than his ancient master. Sancho Panza has been elevated to knighthood in his heart and

Quixote often dismounts in order that his equerry can rest in the saddle. Democracy has been taken in stride by Don Quixote and Sancho Panza as something forever implicit in the romantic heart, which is the true heart of man. Their language has changed. It is simplified. Now a syllable suffices where a sentence was necessary once. Sometimes they may go for days with only signs exchanged between them, the elevation of a single gaunt finger, slightly crooked at both joints, a cock of the head as it climbs into silhouette against a bank of gray cloud, the heavenward roll of the eyes, blue in the case of Quixote, dark brown in Sancho's. By silent agreement they will stop for the night, and now it is not unusual for both heads to rest in the padded crook of the saddle nor for the weatherworn hands to intertwine in slumber. Distance and time have purified their manners. Their customs are private. Sometimes they may fall out. That, too, is romantic. But somehow the roads they take in different directions always manage to cross again somewhere, and at the next encounter they are bashful as girls and each one wishes to take the smaller share of the wretched fish or chop, ceremonially prepared in honor of the reunion. And what of their deaths? They meet beyond the grave. Each one observes that the other is older and thinner but neither is so unkind as to comment upon it even to himself, for love of this kind is also a lunatic thing. Birds know them and understand them better than men. Have you ever seen the skeleton of a bird? If you have, you will know how completely they are still flying . . .

Gewinner was solitary nearly always, he gave no evidence of being a very warmhearted person and in all external respects he bore but little resemblance to Quixote. But in his vision was that alchemy of the romantic, that capacity for transmutation somewhere between a thing and the witness of it. The gods used to do that for us. Ceaselessly lamenting women were changed into arboreal shapes and fountains. Masterless hounds became a group of stars. The earth and the sky were full of metamorphosed beings. Behind all of this there must have been some truth. Perhaps it was actually the only truth. Things may be only what we change them into, now that we have taken over this former prerogative of the divine.

It may be remembered, if it isn't forgotten, that Violet once received a message by carrier pigeon from her school chum Gladys and that, on that occasion, she asked Gewinner if he would like to receive a message from Gladys dispatched in the same quaint manner. At that time Gewinner could not imagine what the message might be. More recently, a number of pigeons had delivered a corresponding number of messages to the two conspirators, Violet and Gewinner, in the Pearce castle, and Gewinner sometimes, and sometimes Violet, had sent the pigeons back with answers to their dispatcher, Gladys, who was now, it so happened, employed as a carhop at the Laughing Boy Drive-in. Gewinner had even learned to swallow the incoming messages and found them not distasteful. They came in several flavors, and the importance of the message was signified by the flavor. Messages of routine importance tasted like lemon sherbet while messages of special gravity had a licorice flavor.

Of course the important elements of these messages were not the flavors of the paper on which they were inscribed, but—to avoid a premature disclosure of what was developing among Gewinner and the two young ladies—it is possible to quote the contents of a single message only. This message from Gladys to Gewinner, delivered at dusk by a pigeon white as a dove, gave him this bit of pleasantly romantic advice, if advice you can call it.

Dear Pen Pal and Pigeon Fancier, went the message quotable at this point, it is advisable for me to remind you that the use of the term "knightly quest" instead of "nightly quest" is not just a verbal conceit but a thing of the highest significance in every part of creation, wherever a man in the prison of his body can remember his spirit. Sincerely, Gladys. Then there was a short postscript: Watch the white bird returning!

Gewinner watched the white bird returning, he saw it open its snowy wings but rising straight up without moving them as if it were caught in a sudden, sweeping updraft of wind, and it disappeared in the air as if it were changed to mist.

Only a day or so after she started working at the drive-in, Gladys had taken Billy aside and told him that she was engaged in counterespionage for The Project but that he must mention this fact to no one, including Braden Pearce.

Billy believed her. He was so enamored of Gladys that she could have told him she was God's mother and he would have believed her, but it did seem to Billy that her methods were lacking in the sort of subtlety that counterespionage seemed to call for. She was continually putting through long-distance calls on the public phone at the drive-in, and whenever she had a spare minute, she opened a brief case and pored over photostatic copies of blueprints. At least twice a week she was visited by a man with whiskers that had a false look about them and they talked together in a foreign tongue that sounded like no earthly language, and one evening Billy was startled to see this man with the whiskers remove from his pocket a live bird and give it to Gladys, along with cardboard tags, bits of wire and a little dog-eared book that Billy presumed was a code book. Such methods of counterespionage seemed much too obvious to Billy. They were outdated. That night, when he and Gladys were alone closing up the drive-in, he told her about these misgivings.

Gladys reassured him. We're using these obvious methods, she said, to disarm the enemy spies with the impression we're stupid. And you've got to make up your mind, Billy, whether you trust me or not. You've got to make up your mind about that now, right now, if you want me to go on operating here at the drive-in . . . or change to some other place.

This conference took place in the little office of the drive-in, and it suddenly turned into a very intimate thing between them when she switched off the office light.

Afterward Billy had a very proud and elated feeling. He felt that something big and wonderful was about to happen, and that he, in his own humble and ignorant way, was a partisan in it, chosen to be one.

Father Acheson of St. Mary's Cathedral and the Reverend Doctor Peters of the Methodist Episcopal Church had both been invited to dine at the Pearce residence on the night of Saturday, March 16. This was a sign of the new amity that had sprung up between the two rival pastors. Only a year ago Dr. Peters had been heard to say, I am going to break the Catholic stranglehold on this town, and Father Acheson had remarked that Protestantism and atheism were holding open the door to the wolves of Asia. The peacemaking had been brought about by none other than Braden Pearce who was to be their host at the Saturday night dinner party at the Pearce mansion. Braden had taken a very bold step to bring about this new amity. He had sent each pastor a check for five thousand dollars, payable one month from the date of receipt, and with it a note saying, I want you two fellows to shake hands with each other on the speakers' platform at the next meeting of the Civic Good-Fellowship League, which is to be next Wednesday, and unless you do shake hands and pull together for the common cause of making this a one hundred percent Christian community, why, these two checks are going to be worth just as much as the paper they're written on when you go to cash them.

The device had worked like a charm. The two pastors had not only shaken hands on the speakers' platform but had thrown their arms about each others' necks with such a lavish show of fraternal feeling that there was not a dry eye in the house when they sat back down to the chicken à la king dinner.

Now they were coming together on a special occasion at the peace-maker's home. This occasion was the seventh anniversary of Braden's marriage to Violet. Only Braden's mother knew that this was the last anniversary of that event which would ever be celebrated. What happened that night was that Violet got really good and drunk for the first time since the marriage in spite of the fact that she had only one more than her usual number of cocktails. Mother Pearce had mixed them. A scene occurred at the dinner table. Father Acheson and Dr. Peters were dreadfully embarrassed. They had to pretend that they didn't notice a thing, though Violet was leaning forward so far that her string of pearls was dangling into her soup. Braden would now and then reach out and pinch her arm or pat her shoulders. She would sit up straight for a minute or two, but then she would slump forward again.

At last Mother Pearce rang a bell. Two uniformed attendants came in as though they had been planted right outside the door for Violet's apparent collapse to occur. They picked her up by her legs and shoulders and whisked her out of the dining room. Only Gewinner made any comment on the occurrence.

Violet seems to be tired. That was his comment. Then he rose from his seat at the table and said, Excuse me, please, I'll go check her condition.

Braden muttered something in the nature of a contemptuous vulgarity as Gewinner followed Violet and her assistants out of the room.

It was amazing how Mother Pearce acted as if nothing surprising or irregular had happened. She turned to Dr. Peters and started a conversation about the sad condition of her flower garden.

Last fall, she said, my chrysanthemums withered almost as soon as they bloomed and now my rhododendron and azaleas have turned their toes up to the daisies, but my daisies are as dead as my roses. Of course I know it's the fumes from The Project, and I realize of course that, after all, it's a small sacrifice for anyone to make for anything as big and important to all the world as The Project. Don't you think so, Dr. Peters?

Dr. Peters agreed with her completely. He said that he hadn't had a real bunch of flowers on his altar in such a long time he couldn't remember how long. Then Father Acheson chimed in.

Eastern doesn't seem the same without lilies.

Braden had sat in irritable silence during this exchange of remarks about the flower situation. Now he spoke up strongly.

In my personal opinion, said Braden, it is time and past time for all people in this country, including civilians in no way connected directly or indirectly with government service, to stop thinking about their lilies and daisies and to start thinking about the many grave problems confronting the country all over the world today and getting no better tomorrow in my personal opinion.

Hear, hear, said Dr. Peters, and the other clergyman at the table said, Yes, indeed, while nodding his head in vigorous affirmation.

Braden continued his extemporaneous speech, expressing himself in such uninhibited language that Mother Pearce tried once or twice to catch his eye with an admonitory glance, the effect of which was so totally useless that her eloquent younger son went on expressing himself more forcefully than before.

Everyone knows, said Braden, that before we put Stew Hammersmith in the White House, that house was occupied by a long succession of fools, one fool after another, a continual daisy chain of pussyfooting old fools without a realistic idea of a progressive nature in the whole goddamn lot of them. They were just there sitting while the reds and the blacks and the yellows were pulling fantastic stunts right out from under our feet, but now, in my personal opinion, we've finally got us a crackerjack man up there who can think as realistic as me or you about the many grave problems confronting this country all over the world today and worse tomorrow. And I'm not saying that as a personal opinion, although this crackerjack man is my personal buddy that flies his own plane down here for consultations with me whenever I give him a signal. No, I just happen to know that we've finally got us a man with a head as well as a butt in the White House that can play the big-time game of political power as good or better than he can play golf or shoot craps, and I'm not shitting you, brother.

Interspersed with Braden's speech were a good many idiomatic expressions which are censored out of this transcription of it, since they were only put in to emphasize his points. When he stopped for a moment to take a look at his watch, Mother Pearce got in a word or two.

Oh, son, she interjected, I'm glad you brought up Stew because my incoming mail this morning included a wire from Mag saying that she and Babe were flying down here with Stew when Stew flies down here this weekend. I thought you'd like to know that wonderful piece of news. Isn't that wonderful news?

Yeah, wonderful, good, but, Mama, I wish you'd let me talk for a change. Will you let me talk for a change?

Talk, son, said Mother Pearce, you go right on and talk, but I just thought that you'd like to know that Babe is expecting to do "Babe's Stomp" with you this weekend and Babe and Mag will be in the castle with us.

Wonderful, good, said Braden, and I'm also pleased to know that General Olds and his staff are going to make the scene, too. I guess we all know I'm giving away no secret when I give you my personal opinion that that old war horse has lost his balls in confronting the moral obligations of this country all over the world, and I don't mean the balls in his golf bag. What I mean is, he's a goddamn pacifist fool that favors us reaching some understanding in Wah Sing Mink and Krek Cow Walla, but after this top-level conference this weekend at The Project, two and two is going to be added together and if old Olds don't know what they add up to, why, by my liver and lights, sitting here at this table, he'd better say four is the sum of two plus two unless he wants to admit that he never learned to count past three in his life.

Son, said Mother Pearce, I want to ask you two favors. Don't use excitable language and save out some time for some fun with the ladies while they're down here. I'm going to throw another terrific clambake at the Diamond Brite and an Indian chief is coming to wrestle an alligator but I know Babe won't take her eyes off the door till you come through it.

Yeah, she's a red-blooded girl, but right now let me get back to what I was saying.

What he was saying went on for another half-hour while the cherries jubilee and coffee were served and the finger bowls set in position around the table.

Mother Pearce got up first. She rose from her seat with a graceful, sweeping movement and said to the gentlemen, Will you gentlemen excuse us?

She had apparently forgotten that Violet had already gone, which isn't a matter of much surprise since she had counted out Violet to begin with, and it surely caused her no grief that Gewinner had taken a fast count too. Now she swept out, a regal figure as she strode from the dining hall toward the library, where she would soon be served a little postprandial drink in the nature of brandy.

Violet, on her way out! Gewinner, on his way out!

That's what she thought to herself as she paraded as if before cheering throngs into the room of a thousand books never opened. It was generally a quiet room but this evening the glass doors on to the conservatory were open and at one end of the conservatory was a large aviary of parakeets and lovebirds and canaries, all of which were now in a state of excitement and making a great commotion. Mrs. Pearce supposed they had heard her approaching and were expressing their delight. She paid the birds two calls a day, one after breakfast and another before dinner, and she would sit with them for a while, talking baby talk and making kissing sounds at them. They always responded to her visits with much chatter and flurry but this evening, hearing her approach, they were downright delirious.

Yes, they do adore me, she remarked to herself. I'll go in there and pay them a little call to settle them down for the night. So she went on through the library into the conservatory. The first thing she noticed there was that the air was quite chilly—and no wonder, the glass doors onto the garden were wide open. Now who did that? she asked herself crossly as she went to close the doors, but before she could close them, wings flapped over her head and a pigeon flew out. What was that, a pigeon? she asked out loud, and to her surprise she was answered by Gewinner whose presence in the conservatory she hadn't noticed till then. He was standing among the tall ferns by the aviary.

Yes, that was a pigeon, Mother, he said, that was a carrier pigeon that delivered a message to me from a young lady named Gladys who works over at the drive-in. It seems she has something like what they call a happening planned for the evening and the pigeon brought me an invitation to it.

Well, why don't you go? urged his mother, secretly meaning why don't you go and stay gone. She was tired of the mocking nonsense that Gewinner talked to her, the few times he talked at all to her. She'd better get him off on his travels again, yes, at all costs. But what the devil was this? she exclaimed to herself, as Violet appeared in the library, looking as sober as if she'd never heard of a martin that wasn't a bird, and dressed as if for travel and carrying a flight bag.

Why, Violet, said Mother Pearce, are you going too?

Violet gave her only the slightest of glances, and spoke past her to Gewinner.

I took a couple of bennies, I'm all straightened out for the clambake.

Good, our invitations just came from the haw-haw drive-in. Everything's A-OK, and timed to the dot and the dash, so there's not a moment to lose.

What shit is this? thought Mother Pearce, almost out loud, but they'd gone rushing past her, out the open doors to the garden and the garage.

Well, I swan, perhaps they're eloping together, wouldn't that be something too good to believe!

Your brandy, madam.

Oh, thank you, Joseph, she replied to the butler's announcement, and then she added, Close the doors to the garden. Parakeets and lovebirds catch pneumonia and wake up dead overnight. Good night, birdies, sleep tight, she crooned to the aviary as she went to her brandy—that she would drink to the providential way that everything seemed to be going in the long sweet and mellow autumn of her existence.

At about the time that Violet and Gewinner left the Pearce mansion the Laughing Boy Drive-in received from The Project an order for a quart container of coffee and a dozen barbecue sandwiches, this order to be delivered by Billy himself and not just delivered to a guard at the gates but brought by Billy personally to the Golden Room in the administration building, an order so extraordinary that Billy tingled all over with elation, there being no way to explain it except as a giant step up in The Project world in reward for his dedication.

There was a problem, though. He had sent everyone home that evening but the new girl, Gladys; they were alone at the drive-in.

How fast can you knock out a dozen barbecue sandwiches? he asked her.

To his amazement, she smiled bewitchingly at him and said, They're ready already!

One more problem: no locomotion, no wheels. His car had stalled on his way to the drive-in that morning and was still on the critical list at the Always Jolly Garage.

In no time flat Gladys had the quart of famously good coffee ready in a container and the barbecued sandwiches, steaming hot, in a glazed paper package.

Gladys, you're incredible, said Billy. Now get me a taxi.

Oh, that's not necessary, said Gladys. Mrs. Braden Pearce has just driven up outside.

Sure enough, she had. And Billy was so excited and elated he hardly noticed that Gewinner was in the car too, and in the driver's seat.

Come on, let's go, Billy, no hard feelings, Gewinner called out.

This was the sort of appeal to simple good fellowship between two men that Billy never resisted.

Wonderful! Coming, he shouted. They fairly jumped in the car and Billy hardly even noticed that Gladys had jumped in with him. What a carhop! She had her hand on his knee and the fingers were creeping up from there to a higher position. Gewinner gunned the car and off it sped toward The Project.

Just before they got there, Billy said to Gladys, Do you hear something ticking?

Gladys said, Ticking, ticking?

Gewinner said, The engine needs a checkup.

Violet said, Tomorrow.

And the hand of Gladys was making such intimate advances that Billy pushed it reluctantly away and said, Wait till we—

Here we are, said Gewinner. And yes they were, they had now arrived at the main gate of The Project and were being accosted by sentries and barking dogs.

Violet leaned over Gewinner and shouted, I'm Mrs. Braden Pearce, my husband is expecting us, let us in!

The sentries seemed distracted by some kind of electric signal going beep-beep, more and more emphatically, from various parts of the grounds. One of the sentries waved the car along, but Billy had scrambled out with the sandwiches and quart container of coffee and was allowed to proceed on his innocent mission as the car sped on with Gewinner, Violet and Gladys.

Billy was aware that something must be going mighty wrong in the grounds of The Project. The electronic sound had become one continual scream and lights had started flashing and changing in color as Billy advanced on his errand. The lights flashed yellow, then red, then a lurid purplish color that seemed to penetrate all the vacant spaces of the sky and the areas between the concrete buildings and fortifications. Now people were running around and shouting at each other so hysterically that Billy couldn't make out what they were shouting. But Billy had the temperament of the perfect soldier and he knew that all he had to do was to follow out his instructions, which were to come to the administration building of The Project with this quart container of drive-in coffee. This he was doing and this he would go on doing no matter what happened. Nothing would stop him, not if all hell broke loose . . . but it sure did look like something had gone really wrong at The Project. He thought maybe he might ask somebody, but nobody was moving at a slow enough pace to be asked a question, so Billy just went on with his errand. Then a silence fell . . . broken almost immediately by a great voice that sounded like a recording. The voice announced: Our system has detected the approach of—

That was all Billy heard of the announcement, for his attention was caught again by a sound of ticking, and since he was now alone, no one for several yards around him, he heard it much more clearly . . . and, for gosh sakes, it seemed to be coming from—

He opened the lid of the coffee container and reached his hand into the scalding brown liquid and drew out the metal cube that was now, obviously, the source of the ticking sound, and held the cube in front of his astonished baby-blue eyes for a second or two before—

Well, before it *went off*, and everything went off with it . . .

Yes, everything went off with it except the getaway spaceship which fortunately rose from its pad just long enough before the big boom at The Project to be in weightless ozone by the time of that far-reaching event. The ship bearing Gewinner, Gladys and Violet was called the Ark of Space—a reassuring touch of romanticism—and its destination is still secret to its passengers three and may still be secret to them for a long time to come.

It doesn't matter. They're so far away now that their watches are timed by light-years. In weightless ozone the concern with time is steadily left behind. Sometimes Gewinner strays from the cabin to the pilots' compartment, which is occupied by three astronauts in the full glitter of youth. They are amused by Gewinner's visits. Stories are swapped back and forth between Gewinner and the radiant young navigator, stories about the knightly quest as both have known it in their different ways. Sometimes a flock of stars will go past like fireflies in a child's twilight, and for a moment or two the Ark of Space will be flooded with light that makes Gewinner smile and say, It's bedtime—meaning it's morning.

And once, and once only, the communication system picked up a rhapsodic music, something like what the Good Gray Poet of Paumanok must have had in mind when he shouted, "Thou Vast Rondure, Swimming in Space." This music was interrupted and silenced by a voice so mighty that it made the ship tremble. Gewinner, at that moment, was in the pilots' compartment, and still having little command of their language, he didn't know, couldn't guess, what the mighty voice was saying, so he inquired of his closest friend, the radiant young navigator, what was the message, what was the shouting about?

The navigator said, Oh, many things that don't concern you particularly, but one thing that does, you've at last and at least been cleared for landing with us—of course for a term of probation.

Ah, good, said Gewinner, to whom the possibility that he might not be accepted had never occurred.

But what, he asked, what about this?

He touched his white silk scarf which had made so many festivals of nights on the planet Earth, far behind them.

Will this be admitted with me?

Why certainly, yes, of course, the young navigator assured him. It will be accepted and highly valued as a historical item in our Museum of Sad Enchantments in Galaxies Drifting Away.

Gewinner was about to dispute this disposition of his scarf, when the junior pilot sprang up, smiling and stretching, and yelled out, Champagne! Celebration!

Then all laughed and sang and joked together and offered toast after toast to each other and to the felicity waiting for them when they eventually reach the spot marked X on the chart of time without end.

1965 (Published 1966)

A Recluse and His Guest

The tall and angular person—man or woman?—had come into town not by the road (which the winter had made nearly impassable for months) but northward through the Midnight Forest, which was still more impassable.

"I understand that you came here through the forest."

"That I did."

"You weren't afraid of being attacked by wolves?"

"No, because, you see, I had smeared my leather wrappings with an oil that is repellent to wolves. They smell this oil and go in other directions without looking back."

"You were coming from—"

"Vladnik."

"Oh, from Vladnik. That explains why you—"

"Couldn't come by the road but had to struggle through the Midnight Forest, losing my way several times. Oh, I doubt that ever in my travels I've had a worse time of it."

"Why did you leave Vladnik?"

"In Vladnik I was the guest of a tradesman who suddenly found it inconvenient for me to stay with him any longer."

(This is part of a conversation that the woman had with someone a few weeks after she arrived in the icy seaport of Staad.)

The woman had eyes the color of the ice in the harbor and her hair, close-cropped, was so fair that it seemed to be gray.

An earlier conversation that she had with a baker—he gave her a loaf of bread—should not be omitted.

"Do you know of a man in Staad, I mean a man who's not married, of course, who might take me in for a while?"

"Well, now, I don't know," said the baker. "No, I don't know of any, unless you'd stay with a recluse."

"I never turn back," said the woman, "and before me in Staad, what is there but the ice in the harbor?"

"This recluse is not much different from the ice in the harbor."

"Thank you for the bread. I was very hungry. Now would you please tell me how I can find the house of this recluse?"

"Let's see, where is it? I think if you go down the road and take the second turn to the left, you'll find the house of the recluse. You'll recognize it by the windows; he keeps them boarded up in winter. But as for your luck there, don't count on it much or even a little. He hasn't let anyone in since the death of his mother and he goes out only now and then to buy necessary provisions."

"Thank you. I'll try my luck there."

It takes a great deal of patience to enter the home of a recluse. The recluse did not admit the woman that morning, but she was patient. She stayed on his porch till evening, and during the time between morning and evening, she swept the snow off his porch with birch branches; and from time to time, during her wait for a meeting with the recluse and a possible acceptance, she sang loudly in a hoarse voice that could have been the voice of a man or a woman.

Evening came on, as bitterly cold as a heart that has never felt love nor even friendship. Then, surprisingly, the recluse opened his door an inch or two and the woman addressed him with a torrent of words.

This went on for an hour before the recluse admitted her into his house.

At the Black Crown tavern that night, the matter was mentioned and discussed a bit.

"I understand that the recluse has taken in somebody who crossed the Midnight Forest from Vladnik."

"A man or a woman?"

"A man."

"No, a woman."

"If it's an adult human being, it must be one or the other, unless it's an apparition."

"It's a woman who seems like an apparition because she's so tall and she moves without bending her knees."

"You mean she stalks?"

"This apparition that you say is a woman swept the snow off the porch of the recluse with birch branches and she waited all day for the recluse to let her in."

"Perhaps the recluse has taken sick and sent for a relative to care for him."

"Yes, well, personally, I—"

"You say she did get in?"

"Finally."

"Strange things happen sometimes, and sometimes they happen as often as things that aren't strange at all."

Now a few days had passed and the stalking woman seemed to have settled in with the recluse, at least for a while.

Changes began to take place in the house of the recluse. The windows were unboarded and the glass panes were washed.

Snow was swept off the stone walk between the porch and the side road.

A wash line was strung between two birch trees and washed garments were hung along it.

The recluse was seen moving about the yard of the house as if he have never looked at it from the outside before.

After some days, the senior councilor of the town paid an official visit to the recluse and his mysterious visitor.

At the Black Crown tavern that night, it was said that the councilor had asked the stalking woman: "What is your occupation; that is, if you have any?" And the woman had replied that she was a traveler.

"Yes, I heard about that, and I also heard that the woman gave the councilor a cup of good coffee and a piece of freshly baked bread with butter and honey on it."

"Is it true that the recluse was taken with a serious illness and sent for a relative to nurse him?"

"That I don't know."

"Who cares?"

A few days later, the recluse came out of his house in an old leather suit and old boots brightly polished. Then people remembered that his name was Klaus. He was with his elderly dog, which he led on a piece of rope. They entered the tavern, where the recluse had two glasses of mulled cherry wine and the elderly dog sat by him, looking astonished.

"It's the woman," said the tavern-keeper, and no one disagreed with him.

How old was the woman?

She was not really so old, but years of wandering through northern countries had aged her face. This look of age in her face began to disappear now that she had settled comfortably into a place.

Every morning she said to the recluse: "May I stay here, or must I continue my travels?"

He would say: "Stay awhile longer."

She washed his dog, which was twelve years old and had never been washed.

She persuaded the recluse to buy a lively young hen that would soon give them eggs.

Not long after, she persuaded the recluse to buy a she-goat that gave them milk.

She knew the fear that the recluse had of change; but gradually, she began to liven and brighten things up.

It was a great day for the woman when the hen laid its first egg. She brought it into the living room, where the recluse was sitting.

"Look, Klaus! The hen is laying!"

After a month or so, eight furious dogs, hardly visible through the frost of their breath, hauled into town a sledge-load of merchandise and mail from the capital, and a letter was delivered to the house of the recluse.

"I have happened to hear that the woman Nevrika is staying at your house. Tell her that I am willing to let her come back to mine."

To this invitation of limited cordiality, the woman shook her head.

"I know the man who wrote this. He was not kind as you are and certainly not so handsome. Besides, in my travels, I never return to a place I have been before."

"Well, then, under the circumstances, I would say it's better for you to stay here awhile."

She said simply: "Thank you," but her voice was very definitely the voice of a woman and she went directly into the kitchen and brought him out several thick slices of blood sausage.

The next day, she persuaded the recluse to have his stove repaired, since it smoked nearly enough to suffocate them.

A few days later, she persuaded the recluse to buy checkered curtains, red and white, for the unboarded windows.

"Appearances are important to drive a depression away."

He began to call her Nevrika, instead of woman, and when he did that first, her face turned almost young. In her throat, there was a quiet sound, almost like weeping.

A few days later, she went out onto the streets with him and she walked with her arm through his, nodding pleasantly to strangers but making it clear that she was the woman of Klaus, who was no longer a recluse.

Some days later, when she opened the back door to call the goat in for milking, a goose with its feathers glittering with ice flew into the house. Klaus killed it. She plucked and stuffed and cooked it, and the meal was delicious and they smiled at each other, shyly.

A few days later, a yearly festival to welcome the spring season was given at the city hall.

Nevrika urged Klaus to attend it.

He said to Nevrika: "You would have to go, too, and you haven't the proper clothes for it, since all the clothes you have are strips of cloth and leather that you wind about yourself."

"It doesn't matter," she said, "they will understand."

And it seemed that they did.

At the festival, he drank several glasses of fuming dark wine and when they went home, she had to hold him straight and dissuade him from shouting.

On the way back to the house, a loose tile fell from the projecting roof of a two-story building and struck Klaus on the head.

"This is my end," he shouted, but she held him upright until his terror of the injury, which wasn't at all important, had passed away and they could go on to the house.

Still, every morning, she would ask him: "May I stay here, or must I continue my travels?"

He never said, "I need you," but still said, "Stay awhile longer."

Now, by this time, it was spring, and the solid, thick ice in the harbor, great slabs of it, gray as nightfall, began to move out to sea.

Klaus said to the woman one morning: "I want to continue my life as it was before you came here."

Her face turned old again. She was silent for a while, and then she asked, in a whisper: "Have I done something wrong?"

He said: "You persuaded me to go out to the festival and on the way back, I was hit on the head by a tile from the roof of a building."

"Oh," she cried out, "how I wish the tile had struck my head, not yours. I would rather it had struck my head than yours, even if it had broken my skull like the shell of an egg."

The recluse interpreted this outcry as a trick.

"Be that as it may," he said to the woman, "it was my head that it struck."

"Klaus, don't you remember it only gave you a little cut, like a scratch, and I rubbed it with ointment that took the sting out of it?"

"When accidents start to happen," said the recluse, "there is no end to them. One comes after another, till the beams of your roof fall on you."

"Klaus, it would take me a day to tell you the accidents I have had in my travels."

"I don't want to hear about them, they're no concern of mine."

She got up from her chair with her mouth open, as if to speak.

The recluse said: "Close your mouth. There's nothing to discuss."

She didn't sit back down. She put her coffee cup back in the kitchen, and when she returned to the living room she circled about it, wringing her large-knuckled hands, now and then stopping a moment to look at his face, which showed no alteration.

She staggered against the furniture and once fell to the floor, but the look of his face remained as it was.

"You'll think this over, won't you?"

"I have thought it over," said the recluse, "and I am determined to continue my life as it was before you came here."

"Won't you have some more coffee?"

"I want nothing that you've prepared in my kitchen; I want you to stay out of my kitchen today and I want you out of my house by this evening."

The room was dim. She leaned toward the recluse to peer at his face with her great bluish-gray eyes.

No change in the set look of his face, the face of a recluse.

She went on circling about the recluse with her mouth open.

"If your mouth is open to speak, I advise you to close it, and you will also oblige me if you wouldn't walk about the room, staring at things with your unnatural eyes."

"Klaus, let me—"

"Let you what?"

"Let me bake you a mandarin cake with sugar and cinnamon sprinkled on it."

"I want you to stay out of my kitchen with your poisonous spices."

She sat down slowly in a chair near him.

"Move your chair away."

"Away where?"

"Farther from mine."

She moved her chair twice before he was satisfied with its position.

Now and then, she would turn her head a little to look at the face of the recluse.

"Will you please stop looking at me with your unnatural eyes?"

"What shall I look at?"

"Turn your chair around and look at the wall."

"Oh, I wish that—"

She didn't complete the sentence and he didn't ask her to complete it.

After a bit of silence between them, she said: "Klaus, did you say you wanted me out of the house by this evening?"

"I said by this evening. No later."

After another bit of silence between them, he said to her: "Aren't you tired of your wanderings here and there on the earth?"

"Oh, you know, Klaus, how tired I was of my travels long before I came here."

"Well, then, I would say it's best to put an end to them."

"Could you, do you mean that I can stay on here awhile?"

"No, that's not what I meant. I meant that this evening, after the street lamps have been turned out, we will go to the harbor and there, at the harbor, you will sit yourself on a piece of ice that is being washed to sea."

She cried out a little and started to rise from her chair, then sat back down.

"Oh, but Klaus, the people of the town, now that most of them know me, would wonder about me."

"Don't let that concern you. If I am questioned about your disappearance, I will say that you suddenly felt restless and decided to continue your travels."

"But why must I go to sea on a piece of ice?"

"A piece of ice is where your travels were always leading you."

She said: "Is it cold in the room?"

"No, the room is warm."

An exhausted silence fell between them and lasted for several minutes, counted by the clock on the mantel of the fireplace.

Then she said: "The ice in the harbor is dark as nighttime."

He said: "The color of the ice is not a relevant matter."

The clock counted off a few more silent minutes. Then she began to sing in her hoarse voice, as much like a man's as a woman's, a hymn of the Knowledgist Church, to which he had once belonged.

"You will oblige me by not singing that hymn of the Knowledgist Church that no man in his right senses doesn't despise."

"I agree with you, Klaus."

An interval of silence. Then, in a strained voice, she said: "Klaus, let's go to the fish market now, before it's crowded, and buy a good trapler for dinner. There's nothing you like better than a trapler, and you know how well I can cook one."

"Is it possible you've heard and understood nothing I've said to you?"

"You said that for dinner tonight you wanted a good trapler."

"I haven't mentioned a trapler to you this morning, and as for your cooking anything in my kitchen, if you take a single step toward it, I will strike you over the head with this shovel by my chair."

"I'll take not a step toward the kitchen if you'd rather I didn't."

"I am determined you won't."

"I won't."

There followed another interval of silence before she spoke.

"Klaus, I think you're right. All of my travels have led me, in a wandering way, to the ice in the harbor. Oh, I know I'll feel the cold for a while, but then I will fall asleep and I think that it will be soon. When you've traveled as much as I have, you reach the end of your travels, and perhaps it should be at a place that's on the sea. Soon, in a week or two, the spring sun will glitter on what's left of the ice in the harbor. Look at it, Klaus, through your unboarded windows and from the streets, and—"

She didn't say, "Think of me," for her travels had taught her, almost from the very first step, that any appeal to sentiment is met with either the resentment that is spoken out or the resentment that hides behind boarded windows.

(*Published 1970*)

Happy August the Tenth

The day had begun unpleasantly at breakfast, in fact it had gotten off on a definitely wrong foot before breakfast when Horne had popped her head into the narrow "study" which served as Elphinstone's bedroom for that month and the next of summer, and she, Horne, had shrieked at her, Happy August the Tenth! and then had popped out again and slammed the door shut, ripping off Elphinstone's sleep which was at best a shallow and difficult sleep and which was sometimes practically no sleep at all.

The problem was that Horne, by long understanding between the two ladies, had the air-conditioned master bedroom for the months of August and September, Elphinstone having it the other months of the year. Superficially this would appear to be an arrangement which was more than equitable to Elphinstone. It had been amicably arranged between the ladies when they had taken occupancy of the apartment ten years ago, but things that have been amicably arranged that long ago may become onerous to one or the other of the consenting parties as time goes on and, looking back now at this arrangement between them, Elphinstone suspected that Horne, being a New Yorker born and bred, must have known that she was going to enjoy the air-conditioner during the really hot, hot part of the summer. In fact, if Elphinstone's recollection served her correctly, Horne had admitted that August was usually the hottest month in Manhattan and that September was rarely inclined to cool it, but she, Horne, had reminded Elphinstone that she had her mother's cool summer retreat, Shadow Glade, to visit whenever she wished and Horne had also reminded her that she did not have to waken early in summer or in any season, since she was self-employed, more or less, as a genealogical consultant, specializing in

F.F.V.'s, while she, Horne, had to adhere to a rather strict office schedule.

During these ruminations, Elphinstone had gotten up and gone to the bathroom and was now about to appear with ominous dignity (she hoped) in the living room at the back of their little fifth-floor brownstone apartment on East Sixty-first Street. Elphinstone knew that she was not looking well for she had glanced at the mirror. Middle age was not approaching on stealthy little cat feet this summer but was bursting upon her as peremptorily as Horne had shrieked her into August the Tenth.

What is August the Tenth? she asked Horne in a deceptively casual tone as she came into the living room for coffee.

Horne chuckled and said, August the Tenth is just August the Tenth.

Then you had no reason at all to wake me up at this hour?

I woke you up early because you told me last night to wake you up as soon as I woke up because Doc Schreiber had switched your hour to nine o'clock today in order to observe your state of mind in the morning.

Well, he is not going to observe it this morning after my third consecutive night with no sleep.

You don't think he ought to observe your awful morning depression?

My morning depressions are related only to prolonged loss of sleep and not to any problems I'm working out with Schreiber, and I am not about to pay him a dollar a minute to occupy that couch when I'm too exhausted to speak a mumbling word to the man.

You might be able to catch a few extra winks on the couch, Horne suggested lightly. And you know, Elphinstone, I'm more and more convinced that your chronic irritability which has gotten much worse this summer is an unconscious reaction to the Freudian insult. You are an Aries, dear, and Aries people, especially with Capricorn rising, can only benefit from Jung. I mean for Aries people it's practically Jung or nothing.

Elphinstone felt a retort of a fulminous nature boiling in her breast but she thought it best, in her exhausted state, to repress it, so she switched the subject to their Panamanian parrot, Lorita, having observed that Lorita was not in her indoor cage.

Where have you put Lorita? she demanded as sharply as if she suspected her friend of having wrung the bird's neck and thrown it into the garbage-disposal unit.

Lorita is on her travels, said Horne briskly.

I don't think Lorita ought to go on her travels till you have gone to your office, Elphinstone grumbled, since you move around so fast in the morning that you are likely to crush her underfoot.

I move rapidly but not blindly, dear, and anyhow Lorita's gone to sit in her summer palace.

Lorita's summer palace was a very spacious and fancy cage that had been set up for her on the little balcony outside the double French doors, and there she was, in it, sitting.

Someday, said Elphinstone darkly, that bird is going to discover that she can fly, and then good-bye, Lorita!

You're full of dire predictions this morning, said Horne. Old Doc Schreiber is going to catch an earful, I bet!

Both were now sipping their coffee, side by side on the little ivory-satin-covered love seat that faced the television and the balcony and the backs of brownstone buildings on East Sixtieth Street. It was a pleasant view with a great deal more foliage than you usually see in Manhattan outside the park. The TV was on. A public-health official was talking about the increased incidence of poliomyelitis in New York that summer.

When are you going for your polio shots? asked Horne.

Elphinstone declared that she had decided not to have the polio shots this summer.

Are you mad? asked Horne.

No, just over forty, said Elphinstone.

What's that got to do with it?

I'm out of the danger zone, Elphinstone boasted.

That's an exploded theory. The man just said there is no real age limit for polio nowadays.

Horne, you will take any shot or pill in existence, Elphinstone said, but for a very odd reason. Not because you are really scared of illness or mortality, but because you have an unconscious death wish and feel so guilty about it that you are constantly trying to convince yourself that you are doing everything possible to improve your health and to prolong your life.

They were talking quietly but did not look at each other as they talked, which was not a good sign for August the Tenth nor for the flowers of friendship.

Yes, that *is* a "very odd reason," a very odd one, indeed! Why should I have a death wish?

Their voices had become low and shaky.

Yesterday evening, Horne, you looked out at the city from the balcony and you said, My God, what a lot of big tombstones, a necropolis with brilliant illumination, the biggest tombstones in the world's biggest necropolis. I repeated this remark to Dr. Schreiber and told him it had upset me terribly. He said, "You are living with, you are sharing your life with, a very sick person. To see great architecture in a great city and call it tombstones in a necropolis is a symptom of a deep psychic disturbance, deeper than yours, and though I know how much you value this companion, I have to warn you that this degree of nihilism and this death wish is not what you should be continually exposing yourself to, during this effort you're making to climb back out of the shadows. I can only encourage you to go on with this relationship provided that this sick person will take psychotherapy, too. But I doubt that she will do this, since she doesn't want to climb up, she wants to move in the opposite direction. And this," he said, "is made very clear by what you've told me about her present choice of associates."

There was a little silence between them, then Horne said: Do you believe that I am an obstacle to your analysis? Because if you do, I want to assure you that the obstacle will remove itself gladly.

Schreiber is chiefly concerned, said Elphinstone, about your new circle of friends because he feels they're instinctively destructive!

Well, said Horne, he hasn't met them and I think it's awfully presumptuous to judge any group of varied personalities without direct personal contact. Of course I have no idea what stories about my friends you may have fed Doc Schreiber.

None, none!—Hardly any . . .

Then how does he know about them? By some sort of divination?

In deep analysis, said Elphinstone portentously, you have to hold nothing back.

But that doesn't mean that what you don't hold back is necessarily true. Does it? Shit, apparently you didn't mean a word of it when you told me you understood how I need to have my own little circle of friends since I'm not accepted by yours.

Elphinstone replied sorrowfully, I have no circle of friends unless you mean my group of old school chums from Sarah Lawrence whom I have lunch with once a month, and very, very occasionally entertain here for a buffet supper and bridge, occasions to which you're always invited, in fact urged to come, but you have declined, except for a single occasion.

Oh, yes, said Horne, you said a few days ago that you not only saw nothing wrong in our having our little separate circle of friends, but you said you thought it was psychologically healthy for us both. You said, if you'd try to remember, that it relieved the tensions between us for each to have her own little social circle, and as for my circle being hostile to you, I can only tell *you*—

Tell me *what*?

That *you* did not accept *them*, you bristled like a hedgehog on the one occasion you honored them with your presence, the single time that you condescended to meet them instead of running out to some dreary get-together of old Sarah Lawrence alumnae.

Another pause occurred in the conversation. Both of them made little noises in their throats and took little sips of coffee and didn't glance at each other: the warm air trembled between them. Even the parrot Lorita seemed to sense the domestic crisis and was making quiet clucking sounds and little musical whistles from her summer palace, as if to pacify the unhappy ladies.

You say I have a death wish, said Horne, resuming the talk between them. I think you are putting the shoe on the wrong foot, dear. My direction is outward toward widening and enriching my contacts with life, but you are obsessed with the slow death of your mother, as if you envied her for it. You hate what you call "my circle of Village hippies" because they're intellectually vital, intensely alive, and dedicated to living, in *here*, and in *here*, and in *here*.

(She touched her forehead, her chest, and her abdomen with her three heres.)

Oh, and all this remarkably diversified vitality is about to explode here again tonight, is it, Horne?

The social climate, said Horne, is likely to be somewhat more animated than you'll find things at Shadow Glade but then the only thing less animated than your mother's is the social climate at your Sarah Lawrence bashes. Elphinstone, why don't you skip this weekend at your mother's and come to my little gathering here tonight and come with a different attitude than you brought to it before, I mean be sweet, natural, friendly, instead of charging the atmosphere with hostility and suspicion, and then I know they would understand you a little better and *you* would understand the excitement that I feel in contact with a group that has some kind of intellectual vitality going for them, and—

What you're implying is that Sarah Lawrence graduates are inevitably and exclusively dim-witted?

I wasn't thinking about Sarah Lawrence graduates, I am nothing to them and they are nothing to me. However, she continued, her voice gathering steam, I do feel it's somewhat ludicrous to make a religion, a fucking mystique, out of having once attended that snobbish institution of smugness!

Well, Horne, if you must know the truth, said Elphinstone, some of the ladies were a bit disconcerted by your lallocropia.

My *what?*

Lallocropia is the psychiatric term for a compulsion to use shocking language, even on the least suitable occasions.

Shit, if I shocked the ladies—

Horne stood up on this line, which was left incomplete because her movement was so abrupt that she spilled some coffee on the ivory-satin cover of the love seat.

Horne cried out wildly when this happened, releasing in her outcry an arsenal of tensions which had accumulated during this black beginning of August the Tenth, and, as if projected by the cry, she made like a bullet for the kitchen to grab a dishcloth and wet it at the faucet; then rushed back in to massage the coffee-stained spot on the elegant love seat with the wet cloth.

Oh, said Elphinstone in a tone more sorrowful than rancorous, I see now why this piece of furniture has been destroyed. You rub this ivory-satin cover, made out of my grandmother's wedding gown, with a wet dishcloth whenever you spill something on it which you do with a very peculiar regularity because of hostility toward—

As a preliminary, yes! said Horne, having heard only the beginning of Elphinstone's rueful indictment. Then, of course, I go over the spot with Miracle Cleanser.

What is Miracle Cleanser?

Miracle Cleanser, said Horne in several breathless gasps, her respiration disturbed by their tension and its explosion, is a marvelous product advertised by Johnny Carson on his "Tonight Show."

I see you are mad, said Elphinstone. Well, I am going to send out this sofa to be covered with coffee-colored burlap.

Of course there's not much I can do to protect my china and glassware from the havoc which I know is impending *ce soir!* The breakage of my Wedgwood and Haviland is a small price to pay for your cultural regeneration these past few months, if six months is a few! And I can't see into the future, but if this place isn't a shambles in—

Why don't you put your goddamn Wedgwood and your Haviland in storage, who wants or needs your goddamn—

Horne, said Elphinstone with a warning vibration in her voice.

Horne replied with that scatological syllable which she used so often in conversations lately, and Elphinstone repeated her friend's surname with even more emphasis.

Christ, Elphinstone, but I mean it. We are sharing a little apartment in which nearly all the space is pre-empted by family relics such as your Wedgwood and your crystal and your silver with your mother's crest on it, everything's mother's or mother's mother's mother's around here so that I feel like a squatter in your family plot in the boneyard, and oh, my God, the bookshelves! Imagine my embarrassment when doctors of letters and philosophy go up to check the books on those shelves and see nothing but all this genealogical crap and think it's my choice of reading matter, *Notable Southern Families Volume I*, *Notable Southern Families Volume II*, *Notable Southern Bullshit* up to the ceiling and down to your Aubusson carpet, shelves and shelves and—

Horne, I believe you know that I am a professional consultant in genealogy and must have my reference books and that I have to work in this room!

Shit, I thought you had it all in your head by this time! Who buggered Governor Dinwiddie in the cranberry bushes, by the Potomac, which tribe scalped Mistress Elphinstone, the Cherokees or the Choctaws, at the—

There's nothing to be ashamed of in a colonial heritage, Horne!

Well, your colonial heritage, Elphinstone, and your family relics have made this place untenable for me! I am going to check into the Chelsea Hotel for the weekend and you'll hear from me later about where to contact me for a reimbursement of my half of the rent money on this Elphinstone sanctuary!

She heard Horne slam the door of the master bedroom and, pricking her ears, she could hear her defecting companion being very busy in there. There was much banging about for ten minutes or so before Horne left for her office and then Elphinstone got up off the ruined love seat and went into the master bedroom for a bit of reconnaissance. It was productive of something in the nature of reassurance. Elphinstone discovered that Horne had packed a few things in a helter-skelter fashion in her Val-pac, had broken the zipper on it, and had left out her toilet articles, even her toothbrush, and so Elphinstone was reasonably certain the half-packed Val-pac was only one of Horne's little childish gestures.

At noon of August the Tenth, Elphinstone phoned the research department of the *National Journal of Social Commentary* which employed Horne and she got Horne on the phone.

Both voices were sad and subdued, so subdued that each had to ask the other to repeat certain things that were said in the long and hesitant phone conversation between them. The conversation was gentle and almost elegiac in tone. Only one controversial topic was brought up, the matter of the polio shots. Elphinstone said, Dear, if it will make you feel better, I'll go for a polio shot. There was a slight pause and a catch in Horne's voice when she replied to this offer.

Dear, she said, you know the horror I have of poliomyelitis since it struck my first cousin Alfie who is still in the iron lung, just his head sticking out, wasted like a death's head, dear, and his lost blue eyes, oh, my God, the look in them when he tries to smile at me, oh, my God, that look!

Both of them started to weep at this point in the conversation and were barely able to utter audible good-byes . . .

But at four o'clock that hot August afternoon there was a sudden change in Elphinstone's mood. Having made an afternoon appointment with her analyst, she recounted with marvelous accuracy the whole morning talk with Horne.

When will you learn, he asked sadly, when a thing is washed up?

He rose from his chair behind the couch on which Elphinstone was stretched, holding a wad of Kleenex to her nostrils; he was terminating the session after only twenty-five minutes of it, thus cheating Elphinstone out of half she paid for it.

Gravely he held the door open for Elphinstone to go forth. She went sobbing into the hot afternoon. It was overcast but blazing.

Nothing, nothing, she thought. She meant she had nothing to do. But when she went home, an aggressive impulse seized her. She went into the master bedroom and completed Horne's packing, very thoroughly, very quickly and neatly, and placed all four pieces of luggage by the bedroom door. Then she went to her own room, packed a zipper bag of weekend things, and cut out to Grand Central Station, taking a train to Shadow Glade where she intended to stay till Horne had taken the radical hint and evacuated the East Sixty-first Street premises for good.

When she arrived at Mama's, Elphinstone found her suffering again from cardiac asthma, having another crisis with a nurse in attendance. She could feel nothing about it, except the usual shameful speculation about Mama's last will and testament: would the estate go mostly to the married sister with three children or had Mama been fair about it and realized that Elphinstone was really the one who needed financial protection over the years to come, or would it all go (oh, God) to the Knowledgist Church and its missionary efforts in New Zealand, which had been Mama's pet interest in recent years. Elphinstone was sickened by this base consideration in her heart, and when Mama's attack of cardiac asthma subsided and Mama got out of bed and began to talk about the Knowledgist faith again, Elphinstone was relieved, and she suddenly told Mama that she thought she, Elphinstone, had better go back to New York, since she had left without letting Horne know that she was leaving, which was not a kind thing to do to such a nervous person as Horne.

I don't understand this everlasting business of Horne, Horne, complained Mama. What the devil is Horne? I've heard nothing but Horne out of you for ten years running. Doesn't this Horne have a Christian name to be called by you? Oh, my God, there's something peculiar about it, I've always thought so. What's it *mean?* I don't know what to imagine!

Oh, Mama, there's nothing for you to imagine, said Elphinstone. We are two unmarried professional women and unmarried professional women address each other by surnames. It's a professional woman's practice in Manhattan, that's all there is to it, Mama.

Oh, said Mama, hmmm, I don't know, well . . .

She gave Elphinstone a little darting glance but dropped the subject of Horne and asked the nurse in attendance to help her onto the potty.

Well, the old lady had pulled through another very serious attack of cardiac asthma and was now inclined to be comforted by little ministrations and also by the successful cheese soufflé which Elphinstone had prepared for their bedside supper.

Then Mama was further comforted and reassured by the doctor's dismissal of the nurse in attendance.

The doctor must think I'm better, she observed to her daughter.

Elphinstone said, Yes, Mama, your face was blue when I got here but now it's almost returned to a normal color.

Blue? said Mama.

Yes, Mama, almost purple. It's a condition called cyanosis.

Oh, my God, Mama sighed, cyna—*what* did you call it?

Observing that her use of such clinical terminology had upset Mama again, Elphinstone made a number of more conventional remarks such as how becoming Mama's little pink bed jacket looked on her now that her face had returned to a normal shade, and she reminded Mama that she had given Mama this bed jacket along with a pair of knitted booties and an embroidered cover for the hot-water bottle on Mama's eighty-fifth birthday.

After a little silence she could not suppress the spoken recollection that Mama's other daughter, the married one, Violet, had completely ignored Mama's birthday, as had the grandchildren Charlie and Clem and Eunice.

But Mama was no longer attentive, her sedation had begun to work on her now, and the slow and comparatively placid rise and fall of her huge old bosom suggested to Elphinstone the swells and lapses of an ocean that was subsiding from the violence of a typhoon.

It's wonderful how she keeps fighting off Mr. Black, said Elphinstone to herself. (Mr. Black was her private name for The Reaper.)

Lacey, said Elphinstone to her Mama's housekeeper, has Mama received any visits from her lawyer lately?

The old housekeeper had prepared a toddy of hot buttered rum for Elphinstone and given her the schedule of morning trains to Manhattan.

Sipping the toddy, Elphinstone felt reassured about Mama's old housekeeper. She'd sometimes suspected Lacey of having a sly intention of surviving Mama and so receiving some portion of Mama's estate, but now, this midnight, it was clearly apparent to Elphinstone that the ancient housekeeper was really unlikely to last as long as Mama. She had asthma, too, as well as rheumatoid arthritis with calcium deposits in the spine so that she walked bent over like a bow, in fact her physical condition struck Elphinstone as being worse than Mama's although she, Lacey, continued to work and move around with it, having that sort of animal tenacity to the habit of existence which Elphinstone was not quite certain that she respected either in Mama or in Mama's old housekeeper.

She can't hang on forever, Elphinstone murmured, half aloud.

What's that, Miss? inquired the housekeeper.

I said that Mama is still obsessed with the Knowledgist Church in spite of the fact it never got out of New Zealand where it originated a year before Mama's conversion, on her visit to Auckland with Papa when he failed to recuperate from the removal of his prostate in 1912 . . .

What?

Nothing, she replied gently to the housekeeper's question. Then she raised her voice and said, *Will you please call me a cab now?*

What?

Cab! Call! Now!

Oh . . .

Yes, I've decided not to wait for the morning train to Manhattan but to return in a taxi. It will be expensive, but—

The sentence, uncompleted, would have been, if completed, to the effect that she intended to surprise Horne in the midst of a Babylonian revel with her N.Y.U. crowd, and she was thinking particularly of a remark she would make to the red-bearded philosophy prof.

Are you an advocate of women's lib, she would ask, for strictly personal reasons?

A slow smile grew on her face as she descended the stairs to the entrance hall of Mama's summer haven.

Hmmm, she reflected.

Her mood was so much improved by her masterly stratagem that she slipped a dollar bill into Lacey's old lizard-chill fingers at the door.

The cab was there.

Told that the fare to Manhattan would probably amount to about eighty dollars, Elphinstone angrily dismissed the driver, but before he had turned onto the highway from the drive she called him back in a voice like a clap of thunder.

It had occurred to Elphinstone that eighty dollars was less than half the cost of two sessions with Schreiber and she suspected so strongly that she was nearly certain that on the early morning of August the Eleventh her little home would be exorcised forever of the demonology and other mischiefs related to that circle from N.Y.U. as well as—

Yes, Horne will attempt to stick to me like a tar baby, but we'll see about that!

When Elphinstone admitted herself by latchkey to the Sixty-first Street apartment, she was confronted by a scene far different from that which she had anticipated all of the long and costly way home.

No revel was in progress, no sign of disorder was to be seen in the Horne-Elphinstone establishment.

Horne? Where *is* she? Oh, there!

Horne was seated in sleep on the ruinously stained love seat. She was facing the idiot box. It was still turned on, although it was after "The Tonight Show" had been wrapped up and even the "Late-Late Movie." The screen was just a crazy white blaze of light with little swirling black dots on it, it was like a negative film clip of a blizzard in some desolate country and it was accompanied, soundwise, by a subdued static roar. Why, my God, it was just like the conscious and unconscious mental processes of Elphinstone were being played back aloud from a sound track made silently during that prodigal gesture of a cab ride home, Christ Jesus.

Elphinstone studied the small, drooping figure of Horne asleep on the love seat, Horne's soft snoring interspersed with her unintelligible murmurs. Before her, on the little cocktail table, was half a bottle of Jack Daniel's Black Label and a single tumbler.

Apparently Horne had drunk herself to sleep in front of that idiot box, quite, quite alone . . .

Elphinstone was in the presence of a mystery.

She checked with their answering service, requesting all messages for herself and Horne, too.

The single one which she had received was from a Sarah Lawrence graduate who was canceling a luncheon appointment because of a touch of the flu. The single message for Horne was more interesting. It said, with a brevity that struck Elphinstone as insulting, Sorry, no show, Sandy Cutsoe.

(The name was that of the red-bearded philosophy prof from the poison-ivy-league school.)

Sympathy for the small and abandoned person on the love seat entered Elphinstone's heart like the warm, peaceful drunkenness that comes from wine. She turned off the TV set, that negative film clip of a snowstorm at night in some way-off empty country, and then it was quite dark in the room and it was silent except for Horne's soft snores and murmurings and the occasional sleepy clucks of the parrot, still in her summer palace on the balcony where she might as well stay the night through.

Ah me, said Elphinstone, we've gotten through August the Tenth, that much is for sure anyhow . . .

She did, then, a curious thing, a thing which she would remember with embarrassment and would report to Schreiber on Monday in hope of obtaining some insight into the deeper meanings that it must surely contain.

She crouched before the love seat and gently pressed a cheek to Horne's bony kneecaps and encircled her thin calves with an arm. In this position, not comfortable but comforting, she watched the city's profile, creep with understandable reluctance into morning, because, my God, yes, Horne's comment did fit those monolithic structures downtown, they truly were like a lot of illuminated tombstones in a necropolis.

The morning light did not seem to care for the city, it seemed to be creeping into it and around it with understandable aversion. The city and the morning were embracing each other as if they'd been hired to perform an act of intimacy that was equally abhorrent to them both.

Elphinstone whispered Happy August the Eleventh to Horne's knee-caps in a tone of condolence, and the day after tomorrow, no, after today, on Monday, she would begin her polio shots despite her childish dread of the prick of a needle.

August 1970 (Published 1971)

The Inventory at Fontana Bella

In the early autumn of her one hundred and second year the Principessa Lisabetta von Hohenzalt-Casalinghi was no longer able to tell light from dark, thunder from a footfall nor the texture of wool from satin. Yet she still got about with amazing agility. She danced to imaginary schottisches, polkas and waltzes with imaginary partners. She gave commands to household domestics in a voice whose volume would shame a drill sergeant. Having once been drawn through Oriental streets in rickshas, she had naturally learnt to yell "Chop, chop!" and she now exercised that command to make haste at the end of each order she shouted and these orders were given all but continually while she was awake and sometimes she would even shout "Chop, chop!" in her sleep.

Early in October, close to midnight, the Principessa sat bolt upright in her bed, breaking out of sleep as a sailfish from water.

"Sebastiano!" she cried, at the same instant of the cry pressing a hard fist to her groin.

Sebastiano was the name of her fifth and last husband who had now been dead for fifty years, and she had clutched her groin because in her dream she had felt the ecstasy of his penetration, a thing which had remained in her recollection more obsessively even than her commands to make haste.

Immediately after the outcry "Sebastiano," she slammed her fist down again, not on her nostalgic groin but upon the electric buttons that were on her bedside table, all eight of them were slammed down by her fist, hard and repeatedly and with continual cries of "Chop, chop!"

It was her resident physician who first responded, thinking that she had finally been stricken by a cardiac seizure.

478 TENNESSEE WILLIAMS: COLLECTED STORIES

"*Cristo*, no, this creature is immortal!" he shouted involuntarily as he entered Lisabetta's huge bedchamber and observed her standing naked by the bed in a state of existence that seemed to be nuclear powered, her blind eyes blazing with preternatural light.

In a number of minutes others assembled and were equally astounded by this phenomenon of vitality in so ancient a being.

"Preparations at once, chop chop. Fastest boat, *motoscafo* with the Rolls engine for lake crossing to Fontana Bella! Party including as follows. *Senta!* Secretaries, business and personal, upstairs and downstairs maids, especially Mariella who remembers Fontana Bella as well as I do. Lawyer, of course, not the old one gone blind but the young one with long beard that speaks High German, the curator of my museum, and of course my bookkeeper because the purpose of this trip is to finally hold, to conduct, an inventory of treasures at Fontana Bella, assessment of treasures remaining there, priceless art-objects and ancestral paintings, all, all valuables kept there, so get to it, chop, chop, teeth in, clothes on, off to Fontana Bella."

The crossing was not so tedious as most of the party had anticipated. The lawyer was soon engaged in the defloration of a very young chambermaid, first with his fingers and then with his tongue and, climactically, with his organ of gender, and the chambermaid's moans and cries were finally heard and mistaken by the Principessa for a noisy sea gull flying over the boat and she ordered it shot down at once. This provoked considerable merriment among the passengers: and then the curator of the Principessa's private gallery, brought along to assess the canvases at Fontana Bella, began to tell a story about a rather well-known and gifted Roman painter who had been recently transferred to an insane asylum in Zurich.

"Dear Florio," said the curator, "he could only set to work under very peculiar conditions. He had to have a barely pubescent youth in his studio. No, no, not as a model, no, not that, just as a sort of excitant to his creative juices, you see, but what's so amusing about it is that this nubile youth, picked up on the Spanish Steps by Florio's secretary, always had to be discovered naked in an alcove of the studio, a curtained alcove, with a peacock's feather inserted in his rectum, oh, no, not all the way in, just in far enough to hold it in place, and the alcove was kept curtained until Florio was seated at his easel. And then the curtain of the alcove would be drawn open by the secretary and he and Florio would utter ecstatic cries at the sight of the boy with the peacock's gorgeous tail feather up his bum and Florio then would cry out, *Ah, che bella sorpresa, un pavone in casa mia!*"

(Which meant, What a lovely surprise, a peacock in my house!)

Then the boy would be paid nicely and dismissed from the house and Florio would start to paint like the madman he was.

At this story, there was general laughter loud enough to be heard by Lisabetta.

"*Silenzio,*" she shouted and began to strike about her with her parasol. She managed to hit only the head of her poodle and when it barked at her in protest, she said: "You flatter me, sir, but we must wait upon another occasion!"

Then she fell asleep.

When the Principessa woke, she was in bed at Fontana Bella and it was again midnight.

She sprang up and shouted into a closet door, "Mariella, dress me, I want on woolens this morning, this is the north shore of Lago Maggiore, not the south, and there's no more disgusting affliction than a summer cold in the head. *Subito,* get them all up, the inventory is going to commence at once!"

Then she stood in the center of the bedroom, lifting legs to step into imaginary woolens and extending arms for the fur jacket which she thought was being put on her. She was quite impatient as the imaginary maid, Mariella, who had been dead for twenty years or more, did not seem to be following instructions with sufficient rapidity.

"Mariella," she shouted. "Teeth in, teeth in! Chop, chop!"

She opened her mouth for the dentures to be inserted.

"Hah, ring a bell, now *andiamo!*"

She then started across the great chamber, knocking over a couple of chairs which she mistook for assistant maids who were slow to get out of her way, and by an act of providence she walked straight to the door upon the hall.

The upper floor of Fontana Bella was still remarkably clear in her head since it was the floor on which she had lain with her great love, Sebastiano. She found the top of the grand staircase as if she had full possession of her sight and she descended it without a false step, at one point crying out, "Hands off me, I can't stand to be touched by anyone but a lover!"

The lower floor of Fontana Bella was more distinct in her mind than any part of her residence on the southern shore of Lago Maggiore and yet it was not as certain as she assumed it to be and at the foot of the stairs she made a wrong turn which brought her outdoors upon an enormous balustraded terrace that faced the gloomy lake that starless midnight.

"*Tutte qui?* All present for inventory? Chop, chop!"

Old ladies have a way, you know, of acquiring prejudice of race and class and gender, so it wasn't surprising that Lisabetta had turned somewhat against members of the Hebrew race, mostly through a paranoid senility.

"If there's a Jew at the inventory," she shouted, "I want him to keep a shut mouth. Not a word out of him during the inventory. I know they're an ancient race but not all ancient races are necessarily noble!"

This struck her as a witty observation and she gave forth a great peal of laughter to which some storks at a far end of the terrace responded with squawks and wing-flapping which Lisabetta interpreted as a flight of Jews from her presence.

"Gone, good! Proceed with the inventory, chop, chop! Oh, Christ, oh, wait, I have to relieve my bowels, put two screens about me and bring me a pot! Chop chop!"

She lowered herself to a squatting position until the windy disturbance in her bowels had subsided and then she stood up and remarked, "These things do happen, you know. It's a natural occurrence when there's so much agitation.

"Doctor, Doctor? Please examine my stool, each morning's stool ought to be examined, it's the key to existence. Now, then, that's over, on with the inventory!"

Lisabetta felt herself surrounded by the party which had accompanied her from the southern shore, that is, all but the possible Jews she'd ordered away.

"Ready? Ready? *Va bene!*"

She began to conduct the inventory, now, and it continued for seven hours. Her memory of her possessions at Fontana Bella was quite remarkable, as remarkable as her endurance.

It was an hour before daybreak when her truant party of attendants returned from the nearby casino but the Principessa was still on the terrace, pacing up and down it, naked in the gray moonlight. From a distance they heard her shouting, "Gold plate, service for eight! In the vault, yes, get the keys! Has the Jew made off with the keys? What, what? Don't shout, I cannot put up with this rushing about and shouting, hands off, I've told you and told you that I abhor the touch of anyone but a lover! You, you there, come here and explain something to me!"

She seemed to be pointing at the Neapolitan lawyer who was the first to approach her on the terrace, the rest standing back in attitudes of indifference and fatigue.

The lawyer was lively as ever. He went up close to the Principessa and shouted directly into her relatively good ear, *"Che volete, cara?"*

The old lady wheeled about to strike at him and the motion made her dizzy. She became disoriented but she was swift as ever as she rushed to the end of the terrace above which the storks were nesting, their patience exhausted by the disturbance beneath them. A great white female stork, alarmed for the safety of her young ones, flapped down from the roof onto Lisabetta to engage her in combat. It dove repeatedly at her head and her breast and abdomen, inflicting wounds with its beak and blows with its wings till the old lady toppled over and fell on the terrace pavement. Her naked and withered arms made frantic attempts to embrace the matron stork. At last she caught hold of its beak and would not let go. She divided her limbs and finally, she forced the stork's beak to penetrate her vagina. It stabbed and stabbed at her uterine passage, and still she kept calling out "Sebastiano" in a loud voice and *"Amore"* in a soft voice.

The lawyer caught hold of the stork's legs and tore it away from the lady. He held the bird up and announced, "The stork is dead, suffocated inside her, and still she's calling it lover!"

It was not voluntarily, nor even wittingly, that the Principessa returned across the lake the following day. The Neapolitan lawyer invented a story to entice the lady away from Fontana Bella: he told her that the owner of the nearby casino had arranged that evening a great gala in honor of her return to the province.

"All the walls of the gaming room are covered with talisman roses," the lawyer told her, "and your name is spelled out in camellias above the grand entrance."

When finally this invention had gotten through her left eardrum it did not surprise Lisabetta at all.

"Ah, well, I'll make an appearance, I suppose it is a case of *noblesse oblige*."

The party got her seated among cushions in the stern of the *motoscafa* informing her it was a Mercedes limousine, and so the return voyage began.

The lake surface that day was smooth as glass and the sky was radiant.

"Perhaps a few turns of the wheel and some rolls of the dice, then home, chop chop, to continue the inventory. So many valuables are still not accounted for, and then, of course, you know—Mariella, cologne!"

A chambermaid passed a handkerchief to her. After a few sniffs of it, she resumed her talk, which seemed now to have gone into the babblings of delirium.

"If the moon were not clouded over, even if some stars were out, you would see behind Fontana Bella a bare hill with a bare tree on it. It ceased to leaf and to blossom when my last lover died."

That preface to her narrative was accurate in regard to the presence of the bare tree on the bare hill behind the villa.

"Sebastiano died as his name-saint died," she continued. "He was chained to a tree and his incomparable young body was transfixed by five arrows. I had five brothers, you know, one for each arrow that pierced him. They're dead now, I trust. No complaints, no demands from them lately. A family and a lover should never meet when a huge fortune's involved and questions of its division are involved, too, since there is no limit at all to the fantasies of hatred when great wealth is involved. First they tried to get His Holiness to annul my marriage to Sebastiano. Got nowhere with that and so resorted to arrows and, well that was that. For them, emigration. For me a period in a convent. Oh, I tell you I have been a few places and I have done a few things and while I was in that convent I learned there are uses for candles beside the illumination of chapel altar and supper table, but it was *faute de mieux*, as the frogs put it, don't they?"

She fell into silent musing for a few moments: then, after a slight, bitter laugh, she spoke again.

"All good doctors," she said, "have telephone numbers that contain no more than one or two digits and the rest is all zeros, you know."

"Yes, and all good morticians," observed the lawyer, "have telephone numbers consisting of nothing but zero, zero, ad infinitum."

The curator of the museum was asked if he recalled any more amusing anecdotes about that Roman painter now confined to the asylum in Zurich.

"Well, yes, now, the last time I visited poor Florio, he seemed to have recovered completely. He kept assuring me that his aberrations were all gone under the excellent treatment at the retreat and he begged me to get his relatives in Rome to have him released, and I, being convinced that he really was quite well, embraced him and started for the gate and I had almost reached it when I was struck on the back of the head by a large piece of concrete paving that almost gave me a concussion but I

managed to turn about and there was Florio behind me. And he had
quite obviously thrown the missile. 'Don't forget now,' he shouted, 'I'm
the sanest man in the world!' "

The passengers were laughing at this tale when Lisabetta leaned
abruptly forward from her mound of pillows.

"Ah!"

With this exclamation, she struck a fist to her groin as if unbearably
pained there but on the reptilian face of the Principessa was a look of
ecstasy that outshone the glassy lake surface on that brightest of
autumn mornings.

The Neapolitan lawyer, seated nearest her in the boat, seized her
wrist and then, discovering no pulse, turned to the party and said, "A
miracle has happened, the lady is dead."

This announcement caused one or two of the passengers to cross
themselves, perhaps while reflecting upon the difficulty of seeking new
employment, but, understandably, most of the others in the boat were
moved to much less solemn expressions of feeling.

July 1972 (Published 1973)

Miss Coynte of Greene

Miss Coynte of Greene was the unhappily dutiful caretaker of a bed-ridden grandmother. This old lady, the grandmother whom Miss Coynte addressed as *Mère* and sometimes secretly as *merde*, had outlived all relatives except Miss Coynte, who was a single lady approaching thirty.

The precise cause of Miss Coynte's grandmother's bed-ridden condition had never been satisfactorily explained to Miss Coynte by their physician in Greene, and Miss Coynte, though not particularly inclined to paranoia, entertained the suspicion that the old lady was simply too lazy to get herself up, even to enter the bathroom.

"What is the matter with *Mère*, Dr. Settle?"

"Matter with your grandmother?" he would say reflectively, looking into the middle distance. "Well, frankly, you know, I have not exactly determined anything of an organic nature that really accounts for her staying so much in bed."

"Dr. Settle, she does not stay so much in bed, but she stays constantly in it, if you know what I mean."

"Oh, yes, I know what you mean . . ."

"Do you know, Dr. Settle, that I mean she is what they call 'incontinent' now, and that I have to spend half my time changing the linen on the bed?"

Dr. Settle was not unsettled at all by this report.

"It's one of a number of geriatric problems that one has to accept," he observed dreamily as he made toward the downstairs door. "Oh, where did I put my hat?"

"You didn't have one," replied Miss Coynte rather sharply.

He gave her a brief, somewhat suspicious glance, and said, "Well, possibly I left it in the office."

"Yes, possibly you left your head there, too."

"What was that you said?" inquired the old doctor, who had heard her perfectly well.

"I said that Chicken Little says the sky is falling," replied Miss Coynte without a change of expression.

The doctor nodded vaguely, gave her his practiced little smile and let himself out the door.

Miss Coynte's grandmother had two major articles on her bedside table. One of them was a telephone into which she babbled all but incessantly to anyone she remembered who was still living and of a social echelon that she regarded as speakable to, and the other important article was a loud-mouthed bell that she would ring between phone talks to summon Miss Coynte for some service.

Most frequently she would declare that the bed needed changing, and while Miss Coynte performed this odious service, *Mère* would often report the salient points of her latest phone conversation.

Rarely was there much in these reports that would be of interest to Miss Coynte, but now, on the day when this narrative begins, *Mère* engaged her granddaughter's attention with a lively but deadly little anecdote.

"You know, I was just talking to Susie and Susie told me that Dotty Reagan, you know Dotty Reagan, she weighs close to three hundred pounds, the fattest woman in Greene, and she goes everywhere with this peculiar little young man who they say is a fairy, if you know what I mean."

"No, *Mère*, can you swing over a little so I can change the sheet?"

"Well, anyway, Dotty Reagan was walking along the street with this little fairy who hardly weighs ninety pounds, a breeze would blow him away, and they had reached the drugstore corner, where they were going to buy sodas, when Dotty Reagan said to the fairy, 'Catch me, I'm going to fall,' and the little fairy said to her, 'Dotty, you're too big to catch,' and so he let her fall on the drugstore corner."

"Oh," said Miss Coynte, still trying to tug the soiled sheet from under her grandmother's massive and immobile body on the brass bed.

"Yes, he let her fall. He made no effort to catch her."

"Oh," said Miss Coynte again.

"Is that all you can say, just 'Oh'?" inquired her grandmother.

Miss Coynte had now managed by almost superhuman effort to get the soiled bed sheet from under her grandmother's great swollen body.

"No, I was going to ask you if anything was broken, I mean like a hipbone, when Dotty Reagan fell."

A slow and malicious smile began to appear on the face of Miss Coynte's grandmother.

"The coroner didn't examine the body for broken bones," the grandmother said, "since Dotty Reagan was stone-cold dead by the time she hit the pavement of the corner by the drugstore where she had intended to have an ice-cream soda with her fairy escort who didn't try to catch her when she told him that she was about to fall."

Miss Coynte did not smile at the humor of this story, for, despite her condition, an erotic, not a frigid, spinster approaching thirty, she had not acquired the malice of her grandmother, and, actually, she felt a sympathy both for the defunct Dotty Reagan and for the ninety-pound fairy who had declined to catch her.

"Were you listening to me or was I just wasting my breath as usual when I talk to you?" inquired her grandmother, flushing with anger.

"I heard what you said," said Miss Coynte, "but I have no comment to make on the story except that the little man with her would probably have suffered a broken back, if not a fracture of all bones, if Miss Dotty Reagan had fallen on top of him when he tried to catch her."

"Yes, well, the fairy had sense enough not to catch her and so his bones were not fractured."

"I see," said Miss Coynte. "Can you lie on the rubber sheet for a while till I wash some clean linen?"

"Be quick about it and bring me a bowl of strawberry sherbet and a couple of cookies," ordered the grandmother.

Miss Coynte got to the door with the soiled sheet and then she turned on her grandmother for the first time in her ten years of servitude and she said something that startled her nearly out of her wits.

"How would you like a bowl full of horseshit?" she said to the old lady, and then she slammed the door.

She had hardly slammed the door when the grandmother began to scream like a peacock in heat; she let out scream after scream, but Miss Coynte ignored them. She went downstairs and she did not wash linen for the screaming old lady. She sat on a small sofa and listened to the screams. Suddenly, one of them was interrupted by a terrific gasp.

"Dead," thought Miss Coynte.

She breathed an exhausted sigh. Then she said, "Finally."

She relaxed on the sofa and soon into her fancy came that customary flood of erotic imagination.

Creatures of fantasy in the form of young men began to approach her through the room of the first floor, cluttered with furnishings and bric-a-brac inherited from the grandmother's many dead relatives. All of these imaginary young lovers approached Miss Coynte with expressions of desire.

They exposed themselves to her as they approached, but never having seen the genitals of a male older than the year-old son of a cousin, Miss Coynte had a very diminutive concept of the exposed organs. She was easily satisfied, though, having known, rather seen, nothing better.

After a few hours of these afternoon fantasies, she went back up to her grandmother. The old lady's eyes and mouth were open but she had obviously stopped breathing . . .

Much of human behavior is, of course, automatic, at least on the surface, so there should be no surprise in Miss Coynte's actions following upon her grandmother's death.

About a week after that long-delayed event, she leased an old store on Marble Street, which was just back of Front Street on the levee, and she opened a shop there called The Better Mousetrap. She hired a black man with two mules and a wagon to remove a lot of the inherited household wares, especially the bric-a-brac, from the house, and then she advertised the opening of the shop in the daily newspaper of Greene. In the lower left-hand corner of the ad, in elegant Victorian script, she had her name, Miss Valerie Coynte, inserted, and it amazed her how little embarrassment she felt over the immodesty of putting her name in print in a public newspaper.

The opening was well attended, the name Coynte being one of historical eminence in the Delta. She served fruit punch from a large cut-glass bowl with a black man in a white jacket passing it out, and the next day the occasion was written up in several papers in that part of the Delta. Since it was approaching the Christmas season, the stuff moved well. The first stock had to be almost completely replaced after the holiday season, and still the late *Mère*'s house was almost overflowing with marketable antiquities.

Miss Coynte had a big publicity break in late January, when the *Memphis Commercial Appeal* did a feature article about the success of her enterprise.

It was about a week after this favorable write-up that a young man employed as assistant manager of the Hotel Alcazar crossed the street to the shop to buy a pair of antique silver salt and pepper shakers as a silver-wedding-anniversary gift for the hotel's owner, Mr. Vernon T. Silk, who was responsible for the young man's abrupt ascendancy from a job as bellhop to his present much more impressive position at the hotel.

More impressive it certainly was, this new position, but it was a good deal less lucrative, for the young man, Jack Jones, had been extraordinarily well paid for his services when he was hopping bells. He had been of a thrifty nature and after only six months, he had accumulated a savings account at the Mercantile Bank that ran into four figures, and it was rumored in Greene that he was now preparing to return to Louisiana, buy a piece of land and become a sugarcane planter.

His name, Jack Jones, has been mentioned, and it probably struck you as a suspiciously plain sort of name and I feel that, without providing you with a full-figure portrait of him in color, executed by an illustrator of remarkable talent, you can hardly be expected to see him as clearly as did Miss Coynte when he entered The Better Mousetrap with the initially quite innocent purpose of buying those antique silver shakers for Mr. Vernon Silk's anniversary present.

Mr. Jones was a startlingly personable young man, perhaps more startlingly so in his original occupation as bellhop, not that there had been a decline in his looks since his advancement at the Alcazar but because the uniform of a bellhop had cast more emphasis upon certain of his physical assets. He had worn, as bellhop, a little white mess jacket beneath which his narrow, muscular buttocks had jutted with a prominence that had often invited little pats and pinches even from elderly drummers of usually more dignified deportment. They would deliver these little familiarities as he bent over to set down their luggage and sometimes, without knowing why, the gentlemen of the road would flush beneath their thinning thatches of faded hair, would feel an obscurely defined embarrassment that would incline them to tip Jack Jones at least double the ordinary amount of their tips to a bellhop.

Sometimes it went past that.

"Oh, thank you, suh," Jack would say, and would linger smiling before them. "Is there anything else that I can do for you, suh?"

"Why, no, son, not right now, but—"

"Later? You'd like some ice, suh?"

Well, you get the picture.

There was a certain state senator, in his late forties, who began to spend every weekend at the hotel, and after midnight at the Alcazar, when usually the activities there were minimal, this junior senator would keep Jack hopping the moon out of the sky for one service after another—for ice, for booze and, finally, for services that would detain the youth in the senator's two-room suite for an hour or more.

A scandal such as this, especially when it involves a statesman of excellent family connections and one much admired by his constituency, even mentioned as a Presidential possibility in future, is not openly discussed; but, privately, among the more sophisticated, some innuendoes are passed about with a tolerant shrug.

Well, this is somewhat tangential to Miss Coynte's story, but recently the handsome young senator's wife—he was a benedict of two years' standing but was still childless—took to accompanying him on his weekend visits to the Alcazar.

The lady's name was Alice and she had taken to drink.

The senator would sit up with her in the living room of the suite, freshening her drinks more frequently than she suggested, and then, a bit after midnight, seeing that Alice had slipped far down in her seat, the junior senator would say to her, as if she were still capable of hearing, "Alice, honey, I think it's beddy time for you now."

He would lift her off the settee and carry her into the bedroom, lay her gently upon the bed and slip out, locking the door behind him: Then immediately he would call downstairs for Jack to bring up another bucket of ice.

Now once, on such an occasion, Jack let himself into the bedroom, not the living room door with a passkey, latched the door from inside and, after an hour of commotion, subdued but audible to adjacent patrons of the Alcazar, the senator's lady climbed out naked onto the window ledge of the bedroom.

This was just after the senator had succeeded in forcing his way into that room.

Well, the lady didn't leap or fall into the street. The senator and Jack managed to coax her back into the bedroom from the window ledge and, more or less coincidentally, the senator's weekend visits to the Alcazar were not resumed after that occasion, and it was just after that occasion that Mr. Vernon Silk had promoted Jack Jones to his new position as night clerk at the hotel.

In this position, standing behind a counter in gentleman's clothes, Jack Jones was still an arrestingly personable young man, since he had large, heavy-lashed eyes that flickered between hazel and green and which, when caught by light from a certain angle, would seem to be almost golden. The skin of his face, which usually corresponds to that of the body, was flawlessly smooth and of a dusky-rose color that seemed more suggestive of an occupation in the daytime, in a region of fair weather, than that of a night clerk at the Alcazar. And this face had attracted the attention of Miss Dorothea Bernice Korngold, who had stopped him on the street one day and cried out histrionically to him: "Nijinsky, the face, the eyes, the cheekbones of the dancer Waslaw Nijinsky! Please, please pose for me as *The Spectre of the Rose* or as *The Afternoon of a Faun!*"

"Pose? Just pose?"

"As the *Faun* you could be in a reclining position on cushions!"

"Oh, I see. Hmm: Uh-huh. Now, what are the rates for posing?"

"Why, it depends on the *hours!*"

"Most things do," said Jack.

"When are you *free?*" she gasped.

"Never," he replied, "but I've got afternoons off and if the rates are OK . . ."

Well, you get the picture.

Jack Jones with his several enterprises did as well as Miss Coynte of Greene with her one. Jack Jones had a single and very clear and simple object in mind, which was to return to southern Louisiana and to buy that piece of land, all his own, and to raise sugarcane.

Miss Coynte's purpose or purposes in life were much more clouded over by generations of dissimulation and propriety of conduct, by night and day, than those of Jack Jones.

However, their encounter in The Better Mousetrap had the volatile feeling of an appointment with a purpose; at least one, if not several purposes of importance.

She took a long, long time wrapping up the antique silver shakers and while her nervous fingers were employed at this, her tongue was engaged in animated conversation with her lovely young patron.

At first this conversation was more in the nature of an interrogation.

"Mr. Jones, you're not a native of Greene?"

"No, ma'am, I ain't. Sorry. I mean I'm not."

"I didn't think you were. Your accent is not Mississippi and you don't have a real Mississippi look about you."

"I don't have much connection with Mississippi."

"Oh, but I heard that our junior state senator, I heard it from *Mère*, was preparing you for a political career in the state."

"Senator Sharp was a very fine gentleman, ma'am, and he did tell me one time that he thought I was cut out for politics in the state."

"And his wife, Mrs. Alice Sharp?"

"Mrs. Alice Sharp was a great lady, ma'am."

"But inclined to . . . you know?"

"I know she wanted to take a jump off the fifth-floor window ledge without wings or a parachute, ma'am."

"Oh, then *Mère* was right."

"Is this *Mère* a female hawss you are talking about who was right?"

"Yes, I think so. Tell me. How was Miss Alice persuaded not to jump?"

"Me and the senator caught ahold of her just before she could do it."

"Well, you know, Mr. Jones, I thought that this story of *Mère*'s was a piece of invention."

"If this *Mère* was a female hawss, she done a good deal of talking."

"That she did! Hmm. How long have you been in Greene?"

"I'll a been here six months and a week next Sunday coming."

"Why, you must keep a diary to be so exact about the time you arrived here!"

"No, ma'am, I just remember."

"Then you're gifted with a remarkable memory," said Miss Coynte, with a shaky little tinkle of laughter, her fingers still fussing with the wrapping of the package. "I mean to be able to recall that you came here to Greene exactly six months and a week ago next Sunday."

"Some things do stick in my mind."

"Oh!"

Pause.

"Is there a fly in the shop?"

"Fly?"

"Yes, it sounds to me like a horsefly's entered the shop!"

"I don't see no fly in the shop and I don't hear none either."

Miss Coynte was now convinced of what she had suspected.

"Then I think the humming must be in my head. This has been such a hectic week for me, if I were not still young, I would be afraid that I might suffer a stroke; you know, I really do think I am going to have to employ an assistant here soon. When I began this thing, I hadn't any suspicion that it would turn out to be such a thriving enterprise . . ."

There was something, more than one thing, between the lines of her talk, and certainly one of those things was the proximity of this exotic young man. He was so close to her that whenever she made one of her flurried turns—they were both in front of a counter now—her fingers would encounter the close-fitting cloth of his suit.

"Mr. Jones, please excuse me for being so slow about wrapping up these things. It's just my, my—state of exhaustion, you know."

"I know."

"Perhaps you know, too, that I lost my grandmother yesterday, and—"

"Wasn't it six weeks ago?"

"Your memory *is* remarkable as . . ."

She didn't finish that sentence but suddenly leaned back against the counter and raised a hand to her forehead, which she had expected to feel hot as fire but which was deathly cold to her touch.

"Excuse me if I . . ."

"What?"

"Oh, Mr. Jones," she whispered with no breath in her throat that seemed capable of producing even a whisper, "if there isn't a fly, there must be a swarm of bees in this shop. Mr. Jones, you know, it was a stroke that took *Mère*."

"No, I didn't know. The paper just said she was dead."

"It was a stroke, Mr. Jones. Most of the Coyntes go that way, suddenly, from strokes due to unexpected . . . excitement . . ."

"You mean you feel . . . ?"

"I feel like Chicken Little when the acorn hit her on the head and she said, 'Oh, the sky is falling!' I swear that's how I feel now!"

It seemed to Miss Coynte that he was about to slip an arm about her slight but sinewy waist as she swayed a little toward him, and perhaps he was about to do that, but what actually happened was this: She made a very quick, flurried motion, a sort of whirling about, so that the knuckles of her hand, lifted to just the right level, brushed over the fly of his trousers.

"Oh!" she gasped. "Excuse me!"

But there was nothing apologetic in her smile and, having completed a full turn before him, so that they were again face to face, she heard herself say to him:

"Mr. Jones, you are not completely Caucasian!"

"Not what, did you say?"

"Not completely a member of the white race?"

His eyes opened very wide, very liquid and molten, but she stood her ground before their challenging look.

"Miss Coynte, in Greene nobody has ever called me a nigger but you. You are the first and the last to accuse me of that."

"But what I said was not an accusation, Mr. Jones, it was merely—"

"Take *this!*"

She gasped and leaned back, expecting him to smash a fist in her face. But what he did was more shocking. He opened the fly that she had sensed and thrust into her hand, seizing it by the wrist, that part of him which she defined to herself as his "member." It was erect and pulsing riotously in her fingers, which he twisted about it.

"Now what does Chicken Little say to you, Miss Whitey Mighty, does she still say the sky is falling or does she say it's rising?"

"Chicken Little says the sky is rising straight up to—"

"Your tight little cunt?"

"Oh, Mr. Jones, I think the shop is still open, although it's past closing time. Would you mind closing it for me?"

"Leggo of my cock and I'll close it."

"Please! Do. I can't move!"

Her fingers loosened their hold upon his member and he moved away from her and her fingers remained in the same position and at the same level, loosened but still curved.

The sound of his footsteps seemed to come from some distant corridor in which a giant was striding barefooted away. She heard several sounds besides that; she heard the blind being jerked down and the catch of the latch on the door and the switching off of the two green-shaded lights. Then she heard a very loud and long silence.

"You've closed the shop, Mr. Jones?"

"That's right, the shop is closed for business."

"Oh! No!"

"By no do you mean don't?"

He had his hand under her skirt, which she had unconsciously lifted, and he was moving his light-palmed, dusky-backed, spatulate-fingered hand in a tight circular motion over her fierily throbbing mound of Venus.

"Oh, no, no, I meant do!"

It was time for someone to laugh and he did, softly.

"That's what I thought you meant. Hold still till I get this off you."

"Oh, I can't, how can I?" she cried out, meaning that her excitement was far too intense to restrain her spasmodic motions.

"Jesus," he said as he lifted her onto the counter.

"God!" she answered.

"You have got a real sweet little thing there and I bet no man has got inside it before."

"My Lord, I'm . . ."

She meant that she was already approaching her climax.

"Hold on."

"Can't."

"OK, we'll shoot together."

And then the mutual flood. It was burning hot, the wetness, and it continued longer than even so practiced a stud as Jack Jones had ever known before.

Then, when it stopped, and their bodies were no longer internally engaged, they lay beside each other, breathing fast and heavily, on the counter.

After a while, he began to talk to Miss Coynte.

"I think you better keep your mouth shut about this. Because if you talk about it and my color, which has passed here so far and which has got to pass in this goddamn city of Greene till I go back to buy me a piece of land and raise cane in Louisiana—"

"You are not going back to raise cane in Louisiana," said Miss Coynte with such a tone of authority that he did not contradict her, then or ever thereafter.

It was nearly morning when she recovered her senses sufficiently to observe that the front door of The Better Mousetrap was no longer locked but was now wide open, with the milky luster of street lamps coming over the sill, along with some wind-blown leaves of flaming color.

Her next observation was that she was stretched out naked on the floor.

"Hallelujah!" she shouted.

From a distance came the voice of a sleepy patrolman calling out, "Wha's that?"

Understandably, Miss Coynte chose not to reply. She scrambled to the door, locked it, got into her widely scattered clothes, some of which would barely hold decently together.

She then returned home by a circuitous route through several alleys and yards, having already surmised that her mission in life was certain, from this point onward, to involve such measures of subterfuge.

As a child in Louisiana, Jack Jones had suffered a touch of rheumatic fever, which had slightly affected a valve in his heart.

He was now twenty-five.

Old Doc Settle said to him, "Son, I don't know what you been up to lately, but you better cut down on it, you have developed a sort of noise in this right valve which is probably just functional, not organic, but we don't want to take chances on it."

A month later, Jack Jones took to his bed and never got up again. His last visitor was Miss Coynte and she was alone with him for about half an hour in Greene Memorial Hospital, and then she screamed and when his nurse went in, he was sprawled naked on the floor.

The nurse said, "Dead."

Then she glared at Miss Coynte.

"Why'd he take off his pajamas," she asked her.

Then she noticed that Miss Coynte was wriggling surreptitiously into her pink support hose, but not surreptitiously enough to escape the nurse's attention.

"I don't know what you are talking about," said Miss Coynte, although the nurse had not opened her mouth to speak a word about what Miss Coynte's state of incomplete dress implied.

It is easy to lead a double life in the Delta; in fact it is almost impossible not to.

Miss Coynte did not need to be told by any specialist in emotional problems that the only way to survive the loss of a lover such as Jack Jones had been before his collapse was to immediately seek out another; and so in the weekend edition of *The Greene Gazette*, she had inserted a small classified ad that announced very simply, "Colored male needed at The Better Mousetrap for heavy delivery service."

Bright and early on Monday morning, Sonny Bowles entered the shop in answer to this appeal.

"Name, please?" inquired Miss Coynte in a brisk and businesslike voice, sharply in contrast to her tone of interrogation with the late Jack Jones.

Her next question was: "Age?"

The answer was: "Young enough to handle delivery service."

She glanced up at his face, which was almost two feet above her own, to assure herself that his answer had been as pregnant with double meaning as she had hoped.

What she saw was a slow and amiable grin. She then dropped her eyes and said: "Now, Mr. Bowles, uh, Sonny, I'm sure that you understand that 'delivery service' is a rather flexible term for all the services that I may have in mind."

Although she was not at all flurried, she made one of her sudden turns directly in front of him, as she had done that late afternoon when she first met the late Jack Jones, and this time it was not her knuckles but her raised finger tips that encountered, with no pretense of accident whatsoever, the prominent something behind the vertical parabola of Sonny Bowles's straining fly.

Or should we say "Super Fly"?

He grinned at her, displaying teeth as white as paper.

Sonny turned off the green-shaded lights himself and locked the shop door himself, and then he hopped up on the counter and sat down and Miss Coynte fell to her knees before him in an attitude of prayer.

Sonny Bowles was employed at once by Miss Coynte to make deliveries in her little truck and to move stock in the store.

The closing hours of the shop became very erratic. Miss Coynte had a sign printed that said OUT TO LUNCH and that sign was sometimes hanging in the door at half past eight in the morning.

"I have little attacks of migraine," Miss Coynte explained to people, "and when they come on me, I have to put up the lunch sign right away."

Whether or not people were totally gullible in Greene, nothing was said in her presence to indicate any suspicion concerning these migraine attacks.

The Better Mousetrap now had four branches, all prospering, for Miss Coynte had a nose for antiquities. As soon as a family died off and she heard about it, Sonny Bowles would drive her to the house in her new Roadmaster. She would pretend to be offering sincere condolences to relatives in the house, but all the while her eyes would be darting about at objects that might be desirable in her shops. And so she throve.

Sonny had a light-blue uniform with silver buttons when he drove her about.

"Why, you two are inseparable," said a spiteful spinster named Alice Bates.

This was the beginning of a feud between Miss Bates and Miss Coynte which continued for two years. Then one midnight Miss Bates's house caught fire and she burned alive in it and Miss Coynte said, "Poor Alice, I warned her to stop smoking in bed, God bless her."

One morning at ten Miss Coynte put up her OUT TO LUNCH sign and locked the door, but Sonny sat reading a religious booklet under one of the green-shaded lamps and when Miss Coynte turned the lamp off, he turned it back on.

"Sonny, you seem tired," remarked Miss Coynte.

She opened the cash register and gave him three twenty-dollar bills.

"Why don't you take a week off," she suggested, "in some quiet town like Memphis?"

When Sonny returned from there a week later, he found himself out of a job and he had been replaced in The Better Mousetrap by his two younger brothers, a pair of twins named Mike and Moon.

These twins were identical.

"Was that you, Mike," Miss Coynte would inquire after one of her sudden lunches, and the answer was just as likely to be:

"No, ma'am, this is Moon, Miss Coynte."

Mike or Moon would drive her in her new yellow Packard every evening that summer to the Friar's Point ferry and across it to a black community called Tiger Town, and specifically to a night resort called Red Dot. It would be dark by the time Mike or Moon would deliver Miss Coynte to this night resort and before she got out of the yellow Packard, she would cover her face with dark face powder and also her hands and every exposed surface of her fair skin.

"Do I pass inspection," she would inquire of Mike or Moon, and he would laugh his head off, and Miss Coynte would laugh along with him as he changed into his Levis and watermelon-pink silk shirt in the Packard.

Then they would enter and dance.

You know what wonderful dancers the black people are, but after a week or so, they would clear the floor to watch Miss Coynte in the arms and hands of Mike or Moon going through their fantastic gyrations on the dance floor of Red Spot.

There was a dance contest in September with a dozen couples participating, but in two minutes the other couples retired from the floor as Miss Coynte leapt repeatedly over the head of Mike or Moon, each time swinging between his legs and winding up for a moment in front of him and then going into the wildest circular motion about him that any astral satellite could dream of performing in orbit.

"Wow!"

With this exclamation Miss Coynte was accustomed to begin a dance and to conclude it also.

"Miss Coynte?"

"Yes?"

"This is Reverend Tooker."

She hung up at once and put the OUT TO LUNCH sign on the shop door, locked it up, and told Mike and Moon, "Our time is probably about to expire in Greene, at least for a while."

"At least for a while" did not mean right away. Miss Coynte was not a lady of the new South to be demoralized into precipitate flight by such a brief and interrupted phone call from a member of the Protestant clergy.

Still, she was obliged, she thought, to consider the advisability of putting some distance between herself and the small city of Greene sometime in the future, which might be nearer than farther.

One morning while she was out to lunch but not lunching, she put through a call to the chamber of commerce in Biloxi, Mississippi.

She identified herself and her name was known, even there.

"I am doing research about the racial integration of Army camps in the South and I understand that you have a large military base just outside Biloxi, and I wonder if you might be able to inform me if enlisted or drafted blacks are stationed at your camp there?"

Answer: "Yes."

"Oh, you said yes, not no. And that was the only question I had to ask you."

"Miss Coynte," drawled the voice at the other end of the phone line, "we've got this situation of integration pretty well under control, and if you'll take my word for it, I don't think that there's a need for any research on it."

"Oh, but, sir, my type of research is not at all likely to disturb your so-called control; if I make up my mind to visit Biloxi this season."

Enough of that phone conversation.

However . . .

The season continued without any change of address for Miss Coynte. The season was late autumn and leaves were leaving the trees, but Miss Coynte remained in Greene.

However, changes of the sort called significant were manifesting themselves in the lady's moods and conditions.

One hour past midnight, having returned from Red Dot across the river, Miss Coynte detained her escorts, Mike and Moon, on the shadowy end of her long front veranda for an inspired conversation.

"Not a light left in the town; we've got to change that to accomplish our purpose."

"Don't you think," asked Mike or Moon, "that—"

The other twin finished the question, saying: "Dark is better for us?"

"Temporarily only," said Miss Coynte. "Now, you listen to me, Mike and Moon! You know the Lord intended something when he put the blacks and whites so close together in this great land of ours, which hasn't yet even more than begun to realize its real greatness. Now, I want you to hear me. Are you listening to me?"

"Yes, ma'am," said Mike or Moon.

"Well, draw up closer," and, to encourage them toward this closer proximity to her, she reached out her hands to their laps and seized their members like handles, so forcibly that they were obliged to draw their chairs up closer to the wicker chair of Miss Coynte.

"Someday after our time," she said in a voice as rich as a religious incantation, "there is bound to be a great new race in America, and this is naturally going to come about through the total mixing together of black and white blood, which we all know is actually red, regardless of skin color!"

All at once, Miss Coynte was visited by an apparition or vision.

Crouched upon the front lawn, arms extended toward her, she saw a crouching figure with wings.

"Lord God Jesus!" she screamed. "Look there!"

"Where, Miss Coynte?"

"Annunciation, the angel!"

Then she touched her abdomen.

"I feel it kicking already!"

The twin brothers glanced at each other with alarm.

"I wonder which of you made it, but never mind that. Since you're identical twins, it makes no difference, does it? Oh! He's floating and fading . . ."

She rose from her chair without releasing their genitals, so that they were forced to rise with her.

Her face and gaze were uplifted.

"Good-bye, good-bye, I have received the Announcement!" Miss Coynte cried out to the departing angel.

Usually at this hour, approaching morning, the twins would take leave of Miss Coynte, despite her wild protestations.

But tonight she retained such a tight grip on their genital organs that they were obliged to accompany her upstairs to the great canopied bed in which *Mère* had been murdered.

There, on the surface of a cool, fresh linen sheet, Miss Coynte enjoyed a sleep of profound temporary exhaustion, falling into it without a dread of waking alone in the morning, for not once during her sleep did she release her tight hold on the handles the twins had provided—or surrendered?—win or lose being the name of all human games that we know of; sometimes both, unnamed.

Now twenty years have passed and that period of time is bound to make a difference in a lady's circumstances.

Miss Coynte had retired from business, and she was about to become a grandmother. She had an unmarried daughter, duskily handsome, named Michele Moon, whom she did not admit was her daughter but whom she loved dearly.

From birth we go so easily to death; it is really no problem unless we make it one.

Miss Coynte now sat on the front gallery of her home and, at intervals, her pregnant daughter would call out the screen door, "Miss Coynte, would you care for a toddy?"

"Yes, a little toddy would suit me fine," would be the reply.

Having mentioned birth and death, the easy progress between them, it would be unnatural not to explain that reference.

Miss Coynte was dying now.

It would also be unnatural to deny that she was not somewhat regretful about this fact. Only persons with suicidal tendencies are not a little regretful when their time comes to die, and it must be remembered what a full and rich and satisfactory life Miss Coynte had had. And so she is somewhat regretful about the approach of that which she could not avoid, unless she were immortal. She was inclined, now, to utter an occasional light sigh as she sipped a toddy on her front gallery.

Now one Sunday in August, feeling that her life span was all but completed, Miss Coynte asked her illegitimate pregnant and unmarried daughter to drive her to the town graveyard with a great bunch of late-blooming roses.

They were memory roses, a name conferred upon them by Miss Coynte, and they were a delicate shade of pink with a dusky center.

She hobbled slowly across the graveyard to where Jack Jones had been enjoying his deserved repose beneath a shaft of marble that was exactly the height that he had reached in his lifetime.

There and then Miss Coynte murmured that favorite saying of hers, "Chicken Little says the sky is falling."

Then she placed the memory roses against the shaft.

"You were the first," she said with a sigh. "All must be remembered, but the first a bit more definitely so than all the others."

A cooling breeze stirred the rather neglected grass.

"Time," she remarked to the sky.

And the sky appeared to respond to her remark by drawing a diaphanous fair-weather cloud across the sun for a moment with a breeze that murmured lightly through the graveyard grasses and flowers.

So many have gone before me, she reflected, meaning those lovers whom she had survived. Why, only one that I can remember hasn't gone before, yes, Sonny Bowles, who went to Memphis in the nick of time, dear child.

Miss Coynte called down the hill to the road, where she had left the pregnant unmarried daughter in curiously animated conversation with a young colored gatekeeper of the cemetery.

There was no response from the daughter, and no sound of conversation came up the hill.

Miss Coynte put on her farsighted glasses, the lenses of which were almost telescopic, and she then observed that Michele Moon, despite her condition, had engaged the young colored gatekeeper in shameless sexual play behind the family crypt of a former governor.

Miss Coynte smiled approvingly.

"It seems I am leaving my mission in good hands," she murmured.

When she had called out to her daughter, Michele Moon, it had been her intention to have this heroically profligate young lady drive her across town to the colored graveyard with another bunch of memory roses to scatter about the twin angels beneath which rested the late Mike and Moon, who had died almost as closely together in time as they had been born, one dying instantly as he boarded the ferry on the Arkansas side and the other as he disembarked on the Mississippi side with his dead twin borne in his arms halfway up the steep levee. Then she had intended to toss here and there about her, as wantonly as Flora scattered blossoms to announce the vernal season, roses in memory of that incalculable number of black lovers who had crossed the river with her from Tiger Town, but of course this intention was far more romantic than realistic, since it would have required a truckload of memory roses to serve as an adequate homage to all of those whom she had enlisted in "the mission," and actually, this late in the season, there were not that many memory roses in bloom.

Miss Coynte of Greene now leaned, or toppled, a nylon-tip pen in her hand, to add to the inscriptions on the great stone shaft one more, which would be the relevant one of the lot. This inscription was taking form in her mind when the pen slipped from her grasp and disappeared in the roses.

Mission was the first word of the intended inscription. She was sure that the rest of it would occur to her when she had found the pen among the memory roses, so she bent over to search among them as laboriously as she now drew breath, but the pen was not recovered— nor was her breath when she fell.

In her prone position among the roses, as she surrendered her breath, the clouds divided above her and, oh my God, what she saw—

Miss Coynte of Greene almost knew what she saw in the division of clouds above her when it stopped in her, the ability to still know or even to sense the approach of—

Knowledge of—

Well, the first man or woman to know anything finally, absolutely for sure has yet to be born in order to die on this earth. This observation is not meant to let you down but, on the contrary, to lift your spirit as the Paraclete lifted itself when—

It's time to let it go, now, with this green burning inscription: *En avant!* or "Right on!"

November 1972 (Published 1973)

Sabbatha and Solitude

"In your earlier work," wrote a former editor of the famed poetess Sabbatha Veyne Duff-Collick, "you had a certain wry touch of astringency to your flights of personal lyricism, and being such a close friend as well as your editor, whilom, I cannot help but admit to you that I am distressed to discover that that always redeeming grace of humor which, in this skeptical age, must underlie the agonies of a romanticist has somehow withheld its delicate influence on these new sonnets, admirable though they . . ."

"Why, this old fart has gone *senile,*" Sabbatha shrieked to her audience of one, a young man whose Mediterranean aspects of character and appearance had magically survived his past ten years of sharing life with Sabbatha in her several retreats.

"Oh, he says you're senile?" the young man murmured with no evidence of surprise.

"I say *he* is, read *this!*—since you didn't *listen!*"

She crumpled the letter from the senior editor of Hark and Smothers and tossed it at Giovanni like a rock at a dangerous assailant, but it was only a crumpled sheet of paper and did him no injury except to distract him from certain private reflections. He was lying on his back before the open stone fireplace, his black-curled head on a throw-away pillow, he was becomingly undressed to the skin, and the fingers of a hand were scratching at the crispy bush over his genitals.

"Johnny, Johnny, Giovanni, for God's sake are you infested with lice?"

"How could I get crabs in this old birdhouse of yours unless I had 'em shipped in from—Bangor?"

Giovanni emphasized and lingered over the name of that city because those unspoken reflections which she had interrupted had to do with the city, well, not so much with the city itself but with a certain frolicsome night place in that city which was frequented mostly by men employed at gathering shellfish and who were presently barred from that employment by a phenomenon of the Maine coast that was called "the red tide," and this red tide was not a political incursion but a form of marine flora which made the shellfish inedible and therefore unmarketable when it made its appearance in the waters. This phenomenon was an economic disaster for the men who frequented the night place in Bangor but it had an appealing aspect to Giovanni, in that it would certainly increase the cordiality of his reception at the waterfront bar if he should drop in there again while the "red tide" was polluting the waters: the difficulty was that the name of the place had slipped his mind and he had discovered it one night which remained quite vivid in his recollection despite a state of drunkenness that approached a mental blackout. The experiences of the night were as memorable as any in his thirty-five years and yet the name of the place and the name of the street of the place and even the general locality of the place had somehow refused to surface in his memory, which was an extremely exasperating thing to him for the night which he had spent there stood out as boldly as the Star of Bethlehem over the many, many nights of shared solitude with Sabbatha in her several retreats from the world.

Now all of a sudden the name of the night place in Bangor, Maine, flashed on the screen of his recollection with such a startling effect that he jumped up and shouted it out.

"*Sea Hag!*"

"How *dare* you!" screamed Sabbatha, thinking that he was addressing her by this name.

Of course Giovanni had addressed her by many equally unflattering names in the course of their present long winter retreat, and sometimes just as loudly, but she was not at this moment in a humor to tolerate any further abuse than she had suffered in the rejections of her new sonnet sequence by Hark and Smothers and a number of others.

Sabbatha retaliated to the presumed insult by kicking Giovanni's very well-turned backside with the toe of her slipper but this resulted in nothing but a stab of pain in her arthritic ankle- and knee-joints, since her slipper was a bedroom slipper of soft material and Giovanni was too comfortably insulated where she kicked him to be jolted out of his elation over remembering the memorable night place by name.

He merely looked at Sabbatha with a sort of wolfish grin and repeated the name to fix it more sharply in his mind: "Sea Hag!"

"Son of a bitch!" she retorted, "Sea hag your ass!"

"My ass is homesick, Sabby, and this birdhouse is not the home of
my ass . . ."

He was now on his feet to get the rum bottle and slosh more rum in
his tea and he drank it down chug-a-lug and then he finally turned his
attention to her latest letter of rejection. He dropped back down by the
fireplace and uncrumpled the letter she'd thrown at him. He read it by
firelight and as he read it a mocking smile grew pleasurably over his
face, which was the face of a juvenile satyr.

The firelight was dimming.

"Christ, don't you see the fire is dying out?" she demanded.

"Throw more faggots in it!"

"*You* do that!"

"Cool it, lady, don't work yourself into a seizure."

He built the fire up a bit and then finished reading the letter.

"Well? No reaction? To that piece of shit?"

"There's no shit in this letter and that's what you hate about it,"
Giovanni told her. "All he says is you've got no humor about yourself
anymore and he's saying also that what you're turning out now is a
bunch of old repeats that no one requests anymore but that you keep
on repeating."

Now from his indolent attitude before the fireplace, he sprung up
quick as a cat to snatch seven other letters of rejection from Sabbatha's
writing table in an alcove.

Some of the letters were scarcely more than perfunctory though all
were penned or dictated by "dearest," "darling" or "beloved" someone
out of her professional past which had always been dangerously involved with her social past, due to the ingenuousness of her earlier
nature.

"Don't," she screamed at Giovanni as if threatened by gang rape.

"Listen, shut up and listen and I'll translate these 'no-thank-you-
Ma'ams' into what's back of the bullshit!"

(For a foreigner, Giovanni had picked up a startling fluency in the use
of rough American idiom, mostly through his fondness for waterfront
bars.)

She tried to climb up his body to get the dreadful letters from his
grasp but he gave her the knee and she slid off him, painfully to her.

"I will not hear them, I have never descended to . . . !"

(To what? In pursuit of what? Her moment of uncertainty and her wild glare into nothing gave him a cutting edge that he used with abandon.)

"Sabby, you'd descend to the asshole of a mole and imagine that you were rimming Apollo and you know it well as I know it!"

"*What, what, what, what, what?*"

(With each "what" she had crawled a pace toward the door, she was now scrambling toward it, almost.)

But all of her motions, now, were subject to arthritis, so she was still short of the door when she collapsed and rolled onto her back and cried out: "*Time!*"

"Yeh, yeh, time has fucked you, with its fickle finger, let's face it, Sabby!"

She managed to get the door open.

"I shall go out and stay out till you've drunk yourself into oblivion as usual, and then I shall make the—necessary arrangements . . ."

What these arrangements might be was a speculation lost in her dizzy flight from the cottage called "Sabbatha's Eyrie."

Sabbatha's Eyrie was one and a half stories of weathered shingles, all mottled white and gray as a sea gull's wings or as her own chestnut hair became when she neglected the beauty shop for a full season as she had done during these past few months of relentless work upon her new sonnet sequence. It stood, the Eyrie, upon the height of the highest and craggiest promontory on that section of New England seacoast. Among its appropriately lyrical assets was a pure narrow brook and it was to this brook that she now took flight, unconsciously hoping that its subdued murmurs of excitement would evoke voices from the past, the sort of excited whispers that she used to hear, for instance, when she would enter a certain little French restaurant in the Village, when Sabbatha was a pre-eminent figure in the literary world and the world of fashion as well.

Oh, yes, the pine wood through which she fled toward the brook was already full of voices, all in reference to her.

"Christ, I must be a little drunk," she admitted to herself as she staggered among those trees which she thought of sometimes as her "sylvan grove," and she was literally toppling from the support of one tree to that of another, and, oh, less than ten years ago, just after the importation of Giovanni from Italy, she had used to run like a nymph in her flowing white nightdress through these woods, crying back to him, "Catch me if you can!"

And of course he could but he didn't. In fact she would often find that he had returned to bed when she returned, winded, to Sabbatha's Eyrie. "Sleep, darling," she would whisper a little crossly and certainly not sincerely, for she would make sure that her wanton caresses interrupted his sleep. She particularly liked to gather his testicles in her hand and to squeeze them spasmodically.

"*Senta!*" he'd shout. "You are not milking a cow!"

"The moon is bone white at daybreak," she would whisper with her tongue in his ear, and often, after some such remark as that, she would scramble from bed to compose a sonnet beginning with such a line.

In a lecture at Vassar, or rather at the conclusion of her lecture when the students were invited to ask her questions, one young lady there had inquired impertinently if she didn't feel that there was too much erotic material in her sonnets.

"Whatever's included in life," she had shot back at the girl, "must be included in art, and if there is eroticism in my work, it is because my existence does not reject it!"

Her head was full of memory tonight, and effect of red wine.

"I must chill my veins in the spring," she advised herself. "I must go back to Giovanni chill and damp from the spring and have him dry me off with one of the big rough towels, and all things will be as they were . . ."

How were they, that was the question, but it was not a question to be entertained at this moment. Her erratic course through the pine woods had now brought her to the spring.

"I can still walk barefooted through cold water, over rough stones," she assured herself. Then she flung off her felt bedroom slippers and stepped into the rapid, murmurous current of the brook.

Tonight it was practically babbling those voices out of the past.

She heard excitedly amplified whispers such as she used to hear in her favorite little French restaurant in the Village before she'd imported Giovanni (and Sabbatha's Eyrie to keep him in), yes, quite a while before then, at least twenty years.

In those days she had always been escorted by a bevy of very young men, and she had marched into the restaurant, oh, yes, it was called *L'Escargot Fou*, ahead of her feverishly animated escorts, and at once, in those early days, a few moments of hush would descend upon "the mad snail," as she called it.

Then, as she was seated at her corner table, voices would become audible, exclaiming about her.

"That striking woman, who is she?"

"Christ, don't you know her? Sabbatha Veyne Duff-Collick?"

"I *thought* so, but wasn't quite sure! Are these young men all her *lovers?*"

"Yes, of course, she's the most profligate artist since Isadora Duncan."

"She does move like a dancer, she has a dancer's gestures, and what a distinguished profile with that long mane of chestnut hair."

And then they would talk about other matters which concerned themselves, but seated among her bevy of youths in a corner, she knew that they were all really talking so loudly in order that she could hear them, and she would smile indulgently to herself at their innocent folly.

But, oh, my God, there was that final visit to "the mad snail" when she had entered to find her usual table usurped by some very scrubby and bearded young men, not at all the sort that she went about with.

"Maître," she had said, "my table is occupied by strangers tonight. Would you please remove them for me?"

"Oh, madam," the maître replied, "that is the young poet Ginsberg with two others, they can't be moved, I'm afraid they'd make a scene if I asked them to give up the table. You see, they're very, very fashionable just now. They've been on the covers of several big magazines lately."

"Why, one of those obscene barbarians is seated in the very chair that has the bronze plate with my *name* engraved on it! Always reserved for *meeeee!*"

"Plate? Bronze? Engraved?" the maître repeated in a mock tone of incredulity. Then his face assumed a look of recollection and he said, "Oh, you must mean the chair that collapsed and couldn't be repaired, it did have an old piece of metal on the back, but it's gone to the junkyard now."

"You must be new here to speak to me in this insolent way."

"I've not been around as long as some of our patrons, but as they say about brooms, a new one sweeps clean, madam."

At this she had drawn herself up and thrown her head back so far that she seemed to be inspecting the ceiling.

"I wouldn't speak of cleanliness, I would avoid that subject in view of your new clientele! Come along, *mes amis!* When an eating place turns into a trough for swine, I . . ."

She didn't complete this statement for the group of poets who had confiscated her table burst into howls of derision: her young men shepherded her quickly onto the street.

"*Cochons!*" she screamed.

The streets of the Village spun brilliantly about her for a moment before everything went black. When she came to, she had only one young man with her: they were in a taxi, headed uptown. He was a very slight young man with great sorrowful eyes, and he carried a small beaded bag.

"Oh, Sabbatha," he whispered, "didn't God tell you that things turn out this way?"

"I have received no information from God except that I am alive and capable of decision. Tomorrow I am going to Paris and then to Venice and then to The Eternal City of Rome."

"Will you take me with you?"

She sighed and permitted her hand to fall into his lap. And there she made a discovery of less than minimal requirements for a long-term companion.

"My dear," she murmured, "how dreadful it must be for you."

He understood her meaning and after a moment or two he said to her: "I have some male friends of your age or thereabouts who have admired the size and color of my eyes."

"God help you, dear, in this world. God help your large eyes, these friends will gouge them out."

And they both began to cry quietly together with clasped hands.

At the dockside in Cherbourg, many cameras were focused on Sabbatha as she disembarked and the effect was exhilarating to her.

Apparently Europe was not yet aware of her declining prestige or it had more respect for work not favored by trivial fashion.

A journalist in Rome . . .

"How does it feel to be the most celebrated female poet since Sappho?"

"Of Sappho's work," she replied, looking into space, "there remain only fragments, such as . . ."

At the moment she couldn't think of any.

"Miss Duff-Collick, your work is sometimes compared to . . ."

"Oh, yes, I know whom you mean and, actually, I did rather like the one about some birds and beasts. How did it go? Something about entertaining no charitable hope. And it rhymed with *antelope*! . . . I've always liked wild animals in their natural habitats, not domestic ones or the pathetic creatures in zoos. I detest confinement, you know . . ."

"Your work in the sonnet form has naturally suggested to some critics the influence of Elizabeth Barrett Browning."

"My dear young man," she laughed. "My influence on Mrs. Browning must have been rather slight since she succumbed to consumption long before I was born."

This interview was taking place in a little *taverna* where the Via Margutta angles sharply into the Piazza di Spagna. There were three young journalists and there was also the young painter Giovanni. He had been in the *taverna* when she and the newspaper people entered and she had greeted him as if she knew him well the moment that she first saw him and had invited him to join the group at her table.

She sensed that her behavior was leading her into public embarrassment. She even suspected that she might be going a little crazy but the thought gave her no alarm: in fact, it exhilarated her as the flash bulbs had when she arrived in Europe.

She had arranged the seating at the table and placed Giovanni next to her.

"You've found some one you know?"

"Oh, yes, I'm sure we've known each other forever."

She decided to expand upon that typically histrionic remark.

"All of my first encounters with people are like that, as if I'd known and hated them forever or as if I'd known and loved them since before I was born."

The journalists exchanged inscrutable glances but she paid no heed.

She had a hand on Giovanni's arm and then on his knee and she made certain that the newspaper people observed this exhibition of poetic license or whatever it might be termed.

They all drank golden Frascati out of big carafes.

Going mad can have a certain elation to it if you don't fight it, if you just pull out all the stops, heedless of consequence.

Sabbatha knew this was happening to her and offered no resistance, with flash cameras popping in her face while pencils scribbled comments for press release, here in a Roman *taverna* so close to the house in which John Keats had written of love and death in lines which almost approached the intensity of her own.

For ten years she had been much out of the public eye and, phonetically, there is slight difference between the noun "decade" and the adjective "decayed," just an accent placed on the first syllable or the second.

Then came a devastatingly brutal question from the young journalist with the most innocent and deferential air.

"Does it disturb you much, Miss Duff-Collick, that your most celebrated poem was written while you were still at the female college of Bryn Mawr?"

The heavy carafe felt very light in her hand as she lifted it from the table and shattered it over the head of the young man who had stabbed her with that insufferable question.

By midnight she had proposed to Giovanni that he remain with her permanently.

He told her that he was a poor young student of painting whose survival depended upon the interest of an elderly patron. But, as Sabbatha guessed, this plaint was only a token of reluctance . . .

(In those days all the young and impoverished Romans dreamt of being spirited off to the States.)

At daybreak they engaged a horse-drawn vehicle, a fiacre with a hunchback driver.

She touched the driver's hump for luck which made him furious. He turned about and shouted in her face, "*Che vecchia strega, che stronza!*"

"What did he say? Something impertinent to me?"

"He called you a witch," said Giovanni, discreet enough that first night between them, not to translate the scatalogical portion of the old man's invective.

"I'll show him when we get to San Pietro!"

At Saint Peter's Square she had Giovanni direct the hunchback to drive about the twin fountains and when he hesitated to comply Sabbatha scrambled over the partition between passengers and driver and wrenched the reins from the driver's hands.

He leapt out of the carriage and started shouting, "*Polizia!*"

Sabbatha stood up like a Roman charioteer, tore her blouse open to expose her rather flat and pendulous breasts and drove the horses round and round the fountains till she was drenched in the winy spray and was almost restored to sobriety.

But this incident proved to be one touch of poetic license too much for public tolerance in The Eternal City.

The next morning it was reported scathingly in *Il Messagero* that a demented female tourist, with a much younger male companion of questionable morales, had made a *"figura bruta"* in the sacred square and that she would be well advised to indulge her inebriate fancies in some other province if not in a madhouse.

Once again, then, and for the last time in her European sojourn, she was confronted by cameras and reporters. It was when she came out of the lift at the Academy.

"About the scandal?" they asked her.

"All truth is a scandal," she informed them in ringing tones, "and all art is an indiscretion!"

With this outcry she had tossed her hair in their faces and lifted her arms in a gesture which she thought the cameras would interpret as an unfettered condition of spirit as strikingly as the camera of Genthe had captured for posterity the classic pose of Isadora Duncan among the columns of the Acropolis: but evidently there was a difference both in the subject and in the photographic craft or intention, for what appeared next day in the papers of Rome suggested nothing more nor less than the abandoned posturing of a middle-aged female, three or four sheets to the wind.

A day later she left Rome with Giovanni who recognized her manic condition quite clearly, now, but was adhered to the lady as a postage stamp to an incoherent postcard.

In the early days of film-making the copulation of lovers could only be suggested by some such device as cutting from a preliminary embrace to a bee hovering over the chalice of a lily: and there is probably a similar bit of artifice involved in bringing up so much of Sabbatha's past history through the murmurs of the spring that cascaded beneath her Eyrie.

In any case, those evocative murmurs of the spring were now invaded and quite overwhelmed by another sound, the starting of a motor which was that of Giovanni's sports car, the Triumph she'd given him on his thirty-fifth birthday that summer. It was roaring into motion.

At its first noise she had cried out, "Giovanni!" and had made a staggering rush to intercept the car in the drive winding down from her Eyrie, but of course wasn't quick enough to throw herself across the drive before the car had passed over the wooden bridge and was beyond interception: indeed, she wondered if, had she been able to throw herself in the car's way, he might not have driven it straight over her prostrate body, and gone on speeding away.

The sound of the motor receded and receded, now, until it faded under the *tristesse* of the brook, and Sabbatha and solitude had at last joined forces truly, if forces is the right word for it.

The first night that Sabbatha found herself unable to ascend the stairs to the bedroom in a reasonably vertical state, in other words as a biped, but had to mount them on all fours if she wished to sleep in bed, she assumed with some logic that she was entering upon a downstairs existence at Sabbatha's Eyrie. She realized that her curvature of the spine which now made it difficult to reach objects on a mantel or kitchen shelf without the precarious expedient of climbing onto a tabletop or a chair, articles of furniture that seemed to resent her efforts to climb on them as female animals not in heat resent the advances of the tumescent males of their species, it occurred to her that death in solitude was not an unlikely or remote prospect, and this reflection was entertained by the lady with mixed emotions.

Death in solitude, she remarked to herself, rolling her sea-green eyes from side to side in their sockets, set rather close together on either side of her almost too prominent nose.

Names of poets and poetesses who had died alone, completely alone or virtually alone, passed through her mind. It was a roll call of honor: it included such names as Thomas Chatterton who had hung himself alone in his garret to escape debtor's prison, it included the minor but not ungifted poetess Sara Teasdale who had cut her wrists in a bathtub, presumably behind a locked door without bath attendants, it included that eccentric spinster poetess, somewhere between minor and major, who had died alone in agony from a deliberate O.D. of some lysergic acid, and now it seemed to Sabbatha that death in solitude was the preordained fate of almost any self-respecting poet or poetess.

On hands and knees she had reached the telephone stand on the stair landing when this sad but uplifting conviction took hold of her.

She was just barely able to haul the phone off its stand and from a prostrate condition she put through a long-distance call to one of her once-young male escorts in Manhattan. He was still living there and was now employed as a society reporter for the leading newspaper. The call was put through with difficulty and through his answering service. It took her almost an hour and a great deal of shrieking and growling to track him down at the residence of the Fourth Duchess of Argyle, and when she finally had him on the wire, she could scarcely make her voice, strong as it remained, heard through the hysteria of supper guests of the Duchess, all high on grass or booze with rock music. The former young escort kept pretending to think, or did actually think, that he was receiving a crank call; she only succeeded in confirming her identity to him by reciting the sextet of a sonnet which he had once pronounced her most exquisite accomplishment of all.

"Oh, yes, then it *is* you, Sabbatha. How *goes* it?"

"My darling, I am preparing myself for death in complete solitude which is why I am calling to beg you to . . . *wait! I'm all choked up!* Preston, I know that important newspapers keep a file of obituaries of well-known persons, especially when the person's health is known to be failing. Now, Preston, this is dreadfully vain of me but I can't help but want to know what is going to be printed about me when I. . . . Do you understand, darling? And could you very, very privately obtain a copy of my obituary from these secret files called obits? Please, please I can't explain how or why it would matter so much to me, but somehow it does, it really and truly does, so for old time's sake, would you, could you, please, do this for me, dearest?"

"Sabbatha, you are breaking my heart," he said rather matter-of-factly. "Why just last month I saw a little squib for your new book of verse, *The Bride's Bouquet*, cute title. And now you want me to sneak your obit out of the files? My God, you've broken my rice bowl! I have to blow my mind with another joint, baby. Take care, *ciao, bambina!*"

He had hung up with a bang, but a few days later a letter arrived whose envelope bore the masthead of his newspaper.

Thus far this top-secret letter had remained unopened at the Eyrie but she knew precisely where it was, she'd put it under a box of Twining's Formosa Oolong tea bags in the breakfast nook.

It took considerable time and effort for her to retrieve it since the chair fell over several times before she could successfully mount it.

It also took her quite a while to get the obit into the living (or dying) room where she had intended to read it by firelight which she had somehow imagined might improve her reaction to its content.

But nothing could have assuaged her shock when she saw that the clipping was less than half a column in length and included no photograph of her and that it had even dared to omit one 'b' from Sabbatha and the hyphen between Duff and Collick.

Fuck them all! she decided. *Fuck them all, past, present and future!*

She flung the obit into the appropriately dying embers where it revived a slight and brief conflagration before going up in smoke—as human vanity must either side of—

The nocturnal *fiasco* of California *Chianti* served Sabbatha now as a measure of the hours before detested daylight crept between the locked shutters of her Eyrie. When the bottle was half empty it would be about midnight and when there were only two or three inches left in it, she knew that she might at any instant expect the crow of a distant cock to warn her that it was time to chug-a-lug the remaining vino and bury her face in the nest of cushions she'd hauled down from the sofa several months ago to provide her with pillow and mattress.

Beside this disordered bed before the fireplace were the implements of her trade, the notebooks and pencils, now that the arthritic condition of her joints had obliged her to give up the Underwood portable whose ribbon, anyway, had faded to a point where a typed page had become barely legible.

It is hardly fair to speak of notebooks and pencils as the implements of her trade, and yet that's how she thought of them: she had come to think of the composition of Elizabethan and Petrarchan sonnets as a trade in the sense that the trade of Jesus of Nazareth had been carpentry. Notebooks and pencils, hammers and nails: in the end, crucifixion, an honorable though God-awful painful way to get out of mortal existence.

Going out alone, prostrate before a dead fire, Father, why hast Thou?

The distant cock had crowed and she had stretched out a hand curved as a hook toward the nearly empty *fiasco* and had upset it so that the remnant of wine was spilt upon a cushion.

Quickly, with a famished "hah," she pressed her mouth to the purple pool and lapped it up with her tongue. "Hah," she said once more, and was about to bury her head in the moist pillow when into her mind flashed the final quatrain of what must have been an early lyric of hers since she couldn't remember its title nor the preceding lines of it.

She clutched at a pencil and made a trembling tight fist of her hand about that implement to scrawl into the nearest notebook this bit of verse that bore so clearly the stamp of her springtime vigor of expression.

> *In masks outrageous and austere*
> *The years go by in single file*
> *Yet none has merited my fear*
> *And none has quite escaped my smile.*

She waited and waited till the blue of daybreak slit through the shutters for the rest to come back to her: it would, and indeed it did, and the fact that she remembered the fact that it was a fragment of a poem by Miss Elinor Wylie was a fact that completely escaped her smile and almost merited her afternoon-long depression.

Curvature of the spine!

The physical being pointing itself remorsely back toward earth.

More and more bending itself back that way, as if the earth had flung a welcoming door wide open for its timorous guest.

Clearly things had not followed an ascending line at Sabbatha's Eyrie during her time of all but total seclusion. She had not heard from Giovanni, not at all directly, but last week a bank official in Bangor had informed her by mail that a young man of a foreign extraction had been forging checks on her name there. He claimed, said this official, to be her husband but admitted that they were now permanently separated: and there had been other complaints about him of a nature that the bank official preferred not to discuss with a lady. He did tell Sabbatha that the young man had been jailed several times and hospitalized also. Of course the bank was interested only in the matter of the forged checks. Did she wish to have him prosecuted? They understood that he was not actually her husband but a former employee, and, given her approval of such action, they could have him put away for at least a year, maybe more.

She got through to the bank by telephone and told them that the young man was not a former employee but her husband by common law.

How large were the checks, she inquired, and for what had the gifted but unbalanced young man been hospitalized, was it a serious condition or—

"Madam," said the official, "I doubt that a lady would care for specific information of this nature."

"All truth," Sabbatha told him, "is scandal. Why not?"

He may or may not have understood this epigrammatic comment on "truth" but it was obvious to him that her voice was deep in drink . . .

How to go on? You go on, in solitude, implements of the trade turned treacherous to you or you to them, cocks crowing thrice before daybreak, detestable as a jail-keeper to the condemned, the whole bit, on you go with it, don't you?

"Oh, my Lord, I don't believe I ordered my instant freeze-dried from Hollow Market and I've run completely out. Oh, my Lord, oh, *shit* . . ."

She said this aloud, not having heard the approach of a taxi from the village, the shutting of its door and the opening of the front door of the Eyrie behind her aching back.

"Sabbatha, that's the first time I ever heard you say shit."

It was the voice of Giovanni, or was she out of her senses?

She rolled over with a crunching sound in her pelvis and there above her stood—no, not Giovanni but the ghost of him, it seemed! He looked ethereal, but not poetically so, and his youthful appearance was gone.

"Oh, my Lord, is that really *you*, Giovanni?"

"Is that really *you*, Sabbatha?"

Very slowly, it must have taken a full minute, they came to accept the present realities of each other's condition without further speech between them.

When she spoke again she said to him: "I understand you have been ill and hospitalized since you left me?"

"Yes, fucked too much," he answered. "It's possible, you know, to get too much of a good thing sometimes."

Again the conversation between them stopped for close to a minute.

"I didn't understand what you said about your illness."

"I developed a fistula," he said.

"A what did you say you developed?"

He threw off his coat and crouched in front of her and repeated the word to her loudly, separating the syllables.

"I've never heard of that. Fist full of what did you say?

He grinned at her then.

"I didn't say fist full of nothing. I said a fistula which is a perforation of the mucous membrane that lines the rectum and I got it from being gang-banged in Bangor, ten cocks up my ass in one night and one of them a yard long. Now did you hear me, did you understand me that time?"

"I don't know medical terms, you know, dear," said Sabbatha. "I'm afraid I've finished the wine but there's some rum in the kitchen and some tea bags and why don't you take off those wet things and dry off in front of the fire."

"The fire's out," he told her.

"Oh, well, if it's burned out there's dry logs and pine cones under the shed. You fix your drink and undress and I'll crawl out for the wood."

She did start to crawl but he stopped her.

"Jesus, woman, have you turned into a snake?"

"Giovanni, I am the Serpent of the Nile," she replied. "And you are Anthony but our fleet has been defeated and scuttled in the harbor of Alexandria."

Apparently some of her old wry humor had returned.

She twisted her neck, which made a creaking noise, and cried out, "Charmine, fetch me the ass!"

After a moment she smiled sleepily and corrected herself: "I meant the asp, of course, dear."

June 1973 (Published 1973)

Completed

Although Miss Rosemary McCool was approaching the age of twenty she had yet to experience her first menstruation. This was surely a circumstance that might have given pause to her widowed mother's intention that season of presenting her daughter, an only child, to the society of Vicksburg, Mississippi, since presenting a girl to society amounts to publicly announcing that she is now eligible for union in marriage and the bearing of offspring.

This being the situation you might suspect the widow McCool of harboring a marked degree of duplicity or delusion in her nature, but such a suspicion, like many suspicions about genteel Southern matrons, would not be fair to the widow, for Rosemary's mother was so caught up in her multitude of social and civic and cultural activities throughout the southern Delta, all of which seemed important to her as the world itself and human life in the world, that it simply seemed to the widow that it was socially meet and proper for her daughter to make a debut and what, then, should deter it.

Of course, "Miss Sally" McCool could not be described as a very devoted and conscientious mother. In fact every time her eyes rested briefly on her daughter, she had to repress a look of trouble and disappointment, if not of personal aggrievement. Even for Miss Sally McCool it was impossible not to admit that Rosemary was an odd-looking girl, very pale and gangling and certainly not endowed with an aura of being much involved with a world of externals. She had the face, especially the eyes, of a frightened little girl, and her Aunt Ella, the widow's older sister, was the only person to whom Rosemary could speak in a voice much above a whisper. This vocal inhibition had naturally been a detriment to her in the Vicksburg high school, such a considerable detriment, in fact, that during her last year there the superintendent had called on the widow McCool and after a lot of effusive guff about her daughter's sweet and charming nature, had announced that Rosemary was simply not suited for the sort of schooling that the high school could give her and that it was his opinion that she should be transferred to a small private school which was called Mary, Help a Christian.

Miss Sally had stared at him open mouthed for a minute without producing a sound except a slight gasp.

He had returned the stare without flinching and had interrupted the silence with a sympathetic remark.

"I know that this suggestion must come to you as a bit of a shock, Miss Sally, but I can assure you personally that this precious young girl of yours is just not adjusting at all to her teachers and schoolmates at Vicksburg High. I'm sorry, Miss Sally, but nobody at the high school knows what to make of the child and I would be very dishonest if I didn't report this to you, privately, here in your house, and suggest Mary, Help a Christian as the best if not only solution I can think of."

The discussion continued a good deal further than that but it resulted exactly as the Vicksburg High superintendent had intended it should and Rosemary was transferred almost at once to Mary, Help a Christian. However, even there, with teachers trained and accustomed to dealing with problem students, Rosemary had shown no improvement in adjustment. While many of the students were irrepressibly outspoken, Rosemary still could not be asked a question by a teacher but had to be graded entirely upon her written work. Of course some of the teachers ignored this vocal inhibition and would sometimes ask her a question. On these awful occasions Rosemary would crouch low in her seat, breathe noisily and raise a trembling hand to her lips as if to indicate that she was a mute. Her written work was not much help in the matter. Her essays were childishly written, her spelling was atrocious, and her handwriting barely legible due to a nervous tremor of her fingers. A condition like this ought to have met with some sympathy but there was something about Rosemary that drew no sympathy toward her, neither among her elders, nor those of her own generation or younger. Not only did she fail to make any friends, she barely made any acquaintances. She seemed determined and destined to slip through the world as an all but unseen and unheard being.

This is harking back half a year, but it is too pertinent to her history to be excluded. Once in her English class at Mary, Help a Christian, she submitted a long, laborious and illegible essay on the assigned subject "My Purpose in Life." This essay was rejected by the English teacher, it was returned to Rosemary with a note that demanded she condense it to a few sentences, write it in print, and adhere precisely to the assigned subject. Miss Rosemary did exactly that. In very large printed letters she wrote not just a few sentences but one sentence only, which sentence was shakily printed out as follows: "I HAVE NO PURPOSE IN LIFE EXCEP COMPLETE IT QUIK AS POSIBLE FOR ALL CON-SERNED IF ANY BESIDE MY ANT ELLA."

Reading this one-sentence essay on Rosemary's purpose in life, the English teacher marked it A plus and added the marginal question: "Who is your 'Ant' Ella?"

Now about Rosemary's sexual malfunction, her failure to menstru-ate as she neared twenty and her presentation to society in the Grand Hotel ballroom of Vicksburg, this was a considerable peculiarity but it remained a thing that neither Miss Sally nor her daughter had ever discussed. Miss Sally was a Southern lady of the sort that considered such matters outside the pale of discussion, even between a mother and a daughter who was her only child, and so she sailed right ahead with her plans for the girl's presentation to society.

The occasion came off, in the sense that it occurred, but it was not only a pathetic affair but a distinctly bizarre one. It was attended mostly by Miss Sally's middle-aged club-women associates and they attended it as if it were a spectator sport.

Whispering on the sidelines, they said such things as this:

"Imagine bringing out a girl like that one!"

"I have never known a girl more suited for staying in!"

Of course, there was a cluster of younger folks in the ballroom but most of them suggested rare species of birds.

The local society editor was there and her comment wasn't whis-pered.

"I don't know how on earth I am going to write this thing up."

This "thing" in the hotel ballroom didn't last very long: it was cut short by an encounter between Rosemary and a skinny young man of whom it was rumored that he suffered from a physiological deficiency that was somewhat analogous to hers. He was called Pip or Pippin, as a nickname, and his rumored deficiency was that his testes had never descended and that this was the reason he spoke in such a high, thin voice and had never shaved in his twenty-two years.

But Pippin was a young man as animated as Rosemary was reserved, and when the colored band struck up their opening number, which was "Beale Street Blues," he rushed over to Rosemary as if shot out of a cannon, shrieking "May I have the pleasure?" and before she had a chance to deny him the pleasure, he clutched her about the waist and attempted violently to move the girl onto the dance floor.

"*Let! Me! Go!*" she screamed.

It was a preposterous incident to occur at a debut party, and the party began to break up at once.

Rosemary was silently furious with her mother for having inflicted this embarrassment on her and had gone to her Aunt Ella's house with no intention of returning home ever.

Aunt Ella had always provided Rosemary with a retreat in times of crisis. She was Miss Sally's much older sister and she called Rosemary "dear child." She occupied a little frame house on the outskirts of town, and was attended by a Negro woman whose voice was soft as a dove's. At Aunt Ella's everything was soft, the lights, the beds, the voices: Aunt Ella had no doorbell and no telephone, she'd had them removed long ago from her weathered blue-shuttered frame residence as abscessed teeth are removed to avoid a poisoning of the system. She also received no publications of any kind, not even the town newspaper, her excuse being that she didn't wish to be informed of changes in the world since she suspected that there was nothing good in them. The shutters were kept almost completely closed day and night and although the house had once been wired for electric current, Miss Ella had permitted all the light bulbs except the one in the kitchen to burn out and had never replaced them since she preferred the light of oil lamps and candles. Receiving no news of births, marriages or deaths, she would refer to middle-aged matrons and grandmothers by their maiden names and she would speak of the dead as if they were still living, which she usually supposed them to be. Her connection with the world was elderly black Susie who did all her marketing for her, and if Susie received any reports of goings on abroad, she was wise enough to maintain a silence about them in Aunt Ella's presence.

"Child, Rosemary, whenever you're tired of that idiotic social business at Sister's, just pack a bag and move out here with old Susie and me. The whole upstairs is vacant. I can't climb steps any more but Susie can get it ready whenever you want it and there's also your Grandfather Cornelius Dunphy's comfortable little room which he occupied down here when he couldn't climb steps any more and, you know, Rosemary, dear child, it's been fifty years since I've received a postcard from him at that veteran's hospital in Jackson so I have a suspicion that since he was over sixty when he went there, he may be resting now with Grandmother on Cedar Hill. Your mother may know about that if she knows about anything but pieces of local gossip not fit for a lady to know . . ."

Rosemary had heard variations of this soft monotone, so much like the sound a moth makes against a screen at dusk, so repeatedly that she could whisper it to herself like a memorized psalm, and there were times when it was seductive to her . . .

There is much to be said for the exclusion of violent sound from the world. Aunt Ella's house was not far from the airport but Aunt Ella did not seem to know about the airport and when she heard a plane fly over she would call out softly, "Susie, fasten the shutters tight, there's going to be a thunder shower, I reckon."

"Yais, Miss Ella, I'll do that, don't you worry."

(But of course she didn't and Miss Ella may well have known that she didn't, since once, in Rosemary's presence, she had given a little wink right after this warning about the approach of a thunder shower.)

Once a week, Sunday nights, Rosemary had supper at Aunt Ella's. There was not much variation on these Sunday evening suppers, there would always be boiled chicken with dumplings, cooked till the chicken meat was falling off the bones in deference to Aunt Ella's chronic gastritis and badly fitted dentures, a bowl full of turnip greens seasoned with salt pork, sticks of lightly toasted corn pone, and either blancmange for dessert or floating island, all of it soft and monotonous as Aunt Ella's talk. The table linen and silver were of lovely quality and Aunt Ella's talk was nearly always about the goodness of The Holy Mother and discrepancies which she had noted in the Scriptures according to the Apostles.

One Sunday evening supper Rosemary had brought up a concern of her own. It had to do with a comic valentine she had received which addressed her as "Miss Priss."

"Oh, dear child," Aunt Ella had interrupted, raising a hand as if to dismiss an intruder, "some people do such things, why, once your Grandfather Cornelius Dunphy, drinking wine at supper, raised his glass to me and said, 'Here's to your everlasting virginity, old Miss, if you know what I mean,' and, well, I knew what he meant, you'd be surprised how much I have managed to know in the way of unwelcome as well as welcome knowledge in the course of my seventy-five or six years on this evil planet, so I simply bowed to him slightly and raised my glass of ice water and said, 'Why, thank you, Sir, I have every reason to hope that my maiden state will continue to defy whatever conspiracy may be offered against it,' and I must say that gave him quite a good, long laugh. Oh, dear, it was just a week later that he left the house for that Veterans' Place in Jackson from which he never returned and has sent me no written message. Oh, I do trust that he has mended his ways, that is, if he isn't now resting on Cedar Hill with your saintly Grandmother, and now, dear child, if you will push my wheel-chair into the parlor, we'll allow Susie to clear the supper dishes and tidy up the kitchen."

Sometimes out of these soft monotones at Aunt Ella's there would emerge a note of philosophy that was far from superficial.

"Now, dear child," she'd once said, "the more that the world outside is excluded, the more the interior world has space in which to increase. Some spinsters enter convents to find this out, but I regard my house as a place of devotion to all that I hold dear, and every evening, soon as I see blackness through the shutters and take my little tablet of morphine, I have Susie set a rocking chair by the bedside and I want you to know that Our Lady has never failed to enter the bedroom almost immediately after Susie goes out. She comes in and She sits down in Her rocker as if it were Her throne in Heaven, and She turns to me and smiles at me so sweetly, lifting her right hand in benediction, that I close my eyes on tears of indescribable peace and happiness, no matter what pains afflict me, and then I drift into sleep. She never leaves till I do . . ."

Soon after Rosemary's reluctant return to her mother's house, she experienced her first menstrual period. When she suddenly found her bed sheets stained with this initial sign of fertility, she had run sobbing out of the house, all the way to Aunt Ella's on foot, through alleys mostly, until she had reached the outskirts of town, and she had arrived before Aunt Ella had slept off her morphine. She had run into Aunt Ella's bedroom and collapsed into the chair reserved for Our Lady's nocturnal visits and had cried out to Aunt Ella, "Oh, Aunt Ella, I'm bleeding!"

"Child, get out of Our Lady's chair," was Aunt Ella's drugged response to this outcry.

Black Susie was now looming in the doorway.

"Miss Ella, the child says she's bleeding."

Miss Ella rose up slowly on her mound of pillows as if reluctantly emerging from a protective state.

"Is she out of Our Lady's chair, Susie?"

"Yes, Ma'am, she's out of the chair and leaning against the wall and shaking all over."

"Well, now, what's wrong with her now?"

"Aunt Ella, I'm bleeding to death!"

"What did she say, Susie? Her voice is so different I can't tell what she's saying."

"She says she's bleeding to death."

"I don't see any cut on her."

"It's not on my face, it's—!"

"Where are you bleeding from, child?"

Rosemary felt as she had felt in a classroom at Mary, Help a Christian when she was asked a question that demanded a spoken answer and she couldn't give one, and so she resorted to gestures, she covered her eyes with one hand, then slowly and tremulously lowered the other hand to her groin.

Miss Ella was now rising out of her opiate cloud.

"Oh, there, she means there. Is this for the first time, child?"

Rosemary nodded her head several desperate times.

"What did she say, Susie?"

"She nodded her head, Miss Ella. I reckon she means she never had it before."

"How old are you, child?" asked Aunt Ella.

Susie answered for her: "She's about twenty, Miss Ella."

"Yes, well, peculiar. Isn't it like my fool sister never to have warned her of the curse which usually afflicts a female person five or six years before twenty."

"We know Miss Sally," said Susie, in her dove-soft voice.

"Yes, we know her too well. I think she gave this child a debut party on the roof of a hotel, which upset her like this, I think you told me so, Susie."

"No, Miss Ella, not me, I never tell you nothing to make you worry."

"Then I reckon Our Lady must have told me, but what I want you to do is draw a warm bath for her while I explain the curse to her and then I want you to go to a store that has that package of gauze that is used to cope with it."

"Don't worry, I will, Miss Ella."

When Susie had left the bedroom, Aunt Ella drew a long breath.

"Dear child, this thing, the curse, without it the world would not continue and personally I think that would be a blessing instead of a curse. But we can discuss that later. What you do now is go and take a warm bath while Susie fetches the gauze, the, the—gauze . . ."

The morphine drew her comfortably back into sleep and, hearing the water running in the bathroom, gently, soothingly, slowly, Rosemary moved that way.

When Susie returned with the gauze pad, she helped Rosemary to secure it, performing this help so discreetly that Rosemary didn't suffer too much embarrassment from it. Then she led Rosemary into that downstairs bedroom once occupied by Cornelius Dunphy. There was lovely fresh linen on the four-poster and four large snowy pillows. But what Rosemary most noticed in the room was that a rocker had been set beside the bed, in just the position, at the same angle, of the rocker in Aunt Ella's bedroom, the one reserved for the nightly visits of Our Lady.

Susie closed the shutters more firmly.

"Now, child, get into bed and I'll be back in a minute with a glass of warm milk and one of your Aunt Ella's tablets."

And it was not until Susie's departing footsteps faded from hearing that Rosemary knew what had happened to her. Aunt Ella had taken her captive. For a moment she thought of resisting. Then one of those jet planes flew over the house and when Susie came back with the milk and the tablet, Rosemary said: "A thunderstorm is coming."

"Yes, child, but don't you worry about it, it'll pass over soon, it's already passing over. Now wash down your tablet with this warm milk and don't be surprised if that Lady who visits your Aunt comes in here to set a while with you in this rocker your Aunt Ella had me put by the bed."

She tucked Rosemary into the bed and padded to the door very quietly. As she opened it she smiled at the captive maiden and said, "Miss Ella will expect you to stay for supper when you wake up, and, honey, I don't think she'd mind you staying on here for good."

November 1973 (Published 1974)

Das Wasser Ist Kalt

Seated opposite her in the second-class compartment of the *Rapido* from Rome to Naples was a youngish American woman who kept exchanging looks with Barbara which were obviously relevant to the two young Italian officers between whose muscular thighs the woman was tightly sandwiched. Barbara knew that this female compatriot was intending to start a conversation with her and despite her loneliness, Barbara wanted to avoid it. On the other hand, she would have liked very much to have tried out her bits of Italian with the young officers, and so she pretended not to observe the woman's glances and allowed her eyes to encounter the officers' as often as she could without being downright flirtatious about it.

The American woman across from Barbara was now speaking in a disagreeably shrill, Midwestern voice:

"These two soldiers know each other, they came in here talking together, and yet one of them sat down on one side of me and the other sat down on the other side of me and as you can see—"

"I beg your pardon," said Barbara, "but these young men are not soldiers but officers and I think it's a mistake to assume that they don't understand any English."

"I just hope they do!" snapped the Midwestern lady.

"Why?" enquired Barbara.

"Don't you see how I'm being squeezed between them, why it's simply outrageous, each of them is pressing a knee against me. Oh, I should have known it was a mistake to go on ahead of my husband to Naples. You see, he was expecting a phone call there from a partner in his real-estate firm in Topeka and has no trust at all in phone calls being transferred to—"

"Oh, what a lovely landscape!" exclaimed Barbara to shut the woman up.

"Hmpf," was the woman's response, and there ensued a suspension of conversation between them for which Barbara was grateful.

The Italian officers exchanged slight laughing sounds, just barely audible. Then one of them leaned across the woman between them and offered the other officer a cigarette; in doing so, he permitted the motion of the *Rapido* to sway his shoulder against the Topeka woman's tight-bra'd bosom.

"Don't you dare!" shrilled the woman.

Still leaning against her, the officer looked into her face with an almost comical air of surprise.

The woman gave him a definite shove.

Then he said, "*Scusa, scusa, Signora,*" but with a smile that Barbara had to concede was fairly impertinent, since it was both sensual and mocking.

"I think," said Madam Topeka, "that I will call the conductor!"

"Aren't you taking it a bit too seriously?" Barbara said to the furious matron.

"Not a bit, not a bit, I'm sick of it, I get it all the time in this country."

"Count your blessings," thought Barbara, and to her astonishment she found that she had spoken this thought aloud.

"Well!"

"Yes?"

"Perhaps it would please *you* to be seated between them."

"Actually, yes, it would."

At this point Barbara removed from her purse a little notebook which served her as a travel journal and made a penciled notation in it.

"I am going mad."

It was only four words, the notation, but it took her a while to write it and to consider its truth. When she closed the notebook, the compatriot woman had extricated herself from her seat between the two officers and taken a position in the corridor, and one of the young officers had risen and was leaning out of the open window of the compartment with a beatific smile as if the sunset view had totally removed him from any carnal connection with things on earth.

The other young officer was smiling at Barbara. One of his hands had dropped between his thighs. It was not displeasing to her, the way the large fingers of the hand, big-knuckled and hairless, occasionally curved inward to touch his groin very lightly.

Am I really going mad? she thought to herself, which is the only way to think on such a subject.

The officer looking out the window now turned from the sunset to face her.

"*Lei è sola, Signorina?*"

"Ah, *si, sola. Io sono sola per questo—*"

(She started to say "*momento*" but stopped just short, substituting a smile for the word.)

"English?"

"No, I'm American, from Georgia."

"Georgia is?"

"Yes, it definitely is. Otherwise it escapes definition."

"*Parla italiano?*" he enquired, looking puzzled.

"*Un poco, un pochino!*" she answered brightly, lifting a little English-Italian phrase book from beside her.

"Oh, you study."

"Yes."

"*Dove vai?*"

"Does that mean where am I going?"

"Yes, where?"

"I am going to Naples for the night and leaving tomorrow for Positano where I hope to stay for the rest of the summer."

The officer seemed to understand most of the statement.

"Positano, *bello.*"

"Yes, I've heard it's lovely with wonderful swimming."

"You like swim?"

She reverted to Italian, saying, "*Si, mi piace molto.*"

"Water cold, *ancora.*"

She was about to say that she liked cold water, that she found it stimulating, but the *Rapido* emitted a very loud whistle and then made a violent jolting motion, and Barbara cried out as the jolt of the train shot a dreadful pain up her spine.

Solicitously, the officer touched her shoulder.

"Nothing, nothing," she whispered, and surreptitiously took a codeine tablet . . .

She was not quite certain whether it was two or three days later that she was seated at a small table, preparing to write some postcards that bore scenes of Positano and the Amalfi Drive. This haziness about time would be a troubling matter if she allowed herself to consider it. She did have the option of attributing it to the sedative tablets that she had kept herself under since that shocking return of her spinal affliction on the train to Naples.

This morning had brought the first relief without tablets. Of course she couldn't be confident that the relief would last long, but that was another matter that it was better not to consider. And so she started her postcards.

"From my breakfast balcony I look down upon a veritable sea of bougainvillea."

She read that over before continuing the message and she decided that it sounded a bit too prettily spinsterish: it might be what the heroine of an early E. M. Forster novel would put on a postcard from Italy, and she was not like that, at least she hoped that she wasn't. Still, she had only half a dozen cards and the pictorial side of this one was too good to waste: it was a picture of a medium-sized dog of no specific breed, seated with its jaws hanging open on the verge of a sea cliff along the Amalfi Drive and beneath the dog was a caption that said *Il Cane Incantato Della Divina Costiera*, which meant "The dog enchanted by the divine coast." What made it so funny was that the dog had a look of shocked stupefaction, more as if it were staring into the pit of hell than at anything divinely enchanting. Well, it would do for Miss Frelich, she'd miss the humor of it but she would not be at all put off by the reference to the "veritable sea of bougainvillea" observed from the breakfast balcony.

Doggedly she went on with the postcard message.

"I am not sure whether I have been enjoying 'Il Dolce Farniente' for two days or three in this charming little *pensione* close to the beach. The continual murmur of the sea is working a miracle on my insomnia. I slept three hours last night, which is almost record-breaking for this difficult past year."

She heard a knock at the bedroom door, so at this point she hastily scribbled, "affectionate regards, Barbara." And then she drew her dressing robe more decorously about her thin breasts and called out, "*Avanti.*"

The young man, hardly more than a boy, who had delivered the breakfast tray had now returned to remove it. She observed something that was a bit too much. The fly of his trousers was almost half unzipped.

"*Prego,*" she said coldly when he asked permission to remove the tray. Then, as he leaned over to lift the tray, she made the still more disturbing discovery that the fly of the trousers was not unzipped at all, that the momentarily exposed metal had merely caught the light in a way which had given her that mistaken impression. And it was alarming that the gleam of a metal zipper should have caused her to think it unzipped. Why, my Lord, it was a betrayal of latent sexuality of an almost hysterical nature. She felt she had to say something to the young waiter to compensate for the coldness of the *"Prego"* with which she'd received him.

"Che bella giornata!" she exclaimed with a flurry of fingers among the gauzy material which she had drawn closer about her breasts.

"Un po' di sirocco ancora," he answered.

"Po de what?" she enquired.

"Sirocco, il vento d'africa."

"Oh, *d'africa, sirocco, sì, sì!"*

He lingered with the tray between them.

"Il vento d'africa porta sabbia della Sahara."

"De what? Oh, Sahara!"

He rubbed thumb and middle finger tight together.

"Molto fin e rossa!"

"Sì, sì, fine red sand from the Sahara is blown in by the sirocco!"

"Tutto è coperto con questa sabbia rossa."

Then he jerked his head with a grin that exposed perfect young teeth between rose lips set in the smooth olive of his skin. And as he turned to move away, she felt, and it made her shudder with a reaction that she'd rather not classify at the moment, the slight brush of his hips against her shoulder, oh, my Lord, so intimate, so warm, or did she imagine that soft brushing warmth of him, too? A vision of him unclothed sprang into her mind. It lingered, despite her shamed resistance, till he'd left the room, and she recalled how she'd unwillingly noticed in Rome how the young men strolling about had so often a hand thrust in a pocket and seemed to be feeling their privates, unconsciously masturbating a little as they moved in pairs across the piazza on which her *pensione* had been located. And then her recollection went back further, way back to nine summers ago when she had spent a week in Manhattan and visited each morning the big Fifth Avenue library, assembling further material on the French poets Rimbaud, Verlaine and Baudelaire whose works had been the subject of her Master's thesis. It had been a successful thesis although Miss Lily had gossiped about her interest in decadent French poets instead of wholesome American poets of the Southern states. However, this was not what her recollection of the stay in Manhattan was centered upon but on a thoroughly non-scholastic thing, an experience in a subway she'd taken at Columbus Circle intending to visit the Battery, where she had hoped to see the aquarium and the Statue of Liberty. On the subway she had sat in a car that was sparsely occupied and which had continued to empty as it neared the Battery till finally there was no one in it but a drugged-looking young man of Latin appearance. He had gotten up as if about to get off in the lower Village, but when the train pulled out of the stop he had lurched over to her bench, breathed in her face, examining it with his unfocused eyes as if searching for something of value which he'd lost, and then he had leaned further toward her and inserted his hot hand under her skirt and for some reason she had not cried out as he worked his fingers under her panties and had started manipulating her vagina. This action had paralyzed her. She had remained in a slightly slouched position through several stops of the subway train while the manipulating young fingers slowly inserted themselves, worked themselves into her spasmodically constricting and opening uterus, massaging the passage to moistness and finally to an ecstasy of wet burning.

It was he who got off the subway train first, winking at her and sniffing his fingers as he stumbled to the dividing doors of the car and saying to her, "Baby, I'm going to lick your cum off my fingers, man, I like the smell of it, so long, Babe."

Then he was out and the train was moving again. She had then, finally, given a little cry of protest . . .

Never, never before had nearly such a shameful experience happened to her. It must have been the result of that research into the lives of those decadent poets, they must have possessed her senses and debauched them.

Still immobilized, she'd stayed slouched on the bench till a conductor passed through the car, sleepily calling out, "Change here for Coney Island."

"Coney Island, I planned to take that in but not in the evening, alone," she remarked to herself as she staggered up and called to the conductor, "How can I get back to Columbus Circle, I'm a stranger in town!"

Well, the genial and personable waiter still in his flower of adolescence had quit the room while she was engaged in mentally divesting him of his securely zipped trousers and then she'd returned to that subway trip nine summers past and she was still seated on her breakfast balcony. She had no impulse at all to get up now and lock the door of her bedroom, in fact she almost considered calling room service again to ask for another *caffe-latte con spuma d'arancia*. And why not, indeed? She needed a bit more coffee to get herself going today. "Don't think about it, just do it" was excellent self-advice. She picked up the bedside phone. After a good deal of buzzing, clicking and clacking an impatient voice said, "*Pronto?*" It was a female voice, not only impatient but supercilious-sounding. She'd noticed that girl on the switchboard when she checked in the *pensione* and hadn't liked the look of her, oh, she was pretty all right in her commonplace fashion and would doubtless be acceptable as a sort of second-string bunny at those Playboy clubs she'd heard of, but her glance, lifting from a book of colored comics, had been disparaging when Barbara, addressing the desk clerk, had asked for a *"singolo con bagno sul mare"* and the girl had giggled when the impertinent clerk had replied in English, "We don't have rooms on the sea."

"Of course I meant facing the sea, not floating on it," she had retorted crisply. "I wired from Rome for a room that would face the sea."

"Rooms on the sea are occupied. You will have to look at the mountains."

The switchboard girl had giggled again and lifted her colored comics.

"Oh, I did hope to escape comic books when I left the States. My students in junior college brought them into the classroom, till prohibited strictly."

The clerk's comprehension of English hadn't seemed to encompass remarks not related to occupied or vacant rooms facing the mountains or sea and the girl on the switchboard was back into comics too deeply to be distracted even by the insistent buzz of—

"*Pronto!*"

The girl's voice was downright insolent, now, and Barbara had to swallow before she could ask for room service.

"*Io voglio—caffe-latte—con spuma d'arancia, per—favore!*"

She had deliberately separated the words, acquired from her phrase book, as if she were addressing a moron, which the girl probably was.

The probable moron muttered something quite unintelligible but very harsh in sound.

Barbara slammed down the phone receiver and turned to face the mirror over the bureau.

Oh, my Lord, she was unfastening the two top buttons of her diaphanous dressing gown and, Oh, my Holy Saviour, she was bending painfully to slip down and step out of her support hose, why, she would be as nearly nude to the young waiter's eyes, when he returned with the second breakfast tray, as Isadora Duncan was said to have been when posing for Genthe among the columns of the Acropolis.

"Hah! What of it? I am a normal woman aside from my afflictions and my desire is a totally natural thing!"

After a wait of twenty minutes there was the knock at the door.

"Avanti, per favore."

And into the room entered not the enchanting youth but a stout man of middle years in a grease-stained apron.

His eyes, as greasy as his apron, took mocking but lascivious account of her diaphanous dressing gown.

"Where is the young man?" she blurted out before she could stop herself.

"Non capito," said Mr. Grease as he rolled his eyes toward the bed.

She pointed furiously toward the balcony and snatched a rumpled sheet off the bed to protect her from his kitchen gaze . . .

Now she was looking out not at the "veritable sea of bougainvillea," which made her seasick, but at the menacing profile of the mountains.

They seemed to have a personal attitude toward her, less favorable than the switchboard girl's and the desk clerk's.

She snatched toward her another postcard.

"I can't begin to tell you what a marvelous improvement I feel on this divine coast, the early morning pale blue of the water almost exactly matches the early morning pale blue of the mountains—"

She'd meant to say of the sea, but never mind, postcards aren't literature.

"How can I ever thank you for—"

Shit!

Did she say that very Mitford "U" word and if she hadn't, who had? She shoved the postcard away.

"How embarrassing!" she said softly, aloud, and she meant the collection of money her colleagues at the junior college had made to give her this trip abroad. Embarrassing but providential it was, since she had used up all her sick leave, taking off the fall semester, all of it, at the Atlanta Clinic and then resting at Cousin Ida's.

She was obliged now to assure them that their munificence had been justified: must report to them nothing of her declining vigor and the

increasing complaint in her knee joints when she mounted and descended the many steps in this village between extinct volcanos and
clear, cold sea.

It was still much too early to begin the painful descent from hotel to
beach for a therapeutic dip before lunch. So what to do? She had no
inclination, now, to continue writing postcards, what she felt like was
retreating to bed agian and studying her phrase book.

Getting up, she noticed that she moved more freely with hardly any
premonitory twinges in her knee joints.

"You sweet, pretty thing, you, have a wonderful time!"

Who'd said that at the farewell, the bon voyage party?

Oh, yes, naturally Daisy, and the others had nodded brightly, embraced her and bestowed kisses on her blushing cheeks.

Now where was the phrase book? Oh. On the natural place for it to
be, on the little bedside table.

How good to lie down again! Would it be good to get up?

No, it wasn't, very, but two hours later she forced herself out of bed
and prepared to make her solitary appearance on the holiday-crowded
beach.

As she had arrived only a day or two before, her clothes were still a
bit creased from the Val-pac which had been presented to her at the
going-away party given her by the faculty of Georgia Junior College.
The piece of luggage was the most prominent single gift in the shower,
that is, aside from the cash endowment, and it had been presented to
her by the head of the English department, the one Ph.D. on the junior
college faculty, a gentleman in his early fifties with the impressive
name of Dr. Horace Leigh Fisher, a collateral cousin of hers on the
maternal side of her family. It had obviously not been newly purchased:
in fact, that spiteful Miss Lily had whispered to her, "The doctor's wife
told me he was giving you his own Val-pac and buying himself a new
one. Now isn't that precious of him. So much more personal, huh?"

Of course Barbara knew how to hold her own with Miss Lily and she
had smiled sweetly at the spiteful prune and whispered back, "*C'est en
famille tu sais!*"—Miss Lily taught French and resented the use of that
language by other faculty members, as though she had established a
proprietorship on the tongue because she taught it.

Well, Barbara picked out a pink frock, a sort of watermelon pink with
dainty white cuffs and a Peter Pan collar, and hung it in the bathroom
and turned on the hot water to steam out the creases while she
completed her toilette. Since this would be her first appearance on the

beach, it was momentous. She placed various beach things in an embroidered reticule that dated back fifty years, a gift from old Cousin Ida. In it she put her suntan lotion, her espadrilles, her reading glasses and a novella by Muriel Spark. There was something sad about this little colleciton: it spelled out "solitude" but then what didn't these days, and at this reflection, she began to apply a decorous bit of makeup to her face. To each of her high cheekbones she applied an almost imperceptible dab of pale rouge, to her lips she applied first a natural lipstick, then rubbed it off and with a sort of defiant vehemence put on the tango red. That outrageous touch removed whatever was decorous from the preparations and she snatched up the little container of false eyelashes that were, God knows, intended only for after-dark occasions. Oh, the hell with it, she thought, and with trembling fingers she put them on. They were only medium length and they did set off her best feature, which was her eyes, rather large and clear and innocent-looking.

Innocent-looking? Well there are several interpretations of the word "innocent." An innocent look could be a guileful look, one that pretended to represent an ingenuousness of nature that didn't quite exist. Oh, yes, she could remember when that innocent look had been a genuine thing, and it lingered on and on, a perennial nonstop thing, as useful now as ever, despite a touch of dissimulation in it at times.

Oh, Lord, the watermelon pink! She rushed from the dressing table to the bathroom door and when she threw it open she was nearly bowled over by the outpouring of steam. Holding a hand to nose and mouth, she fumbled for the frock on the wire hanger and fled with it back to the bedroom and found that it was wet to the point that it would cling to her body if she wore it.

Well, why not, let it cling! A phrase came into her mind which she'd heard the boys and girls use at the junior college, "Let it all hang out!"

After all, when she'd put on the tango red instead of the natural lipstick, there was hardly any point in retreating to anything like decorum . . .

Her knee joints ached as she passed with a soulful expression toward a row of cabanas, but she allowed nothing in her sinuous walk to betray the discomfort of it.

She had learned the present tense of "I wish."

To the man in charge of the cabanas she said slowly and carefully, "*Io voglio una cabana, prego!*"

His answer threw her off.

"Tutte sono occupate oggi."

She guessed that *"occupate"* meant occupied but the rest of the answer wasn't clear, and so she continued to wait and to smile. At last he smiled back and said:

"Forse c'è una, aspet'."

He rushed away and in a few moments returned saying, this time in pidgin English, "I find one for Signorina, number feefty!"

He made a gesture that meant for her to follow and she nodded brightly and followed. To her bafflement this cabana number fifty was placed between numbers sixteen and eighteen and, seeing her puzzled look, the cabana man said, "In Italy seventeen bad luck so we call this feefty."

"Ah," she murmured as he opened the door of the little cabana for her.

Ridiculous, she thought as she entered the dim cubicle, meaning her reluctance to occupy anything thought unlucky. Then she remembered that in America the thirteenth floor of a hotel was sometimes counted as the fourteenth although it was directly above the twelfth, so she latched the door of the cabana and changed into a swimsuit that had a bare midriff and was pale blue to match her eyes, a gift from the notorious teacher of physics who, it was rumored, had enjoyed sexual relations with nearly a dozen of the younger female faculty members but despite this scandal, retained his post because he had, for political reasons, offered himself now and then to Dr. Boxer's wife, a rather plump matron pushing forty behind her, and Dr. Boxer was President of the junior college in Macon and completely under the dominance of his wife.

Now, then, she was ready, she guessed, and out she went into the noonday glare of the Divina Costiera with which that dog on the postcard had been so enchanted.

She rented a beach chair with umbrella in the first row facing the sea but she didn't sit down, she pulled on her florally decorated swim cap and waded into the smooth, clear water with an alacrity that disguised her painful joints.

"Ouuu!" she cried aloud, for the sea felt almost icy.

At the same moment she lost her balance and would have fallen clumsily into the water if someone hadn't caught hold of her by the elbow.

"Ahhh!" she exclaimed as she faced him. Of course the exclamation was involuntary but it was well justified by her rescuer's appearance. He was obviously of a northern clime, tall, blond-balding and with a musculature that compensated for some excess weight.

"*Grazie, grazie, l'acqua!*"

"*Ja, ja, das Wasser ist kalt!*"

"Oh, excuse me, you're German!"

Now she was in the water up to her waist and he was up to his— goodness! Crotch was the word that had almost entered her mind, and with a graceful out-spread of arms, she fell into the water and for some reason, which she didn't explain to herself, she began to make choking sounds and floundering motions as if she had never been in water before although she was really an experienced swimmer.

At once two hands went about her body and one of them was very close to her buttocks and the other between her breasts.

While she continued her spurious gasps, she turned toward him her tango-red smile and cried out, "Donky-shane."

"Do not be frightened. I will not release."

Indeed he did not release!

Within a few minutes the hand between her breasts was firmly cupping one of them and the other had moved to her groin, in fact one of his fingers was pressing at the lips of that orifice which had been entered only once, by the drugged Puerto Rican's licentious—

"Oh, my Lord, how suddenly You have provided!" she exclaimed to herself.

Since he commanded a bit of English as well as a commanding grasp of her body, he gave her some verbal as well as physical instruction in swimming and she was an apt pupil. Her previous swimming had been at "Ladies' Day" at the Macon, Georgia, Y.M.C.A., she had been a regular there, attending both times a week. She had learned how to immerse her head in the pool with each stroke and to expel the bit of water that entered her mouth. It had been at the "Y" pool, diving daintily off the springboard, that she had first felt the stab of pain in her spine, early last fall . . .

Oh, my Lord, it was quite unmistakable now that the German's finger was gently inserting itself between her vaginal lips, and it was also clear that he was guiding her about a protrusion of rocks toward a little cove that was clear and cold and almost deserted, a printed sign over it saying "*Massi Caduti,*" meaning that rocks might fall.

Oh, well, what if rocks fell? Things more important than rocks can fall in a secluded cove of such stimulating clear, cold water . . .

Then a sad thing happened.

A loud female voice called out to him as he was about to conduct her around that outcropping of rocks into the secluded cove.

"Klaus! Klaus!"

"Ja, Liebchen! Ich kommen!"

It was an outraged wife's voice that had called him from the water. He made a quick apology to Barbara and swam ashore to where his *Frau* and three *kinder* were spreading out edibles from a wicker hamper on the dark gray pebbles, not as dark as Barbara's disappointment.

I must forget that incident, she thought as she settled into her beach chair beneath a spangled umbrella and put on her reading glasses.

Miss Spark's new novella, *The Hothouse by the East River*, was much better than her attention to it suggested. Her eyes kept drifting toward the cluster of Germans, all now greedily eating and shouting at each other across their paper plates.

Once Klaus caught her eyes and waved. His *Frau* shouted something to him and snatched his paper plate from him to refill it with potato salad and sausage.

Disappointment always removes one a little from a holiday crowd, and as she started back on her aching knee joints toward the *pensione*, nobody seemed to notice her in the still damply clinging watermelon-pink dress.

It was Italian lunchtime, two-thirty, but she felt a bit nauseous now and ignored the eating places she passed.

Oh, how could she possibly lunch alone!

Is there anything more humiliating in this world than to eat alone?

The night before there had been the *festa* of San Pietro, celebrated a kilometer down the coast with such loud explosives that sleep had been impossible even after the codeine, the Valium and the Nembutal tablets.

Tonight there was another *festa*, closer and still noisier. It was a local *festa*, observed by a village halfway up the mountain behind her hotel and it was a most peculiar type of *festa*. It enacted in fireworks an attempt by the devil to assault the Virgin Mary. Great booming rockets traced the gradual retreat of the Virgin before the presumably lecherous pursuit of his satanic majesty, and of course it always concluded, finally, in the triumph of the lady's virtue but it sure in hell took a long time for this triumph to be accomplished.

Having been warned by the proprietor of Posa Posa *pensione* that this *festa* was to commence at midnight and continue for about four hours, she had purchased on her way back from the beach some ear-stoppers of a gummy substance. At the *pensione* she took a very hot bath, as hot as she could stand it, to ease the ache in her bones, and had put out on her bedside table two tablets of codeine, four Valium tablets and three Nembutals and she had wedged the ear-stoppers very tight into her ears and gone to bed with all the windows closed on the imminent noise of battle between the Virgin and the devil.

Nothing availed.

The contest between the Virgin and Satan, accompanied by appreciative shrieks from onlookers on the terraces below, made sleep the last possibility in Barbara's world of torment.

Toward three in the morning a new symptom manifested itself: her aching limbs began to make convulsive movements, something the doctors back home had not warned her to expect. Three times that night she soaked herself in the tub as hot as she could bear it and the third time, reaching for the bath towel, she fell upon the floor with a cry of anguish.

"Tomorrow I'm going home!" she declared to herself and she meant it. If only it were daytime she could immediately get in touch with the airline which had brought her from the States to Rome.

"Where's my ticket? Have I lost my ticket?"

She found it folded in her Book of Common Prayer and then she found a thing that made her cry out again.

The ticket was a one-way ticket, it did not include *return passage*!

Oh, now, no, such a thing couldn't be, she didn't have on her reading glasses and wasn't seeing the ticket clearly.

"Reading glasses, where?"

She located them, after several minutes of panicky search, in the drawer of the bedside table, pushed back so far that she hadn't seen them the first two times she'd wrenched the drawer open.

Breathless and almost tottering like a crone, she hurried back to examine again the Pan Am ticket, and Lord have mercy, all that existed in the blue Pan Am ticket folder was a carbon copy of a one-way passage from New York to Rome, economy class.

All thought was suspended for some moments, as if she'd received a brain concussion.

Then she found herself, panting, in a seated position, on the straight-back chair on the balcony, and there she admitted the inadmissible realization that her friends at the junior college had not expected her to return from this vacation abroad; or simply couldn't or wouldn't endow her with more than a one-way economy passage . . .

"Nevertheless I shall make it, oh I'll make it all right, I don't know how but I will!"

Now at last, predictably, Our Lady had defeated the devil and the *festa* was over; and since it was late in June, it would soon be daybreak.

The shock of the one-way passage would permit no sleep, and with the sharp fox-teeth of loneliness gnawing away at her heart, she was now seated on the bed with something in her hands. It wasn't the Book of Common Prayer, it was the embroidered reticule that old Cousin Ida had given her at her "going away" party in Macon, and she now recalled that only Cousin Ida had advised her against the holiday abroad.

"Barbara, let me speak to you alone for a minute, let's go over there in a corner and discuss this impulse of yours to visit foreign countries, at this particular time."

She recalled her impatience at the suggestion and also the firm grip of Cousin Ida's hand on her elbow and how, when they had occupied chairs in a remote corner of the room, she had said, "Oh, Cousin Ida, I don't understand why you oppose my plan to travel. Is it because you're afraid that I can't manage alone? Why, I'm about the most independent soul in the world and I am determined to remain that way and simply depend on myself."

Now what had been Cousin Ida's reply to that extravagant statement?

Nothing, at first, but the touch of Cousin Ida's gnarled hand on her own hand that was trembling.

Oh? Now! The words came back to her, now!

"Barbara, to depend on yourself is to depend upon a broken stick. All of us need the devoted support of someone at certain times."

"Whose support, Cousin Ida? Do you mean God's? And you know that I'm agnostic?"

"No, dear, what I mean is—"

The delicate voice of the old lady had waited for the shrill voices of two quarreling faculty members to subside as they, Barbara and Cousin Ida, returned to the buffet table.

Then Cousin Ida had resumed her diffident counsel, and Barbara remembered, now, quite definitely what Cousin Ida had said.

"Just postpone the trip till next summer. Then you'll be stronger and traveling alone in foreign countries will be more practical, dear."

"When they've given me the fare, postpone it, absurd!"

"Yes, I understand, Barbara, I do understand, but—"

She noticed that Cousin Ida was dabbing tears from her eyes.

"Cousin Ida, what *are* you weeping about? It isn't as if I were going away for good. I'm certainly going to get back here days before registration for the fall term."

"Of course," said Cousin Ida. "I'm sure they'll want you back for next term."

"Can you think of any reason why they wouldn't want me back? Why, I don't want to seem immodest but I am really the only one in the English department that has made a reputation in national academic circles. Did you know I received a two-page letter last week from Robert Penn Warren? You know Robert Penn Warren, the greatest living novelist of the South. He wrote me this long letter of appreciation when I had informed him that I was including *All the King's Men* in my required-reading list for my seminar in modern American classics."

"Now that was real nice of him, Barbara, but didn't you cause a little, well, dispute and friction and a little disagreeability among the other English-department members when you refused to include *Gone with the Wind* by that great Georgia lady writer that—?"

"Oh, yes, oh, yes. Naturally I respect Margaret Mitchell as a gifted storyteller but even though she was run down crossing a street in Atlanta, I just couldn't live with my critical conscience if I put that big popular best-seller on my required reading list of American classics just because she was a lady writer of Georgia and her book was made into a film with Clark Gable and Vivien Leigh and it turned into what they call a blockbuster. Those standards are just not my standards, why if I had included that *magnum opus* in my list, I would probably have had to leave out *All the King's Men* by Mr. Robert Penn Warren."

"Honey, if you did what you thought was most honest according to your standards, why, then I say you did right. Now before we go back and mix with the others, I have something to give you. Well, it was actually given me to give you by your doctor in Atlanta. It's the name of a doctor in Rome that you should call this summer if you should have any recurrence of your back trouble, which God willing you won't. Here it is. The name is peculiar but I guess it's Italian."

Cousin Ida had removed from her reticule, then, and handed to Barbara a slip of paper that bore the name "Dottore Emilio Fausto" and that also bore his address and his phone number at a Roman hospital called *"Nostra Signora del Cielo."*

"Thank you, Cousin Ida, but I am going to be much closer to Naples than Rome and I really don't think—"

"Well, what your Atlanta doctor says is that the Roman doctor can recommend a doctor in Naples and I think you ought to take it, just in case."

"Thank you, Cousin Ida. I'll take it with me but I promise you that I won't have the least need of it. So let's go back to the party."

Now how very clear to Barbara was the discreetly veiled meaning of that little talk with Cousin Ida in a private corner of the "bon voyage" party.

Cousin Ida had been weeping because she was really informing her that *Das Wasser* was very cold indeed, and that nobody on the faculty of the Georgia college expected or wanted her back among them for the start of the fall term.

Dawn was breaking not only in her comprehension, now, but over the ominously dark volcanic mountains.

Is it possible that the blood in the arteries of the faculty of the college in—

Well, I suppose, thought Barbara, the answer to that is anybody's guess, if it isn't mine . . .

1973–79 (Published 1982)

Mother Yaws

"**H**ey, Luther'n minister's daughter!"

Barle turned from the stove as if the stove had burned her.

"Did you speak to me, Tom?"

She raised a hand to her cheek.

"Who else around her is a Luther'n minister's daughter?"

"Why, nobody but me."

With the hand not covering her cheek, she was making a number of jerky, startled, purposeless motions, for this was the first time her husband, Tom McCorkle, of Triumph, Tennessee, had addressed her for a good while, possibly several weeks.

"Do you want something, Tom?"

"Yeh, I want to know what you got on your cheek that you put your hand over."

"My cheek?"

"That's right. What's wrong there?"

"You mean on my face?"

"That's right, not on your ass."

Their nearly grown son, Tommy Two, chuckled at this, and the middle girl remarked indifferently, "She got a sore on her face."

"I seen it on her face, too," said the smaller girl, as if not to be outdone.

The boy, Tommy Two, gave his mother one of his contemptuous glances and confirmed his own awareness of the sore on his mother's left cheek by a nod and another little chuckle of amusement.

"Go look at yuhself if you doubt it," said McCorkle.

"Where?"

"There's a lookin' glass in the bedroom. Ain't you ever seen it?"

"You want me to go take a look?"

McCorkle's small eyes sharpened.

"Why the fuck else would I mention that sore on yuh face an' the lookin' glass in the bedroom if I didn't mean to advise you to go take a look at yuhself in that glass?"

Then he turned to the middle girl and said, "She still ain't moved. She don't wanta look in the glass because I reckon she knows what she'll see. I think she already seen it or felt it an' thought nobody would notice, but goddamn if it ain't a punishment to the eye."

"Punishment to the eye," Tommy Two repeated with a mean chuckle.

"Mama, go look at yuhself like Dad tole you," said the middle girl.

"I have looked at myself," said the Lutheran minister's daughter. "I don't want to do it again."

"She looks like a half-butchered hawg," said McCorkle, as he shifted in his chair to let a fart.

"You oughtn't to do that in front of the girls," Barle protested faintly. Then she stumbled out of the kitchen door to the yard, feeling nausea.

"Don't let her put a hand on nothin' in the kitchen," McCorkle warned. "Best she don't touch nothin' till that sore's been looked at."

After she had vomited the coffee, Barle started away from the house in no planned direction.

Tommy Two appeared twice in the back door.

"Dad says don't throw up near the house."

A minute later he called to her: "Dad wants you to come back to the kitchen."

She came back in.

"Have you awready forgot I tole you to go upstairs and take a look at yuhself in the glass?"

"No."

"Then go do it right now."

She backed into a corner of the kitchen.

"Git her out of that corner, but don't touch her—it could be somethin' contagious."

Then Barle moved out of the corner.

"I will go in the bedroom and look in the glass."

She walked out of the kitchen and could be heard slowly mounting the steps in the hall. She was still up there when McCorkle had finished his breakfast and departed for his dry-goods store.

With nothing else to do, the girls picked up an old topic of discussion in the desultory fashion that an object is moved from one position to another for no apparent purpose.

"Mama's name is Barle, but Dad nearly always calls her Luther'n minister's daughter."

"You know why he does that? The Luther'n minister had a brother name Barle that Mama was named for because this brother Barle had a good piece of real estate, a corner lot with a house and a store built on it, and Dad expected this uncle of Mama to leave her the corner property when he died because she was his namesake. But he didn't. He left this corner property to the whore that kept house for him."

"Oh. Yeh."

"So Dad was cheated, he thought, after he married Mama and didn't git the corner lot with the store but had to buy some ground an' put up a building hisself."

"Oh, yeh, that's right. So that's why he calls her Luther'n minister's daughter."

"That's right," said the other.

Later on that morning the two girls began to speculate on why their mother had not returned downstairs.

"Why ain't she come down to clean the breakfast dishes an' feed the yard dog like she always does? It expecks her to. It's lookin' in the door."

"Dawg, git out!" said the girl, and when the dog had reluctantly backed away, she said, "I reckon she is ashame to come back down."

McCorkle took his wife to the depot and put her on a day coach to Gatlinburg, the biggest town in the county, to have a doctor there look at the sore on the face and determine if it was contagious.

The day-coach fare to Gatlinburg cost McCorkle four dollars and eighty-five cents, and he marked down that expense on the first page of a black notebook he had purchased at the five-and-ten on their way to the depot. His wife observed him marking it down and she surmised rightly that the black notebook had been purchased for no other reason than to keep an account of all expenditures that her affliction might cost him.

After closing the notebook, McCorkle said, "A' course you know that if the Gatlinburg doctor says this thing is contagious, you got to go back to the Luther'n minister's house and stay there."

"I don't think Papa would like me to stay there, neither," said Barle.

"I don't give a shit if he likes it or not. That's where you go if they say this thing is contagious, and if the Luther'n minister throws you out, well, then, you take it from there."

"Take what from there, Tom?"

"Your plans for the future, if any."

When Barle arrived at the office of the Gatlinburg doctor, nine other patients were there waiting to see him. All of them looked at her and despite the fact that silence had prevailed among them until she entered, they now began to exchange looks and whispers and to shift the positions of their chairs. One fat, sweaty woman with two children occupied a sofa that couldn't be moved. She stared at Barle with undisguised repugnance, steadily, for about two minutes. Then she sprang up from the sofa. "Don't move," she said to the children, and she went to the inner door and pounded heavily on it till the doctor's nurse appeared.

"Tha's a woman out here with a terrible sore on her face. Nobody wants to be sittin' in the room with her, so why don't you tell her to wait outside on the steps. I got two *children* with me."

She continued speaking to the nurse who had shut the door on the waiting room so the rest of the complaint could not be heard plainly until the door opened again and the fat woman's voice, higher in volume, more vehement in protest, was again very distinct as she told the nurse that either Barle had to wait outside or she, the fat woman, was going to leave with her children, it was one or the other. Then the nurse came out grimly and stood in the center of the room to look at Barle.

"You see what I mean?" the fat woman shouted.

"Yes, I see what you mean. Will you gimme your name, ma'am?" she asked Barle.

Barle was barely able to whisper. "Mrs. McCorkle."

"Where do you live?"

"Triumph."

"What is that on your face?"

"That's what I come to find out."

"What is the history of it?"

"What is the what?"

"How long is it been on your face and has it been there before or is this the first time you had it?"

"Oh. I see. I noticed it beginnin' about two weeks ago."

"Appeared for the first time then?"

"That's right. Never before."

"Well, it looks like nothing I ever seen before, and since these other patients are regular and local, I think you better wait outside till I call you back in."

The other patients raised their voices in agreement with the nurse's suggestion.

Barle stood up.

"Where do you want me to wait?"

"*Outside! She said outside!*" the other patients shouted.

"Can I take my chair with me? I had to git on the train without breakfast, so I'm not feelin' too good."

"Ordinarily no."

Barle was puzzled by this answer. Her head was swimming; she felt she was going to faint.

"Is anyone willin' to carry a chair out for her?" the nurse said.

A man took a blue handkerchief out of his pocket and, using it to protect the hand from contact with the chair, hauled it outside, Barle stumbling after him.

Outside it was hot and yellow and her vision was blurred by sweat running into her eyes, but she noticed that the man had thrown his handkerchief down next to the chair. She bent over, intending to return it to him. But as she bent she blacked out and didn't come to till the nurse was shouting at her from the front door.

"Mizz McCorkle, the doctor will look at you now!"

As Barle entered the office, the nurse stood back a good distance with a look that contained no comfort.

All the patients were gone; the inner door was open.

Barle crossed to it in a slow, irregular way.

"Watch out," the nurse said, but Barle collided with the doorframe and stumbled back a few paces.

Then Barle was inside the office in the doctor's presence, but a table was between them. He pushed his chair back and scrutinized her through his glasses.

"You are Mrs. McCorkle from Triumph?"

"Yes, sir, I am the wife of Tom McCorkle of Triumph and the Lutheran minister's daughter."

"Hmm. Well. I will phone a hospital to see if they've got a bed for you there, because a condition like yours needs several days of examination and tests. You got Blue Cross?"

"I got blue cross! Is *that* what this is?"

"I meant does the government pay your medical expenses?"

"Oh."

"That's not a reply to the question."

"I thought maybe you'd tell me what I got."

"Have you had any mental trouble?" asked the doctor.

"Mental?"

"Trouble thinking?"

"Mr. McCorkle and the Lutheran minister say so."

"The hospital will be able to check on that, too," said the doctor, with his phone in his hand.

An ambulance picked her up and took her to the hospital, where she stayed for a few days. On the last day, a doctor at the hospital sat by her bed and informed her that the eruption on her face was a thing called yaws.

Of course she didn't understand much of what he was saying until he got up. "It's going to be a slow thing," he said. "That's about all we can tell you except it's a rare disease that usually happens in Africa. Have you been in Africa?"

"Africa?"

"The continent of Africa."

"You mean? . ."

"Never mind, Mrs. McCorkle. This is a case that will be written up in medical journals. Do you want your real name and address mentioned in these write-ups?"

"Mizz McCorkle, the Lutheran minister's daughter from Triumph."

When she left the hospital, she was given slips of paper and a printed pamphlet, and she was even taken to the Gatlinburg railway station in a taxi.

"So what you got wrong with you?" McCorkle asked when she returned to Triumph.

"They say it's something called yaws."

"Well, can they do something for it or is it one a' those incurable things that git worse?"

She made a baffled noise in her throat.

"Don't whine about it. We all got to go someday from one thing or another. Now for tonight, I will let you sleep on a pallet downstairs, but tomorrow you're gonna go stay with the Luther'n minister who brought you into this world. Now what did the doctor in Gatlinburg charge you? I want to know all charges connected with this yaws, so I can set them down in the little black book."

"The Gatlinburg doctor put me in a hospital."

"You mean for nothing or is there a charge connected?"

"I asked about that and he said the bill would be mailed."

"Well, have it mailed to your Luther'n minister dad. He was at least half responsible for your coming into the world and your dead mother the other. And he performed the goddamn wedding between us, which I never respected and now I know why, since I was married to *yaws*!"

At this she broke down and cried a little.

This seemed to infuriate McCorkle.

"Git up off the porch, you and your goddamn yaws, and go lie on your pallet and lock the door from inside. I don't want a child of mine to come in the room an' maybe catch this disease which I never even heard of."

He stood back from her farther than the Gatlinburg doctor had as she entered the house and the downstairs storeroom, where an old mattress was thrown in after her.

Dawn the next day, Barle awoke to the sound of the key to the storeroom being turned in the lock. She sat up on the pallet and saw the door swing open a little.

"Is that you, Tom?"

His response didn't come from the hall but from halfway up the stairs. "Yeh, you can come out now and git on your way to the Luther'n minister's house."

"Oh, Tom, I ain't made breakfast yet."

"Don't bother with that. Nobody wants a breakfast that might be infected with yaws. Under a stone on the porch you will find a list of expenses that this thing will cost. Your trip to the doctor and stay in the hospital. Also me and the children's. We all got to be tested to find out if you have given us this yaws."

Barle put on the clothes that she had gone to Gatlinburg in, and then she came out in the hall. "How about the rest of my clothes?" she asked.

"They'll be delivered to the Luther'n minister's later by a nigger."

"Well, good-bye," said Barle.

She got the long list of expenses and started across Triumph to the Lutheran minister's house. She guessed the news of her affliction had been spread about the town. On most of the porches she passed, there were people standing and watching and making comments as she went by.

"Hello," she would say, and, receiving no response, she would say, "Good-bye."

Barle had not expected to be admitted to the Lutheran minister's house, and so it was no surprise to her that on the gate was a large printed note reading: BARLE, YOU CANNOT ENTER.

The Lutheran minister's house was located at the edge of Triumph. There was no building beyond it, just a road that diminished into a trail among tall, coppery weeds. She stood for a while among the weeds, uncertain about whether or not to go farther. Beyond the slope of weeds was a mountain known as Cat's Back. It was the heat of the sun that finally determined Barle to continue on up the slope and into the shade of the woods.

The shade felt good. There was also a clear stream of water. She cupped some in her hands to wash the sweat off her face and sat down to rest for a while. A family of beavers came out of their residence in the stream and they all looked at her and made friendly barking sounds.

"Hello," said Barle.

They kept on looking and amiably barking.

She thought to herself, "I guess they don't notice the yaws."

Barle did not count the days in the woods on Cat's Back mountain. But they passed pleasantly for her. She lived on mushrooms and acorns and discovered other edible kinds of nuts and vegetation.

There was a lot of wildlife on Cat's Back, but none of it seemed to regard her as a victim of yaws. She would imagine that the birds were conversing with her in a friendly fashion, and she talked to the beavers and the raccoons.

She reckoned she had until late fall or winter to survive on Cat's Back—and she was almost right about that. But the time she'd allotted herself was cut slightly short when she heard a mewing sound and noticed some baby wildcats playing around some great rocks. She smiled and went up to them.

The mother wildcat came out of nowhere right down on her.

"Please, please," she said, but it was over with quickly.

(Published 1977)

The Killer Chicken and the Closet Queen

A t thirty-seven Stephen Ashe was the youngest member of the Wall Street law firm of Webster, Eggleston, Larrabee and Smythe. He was quite as important a member as any of the four whose surnames comprised the firm's title and the name Ashe was not included only because it was felt that five names to the title would overload it. The oldest member, fifty-nine-year-old Nathaniel Webster the Fifth, was on his way out, having suffered a stroke the day of President Nixon's resignation and another on the night of his wedding to his nephew's adolescent widow from the Arkansas Ozarks. The day that he mistook Larrabee for Smythe in the elevator ascending to the firm's thirty-second floor offices in the Providential Building, Jerry Smythe had slipped a business card of the firm into Stephen Ashe's pocket as they went down the elevator for lunch that day, giving Stephen a smiling wink and a slight pat on the butt. When Stephen looked at the card he saw that the name Webster had been scratched and the name Ashe appended to the three remaining, printed on it with a ballpoint pen.

In the next few days the same conniving winks and little butt-pats had been delivered to Stephen by Jack Larrabee and Ralph Eggleston, and so it was now fully apparent to Stephen that there was no dissident voice on the matter, that is, none excepting that of the senior gentleman who was on his way out. Of course it was a bit unnerving the way that Nat Webster hung in. A workday never passed at the law firm without Nat, secretly known as the old hound dog, shouting out exuberantly, his door having banged open, "Pressure down five more points, I'm in the clear!"

Stephen and Jerry Smythe went directly from work every evening to the Ivy League Club, for a splash in the pool, a massage, and a sauna.

They each had an interest in keeping physically fit; both were under forty and on good days or evenings didn't look like they'd been out of law school for more than a couple of years. They undressed in the same cubicle at the club. Smythe would wait until Stephen had found a cubicle that was vacant and gone in it and then Smythe would enter it, too, and as they undressed together, Stephen could hardly ignore how frequently Smythe's hands would brush against his thighs and, once or twice, even his crotch.

They had their massages on adjoining tables and Stephen's was administered by a good-looking young Italian, and whenever this masseur's fingers worked up Stephen's thighs, Stephen would get an erection. He tried to resist it but he couldn't. The Italian would chuckle a little under his breath but Smythe would make a loud, jocular comment, such as, "Hey, Steve, who're you thinking of?"

One Friday evening Stephen replied, "I was thinking of Nat Webster's little teen-age wife."

"Oh, did I tell you, she's got her kid brother up here, he was staying with Nat and her but Nat threw him out on his ass last weekend."

"Why'd Nat throw him out?"

"Found out he was delinquent."

"Delinquent *how?*"

"Jailed for lewd vagrancy, peddling his goodies, you know," said Smythe, his voice lowered to a theatrical whisper.

Stephen wanted, for some reason, to extract more information on the boy's delinquencies but he refrained from pursuing the subject with Smythe because he found himself wondering, as he had sometimes wondered before, if Smythe's freedom of speech and behavior with him were not a kind of espionage. It was altogether possible that Eggleston and Larrabee were using Smythe's closer familiarity with Stephen to delve a bit more into his, Stephen's private life. It was more than altogether possible that this was the case. Stephen remembered a little closed counsel among the partners a few months ago when they had discussed the advisability of discharging a junior accountant on suspicion of homosexual inclinations, a suspicion based on nothing more than the facts that he was still unmarried at thirty-one and was sharing an apartment with a younger man whose photograph had appeared in a magazine advertisement for Marlboro cigarettes.

Stephen had felt himself flushing but had said nothing at this counsel. Smythe had spoken up loudly, saying: "I don't see how it can affect the prestige of the firm one way or another."

Stephen's head lifted involuntarily, it sort of jerked up, and he had seen Smythe's eyes fastened on his flushed face.

"What do *you* say, Steve?" Smythe had asked him, challengingly.

Despising himself a bit, Stephen had cleared his throat and said, "Well, I don't think it's to our advantage to be associated in any way with this sort of deviation from the norm. I mean we don't want to be associated with it even by—"

For a moment he had dried up: then he had completed the sentence too loudly with the word "association!"

"Exactly," Larrabee had said.

The junior accountant had been given two week's notice that day.

Now the Italian masseur had turned Stephen on his belly and was kneading his buttocks.

Smythe was continuing his discussion of Nat Webster's wife's kid brother's precociously colorful past.

"In Arkansas he was involved in the beating up of an old homo who is still in traction in a Hot Springs hospital. Well, the old hound dog told this kid to hit the streets and I understand he is now living at the 'Y'. You know what that means, don't you?"

"Does it mean something besides living at the 'Y'?" Stephen enquired with affected indifference.

At this moment the masseur's fingers entered Stephen's natal cleave, and Stephen said, "Is there any truth in the report that there is going to be a merger between Fuller, Cohen, Stern and the Morris Brothers?"

"Steve, are you in dreamland? Why, the Morris Brothers declared bankruptcy last week, and have flown to Hong Kong!"

"A massage makes me sleepy," said Stephen affecting a great yawn.

One evening in early spring Stephen was viewing an old Johnny Weissmuller film on his bedroom TV set when the persistent ringing of the phone brought him out of a state that verged upon entrancement.

"Aw, let it go," was his first impulse but the phone would not shut up. At length he got up from his vibra-chair, turning the TV set so that he could still admire it while at the phone.

"Yes, yes, what is it?" he shouted with irrepressible annoyance.

"Oh, I'm sorry! Did I interrupt something?"

The precocious little girl voice, reminiscent of Marilyn Monroe's, was recognizable to Stephen instantly. It was Nat Webster's adolescent wife's.

"No, no, not a bit, Maude, not a bit in this world or the next one. In fact I was just about to phone you and Nat and invite you over for Sunday brunch to meet my mother who is flying up from Palm Beach for my birthday."

"You are havin' a *birth*-day?" Maude exclaimed as if amazed that he had ever been born.

"How is Nat doing, Maude?"

"Let's not discuss the condition of Nat," Maude said with abrupt firmness.

"Bad as *that*?"

"It's his lack of concern for the—sorry, I shouldn't be botherin' you about this, but, you know, Steve, you're the only one in the bunch, I mean his Wall Street buddies, that I feel I can open up with. Now, Steve, maybe you've heard about my little brother payin' us a visit from Arkansas."

"It seems to me that Jerry mentioned you had him with you right now."

"Look, Steve, I'm callin' from a coin-box because I didn't want Nat to hear this conversation. You see, a problem has come up."

"Oh?"

"Yes, you see, I think that Nat resents my attachment to this sweet kid brother of mine."

"Oh?"

"Well, I'm not going to drag out the conversation, another party is waitin' outside the booth. But the problem is this. Nat suddenly told me an' Clove, that's my kid brother's name, sweetest, cutest little sixteen-year-old thing, that there wasn't room enough for him in our eight-room penthouse on Park."

"Oh. A spatial problem."

"Space is not the problem, the problem is that Nat is resentful of youth and natural gay spirits, and that's the reason he handed Clove ten dollars, imagine, one measly ole sawbuck over the breakfast table this week and told him to go and check in at the 'Y'."

Stephen felt a premonitory tightening in his throat. In a guarded tone he remarked that there were a lot of physical advantages to be had at the "Y", the swimming pool and the workout rooms and association with other young Christian kids.

"Steven, you're playin' dumb!" Maude almost shrieked, "Why, everyone knows that 'Y's' are overrun with wolves out for chickens!"

"Wolves? Chickens?"

Stephen gave a totally false little chuckle of incomprehension.

"Quit that, Steve, you can't play dumb with *me*! Now I am comin' straight to the point. I've got to remove little Clove from that kind of temptation that's so unattractive and it occurred to me that you might be able to give Clove a bed at your place, you being the only young bachelor in Nat's crowd, I thought that maybe—well, how *about* it, Steve?"

Stephen took a break on that one, a pause for breath.

"I've got an extra bedroom for Mother's visits, but—"

"Oh, that I didn't know, but if I remember correctly, you've also got a sofa in the livin' room, haven't you, Steve?"

Stephen again was unable to come up with an immediate, natural reply, but that was not necessary.

"Goddamn, hold your hawses!" Maude shouted presumably to the party waiting outside the coin-box. She then lowered her voice a little and said in her reminiscent-of-Monroe tone, "We'll see you Sunday at brunch to meet your mother, she will just love Clove and so will you!"

The phone had been hung up. In a dazed fashion Stephen noted that the nearly nude backside of Johnny Sheffield, son of Tarzan and Jane whom they called Boy, was as close to perfection as, well, his *own*, when he looked at himself in the triplicate mirror in his dressing room, in the right sort of light.

"My God, why is it that—! I do get myself in for—!"

He was still awake when the midnight news came on. There was a photo of Anita Bryant with a banana cream pie on her face.

"—thrown by a militant gay with a shout about bigots deserving no less . . ."

"But what will Mom *think*?" Stephen murmured aloud as he switched off the TV and the bed-lamp and cradled his crotch with a hand . . .

Mom's plane was due to be delayed five hours owing to a visibility problem over Kennedy Airport.

Having received this report at Kennedy, Stephen thought about Mom and what her reaction to the situation might be.

"Mom is an old trouper," he thought, "but definitely not one that's about to wait five hours in West Palm Beach for weather to change over Kennedy. I bet if I got on the phone and called her suite at the Royal Shores I'd find she is already back there, yes, I ought to do that."

But he didn't do that right away. Without a conscious thought of so doing, he took out the latest report on Mom's stockholdings on Wall Street.

"This will put her in a bad humor," he thought. "She claims she doesn't keep up with things like stock fluctuations although I know she watches them like a hawk. She won't admit that she knows the Dow Jones has slipped almost forty points in the last two months. But it's just on paper. I'll tell her again 'Just trust me, Mom, you know it is just on paper, your net worth is still a million over what it was when Dad left us.'"

He would give her this pitch on the ride back from J.F.K. and she would maintain a reproachful silence for the next several minutes. Then she would make some politely withering remark, something like: "Son, you must know that nobody's net worth is what it is on paper, not since they forced Richard Nixon to resign and put that peanut-vendor in the White House."

"All right, I couldn't agree with you more, but you must remember, Mom, that even with an economic situation unfavorable as it is, you have not only a portfolio of stockholdings worth more than three million but nearly as much in the Manhattan Chemical Bank, I mean in your savings account alone, and as for your holdings in Switzerland, Mom—"

"Stephen, I can't imagine what you are talking about!"

Mom always pretended she hadn't the least idea that the bulk of her fortune was in diamonds and gold bricks in the vault of a bank in Zurich.

Stephen found himself standing, although he didn't remember getting up. He also found that he had sweated through his shirt, and he heard himself saying in a strident whisper, "Christ Almighty, does she think she can take it all with her?"

He was now in a phone booth, calling Mom's suite at the Royal Shores of Palm Beach.

"Thank God, Precious, you didn't wait, you went home."

"Naturally, Stephen, I knew you wouldn't expect me to wait in West Palm Beach for five hours or even one."

"No, no, Mom, I just wanted to be sure. So what *are* your travel plans now?"

"I may be a little late for your Sunday brunch. Why don't you change it to a buffet supper? Would that put you out too much?"

"I'd just have to call up about a dozen people."

"You mean it *would* be too much, then?"

"Precious, has anything for *you* ever been too much for *me*, Mom?"

"Stephen, as we both know, you have always been a paragon of filial devotion. Then it is understood. If you're tied up with preparations for the buffet supper, just have a limousine waiting at Idlewild to meet me."

"Mom, it's not Idlewild any more, it is Kennedy Airport."

"To *me* it remains *Idlewild*. Understood?"

"Oh, yes, Precious, I understand completely, I was just afraid that—"

"And, Stephen, one thing more."

Her voice had dropped to a level that was still firm but slightly less militant.

"What thing, Mother?"

"I trust not a thing but a person. This Miss Sue Coffin whom you mention to me as a young woman, well, she couldn't be still too young, that you are perennially 'going out' with, as you put it, as if you thought I could not see through euphemisms, however transparent. Are you still going out with *Miss* Sue Coffin whom, for fifteen years, now, Stephen, since we buried your dear father, you have described to me as a successful young career woman in some sort of promotional field?"

"Oh, yes, *her*! I am still seeing Sue Coffin, oh, yes, I see her regularly, Mom."

"I presume that you mean upon a nightly basis. Now, Son, I have become increasingly disturbed by the fact that you have been 'going out' for fifteen years, slightly more than fifteen, I believe, with this young woman whom I have yet to enjoy the possible pleasure of meeting. Stephen? When I fly up to Manhattan for the buffet I shall expect to be granted that pleasure and an opportunity to discuss this situation with her in private, and before I hang up I wish to know if she is connected with the Nantucket Island Coffins with which all the socially acceptable Coffins are connected?"

"Oh, now, Mom, I wouldn't be going out all this time with a Miss Coffin that wasn't a socially acceptable one, you know that, I wouldn't dream of it, ever!"

"Son, this extra-marital alliance with a woman, socially acceptable as the Nantucket Coffins, must be legalized, Stephen, and I insist that she be produced, that she be presented to me at the buffet on Sunday. Now I'm exhausted, there's nothing more to discuss. I love you, Stephen. Good night."

Produce her, produce her, produce her, out of a hat or a sleeve, why, my God, Sue Coffin is—

Yes, there had, indeed, been a fleeting association of a slightly intimate nature between a Miss Sue Coffin and Stephen but that association had been terminated long since when she had married an advertising executive for whom she'd worked and they'd moved to San
Francisco, why, even Christmas cards from her no longer came in, the
last card he'd received from her was an engraved one bearing her
married name and announcing the birth of twins, giving the date of
their nativity and their weight at that occasion and a scribbled statement from Sue Coffin Merriwether saying "Proud mother is happy as
a lark! Fond greetings, Sue."

Not happily as a lark did Stephen emerge from the phone booth, in
fact he staggered from its stifling enclosure as though about to collapse. A discreet hand clasped his elbow, steering him toward a door
marked EXIT beyond which possibly there existed some reviving fresh
air . . .

On the long ride home Stephen's usually well-ordered mind seemed to
be getting the wrong sort of feedback for the input. It was not continuing along a chosen groove but was abruptly skipping onto a series of
little tangents. It was as if somebody had monkeyed with a perfectly
but too delicately tooled computer. No matter how finely a machine of
this sort is tooled, even if it is hand-tooled by artist-craftsmen—

"Wow!" said Stephen aloud. He said it loudly enough for the chauffeur from the rental limousine service to glance back and enquire,
"Something wrong, Sir?"

"No, no, no, just—"

(Just what, and why three "no's"? Must be really upset: have a
feverish feeling.)

He knew how to take his own pulse and the hands of his watch were
luminous so he could time it. He was alarmed at how it was racing. One
hundred and twenty a minute!

The new rental limousines were equipped with liquor cabinets. Why
did Stephen open it so stealthily, since he had already pressed the
button that shut him off, sound-wise, from the chauffeur?

I guess I must be afraid of getting a liquor problem like Dad's.

He was trying to remember what he had been thinking about when
he had silently uttered "Wow" a short while ago as he had followed the
chauffeur out of Kennedy. Was it because the chauffeur's elegantly
tapered back was—

Wow!

In the liquor cabinet was a half-full bottle of bourbon, a good brand of it, Old Nick. Stephen helped himself to half a tumbler and by the time they were passing serenely into the outskirts of Queens, the other side of LaGuardia, Stephen had, with no conscious plan to, lowered the soundproof panel between himself and the chauffeur.

He knew that he was in a dreamlike, an almost trancelike condition.

"What's your name?" he asked the chauffeur in a slurred voice.

"Tony," said the chauffeur.

"Ah, Italian, are you?"

"That's right."

"Love Italy," said Stephen, "beautiful, beautiful country, beautiful people. You know—"

"Know what, Sir?"

"I've got a mother."

"Me, too. I got a helluva Mama."

There was something soothing, almost caressing, about the voice of the young Italian chauffeur, and in response to those qualities in it, Stephen sloshed some more Old Nick into the tumbler which he had just drained.

"You've got a helluva Mama and I've got one hell of a Mom. Do you notice the difference?"

"Not sure what you mean, Sir."

"How much time have you got for me to explain?"

"My time is yours, at your expense, but it's yours."

The voice of the young Italian chauffeur had undergone an indefinable change.

"Well, taking you at your word's value," said Stephen, "drive off the highway at the next turn and let's have a little talk. About Moms and Mamas."

Stephen felt a slight lurch as the limousine turned off the highway but felt nothing more until the car had stopped.

Through eyes with lids that drooped, Stephen looked about.

The personable young chauffeur had parked the limousine in a place to which the nearest lighted building was at least half a block away.

Without invitation from Stephen, the chauffeur now entered the back seat of the limo and sat rather close to Stephen. He was not only young and good-looking but there was a redolence about him, a musky fragrance.

After a few moments' silence, he said to Stephen, "The next move's up to you."

"Strange remark," Stephen said in his slurred voice, now very deeply slurred.

Another few moments of silence but not altogether inactive. The Italian's left knee had swung open to encounter Stephen's right knee.

There was a wild clicking on and off of multi-colored buttons inside Stephen's head, along with electronic noises. This disturbance suddenly descended to his stomach and he began to make retching sounds.

"If you're gonna puke, stick your head out the window. Not so far, okay, I'm holding your ass."

When Stephen had vomited, he sprawled back into the lap of the chauffeur. After swabbing his mouth and chin with his monogrammed handkerchief of fine Irish linen, a customary sort of adjustment to his position in the world took precedence over all other circumstances, and to the chauffeur, still holding him on his lap, he said in a tone inherited from his mother, "Young man, I believe you are taking liberties with my person!"

"Me? Liberties? Person?"

"Yes, I am a *person*. In fact, I am a member of the Wall Street law firm of Webster, Eggleston, Larrabee and Smythe. I am in Register, Social, and headed for Dun and Bradstreet's."

"*Marrone!*" said the chauffeur. "Didn't you tell me to drive off the highway at the next turnoff?"

"If I did, I assure you it was to have a discussion of our respective mothers, not to be subjected to liberties with my—person . . ."

"Blow that out of your ass!" said the now-outraged Italian, as he dumped Stephen off his lap and opened the back door of the rental limousine.

"The person you are is a goddamn closet queen."

"And what is a closet queen, that curious expression?"

The chauffeur grinned.

"A queen in a closet with a broomstick up his butt," replied the chauffeur, slamming the back door shut and returning to the wheel.

Of course this bizarre experience was somewhat blurred in his recollection when Stephen woke late the next morning with a violent headache. He recalled only that a rental limousine chauffeur had made suggestions to him of a presumptuous nature on the drive back from the airport.

It was, when he woke, much too late to call off the Sunday brunch: in fact, there was barely time to prepare the Bloody Marys. He had all the ingredients for Eggs Benedict and since old Nat's young bride was on the guest list, Stephen was confident he could engage her as an assistant chef.

He was just out of the needle-sharp shower, drying off vigorously, and reaching for his paisley silk robe when the doorbell rang.

"Just a mo!" he shouted in the hall as he got himself into the robe and secured about his throat a snowy new scarf, arranging it as an ascot.

The bell rang again and again he called out "Just a mo" as he inspected himself in the full-length mirror on the door's interior surface.

He inspected himself two ways, head on and in profile, and was far from displeased, particularly by the way that the paisley silk so gracefully delineated, in profile, the masculine but prominent buttocks that Dame Nature had gifted him with.

"It's me, it's Maude. I came a little early because I thought you might need a woman's hand in the kitchen."

But Stephen was not looking at her, he was looking at her companion, a boy in blue jeans, no taller than Maude but with a—

Again the word "Wow!" exploded in Stephen's head.

"Oh, this is my kid brother, Clove," Maude was saying. "I just stopped off at the 'Y' to pick him up 'cause it's important you and him get to know each other before the others get here, especially Nat."

(Wow!)

"Now you two just leave the kitchen to me an' go get to know each other. Oh. Is your Mom up from Palm Beach?"

"Plane—delayed—she—"

"What a bitch," Maude said with great cheer in her voice. "I mean the plane delay."

Stephen found that he had not gone into the living room, as he had naturally intended, but had returned to the bedroom. He heard the door being closed, not by himself.

"Sis is right, we should get to know each other if you're gonna put me up here."

Stephen found himself rattling a bit, uttering words without due process of thought.

"I think I must be sort of unnerved this morning."

"Over your Mom coming up to check on you, huh?"

"There's nothing for her to check on, nothing at all, but her visits disturb the routine. Hey, now, what are you doing?"

"Feelin' the material," said the boy, Clove, breathing on Stephen's neck and running his hot little hand down the gracefully, just-enough-swaybacked curvature of Stephen's spine and right onto that ellipsis of his posterior which Stephen had only a few minutes past admired with such satisfaction in the mirror-back of the front door.

"Good stuff, whacha call it?"

"I just had time to put on my silk robe, and this white cravat, before your sister and you arrived at the door."

Maude's kid brother's hot little hand was still feeling the material, as he had put it, but with increased pressure.

"Would you mind going into the kitchen to bring me a Bloody Mary, a—double?"

"Now you're talkin', baby. I'll bring both of us doubles, and when I come back, you are gonna forget all about your Mom's check on yuh."

A cunning idea abruptly occurred to Stephen.

"Clove?"

The boy glanced back at Stephen from the door.

In a husky whisper, Stephen said to him: "Clove, don't ask me why right now, but when Mom arrives, I want you to get her aside and tell her that you are a secret."

"What kinda secret you mean?"

"Clove, I can make it worth your while if you go through with this little conspiracy right. I want you to convince Mom that you are a secret child of mine, born fifteen years ago, and your Mom was a Miss Sue Coffin from Nantucket Island."

Clove's eyes narrowed to a look of shrewd contemplation. He had a definite attraction to deception as a practice in life. Of course he did not comprehend at all the purpose of this particular deceit but that it involved a trick about to be played on someone was immediately appealing.

"Just lemme git all this straight. You are my secret daddy? And my mom, she's also a secret named—"

"A young lady named Sue Coffin who died at your birth, Clove."

"Jeez, this is heavy, but when you say you'll make it worth my while, I reckon that I can handle it for you okay. Now you stay in here, rest on that bed there, and I'll fetch a couple of doubles, I'll be right out and then we can git it together in more detail, Daddy."

As the door opened briefly for Clove's kitchen errand, Stephen heard from near, but as if from far, the doorbell ringing again.

"Never had such a hangover, wow . . ." he murmured to himself, falsely, as he removed the paisley silk robe and toppled onto the bed.

Easily an hour had passed by the time Stephen emerged gradually and uncertainly from his bedroom in which he had ingested easily three and probably more Bloody Marys, fetched him by the Ganymede younger sibling of Nat Webster's adolescent bride from the Arkansas Ozarks.

He did not begin to know what faced him in the living room: he knew only that the entire complement of his colleagues in the Wall Street law firm of Webster, Eggleston, Larrabee and Smythe were there assembled, each with his respective spouse.

"Well, I want you to know—" he heard himself saying, in a slow and slurred voice as he joined the abruptly hushed assemblage.

Nat Webster, the old hound dog, was first to speak up.

"I don't much think you want us to know a goddamn thing which we don't know already."

"I want you to know I passed out in the bedroom and I don't know how it happened."

Nat Webster was on his feet.

"If you'll drop by the office tomorrow about noon, I think your official paper of resignation from the firm will be ready for signature. Is that understood, Ashe?"

Then he marched to the door, calling back "Come on, Maude!"

Maude bestowed a sisterly kiss on Stephen's blanched cheek as she responded languidly to this summons. Then she lisped loudly and sweetly,

"Thanks for putting up Clove, so much better for him than life at the 'Y'."

"Maude!" shouted Nat Webster from the door.

She blew a kiss at the lingering guests and undulated into the hallway.

Eggleston, Larrabee and Smythe were all on their feet now and their wives, conferring together in whispers, were getting into their furs.

Clove had now entered. He closed the fly of his jeans with a loud zip.

Smythe was last to leave the Sunday brunch. He came up close to Stephen, still standing stunned in the living room center, and delivered these comforting words.

"Too bad, boy, you had to blow it like this."

His butt-pat, which followed, was of a fondly valedictory nature.

Vertigo took sudden hold of Stephen, he tottered in several directions, but finally fell backwards into the arms of Clove.

"Bed, bed, before Mom," he heard himself imploring before it all went black.

It could not be said that Stephen emerged altogether from black when he recovered consciousness in his elegantly appointed bachelor bedroom. However the black was not total, unrelieved black, although the room was not lighted by the least lingering vestige of daylight through his dormer windows. Day had withdrawn as completely, and, to Stephen, as precipitately as had his future association with the law firm of Webster, Eggleston, Larrabee and Smythe. Still, as the pupils of his eyes expanded, he could detect those sometimes-comforting little irregular glimmerings of light on the river East, which the windows of the bedroom overlooked, as well as the more assertive challenges to dark that were offered by city-bound Sunday night traffic on the Triboro Bridge.

"Jesus K. Morris BROTHERS!"

This extraordinary exclamation was not provoked by a reassessment of his future with Wall Street and its legal aspects but by a very precisely located physical sensation, one bitch of a pain where he had never experienced one before.

Hard upon this outcry of distress, Stephen heard from the hallway (thank God the door was closed!) the voice of his nearest and dearest still living relative, none other than his mother, her voice, yes, but not at all under its usual cool restraint.

To whom was she talking? Herself or someone other?

Although pitched rather loudly, the voice of Mother was saying something incomprehensible to him.

"Oh, Precious gran'chile, I believe your daddy's awake, now, I heard him in his bedroom, le's go in and—"

"Oh, no, Mother, hello, Mother, no, no, not quite yet, dear!"

"Shun, shun, Shtephen, what a sad but beautiful shtory! Mother's naturally very upshet by the tragedy of poor Sue Coffin but undershtands why you preferred not to shpeak of it. The thing to consider now ish the proper background and shchooling of thish adorable deshendant of an Ashe and a Coffin of the Nantucket Coffins. Thish beautiful shecret of yours, thish darlin' Clove Coffin Ashe ish comin' in there to fetch you shoon as—Oh, Clove, Preshus, I'm shtill sho un-shtrung, thrilled to pieces, of course, but shtill a bit overcome by the shuddenness of it all. Sweetheart, do you think I could have another one of those marvelous ashpirin shubstitutes you gave me when I arrived, and maybe alsho another one of thoshe delishous Merry Marys to wash it down with?"

Then through the hall door, that frontier of a world in which all that remained of his particular reality was confined with Stephen Ashe, came the voice of Clove, its hillbilly coarseness, outright abrasiveness of intonation, hardly recognizably muted and transfigured, as if adapted from a score for a brass instrument to one for a delicate woodwind.

"Mommy, I reckoned you might want seconds and here they are, just stick your tongue out and I'll pop in this new type aspirin and—there! Leave mouth open for Mary!—There, now, slowly, drink all, don't let none spill! Good, huh, Mommy? If the drugstore man was God and the barman was Jesus, they couldn't make 'em better, you can bet your sweet—"

"Shunny, I am afraid that Shun Stephen has neglected your social training. You mustn't pat a lady on her behind, not on such short acquaintansh, regardless of—relashuns!"

But if there was any genuine reproof in Mom's tone, it was immediately cancelled out by her subsequent giggles, coy as a skittish schoolgirl's . . .

Some minutes later, fewer than might be surmised, Stephen had opened the bedroom door just a crack and had called softly: "Son?"

"Yes, Daddy?"

"Shun Stephen!" cried out Mom in her curiously altered voice.

"Mom, I'm sorry you had to discover my little, uh, *secret* like this, but if Son will give me some help in here, I'm not feeling well, Mom. You remember that thing I had called labyrinthitis? Well, it has come back on me, there's been a little recurrence, it, it—affects my equilibrium, and if Sonny will help me in here, I'll, I'll—make myself decent so we can talk this all out together."

Stephen heard the sound of a prolonged and moist osculation in the hall. He swayed backwards a little as Clove entered the door of the dark bedroom. Having swayed in that direction, Stephen went all the way backwards to the little bench beneath the dormer windows, where he soon found Clove beside him.

"You know, at sixteen I'm one helluva lot smarter than you are, Daddy. Your Mom likes Quaalude, Daddy, and she got one in her first Mary."

"Quaa what?"

"Lude."

"Yes, it's all very lewd, it's almost disgustingly lewd."

"You got the wrong spellin', Daddy, but never mind about that. I think that your Mom is already hooked on Quaaludes washed down with a toddy or two. Now, here. You take this other Quaalude and then you go out to your Mom."

"And do what?"

"Shit, you'll know what to do when this big one hits you, washed down with a Merry Mary as your sweet ole Mom calls it!"

Clove thrust the Quaalude into Stephen's slack mouth, then pressed the Mary to his lips.

"Now swallow slowly, Daddy, don't slobber. Which one of the drawers in that bureau is the drawer full of drawers?"

"Bottom drawer."

"Right. Drawers for your bottom in bottom drawer."

Clove got Stephen dressed for his heart-to-heart with Mom in less time than an experienced short-order cook would need to serve up two over lightly with a side of French fries.

"How you feel, how'd it hit you, Daddy?" whispered Clove.

"No problem, no problem at all," Stephen replied with an uncertain air of assurance.

"Must run in the family but it took me to bring it out. Now git with Mom."

He headed Stephen forcibly toward the door.

Mom attempted to rise to her feet to embrace Stephen as he entered the hall but she nearly hit the carpet. Clove caught her buttocks to his groin, and then Stephen witnessed a scene the shock of which even his Quaalude washed down with a double Mary did not insulate him against completely. Mom was now seated in the lap of Clove. Both of them were sobbing, the difference being that Clove was winking and grinning over Mom's shoulder.

Mom made a sound that was "Shun, Shun, Shun," but doubtless was her best effort, under the circumstances, to articulate three times the word "Son."

"Mom, can you hear me?" Stephen shouted.

"Oh, Shun, oh, Shun!"

"Daddy," said Clove, "your Mom is the treasure at the end of the rainbow I've waited for all my life. She understands! You understand, Daddy? Your Mom understands and is so goddamn happy she's speechless!"

Mom did, indeed, appear to be overcome with felicity but she was not only in the arms of the Arkansas chicken but those of narcotized slumber. After a little colloquy between Clove and Stephen, it was agreed that she should be transferred to her suite in the Ritz Tower where she customarily stayed when in Manhattan, Stephen's room for her in his apartment being a matter of fiction.

Endlessly resourceful, Clove prepared Mom for this transference. He put over her blind but half-open eyes his own pair of shades, got her sables about her and hung her crocodile shoulder bag over her slumped shoulder.

"Now, Daddy, git with it. You got to show downstairs when I put her in the limo and you got to tell the driver to git her delivered all the way up to her room at this fat cat hotel where she sacks."

As he was conveying this command to Stephen, his hand was busy inside Mom's shoulder bag, extricating from it some nice bits of green, well-engraved.

"Mom is sharp about money."

"That's why she's loaded with it, but, Daddy, it's got a price, all of it's got a price, that's one piece of education that I took with me out of the Arkansas Ozarks."

Late the next day, after another all-afternoon heart-to-heart among son Stephen and Mom and this treasure of an offspring Clove Coffin Ashe, Mom was carefully deposited on a jet to Palm Beach, blowing kisses to "Shun" and his "Lamb" long after the jet was airborne. In her crocodile shoulder bag was a bottle of forty-nine Quaaludes, the fiftieth having been ingested at the start of the highly emotional afternoon and washed down with a Merry Mary and high oh-oh . . .

Stephen and Clove and a tiny French Pug puppy (surprise gift for Mom who associated that breed of canine fondly with dear old Wally Windsor) were sharing a compartment on the Amtrak to Miami which would let them off at Palm Beach. They had chosen rail travel instead of plane because Stephen's infinitely precocious (and improbable) offspring felt that the extra time was needed to prepare his daddy-byadoption for certain ideas, in the nature of projects on the agenda, which had to involve them jointly during their visit with Mom at the Golden Shores.

"I think the porter heard that goddamn dog under the fruit in the basket when he was making up the beds."

"If he heard the dog in the basket, the memory of it was completely erased by that twenty bucks I got you to give him on his way out."

"Clove, you don't seem to recognize the fact that I'm an unemployed man, I can't be that loose with money."

"With all the money you got comin' in to you?"

"Money from where, Clove?"

"Man, you know and I know that your Mom is sittin' on one helluva bundle and I don't mean her fat ass."

"Clove, you don't know how close Mom is with her money, why, she—"

"Daddy, don't give me that jive, what I don't know is yet to be known by sweet Jesus. Now you jus' stick out your tongue for this lewd pill. Tha's right. Now drink this shot of Wild Turkey. Tha's right. —Feel better? Feel good? Like when I'm teaching you the Arkansas Ozark way?"

Attempting to nod, Stephen moved his head in an elliptical way.

"Now, then, Daddy, jus' lissen, don't bother to speak. Your Mom is down there sittin' on this helluva bundle and high as the moon on her lewds, and what is more important to me and to you, Mom is afflicted with *tragic sickness!*"

"Sickness, tragic? I don't follow you, Clove. All that's ever been wrong with Mom is an occasional little asthmatic condition which allergy specialists say is just a touch of rose fever, so she had to insist that the gardener at Golden Shores dispose of all rosebushes on the five-acre grounds."

"Shay-*it!*" Clove said with a slightly savage chuckle.

"Clove, you must not indulge in vulgarisms of this nature while you're—"

"Comfo'ting Mom through the last stage of her tragic asthma condition, Daddy?"

At this point his *fils-adoptif* had somewhat diverted Stephen from the kid's Dogpatch drawl by the slow removal of Clove's fine-textured flesh-colored briefs.

Dear God, thought Stephen, You must have said *Let there be Clove* before You said *Let there be light*, because what this Arkansas Ozark kid is now unveiling surely equals or takes precedence over all other works and wonders that You performed in Your six days of creation!

Unconsciously Stephen Ashe crossed a few paces to secure the lock on the compartment door of the Amtrak southbound to Mom. And he thought it best not to comprehend fully what Clove was speaking, now, his words timed with the gradual removal of his briefs.

"Daddy, I've told you but I'll tell you once more," Clove was saying. "You got to come out of the closet, I mean all the way out and for good, and you got to lock the door of it behind you and forget that the goddamn closet ever existed, because—now you hear *this!*—You are alone on this Amtrak with a *killer chicken!* An' when this chicken infawms you that Mom is afflicted with a tragic sickness, you better rate this chicken's word higher than words out of any medical mouth in the world."

Clackety-clack went the wheels of the Amtrak, rhythmically unchanging over its roadbed, but Stephen heard nothing but a hum in his ears as faint as the late-night music of the river named East in the passive view of which the ravishment of his often-patted backside had occurred between a Sunday brunch and Mom's oddly catered buffet.

"Clove, I didn't quite catch what you've been talking about and maybe it's better that way."

Clove's response was only an ineffably innocent smile, but from the wicker basket of Hammacher Schlemmer's Garden of Eden department, from under the apples, bananas, peaches and seedless grapes, the French Pug puppy uttered a sound, a little "Woof-woof" which had to pass for a note of moral protest in the absence of any other more consequential to events proceeding in this world whose one and only crisis is not the depletion of its energy resources.

November 1977 (Published 1978)

Bibliographical Notes

THE ACCENT OF A COMING FOOT. Written in March 1935, not previously published. This version is from a manuscript of early writings, *Pieces of my Youth*, put together by Williams in the mid-seventies but never published. In that manuscript the following note accompanied the story:

It was immediately after the conclusion of this story, one of those which I wrote in the evenings after my days at the Continental Branch of the International Shoe Company in St. Louis, that I suffered my first heart attack. As I rose from my worktable in my cubbyhole room in the apartment we were crammed into at 6254 Enright St., in the unfashionable suburb of University City, I found that my heart was pounding and skipping beats. Something more than cups of black coffee, something too close to myself in the character of Bud and the tension of Catharine, triggered this first cardiac seizure. Persons suffering from an attack of this sort always feel an instinct to rush outside. It should be restrained but it wasn't. Everyone was asleep in the apartment but me. I rushed down the back fire escape and I went wildly along the midnight street, quickening my pace as my pulse quickened. I must have rushed for miles, all the way from the suburb to Union Boulevard deep into St. Louis. It was March: the trees along the streets were beginning to bud. With characteristic romanticism, I kept looking up at those green bits of life emerging again and somehow it was this that quieted my panic and my tachycardia subsided.

Later that week, after work, I went secretly to a doctor who informed me that I did, indeed, have a defective heart. Shortly afterwards a second attack occured which hospitalized me for a week and which had one great compensation—it released me from the shoe business in which I'd been trapped for three years . . .

The title is a quote from Emily Dickinson.

THE ANGEL IN THE ALCOVE. Written in October 1943 in Santa Monica, published in 1948 in the collection *One Arm*. This story is a partial basis for the play *Vieux Carré*.

BIG BLACK: A MISSISSIPPI IDYLL. Written 1931/32, not previously published. This story won an honorable mention in the Mahan Contest run by the University of Missouri English Department. (The contest is still a yearly event.) A copy of the typescript was supplied by the University of Missouri Archives.

CHRONICLE OF A DEMISE. Published in 1948 in the collection *One Arm*.

THE COMING OF SOMETHING TO THE WIDOW HOLLY. Begun in 1943, published in 1953 in *ND Fourteen—New Directions in Prose & Poetry*, included in the collection *Hard Candy* (1954).

COMPLETED. Written in November 1973, published in 1974 in the collection *Eight Mortal Ladies Possessed*.

THE DARK ROOM. Written c. 1940, not previously published. A copy of the typescript was supplied by the Harry Ransom Research Center, The University of Texas at Austin.

DAS WASSER IST KALT. Written during the period 1973–79, published in 1982 in *Antaeus*, not previously collected.

DESIRE AND THE BLACK MASSEUR. Begun in March 1942, finished in April 1946, published in 1948 in the collection *One Arm*.

THE FIELD OF BLUE CHILDREN. Written in 1937, published in 1939 in *Story* magazine, included in the collection *One Arm* (1948).

GIFT OF AN APPLE. Written c. 1936, not previously published. A copy of the typescript was supplied by the Harry Ransom Humanities Research Center, The University of Texas at Austin.

"GRAND." Published in a limited edition (House of Books, Ltd.) in 1964, included in the collection *The Knightly Quest* (1966).

HAPPY AUGUST THE TENTH. Probably begun in 1957 but mainly written in August 1970, published in *Antaeus* in 1971, reprinted in *Esquire* and *Best American Short Stories of 1973*, included in the collection *Eight Mortal Ladies Possessed* (1974).

HARD CANDY. Begun in Rome, August 1949, finished in March 1953, published in 1954 in the collection, *Hard Candy*. This story is really a variation of the earlier "The Mysteries of the Joy Rio."

THE IMPORTANT THING. Published in *Story* in 1945, included in the collection *One Arm* (1948).

IN MEMORY OF AN ARISTOCRAT. Written c. 1940, not previously published. A copy of the typescript was supplied by the Harry Ransom Humanities Research Center, The University of Texas at Austin.

THE INTERVAL. Written in September/October 1945, not previously published. This version is from the *Pieces of my Youth* manuscript where several variant endings are given; the ending used is dated October 1945.

THE INVENTORY AT FONTANA BELLA. Written in July 1972, published in *Playboy* in 1973, included in the collection *Eight Mortal Ladies Possessed* (1974).

THE KILLER CHICKEN AND THE CLOSET QUEEN. Written in November 1977, published in 1978 in *Christopher Street*, not previously collected.

THE KINGDOM OF EARTH. Begun in 1942 in Macon, Georgia, published in 1954 in the limited edition of the collection, *Hard Candy*, included in the trade edition of *The Knightly Quest* (1966). This story is the basis for the play *The Kingdom of Earth* or *The Seven Descents of Myrtle*.

THE KNIGHTLY QUEST. Begun in 1949 but mainly written in 1965, published in

1966 in the collection *The Knightly Quest*. This long story is a partial basis for the unpublished play *The Red Devil Battery Sign*.

A LADY'S BEADED BAG. Published in 1930 in the magazine *The Columns*.

THE MALEDITION. Begun in the summer of 1941, published in 1945, included in the collection *One Arm* (1948).

MAMA'S OLD STUCCO HOUSE. Published in the January 1965 issue of *Esquire*, included in the collection *The Knightly Quest* (1966).

MAN BRING THIS UP ROAD. Written in Italy in the summer of 1953, published in 1959 in *Mademoiselle*, included in the collection *The Knightly Quest* (1966). This story is the basis for the play *The Milk Train Doesn't Stop Here Anymore* and the filmscript *Boom!*

THE MAN IN THE OVERSTUFFED CHAIR. Written c. 1960, published in December 1980 in *Antaeus*, not previously collected.

THE MATTRESS BY THE TOMATO PATCH. Written in 1953 (refers to an incident c. 1943), published in 1954 in the collection *Hard Candy*.

MISS COYNTE OF GREENE. Written in November 1972, published in 1973 in *Playboy*, included in the collection *Eight Mortal Ladies Possessed* (1974).

MOTHER YAWS. Published in 1977 in *Esquire*, not previously collected.

THE MYSTERIES OF THE JOY RIO. Written in 1941 in New Orleans, published in 1954 in the collection *Hard Candy*.

THE NIGHT OF THE IGUANA. Begun in April 1946 in New Orleans (based on an incident in Acapulco in September 1940), finished in February 1948 in Rome, published in 1948 in the collection *One Arm*. This story is a partial basis for the play *The Night of the Iguana*.

ONE ARM. Begun in May 1942 in New York, revised in 1943 in Santa Monica, but not finished until 1945 in Dallas, published in 1948 in the collection *One Arm*. This story is the basis for the unproduced screenplay of the same title.

ORIFLAMME. Written in January 1944 (based on the 1937 unpublished story, "The Red Part of a Flag"), published in 1974 in *Vogue*, included in the collection *Eight Mortal Ladies Possessed* (1974).

THE POET. Published in 1948 in the collection *One Arm*.

PORTRAIT OF A GIRL IN GLASS. Begun in February 1941 in Key West, finished in June 1943 in Santa Monica, published in 1948 in the collection *One Arm*. This story is the basis of the play *The Glass Menagerie*.

A RECLUSE AND HIS GUEST. Published in 1970 in *Playboy*, not previously collected.

THE RESEMBLANCE BETWEEN A VIOLIN CASE AND A COFFIN. Written in October 1949, published in 1950 in *Flair*, reprinted in *Best American Short Stories of 1951*, included in the collection *Hard Candy* (1954).

RUBIO Y MORENA. Published in 1948 in *Partisan Review*, reprinted in 1949 in *New Directions In Prose and Poetry Number Eleven*, included in the collection *Hard Candy* (1954).

SABBATHA AND SOLITUDE. Written in June 1973, published in 1973 in *Playgirl*, included in the collection *Eight Mortal Ladies Possessed* (1974).

SAND. Written in April 1936, not previously published.

SOMETHING ABOUT HIM. Published in 1946 in *Mademoiselle*, not previously reprinted.

SOMETHING BY TOLSTOI. Written 1930/31, not previously published. This story won an honorable mention in the Mahan Contest at the University of Missouri (see comments under "Big Black"). A copy of the typescript was supplied by the University of Missouri Archives.

TEN MINUTE STOP. Written c. 1936, not previously published. A copy of the typescript was supplied by the Harry Ransom Humanities Research Center, The University of Texas at Austin.

TENT WORMS. Written c. 1945 (in the *Pieces of my Youth* manuscript), published in 1980 in *Esquire*, not previously collected.

THREE PLAYERS OF A SUMMER GAME. Written in Venice and Rome, summer 1951, revised and finished in April 1952, published in 1952 in *The New Yorker*, reprinted in *Best American Short Stories of 1953*, included in the collection *Hard Candy* (1954). This story is the basis for the play *Cat on a Hot Tin Roof*.

TWENTY-SEVEN WAGONS FULL OF COTTON. Written in 1935, published in 1936 in *Manuscript* magazine, not previously collected. This story is the basis for the one-act play of the same title and is a partial basis for the filmscript *Baby Doll*.

TWO ON A PARTY. Begun in London, finished in New Orleans 1951/52, published in 1954 in the collection *Hard Candy*.

THE VENGEANCE OF NITOCRIS. Published in 1928 in *Weird Tales*. In his "Foreword" to *Sweet Bird of Youth* (originally published in *The New York Times*, Sunday, March 8, 1959), Tennessee Williams writes:

> In my first published work, for which I received the big sum of thirty-five dollars, a story published in the July or August issue of *Weird Tales* in the year 1928, I drew upon a paragraph in the ancient histories of Herodotus to create a story of how the Egyptian queen, Nitocris, invited all of her enemies to a lavish banquet in a subterranean hall on the shores of the Nile, and how, at the height of this banquet, she excused herself from the table and opened sluice gates admitting the waters of the Nile into the locked banquet hall, drowning her unloved guests like so many rats.
>
> I was sixteen when I wrote this story, but already a confirmed writer, having entered upon this vocation at the age of fourteen, and, if you're well acquainted with my writings since then, I don't have to tell you that it set the keynote for most of the work that has followed.

THE VINE. Begun in Laguna Beach in 1939, revised and finished in 1944 in Clayton, Missouri, published in 1954 in *Mademoiselle*, included in the collection *Hard Candy* (1954). This story won the Benjamin Franklin Magazine Award for Excellence in 1955.

THE YELLOW BIRD. Published in 1947 in *Town and Country*, included in the collection *One Arm* (1948). This story is a partial basis for the plays *Summer and Smoke* and *The Eccentricities of a Nightingale*.